65
GREAT TALES
OF THE
SUPERNATURAL

Edited by Mary Danby

Sundial

This edition first published in Great Britain in 1979 by:
Sundial Publications Limited
59 Grosvenor Street
London W1
in collaboration with:
William Heinemann Limited
15–16 Queen Street
London W1
and
Martin Secker & Warburg Limited
54 Poland Street
London W1

ISBN 0 904230 99 6

Filmset in Great Britain by
Northumberland Press Ltd, Gateshead,
Tyne and Wear
Second Impression   1980

Printed in the United States of America

ACKNOWLEDGEMENTS

The Editor gratefully acknowledges permission to reprint copyright material to the following: Robert Aickman for Ringing the Changes, from 'Dark Entries'. Charles Lavell Ltd., Authors' Agents, for My Adventure in Norfolk by A. J. Alan. The Estate of the late E. F. Benson, and A. P. Watt Ltd., for The Bus Conductor. Sir Charles Birkin for Little Boy Blue, from 'The Smell of Evil'. The Public Trustee and the Garnstone Press for Keeping His Promise by Algernon Blackwood. Stella Jonckheere for Kecksies, from 'The Bishop of Hell and Other Stories' by Marjorie Bowen. William Heinemann Ltd. for Couching at the Door by D. K. Broster. The Author and David Higham Associates Ltd. for Don't You Dare, from the book of that name published by the Hutchinson Publishing Group Ltd. The Author for A Vindictive Woman; © R. Chetwynd-Hayes 1979. The Author for The Horror Under Penmire; © Adrian Cole 1974. The Engelmayer Puppets is © Mary Danby 1979. Susan Dickinson for The House of Balfother, from 'Dark Encounters' by William Croft Dickinson, published by the Harvill Press 1963; © the Estate of William Croft Dickinson 1963. The Owners of the Copyright – Baskervilles Investments Ltd. – John Murray Ltd. and Jonathan Cape Ltd. for The Brown Hand by Sir Arthur Conan Doyle. Curtis Brown Ltd., London, as Agent for the Author, for The Apple Tree by Daphne du Maurier. Celia Fremlin and Victor Gollancz Ltd. for Don't Tell Cissie, from 'By Horror Haunted'. A. D. Peters & Co. Ltd. for The Horsehair Trunk by Davis Grubb. John Halkin and Michael Bakewell Associates Ltd. for Bobby; © John Halkin. Curtis Brown Ltd., London, as Agent for the Author, for Ghost of Honour by Pamela Hansford-Johnson. Hamish Hamilton Ltd., London, for Monkshood Manor, from 'The Complete Short Stories of L. P. Hartley'. J. M. Dent & Sons Ltd. for The Ankardyne Pew, from 'Midnight Tales' by W. F. Harvey. The Author for Those Lights and Violins; © Dorothy K. Haynes 1979. Arkham House Publishers, Inc., Sauk City, Wisconsin, U.S.A. for The Whistling Room by William Hope Hodgson, from 'Carnacki, the Ghost Finder'. Robert Holdstock and A. P. Watt Ltd. for Magic Man; © Robert Holdstock 1976. David Higham Associates Ltd. for A Night at a Cottage, from 'A Moment of Time' by Richard Hughes, published by Chatto & Windus Ltd. Curtis Brown Ltd., London, as Agent for the Author, for South Sea Bubble by Hammond Innes. The Society of Authors as the literary representative of the Estate of W. W. Jacobs for The Monkey's Paw. Edward Arnold (Publishers) Ltd. for Lost Hearts by M. R. James, from 'Ghost Stories of an Antiquary'. William Heinemann Ltd. for Carnival on the Downs by Gerald Kersh, from 'Men Without Bones'. The National Trust, the Macmillan Co. of London and Basingstoke, and A. P. Watt Ltd. for The Mark of the Beast by Rudyard Kipling, from 'Life's Handicap'. Nigel Kneale and Douglas Rae (Management) Ltd. for Minuke. The Author for For the Love of Pamela; © Kay Leith 1974. A. M. Heath & Co. Ltd. for The Moon-Bog by H. P. Lovecraft. The Author for A Fair Lady; © Roger Malisson 1979. The Author for The Master of Blas Gwynedd; © Joyce Marsh 1977. Hugh Noyes (for the Executors of the Alfred Noyes Literary Estate) and John Murray (Publishers) Ltd. for Midnight Express. The Author for Mary; © Roger B. Pile 1978. A. D. Peters & Co. Ltd., for A Story of Don Juan by V. S. Pritchett. Elaine Greene Ltd. for A Woman Seldom Found; © William Sansom 1963. The Author and Harvey Unna & Stephen Durbridge Ltd. for Travelling Light; © Bernard Taylor 1979. The Author and Harvey Unna & Stephen Durbridge Ltd. for The Deathly Silence;

ACKNOWLEDGEMENTS

© *Rosemary Timperley 1979. The Author for* Guest Room, © *Tim Vicary 1976. Curtis Brown Ltd., London, for* The Triumph of Death *by H. Russell Wakefield. Sir Rupert Hart-Davis for* Mrs Lunt *by Hugh Walpole. Elizabeth Walter for* The Hollies and the Ivy, *from 'Dead Woman', published by Collins & Harvill Press 1975. The Estate of the late H. G. Wells, and A. P. Watt Ltd. for* The Red Room. *Constable & Co. Ltd. for* All Souls', *from 'The Ghost Stories of Edith Wharton'. The Estate of the late Dennis Wheatley, Hutchinson Publishing Group Ltd. and A. P. Watt Ltd. for* The Case of the Long-Dead Lord.

Every effort has been made to trace the owners of the copyright material in this book. In the case of any question arising as to the use of any such material, the Editor would be pleased to receive notification of this.

Contents

CONTENTS

CONTENTS

Ringing the Changes
Robert Aickman

He had never been among those many who deeply dislike church bells, but the ringing that evening at Holihaven changed his view. Bells could certainly get on one's nerves he felt, although he had only just arrived in the town.

*　　*　　*

He had been too well aware of the perils attendant upon marrying a girl twenty-four years younger than himself to add to them by a conventional honeymoon. The strange force of Phrynne's love had borne both of them away from their previous selves; in him a formerly haphazard and easy-going approach to life had been replaced by much deep planning to wall in happiness; and she, though once thought cold and choosy, would now agree to anything as long as she was with him. He had said that if they were to marry in June, it would be at the cost of not being able to honeymoon until October. Had they been courting longer, he had explained, gravely smiling, special arrangements could have been made; but, as it was, business claimed him. This, indeed, was true; because his business position was less influential than he had led Phrynne to believe. Finally, it would have been impossible for them to have courted longer, because they had courted from the day they met, which was less than six weeks before the day they married.

'"A village",' he had quoted as they entered the branch line train at the junction (itself sufficiently remote), '"from which (it was said) persons of sufficient longevity might hope to reach Liverpool Street".' By now he was able to make jokes about age, although perhaps he did so rather too often.

'Who said that?'

'Bertrand Russell.'

She had looked at him with her big eyes in her tiny face.

'Really.' He had smiled confirmation.

'I'm not arguing.' She had still been looking at him. The romantic gas light in the charming period compartment had left him uncertain

whether she was smiling back or not. He had given himself the benefit of
the doubt, and kissed her.

The guard had blown his whistle and they had rumbled out into the
darkness. The branch line swung so sharply away from the main line
that Phrynne had been almost toppled from her seat.

'Why do we go so slowly when it's so flat?'

'Because the engineer laid the line up and down the hills and valleys
such as they are, instead of cutting through and embanking over them.'
He liked being able to inform her.

'How do you know? Gerald! You said you hadn't been to Holihaven
before.'

'It applies to most of the railways in East Anglia.'

'So that even though it's flatter, it's slower?'

'Time matters less.'

'I should have hated going to a place where time mattered or
that you'd been to before. You'd have had nothing to remember me
by.'

He hadn't been quite sure that her words exactly expressed her
thoughts, but the thought had lightened his heart.

*   *   *

Holihaven station could hardly have been built in the days of the town's
magnificence, for they were in the Middle Ages; but it still implied
grander functions than came its way now. The platforms were long
enough for visiting London expresses, which had since gone elsewhere;
and the architecture of the waiting rooms would have been not
insufficient for occasional use by foreign royalty. Oil lamps on perches
like those occupied by macaws, lightened the uniformed staff, who
numbered two and, together with every native of Holihaven, looked like
storm-habituated mariners.

The station-master and porter, as Gerald took them to be, watched
him approach down the platform with a heavy suitcase in each hand
and Phrynne walking deliciously by his side. He saw one of them address
a remark to the other, but neither offered to help. Gerald had to put
down the cases in order to give up their tickets. The other passengers had
already disappeared.

'Where's the Bell?'

Gerald had found the hotel in a reference book. It was the only one
allotted to Holihaven. But as Gerald spoke, and before the ticket-
collector could answer, the sudden deep note of an actual bell rang
through the darkness. Phrynne caught hold of Gerald's sleeve.

Ignoring Gerald, the station-master, if such he was, turned to his
colleague. 'They're starting early.'

'Every reason to be in good time,' said the other man.

The station-master nodded, and put Gerald's tickets indifferently in his jacket pocket.

'Can you please tell me how I get to the Bell Hotel?'

The station-master's attention returned to him. 'Have you a room booked?'

'Certainly.'

'Tonight?' The station-master looked inappropriately suspicious.

'Of course.'

Again the station-master looked at the other man.

'It's them Pascoes.'

'Yes,' said Gerald. 'That's the name. Pascoe.'

'We don't use the Bell,' explained the station-master. 'But you'll find it in Wrack Street.' He gesticulated vaguely and unhelpfully. 'Straight ahead. Down Station Road. Then down Wrack Street. You can't miss it.'

'Thank you.'

As soon as they entered the town, the big bell began to boom regularly.

'What narrow streets!' said Phrynne.

'They follow the lines of the medieval city. Before the river silted up, Holihaven was one of the most important seaports in Great Britain.'

'Where's everybody got to?'

Although it was only six o'clock, the place certainly seemed deserted.

'Where's the hotel got to?' rejoined Gerald.

'Poor Gerald! Let me help.' She laid her hand beside his on the handle of the suitcase nearest to her, but as she was about fifteen inches shorter than he, she could be of little assistance. They must already have gone more than a quarter of a mile. 'Do you think we're in the right street?'

'Most unlikely, I should say. But there's no one to ask.'

'Must be early closing day.'

The single deep notes of the bell were now coming more frequently.

'Why are they ringing that bell? Is it a funeral?'

'Bit late for a funeral.'

She looked at him a little anxiously.

'Anyway it's not cold.'

'Considering we're on the east coast it's quite astonishingly warm.'

'Not that I care.'

'I hope that bell isn't going to ring all night.'

She pulled on the suitcase. His arms were in any case almost parting from his body. 'Look! We've passed it.'

They stopped, and he looked back. 'How could we have done that?'

'Well, we have.'

She was right. He could see a big ornamental bell hanging from a bracket attached to a house about a hundred yards behind them.

They retraced their steps and entered the hotel. A woman dressed in a navy blue coat and skirt, with a good figure but dyed red hair and a face ridged with make-up, advanced upon them.

'Mr and Mrs Banstead? I'm Hilda Pascoe. Don, my husband, isn't very well.'

Gerald felt full of doubts. His arrangements were not going as they should. Never rely on guide-book recommendations. The trouble lay partly in Phrynne's insistence that they go somewhere he did not know. 'I'm sorry to hear that,' he said.

'You know what men are like when they're ill?' Mrs Pascoe spoke understandingly to Phrynne.

'Impossible,' said Phrynne. 'Or very difficult.'

'Talk about "Woman in our hours of ease".'

'Yes,' said Phrynne. 'What's the trouble?'

'It's always been the same trouble with Don,' said Mrs Pascoe; then checked herself. 'It's his stomach,' she said. 'Ever since he was a kid, Don's had trouble with the lining of his stomach.'

Gerald interrupted. 'I wonder if we could see our rooms?'

'So sorry,' said Mrs Pascoe. 'Will you register first?' She produced a battered volume bound in peeling imitation leather. 'Just the name and address.' She spoke as if Gerald might contribute a résumé of his life.

It was the first time he and Phrynne had ever registered in an hotel; but his confidence in the place was not increased by the long period which had passed since the registration above.

'We're always quiet in October,' remarked Mrs Pascoe, her eyes upon him. Gerald noticed that her eyes were slightly bloodshot. 'Except sometimes for the bars, of course.'

'We wanted to come out of the season,' said Phrynne soothingly.

'Quite,' said Mrs Pascoe.

'Are we alone in the house?' enquired Gerald. After all the woman was probably doing her best.

'Except for Commandant Shotcroft. You won't mind him, will you? He's a regular.'

'I'm sure we shan't,' said Phrynne.

'People say the house wouldn't be the same without Commandant Shotcroft.'

'I see.'

'What's that bell?' asked Gerald. Apart from anything else, it really was much too near.

Mrs Pascoe looked away. He thought she looked shifty under her entrenched make-up. But she only said 'Practice.'

'Do you mean there will be more of them later?'

She nodded. 'But never mind,' she said encouragingly. 'Let me show you to your room. Sorry there's no porter.'

Before they had reached the bedroom, the whole peal had commenced.

'Is this the quietest room you have?' enquired Gerald. 'What about the other side of the house?'

'This *is* the other side of the house. Saint Guthlac's is over there.' She pointed out through the bedroom door.

'Darling,' said Phrynne, her hand on Gerald's arm, 'they'll soon stop. They're only practising.'

Mrs Pascoe said nothing. Her expression indicated that she was one of those people whose friendliness has a precise and never exceeded limit.

'If *you* don't mind,' said Gerald to Phrynne, hesitating.

'They have ways of their own in Holihaven,' said Mrs Pascoe. Her undertone of militancy implied, among other things, that if Gerald and Phrynne chose to leave, they were at liberty to do so. Gerald did not care for that either: her attitude would have been different, he felt, had there been anywhere else for them to go. The bells were making him touchy and irritable.

'It's a very pretty room,' said Phrynne. 'I adore four-posters.'

'Thank you,' said Gerald to Mrs Pascoe. 'What time's dinner?'

'Seven-thirty. You've time for a drink in the bar first.'

She went.

'We certainly have,' said Gerald when the door was shut. 'It's only just six.'

'Actually,' said Phrynne, who was standing by the window looking down into the street, 'I *like* church bells.'

'All very well,' said Gerald, 'but on one's honeymoon they distract the attention.'

'Not mine,' said Phrynne simply. Then she added, 'There's still no one about.'

'I expect they're all in the bar.'

'I don't want a drink. I want to explore the town.'

'As you wish. But hadn't you better unpack?'

'I ought to, but I'm not going to. Not until after I've seen the sea.'

Such small shows of independence in her enchanted Gerald.

Mrs Pascoe was not about when they passed through the lounge, nor was there any sound of activity in the establishment.

Outside, the bells seemed to be booming and bounding immediately over their heads.

'It's like warriors fighting in the sky,' shouted Phrynne. 'Do you think the sea's down there?' She indicated the direction from which they had previously retraced their steps.

'I imagine so. The street seems to end in nothing. That would be the sea.'

'Come on. Let's run.' She was off, before he could even think about it. Then there was nothing to do but run after her. He hoped there were not eyes behind blinds.

She stopped, and held wide her arms to catch him. The top of her head hardly came up to his chin. He knew she was silently indicating that his failure to keep up with her was not a matter for self-consciousness.

'Isn't it beautiful?'

'The sea?' There was no moon; and little was discernible beyond the end of the street.

'Not only.'

'Everything but the sea. The sea's invisible.'

'You can smell it.'

'I certainly can't hear it.'

She slackened her embrace and cocked her head away from him.

'The bells echo so much, it's as if there were two churches.'

'I'm sure there are more than that. There always are in old towns like this.' Suddenly he was struck by the significance of his words in relation to what she had said. He shrank into himself, tautly listening.

'Yes,' cried Phrynne delightedly. 'It *is* another church.'

'Impossible,' said Gerald. 'Two churches wouldn't have practice ringing on the same night.'

'I'm quite sure. I can hear one lot of bells with my left ear, and another lot with my right.'

They had still seen no one. The sparse gas lights fell on the furnishings of a stone quay, small but plainly in regular use.

'The whole population must be ringing the bells.' His own remark discomfited Gerald.

'Good for them,' she took his hand. 'Let's go down on the beach and look for the sea.'

They descended a flight of stone steps at which the sea had sucked and bitten. The beach was as stony as the steps, but lumpier.

'We'll just go straight on,' said Phrynne. 'Until we find it.'

Left to himself, Gerald would have been less keen. The stones were very large and very slippery, and his eyes did not seem to be becoming accustomed to the dark.

'You're right, Phrynne, about the smell.'

'Honest sea smell.'

'Just as you say.' He took it rather to be the smell of dense rotting weed; across which he supposed they must be slithering. It was not a smell he had previously encountered in such strength.

Energy could hardly be spared for thinking, and advancing hand in hand was impossible.

After various random remarks on both sides and the lapse of what seemed a very long time, Phrynne spoke again. 'Gerald, where is it? What sort of seaport is it that has no sea?'

She continued onwards, but Gerald stopped and looked back. He had thought the distance they had gone overlong, but was startled to see how great it was. The darkness was doubtless deceitful, but the few lights on the quay appeared as on a distant horizon.

The far glimmering specks still in his eyes, he turned and looked after Phrynne. He could barely see her. Perhaps she was progressing faster without him.

'Phrynne! Darling!'

Unexpectedly she gave a sharp cry.

'Phrynne!'

She did not answer.

'Phrynne!'

Then she spoke more or less calmly. 'Panic over. Sorry, darling. I stood on something.'

He realized that a panic it had indeed been; at least in him.

'You're all right?'

'Think so.'

He struggled up to her. 'The smell's worse than ever.' It was overpowering.

'I think it's coming from what I stepped on. My foot went right in, and then there was the smell.'

'I've never known anything like it.'

'Sorry darling,' she said gently mocking him. 'Let's go away.'

'Let's go back. Don't you think?'

'Yes,' said Phrynne. 'But I must warn you I'm very disappointed. I think that seaside attractions should include the sea.'

He noticed that as they retreated, she was scraping the sides of one shoe against the stones, as if trying to clean it.

'I think the whole place is a disappointment,' he said. 'I really must apologize. We'll go somewhere else.'

'I like the bells,' she replied, making a careful reservation.

Gerald said nothing.

'I don't want to go somewhere where you've been before.'

The bells rang out over the desolate unattractive beach. Now the sound seemed to be coming from every point along the shore.

'I suppose all the churches practise on the same night in order to get it over with,' said Gerald.

'They do it in order to see which can ring the loudest,' said Phrynne.

'Take care you don't twist your ankle.'

The din as they reached the rough little quay was such as to suggest that Phrynne's idea was literally true.

*   *   *

The Coffee Room was so low that Gerald had to dip beneath a sequence of thick beams.

'Why "Coffee Room"?' asked Phrynne, looking at the words on the door. 'I saw a notice that coffee will only be served in the lounge.'

'It's the *lucus a non lucendo* principle.'

'That explains everything. I wonder where we sit.' A single electric lantern, mass produced in an antique pattern, had been turned on. The bulb was of that limited wattage which is peculiar to hotels. It did little to penetrate the shadows.

'The *lucus a non lucendo* principle is the principle of calling white black.'

'Not at all,' said a voice from the darkness. 'On the contrary. The word black comes from an ancient root which means "to bleach".'

They had thought themselves alone, but now saw a small man seated by himself at an unlighted corner table. In the darkness he looked like a monkey.

'I stand corrected,' said Gerald.

They sat at the table under the lantern.

The man in the corner spoke again. 'Why are you here at all?'

Phrynne looked frightened, but Gerald replied quietly. 'We're on holiday. We prefer it out of the season. I presume you are Commandant Shotcroft?'

'No need to presume.' Unexpectedly the Commandant switched on the antique lantern which was nearest to him. His table was littered with a finished meal. It struck Gerald that he must have switched off the light when he heard them approach the Coffee Room. 'I'm going anyway.'

'Are we late?' asked Phrynne, always the assuager of situations.

'No, you're not late,' called the Commandant in a deep moody voice. 'My meals are prepared half an hour before the time the rest come in. I don't like eating in company.' He had risen to his feet. 'So perhaps you'll excuse me.'

Without troubling about an answer, he stepped quickly out of the Coffee Room. He had cropped white hair; tragic, heavy-lidded eyes; and a round face which was yellow and lined.

A second later his head reappeared round the door.

'Ring,' he said; and again withdrew.

'Too many other people ringing,' said Gerald. 'But I don't see what else we can do.'

The Coffee Room bell, however, made a noise like a fire alarm.

Mrs Pascoe appeared. She looked considerably the worse for drink.

'Didn't see you in the bar.'

'Must have missed us in the crowd,' said Gerald amiably.

'Crowd?' enquired Mrs Pascoe drunkenly. Then, after a difficult pause, she offered them a hand-written menu.

They ordered; and Mrs Pascoe served them throughout. Gerald was apprehensive lest her indisposition increase during the course of the meal; but her insobriety, like her affability, seemed to have an exact and definite limit.

'All things considered, the food might be worse,' remarked Gerald, towards the end. It was a relief that something was going reasonably well. 'Not much of it, but at least the dishes are hot.'

When Phrynne translated this into a compliment to the cook, Mrs Pascoe said, 'I cooked it all myself, although I shouldn't be the one to say so.'

Gerald felt really surprised that she was in a condition to have accomplished this. Possibly, he reflected with alarm, she had had much practice under similar conditions.

'Coffee is served in the lounge,' said Mrs Pascoe.

They withdrew. In a corner of the lounge was a screen decorated with winning Elizabethan ladies in ruffs and hoops. From behind it, projected a pair of small black boots. Phrynne nudged Gerald and pointed to them. Gerald nodded. They felt constrained to talk about things which bored them.

The hotel was old and its walls thick. In the empty lounge the noise of the bells would not prevent conversation being overheard, but still came from all around, as if the hotel were a fortress beleaguered by surrounding artillery.

After their second cups of coffee, Gerald suddenly said he couldn't stand it.

'Darling, it's not doing us any harm. I think it's rather cosy.' Phrynne subsided in the wooden chair with its sloping back and long mud-coloured mock-velvet cushions; and opened her pretty legs to the fire.

'Every church in the town must be ringing its bells. It's been going on for two and a half hours and they never seem to take the usual breathers.'

'We wouldn't hear. Because of all the other bells ringing. I think it's nice of them to ring the bells for us.'

Nothing further was said for several minutes. Gerald was beginning to realize that they had yet to evolve a holiday routine.

'I'll get you a drink. What shall it be?'

'Anything you like. Whatever *you* have.' Phrynne was immersed in female enjoyment of the fire's radiance on her body.

Gerald missed this, and said 'I don't quite see why they have to keep the place like a hothouse. When I come back, we'll sit somewhere else.'

'Men wear too many clothes, darling,' said Phrynne drowsily.

Contrary to his assumption, Gerald found the lounge bar as empty as everywhere else in the hotel and the town. There was not even a person to dispense.

Somewhat irritably Gerald struck a brass bell which stood on the counter. It rang out sharply as a pistol shot.

Mrs Pascoe appeared at a door among the shelves. She had taken off her jacket, and her make-up had begun to run.

'A cognac, please. Double. And a Kummel.'

Mrs Pascoe's hands were shaking so much that she could not get the cork out of the brandy bottle.

'Allow me.' Gerald stretched his arm across the bar.

Mrs Pascoe stared at him blearily. 'O.K. But I must pour it.'

Gerald extracted the cork and returned the bottle. Mrs Pascoe slopped a far from precise dose into a balloon.

Catastrophe followed. Unable to return the bottle to the high shelf where it resided. Mrs Pascoe placed it on a waist-level ledge. Reaching for the alembic of Kummel, she swept the three-quarters full brandy bottle onto the tiled floor. The stuffy air became fogged with the fumes of brandy from behind the bar.

At the door from which Mrs Pascoe had emerged appeared a man from the inner room. Though still youngish, he was puce and puffy, and in his braces, with no collar. Streaks of sandy hair laced his vast red scalp. Liquor oozed all over him, as if from a perished gourd. Gerald took it that this was Don.

The man was too drunk to articulate. He stood in the doorway, clinging with each red hand to the ledge, and savagely struggling to flay his wife with imprecations.

'How much?' said Gerald to Mrs Pascoe. It seemed useless to try for the Kummel. The hotel must have another bar.

'Three and six,' said Mrs Pascoe, quite lucidly; but Gerald saw that she was about to weep.

He had the exact sum. She turned her back on him and flicked the cash register. As she returned from it, he heard the fragmentation of glass as she stepped on a piece of the broken bottle. Gerald looked at her husband out of the corner of his eye. The sagging, loose-mouthed figure made him shudder. Something moved him.

'I'm sorry about the accident,' he said to Mrs Pascoe. He held the balloon in one hand, and was just going.

Mrs Pascoe looked at him. The slow tears of desperation were edging down her face, but she now seemed quite sober. 'Mr Banstead,' she said in a flat, hurried voice. 'May I come and sit with you and your wife in the lounge? Just for a few minutes.'

'Of course.' It was certainly not what he wanted, and he wondered what would become of the bar, but he felt unexpectedly sorry for her, and it was impossible to say no.

To reach the flap of the bar, she had to pass her husband. Gerald saw her hesitate for a second; then she advanced resolutely and steadily, and looking straight before her. If the man had let go with his hands, he would have fallen; but as she passed him, he released a great gob of spit. He was far too incapable to aim, and it fell on the side of his own trousers. Gerald lifted the flap for Mrs Pascoe and stood back to let her precede him from the bar. As he followed her, he heard her husband maundering off into unintelligible inward searchings.

'The Kummel!' said Mrs Pascoe, remembering in the doorway.

'Never mind,' said Gerald. 'Perhaps I could try one of the other bars?'

'Not tonight. They're shut. I'd better go back.'

'No. We'll think of something else.' It was not yet nine o'clock, and Gerald wondered about the Licensing Justices.

But in the lounge was another unexpected scene. Mrs Pascoe stopped as soon as they entered, and Gerald, caught between two imitation-leather armchairs, looked over her shoulder.

Phrynne had fallen asleep. Her head was slightly on one side, but her mouth was shut, and her body no more than gracefully relaxed, so that she looked most beautiful, and, Gerald thought, a trifle unearthly, like a dead girl in an early picture by Millais.

The quality of her beauty seemed also to have impressed Commandant Shotcroft; for he was standing silently behind her and looking down at her, his sad face transfigured. Gerald noticed that a leaf of the pseudo-Elizabethan screen had been folded back, revealing a small cretonne-covered chair, with an open tome face downward in its seat.

'Won't you join us?' said Gerald boldly. There was that in the Commandant's face which boded no hurt. 'Can I get you a drink?'

The Commandant did not turn his head, and for a moment seemed unable to speak. Then in a low voice he said, 'For a moment only.'

'Good,' said Gerald. 'Sit down. And you, Mrs Pascoe.' Mrs Pascoe was dabbing at her face. Gerald addressed the Commandant. 'What shall it be?'

'Nothing to drink,' said the Commandant in the same low mutter. It occurred to Gerald that if Phrynne awoke, the Commandant would go.

'What about you?' Gerald looked at Mrs Pascoe, earnestly hoping she would decline.

'No thanks.' She was glancing at the Commandant. Clearly she had not expected him to be there.

Phrynne being asleep, Gerald sat down too. He sipped his brandy. It was impossible to romanticize the action with a toast.

The events in the bar had made him forget about the bells. Now, as they sat silently round the sleeping Phrynne, the tide of sound swept over him once more.

'You mustn't think,' said Mrs Pascoe, 'that he's always like that.' They all spoke in hushed voices. All of them seemed to have reason to do so. The Commandant was again gazing sombrely at Phrynne's beauty.

'Of course not.' But it was hard to believe.

'The licensed business puts temptations in a man's way.'

'It must be very difficult.'

'We ought never to have come here. We were happy in South Norwood.'

'You must do good business during the season.'

'Two months,' said Mrs Pascoe bitterly, but still softly. 'Two and a half at the very most. The people who come during the season have no idea what goes on out of it.'

'What made you leave South Norwood?'

'Don's stomach. The doctor said the air would do him good.'

'Speaking of that, doesn't the sea go too far out? We went down on the beach before dinner, but couldn't see it anywhere.'

On the other side of the fire, the Commandant turned his eyes from Phrynne and looked at Gerald.

'I wouldn't know,' said Mrs Pascoe. 'I never have time to look from one year's end to the other.' It was a customary enough answer, but Gerald felt that it did not disclose the whole truth. He noticed that Mrs Pascoe glanced uneasily at the Commandant, who by now was staring neither at Phrynne nor at Gerald but at the toppling citadels in the fire.

'And now I must get on with my work,' continued Mrs Pascoe, 'I only came in for a minute.' She looked Gerald in the face. 'Thank you,' she said, and rose.

'Please stay a little longer,' said Gerald, 'Wait till my wife wakes up.' As he spoke, Phrynne slightly shifted.

'Can't be done,' said Mrs Pascoe, her lips smiling. Gerald noticed that all the time she was watching the Commandant from under her lids, and she knew that were he not there, she would have stayed.

As it was, she went. 'I'll probably see you later to say goodnight. Sorry the water's not very hot. It's having no porter.'

The bells showed no sign of flagging.

When Mrs Pascoe had closed the door, the Commandant spoke.

'He was a fine man once. Don't think otherwise.'

'You mean Pascoe?'

The Commandant nodded seriously.

'Not my type,' said Gerald.

'D.S.O. and bar. D.F.C. and bar.'

'And now bar only. Why?'

'You heard what she said. It was a lie. They didn't leave South Norwood for the sea air.'

'So I supposed.'

'He got into trouble. He was fixed. He wasn't the kind of man to know about human nature and all its rottenness.'

'A pity,' said Gerald. 'But perhaps, even so, this isn't the best place for him?'

'It's the worst,' said the Commandant, a dark flame in his eyes. 'For him or anyone else.'

Again Phrynne shifted in her sleep: this time more convulsively, so that she nearly woke. For some reason the two men remained speechless and motionless until she was again breathing steadily. Against the silence within, the bells sounded louder than ever. It was as if the tumult were tearing holes in the roof.

'It's certainly a very noisy place,' said Gerald, still in an undertone.

'Why did you have to come tonight of all nights?' The Commandant spoke in the same undertone, but his vehemence was extreme.

'This doesn't happen often?'

'Once every year.'

'They should have told us.'

'They don't usually accept bookings. They've no right to accept them. When Pascoe was in charge they never did.'

'I expect that Mrs Pascoe felt they were in no position to turn away business.'

'It's not a matter that should be left to a woman.'

'Not much alternative surely?'

'At heart, women are creatures of darkness all the time.' The Commandant's seriousness and bitterness left Gerald without a reply.

'My wife doesn't mind the bells,' he said after a moment. 'In fact she rather likes them.' The Commandant really was converting a nuisance, though an acute one, into a melodrama.

The Commandant turned and gazed at him. It struck Gerald that what he had just said in some way, for the Commandant, placed Phrynne also in a category of the lost.

'Take her away, man,' said the Commandant, with scornful ferocity.

'In a day or two perhaps,' said Gerald, patiently polite. 'I admit that we are disappointed with Holihaven.'

'Now. While there's still time. This *instant*.'

There was an intensity of conviction about the Commandant which was alarming.

Gerald considered. Even the empty lounge, with its dreary decorations and commonplace furniture, seemed inimical. 'They can hardly go on practising all night,' he said. But now it was fear that hushed his voice.

'Practising!' The Commandant's scorn flickered coldly through the overheated room.

'What else?'

'They're ringing to wake the dead.'

A tremor of wind in the flue momentarily drew on the already roaring fire. Gerald had turned very pale.

'That's a figure of speech,' he said, hardly to be heard.

'Not in Holihaven.' The Commandant's gaze had returned to the fire.

Gerald looked at Phrynne. She was breathing less heavily. His voice dropped to a whisper. 'What happens?'

The Commandant also was nearly whispering. 'No one can tell how long they have to go on ringing. It varies from year to year. I don't know why. You should be all right up to midnight. Probably for some while after. In the end the dead awake. First one or two, then all of them. Tonight even the sea draws back. You have seen that for yourself. In a place like this there are always several drowned each year. This year there've been more than several. But even so that's only a few. Most of them come not from the water but from the earth. It is not a pretty sight.'

'Where do they go?'

'I've never followed them to see. I'm not stark staring mad.' The red of the fire reflected in the Commandant's eyes. There was a long pause.

'I don't believe in the resurrection of the body,' said Gerald. As the hour grew later, the bells grew louder. 'Not of the body.'

'What other kind of resurrection is possible? Everything else is only theory. You can't even imagine it. No one can.'

Gerald had not argued such a thing for twenty years. 'So,' he said, 'you advise me to go. Where?'

'Where doesn't matter.'

'I have no car.'

'Then you'd better walk.'

'With her?' He indicated Phrynne only with his eyes.

'She's young and strong.' A forlorn tenderness lay within the Commandant's words. 'She's twenty years younger than you and therefore twenty years more important.'

'Yes,' said Gerald. 'I agree ... What about you? What will you do?'

'I've lived here some time now. I know what to do.'

'And the Pascoes?'

'He's drunk. There is nothing in the world to fear if you're thoroughly drunk. D.S.O. and bar. D.F.C. and bar.'

'But you're not drinking yourself?'

'Not since I came to Holihaven. I lost the knack.'

Suddenly Phrynne sat up. 'Hallo,' she said to the Commandant; not yet fully awake. Then she said, 'What fun! The bells are still ringing.'

The Commandant rose, his eyes averted. 'I don't think there's anything more to say,' he remarked, addressing Gerald. 'You've still got time.' He nodded slightly to Phrynne, and walked out of the lounge.

'What have you still got time for?' asked Phrynne, stretching. 'Was he trying to convert you? I'm sure he's an Anabaptist.'

'Something like that,' said Gerald, trying to think.

'Shall we go to bed? Sorry, I'm so sleepy.'

'Nothing to be sorry about.'

'Or shall we go for another walk? That would wake me up. Besides the tide might have come in.'

Gerald, although he half-despised himself for it, found it impossible to explain to her that they should leave at once; without transport or a destination; walk all night if necessary. He said to himself that probably he would not go even were he alone.

'If you're sleepy, it's probably a *good* thing.'

'Darling!'

'I mean with these bells. God knows when they will stop.' Instantly he felt a new pang of fear at what he had said.

Mrs Pascoe had appeared at the door leading to the bar, and opposite to that from which the Commandant had departed. She bore two steaming glasses on a tray. She looked about, possibly to confirm that the Commandant had really gone.

'I thought you might both like a nightcap. Ovaltine, with something in it.'

'Thank you,' said Phrynne. 'I can't think of anything nicer.'

Gerald set the glasses on a wicker table, and quickly finished his cognac.

Mrs Pascoe began to move chairs and slap cushions. She looked very haggard.

'Is the Commandant an Anabaptist?' asked Phrynne over her shoulder. She was proud of her ability to outdistance Gerald in beginning to consume a hot drink.

Mrs Pascoe stopped slapping for a moment. 'I don't know what that is,' she said.

'He's left his book,' said Phrynne, on a new tack.

'I wonder what he's reading,' continued Phrynne. 'Foxe's *Lives of the Martyrs,* I expect.' A small unusual devil seemed to have entered into her.

But Mrs Pascoe knew the answer. 'It's always the same,' she said contemptuously. 'He only reads one. It's called *Fifteen Decisive Battles of the World.* He's been reading it ever since he came here. When he gets to the end, he starts again.'

'Should I take it up to him?' asked Gerald. It was neither courtesy nor inclination, but rather a fear lest the Commandant return to the lounge: a desire, after those few minutes of reflection, to cross-examine.

'Thanks very much,' said Mrs Pascoe, as if relieved of a similar apprehension. 'Room One. Next to the suit of Japanese armour.' She went on tipping and banging. To Gerald's inflamed nerves, her behaviour seemed too consciously normal.

He collected the book and made his way upstairs. The volume was bound in real leather, and the top of its pages were gilded: apparently a presentation copy. Outside the lounge, Gerald looked at the fly-leaf: in a very large hand was written 'To my dear Son, Raglan, on his being honoured by the Queen. From his proud Father, B. Shotcroft, Major-General.' Beneath the inscription a very ugly military crest had been appended by a stamper of primitive type.

The suit of Japanese armour lurked in a dark corner as the Commandant himself had done when Gerald had first encountered him. The wide brim of the helmet concealed the black eyeholes in the headpiece; the moustache bristled realistically. It was exactly as if the figure stood guard over the door behind it. On this door was no number, but, there being no other in sight, Gerald took it to be the door of Number One. A short way down the dim empty passage was a window, the ancient sashes of which shook in the din and blast of the bells. Gerald knocked sharply.

It there was a reply, the bells drowned it; and he knocked again. When to the third knocking there was still no answer, he gently opened the door. He really had to know whether all would, or could be well if Phrynne, and doubtless he also, were at all costs to remain in their room until it was dawn. He looked into the room and caught his breath.

There was no artificial light, but the curtains, if there were any, had been drawn back from the single window, and the bottom sash forced up as far as it would go. On the floor by the dusky void, a maelstrom of sound, knelt the Commandant, his cropped white hair faintly catching the moonless glimmer, as his head lay on the sill, like that of a man about to be guillotined. His face was in his hands, but slightly sideways, so that Gerald received a shadowy distorted idea of his expression. Some might have called it ecstatic, but Gerald found it agonized. It frightened him more than anything which had yet happened. Inside the room the bells were like plunging roaring lions.

He stood for some considerable time quite unable to move. He could not determine whether or not the Commandant knew he was there. The Commandant gave no direct sign of it, but more than once he writhed and shuddered in Gerald's direction, like an unquiet sleeper made more unquiet by an interloper. It was a matter of doubt whether Gerald should leave the book; and he decided to do so mainly because the thought of further contact with it displeased him. He crept into the room and softly laid it on a hardly visible wooden trunk at the foot of the plain metal bedstead. There seemed no other furniture in the room. Outside the door, the hanging mailed fingers of the Japanese figure touched his wrist.

He had not been away from the lounge for long, but it was long enough for Mrs Pascoe to have begun to drink again. She had left the tidying up half completed, or rather the room half disarranged; and was leaning against the over-mantel, drawing heavily on a dark tumbler of whisky. Phrynne had not yet finished her Ovaltine.

'How long before the bells stop?' asked Gerald as soon as he opened the lounge door. Now he was resolved that, come what might, they must go. The impossibility of sleep should serve as an excuse.

'I don't expect Mrs Pascoe can know any more than we can,' said Phrynne.

'You should have told us about this – this annual event before accepting our booking.'

Mrs Pascoe drank some more whisky. Gerald suspected that it was neat. 'It's not always the same night,' she said throatily, looking at the floor.

'We're not staying,' said Gerald wildly.

'Darling!' Phrynne caught him by the arm.

'Leave this to me, Phrynne.' He addressed Mrs Pascoe. 'We'll pay for the room, of course. Please order me a car.'

Mrs Pascoe was now regarding him stonily. When he asked for a car, she gave a very short laugh. Then her face changed, she made an effort, and she said, 'You mustn't take the Commandant so seriously, you know.'

Phrynne glanced quickly at her husband.

The whisky was finished. Mrs Pascoe placed the empty glass on the plastic over-mantel with too much of a thud. 'No one takes Commandant Shotcroft seriously,' she said. 'Not even his nearest and dearest.'

'Has he any?' asked Phrynne. 'He seemed so lonely and pathetic.'

'He's Don and I's mascot,' she said, the drink interfering with her grammar. But not even the drink could leave any doubt about her rancour.

'I thought he had personality,' said Phrynne.

'That and a lot more no doubt,' said Mrs Pascoe. 'But they pushed him out, all the same.'

'Out of what?'

'Cashiered, court-martialled, badges of rank stripped off, sword broken in half, muffled drums, the works.'

'Poor old man. I'm sure it was a miscarriage of justice.'

'That's because you don't know him.'

Mrs Pascoe looked as if she were waiting for Gerald to offer her another whisky.

'It's a thing he could never live down,' said Phrynne, brooding to herself, and tucking her legs beneath her. 'No wonder he's so queer if all the time it was a mistake.'

'I just told you it was not a mistake,' said Mrs Pascoe insolently.

'How can we possibly know?'

'*You* can't. *I* can. No one better.' She was at once aggressive and tearful.

'If you want to be paid,' cried Gerald, forcing himself in, 'make out your bill. Phrynne, come upstairs and pack.' If only he hadn't made her unpack between their walk and dinner.

Slowly Phrynne uncoiled and rose to her feet. She had no intention of either packing or departing, but nor was she going to argue, 'I shall need your help,' she said, softly. 'If I'm going to pack.'

In Mrs Pascoe there was another change. Now she looked terrified. 'Don't go. Please don't go. Not now. It's too late.'

Gerald confronted her. 'Too late for what?' he asked harshly.

Mrs Pascoe looked paler than ever. 'You said you wanted a car,' she faltered. 'You're too late.' Her voice trailed away.

Gerald took Phrynne by the arm. 'Come on up.'

Before they reached the door, Mrs Pascoe made a further attempt. 'You'll be all right if you stay. Really you will.' Her voice, normally somewhat strident, was so feeble that the bells obliterated it. Gerald observed that from somewhere she had produced the whisky bottle and was refilling her tumbler.

With Phrynne on his arm he went first to the stout front door. To his surprise it was neither locked nor bolted, but opened at a half-turn of the handle. Outside the building the whole sky was full of bells, the air an inferno of ringing.

He thought that for the first time Phrynne's face also seemed strained and crestfallen. 'They've been ringing too long,' she said, drawing close to him. 'I wish they'd stop.'

'We're packing and going. I needed to know whether we could get out this way. We must shut the door quietly.'

It creaked a bit on its hinges, and he hesitated with it half shut, uncertain whether to rush the creak or to ease it. Suddenly, something dark and shapeless, with its arm seeming to hold a black vesture over its head, flitted, all sharp angles, like a bat, down the narrow ill-lighted street, the sound of its passage audible to none. It was the first being that either of them had seen in the streets of Holihaven; and Gerald was acutely relieved that he alone had set eyes upon it. With his hand trembling, he shut the door much too sharply.

But no one could possibly have heard, although he stopped for a second outside the lounge. He could hear Mrs Pascoe now weeping hysterically; and again was glad that Phrynne was a step or two ahead of him. Upstairs the Commandant's door lay straight before them. They had to pass close beside the Japanese figure, in order to take the passage to the left of it.

But soon they were in their room, with the key turned in the big rim lock.

'Oh God,' cried Gerald, sinking on the double bed. 'It's pandemonium.' Not for the first time that evening he was instantly more frightened than ever by the unintended appositeness of his own words.

'It's pandemonium all right,' said Phrynne, almost calmly. 'And we're not going out in it.'

He was at a loss to divine how much she knew, guessed, or imagined; and any word of enlightenment from him might be inconceivably dangerous. But he was conscious of the strength of her resistance, and lacked the reserves to battle with it.

She was looking out of the window into the main street. 'We might *will* them to stop,' she suggested wearily.

Gerald was now far less frightened of the bells continuing than of their ceasing. But that they should go on ringing until day broke seemed hopelessly impossible.

Then one peal stopped. There could be no other explanation for the obvious diminution in sound.

'You see!' said Phrynne.

Gerald sat up straight on the side of the bed.

Almost at once further sections of sound subsided, quickly one after the other, until only a single peal was left, that which had begun the ringing. Then the single peal tapered off into a single bell. The single bell tolled on its own, disjointedly, five or six or seven times. Then it stopped, and there was nothing.

Gerald's head was a cave of echoes, mountingly muffled by the noisy current of his blood.

'Oh goodness,' said Phrynne, turning from the window and stretching her arms above her head. 'Let's go somewhere else tomorrow.' She began to take off her dress.

Sooner than usual they were in bed, and in one another's arms. Gerald had carefully not looked out of the window, and neither of them suggested that it should be opened, as they usually did.

'As it's a four-poster, shouldn't we draw the curtains?' asked Phrynne. 'And be really snug? After those damned bells?'

'We should suffocate.'

'They only drew the curtains when people were likely to pass through the room.'

'Darling, you're shivering. I think we *should* draw them."

'Lie still instead, and love me.'

But all his nerves were straining out into the silence. There was no sound of any kind, beyond the hotel or within it; not a creaking floorboard or a prowling cat or a distant owl. He had been afraid to look at his watch when the bells stopped, or since; the number of the dark hours before they could leave Holihaven weighed on him. The vision of the Commandant kneeling in the dark window was clear before his eyes, as if the intervening panelled walls were made of stage gauze; and the thing he had seen in the street darted on its angular way back and forth through memory.

Then passion began to open its petals within him, layer upon slow layer; like an illusionist's red flower which, without soil or sun or sap, grows as it is watched. The languor of tenderness began to fill the musty room with its texture and perfume. The transparent walls became again opaque, the old man's vaticinations mere obsession. The street must have been empty, as it was now; the eye deceived.

But perhaps rather it was the boundless sequacity of love that deceived, and most of all in the matter of the time which had passed since the bells stopped ringing; for suddenly Phrynne drew very close to him, and he heard steps in the thoroughfare outside, and a voice calling. These were loud steps, audible from afar even through the shut window; and the voice had the possessed stridency of the street evangelist.

'The dead are awake!'

Not even the thick bucolic accent, the guttural vibrato of emotion, could twist or mask the meaning. At first Gerald lay listening with all his body, and concentrating the more as the noise grew; then he sprang from the bed and ran to the window.

A burly, long-limbed man in a seaman's jersey was running down the street, coming clearly into view for a second at each lamp, and between them lapsing into a swaying lumpy wraith. As he shouted his joyous message, he crossed from side to side and waved his arms like a negro. By flashes, Gerald could see that his weatherworn face was transfigured.

'The dead are awake!'

Already, behind him, people were coming out of their houses, and descending from the rooms above shops. There were men, women, and children. Most of them were fully dressed, and must have been waiting in silence and darkness for the call; but a few were dishevelled in night attire or the first garments which had come to hand. Some formed themselves into groups, and advanced arm in arm, as if towards the conclusion of a Blackpool beano. More came singly, ecstatic and waving their arms above their heads, as the first man had done. All cried out, again and again, with no cohesion or harmony. 'The dead are awake! The dead are awake!'

Gerald became aware that Phrynne was standing behind him.

'The Commandant warned me,' he said brokenly. 'We should have gone.'

Phrynne shook her head and took his arm. 'Nowhere to go,' she said. But her voice was soft with fear, and her eyes blank. 'I don't expect they'll trouble *us*.'

Swiftly Gerald drew the thick plush curtains, leaving them in complete darkness. 'We'll sit it out,' he said, slightly histrionic in his fear. 'No matter what happens.'

He scrambled across to the switch. But when he pressed it, light did not come. 'The current's gone. We must get back into bed.'

'Gerald! Come and help me.' He remembered that she was curiously vulnerable in the dark. He found his way to her, and guided her to the bed.

'No more love,' she said ruefully and affectionately, her teeth chattering.

He kissed her lips with what gentleness the total night made possible.

'They were going towards the sea,' she said timidly.

'We must think of something else.'

But the noise was still growing. The whole community seemed to be passing down the street, yelling the same dreadful words again and again.

'Do you think we can?'

'Yes,' said Gerald. 'It's only until tomorrow.'

'They can't be actually dangerous,' said Phrynne. 'Or it would be stopped.'

'Yes, of course.'

By now, as always happens, the crowd had amalgamated their utterances and were beginning to shout in unison. They were like agitators bawling a slogan, or massed trouble-makers at a football match. But at the same time the noise was beginning to draw away. Gerald suspected that the entire population of the place was on the march.

Soon it was apparent that a processional route was being followed. The tumult could be heard winding about from quarter to quarter; sometimes drawing near, so that Gerald and Phrynne were once more seized by the first chill of panic, then again almost fading away. It was possibly this great variability in the volume of the sound which led Gerald to believe that there were distinct pauses in the massed shouting; periods when it was superseded by far, disorderly cheering. Certainly it began also to seem that the thing shouted had changed; but he could not make out the new cry, although unwillingly he strained to do so.

'It's extraordinary how frightened one can be,' said Phrynne, 'even when one is not directly menaced. It must prove that we all belong to one another, or whatever it is, after all.'

In many similar remarks they discussed the thing at one remove. Experience showed that this was better than not discussing it at all.

In the end there could be no doubt that the shouting had stopped, and that now the crowd was singing. It was no song that Gerald had ever heard, but something about the way it was sung convinced him that it was a hymn or psalm set to an out of date popular tune. Once more the crowd was approaching; this time steadily, but with strange, interminable slowness.

'What the hell are they doing now?' asked Gerald of the blackness, his nerves wound so tight that the foolish question was forced out of them.

Palpably the crowd had completed its peregrination, and was returning up the main street from the sea. The singers seemed to gasp and fluctuate, as if worn out with gay exercise, like children at a party. There was a steady undertow of scraping and scuffling. Time passed and more time.

Phrynne spoke. 'I believe they're *dancing.*'

She moved slightly, as if she thought of going to see.

'No, no,' said Gerald, and clutched her fiercely.

There was a tremendous concussion on the ground floor below them. The front door had been violently thrown back. They could hear the hotel filling with a stamping, singing mob.

Doors banged everywhere, and furniture was overturned, as the beatic throng surged and stumbled through the involved darkness of the old building. Glasses went and china and Birmingham brass warming pans. In a moment, Gerald heard the Japanese armour crash to the boards. Phrynne screamed. Then a mighty shoulder, made strong by the sea's assault, rammed at the panelling and their door was down.

'*The living and the dead dance together.*

Now's the time. Now's the place. Now's the weather.'

At last Gerald could make out the words.

The stresses in the song were heavily beaten down by much repetition.

Hand in hand, through the dim grey gap of the doorway, the dancers lumbered and shambled in, singing frenziedly and brokenly; ecstatic but exhausted. Through the stuffy blackness they swayed and shambled, more and more of them, until the room must have been packed tight with them.

Phrynne screamed again. 'The smell. Oh, God, the smell.'

It was the smell they had encountered on the beach; in the congested room, no longer merely offensive, but obscene, unspeakable.

Phrynne was hysterical. All self-control gone, she was scratching and tearing, and screaming again and again. Gerald tried to hold her, but one of the dancers struck him so hard in the darkness that she was jolted out of his arms. Instantly it seemed that she was no longer there at all.

The dancers were thronging everywhere, their limbs whirling, their lungs bursting with the rhythm of the song. It was difficult for Gerald even to call out. He tried to struggle after Phrynne, but immediately a blow from a massive elbow knocked him to the floor, an abyss of invisible trampling feet.

But soon the dancers were going again: not only from the room, but, it seemed, from the building also. Crushed and tormented though he was, Gerald could hear the song being resumed in the street, as the various frenzied groups debouched and reunited. Within, before long there was nothing but the chaos, the darkness, and the putrescent odour. Gerald felt so sick that he had to battle with unconsciousness. He could not think or move, despite the desperate need.

Then he struggled into a sitting position, and sank his head on the torn sheets of the bed. For an uncertain period he was insensible to everything: but in the end he heard steps approaching down the dark passage. His door was pushed back, and the Commandant entered gripping a lighted candle. He seemed to disregard the flow of hot wax which had already congealed on much of his knotted hand.

'She's safe. Small thanks to you.'

The Commandant stared icily at Gerald's undignified figure. Gerald tried to stand. He was terribly bruised, and so giddy that he wondered if this could be concussion. But relief rallied him.

'Is it thanks to *you?*'

'She was caught up in it. Dancing with the rest.' The Commandant's eyes glowed in the candlelight. The singing and the dancing had almost died away.

Still Gerald could do no more than sit upon the bed. His voice was low and indistinct, as if coming from outside his body. 'Were they ... were some of them ...'

The Commandant replied, more scornful than ever of his weakness. 'She was between two of them. Each had one of her hands.'

Gerald could not look at him. 'What did you do?' he asked in the same remote voice.

'I did what had to be done. I hope I was in time.' After the slightest possible pause he continued. 'You'll find her downstairs.'

'I'm grateful. Such a silly thing to say, but what else is there?'

'Can you walk?'

'I think so.'

'I'll light you down.' The Commandant's tone was as uncompromising as always.

There were two more candles in the lounge, and Phrynne, wearing a woman's belted overcoat which was not hers, sat between them, drinking. Mrs Pascoe, fully dressed but with eyes averted, pottered about the wreckage. It seemed hardly more than as if she were completing the task which earlier she had left unfinished.

'Darling, look at you!' Phrynne's words were still hysterical, but her voice was as gentle as it usually was.

Gerald, bruises and thoughts of concussion forgotten, dragged her into his arms. They embraced silently for a long time; then he looked into her eyes.

'Here I am,' she said, and looked away. 'Not to worry.'

Silently and unnoticed, the Commandant had already retreated.

Without returning his gaze, Phrynne finished her drink as she stood there. Gerald supposed that it was one of Mrs Pascoe's concoctions.

It was so dark where Mrs Pascoe was working that her labours could have been achieving little; but she said nothing to her visitors, nor they to her. At the door Phrynne unexpectedly stripped off the overcoat and threw it on a chair. Her nightdress was so torn that she stood almost naked. Dark though it was, Gerald saw Mrs Pascoe regarding Phrynne's pretty body with a stare of animosity.

'May we take one of the candles?' he said, normal standards reasserting themselves in him.

But Mrs Pascoe continued to stand silently staring; and they lighted themselves through the wilderness of broken furniture to the ruins of their bedroom. The Japanese figure was still prostrate, and the Commandant's door shut. And the smell had almost gone.

*   *   *

Even by seven o'clock the next morning surprisingly much had been done to restore order. But no one seemed to be about, and Gerald and Phrynne departed without a word.

In Wrack Street a milkman was delivering, but Gerald noticed that his cart bore the name of another town. A minute boy whom they encountered later on an obscure purposeful errand might, however, have been indigenous; and when they reached Station Road, they saw a small plot of land on which already men were silently at work with spades in their hands. They were as thick as flies on a wound, and as black. In the darkness of the previous evening, Gerald and Phrynne had missed the place. A board named it the New Municipal Cemetery.

In the mild light of an autumn morning the sight of the black and silent toilers was horrible; but Phrynne did not seem to find it so. On the contrary, her cheeks reddened and her soft mouth became fleetingly more voluptuous still.

She seemed to have forgotten Gerald, so that he was able to examine her closely for a moment. It was the first time he had done so since the night before. Then, once more, she became herself. In those previous seconds Gerald had become aware of something dividing them which neither of them would ever mention or ever forget.

My Adventure in Norfolk
A. J. Alan

I don't know how it is with you, but during February *my* wife generally says to me: 'Have you thought at all about what we are going to do for August?' And, of course, I say 'No,' and then she begins looking through the advertisements of bungalows to let.

Well, this happened last year, as usual, and she eventually produced one that looked possible. It said: 'Norfolk – Hickling Broad – Furnished Bungalow – Garden – Garage, Boathouse,' and all the rest of it—— Oh – *and* plate and linen. It also mentioned an exorbitant rent. I pointed out the bit about the rent, but my wife said: 'Yes, you'll have to go down and see the landlord, and get him to come down. They always do.' As a matter of fact, they always don't, but that's a detail.

Anyway, I wrote off to the landlord and asked if he could arrange for me to stay the night in the place to see what it was really like. He wrote back and said: 'Certainly,' and that he was engaging Mrs So-and-so to come in and 'oblige me', and make up the beds and so forth.

I tell you, we do things thoroughly in our family – I have to sleep in all the beds, and when I come home my wife counts the bruises and decides whether they will do or not.

At any rate, I arrived, in a blinding snowstorm, at about *the* most desolate spot on God's earth. I'd come to Potter Heigham by train, and been driven on – (it was a good five miles from the station). Fortunately, Mrs Selston, the old lady who was going to 'do' for me, was there, and she'd lighted a fire, and cooked me a steak, for which I was truly thankful.

I somehow think the cow, or whatever they get steaks off, had only died that morning. It was very – er – obstinate. While I dined, she talked to me. She *would* tell me all about an operation her husband had just had. *All* about it. It was almost a lecture on surgery. The steak was rather underdone, and it sort of made me feel I was illustrating her lecture. Anyway, she put me clean off my dinner, and then departed for the night.

I explored the bungalow and just had a look outside. It was, of course, very dark, but not snowing quite so hard. The garage stood about fifteen yards from the back door. I walked round it but didn't go in. I also went down to the edge of the broad, and verified the boathouse. The whole place looked as though it might be all right in the summertime, but just then it made one wonder why people ever wanted to go to the North Pole.

Anyhow, I went indoors, and settled down by the fire. You've no idea how quiet it was; even the water-fowl had taken a night off – at least, they weren't working.

At a few minutes to eleven I heard the first noise there'd been since Mrs What's-her-name – Selston – had cleared out. It was the sound of a car. If it had gone straight by I probably shouldn't have noticed it at all, only it didn't go straight by; it seemed to stop farther up the road, before it got to the house. Even that didn't made much impression. After all, cars *do* stop.

It must have been five or ten minutes before it was borne in on me that it hadn't gone on again. So I got up and looked out of the window. It had left off snowing, and there was a glare through the gate that showed that there were headlamps somewhere just out of sight. I thought I might as well stroll out and investigate.

I found a fair-sized limousine pulled up in the middle of the road about twenty yards short of my gate. The light was rather blinding, but when I got close to it I found a girl with the bonnet open, tinkering with the engine. Quite an attractive young female, from what one could see, but she was so muffled up in furs that it was rather hard to tell.

I said:

'Er – good evening – anything I can do?'

She said she didn't know what was the matter. The engine had just stopped, and wouldn't start again. And it *had*! It wouldn't even turn, either with the self-starter or the handle. The whole thing was awfully hot, and I asked her whether there was any water in the radiator. She didn't see why there shouldn't be, there always had been. This didn't strike me as entirely conclusive. I said, we'd better put some in, and see what happened. She said, why not use snow? But I thought not. There was an idea at the back of my mind that there was some reason why it was unwise to use melted snow, and it wasn't until I arrived with a bucketful that I remembered what it was. Of course – goitre.

When I got back to her she'd got the radiator cap off, and inserted what a Danish friend of mine calls a 'funeral'. We poured a little water in . . . Luckily I'd warned her to stand clear. The first tablespoonful that went in came straight out again, red-hot, and blew the 'funeral' sky-high. We waited a few minutes until things had cooled down a bit, but it was no go. As fast as we poured water in it simply ran out again into the road underneath. It was quite evident that she'd been driving with the radiator bone dry, and that her engine had seized right up.

I told her so. She said:

'Does that mean I've got to stop here all night?'

I explained that it wasn't as bad as all that; that is, if she cared to accept the hospitality of my poor roof (and it *was* a poor roof – it let the wet in). But she wouldn't hear of it. By the by, she didn't know the – er – circumstances, so it wasn't that. No, she wanted to leave the car where it was and go on on foot.

I said:

'Don't be silly, it's miles to anywhere.'

However, at that moment we heard a car coming along the road, the same way as she'd come. We could see its lights, too, although it was a very long way off. You know how flat Norfolk is – you can see a terrific distance.

I said:

'There's the way out of all your troubles. This thing, whatever it is, will give you a tow to the nearest garage, or at any rate a lift to some hotel.'

One would have expected her to show some relief, but she didn't. I began to wonder what she jolly well *did* want. She wouldn't let me help her to stop where she was, and she didn't seem anxious for anyone to help her to go anywhere else.

She was quite peculiar about it. She gripped hold of my arm, and said:

'What do you think this is that's coming?'

I said:

'I'm sure I don't know, being a stranger in these parts, but it sounds like a lorry full of milk cans.'

I offered to lay her sixpence about it (this was before the betting tax came in). She'd have had to pay, too, because it *was* a lorry full of milk cans. The driver had to pull up because there wasn't room to get by.

He got down and asked if there was anything he could do to help. We explained the situation. He said he was going to Norwich, and was quite ready to give her a tow if she wanted it. However, she wouldn't do that, and it was finally decided to shove her car into my garage for the night, to be sent for next day, and the lorry was to take her along to Norwich.

Well, I managed to find the key of the garage, and the lorry-driver – Williams, his name was – and I ran the car in and locked the door. This having been done – (ablative absolute) – I suggested that it was a very cold night. Williams agreed, and said he didn't mind if he did. So I took them both indoors and mixed them a stiff whisky and water each. There wasn't any soda. And, naturally, the whole thing had left *me* very cold, too. I hadn't an overcoat on.

Up to now I hadn't seriously considered the young woman. For one thing it had been dark, *and* there had been a seized engine to look at. Er – I'm afraid that's not a very gallant remark. What I mean is that to anyone with a mechanical mind a motor car in that condition is much more interesting than – er – well, it *is* very interesting – but why labour the point? However, in the sitting-room, in the lamplight, it was possible to get more of an idea. She was a little older than I'd thought, and her eyes were too close together.

Of course, she wasn't a – how shall I put it? Her manners weren't quite easy and she was careful with her English. *You* know. But that wasn't it. She treated us with a lack of friendliness which was – well, we'd done nothing to deserve it. There was a sort of vague hostility and suspicion, which seemed rather hard lines, considering. Also, she was so anxious to keep in the shadow that if I hadn't moved the lamp away she'd never have got near the fire at all.

And the way she hurried the wretched Williams over his drink was quite distressing; and foolish, too, as *he* was going to drive, but that was her – funnel. When he'd gone out to start up his engine I asked her if she was all right for money, and she apparently was. Then they started off, and I shut up the place and went upstairs.

There happened to be a local guide-book in my bedroom, with maps in it. I looked at these and couldn't help wondering where the girl in the car had come from; I mean my road seemed so very unimportant. The sort of road one might use if one wanted to avoid people. If one were driving a stolen car, for instance. This was quite a thrilling idea. I thought it might be worth while having another look at the car. So I once more unhooked the key from the kitchen dresser and sallied forth into the snow. It was as black as pitch, and so still that my candle hardly flickered. It wasn't a large garage, and the car nearly filled it. By the by, we'd backed it in so as to make it easier to tow it out again.

The engine I'd already seen, so I squeezed past along the wall and opened the door in the body part of the car. At least, I only turned the handle, and the door was pushed open from the inside and – something – fell out on me. It pushed me quite hard, and wedged me against the wall. It also knocked the candle out of my hand and left me in the dark – which was a bit of a nuisance. I wondered what on earth the thing was – barging into me like that – so I felt it, rather gingerly, and found it was a man – a dead man – with a moustache. He'd evidently been sitting propped up against the door. I managed to put him back, as decorously as possible, and shut the door again.

After a lot of grovelling about under the car I found the candle and lighted it, and opened the opposite door and switched on the little lamp in the roof – and then – oo-er!

Of course, I had to make some sort of examination. He was an extremely tall and thin individual. He must have been well over six feet three. He was dark and very cadaverous looking. In fact, I don't suppose he'd ever looked so cadaverous in his life. He was wearing a trench coat.

It wasn't difficult to tell what he'd died of. He'd been shot through the back. I found the hole just under the right scrofula, or scalpel – what is shoulder-blade, anyway? Oh, clavicle – stupid of me – well, that's where it was, and the bullet had evidently gone through into the lung. I say 'evidently', and leave it at that.

There were no papers in his pockets, and no tailor's name on his clothes, but there was a note-case, with nine pounds in it. Altogether a most unpleasant business. Of course, it doesn't do to question the workings of Providence, but one couldn't help wishing it hadn't happened. It was just a little mysterious, too – er – who had killed him? It wasn't likely that the girl had or she wouldn't have been joy-riding about the country with him; and if someone else had murdered him why hadn't she mentioned it? Anyway, she hadn't and she'd gone, so one couldn't do anything for the time being. No telephone, of course. I just locked up the garage and went to bed. That was two o'clock.

Next morning I woke early, for some reason or other, and it occurred to me as a good idea to go and have a look at things – by daylight, and before Mrs Selston turned up. So I did. The first thing that struck me was that it had snowed heavily during the night, because there were no wheel tracks or footprints, and the second was that I'd left the key in the garage door. I opened it and went in. The place was completely empty. No car, no body, no nothing. There was a patch of grease on the floor where I'd dropped the candle, otherwise there was nothing to show I'd been there before. One of two things must have happened: either some people had come along during the night and taken the car away, or else I'd fallen asleep in front of the fire and dreamt the whole thing.

Then I remembered the whisky glasses.

They should still be in the sitting-room. I went back to look, and they were, all three of them. So it *hadn't* been a dream and the car *had* been fetched away, but they must have been jolly quiet over it.

The girl had left her glass on the mantelpiece, and it showed several very clearly defined finger-marks. Some were mine, naturally, because I'd fetched the glass from the kitchen and poured out the drink for her, but hers, her finger-marks, were clean, and mine were oily, so it was quite easy to tell them apart. It isn't necessary to point out that this glass was very important. There'd evidently been a murder, or something of that kind, and the girl must have known all about it, even if she hadn't actually done it herself, so anything she had left in the way of evidence ought to be handed over to the police; and this was all she *had* left. So I packed it up with meticulous care in an old biscuit box out of the larder.

When Mrs Selston came, I settled up with her and came back to town. Oh, I called on the landlord on the way and told him I'd 'let him know' about the bungalow. Then I caught my train, and in due course drove straight to Scotland Yard. I went up and saw my friend there. I produced the glass and asked him if his people could identify the marks. He said, 'Probably not,' but he sent it down to the fingerprint department and asked me where it came from. I said: 'Never you mind; let's have the identification first.' He said: 'All right.'

They're awfully quick, these people – the clerk was back in three minutes with a file of papers. They knew the girl all right. They told me her name and showed me her photograph; not flattering. Quite an adventurous lady, from all accounts. In the early part of her career she'd done time twice for shoplifting, chiefly in the book department. Then she'd what they call 'taken up with' a member of one of those race gangs one sometimes hears about.

My pal went on to say that there'd been a fight between two of these gangs, in the course of which her friend had got shot. She'd managed to get him away in a car, but it had broken down somewhere in Norfolk. So she'd left it and the dead man in someone's garage, and had started off for Norwich in a lorry. Only she never got there. On the way the lorry had skidded, and both she and the driver – a fellow called Williams – had been thrown out, and they'd rammed their heads against a brick wall, which everyone knows is a fatal thing to do. At least, it was in their case.

I said: 'Look here, it's all very well, but you simply can't know all this; there hasn't been time – it only happened last night.'

He said: 'Last night be blowed! It all happened in February 1919. The people you've described have been dead for years.'

I said: 'Oh!'

And to think that I might have stuck to that nine pounds!

The Leaden Ring
S. Baring-Gould

'It is not possible, Julia. I cannot conceive how the idea of attending the county ball can have entered your head after what has happened. Poor young Hattersley's dreadful death suffices to stop that.'

'But, Aunt, Mr Hattersley is no relation of ours.'

'No relation – but you know that the poor fellow would not have shot himself if it had not been for you.'

'Oh, Aunt Elizabeth, how can you say so, when the verdict was that he committed suicide when in an unsound condition of mind? How could I help his blowing out his brains, when those brains were deranged?'

'Julia, do not talk like this. If he did go off his head, it was you who upset him by first drawing him on, leading him to believe that you liked him, and then throwing him over as soon as the Hon. James Lawlor appeared on the *tapis*. Consider: what will people say if you go to the assembly?'

'What will they say if I do not go? They will immediately set it down to my caring deeply for James Hattersley, and they will think that there was some sort of engagement.'

'They are not likely to suppose that. But really, Julia, you were for a while all smiles and encouragement. Tell me, now, did Mr Hattersley propose to you?'

'Well – yes, he did, and I refused him.'

'And then he went and shot himself in despair. Julia, you cannot with any face go to the ball.'

'Nobody knows that he proposed. And precisely because I do go everyone will conclude that he did not propose. I do not wish it to be supposed that he did.'

'His family, of course, must have been aware. They will see your name among those present at the assembly.'

'Aunt, they are in too great trouble to look at the paper to see who were at the dance.'

'His terrible death lies at your door. How you can have the heart, Julia ...'

'I don't see it. Of course, I feel it. I am awfully sorry, and awfully sorry for his father, the admiral. I cannot bring him to life again. I wish that when I rejected him he had gone and done as did Joe Pomeroy, marry one of his landlady's daughters.'

'There, Julia, is another of your deliquencies. You lured on young Pomeroy till he proposed, then you refused him, and in a fit of vexation and mortified vanity he married a girl greatly beneath him in social position. If the *ménage* proves a failure you will have it on your conscience that you have wrecked his life and perhaps hers as well.'

'I cannot throw myself away as a charity to save this man or that from doing a foolish thing.'

'What I complain of, Julia, is that you encouraged young Mr Pomeroy till Mr Hattersley appeared, whom you thought more eligible, and then you tossed him aside; and you did precisely the same with James Hattersley as soon as you came to know Mr Lawlor. After all, Julia, I am not so sure that Mr Pomeroy has not chosen the better part. The girl, I dare say, is simple, fresh, and affectionate.'

'Your implication is not complimentary, Aunt Elizabeth.'

'My dear, I have no patience with the young lady of the present day, who is shallow, self-willed, and indifferent to the feelings and happiness of others, who craves excitement and pleasures, and desires nothing that is useful and good. Where now will you see a girl like Viola's sister, who let concealment, like a worm i' the bud, feed on her damask cheek? Nowadays a girl lays herself at the feet of a man if she likes him, turns herself inside out to let him and all the world read her heart.'

'I have no relish to be like Viola's sister, and have my story – a blank. I never grovelled at the feet of Joe Pomeroy or James Hattersley.'

'No, but you led each to consider himself the favoured one till he proposed, and then you refused him. It was like smiling at a man and then stabbing him to the heart.'

'Well – I don't want people to think that James Hattersley cared for me – I certainly never cared for him – nor that he proposed; so I shall go to the ball.'

Julia Demant was an orphan. She had been kept at school till she was eighteen, and then had been removed just at the age when a girl begins to take an interest in her studies, and not to regard them as drudgery. On her removal she had cast away all that she had acquired, and had been plunged into the whirl of Society. Then suddenly her father died – she had lost her mother some years before – and she went to live with her aunt, Miss Flemming. Julia had inherited a sum of about five hundred pounds a year, and would probably come in for a good estate and funds as well on the death of her aunt. She had been

flattered as a girl at home, and at school as a beauty, and she certainly
thought no small bones of herself.

Miss Flemming was an elderly lady with a sharp tongue, very
outspoken, and very decided in her opinions; but her action was weak,
and Julia soon discovered that she could bend the aunt to do anything
she willed, though she could not modify or alter her opinions.

In the matter of Joe Pomeroy and James Hattersley, it was as Miss
Flemming had said. Julia had encouraged Mr Pomeroy, and had only
cast him off because she thought better of the suit of Mr Hattersley, son
of an admiral of that name. She had seen a good deal of young
Hattersley, had given him every encouragement, had so entangled him,
that he was madly in love with her; and then, when she came to know
the Hon. James Lawlor, and saw that he was fascinated, she rejected
Hattersley with the consequences alluded to in the conversation above
given.

Julia was particularly anxious to be present at the county ball, for
she had been already booked by Mr Lawlor for several dances, and she
was quite resolved to make an attempt to bring him to a declaration.

On the evening of the ball Miss Flemming and Julia entered the
carriage. The aunt had given way, as was her wont, but under protest.

For about ten minutes neither spoke, and then Miss Flemming said,
'Well, you know my feelings about this dance. I do not approve. I
distinctly disapprove. I do not consider your going to the ball in good
taste, or, as you would put it, in good form. Poor young Hattersley ...'

'Oh, dear Aunt, do let us put young Hattersley aside. He was buried
with the regular forms, I suppose?'

'Yes, Julia.'

'Then the rector accepted the verdict of the jury at the inquest. Why
should not we? A man who is unsound in his mind is not responsible for
his actions.'

'I suppose not.'

'Much less, then, I who live ten miles away.'

'I do not say that you are responsible for his death, but for the
condition of mind that led him to do the dreadful deed. Really, Julia,
you are one of those into whose head or heart only by a surgical
operation could the thought be introduced that you could be in the
wrong. A hypodermic syringe would be too weak an instrument to effect
such a radical change in you. Everyone else may be in the wrong, you –
never. As for me, I cannot get young Hattersley out of my head.'

'And I,' retorted Julia with asperity, for her aunt's words had stung
her – 'I, for my part, do not give him a thought.'

She had hardly spoken the words before a chill wind began to pass
round her. She drew the Barege shawl that was over her bare shoulders
closer about her, and said, 'Auntie! is the glass down on your side?'

'No, Julia; why do you ask?'

'There is such a draught.'

'Draught! – I do not feel one; perhaps the window on your side hitches.'

'Indeed, that is all right. It is blowing harder and is deadly cold. Can one of the front panes be broken?'

'No. Rogers would have told me had that been the case. Besides, I can see that they are sound.'

The wind of which Julia complained swirled and whistled about her. It increased in force; it plucked at her shawl and slewed it about her throat; it tore at the lace on her dress. It snatched at her hair, it wrenched it away from the pins, the combs that held it in place; one long tress was lashed across the face of Miss Flemming. Then the hair, completely released, eddied up above the girl's head, and the next moment was carried as a drift before her, blinding her. Then – a sudden explosion, as though a gun had been fired into her ear; and with a scream of terror she sank back among the cushions. Miss Flemming, in great alarm, pulled the check-string, and the carriage stopped. The footman descended from the box and came to the side. The old lady drew down the window and said: 'Oh! Phillips, bring the lamp. Something has happened to Miss Demant.'

The man obeyed, and sent a flood of light into the carriage. Julia was lying back, white and senseless. Her hair was scattered over her face, neck, and shoulders; the flowers that had been stuck in it, the pins that had fastened it in place, the pads that had given shape to the convolutions lay strewn, some on her lap, some in the rug at the bottom of the carriage.

'Phillips!' ordered the old lady in great agitation, 'tell Rogers to turn the horses and drive home at once; and you run as fast you can for Dr Crate.'

A few minutes after the carriage was again in motion, Julia revived. Her aunt was chafing her hand.

'Oh, Aunt!' she said, 'are all the glasses broken?'

'Broken – what glasses?'

'Those of the carriage – with the explosion.'

'Explosion, my dear!'

'Yes. That gun which was discharged. It stunned me. Were you hurt?'

'I heard no gun – no explosion.'

'But I did. It was as though a bullet had been discharged into my brain. I wonder that I escaped. Who can have fired at us?'

'My dear, no one fired. I heard nothing. I know what it was. I had the same experience many years ago. I slept in a damp bed, and awoke stone deaf in my right ear. I remained so for three weeks. But one night when I was at a ball and was dancing, all at once I heard a report as of a pistol in my right ear, and immediately heard quite clearly again. It was wax.'

'But, Aunt Elizabeth, I have not been deaf.'

'You have not noticed that you were deaf.'

'Oh! but look at my hair; it was that wind that blew it about.'

'You are labouring under a delusion, Julia. There was no wind.'

'But look – feel how my hair is down.'

'That has been done by the motion of the carriage. There are many ruts in the road.'

They reached home, and Julia, feeling sick, frightened and bewildered, retired to bed. Dr Crate arrived, said that she was hysterical, and ordered something to soothe her nerves. Julia was not convinced. The explanation offered by Miss Flemming did not satisfy her. That she was a victim to hysteria she did not in the least believe. Neither her aunt, nor the coachman, nor Phillips had heard the discharge of a gun. As to the rushing wind, Julia was satisfied that she had experienced it. The lace was ripped, as by a hand, from her dress, and the shawl was twisted about her throat; besides, her hair had not been so slightly arranged that the jolting of the carriage would completely disarrange it. She was vastly perplexed over what she had undergone. She thought and thought, but could get no nearer to a solution of the mystery.

Next day, as she was almost herself again, she rose and went about as usual.

In the afternoon the Hon. James Lawlor called and asked after Miss Flemming. The butler replied that his mistress was out making calls, but that Miss Demant was at home, and he believed was on the terrace. Mr Lawlor at once asked to see her.

He did not find Julia in the parlour or on the terrace, but in a lower garden to which she had descended to feed the goldfish in the pond.

'Oh! Miss Demant,' said he, 'I was so disappointed not to see you at the ball last night.'

'I was very unwell; I had a fainting fit and could not go.'

'It threw a damp on our spirits – that is to say, on mine. I had you booked for several dances.'

'You were able to give them to others.'

'But that was not the same to me. I did an act of charity and self-denial. I danced instead with the ugly Miss Burgons and with Miss Pounding, and that was like dragging about a sack of potatoes. I believe it would have been a jolly evening, but for that shocking affair of young Hattersley which kept some of the better sort away. I mean those who knew the Hattersleys. Of course, for me that did not matter, we were not acquainted. I never even spoke with the fellow. You knew him, I

believe? I heard some people say so, and that you had not come because
of him. The supper, for a subscription ball, was not atrociously bad.'

'What did they say of me?'

'Oh! – if you will know – that you did not attend the ball because
you liked him very much, and were awfully cut up.'

'I – I! What a shame that people should talk! I never cared a rush for
him. He was nice enough in his way, not a bounder, but tolerable as
young men go.'

Mr Lawlor laughed. 'I should not relish to have such a qualified
estimate made of me.'

'Nor need you. You are interesting. He became so only when he had
shot himself. It will be by this alone that he will be remembered.'

'But there is no smoke without fire. Did he like you – much?'

'Dear Mr Lawlor, I am not a clairvoyante, and never was able to see
into the brains or hearts of people – least of all of young men. Perhaps it
is fortunate for me that I cannot.'

'One lady told me that he had proposed to you.'

'Who was that? The potato-sack?'

'I will not give her name. Is there any truth in it? Did he?'

'No.'

At the moment she spoke there sounded in her ear a whistle of wind,
and she felt a current like a cord of ice creep round her throat,
increasing in force and compression; her hat was blown off, and next
instant a detonation rang through her head as though a gun had been
fired into her ear. She uttered a cry and sank upon the ground.

James Lawlor was bewildered. His first impulse was to run to the
house for assistance; then he considered that he could not leave her lying
on the wet soil, and he stooped to raise her in his arms and to carry her
within. In novels young men perform such a feat without difficulty; but
in fact they are not able to do it, especially when the girl is tall and big-
boned. Moreover, one in a faint is a dead weight. Lawlor staggered
under his burden to the steps. It was as much as he could perform to
carry her up to the terrace, and there he placed her on a seat. Panting,
and with his muscles quivering after the strain, he hastened to the
drawing-room, rang the bell, and when the butler appeared, he gasped:
'Miss Demant has fainted; you and I and the footman must carry her
within.'

'She fainted last night in the carriage,' said the butler.

When Julia came to her senses, she was in bed attended by the
housekeeper and her maid. A few moments later Miss Flemming
arrived.

'Oh, Aunt! I have heard it again.'

'Heard what, dear?'

'The discharge of a gun.'

'It is nothing but wax,' said the old lady. 'I will drop a little sweet-oil into your ear, and then have it syringed with warm water.'

'I want to tell you something – in private.'

Miss Flemming signed to the servants to withdraw.

'Aunt,' said the girl, 'I must say something. This is the second time that this has happened. I am sure it is significant. James Lawlor was with me in the sunken garden, and he began to speak about James Hattersley. You know it was when we were talking about him last night that I heard that awful noise. It was precisely as if a gun had been discharged into my ear. I felt as if all the nerves and tissues of my head were being torn, and all the bones of my skull shattered – just what Mr Hattersley must have undergone when he pulled the trigger. It was an agony for a moment perhaps, but it felt as if it lasted an hour. Mr Lawlor had asked me point blank if James Hattersley had proposed to me, and I said, "No." I was perfectly justified in so answering, because he had no right to ask me such a question. It was an impertinence on his part, and I answered him shortly and sharply with a negative.

'But actually James Hattersley proposed twice to me. He would not accept a first refusal, but came next day bothering me again, and I was pretty curt with him. He made some remarks that were rude about how I had treated him, and which I will not repeat, and as he left, in a state of great agitation, he said, "Julia, I vow that you shall not forget this, and you shall belong to no one but me, alive or dead." I considered this great nonsense, and did not accord it another thought. But, really, these terrible annoyances, this wind and the bursts of noise, do seem to me to come from him. It is just as though he felt a malignant delight in distressing me, now that he is dead. I should like to defy him, and I will do it if I can, but I cannot bear more of these experiences – they will kill me.'

Several days elapsed.

Mr Lawlor called repeatedly to enquire, but a week passed before Julia was sufficiently recovered to receive him, and then the visit was one of courtesy and of sympathy, and the conversation turned upon her health, and on indifferent themes.

But some few days later it was otherwise. She was in the conservatory alone, pretty much herself again, when Mr Lawlor was announced.

Physically she had recovered, or believed that she had, but her nerves had actually received a severe shock. She had made up her mind that the phenomena of the circling wind and the explosion were in some mysterious manner connected with Hattersley.

She bitterly resented this, but she was in mortal terror of a recurrence; and she felt no compunction for her treatment of the unfortunate young man, but rather a sense of deep resentment against him. If he were dead, why did he not lie quiet and cease from vexing her?

To be a martyr was to her no gratification, for hers was not a martyrdom that provoked sympathy, and which could make her interesting.

She had hitherto supposed that when a man died there was an end of him; his condition was determined for good or for ill. But that a disembodied spirit should hover about and make itself a nuisance to the living, had never entered into her calculations.

'Julia – if I may be allowed so to call you——' began Mr Lawlor, 'I have brought you a bouquet of flowers. Will you accept them?'

'Oh!' she said, as he handed the bunch to her, 'how kind of you. At this time of the year they are so rare, and Aunt's gardener is so miserly that he will spare me none for my room but some miserable bits of geranium. It is too bad of you wasting your money like this upon me.'

'It is no waste, if it affords you pleasure.'

'It is a pleasure. I dearly love flowers.'

'To give you pleasure,' said Mr Lawlor, 'is the great object of my life. If I could assure you happiness – if you would allow me to hope – to seize this opportunity, now that we are alone together ...'

He drew near and caught her hand. His features were agitated, his lips trembled, there was earnestness in his eyes.

At once a cold blast touched Julia and began to circle about her and to flutter her hair. She trembled and drew back. That paralysing experience was about to be renewed. She turned deadly white, and put her hand to her right ear. 'Oh, James! James!' she gasped. 'Do not, pray do not speak what you want to say, or I shall faint. It is coming on. I am not yet well enough to hear it. Write to me and I will answer. For pity's sake do not speak it.' Then she sank upon a seat – and at that moment her aunt entered the conservatory.

On the following day a note was put into her hand, containing a formal proposal from the Hon. James Lawlor; and by return of post Julia answered with an acceptance.

There was no reason whatever why the engagement should be long; and the only alternative mooted was whether the wedding should take place before or after Easter. Finally, it was settled that it should be celebrated on Shrove Tuesday. This left a short time for the necessary preparations, Miss Flemming would have to go to town with her niece concerning a trousseau, and a trousseau is not turned out rapidly any more than an armed cruiser.

There is usually a certain period allowed to young people who have become engaged to see much of each other, to get better acquainted with one another, to build their castles in the air, and to indulge in little passages of affection, vulgarly called 'spooning'. But in this case the spooning had to be curtailed and postponed.

At the outset, when alone with James, Julia was nervous. She feared a recurrence of those phenomena that so affected her. But, although every now and then the wind curled and soughed about her, it was not violent, nor was it chilling; and she came to regard it as a wail of discomfiture. Moreover, there was no recurrence of the detonation, and she fondly hoped that with her marriage the vexation would completely cease.

In her heart was deep down a sense of exultation. She was defying James Hattersley and setting his prediction at naught. She was not in love with Mr Lawlor; she liked him, in her cold manner, and was not insensible to the social advantage that would be hers when she became the Honourable Mrs Lawlor.

The day of the wedding arrived. Happily it was fine. 'Blessed is the bride the sun shines on,' said the cheery Miss Flemming; 'an omen, I trust, of a bright and unruffled life in your new condition.'

All the neighbourhood was present at the church. Miss Flemming had many friends. Mr Lawlor had fewer present, as he belonged to a distant county. The church path had been laid with red cloth, the church decorated with flowers, and a choir was present to twitter 'The voice that breathed o'er Eden'.

The rector stood by the altar, and two cushions had been laid at the chancel steps. The rector was to be assisted by an uncle of the bridegroom who was in Holy orders; the rector, being old-fashioned, had drawn on pale grey kid gloves.

First arrived the bridegroom with his best man, and stood in a nervous condition balancing himself first on one foot, then on the other, waiting, observed by all eyes.

Next entered the procession of the bride, attended by her maids, to the 'Wedding March' in *Lohengrin*, on a wheezy organ. Then Julia and her intended took their places at the chancel step for the performance of the first portion of the ceremony, and the two clergy descended to them from the altar.

'Wilt thou have this woman to thy wedded wife?'

'I will.'

'Wilt thou have this man to thy wedded husband?'

'I will.'

'I, James, take thee, Julia, to my wedded wife, to have and to hold ...' and so on.

As the words were being spoken, a cold rush of air passed over the clasped hands, numbing them, and began to creep round the bride, and to flutter her veil. She set her lips and knitted her brows. In a few moments she would be beyond the reach of these manifestations.

When it came to her turn to speak, she began firmly: 'I, Julia, take thee, James ...' but as she proceeded the wind became fierce; it raged about her, it caught her veil on one side and buffeted her cheek, it switched the veil about her throat, as though strangling her with a drift of snow contracting into ice. But she persevered to the end.

Then James Lawlor produced the ring, and was about to place it on her finger with the prescribed words: 'With this ring I thee wed ...' when a report rang in her ear, followed by a heaving of her skull, as though the bones were being burst asunder, and she sank unconscious on the chancel step.

In the midst of profound commotion, she was raised and conveyed to the vestry, followed by James Lawlor, trembling and pale. He had slipped the ring back into his waistcoat pocket. Dr Crate, who was present, hastened to offer his professional assistance.

In the vestry Julia rested in a Glastonbury chair, white and still, with her hands resting in her lap. And to the amazement of those present, it was seen that on the third finger of her left hand was a leaden ring, rude and solid as though fashioned out of a bullet. Restoratives were applied, but fully a quarter of an hour elapsed before Julia opened her eyes, and a little colour returned to her lips and cheek. But, as she raised her hands to her brow to wipe away the damp that had formed on it, her eye caught sight of the leaden ring, and with a cry of horror she sank again into insensibility.

The congregation slowly left the church, awestruck, whispering, asking questions, receiving no satisfactory answers, forming surmises all incorrect.

'I am very much afraid, Mr Lawlor,' said the rector, 'that it will be impossible to proceed with the service today; it must be postponed till Miss Demant is in a condition to conclude her part, and to sign the register. I do not see how it can be gone on with today. She is quite unequal to the effort.'

The carriage which was to have conveyed the couple to Miss Flemming's house, and then, later, to have taken them to the station for their honeymoon, the horses decorated with white rosettes, the whip adorned with a white bow, had now to convey Julia, hardly conscious, supported by her aunt, to her home.

No rice could be thrown. The bell-ringers, prepared to give a joyous peal, were constrained to depart.

The reception at Miss Flemming's was postponed. No one thought of attending. The cakes, the ices, were consumed in the kitchen.

The bridegroom, bewildered, almost frantic, ran hither and thither, not knowing what to do, what to say.

Julia lay as a stone for fully two hours; and when she came to herself could not speak. When conscious, she raised her left hand, looked on the leaden ring, and sank back into senselessness.

Not till late in the evening was she sufficiently recovered to speak, and then she begged her aunt, who had remained by her bed without stirring, to dismiss attendants. She desired to speak with her alone. When no one was in the room with her, save Miss Flemming, she said in a whisper: 'Oh, Aunt Elizabeth! Oh, Auntie! Such an awful thing has happened. I can never marry Mr Lawlor, never. I have married James Hattersley; I am a dead man's wife. At the time that James Lawlor was making the responses, I heard a piping voice in my ear, an unearthly voice, saying the same words. When I said: "I, Julia, take you, James, to my wedded husband" – you know Mr Hattersley is James as well as Mr Lawlor – then the words applied to him as much or as well as to the other. And then, when it came to the giving of the ring, there was the explosion in my ear, as before – and the leaden ring was forced on to my finger, and not James Lawlor's golden ring. It is of no use my resisting any more. I am a dead man's wife, and I cannot marry James Lawlor.'

Some years have elapsed since that disastrous day and that incomplete marriage.

Miss Demant is Miss Demant still, and she has never been able to remove the leaden ring from the third finger of her left hand. Whenever the attempt has been made, either to disengage it by drawing it off or by cutting through it, there has ensued that terrifying discharge as of a gun into her ear, causing insensibility. The prostration that has followed, the terror it has inspired, have so affected her nerves, that she has desisted from every attempt to rid herself of the ring.

She invariably wears a glove on her left hand, and it is bulged over the third finger, where lies the leaden ring.

She is not a happy woman, although her aunt is dead and has left her a handsome estate. She has not got many acquaintances. She has no friends; for her temper is unamiable, and her tongue is bitter. She supposes that the world, as far as she knows it, is in league against her.

Towards the memory of James Hattersley she entertains a deadly hate. If an incantation could lay his spirit, if prayer could give him repose, she would have recourse to none of these expedients, even though they might relieve her, so bitter is her resentment. And she harbours a silent wrath against Providence for allowing the dead to walk and to molest the living.

The Bus Conductor

E. F. Benson

My friend, Hugh Grainger, and I had just returned from a two days' visit to the country, where we had been staying in a house of sinister repute which was supposed to be haunted by ghosts of a peculiarly fearsome and truculent sort. The house itself was all that such a house should be, Jacobean and oak-panelled, with long dark passages and high vaulted rooms. It stood also, very remote, and was encompassed by a wood of sombre pines that muttered and whispered in the dark, and all the time that we were there a south-westerly gale with torrents of scolding rain had prevailed, so that by day and night weird noises moaned and fluted in the chimneys, a company of uneasy spirits held colloquy among the trees, and sudden tattooes and tappings beckoned from the window panes. But in spite of these surroundings, which were sufficient in themselves, one would almost say, to spontaneously generate occult phenomena, nothing of any description had occurred. I am bound to add, also, that my own state of mind was peculiarly well adapted to receive or even to invent the sights and sounds we had gone to seek, for I was, I confess, during the whole time that we were there, in a state of abject apprehension, and lay awake both nights through hours of terrified unrest, afraid of the dark, yet more afraid of what a lighted candle might show me.

Hugh Grainger, on the evening after our return to town, had dined with me, and after dinner our conversation, as was natural, soon came back to these entrancing topics.

'But why you go ghost-seeking I cannot imagine,' he said, 'because your teeth were chattering and your eyes starting out of your head all the time you were there, from sheer fright. Or do you like being frightened?'

Hugh, though generally intelligent, is dense in certain ways; this is one of them.

'Why, of course I like being frightened,' I said. 'I want to be made to creep and creep and creep. Fear is the most absorbing and luxurious of emotions. One forgets all else if one is afraid.'

'Well, the fact that neither of us saw anything,' he said, 'confirms what I have always believed.'

'And what have you always believed?'

'That these phenomena are purely objective, not subjective, and that one's state of mind has nothing to do with the perception that perceives them, nor have circumstances or surroundings anything to do with them either. Look at Osburton. It has had the reputation of being a haunted house for years, and it certainly has all the accessories of one. Look at yourself, too, with all your nerves on edge, afraid to look round or light a candle for fear of seeing something! Surely there was the right man in the right place then, if ghosts are subjective.'

He got up and lit a cigarette, and looking at him – Hugh is about six feet high, and as broad as he is long – I felt a retort on my lips, for I could not help my mind going back to a certain period in his life, when, from some cause which, as far as I knew, he had never told anybody, he had become a mere quivering mass of disordered nerves. Oddly enough, at the same moment and for the first time, he began to speak of it himself.

'You may reply that it was not worth my while to go either,' he said, 'because I was so clearly the wrong man in the wrong place. But I wasn't. You for all your apprehensions and expectancy have never seen a ghost. But I have, though I am the last person in the world you would have thought likely to do so, and, though my nerves are steady enough again now, it knocked me all to bits.'

He sat down again in his chair.

'No doubt you remember my going to bits,' he said, 'and since I believe that I am sound again now, I should rather like to tell you about it. But before I couldn't; I couldn't speak of it at all to anybody. Yet there ought to have been nothing frightening about it; what I saw was certainly a most useful and friendly ghost. But it came from the shaded side of things; it looked suddenly out of the night and the mystery with which life is surrounded.

'I want first to tell you quite shortly my theory about ghost-seeing,' he continued, 'and I can explain it best by a simile, an image. Imagine then that you and I and everybody in the world are like people whose eye is directly opposite a little tiny hole in a sheet of cardboard which is continually shifting and revolving and moving about. Back to back with that sheet of cardboard is another, which also, by laws of its own, is in perpetual but independent motion. In it, too, there is another hole, and when, fortuitously it would seem, these two holes, the one through which we are always looking, and the other in the spiritual plane, come opposite one another, we see through, and then only do the sights and sounds of the spiritual world become visible or audible to us. With most people these holes never come opposite each other during their life. But at the hour oi death they do, and then they remain stationary. That, I fancy, is how we "pass over".

'Now, in some natures, these holes are comparatively large, and are constantly coming into opposition. Clairvoyants, mediums, are like that. But, as far as I knew, I had no clairvoyant or mediumistic powers at all. I therefore am the sort of person who long ago made up his mind that he never would see a ghost. It was, so to speak, an incalculable chance that my minute spyhole should come into opposition with the other. But it did; and it knocked me out of time.'

I had heard some such theory before, and though Hugh put it rather picturesquely, there was nothing in the least convincing or practical about it. It might be so, or again it might not.

'I hope your ghost was more original than your theory,' said I, in order to bring him to the point.

'Yes, I think it was. You shall judge.'

I put on more coal and poked up the fire. Hugh has got, so I have always considered, a great talent for telling stories, and that sense of drama which is so necessary for the narrator. Indeed before now, I have suggested to him that he should take this up as a profession, sit by the fountain in Piccadilly Circus, when times are, as usual, bad, and tell stories to the passers-by in the street. Arabian fashion, for reward. The most part of mankind, I am aware, do not like long stories, but to the few, among whom I number myself, who really like to listen to lengthy accounts of experiences, Hugh is an ideal narrator. I do not care for his theories, or for his similes, but when it comes to facts, to things that happened, I like him to be lengthy.

'Go on, please, and slowly,' I said. 'Brevity may be the soul of wit, but it is the ruin of story-telling. I want to hear when and where and how it all was, and what you had for lunch and where you had dined and what——'

Hugh began:

'It was June 24th, just eighteenth months ago,' he said. 'I had let my flat, you may remember, and came up from the country to stay with you for a week. We had dined alone here——'

I could not help interrupting.

'Did you see the ghost here?' I asked. 'In this square little box of a house in a modern street?'

'I was in the house when I saw it.'

I hugged myself in silence.

'We had dined alone here in Graeme Street,' he said, 'and after dinner I went out to some party, and you stopped at home. At dinner your man did not wait, and when I asked where he was, you told me he was ill, and, I thought, changed the subjected rather abruptly. You gave me your latch-key when I went out, and on coming back, I found you had gone to bed. There were, however, several letters for me, which required answers. I wrote them there and then, and posted them at the pillar-box opposite. So I suppose it was rather late when I went upstairs.

'You had put me in the front room, on the third floor, overlooking the street, a room which I thought you generally occupied yourself. It was a very hot night, and though there had been a moon when I started to my party, on my return the whole sky was cloud-covered, and it both looked and felt as if we might have a thunderstorm before morning. I was feeling very sleepy and heavy, and it was not till after I had got into bed that I noticed by the shadows of the window frames on the blind that only one of the windows was open. But it did not seem worth while to get out of bed in order to open it, though I felt rather airless and uncomfortable, and I went to sleep.

'What time it was when I awoke I do not know, but it was certainly not yet dawn, and I never remembered being conscious of such an extraordinary stillness as prevailed. There was no sound either of foot-passengers or wheeled traffic; the music of life appeared to be absolutely mute. But now, instead of being sleepy and heavy, I felt, though I must have slept an hour or two at most, since it was not yet dawn, perfectly fresh and wide awake, and the effort which had seemed not worth making before, that of getting out of bed and opening the other window, was quite easy now, and I pulled up the blind, threw it wide open, and leaned out, for somehow I parched and pined for air. Even outside the oppression was very noticeable, and though, as you know, I am not easily given to feel the mental effects of climate, I was aware of an awful creepiness coming over me. I tried to analyse it away, but without success; the past day had been pleasant, I looked forward to another pleasant day tomorrow, and yet I was full of some nameless apprehension. I felt, too, dreadfully lonely in this stillness before the dawn.

'Then I heard suddenly and not very far away the sound of some approaching vehicle; I could distinguish the tread of two horses walking at a slow foot's pace. They were, though yet invisible, coming up the street, and yet this indication of life did not abate that dreadful sense of loneliness which I have spoken of. Also in some dim unformulated way that which was coming seemed to me to have something to do with the cause of my oppression.

'Then the vehicle came into sight. At first I could not distinguish what it was. Then I saw that the horses were black and had long tails, and that what they dragged was made of glass, but had a black frame. It was a hearse. Empty.

'It was moving up this side of the street. It stopped at your door.

'Then the obvious solution struck me. You said at dinner that your man was ill, and you were, I thought, unwilling to speak more about his illness. No doubt, so I imagined now, he was dead, and for some reason, perhaps because you did not want me to know anything about it, you were having the body removed at night. This, I must tell you, passed through my mind quite instantaneously, and it did not occur to me how unlikely it really was, before the next thing happened.

'I was still leaning out of the window, and I remember also wondering, yet only momentarily, how odd it was that I saw things – or rather the one thing I was looking at – so very distinctly. Of course, there was a moon behind the clouds, but it was curious how every detail of the hearse and the horses was visible. There was only one man, the driver, with it, and the street was otherwise absolutely empty. It was at him I was looking now. I could see every detail of his clothes, but from where I was, so high above him, I could not see his face. He had on grey trousers, brown boots, a black coat buttoned all the way up, and a straw hat. Over his shoulder there was a strap, which seemed to support some sort of little bag. He looked exactly like – well, from my description what did he look exactly like?'

'Why – a bus conductor,' I said instantly.

'So I thought, and even while I was thinking this, he looked up at me. He had a rather long thin face, and on his left cheek there was a mole with a growth of dark hair on it. All this was as distinct as if it had been noonday, and as if I was within a yard of him. But – so instantaneous was all that takes so long in the telling – I had not time to think it strange that the driver of a hearse should be so unfunereally dressed.

'Then he touched his hat to me, and jerked his thumb over his shoulder.'

'"Just room for one inside, sir," he said.

'There was something so odious, so coarse, so unfeeling about this that I instantly drew my head in, pulled the blind down again, and then, for what reason I do not know, turned on the electric light in order to see what time it was. The hands of my watch pointed to half past eleven.

'It was then for the first time, I think, that a doubt crossed my mind as to the nature of what I had just seen. But I put out the light again, got into bed, and began to think. We had dined; I had gone to a party, I had come back and written letters, had gone to bed and had slept. So how could it be half past eleven? ... Or – *what* half past eleven was it?

'Then another easy solution struck me; my watch must have stopped. But it had not; I could hear it ticking.

'There was stillness and silence again. I expected every moment to hear muffled footsteps on the stairs, footsteps moving slowly and smally under the weight of a heavy burden, but from inside the house there was no sound whatever. Outside, too, there was the same dead silence, while the hearse waited at the door. And the minutes ticked on and ticked on, and at length I began to see a difference in the light in the room, and knew that the dawn was beginning to break outside. But how had it happened then that if the corpse was to be removed at night it had not gone, and that the hearse still waited, when morning was already coming?

'Presently I got out of bed again, and with the sense of strong physical shrinking, I went to the window and pulled back the blind. The dawn was coming fast; the whole street was lit by that silver hueless light of morning. But there was no hearse there.

'Once again I looked at my watch. It was just a quarter past four. But I would swear that not half an hour had passed since it had told me that it was half past eleven.

'Then a curious double sense, as if I was living in the present and at the same moment had been living in some other time, came over me. It was dawn on June 25th, and the street, as natural, was empty. But a little while ago the driver of a hearse had spoken to me, and it was half past eleven. What was that driver, to what plane did he belong? And again *what* half past eleven was it that I had seen recorded on the dial of my watch?

'And then I told myself that the whole thing had been a dream. But if you ask me whether I believed what I told myself, I must confess that I did not.

'Your man did not appear at breakfast next morning, nor did I see him again before I left that afternoon. I think if I had, I should have told you about all this, but it was still possible, you see, that what I had seen was a real hearse, driven by a real driver, for all the ghastly gaiety of the face that had looked up to mine and the levity of his pointing hand. I might possibly have fallen asleep soon after seeing him, and slumbered through the removal of the body and the departure of the hearse. So I did not speak of it to you.'

*   *   *

There was something wonderfully straightforward and prosaic in all this; here were no Jacobean houses oak-panelled and surrounded by weeping pine trees, and somehow the very absence of suitable surroundings made the story more impressive. But for a moment a doubt assailed me.

'Don't tell me it was all a dream,' I said.

'I don't know whether it was or not. I can only say that I believe myself to have been wide awake. In any case the rest of the story is – odd.

'I went out of town again that afternoon,' he continued, 'and I may say that I don't think that even for a moment did I get the haunting sense of what I had seen or dreamed that night out of my mind. It was present to me always as some vision unfulfilled. It was as if some clock had struck the four quarters, and I was still waiting to hear what the hour would be.

'Exactly a month afterwards I was in London again, but only for the day. I arrived at Victoria about eleven, and took the underground to Sloane Square in order to see if you were in town and would give me lunch. It was a baking hot morning, and I intended to take a bus from the King's Road as far as Graeme Street. There was one standing at the corner just as I came out of the station, but I saw that the top was full, and the inside appeared to be full also. Just as I came up to it the conductor who, I suppose, had been inside, collecting fares or what not, came out on to the step within a few feet of me. He wore grey trousers, brown boots, a black coat buttoned, a straw hat, and over his shoulder was a strap on which hung his little machine for punching tickets. I saw his face, too; it was the face of the driver of the hearse, with a mole on the left cheek. Then he spoke to me, jerking his thumb over his shoulder.

'"Just room for one inside, sir," he said.

'At that a sort of panic-stricken terror took possession of me, and I knew I gesticulated wildly with my arms, and cried, "No, no!" But at that moment I was living not in the hour that was then passing, but in that hour which had passed a month ago, when I leaned from the window of your bedroom here just before the dawn broke. At this moment, too, I knew that my spyhole had been opposite the spyhole into the spiritual world. What I had seen there had some significance, now being fulfilled, beyond the significance of the trivial happenings of today and tomorrow. The powers of which we know so little were visibly working before me. And I stood there on the pavement shaking and trembling.

'I was opposite the post office at the corner, and just as the bus started my eye fell on the clock in the window there. I need not tell you what the time was.

'Perhaps I need not tell you the rest, for you probably conjecture it, since you will not have forgotten what happened at the corner of Sloane Square at the end of July, the summer before last. The bus pulled out from the pavement into the street in order to get round a van that was standing in front of it. At that moment there came down the King's Road a big motor going at a hideously dangerous pace. It crashed full into the bus, burrowing into it as a gimlet burrows into a board.'

He paused.

'And that's my story,' he said.

The Middle Toe of the Right Foot
Ambrose Bierce

It is well known that the old Manton house is haunted. In all the rural district near about, and even in the town of Marshall, a mile away, not one person of unbiased mind entertains a doubt of it; incredulity is confined to those opinionated people who will be called 'cranks' as soon as the useful word shall have penetrated the intellectual demesne of the Marshall *Advance*. The evidence that the house is haunted is of two kinds: the testimony of disinterested witnesses who have had ocular proof, and that of the house itself. The former may be disregarded and ruled out on any of the various grounds of objection which may be urged against it by the ingenious; but facts within the observation of all are fundamental and controlling.

In the first place, the Manton house has been unoccupied by mortals for more than ten years, and with its outbuildings is slowly falling into decay – a circumstance which in itself the judicious will hardly venture to ignore. It stands a little way off the loneliest reach of the Marshall and Harriston road, in an opening which was once a farm and is still disfigured with strips of rotting fence and half covered with brambles overrunning a stony and sterile soil long unacquainted with the plough. The house itself is in tolerably good condition, though badly weather-stained and in dire need of attention from the glazier, the smaller male population of the region having attested in the manner of its kind its disapproval of dwellings without dwellers. The house is two stories in height, nearly square, its front pierced by a single doorway flanked on each side by a window boarded up to the very top. Corresponding windows above, not protected, serve to admit light and rain to the rooms of the upper floors. Grass and weeds grow pretty rankly all about, and a few shade trees, somewhat the worse for wind and leaning all in one direction, seem to be making a concerted effort to run away. In short, as the Marshall town humourist explained in the columns of the *Advance*, 'the proposition that the Manton house is badly haunted is the only logical conclusion from the premises.' The fact that in this dwelling Mr Manton thought it expedient one night some ten years ago to rise and cut the throats of his wife and two small children, removing at once to another part of the country, has no doubt done its share in directing public attention to the fitness of the place for supernatural phenomena.

To this house, one summer evening, came four men in a waggon. Three of them promptly alighted, and the one who had been driving hitched the team to the only remaining post of what had been a fence. The fourth remained seated in the waggon. 'Come,' said one of his companions, approaching him, while the others moved away in the direction of the dwelling – 'this is the place.'

The man addressed was deathly pale and trembled visibly. 'By God!' he said harshly, 'this is a trick, and it looks to me as if you were in it.'

'Perhaps I am,' the other said, looking him straight in the face and speaking in a tone which had something of contempt in it. 'You will remember, however, that the choice of place was, with your own assent, left to the other side. Of course if you are afraid of spooks——'

'I am afraid of nothing,' the man interrupted with another oath, and sprang to the ground. The two of them joined the others at the door, which one of them had already opened with some difficulty, caused by rust of lock and hinge. All entered. Inside it was dark, but the man who had unlocked the door produced a candle and matches and made a light. He then unlocked a door on their right as they stood in the passage. This gave them entrance to a large, square room, which the candle but dimly lighted. The floor had a thick carpeting of dust, which partly muffled their footfalls. Cobwebs were in the angles of the walls and depended from the ceiling like strips of rotting lace, making undulatory movements in the disturbed air. The room had two windows in adjoining sides, but from neither could anything be seen except the rough inner surfaces of boards a few inches from the glass. There was no fireplace, no furniture; there was nothing. Besides the cobwebs and the dust, the four men were the only objects there which were not a part of the architecture. Strange enough they looked in the yellow light of the candle. The one who had so reluctantly alighted was especially 'spectacular' – he might have been called sensational. He was of middle age, heavily built, deep-chested and broad-shouldered. Looking at his figure, one would have said that he had a giant's strength; at his face, that he would use it like a giant. He was clean shaven, his hair rather closely cropped and grey. His low forehead was seamed with wrinkles above the eyes, and over the nose these became vertical. The heavy black brows followed the same law, saved from meeting only by an upward turn at what would otherwise have been the point of contact. Deeply sunken beneath these, glowed in the obscure light a pair of eyes of uncertain colour, but, obviously enough, too small. There was something forbidding in their expression, which was not bettered by the cruel mouth and wide jaw. The nose was well enough, as noses go; one does not expect much of noses. All that was sinister in the man's face seemed accentuated by an unnatural pallor – he appeared altogether bloodless.

The appearance of the other men was sufficiently commonplace: they were such persons as one meets and forgets that one met. All were younger than the man described, between whom and the eldest of the others, who stood apart, there was apparently no kindly feeling. They avoided looking at one another.

'Gentlemen,' said the man holding the candle and keys, 'I believe everything is right. Are you ready, Mr Rosser?'

The man standing apart from the group bowed and smiled.

'And you, Mr Grossmith?'

The heavy man bowed and scowled.

'You will please remove your outer clothing.'

Their hats, coats, waistcoats and neckwear were soon removed and thrown outside the door, in the passage. The man with the candle now nodded, and the fourth man – he who had urged Mr Grossmith to leave the waggon – produced from the pocket of his overcoat two long, murderous-looking bowie knives, which he drew from the scabbards.

'They are exactly alike,' he said, presenting one to each of the two principals – for by this time the dullest observer would have understood the nature of this meeting. It was to be a duel to the death.

Each combatant took a knife, examined it critically near the candle and tested the strength of blade and handle across his lifted knee. Their persons were then searched in turn, each by the second of the other.

'If it is agreeable to you, Mr Grossmith,' said the man holding the light, 'you will place yourself in that corner.'

He indicated the angle of the room farthest from the door, to which Grossmith retired, his second parting from him with a grasp of the hand which had nothing of cordiality in it. In the angle nearest the door Mr Rosser stationed himself and, after a whispered consultation, his second left him, joining the other near the door. At that moment the candle was suddenly extinguished, leaving all in profound darkness. This may have been done by a draught from the open door; whatever the cause, the effect was appalling!

'Gentlemen,' said a voice which sounded strangely unfamiliar in the altered condition affecting the relations of the senses, 'gentlemen, you will not move until you hear the closing of the outer door.'

A sound of trampling ensued, the closing of the inner door, and finally the outer one closed with a concussion which shook the entire building.

A few minutes later a belated farmer's boy met a waggon which was being driven furiously towards the town of Marshall. He declared that behind the two figures on the front seat stood a third with its hands upon the bowed shoulders of the others, who appeared to struggle vainly to free themselves from its grasp. This figure, unlike the others, was clad in white, and had undoubtedly boarded the waggon as it passed the haunted house. As the lad could boast a considerable former experience with the supernatural thereabout, his word had the weight justly due to the testimony of an expert. The story eventually appeared in the *Advance*, with some slight literary embellishments and a concluding intimation that the gentlemen referred to would be allowed the use of the paper's columns for their version of the night's adventure. But the privilege remained without a claimant.

* * *

The events which led up to this 'duel in the dark' were simple enough. One evening three young men of the town of Marshall were sitting in a quiet corner of the porch of the village hotel, smoking and discussing such matters as three educated young men of a Southern village would naturally find interesting. Their names were King, Sancher and Rosser. At a little distance, within easy hearing but taking no part in the conversation, sat a fourth. He was a stranger to the others. They merely knew that on his arrival by the stage coach that afternoon he had written in the hotel register the name Robert Grossmith. He had not been observed to speak to anyone except the hotel clerk. He seemed, indeed, singularly fond of his own company – or, as the *personnel* of the *Advance* expressed it, 'grossly addicted to evil associations.' But then it should be said in justice to the stranger that the *personnel* was himself of a too convivial disposition fairly to judge one differently gifted, and had, moreover, experienced a slight rebuff in an effort at an 'interview'.

'I hate any kind of deformity in a woman,' said King, 'whether natural or – or acquired. I have a theory that any physical defect has its correlative mental and moral defect.'

'I infer, then,' said Rosser, gravely, 'that a lady lacking the advantage of a nose would find the struggle to become Mrs King an arduous enterprise.'

'Of course you may put it that way,' was the reply; 'but, seriously, I once threw over a most charming girl on learning, quite accidentally, that she had suffered amputation of a toe. My conduct was brutal, if you like, but if I had married that girl I should have been miserable and should have made her so.'

'Whereas,' said Sancher, with a light laugh, 'by marrying a gentleman of more liberal views she escaped with a cut throat.'

'Ah, you know to whom I refer! Yes, she married Manton, but I don't know about his liberality; I'm not sure but he cut her throat because he discovered that she lacked that excellent thing in woman, the middle toe of the right foot.'

'Look at that chap!' said Rosser in a low voice, his eyes fixed upon the stranger.

That person was obviously listening intently to the conversation.

'That's an easy one,' Rosser replied, rising. 'Sir,' he continued, addressing the stranger, 'I think it would be better if you would remove your chair to the other end of the verandah. The presence of gentlemen is evidently an unfamiliar situation to you.'

The man sprang to his feet and strode forward with clenched hands, his face white with rage. All were now standing. Sancher stepped between the belligerents.

'You are hasty and unjust,' he said to Rosser; 'this gentleman has done nothing to deserve such language.'

But Rosser would not withdraw a word. By the custom of the country and the time, there could be but one outcome to the quarrel.

'I demand the satisfaction due to a gentleman,' said the stranger, who had become more calm. 'I have not an acquaintance in this region. Perhaps you, sir,' bowing to Sancher, 'will be kind enough to represent me in this matter.'

Sancher accepted the trust – somewhat reluctantly, it must be confessed, for the man's appearance and manner were not at all to his liking. King, who during the colloquy had hardly removed his eyes from the stranger's face, and had not spoken a word, consented with a nod to act for Rosser, and the upshot of it was that, the principals having retired, a meeting was arranged for the next evening. The nature of the arrangements has been already disclosed. The duel with knives in a dark room was once a commoner feature of South-western life than it is likely to be again. How thin a veneering of 'chivalry' covered the essential brutality of the code under which such encounters were possible, we shall see.

*   *   *

In the blaze of a midsummer noonday, the old Manton house was hardly true to its traditions. It was of the earth, earthy. The sunshine caressed it warmly and affectionately, with evident unconsciousness of its bad reputation. The grass greening all the expanse in its front seemed to grow, not rankly, but with a natural and joyous exuberance, and the weeds blossomed quite like plants. Full of charming lights and shadows, and populous with pleasant-voiced birds, the neglected shade trees no longer struggled to run away, but bent reverently beneath their burdens of sun and song. Even in the glassless upper windows was an expression of peace and contentment, due to the light within. Over the stony fields the visible heat danced with a lively tremor incompatible with the gravity which is an attribute of the supernatural.

Such was the aspect under which the place presented itself to Sheriff Adams and the two other men who had come out from Marshall to look at it. One of these men was Mr King, the sheriff's deputy; the other, whose name was Brewer, was a brother of the late Mrs Mantôn. Under a beneficent law of the State relating to property which has been for a certain period abandoned by its owner, whose residence cannot be ascertained, the sheriff was the legal custodian of the Manton farm and the appurtenances thereunto belonging. His present visit was in mere perfunctory compliance with some order of a court in which Mr Brewer had an action to get possession of the property as heir to his deceased sister. By a mere coincidence the visit was made on the day after the night that Deputy King had unlocked the house for another and very different purpose. His presence now was not of his own choosing: he had been ordered to accompany his superior, and at the moment could think of nothing more prudent than simulated alacrity in obedience. He had intended going anyhow, but in other company.

Carelessly opening the front door, which to his surprise was not locked, the sheriff was amazed to see, lying on the floor of the passage into which it opened, a confused heap of men's apparel. Examination showed it to consist of two hats, and the same number of coats, waistcoats and scarves, all in a remarkably good state of preservation, albeit somewhat defiled by the dust in which they lay. Mr Brewer was equally astonished, but Mr King's emotion is not on record. With a new and lively interest in his own actions, the sheriff now unlatched and pushed open a door on the right, and the three entered. The room was apparently vacant – no; as their eyes became accustomed to the dimmer light, something was visible in the farthest angle of the wall. It was a human figure – that of a man crouching close in the corner. Something in the attitude made the intruders halt when they had barely passed the threshold. The figure more and more clearly defined itself. The man was on one knee, his back in the angle of the wall, his shoulders elevated to the level of his ears, his hands before his face, palms outward, the fingers spread and crooked like claws; the white face turned upward on the retracted neck had an expression of unutterable fright, the mouth half open, the eyes incredibly expanded. He was stone dead – dead of terror! Yet, with the exception of a knife, which had evidently fallen from his own hand, not another object was in the room.

In the thick dust which covered the floor were some confused footprints near the door and along the wall through which it opened. Along one of the adjoining walls, too, past the boarded-up windows, was the trail made by the man himself in reaching his corner. Instinctively in approaching the body the three men now followed that trail. The sheriff grasped one of the out-thrown arms; it was as rigid as iron, and the application of a gentle force rocked the entire body without altering the relation of its parts. Brewer, pale with terror, gazed intently into the distorted face. 'God of mercy!' he suddenly cried, 'it is Manton!'

'You are right,' said King, with an evident attempt at calmness: 'I knew Manton. He then wore a full beard and his hair long, but this is he.'

He might have added: 'I recognized him when he challenged Rosser. I told Rosser and Sancher who he was before we played him this horrible trick. When Rosser left this dark room at our heels, forgetting his clothes in the excitement, and driving away with us in his shirt – all through the discreditable proceedings we knew whom we were dealing with, murderer and coward that he was!'

But nothing of this did Mr King say. With his better light he was trying to penetrate the mystery of the man's death. That he had not once moved from the corner where he had been stationed, that his posture was that of neither attack nor defence, that he had dropped his weapon, that he had obviously perished of sheer terror of something that he *saw* – these were circumstances which Mr King's disturbed intelligence could not rightly comprehend.

Groping in intellectual darkness for a clue to his maze of doubt, his gaze directed mechanically downward, as is the way of one who ponders momentous matters, fell upon something which, there, in the light of day, and in the presence of living companions, struck him with an invincible terror. In the dust of years that lay thick upon the floor – leading from the door by which they had entered, straight across the room to within a yard of Manton's crouching corpse – were three parallel lines of footprints – light but definite impressions of bare feet, the outer ones those of small children, the inner a woman's. From the point at which they ended they did not return; they pointed all one way. Brewer, who had observed them at the same moment, was leaning forward in an attitude of rapt attention, horribly pale.

'Look at that!' he cried, pointing with both hands at the nearest print of the woman's right foot, where she had apparently stopped and stood. 'The middle toe is missing – it was Gertrude!'

Gertrude was the late Mrs Manton, sister to Mr Brewer.

Little Boy Blue
Charles Birkin

Moira Latten had not herself stayed at Stonethorpe. When, as a child, she had first been taken for a holiday to Cleeness, the house had been pointed out to her, and on subsequent occasions she had gone there to tea. It was her mother who, in her youth, used to be sent to the Misses Wallace to recuperate after various infantile ailments, under the care of the three kindly ladies who owned the house, which they let out as lodgings.

Stonethorpe was one of a row of semi-detached Victorian villas that faced the sea. There was a road which separated their neat and formal front gardens from the bowling green, now seldom used, behind which lay the sandhills and the beach.

Cleeness had expanded a good deal since the war, but the expansion had taken place at the other end of the town, beyond the shopping centre and the clock tower and the Amusement Park, until it had petered out at the new Butlin's Holiday Camp, and the vicinity in which Stonethorpe was situated was hardly changed. It had become more of a backwater and it was shabbier, but otherwise it had remained much the same as when Moira had last seen it.

For several years, when her two children were growing up, Moira's mother, Mrs Soskin, had chosen to take a bungalow in Cleeness for the summer, preferring it to the more select resorts. It had usually been the same bungalow, The Look Out, and it had been rambling and white stuccoed and had stood on the edge of the sandhills, surrounded by a defeatist garden in which practically nothing but seathrift and marigolds and surges of nasturtiums would grow. To remedy this floral sparsity there was a lot of gravel drive lined with whitewashed boulders. The town was on a bleak part of the Lincolnshire coast and was considered to be bracing, and certainly the bathing there had been more of an endurance test than a genuine pleasure, necessitating as it did brisk rubs down with towels and reviving cups of Bovril which had been forced between chattering teeth.

Moira had retained a strange nostalgia for these somewhat Spartan holidays and so, with the passage of time, when her own son, Oliver, had been recovering from a severe attack of measles, she had remembered the Misses Wallace's establishment and had written on chance to enquire if they still received guests. Their reply had said that they did so on occasion, but since they were well advanced in years they could no longer undertake to provide dinner at night.

Moira and Oliver arrived at Stonethorpe late on a Friday afternoon, and immediately upon entering the house, so unchanged was the atmosphere that Moira had felt that she had stepped back not only into her own nursery days but even into those of her mother. They were the sole visitors and had been given the front sitting-room for their exclusive use, and the room across the hall was to be set aside for the serving of their meals. Their bedrooms on the first floor faced the sea and were adjacent to the only bathroom.

Miss Dolly Wallace had been delighted to see her. Yes, she well remembered the days when they used to meet, when Moira had been 'so high'. And how was dear Mrs Soskin? Keeping in good health, she hoped. How time flew! It seemed like yesterday! She and her sister Connie had been saying so last night, and to imagine that Moira herself now had a child of her own, and such a big boy for eight. Quite the little man! No doubt Moira had heard that they had lost their sister Annie? She had been the youngest of the family, seventy-one, and the first of them to go. It only went to show, didn't it? Moira must come down after tea and have a word with Connie. She was keeping very well really, had retained all her faculties, but nowadays could not manage the stairs.

Yes, it was strange to think that between them they had run the house for close on eighty years, ever since Mrs Wallace had been brought to Stonethorpe as a bride by her husband in 1888 when it had been newly built, and all their family had been born there. Until a short while back the management of the establishment had been no trouble, but finally they had been reduced to a single girl as staff, and now they had no one. Girls could pick and choose, couldn't they, and they didn't seem to fancy domestic work.

Miss Wallace patted Oliver on the shoulder and told him to make himself at home and then left Moira to settle in, telling her that tea would be ready in ten minutes and that there would also be a snack at a quarter past seven.

Oliver adored Cleeness. It had all the basic requirements for a boy of his age. Miles of sands studded with rockpools, and the dunes in which he could dig caves and roll down their sides. It was the beginning of May, and except for Saturdays and Sundays the beach was practically empty. Spring had come late, but when it had arrived it had been an exceptionally warm one, and paddling and sunbathing could be indulged in as well as the building of sandcastles for the incoming tide to attack and obliterate. They spent nearly all their day in the open air, and right from the start Oliver's strength had improved.

Moira had planned to stay at Cleeness for two weeks. She did not mind the uneventfulness of the routine, for in the evenings she was able to continue with her work. She was a contributor to several of the women's magazines for which she wrote articles and short stories, and she was glad to be freed from all domestic chores.

It was at the end of their fourth day that Oliver had come running in to her in a state of gleeful gratification. Since Stonethorpe commanded the bowling green and sand dunes Moira used to allow him to go out by himself after tea, with the proviso that he should not stray too far, and that at half past six she would emerge to retrieve him. On this Tuesday evening, pink with excitement, he came jumping down the sandhills with the news that he had made a friend. His name was Sammy and, being seven and a half, he was a year younger than Oliver. He was staying nearby, although he had not mentioned the name of the house. Moira must come immediately and meet him, and could he please ask him to lunch tomorrow?

'Of course you can, darling,' Moira said. 'We'll go and find him now and invite him, and I'll see if Miss Wallace will give us chops and ice cream.'

Oliver led the way, pulling her along behind him in his eagerness, but there was no sign of Sammy and the happy anticipation faded from his face. 'You'll meet him again in the morning,' said Moira comfortingly. 'We've got the beach almost to ourselves, so you can't miss him and you'll be able to ask him then.'

After Oliver had had his bath and was in bed Moira went up to his room to say goodnight to him and, as always, he was loath to let her go, choosing for delaying tactics, to give her a detailed account of his encounter with Sammy. 'He's going away to boarding school next term, and he lives at Uxton, which is a village outside Nottingham, and he has sixpence a week pocket money – which I don't think is very much, do you? – and he wears a sailor suit with a ribbon on the hat saying H.M.S. *Valiant*, which I think is rather babyish and I told him so and he didn't seem to mind a bit and said lots of boys have them and that I was dotty, and he's got a bucket and a wooden spade, and his father's got a big grocer's shop, and there's an older sister who's called Mavis.' Oliver paused for breath before he went on: 'He knows an awful lot, the names of all the different kinds of seaweed and shells and anemones, and all about the tides and the stars, and he told me a story about a ghost ship called the Marie something or other, and he collects stamps and fossils and his mother makes him go to dancing class and he can't swim yet.' Oliver sounded rather reassured by his lack of this latter accomplishment.

Moira laughed. 'Neither can I,' she said, 'and neither can you! Maybe there are some baths in the town where you and Sammy could have lessons. I'll find out. It's still a bit cold for the sea.' She bent down to receive his hug. 'I'm so pleased you've made a friend. There're another ten days during which you can play together. Goodnight darling. Sleep tight!'

Her hand was on the door-knob when Oliver was in full spate again. 'And he knows all the songs the pierrots sing. They have competitions for the children. I've never seen any pierrots. Can we go one day?'

'If you like,' said Moira. 'They used to be an attraction in every seaside town, but I thought they'd been dropped these days except on the big piers. We'll go on Friday if you want to. I wonder where they are? I expect on the other side of the Amusement Park.'

Oliver held out his arms and she could not resist going back to give him another kiss. 'Goodnight, Mummy,' he said. 'It is all rather super, isn't it?'

Wednesday, however, brought a disappointment. It was a glorious morning and a few people made their appearance on the sands, but Sammy was not amongst them. Oliver spent most of the morning and afternoon looking for him but without success. A small girl with rabbit teeth and spectacles, by the name of Freda, tried to scrape acquaintance, but it was not the same thing and he gave her no encouragement. Oliver experienced a sense of anti-climax. Perhaps Sammy's mother had been called back suddenly to Uxton and had taken him with her and he would never meet him again.

Moira was delighted by Oliver's progress. He was already a different child from the pallid little boy of the previous week. Cleeness, she thought gratefully, must indeed be as health-giving as its publicity claimed, and at this, the quiet end, it was really ideal for children. No dangerous currents, no steep cliffs and no traffic except for an occasional tradesman's van. There were, it is true, buried strands of rusted barbed wire concealed amongst the hummocks, relics of forgotten defences erected against invasion by the Germans in World War One, and there were, too, some scattered patches of quicksand when the tide was out, but all the residents knew their exact locations and they look care to brief the visitors so that they could keep away from them. Otherwise there were no perils for the unwary.

Sammy's withdrawal from Oliver's life lasted until Sunday evening and then, when the last of the trippers were trailing back to their cars, Oliver found him again. He was solemn and shy and was unwilling to say where he had been or why he had kept away from the beach, and Oliver forbore from pressing him. Parents, as he knew himself, could be odd and unpredictable and their actions difficult of explanation, and he did not wish to cause him embarrassment by persistent questioning.

It was Sammy's suggestion that they should leave the dunes and, as the tide was turning, build a castle near the water line which they could strengthen and defend defiantly and breathlessly against the siege of the waves. He proved to be an expert builder and under his tuition a most intricate and impressive fortress was constructed which they decorated with a pattern of pebbles and oyster shells.

When Moira came across the dunes to collect Oliver she was rather vexed at being forced to walk for such a long way before she could shout to him. He was a tiny dot between the arc of the sky and desolate sweep of the sands. He came to her reluctantly. His shorts and gym shoes were soaked, and he made no protest when his mother told him that he had gone beyond their agreed boundary and that he had stayed out too late.

Rather to his surprise she did not include Sammy in these strictures and, since Oliver saw that she was annoyed, and suspected that if prompted she would probably put the blame on to Sammy for having led him astray, he neither looked back nor referred to him, especially as his friend had shown small pleasure on receiving the invitation to lunch at Stonethorpe, but instead had said firmly that it would be better if they were to meet each other away from the company of grown-ups, who were frequently bent on spoiling everything. His veiled ultimatum had implied that if their friendship were to continue it would have to be a secret one, and on his own terms, with no adult interference.

As Oliver volunteered nothing more after this concerning Sammy, Moira had taken it for granted that the boy must have left Cleeness, and had decided that it would be wiser not to make enquiries through Miss Wallace how he could be traced, for Oliver did not seem to miss him. In fact he appeared perfectly content and self-sufficient. When they came back to the house he sat bright-eyed and smiling and seemed vaguely constipated with some suppressed and unshared pleasure. He could hardly wait to finish his tea before rushing off to resume his interrupted play, but she could not help but wonder why it was that he so preferred the evenings when the warmth of the sun had gone and there was very often a chill wind.

*   *   *

On Sunday night Moira sighed and put the cover on her typewriter. She crushed out her cigarette. There were already half a dozen stubs in the ashtray. It was ten o'clock and the article which she had just finished was abysmal in its banality. It epitomized all the dreary and rehashed triteness that she had read so often and at which she had so readily mocked. Tomorrow she would make herself tear it up and start afresh. She should have thrown it away at once but here and there there had been a phrase or two which had pleased her and which she considered might have some future potential.

Miss Wallace's over-furnished sitting-room was stuffy, for one of the by-products of the dislike of girls for domestic service had been the replacement of the open fire which had formerly blazed there by a cheerless, but labour-saving arrangement of electric logs which she had switched on. This was made to appear even more unwelcoming by the background of black tiles with hand painted water-lilies that had surrounded the old grate. Moira lit another cigarette and thought that she would walk to the gate for a breath of fresh air before going up to bed.

She stood looking out on to the deserted road and wondered how Jeremy was making out while she and Oliver were at Cleeness. On the whole their marriage had been a happy one, but when, for one reason or another, they had to be apart, they were both tacitly relieved, although their subsequent reunions were appreciated by both.

The night was as warm as June and a full moon hung in a sky of light grey silk, and while Moira lingered by the gate, unwilling to go in, she heard Oliver's voice speaking cautiously and quietly as if he did not want to be overheard. 'All right, Sammy,' he was saying. 'I'll be there, and I'll bring some sweets and my sailing boats. I've got two and they're super and so there'll be one each. Same place. Same time.'

Moira looked quickly over her shoulder. Naturally there was no one there. Little boys wouldn't be allowed out so late at night. Oliver must be talking in his sleep, and his bed was pushed up against the open window which made her able to hear him. Or else he was awake and playing – which was very naughty of him. He ought to have been asleep hours ago. She glanced up at the facade and caught the flash of a striped pyjama sleeve as it was whisked back behind a curtain. She returned to the house and hurried up the stairs. Oliver was fast asleep. She scrutinized the heart-breakingly innocent face and the closed eyes with their fingers of dark lashes. Or was he just pretending? Moira tucked in the sheets and he did not stir, and closing the door softly behind her she went on to her own room. Tomorrow would be their final day. It was so hard to remember how vivid the games of childhood had been and how real the imaginary companions. Perhaps he had been missing Sammy all the time and had been putting up a brave front.

She smiled wistfully as she started to undress, for so soon it would be childhood's end.

*   *   *

It was the following evening, and Moira straightened up from her packing. It was all finished except for the few things which they would need in the morning. She looked with a jaundiced eye at the collection of souvenirs which Oliver had painstakingly accumulated during their stay, limpet-spotted strands of bladder-weed, smoothly frosted fragments of glass of white, blue, green and brown, which had been ground by the action of the waves until they had acquired the beauty of uncut jewels. There were scallop and razor shells, and some with exquisite pink shading that had housed minute bivalves such as she clearly remembered having collected during her own long ago foragings. In a bucket there were other shells containing live or moribund winkles and whelks, which would promptly die and smell to high heaven, but she knew that Oliver would insist on taking them all back with him to his home near Guildford.

She saw from the Mickey Mouse watch by Oliver's bed that it was almost seven. As their holiday was finishing she had asked Miss Wallace if she would put back their supper until a quarter to eight as a treat for Oliver, so she would not have to chase him up yet but could leave him to enjoy the extra time. She closed the cases and went down the precipitous stairs with their worn oilcloth and into the sombre hall that was dominated by the ponderously ticking grandfather clock and the big brass gong, and which always smelled of yesterday's roast mutton and cabbage.

As she entered the sitting-room Miss Wallace came up from the basement with a bulky album cradled in her arms. 'Oh, there you are, Mrs Latten!' she exclaimed. 'While I was having a turn-out yesterday I came across this book of photographs and Connie said I must show it to you, so I've brought it up as she suggested. There's a sweet one of you taken when you used to come to see us as a little slip of a thing.' Miss Wallace followed Moira into the room and dumped the heavy book on to the tablecloth. 'It's quite a comprehensive record of our lives here,' she said. 'My parents began it and after they died we three girls kept it up. Of course these are only a selection in this, from the years 1915 to 1938.' She carefully turned the thick gilt-edged leaves.

Moira, who topped her by a head, peered down over her shoulder. 'But what fun!' she said politely.

'There!' said Miss Wallace, pointing in triumph with a wrinkled finger. 'There you are!' She displayed proudly the photograph of a skinny and singularly unprepossessing child who was making hideous grimaces above a shrimping net that she extended towards the camera. 'Connie declares that you haven't changed at all!' enthused Miss Wallace contentedly. 'She told me that she would have known you anywhere. And so would I!' Moira's smile was a trifle bleak. 'And what is more,' Miss Wallace went on, 'in an earlier book I have one of your dear mother when *she* was a kiddy! I'll just pop down and fetch it. It's no trouble,' she said as Moira began to protest, 'only carrying more than one album is too heavy for me. I'm not so young as I was.'

'We none of us are', said Moira automatically.

Miss Wallace gave a primly appreciative laugh. 'You cannot bracket yourself with me, Mrs Latten!' She pattered out of the room, with evident enjoyment, leaving Moira to thumb through the pages.

The dreadful thing was that none of the names that confronted her rang any bell at all, so that it would be hard to show satisfactory enthusiasm. She stared at a forbidding 'Miss Hill and Ivor,' who had probably been staying at Stonethorpe when she had been taken there, but she had retained no recollection of them.

Miss Dolly Wallace returned. The second volume was even more massive than its predecessor, and had once been secured by a large brass lock, but this was now tarnished and hung open disconsolately. She was panting from her exertions and her pince-nez were askew. Her yellowish-white hair was also in need of tidying.

Moira suddenly remembered how much her grandmother had laughed when she had told her of her own early visits to Cleeness, which had always been to Stonethorpe and which had taken place shortly after the turn of the century. The Misses Wallace had been young women then and the personifications of Edwardian respectability but, according to Grandma, their lavatory had, for utilitarian purposes, been stocked with sheaves of neatly cut up newsprint from an obscure Bolshevist publication which had prophesied, and indeed advocated, bloody revolution. 'As if,' the old lady had told her, 'the poor dears would have liked to have packed all of us into tumbrils and sent us off to the guillotine!' Fortunately this economy had long been discontinued and more normal amenities were now provided.

The oldest of the photographs had been printed in that delightfully soft sepia that is now seldom used. These were for the most part stiffly posed tableaux of the Wallace family, steadfastly hypnotized by the lens. Then, with the coming of black and white processing, emerged the more informal 'snaps' of the guests who had come to Stonethorpe on annual holidays. Miss Wallace found the one of Moira's mother and it bore a striking resemblance to that which Moira had been shown of herself. It could not be denied that it was fortunate that the looks of the female members of her family had invariably improved with puberty.

She put the book down and as she did so it fell open at a page which was headed in intricate script: 'Summer Season, 1912'. The lady lodgers of that year had worn long white skirts and busy high-necked blouses. Their hair had been arranged in a fashion which Moira mentally labelled as 'cowpat', or else they had pinned on elaborately trimmed hats. The men had worn choking collars with their blazers and boaters and had displayed a wide variety of moustaches.

In one corner was the picture of a small serious boy in a sailor suit leaning bashfully against the side of a young and pretty woman. The caption underneath read: 'Mrs Mortlock and Sammy. July.'

Miss Wallace could not fail to notice Moira's fascination as she studied it. 'That poor little boy!' she said. 'It might have been yesterday.

Such a tragedy! He was the Mortlocks' only son, and he met his death on the last evening of his stay with us.' She shook her head. 'He was sucked under by the quicksands. A fearful calamity! He had been cautioned about them continually, as all of our visitors are always cautioned, but he managed to give Mrs Mortlock the slip, and in spite of the fact that as soon as he was missed we all of us went out to search for him, it was too late. It was terribly distressing. Poor, poor Mrs Mortlock! I thought she would go out of her mind! Sammy was a charming child who won everybody's heart with his winning ways. Such a friendly little fellow, although in some ways he gave the impression of being shy and lonely – or shall I say reserved? We used to call him Little Boy Blue.' Dolly Wallace was looking back through the long tunnel of the years. 'Such a lovable little fellow,' she repeated. 'I feel haunted by him to this very day, and even after all this time! It's funny but it's true. And so does Connie. He seems so real, he might never have left us.'

It came with dreadful impact to Moira that she had never met Oliver's 'Sammy'. Up to this moment, without troubling to think, she had accepted alternative explanations concerning him. Either he had been granted scant liberty until the evenings, or else he had never had any existence except in Oliver's imagination. He had been a 'dream friend', such as solitary children often invented and adopted. But how could Oliver have dreamed up the sailor suit and coupled it with the correct Christian name? And why had Sammy only come to him at the close of day ... when he would find him alone?

Without a word of explanation to Miss Wallace, Moira hurried out of the sitting-room, brushing past the branched hat-stand in the hallway on her way to the door. She crossed the road and, squeezing through the railings which protected the bowling green, dropped down and ran across the dark patchy grass to the spiked hummocks of the dunes. 'Oliver!' she called. 'Oliver ... where are you?' There was no answer. Driven by a sense of panic urgency she climbed up the hillocks, the loose sand slipping down and filling her shoes.

At the top she paused. The boundless sweep of the deserted beach stretched out before her. Away to her left were the forsaken fantasies of the Amusement Park; the figure-of-eight, the phallic tower embraced by the curving path of the helter-skelter, the Ghost Train, whose gaping fang-fringed entrance was closed by a barrier. The distance dwarfed them all into toys, and they would be untenanted and silent until Whitsun.

'Oliver!' she called again. Her voice in the vast emptiness was thin and tinny. 'Oliver ... where are you?' A strong breeze was blowing in from the sea and it flung her words back to her, flattening her skirt against her body and tangling her hair before her eyes.

Across the expanse of the sand a scattering of gulls, startlingly white, strutted and pecked in search of food, or rode on the swell of the waves before they broke and forced them to take flight, and their plaintive strident cries were both harshly angry and forlorn.

The sea was racing in, flooding over the hard corrugated ridges which the receding waves had carved earlier and which were so painful to hastening naked feet. There was a network of creeks which at low tide became stretches and lakes of sand-locked water, but which swiftly joined together with alarming speed when the tide turned.

At what seemed to her to be an incredible distance the flowing together of the creeks had combined to leave an island around which the encroaching waters lapped and nibbled, and marooned in this low lying hump of sand stood the figure of a little boy. Moira's heart leapt until it seemed to stick in her throat. From where she was standing it must be a quarter of a mile to the water's edge, and beyond that was a stretch of sea which was nearly as wide. She stumbled forward, kicking off her shoes, in the grip of paralysing terror. The cold of the water struck at her ankles and calves as she splashed through the shallows. For a hundred yards the shelving of the beach was gradual, although the water was rising steadily until it became waist high. When she judged herself to be within hailing point of Oliver she shouted his name once more. This time the child, who had been looking out to sea, heard her and turned his head, his delicate arms planted with heroic bravado on his hips as he tried to swivel round.

The island on which he stood had in a few minutes shrunk to half of its former size. 'Stay where you are,' she called, 'and I'll try to get to you.' She staggered into a hollow and almost fell, but managed to struggle to her feet, the salt stinging and smarting in her eyes. Battling on determinedly she realized that very soon she would be out of her depth and would be able to go no further. Oh God, why had she never been made to learn to swim? Oliver was too far away for her to see his expression, but she knew that he must be afraid.

'Sammy brought me out here,' Oliver called. 'He said that we could dig up buried treasure. And now he's gone. He disappeared and left me alone, and then I found that I was surrounded. He disappeared under the sand and left me. I thought he must have found a secret tunnel and had gone to look for the treasure, but I couldn't find one, and I'm frightened.' His voice grew higher. 'The sand is getting all wobbly and shaky. It's up to my knees and I'm stuck. I can't lift my legs. Hurry, Mummy, and find somebody with a boat.' Oliver tried to move round towards her but the effort only made him sink the deeper.

Moira tried to remember what little information she had ever heard about quicksands. You must remain quite still. Best of all you should lie down flat to distribute the weight as evenly as possible. But Oliver was too frightened to do that. If only she had a plank. But there was no plank, and very soon there would be no island. 'Keep still darling,' she shouted. 'I'm going back for help now. Don't try to make a move. I know it's hard, but don't do it. You understand? Whatever happens you must not struggle.' The impossibility of her being able to reach him appalled her. If she could have done so somehow she would have managed to pull him clear. On the horizon a tiny cargo boat was chugging northwards.

She fought desperately back to the shore and ran blindly up the beach and over the dunes to enlist aid, and the knowledge that the water was rising with each passing second pounding like hammers in her brain.

> 'Oh Little Boy Blue
> Come blow on your horn...'

Oliver watched his mother's retreat as she made her way back to dry land. He was afraid, terribly afraid. Right at the beginning, playing and laughing with Sammy, he had not been at all frightened. When the sand had started to quake a little he had regarded it as funny, and had prodded at it jokingly with his spade. Soon afterwards Sammy had dared him to collect the sailing boats which had overturned and had drifted some way out, and he had chased after them, and it was while he was on his way back that his legs had become stuck in the sand and he had not been able to free them, and he had noticed that the sea was all around him and that Sammy was no longer there.

He had sunk up to his thighs. The sea was closing in on him from every side, and through the sands, not six feet away, bubbles were rising, bubbles which grew and pulsated before they burst. The movement he gave was involuntary, and immediately the suction was increased. He must remain absolutely still as his mother had told him to do, until she could return to him with help. She would not fail him, she had never done so. He must be courageous and calm.

Despite his resolutions he pushed down with his hands at the melting sand and it offered no resistance, but when he endeavoured to withdraw them he found that he could not do so. A wave darted in and, having spent itself, gently touched his arm. The wind had turned colder with the fading daylight, and a gull flew low over his head, and the sea began to slap against him in a regular and rhythmic caress. He was being drawn down inexorably by the enveloping sand.

It was as if eager arms were dragging him down, a small boy's insistent arms, arms that were covered by the navy blue sleeves of a sailor suit, and he thought that he could hear Sammy's urgent whisper: 'Come and join me, Ollie. I'm lonely and I want you, and it will not hurt for long.'

He made one last effort to free himself and the sand welled up to his chin and was forcing itself into his mouth and nostrils. He twisted back his head and started to choke and gave a retching spluttering cry as he tried to spit out the sand and water which were suffocating him. All he could see now was the cloud smudged sky. His small round face was stricken. On what, at his age, should have been an unsullied canvas, there was stamped an incredulous horror, the realization of what was about to happen, a hopeless and rebellious despair that no human being, least of all a child, should ever have known.

The ripples lifted his fair hair so that it floated in the sea, and presently the remaining vestige of the sand bar was submerged and the surface of the water was untroubled.

*   *   *

Miss Wallace had kept her head admirably and had rung up the police who were already on their way and who had in turn immediately alerted the Cleeness lifeboat. The two young men with Moira were the Melvilles, who lived in the house next to Stonethorpe, and who were powerful swimmers.

They were standing beside her at the water's edge and, gazing out over the smooth grey waste of the sea, and she realized that she could no longer even be certain of where the island had been. As she scanned the water it seemed that for an instant two children rose above its surface, and that one of them had on a yellow jersey and flannel shorts, while the other was wearing an old-fashioned sailor suit.

Keeping His Promise
Algernon Blackwood

It was eleven o'clock at night, and young Marriott was locked into his room, cramming as hard as he could cram. He was a Fourth Year Man at Edinburgh University and he had been ploughed for this particular examination so often that his parents had positively declared they could no longer supply the funds to keep him there.

His rooms were cheap and dingy, but it was the lecture fees that took the money. So Marriott pulled himself together at last and definitely made up his mind that he would pass or die in the attempt, and for some weeks now he had been reading as hard as mortal man can read. He was trying to make up for lost time and money in a way that showed conclusively he did not understand the value of either. For no ordinary man – and Marriott was in every sense an ordinary man – can afford to drive the mind as he had lately been driving his, without sooner or later paying the cost.

Among the students he had few friends or acquaintances, and these few had promised not to disturb him at night, knowing he was at last reading in earnest. It was, therefore, with feelings a good deal stronger than mere surprise that he heard his doorbell ring on this particular night and realized that he was to have a visitor. Some men would simply have muffled the bell and gone on quietly with their work. But Marriott was not this sort. He was nervous. It would have bothered and pecked at his mind all night long not to know who the visitor was and what he wanted. The only thing to do, therefore, was to let him in – and out again – as quickly as possible.

The landlady went to bed at ten o'clock punctually, after which hour nothing would induce her to pretend she heard the bell, so Marriott jumped up from his books with an exclamation that augured ill for the reception of his caller, and prepared to let him in with his own hand.

The streets of Edinburgh town were very still at this late hour – it was late for Edinburgh – and in the quiet neighbourhood of F—— Street, where Marriott lived on the third floor, scarcely a sound broke the silence. As he crossed the floor, the bell rang a second time, with unnecessary clamour, and he unlocked the door and passed into the little hall-way with considerable wrath and annoyance in his heart at the insolence of the double interruption.

'The fellows all know I'm reading for this exam. Why in the world do they come to bother me at such an unearthly hour?'

The inhabitants of the building, with himself, were medical students, general students, poor Writers to the Signet, and some others whose vocations were perhaps not so obvious. The stone staircase, dimly lighted at each floor by a gas jet that would not turn above a certain height, wound down to the level of the street with no pretence at carpet or railing. At some levels it was cleaner than at others. It depended on the landlady of the particular level.

The acoustic properties of a spiral staircase seem to be peculiar. Marriott, standing by the open door, book in hand, thought every moment the owner of the footsteps would come into view. The sound of the boots was so close and so loud that they seemed to travel disproportionately in advance of their cause. Wondering who it could be, he stood ready with all manner of sharp greetings for the man who dared thus to disturb his work. But the man did not appear. The steps sounded almost under his nose, yet no one was visible.

A sudden queer sensation of fear passed over him – a faintness and a shiver down the back. It went, however, almost as soon as it came, and he was just debating whether he would call aloud to his invisible visitor, or slam the door and return to his books, when the cause of the disturbance turned the corner very slowly and came into view.

It was a stranger. He saw a youngish man, short of figure and very broad. His face was the colour of a piece of chalk, and the eyes, which were very bright, had heavy lines underneath them. Though the cheeks and chin were unshaven and the general appearance unkempt, the man was evidently a gentleman, for he was well dressed and bore himself with a certain air. But, strangest of all, he wore no hat, and carried none in his hand, and although rain had been falling steadily all the evening, he appeared to have neither overcoat nor umbrella.

A hundred questions sprang up in Marriott's mind and rushed to his lips, chief among which was something like 'Who in the world are you?' and 'What in the name of Heaven do you come to me for?' But none of these questions found time to express themselves in words, for almost at once the caller turned his head a little so that the gaslight in the hall fell upon his features from a new angle. Then in a flash Marriott recognized him.

'Field! Man alive! Is it you?' he gasped.

The Fourth Year Man was not lacking in intuition, and he perceived at once that here was a case for delicate treatment. He divined, without any actual process of thought, that the catastrophe often predicted had come at last, and that this man's father had turned him out of the house. They had been at a private school together years before, and though they had hardly met once since, the news had not failed to reach him from time to time with considerable detail, for the family lived near his own, and between certain of the sisters there was great intimacy. Young Field had gone wild later, he remembered hearing about it all – drink, a woman, opium, or something of the sort – he could not exactly call to mind.

'Come in,' he said at once, his anger vanishing. 'There's been something wrong, I can see. Come in, and tell me all about it and perhaps I can help——' He hardly knew what to say, and stammered a lot more besides. The dark side of life, and the horror of it, belonged to a world that lay remote from his own select little atmosphere of books and dreamings. But he had a man's heart for all that.

He led the way across the hall, shutting the front door carefully behind him, and noticed as he did so that the other, though certainly sober, was unsteady on his legs, and evidently much exhausted. Marriott might not be able to pass his examinations, but he at least knew the symptoms of starvation – acute starvation, unless he was much mistaken – when they stared him in the face.

'Come along,' he said cheerfully, and with genuine sympathy in his voice. 'I'm glad to see you. I was going to have a bite of something to eat, and you're just in time to join me.'

The other made no audible reply, and shuffled so feebly with his feet that Marriott took his arm by way of support. He noticed for the first time that the clothes hung on him with pitiful looseness. The broad frame was literally hardly more than a frame. He was as thin as a skeleton. But, as he touched him, the sensation of faintness and dread returned. It only lasted a moment, and then passed off, and he ascribed it not unnaturally to the distress and shock of seeing a former friend in such a pitiful plight.

'Better let me guide you. It's shamefully dark – this hall. I'm always complaining,' he said lightly, recognizing by the weight upon his arm that the guidance was sorely needed, 'but the old cat never does anything except promise.' He led him to the sofa, wondering all the time where he had come from and how he had found out the address. It must be at least seven years since those days at the private school when they used to be such close friends.

'Now, if you'll forgive me for a minute,' he said, 'I'll get supper ready – such as it is. And don't bother to talk. Just take it easy on the sofa. I see you're dead tired. You can tell me about it afterwards, and we'll make plans.'

The other sat down on the edge of the sofa and stared in silence, while Marriott got out the brown loaf, scones and a huge pot of marmalade that Edinburgh students always keep in their cupboards. His eyes shone with a brightness that suggested drugs, Marriott thought, stealing a glance at him from behind the cupboard door. He did not like yet to take a full square look. The fellow was in a bad way, and it would have been so like an examination to stare and wait for explanations. Besides, he was evidently almost too exhausted to speak. So, for reasons of delicacy – and for another reason as well which he could not exactly formulate to himself – he let his visitor rest apparently unnoticed, while he busied himself with the supper. He lit the spirit-lamp to make cocoa, and when the water was boiling he drew up the table with the good things to the sofa, so that Field need not have even the trouble of moving to a chair.

'Now, let's tuck in,' he said, 'and afterwards we'll have a pipe and a chat. I'm reading for an exam, you know, and I always have something about this time. It's jolly to have a companion.'

He looked up and caught his guest's eyes directed straight upon his own. An involuntary shudder ran through him from head to foot. The face opposite him was deadly white and wore a dreadful expression of pain and mental suffering.

'By gad!' he said, jumping up, 'I quite forgot. I've got some whisky somewhere. What an ass I am. I never touch it myself when I'm working like this.'

He went to the cupboard and poured out a stiff glass which the other swallowed at a single gulp and without any water. Marriott watched him while he drank it, and at the same time noticed something else as well – Field's coat was all over dust, and on one shoulder was a bit of cobweb. It was perfectly dry; Field arrived on a soaking wet night without hat, umbrella or overcoat, and yet perfectly dry, even dusty. Therefore he had been under cover. What did it all mean? Had he been hiding in the building? . . .

It was very strange. Yet he volunteered nothing; and Marriott had pretty well made up his mind by this time that he would not ask any questions until he had eaten and slept. Food and sleep were obviously what the poor devil needed most and first – he was pleased with his powers of ready diagnosis – and it would not be fair to press him till he had recovered a bit.

They ate their supper together while the host carried on a running one-sided conversation, chiefly about himself and his exams and his 'old cat' of a landlady, so that the guest need not utter a single word unless he really wished to – which he evidently did not! But, while he toyed with his food, feeling no desire to eat, the other ate voraciously. To see a hungry man devour cold scones, stale oatcake, and brown bread laden with marmalade was a revelation to this inexperienced student who had never known what it was to be without at least three meals a day. He watched in spite of himself, wondering why the fellow did not choke in the process.

But Field seemed to be as sleepy as he was hungry. More than once his head dropped and he ceased to masticate the food in his mouth. Marriott had positively to shake him before he would go on with his meal. A stronger emotion will overcome a weaker, but this struggle between the sting of real hunger and the magical opiate of overpowering sleep was a curious sight to the student, who watched it with mingled astonishment and alarm. He had heard of the pleasure it was to feed hungry men, and watch them eat, but he had never actually witnessed it, and he had no idea it was like this. Field ate like an animal – gobbled, stuffed, gorged. Marriott forgot his reading, and began to feel something very much like a lump in his throat.

'Afraid there's been awfully little to offer you, old man,' he managed to blurt out when at length the last scone had disappeared, and the rapid, one-sided meal was at an end. Field still made no reply, for he was almost asleep in his seat. He merely looked up wearily and gratefully.

'Now you must have some sleep, you know,' he continued, 'or you'll go to pieces. I shall be up all night reading for this blessed exam. You're more than welcome to my bed. Tomorrow we'll have a late breakfast and – and see what can be done – and make plans – I'm awfully good at making plans, you know,' he added with an attempt at lightness.

Field maintained his 'dead sleepy' silence, but appeared to acquiesce, and the other led the way into the bedroom, apologizing as he did so to this half-starved son of a baronet – whose own home was almost a palace – for the size of the room. The weary guest, however, made no pretence of thanks or politeness. He merely steadied himself on his friend's arm as he staggered across the room, and then, with all his clothes on, dropped his exhausted body on the bed. In less than a minute he was to all appearances sound asleep.

For several minutes Marriott stood in the open door and watched him; praying devoutly that he might never find himself in a like predicament, and then fell to wondering what he would do with his unbidden guest on the morrow. But he did not stop long to think, for the call of his books was imperative, and happen what might, he must see to it that he passed that examination.

Having again locked the door into the hall, he sat down to his books and resumed his notes on *materia medica* where he had left off when the bell rang. But it was difficult for some time to concentrate his mind on the subject. His thoughts kept wandering to the picture of that white-faced, strange-eyed fellow, starved and dirty, lying in his clothes and boots on the bed. He recalled their schooldays together before they had drifted apart, and how they had vowed eternal friendship – and all the rest of it. And now! What horrible straits to be in. How could any man let the love of dissipation take such hold upon him?

But one of their vows together Marriott, it seemed, had completely forgotten. Just now, at any rate, it lay too far in the background of his memory to be recalled.

Through the half-open door – the bedroom led out of the sitting-room and had no other door – came the sound of deep, long-drawn breathing, the regular steady breathing of a tired man, so tired that even to listen to it made Marriott almost want to go to sleep himself.

'He needed it,' reflected the student, 'and perhaps it came only just in time!'

Perhaps so; for outside the bitter wind from across the Forth howled cruelly and drove the rain in cold streams against the window-panes, and down the deserted streets. Long before Marriott settled down again properly to his reading, he heard distinctly, as it were, through the sentences of the book, the heavy, deep breathing of the sleeper in the next room.

A couple of hours later, when he yawned and changed his books, he still heard the breathing, and went cautiously up to the door to look round.

At first the darkness of the room must have deceived him, or else his eyes were confused and dazzled by the recent glare of the reading-lamp. For a minute or two he could make out nothing at all but dark lumps of furniture, the mass of the chest of drawers by the wall, and the white patch where his bath stood in the centre of the floor.

Then the bed came slowly into view. And on it he saw the outline of the sleeping body gradually take shape before his eyes, growing up strangely into the darkness, till it stood out in marked relief – the long black form against the white counterpane.

He could hardly help smiling. Field had not moved an inch. He watched him a moment or two and then returned to his books. The night was full of the singing voices of the wind and rain. There was no sound of traffic; no hansoms clattered over the cobbles, and it was still too early for the milk-carts. He worked on steadily and conscientiously, only stopping now and again to change a book, or to sip some of the poisonous stuff that kept him awake and made his brain so active, and on these occasions Field's breathing was always distinctly audible in the room. Outside, the storm continued to howl, but inside the house all was stillness. The shade of the reading-lamp threw all the light upon the littered table, leaving the other end of the room in comparative darkness. The bedroom door was exactly opposite him where he sat. There was nothing to disturb the worker, nothing but an occasional rush of wind against the windows, and a slight pain in his arm.

This pain, however, which he was unable to account for, grew once or twice very acute. It bothered him; and he tried to remember how, and when, he could have bruised himself so severely, but without success.

At length the page before him turned from yellow to grey, and there were sounds of wheels in the street below. It was four o'clock. Marriott leaned back and yawned prodigiously. Then he drew back the curtains. The storm had subsided and the Castle Rock was shrouded in mist. With another yawn he turned away from the dreary outlook and prepared to sleep the remaining few hours till breakfast on the sofa. Field was still breathing heavily in the next room, and he first tiptoed across the floor to take another look at him.

Peering cautiously round the half-opened door his first glance fell upon the bed now plainly discernible in the grey light of morning. He stared hard. Then he rubbed his eyes. Then he rubbed his eyes again and thrust his head farther round the edge of the door. With fixed eyes, he stared harder still, and harder.

But it made no difference at all. He was staring into an empty room.

The sensation of fear he had felt when Field first appeared upon the scene returned suddenly, but with much greater force. He became conscious, too, that his left arm was throbbing violently and causing him great pain. He stood wondering, and staring, and trying to collect his thoughts. He was trembling from head to foot.

By a great effort of the will he left the support of the door and walked forward boldly into the room.

There, upon the bed, was the impress of a body, where Field had lain and slept. There was the mark of the head on the pillow, and the slight indentation at the foot of the bed where the boots had rested on the counterpane. And there, plainer than ever – for he was closer to it – was *the breathing*!

Marriott tried to pull himself together. With a great effort he found his voice and called his friend aloud by name!

'Field! Is that you? Where are you?'

There was no reply; but the breathing continued without interruption, coming directly from the bed. His voice had such an unfamiliar sound that Marriott did not care to repeat his questions, but he went down on his knees and examined the bed above and below, pulling the mattress off finally, and taking the coverings away separately one by one. But though the sounds continued there was no visible sign of Field, nor was there any space in which a human being, however small, could have concealed itself. He pulled the bed out from the wall, but the sound *stayed where it was*. It did not move with the bed.

Marriott, finding self-control a little difficult in his weary condition, at once set about a thorough search of the room. He went through the cupboard, the chest of drawers, the little alcove where the clothes hung – everything. But there was no sign of anyone. The small window near the ceiling was closed; and, anyhow, was not large enough to let a cat pass. The sitting-room door was locked on the inside; he could not have got out that way. Curious thoughts began to trouble Marriott's mind, bringing in their train unwelcome sensations. He grew more and more excited; he searched the bed again till it resembled the scene of a pillow fight; he searched both rooms, knowing all the time it was useless – and then he searched again. A cold perspiration broke out all over his body; and the sound of heavy breathing, all this time, never ceased to come from the corner where Field had lain down to sleep.

Then he tried something else. He pushed the bed back exactly into its original position – and himself lay down upon it just where his guest had lain. But the same instant he sprang up again in a single bound. The breathing was close beside him, almost on his cheek, and between him and the wall! Not even a child could have squeezed into the space.

He went back into his sitting-room, opened the windows, welcoming all the light and air possible, and tried to think the whole matter over quietly and clearly. Men who read too hard, and slept too little, he knew, were sometimes troubled with very vivid hallucinations. Again he calmly reviewed every incident of the night: his accurate sensations; the vivid details; the emotions stirred in him; the dreadful feast – no single hallucination could ever combine all these and cover so long a period of time. But with less satisfaction he thought of the recurring faintness, and curious sense of horror that had once or twice come over him, and then of the violent pains in his arm. These were quite unaccountable.

Moreover, now that he began to analyse and examine, there was one other thing that fell upon him like a sudden revelation: *during the whole time Field had not actually uttered a single word!* Yet, as though in mockery upon his reflections, there came ever from that inner room the sound of the breathing, long-drawn, deep and regular. The thing was incredible. It was absurd.

Haunted by visions of brain fever and insanity, Marriott put on his cap and mackintosh and left the house. The morning air on Arthur's Seat would blow the cobwebs from his brain; the scent of the heather, and above all, the sight of the sea. He roamed over the wet slopes above Holyrood for a couple of hours, and did not return until the exercise had shaken some of the horror out of his bones, and given him a ravening appetite into the bargain.

As he entered he saw that there was another man in the room, standing against the window with his back to the light. He recognized his fellow-student, Greene, who was reading for the same examination.

'Read hard all night, Marriott,' he said, 'and thought I'd drop in here to compare notes and have some breakfast. You're out early?' he added, by way of a question. Marriott said he had a headache and a walk had helped it, and Greene nodded and said, 'Ah!' But when the girl had set the steaming porridge on the table and gone out again, he went on with rather a forced tone, 'Didn't know you had any friends who drank, Marriott?'

This was obviously tentative, and Marriott replied dryly that he did not know it either.

'Sounds just as if some chap were "sleeping it off" in there, doesn't it, though?' persisted the other, with a nod in the direction of the bedroom, and looking curiously at his friend. The two men stared steadily at each other for several seconds, and then Marriott said earnestly:

'Then you hear it too, thank God!'

'Of course I hear it. The door's open. Sorry if I wasn't meant to.'

'Oh, I don't mean that,' said Marriott, lowering his voice. 'But I'm awfully relieved. Let me explain. Of course, if you hear it too, then it's all right; but really it frightened me more than I can tell you. I thought I was going to have brain fever, or something, and you know what a lot depends on this exam. It always begins with sounds, or visions, or some sort of beastly hallucination, and I——'

'Rot!' ejaculated the other impatiently. 'What *are* you talking about?'

'Now, listen to me, Greene,' said Marriott, as calmly as he could, for the breathing man was still plainly audible, 'and I'll tell you what I mean, only don't interrupt.' And thereupon he related exactly what had happened during the night, telling everything, even down to the pain in his arm. When it was over he got up from the table and crossed the room.

'You hear the breathing now plainly, don't you?' he said. Greene said he did. 'Well, come with me, and we'll search the room together.' The other, however, did not move from his chair.

'I've been in already,' he said sheepishly; 'I heard the sounds and thought it was you. The door was ajar – so I went in.'

Marriott made no comment, but pushed the door open as wide as it would go. As it opened, the sound of breathing grew more and more distinct.

'*Someone* must be in there,' said Greene under his breath.

'*Someone* is in there, but *where*?' said Marriott. Again he urged his friend to go in with him. But Greene refused point-blank; said he had been in once and had searched the room and there was nothing there. He would not go in again for a good deal.

They shut the door and retired into the other room to talk it all over with many pipes. Greene questioned his friend very closely, but without illuminating result, since questions cannot alter facts.

'The only thing that ought to have a proper, logical explanation is the pain in my arm,' said Marriott, rubbing that member with an attempt at a smile. 'It hurts so infernally and aches all the way up. I can't remember bruising it, though.'

'Let me examine it for you,' said Greene. 'I'm awfully good at bones in spite of the examiners' opinion to the contrary.' It was a relief to play the fool a bit and Marriott took his coat off and rolled up his sleeve.

'By George, though, I'm bleeding!' he exclaimed. 'Look here! What on earth is this?'

On the forearm, quite close to the wrist, was a thin red line. There was a tiny drop of apparently fresh blood on it. Greene came over and looked closely at it for some minutes. Then he sat back in his chair, looking curiously at his friend's face.

'You've scratched yourself without knowing it,' he said presently.

'There's no sign of a bruise. It must be something else that made the arm ache.'

Marriott sat very still, staring silently at his arm as though the solution of the whole mystery lay there actually written upon the skin.

'What's the matter? I see nothing very strange about a scratch,' said Greene, in an unconvincing sort of voice. 'It was your cuff-links probably. Last night in your excitement——'

But Marriott, white to the very lips, was trying to speak. The sweat stood in great beads on his forehead. At last he leaned forward close to his friend's face.

'Look,' he said, in a low voice that shook a little. 'Do you see that red mark? I mean *underneath* what you call the scratch?'

Greene admitted he saw something or other, and Marriott wiped the place clean with his handkerchief and told him to look again more closely.

'Yes, I see,' returned the other lifting his head after a moment's careful inspection. 'It looks like an old scar.'

'It *is* an old scar,' whispered Marriott, his lips trembling. '*Now* it all comes back to me.'

'All what?' Greene fidgeted on his chair. He tried to laugh, but without success. His friend seemed bordering on collapse.

'Hush! Be quiet, and – I'll tell you,' he said. '*Field made that scar.*'

For a whole minute the two men looked each other full in the face without speaking.

'Field made that scar!' repeated Marriott at length in a louder voice.

'Field! You mean – last night?'

'No, not last night. Years ago – at school, with his knife. And I made a scar in his arm with mine.' Marriott was talking rapidly now.

'We exchanged drops of blood in each other's cuts. He put a drop into my arm and I put one into his——'

'In the name of heaven, what for?'

'It was a boys' compact. We made a sacred pledge, a bargain. I remember it all perfectly now. We had been reading some dreadful book and we swore to appear to one another – I mean, whoever died first swore to show himself to the other. And we sealed the compact with each other's blood. I remember it all so well – the hot summer afternoon in the playground, seven years ago – and one of the masters caught us and confiscated the knives – and I have never thought of it again to this day——'

'And you mean——' stammered Greene.

But Marriott made no answer. He got up and crossed the room and law down wearily upon the sofa, hiding his face in his hands.

Greene himself was a bit nonplussed. He left his friend alone for a little while, thinking it all over again. Suddenly an idea seemed to strike him. He went over to where Marriott still lay motionless on the sofa and roused him. In any case it was better to face the matter, whether there was an explanation or not. Giving in was always the silly exit.

'I say, Marriott,' he began, as the other turned his white face up to him. 'There's no good being so upset about it. I mean – if it's all a hallucination we know what to do. And if it isn't – well, we know what to think, don't we?'

'I suppose so. But it frightens me horribly for some reason,' returned his friend in a hushed voice. 'And that poor devil——'

'But, after all, if the worst is true and – and that chap *has* kept his promise – well, he has; that's all, isn't it?'

Marriott nodded.

'There's only one thing that occurs to me,' Greene went on, 'and that is, are you quite sure that – that he really ate like that – I mean that he actually *ate anything at all?*' he finished, blurting out all his thought.

Marriott stared at him for a moment and then said he could easily make certain. He spoke quietly. After the main shock no lesser surprise could affect him.

'I put the things away myself,' he said, 'after we had finished. They are on the third shelf in that cupboard. No one's touched 'em since.'

He pointed without getting up, and Greene took the hint and went over to look.

'Exactly,' he said, after a brief examination; 'just as I thought. It was partly hallucination, at any rate. The things haven't been touched. Come and see for yourself.'

Together they examined the shelf. There was the brown loaf, the plate of stale scones, the oatcake, all untouched. Even the glass of whisky Marriott had poured out stood there with the whisky still in it.

'You were feeding – no one,' said Greene. 'Field ate and drank nothing. He was not there at all!'

'But the breathing?' urged the other in a low voice, staring with a dazed expression on his face.

Greene did not answer. He walked over to the bedroom, while Marriott followed him with his eyes. He opened the door, and listened.

There was no need for words. The sound of deep, regular breathing came floating through the air. There was no hallucination about that, at any rate. Marriott could hear it where he stood on the other side of the room.

Greene closed the door and came back. 'There's only one thing to do,' he declared with decision. 'Write home and find out about him, and meanwhile come and finish your reading in my rooms. I've got an extra bed.'

'Agreed,' returned the Fourth Year Man; 'there's no hallucination about that exam; I must pass that whatever happens.'

And this was what they did.

It was about a week later when Marriott got the answer from his sister. Part of it he read out to Greene:

'It is curious,' she wrote, 'that in your letter you should have enquired after Field. It seems a terrible thing, but you know only a short while ago Sir John's patience became exhausted, and he turned him out of the house, they say without a penny. Well, what do you think? He has killed himself. At least, it looks like a suicide. Instead of leaving the house, he went down into the cellar and simply starved himself to death... They're trying to suppress it, of course, but I heard it all from my maid, who got it from their footman... They found the body on the 14th, and the doctor said he had died about twelve hours before... He was dreadfully thin...'

'Then he died on the 13th,' said Greene.

Marriott nodded.

'That's the very night he came to see you.'

Marriott nodded again.

Kecksies
Marjorie Bowen

Two young esquires were riding from Canterbury, jolly and drunk, they shouted and trolled, and rolled in their saddles as they followed the winding road across the downs.

A dim sky was overhead and shut in the wide expanse of open country that one side stretched to the sea and the other to the Kentish Weald.

The primroses grew in thick posies in the ditches, the hedges were full of fresh hawthorn green, the new grey leaves of eglantine and honeysuckle, the long boughs of ash with the hard black buds, the wand-like shoots of sallow willow hung with catkins and the smaller red tassels of the nut and birch. Little the two young men heeded of any of these things, for they were in their own country that was thrice familiar; but Nick Bateup blinked across to the distant purple hills and cursed the gathering rain.

'Ten miles more of the open,' he muttered, 'and a great storm blackening upon us.'

Young Crediton, who was more full of wine, laughed drowsily. 'We'll lie at a cottage on the way, Nick – think you I've never a tenant who'll let me share board and bed?' He maundered into singing:

> 'There's a light in the old mill
>   Where the witch weaves her charms,
> But dark is the chamber
>   Where you sleep in my arms.
> Now come you by magic, by trick, or by spell
>   I have you and hold you,
> And love you right well!'

The clouds overtook them like an advancing army; the wayside green looked vivid under the purple threat of the heavens and the birds were all still and silent.

'Split me if I'll be soaked,' muttered young Bateup. 'Knock up one of these boors of thine, Ned – but damn me if I see as much as hut or barn.'

'We come to Banells farm soon – or have we passed it?' answered the other confusedly. 'What's the pother? A bold bird as thou art and scared of a drop of rain?'

'My lungs are not as lusty as thine,' replied Bateup, who was indeed of a delicate build and more carefully dressed in greatcoat and muffler.

'But thy throat is as wide!' laughed Crediton. 'And God help you, you are shawled like an old woman – and as drunk as a Spanish parrot.

> *'Tra la la, my sweeting,*
> *Tra la la, my May,*
> *If now I miss the meeting*
> *I'll come some other day.'*

His companion took no notice of this nonsense, but with as much keenness as his muddled faculties would allow, was looking out for some shelter, for he retained sufficient perception to able him to mark the violence of the approaching storm and the loneliness of the vast stretch of country where the only human habitations appeared to be some few poor cottages far distant in the fields.

Ned lost his good humour and as the first drops of stinging cold rain began to fall, he cursed freely, using the terms common to the pot-houses where he had intoxicated himself on the way from Canterbury.

Urging their tired horses, they came onto the top of the little hill they ascended; immediately before them was the silver ashen skeleton of a blasted oak, polished like worn bone, standing over a small pool of stagnant water (for there had been little rain and much east wind), where a few shivering ewes crouched together from the oncoming storm.

Just beyond this, rising out of the bare field, was a humble cottage of black timber and white plaster and a deep thatched roof. For the rest of the crest of the hill was covered by a hazel copse and then dipped lonely again to the clouded lower levels that now began to slope into the marsh.

'This will shelter us, Nick,' cried Crediton.

' 'Tis a foul place and the boors have a foul reputation,' objected the lord of the manor. 'There are those who swear to seeing the devil's own fizz leer from Goody Boyle's windows – but anything to please thee and thy weak chest.'

They staggered from their horses, knocked open the rotting gate, and leading the beasts across the hard dry grazing field, knocked with their whips at the tiny door of the cottage.

The grey sheep under the grey tree looked at them and bleated faintly; the rain began to fall like straight yet broken darts out of the sombre clouds.

The door was opened by a woman very neatly dressed, with large scrubbed hands, who looked at them with fear and displeasure; for if her reputation was bad, theirs was no better. The lord of the manor was a known roisterer and wild liver who spent his idleness in rakish expeditions with Sir Nicholas Bateup from Bodiam, who was easily squandering a fine property. Neither were believed to be free of bloodshed, and as for honour they were as stripped of that as the blasted tree by the lonely pool was stripped of leaves.

Besides they were both now, as usual, drunk.

'We want shelter, Goody Boyle,' cried Crediton, pushing his way in as he threw her his reins. 'Get the horses into the barn.'

The woman could not deny the man, who could make her homeless in a second; she shouted hoarsely an inarticulate name and a loutish boy came and took the horses, while the two young men stumbled into the cottage, which they filled and dwarfed with their splendour.

Edward Crediton had been a fine young man, and though he was marred with insolence and excess, he still made a magnificent appearance, with his full, blunt features, his warm colouring, the fair hair rolled and curled, and all his bravery of blue broad-cloth, buckskin breeches, foreign lace, top boots, French sword, and gold rings and watch-chains.

Sit Nicholas Bateup was darker and more effeminate, having a cast of weakness in his constitution that betrayed itself in his face; but his dress was splendid to the point of foppishness and his manners even more arrogant and imposing.

Of the two he had the more evil repute; he was unwed and, therefore, there was no check upon his mischief; whereas Crediton had a young wife, whom he loved after his fashion and who checked some of his doings and softened others, and stayed very faithful to him and adored him still after five years of a wretched marriage, as is the manner of some women.

The rain came down with slashing severity; the little cottage panes were blotted with water.

Goody Boyle put logs on the fire and urged them with the bellows. It was a gaunt white room with nothing in it but a few wooden stools, a table, and an eel-catcher's prong.

On the table were large, fair, wax candles.

'What are these for, Goody?' asked Crediton.

'For the dead, sir.'

'You've dead in the house?' cried Sir Nicholas, who was leaning by the fireplace and warming his hands. 'What do you want with dead men in the house, you trollop?'

'It is no dead of mine, my lord,' answered the woman with evil civility, 'but one who took shelter here and died.'

'A curse, witch!' roared Crediton. 'You hear that, Nick? Came here – died. And now you'll put spells on us, you ugly slut——'

'No spells of mine,' answered the woman quietly, rubbing her large clean hands together. 'He had been long ailing and died here of an ague.'

'And who sent the ague?' asked Crediton with drunken gravity. 'And who sent him here?'

'Perhaps the same hand that sent us,' laughed Sir Nicholas. 'Where is your corpse, Goody?'

'In the next room – I have but two.'

'And two too many – you need but a bundle of faggots and a tuft of tow to light it – an arrant witch, a confest witch,' muttered Crediton; he staggered up from the stool. 'Where is your corpse? I've a mind to see if he looks as if he died a natural death.'

'Will you not ask first who it is?' asked the woman, unlatching the inner door.

'Why should I care?'

'Who is it?' asked Sir Nicholas, who had the clearer wits, drunk or sober.

'Robert Horne,' said Goody Boyle.

Ned Crediton looked at her with the eyes of a sober man.

'Robert Horne,' said Sir Nicholas. 'So he is dead at last – your wife will be glad of that, Ned.'

Crediton gave a sullen laugh. 'I'd broken him – she wasn't afraid any longer of a lost wretch cast out to die of ague on the marsh.'

But Sir Nicholas had heard differently; he had been told, even by Ned himself, how Anne Crediton shivered before the terror of Robert Horne's pursuit, and would wake up in the dark crying out for fear of him like a lost child; for he had wooed her before her marriage and persisted in loving her afterwards with mad boldness and insolent confidence, so that justice had been set on him and he had been banished to the marsh, a ruined man.

'Well, sirs,' said Goody Boyle in her thin voice, that had the pinched accents of other parts, 'my lady can sleep of nights now – Robert Horne will never disturb her again.'

'Do you think he ever troubled us?' asked Crediton with a coarse oath. 'I flung him out like an adder that had writhed across the threshold——'

'A wonder he did not put a murrain on thee, Ned. He had fearful ways and a deep knowledge of unholy things.'

'A warlock – God help us!' added the woman.

'The devil's proved an ill master then,' laughed Crediton. 'He could not help Robert Horne into Anne's favour – nor prevent him lying in a cold bed in the flower of his age.'

'The devil,' smiled Sir Nicholas, 'was over busy, Ned, helping *you* to the lady's favour and a warm bed. You were the dearer disciple.'

'Oh, good lords, will you talk less wildly with a lost man's corpse in the house and his soul riding the storm without?' begged Goody Boyle; and she latched again the inner door.

Murk filled the cottage now; waves of shadow flowed over the landscape; without the rain blotted the window and drowned the valley; in the bitter field the melancholy ewes huddled beneath the blasted oak beside the bare pool, the stagnant surface of which was now broken by the quick rain drops; a low thunder grumbled from the horizon and all the young greenery looked livid in the ghastly light of heaven.

'I'll see him,' said Ned Crediton swaggering. 'I'll look at this gay gallant in his last smock – so that I can swear to Anne he has taken his amorous smile to the earthworms – surely.'

'Look as you like,' answered Sir Nicholas, 'glut your eyes with looking——'

'But you'll remember, sirs, that he was a queer man and died queerly, and there was no parson or priest to take the edge off his going or challenge the fiends who stood at his head and feet.'

'Saw you the fiends?' asked Ned curiously.

'Question not what I saw,' muttered the woman. 'You'll have your own familiars, Esquire Crediton.'

She unlatched the inner door again and Ned passed in, bowing low on the threshold.

'Good day, Robert Horne,' he jeered. 'We parted in anger; but my debts are paid now and I greet you well.'

The dead man lay on a pallet bed with a coarse white sheet over him that showed his shape but roughly; the window was by his head and looked blankly onto the rain-bitten fields and dismal sky; the light was cold and colourless on the white sheet and the miserable room.

Sir Nicholas lounged in the doorway; he feared no death but his own, and that he set so far away it was but a dim dread.

'Look and see if it is Robert Horne,' he urged, 'or if the beldame lies.'

And Crediton turned down the sheet. ''Tis Robert Horne,' he said.

The dead man had his chin uptilted, his features sharp and horrible in the setting of the spilled hair on the coarse pillow. Ned Crediton triumphed over him, making lewd jests of love and death and sneering at this great gallant who had been crazed for love and driven by desire, and who now lay impotent.

And Sir Nicholas in the doorway listened and laughed and had his own wicked jeers to add; for both of them had hated Robert Horne as a man who had defied them.

But Goody Boyle stole away with her fingers in her ears.

When these two were weary of their insults they replaced the flap of the sheet over the dead face and returned to the outer room. And Ned asked for drink, declaring that Goody Boyle was a known smuggler and had cellars of rare stuff.

So the lout brought up glasses of cognac and a bottle of French wine, and these two drank grossly, sitting over the fire; and Goody Boyle made excuse for the drink by saying that Robert Horne had given her two gold pieces before he died (not thin pared coins, but thick and heavy) for his funeral and the entertainment of those who should come to his burying.

'What mourners could he hope for?' laughed Ned Crediton. 'The crow and the spider and the death-watch beetle?'

But Goody Boyle told them that Robert Horne had made friends while he had lived an outcast on the marshes; they were no doubt queer and even monstrous people, but they were coming tonight to sit with Robert Horne before he was put in the ground.

'And who, Goody, have warned this devil's congregation of the death of Robert Horne?' asked Sir Nicholas.

She answered him – that Robert Horne was not ill an hour or a day, but for a long space struggled with fits of marsh fever, and in between these bouts of the ague he went abroad like a well man and his friends would come up and see him, and the messenger who came up to enquire after him was Tora, the Egyptian girl who walked with her bosom full of violets.

The storm was in full fury now, muttering low and sullen round the cottage with great power of beating rain.

'Robert Horne was slow in dying,' said Sir Nicholas. 'Of what did he speak in those days?'

'Of a woman, good sir.'

'Of my wife!' cried Ned.

Goody Boyle shook her head with a look of stupidity. 'I know nothing of that. Though for certain he called her Anne, sweet Anne, and swore he would possess her yet – in so many words and very roundly.'

'But he died baulked,' said Ned, swaying on his stool, 'and he'll rot outside holy ground.'

'They'll lay him in Deadman's Field, which is full of old bones none can plough and no sheep will graze,' answered the woman; 'and I must set out to see lame Jonas, who promised to have the grave ready – but maybe the rain has hindered him.'

She looked at them shrewdly as she added: 'That is, gentles, if you care to remain alone with the body of Robert Horne.'

'I think of him as a dead dog,' replied Ned Crediton.

And when the woman had gone, he, being loosened with the French brandy, suggested a gross jest.

'Why should Robert Horne have all this honour, even from rogues and Egyptians? Let us fool them – throwing his corpse out into the byre, and I will lie under the sheet and presently sit up and fright them all with the thought it is the devil!'

Sir Nicholas warmly cheered this proposal and they lurched into the inner chamber, which was dark enough now by reason of a great northern cloud that blocked the light from the window.

They pulled the sheet off Robert Horne and found him wrapped in another that was furled up under his chin, and so they carried him to the back door and peered through the storm for some secret place where they might throw him.

And Ned Crediton saw a dark bed of rank hemlock and cried, 'Cast him into the kecksies!' that being the rustic name for the weed.

So they flung the dead man into the hemlocks, which were scarce high enough to cover him, and to hide the whiteness of the sheet, broke off boughs from the hazel copse and put over him, and went back laughing to the cottage, and there kept a watch out from the front window, and when they saw Goody Boyle toiling along through the rain, Ned took off his hat and coat and sword and folded them away under the bed; then Sir Nicholas wrapped him in the under sheet, so that he was shrouded to the chin, and he lay on the pillow and drew the other sheet over him.

'If thou sleepst, do not snore,' said Nicholas, and went back to the fire and lit his long clay full of Virginian tobacco.

When Goody Boyle entered with her wet shawl over her head, she had two ragged creatures behind her who stared malevolently at the fine gentleman with his fine clothes and dark curls lolling by the fire and watching the smoke rings rise from his pipe.

'Esquire Crediton has ridden for home,' he said, 'but I am not minded to risk the ague.'

And he sipped more brandy and laughed at them, and they, muttering, for they knew his fame, went into the death chamber and crouched round the couch where Sir Nicholas had just laid Ned Crediton under the sheet.

And presently others came up, Egyptians, eel-catchers and the like, outcasts and vagrants who crept in to watch by the corpse.

Sir Nicholas presently rolled after them to see the horror and shriekings for grace there would be when the dead man threw aside his shroud and sat up.

But the vigil went on till the night closed in and the two wax candles were lit, and still Ned Crediton gave no sign, nor did he snore or heave beneath the sheet; and Sir Nicholas became impatient, for the rain was over and he was weary of the foul air and the grotesque company.

'The fool,' he thought (for he kept his wits well even in his cups), 'has gone into a drunken sleep and forgot the joke.'

So he pushed his way to the bed and turned down the sheet, whispering, 'This jest will grow stale with keeping.'

But the words withered on his lips, for he looked into the face of a dead man. At the cry he gave they all came babbling about him and he told them of the trick that had been put upon them.

'But there's devil's work here,' he ended. 'For here is the body back again – or else Ned Crediton dead and frozen into the likeness of the other.' And he flung the sheet end quickly over the pinched face and fair hair.

'And what did ye do with Robert Horne, outrageous dare-fiend that ye be?' demanded an old vagrant.

And the young lord passed the ill words and answered with whitened lips: 'We cast him into yon bed of kecksies.'

And they all beat out into the night, the lout with a lantern.

And there was nothing at all in the bed of kecksies ... and Ned Crediton's horse was gone from the stable.

'He was drunk,' said Sir Nicholas, 'and forgot the part – and fled that moment I was in the outer room.'

'And in that minute did he carry Robert Horne in alone and wrap him up so neatly?' queried Goody Boyle.

'We'll go in,' said another hag, 'and strip the body and see which man it be——'

But Sir Nicholas was in the saddle.

'Let be,' he cried wildly; 'there's been gruesome work enough for tonight – it's Robert Horne you have there – let be. I'll back to Crediton Manor——'

And he rode his horse out of the field, then more quickly down the darkling road, for the fumes of the brandy were out of his brain and he saw clearly and dreaded many things. At the cross-roads when the ghastly moon had suddenly struck free of the retreating clouds he saw Ned Crediton ahead of him riding sharply, and he called out:

'Eh, Ned, what have you made of this jest? This way it is but a mangled folly.'

'What matter now for the jest or earnest?' answered the other. 'I ride home at last.'

Sir Nicholas kept pace with him; he was hatless and wore a shabby cloak that was twisted about him with the wind of his riding.

'Why did not you take your own garments?' asked Sir Nicholas. 'Belike that rag you've snatched up belonged to Robert Horne——'

'If Crediton could steal his shroud, he can steal his cloak,' replied Ned, and his companion said no more, thinking him wrought into a frenzy with the brandy and the evil nature of the joke.

The moon shone clear and cold with a faint stain like old blood in the halo, and the trees, bending in a seaward wind, cast the recent rain that loaded them heavily to the ground as the two rode into the gates of Crediton Manor.

The hour was later than even Sir Nicholas knew (time had been blurred for him since the coming of the storm) and there was no light save a dim lamp in an upper window.

Ned Crediton dropped out of the saddle, not waiting for the mounting-block, and rang the iron bell till it clattered through the house like a madman's fury.

'Why, Ned, why this panic home-coming?' asked Sir Nicholas; but the other answered him not, but rang again.

There were footsteps within and the rattle of chains, and a voice asked from the side window.

'Who goes there?'

And Ned Crediton dragged at the bell and screamed: 'I! The master!'

The door was opened and an old servant stood there, pale in his bedgown.

Ned Crediton passed him and stood by the newel-post, like a man spent yet alert.

'Send someone for the horses,' said Nick Bateup, 'for your master is crazy drunk. I tell you Mathews, he has seen Robert Horne dead tonight——'

Crediton laughed: the long rays of the lamplight showed him pale, haggard, distorted, with tumbled fair hair and a torn shirt under the mantle, and at his wrist a ragged bunch of hemlock thrust into his sash.

'A posy of kecksies for Anne,' he said. The sleepy servants who were already up began to come into the hall, and looked at him with dismay.

'I'll lie here tonight,' said Sir Nicholas; 'bring me lights into the parlour. I've no mind to sleep.'

He took off his hat and fingered his sword and glanced uneasily at the figure by the newel-post with the posy of kecksies.

Another figure appeared at the head of the stairs. Anne Crediton holding her candle, wearing a grey lute-string robe and a lace cap with long ribbons that hung on to her bosom; she peered over the baluster and some of the hot wax from her taper fell onto the oak treads.

'I've a beau pot for you, Anne,' said Crediton, looking up and holding out the hemlocks. 'I've long been dispossessed, Anne, but I've come home at last.'

She drew back without a word and her light flickered away across the landing; Crediton went up after her and they heard a door shut.

In the parlour the embers had been blown to flames and fresh logs put on, and Sir Nicholas warmed his cold hands and told old Mathews, in a sober manner for him, the story of the jest they had striven to put on Goody Boyle and the queer monstrous people from the marsh and the monstrous ending of it, and the strangeness of Ned Crediton; it was not his usual humour to discourse with servants or to discuss his vagrant debaucheries with any, but tonight he seemed to need company and endeavoured to retain the old man, who was not reluctant to stay, though usually he hated to see the dark face and bright clothes of Nick Bateup before the hearth of Crediton Manor.

And as these two talked disconnectedly, as if they would fill the gap of any silence that might fall in the quiet house, there came the wail of a woman, desperate yet sunken.

'It is Mistress Crediton,' said Mathews with a downcast look.

'He ill uses her?'

'God help us, he will use buckles and straps to her, Sir Nicholas.'

A quivering shriek came brokenly down the stairs and seemed to form the word 'mercy'.

Sir Nicholas was an evil man who died unrepentant, but he was not of a temper to relish raw cruelty or crude brutalities to women; he would break their souls but never their bodies. So he went to the door and listened, and old Mathews had never liked him so well as now when he saw the look on the thin, dark face.

For the third time she shrieked and they marvelled that any human being could hold her breath so long; yet it was muffled as if someone held a hand over her mouth.

The sweat stood on the old man's forehead.

'I've never before known her complain, sir,' he whispered. 'She is a very dog to her lord and takes her whip mutely——'

'I know, I know – she adores his hand when it caresses or when it strikes; but tonight, if I know anything of a woman's accents, that is a note of abhorrence——'

He ran up the stairs, the old man panting after him with the snatched-up lantern.

'Which is her chamber?'

'Here, Sir Nicholas.'

The young man struck on the heavy oak panels with the hilt of his sword.

'Madam – Madam Crediton, why are you so ill at ease?'

She moaned from within.

'Open to me. I'll call some of your women – come out———'

Their blood curdled to hear her wails.

'Damn you to hell,' cried Sir Nicholas in a fury. 'Come out, Ned Crediton, or I'll have the door down and run you through.'

The answer was a little break of maniac laughter.

'She has run mad or he,' cried Mathews, backing from the room. 'And surely there is another clamour at the door———'

Again the bell clanged and there were voices and tumult at the door; Mathews went and opened, and Sir Nicholas, looking down the stairs, saw in the moonlight a dirty farm cart, a sweating horse, and some of the patched and rusty crew who had been keeping vigil in Goody Boyle's cottage.

'We've brought Esquire Crediton home,' said one; and the others lifted a body from the cart and carried it through the murky moonlight.

Sir Nicholas came downstairs, for old Mathews could do nothing but cry for mercy.

'It was Edward Crediton,' repeated the eel-catcher, shuffling into the hall, 'clothed all but his coat and hat, and that was under the bed – there be his watches and chains, his seals and the papers in his pockets – and for his visage now, there is no mistaking it.'

They had laid the body on the table where it had so often sat and larked and ate and drunk and cursed; Sir Nicholas gazed, holding up the lantern.

Edward Crediton – never any doubt of that now, though his face was distorted as by the anguish of a sudden and ugly death.

'We never found Robert Horne,' muttered one of the mourners, trailing his foul muddy rags nearer the fire and thrusting his crooked hands to the blaze.

Mathews fell on his knees and tried to pray, but could think of no words.

'Who is upstairs?' demanded Sir Nicholas in a terrible voice. 'Who is with that wretched woman?'

And he stared at the body of her husband.

Mathews, who had loved her as a little child, began gibbering and moaning.

'Did he not say he'd have her? And did not yon fool change places with him? Oh God, oh God, and he has not come to take his place———'

'But Robert Horne was *dead*. I saw him dead,' stammered Sir Nicholas, and set the lantern down, for his hand shook so the flame waved in gusts.

'Eh,' shrieked old Mathews, grovelling on his hands and knees in his bedgown. 'Might not the devil have lent his body back for his own pitchy purposes?'

They looked at him a little, seeing he was suddenly crazed; then Sir Nicholas ran up the stairs with the others at his heels and thundered with his sword, and kicked and shouted outside Anne Crediton's chamber door.

All the foul, muddy, earthy crew cowered on the stairs and chittered together, and in the parlour before the embers old Mathews crouched and huddled and whimpered.

The bedroom door opened and Robert Horne came out and stood and smiled at them, and the young man in his fury fell back and his sword rattled from his hand to the floor.

Robert Horne was a white death, nude to the waist and from there swathed in grave clothes; under the tattered dark cloak he had ridden in was his shroud knotted round his neck; his naked chest gleamed with ghastly dews, and under the waxen polish of his sunken face the decayed blood showed in discoloured patches; he went down the stairs and they hid their faces while his foul whiteness passed.

Sir Nicholas stumbled into the bedchamber. The moonlight showed Anne Crediton tumbled on the bed, dead and staring, with the posy of kecksies on her bare breast and her mouth hung open and her hands clutching at the curtains.

The mourners rode back and picked up Robert Horne's body whence it had returned to the kecksie patch and buried it in unholy ground with great respect, *as one to whom the devil had given his great desire.*

Couching at the Door

D. K. Broster

The first inkling which Augustine Marchant had of the matter was on
one fine summer morning about three weeks after his visit to Prague,
that is to say, in June 1898. In his library at Abbot's Medding he was
reclining, as his custom was when writing his poetry, on the very comfortable sofa near the french windows, one of which was open to the
garden. Pausing for inspiration – he was nearly at the end of his poem,
Salutation to All Unbeliefs – he let his eyes wander round the beautifully
appointed room, with its cloisonné and Satsuma, Buhl and first editions,
and then allowed them to stray towards the sunlight outside. And so,
between the edge of the costly Herat carpet and the sill of the open
window, across the strip of polished oak flooring, he observed what he
took to be a small piece of dark fluff blowing in the draught; and
instantly made a note to speak to his housekeeper about the parlour-
maid. There was slackness somewhere; and in Augustine Marchant's
house no one was allowed to slack but himself.

There had been a time when the poet would not for a moment have
been received, as he was now, in country and even county society –
those days, even before the advent of *The Yellow Book* and *The Savoy*,
when he had lived in London, writing the plays and poems which had
so startled and shocked all but the 'decadent' and the 'advanced',
*Pomegranates of Sin, Queen Theodora and Queen Marozia, The Nights of the
Tour de Nesle, Amor Cypriacus* and the rest. But when, as the 'nineties
began to wane, he inherited Abbot's Medding from a distant cousin
and came to live there, being then at the height of an almost international reputation, Wiltshire society at first tolerated him for his
kinship with the late Lord Medding, and then, placated by the excel-
lence of his dinners and further mollified by the patent staidness of his
private life, decided that, in his personal conduct at any rate, he must
have turned over a new leaf. Perhaps indeed he had never been as
bad as he was painted, and if his writings continued to be no less
scandalously free-thinking than before, and needed to be just as rigidly

kept out of the hands of daughters, well, no country gentleman in the neighbourhood was obliged to read them!

And indeed Augustine Marchant in his fifty-first year was too keenly alive to the value of the good opinion of county society to risk shocking it by any overt doings of his. He kept his licence for his pen. When he went abroad, as he did at least twice a year – but that was another matter altogether. The nose of Mrs Grundy was not sharp enough to smell out his occupations in Warsaw or Berlin or Naples, nor her eyes long-sighted enough to discern what kind of society he frequented even so near home as Paris. At Abbot's Medding his reputation for being 'wicked' was fast declining into just enough of a sensation to titillate a croquet party. He had charming manners, could be witty at moments (though he could not keep it up), still retained his hyacinthine locks (by means of hair restorers), wore his excellently cut velvet coats and flowing ties with just the right air – half poet, half man of the world – and really had, at Abbot's Medding, no dark secret to hide beyond the fact, sedulously concealed by him for five-and-twenty years, that he had never been christened Augustine. Between Augustus and Augustine, what a gulf! But he had crossed it, and his French poems (which had to be smuggled into his native land) were signed *Augustin – Augustin Lemarchant.*

Removing his gaze from the objectionable evidence of domestic carelessness upon the floor, Mr Marchant now fixed it meditatively upon the ruby-set end of the gold pencil which he was using. Rossell & Ward, his publishers, were about to bring out an édition de luxe of *Queen Theodora and Queen Marozia* with illustrations by a hitherto unknown young artist – if they were not too daring. It would be a sumptuous affair in a limited edition. And as he thought of this the remembrance of his recent stay in Prague returned to the poet. He smiled to himself, as a man smiles when he looks at a rare wine, and thought, *Yes, if these blunt-witted Pharisees round Abbot's Medding only knew!* It was a good thing that the upholders of British petty morality were seldom great travellers; a dispensation of – ahem, Providence!

Twiddling his gold pencil between plump fingers, Augustine Marchant returned to his ode, weighing one epithet against another. Except in summer he was no advocate of open windows, and even in summer he considered that to get the most out of that delicate and precious instrument, his brain, his feet must always be kept thoroughly warm; he had therefore cast over them, before settling into his semi-reclining position, a beautiful rose-coloured Indian *sari* of the purest and thickest silk, leaving the ends trailing on the floor. And he became aware, with surprise and annoyance, that the piece of brown fluff or whatever it was down there, travelling in the draught from the window, had reached the nearest end of the *sari* and was now, impelled by the same current, travelling up it.

The master of Abbot's Medding reached out for the silver handbell on the table by his side. There must be more breeze coming in than he had realized, and he might take cold, a catastrophe against which he guarded himself as against the plague. Then he saw that the upward progress of the dark blot – it was about the size of a farthing – could not by any possibility be assigned to any other agency than its own. It was *climbing* up – some horrible insect, plainly, some disgusting kind of almost legless and very hairy spider, round and vague in outline. The poet sat up and shook the *sari* violently. When he looked again the invader was gone. He had obviously shaken it onto the floor, and on the floor somewhere it must still be. The idea perturbed him, and he decided to take his writing out to the summerhouse, and give orders later that the library was to be thoroughly swept out.

Ah! it was good to be out of doors and in a pleasance so delightfully laid out, so exquisitely kept, as his! In the basin of the fountain the sea-nymphs of rosy-veined marble clustered round a Thetis as beautiful as Aphrodite herself; the lightest and featheriest of acacia trees swayed near. And as the owner of all this went past over the weedless turf he repeated snatches of Verlaine to himself about '*sveltes jets d'eau*' and '*sanglots d'extase.*'

Then turning his head to look back at the fountain, he became aware of a little dark brown object about the size of a halfpenny running towards him over the velvet-smooth sward ...

He believed afterwards that he must first have had a glimpse of the truth at that instant in the garden, or he would not have acted so instinctively as he did and so promptly. For, a moment later, he was standing at the edge of the basin of Thetis, his face blanched in the sunshine, his hand firmly clenched. Inside that closed hand something feather-soft pulsated ... Holding back as best he could the disgust and the something more which clutched at him, Augustine Marchant stooped and plunged his whole fist into the bubbling water, and let the stream of the fountain whirl away what he had picked up. Then with uncertain steps he went and sat down on the nearest seat and shut his eyes. After a while he took out his lawn handkerchief and carefully dried his hand with the intaglio ring, dried it, and then looked curiously at the palm. *I did not know I had so much courage*, he was thinking; *so much courage and good sense!* ... I would doubtless drown very quickly.

Burrows, his butler, was coming over the lawn. 'Mr and Mrs Morrison have arrived, sir.'

'Ah, yes; I had forgotten for the moment.' Augustine Marchant got up and walked towards the house and his guests, throwing back his shoulders and practising his famous enigmatic smile, for Mrs Morrison was a woman worth impressing.

(But what had it been exactly? Why, just what it had looked – a tuft of fur blowing over the grass, a tuft of fur! Sheer imagination that it had moved in his closed hand with a life of its own ... Then why had he shut his eyes as he stooped and made a grab at it? Thank God, thank God, it was nothing now but a drenched smear swirling round the nymphs of Thetis!)

'Ah, dear lady, you must forgive me! Unpardonable of me not to be in to receive you!' He was in the drawing-room now, fragrant with its banks of hothouse flowers, bending over the hand of the fashionably attired guest on the sofa, in her tight bodice and voluminous sleeves, with a fly-away hat perched at a rakish angle on her gold-brown hair.

'Your man told us that you were writing in the garden,' said her goggle-eyed husband reverentially.

'*Cher maître*, it is we who ought not to be interrupting your rendezvous with the Muse,' returned Mrs Morrison in her sweet, high voice. 'Terrible to bring you from such company into that of mere visitors!'

Running his hand through his carefully tended locks the *cher maître* replied, 'Between a visit from the Muse and one from beauty's self no true poet would hesitate! – Moreover, luncheon awaits us, and I trust it is a good one.'

He liked faintly to shock fair admirers by admitting that he cared for the pleasures of the table; it was quite safe to do so, since none of them had sufficient acumen to see that it was true.

The luncheon was excellent, for Augustine kept an admirable cook. Afterwards he showed his guests over the library – yes, even though it had not received the sweeping which would not be necessary now – and round the garden; and in the summerhouse was prevailed upon to read some of *Amor Cypriacus* aloud. And Mrs Frances (nowadays Francesca) Morrison was thereafter able to recount to envious friends how the Poet himself had read her stanza after stanza from that most *daring* poem of his; and how poor Fred, fanning himself meanwhile with his straw hat – not from the torridity of the verse but because of the afternoon heat – said afterwards that he had not understood a single word. A good thing, perhaps ...

When they had gone Augustine Marchant reflected rather cynically, *All that was just so much bunkum when I wrote it.* For, ten years ago, in spite of those audacious, glowing verses, he was an ignorant neophyte. Of course, since then ... He smiled, a private, sly, self-satisfied smile. It was certainly pleasant to know oneself no longer a fraud!

Returning to the summerhouse to fetch his poems he saw what he took to be Mrs Morrison's fur boa lying on the floor just by the basket chair which she had occupied. Odd of her not to have missed it on departure – a tribute to his verses perhaps. His housekeeper must send it after her by post. But just at that moment his head gardener approached, desiring some instructions, and when the matter was settled, and Augustine Marchant turned once more to enter the summerhouse, he found that he had been mistaken about the dropped boa, for there was nothing on the floor.

Besides, he remembered now that Mrs Morrison's boa had been a rope of grey feathers, not of dark fur. As he took up *Amor Cypriacus* he asked himself lazily what could have led him to imagine a woman's boa there at all, much less a fur one.

Suddenly he knew why. A lattice in the house of memory had opened, and he remained rigid, staring out at the jets of the fountain rising and falling in the afternoon sun. Yes; of that glamorous, wonderful, abominable night in Prague, the part he least wished to recall was connected – incidentally but undeniably – with a fur boa – a long boa of dark fur ...

He had to go up to town next day to a dinner in his honour. There and then he decided to go up that same night by a late train, a most unusual proceeding, and most disturbing to his valet, who knew that it was doubtful whether he could at such short notice procure him a first-class carriage to himself. However, Augustine Marchant went, and even, to the man's amazement, deliberately chose a compartment with another occupant when he might, after all, have had an empty one.

The dinner was brilliant: Augustine had never spoken better. Next day he went round to the little street not far from the British Museum where he found Lawrence Storey, his new illustrator, working feverishly at his drawings for *Queen Theodora and Queen Marozia*, and quite overwhelmed at the honour of a personal visit. Augustine was very kind to him, and, while offering a few criticisms, highly praised his delineation of those two Messalinas of tenth-century Rome, their long supple hands, their heavy eyes, their full, almost repellent mouths. Storey had followed the same type for mother and daughter, but with a subtle difference.

'They were certainly two most evil women, especially the younger.' he observed ingenuously. 'But I suppose that, from an artistic point of view, that doesn't matter nowadays!'

Augustine, smoking one of his special cigarettes, made a delicate little gesture. 'My dear fellow, Art has nothing whatever to do with what is called "morality"; happily we know that at last! Show me how you thought of depicting the scene where Marozia orders the execution of her mother's papal paramour. Good, very good! Yes, the lines there, even the fall of that loose sleeve from the extended arm, express with clarity what I had in mind. You have great gifts!'

'I have tried to make her look wicked,' said the young man, reddening with pleasure. 'But,' he added deprecatingly, 'it is very hard for a ridiculously inexperienced person like myself to have the right artistic vision. For to you, Mr Marchant, who have penetrated into such wonderful arcana of the forbidden, it would be foolish to pretend to be other than I am.'

'How do you know that I have penetrated into any such arcana?' enquired the poet, half shutting his eyes and looking (though not to the almost worshipping gaze of young Storey) like a great cat being stroked.

'Why, one has only to read you!'

'You must come down and stay with me soon,' were Augustine Marchant's parting words. (He would give the boy a few days' good living, for which he would be none the worse; let him drink some decent wine.) 'How soon do you think you will be able to finish the rough sketches for the rest, and the designs for the *culs de lampe*? A fortnight or three weeks? Good; I shall look to see you then. Goodbye, my dear fellow; I am very, very much pleased with what you have shown me!'

The worst of going up to London from the country was that one was apt to catch a cold in town. When he got back Augustine Marchant was almost sure that this misfortune had befallen him, so he ordered a fire in his bedroom, despite the season, and consumed a *recherché* little supper in seclusion. And, as the cold turned out to have been imaginary, he was very comfortable, sitting there in his silken dressing-gown, toasting his toes and holding up a glass of golden Tokay to the flames. Really *Theodora and Marozia* would make as much sensation when it came out with these illustrations as when it first appeared!

All at once he set down his glass. Not far away on his left stood a big cheval mirror, like a woman's, in which a good portion of the bed behind him was reflected. And, in this mirror, he had just seen the valance of the bed move. There could be no draught to speak of in this warm room, he never allowed a cat in the house, and it was quite impossible that there should be a rat about. If after all some stray cat should have got in it must be ejected at once. Augustine hitched round in his chair to look at the actual bedhanging.

Yes, the topaz-hued silk valance again swung very slightly outward as though it were being pushed. Augustine bent forward to the bellpull to summon his valet. Then the flask of Tokay rolled over on the table as he leaped from his chair instead. Something like a huge, dark caterpillar was emerging very slowly from under his bed, moving as a caterpillar moves, with undulations running over it. Where its head should have been was merely a tapering end smaller than the rest of it, but of like substance. It was a dark fur boa.

Augustine Marchant felt that he screamed, but he could not have done so, for his tongue clave to the roof of his mouth. He merely stood staring, staring, all the blood gone from his heart. Still very slowly, the thing continued to creep out from under the valance, waving that eyeless, tapering end to and fro, as though uncertain where to proceed. *I am going mad, mad, mad!* thought Augustine, and then, with a revulsion, *No, it can't be! It's a real snake of some kind!*

That could be dealt with. He snatched up the poker as the boa-thing, still swaying the head which was no head, kept pouring steadily out from under the lifted yellow frill, until quite three feet were clear of the bed. Then he fell upon it furiously, with blow after blow.

But they had no effect on the furry, spineless thing; it merely gave under them and rippled up in another place. Augustine hit the bed, the floor; at last, really screaming, he threw down his weapon and fell upon the thick, hairy rope with both hands, crushing it together into a mass – there was little if any resistance in it – and hurled it into the fire and, panting, kept it down with shovel and tongs. The flames licked up instantly and, with a roar, made short work of it, though there seemed to be some slight effort to escape, which was perhaps only the effect of the heat. A moment later there was a very strong smell of burned hair, and that was all.

Augustine Marchant seized the fallen flask of Tokay and drained from its mouth what little was left in the bottom ere, staggering to the bed, he flung himself upon it and buried his face in the pillows, even heaping them over his head as if he could thus stifle the memory of what he had seen.

He kept his bed next morning; the supposed cold afforded a good pretext. Long before the maid came in to re-lay the fire he had crawled out to make sure that there were no traces left of – what he had burned there. There were none. A nightmare could not have left a trace, he told himself. But well he knew that it was not a nightmare.

And now he could think of nothing but that room in Prague and the long fur boa of the woman. Some department of his mind (he supposed) must have projected that thing, scarcely noticed at the time, scarcely remembered, into the present and the here. It was terrible to think that one's mind possessed such dark, unknown powers. But not so terrible as if the – apparition – had been endowed with an entirely separate objective existence. In a day or two he would consult his doctor and ask him to give him a tonic.

But, expostulated an uncomfortably lucid part of his brain, you are trying to run with the hare and hunt with the hounds. Is it not better to believe that the thing *had* an objective existence, for you have burned it to nothing? Well and good! But if it is merely a projection from your own mind, what is to prevent it from reappearing, like the phoenix, from the ashes?

There seemed no answer to that, save in an attempt to persuade himself that he had been feverish last night. Work was the best antidote. So Augustine Marchant rose, and was surprised and delighted to find the atmosphere of his study unusually soothing and inspiring, and that day, against all expectation, *Salutation to All Unbeliefs* was completed by some stanzas with which he was not too ill-pleased. Realizing nevertheless that he should be glad of company that evening, he had earlier sent round a note to the local solicitor, a good fellow, to come and dine with him; played a game of billiards with the lawyer afterwards and retired to bed after some vintage port and a good stiff whisky and soda with scarcely a thought of the visitant of the previous night.

He woke at that hour when the thrushes in early summer punctually greet the new day – three o'clock. They were greeting it even vociferously, and Augustine Marchant was annoyed with their enthusiasm. His golden damask window-curtains kept out all but a glimmer of the new day, yet as, lying upon his back, the poet opened his eyes for a moment, his only half-awakened sense of vision reported something swinging to and fro in the dimness like a pendulum of rope. It was indistinct but seemed to be hanging from the tester of the bed. And, wide awake in an instant, with an unspeakable anguish of premonition tearing through him, he felt, next moment, a light thud on the coverlet about the level of his knees. Something had arrived on the bed ...

And Augustine Marchant neither shrieked nor leaped from his bed; he could not. Yet, now that his eyes were grown used to the twilight of the room, he saw it clearly, the fur rope which he had burned to extinction two nights ago, dark and shining as before, rippling with a gentle movement as it coiled itself neatly together in the place where it had struck the bed, and subsided there in a symmetrical round, with only that tapering end a little raised and, as it were, looking at him – only, eyeless and featureless, it could not look. One thought of disgusted relief, that it was not at any rate going to attack him, and Augustine Marchant fainted.

Yet his swoon must have merged into sleep, for he woke in a more or less ordinary fashion to find his man placing his early tea-tray beside him and enquiring when he should draw his bath. There was nothing on the bed.

I shall change my bedroom, thought Augustine to himself, looking at the haggard, fallen-eyed man who faced him in the mirror as he shaved. *No, better still, I will go away for a change. Then I shall not have these – dreams. I'll go to old Edgar Fortescue for a few days; he begged me again not long ago to come any time.*

So to the house of that old Maecenas he went. He was much too great a man now to be in need of Sir Edgar's patronage. It was homage which he received there, both from host and guests. The stay did much to soothe his scarified nerves. Unfortunately the last day undid the good of all the foregoing ones.

Sir Edgar possessed a pretty young wife – his third – and, among other charms of his place in Somerset, an apple orchard underplanted with flowers. And in the cool of the evening Augustine walked there with his host and hostess almost as if he were the Almighty with the dwellers in Eden. Presently they sat down upon a rustic seat (but a very comfortable one) under the shade of the apple boughs, amid the incongruous but pleasant parterres.

'You have come at the wrong season for these apple trees, Marchant,' observed Sir Edgar after a while, taking out his cigar. 'Blossom-time or apple-time – they are showy at either, in spite of the underplanting. What is attracting you on that tree – a titmouse? We have all kinds here, pretty, destructive little beggars!'

'I did not know that I was looking – it's nothing – thinking of something else,' stammered the poet. Surely, surely he had been mistaken in thinking that he had seen a sinuous, dark furry thing undulating like a caterpillar down the stem of that particular apple tree at a few yards' distance?

Talk went on, even his; there was safety in it. It was only the breeze which faintly rustled that bed of heliotrope behind the seat. Augustine wanted desperately to get up and leave the orchard, but neither Sir Edgar not his wife seemed disposed to move, and so the poet remained at his end of the seat, his left hand playing nervously with a long bent of grass which had escaped the scythe.

All at once he felt a tickling sensation on the back of his hand, looked down and saw that featureless snout of fur protruding upward from underneath the rustic bench and sweeping itself backward and forward against his hand with a movement which was almost caressing. he was on his feet in a flash.

'Do you mind if I go in?' he asked abruptly. 'I'm not – feeling very well.'

*　　*　　*

If the thing could follow him it was of no use to go away. He returned to Abbot's Medding looking so much the worse for his change of air that Burrows expressed a respectful hope that he was not indisposed. And almost the first thing that occurred, when Augustine sat down at his writing-table to attend to his correspondence, was the unwinding of itself from one of its curved legs, of a soft, brown, oscillating serpent which slowly waved an end at him as if in welcome ...

In welcome, yes, that was it! The creature, incredible though it was, the creature seemed glad to see him! Standing at the other end of the room, his hands pressed over his eyes – for what was the use of attempting to hurt or destroy it – Augustine Marchant thought shudderingly that, like a witch's cat, a 'familiar' would not, presumably, be ill-disposed towards its master. Its master! Oh, God!

The hysteria which he had been trying to keep down began to mount uncontrollably when, removing his hand, Augustine glanced again towards his writing-table and saw that the boa had coiled itself in his chair and was sweeping its end to and fro over the back, somewhat in the way that a cat, purring meanwhile, rubs itself against furniture or a human leg in real or simulated affection.

'Oh, go away from there!' he suddenly screamed at it, advancing with outstretched hand. 'In the devil's name, get out.'

To his utter amazement, he was obeyed. The rhythmic movements ceased, the fur snake poured itself down out of the chair and writhed towards the door. Venturing back to his writing-table after a moment Augustine saw it coiled on the threshold, the blind end turned towards him as usual, as though watching. And he began to laugh. What would happen if he rang and someone came; would the opening door scrape it aside – would it vanish? Had it, in short, an existence for anyone else but himself?

But he dared not make the experiment. He left the room by the french window, feeling that he could never enter the house again. And perhaps, had it not been for the horrible knowledge just acquired that it could follow him, he might easily have gone away for good from Abbot's Medding and all his treasures and comforts. But of what use would that be – and how should he account for so extraordinary an action? No; he must think and plan while he yet remained sane.

To what, then, could he have recourse? The black magic in which he had dabbled with such disastrous consequences might possibly help him. Left to himself he was but an amateur, but he had a number of books ... There was also that other realm whose boundaries sometimes marched side by side with magic – religion. But how could he pray to a Deity in whom he did not believe? Rather pray to the Evil which had sent this curse upon him, to show him how to banish it. Yet since he had deliberately followed what religion stigmatized as sin, what even the world would label as lust and necromancy, supplication to the dark powers was not likely to deliver him from them. They must somehow be outwitted.

He kept his *grimoires* and books of the kind in a locked bookcase in another room, not in his study; in that room he sat up till midnight. But the spells which he read were useless; moreover, he did not really believe in them. The irony of the situation was that, in a sense, he had only played at sorcery; it had but lent a spice to sensuality. He wandered wretchedly about the room dreading at any moment to see his

'familiar' wreathed round some object in it. At last he stopped at a
small bookcase which held some old forgotten books of his mother's –
Longfellow and Mrs Hemans, *John Halifax, Gentleman*, and a good many
volumes of sermons and mild essays. And when he looked at that
blameless assembly a cloud seemed to pass over Augustine Marchant's
vision, and he saw his mother, gentle and lace-capped as years and years
ago she used to sit, hearing his lessons, in an antimacassared chair. She
had been everything to him then, the little boy whose soul was not
smirched. He called silently to her now, 'Mamma, Mamma, can't you
help me? Can't you send this thing away?'

When the cloud had passed he found that he had stretched out his
hand and removed a big book. Looking at it he saw that it was her
Bible, with *Sarah Amelia Marchant* on the faded yellow flyleaf. Her spirit
was going to help him! He turned over a page or two, and out of the
largish print there sprang instantly at him: *Now the serpent was more subtle
than any beast in the field.* Augustine shuddered and almost put the Bible
back, but the conviction that there was help there urged him to go on.
He turned a few more pages of Genesis and his eyes were caught by this
verse, which he had never seen before in his life:

*And if thou doest well, shalt thou not be accepted? And if thou doest not well,
sin lieth at the door. And unto thee shall be his desire, and thou shalt rule
over him.*

What strange words! What could they possibly mean? Was there
light for him in them? *Unto thee shall be his desire.* That Thing, the loathsome semblance of affection which hung about it ... *Thou shalt rule over
him.* It *had* obeyed him, up to a point ... Was this Book, of all others,
showing him the way to be free? But the meaning of the verse was so
obscure! He had not, naturally, such a thing as a commentary in the
house. Yet, when he came to think of it, he remembered that some pious
and anonymous person, soon after the publication of *Pomegranates of Sin*,
had sent him a Bible in the Revised Version, with an inscription
recommending him to read it. He had it somewhere, though he had
always meant to get rid of it.

After twenty minutes' search through the sleeping house he found it
in one of the spare bedrooms. But it gave him little enlightenment, for
there was scant difference in the rendering, save that for *lieth at the door*,
this version had *coucheth*, and that the margin held an alternative
translation for the end of the verse: *And unto thee is its desire, but thou
shouldst rule over it.*

Nevertheless, Augustine Marchant stood after midnight in this
silent, sheeted guest-chamber repeating, '*But thou shouldst rule over it.*'
And all at once he thought of a way of escape.

*   *   *

It was going to be a marvellous experience, staying with Augustine Marchant. Sometimes Lawrence Storey hoped there would be no other guests at Abbot's Medding; at other times he hoped there would be. A *tête-à-tête* of four days with the great poet – could he sustain his share worthily? For Lawrence, despite the remarkable artistic gifts which were finding their first real flowering in these illustrations to Augustine's poem, was still unspoiled, still capable of wonder and admiration, still humble and almost naïve. It was still astonishing to him that he, an architect's assistant, should have been snatched away, as Ganymede by the eagle, from the lower world of elevations and drains to serve on Olympus. It was not, indeed, Augustine Marchant who had first discovered him, but it was Augustine Marchant who was going to make him famous.

The telegraph poles flitted past the second-class carriage window, and more than one traveller glanced with a certain envy and admiration at the fair, good-looking young man who diffused such an impression of happiness and candour, and had such a charming smile on his boyish lips. He carried with him a portfolio which he never let out of reach of his hand; the oldish couple opposite, speculating upon its contents, might have changed their opinion of him had they seen them.

But no shadow of the dark weariness of things unlawful rested on Lawrence Storey; to know Augustine Marchant, to be illustrating his great poem, to have learned from him that art and morality had no kinship, this was to plunge into a new realm of freedom and enlarging experience. Augustine Marchant's poetry, he felt, had already taught his hand what his brain and heart knew nothing of.

There was a dogcart to meet him at the station, and in the scented June evening he was driven with a beating heart past meadows and hayfields to his destination.

Mr Marchant, awaiting him in the hall, was at his most charming. 'My dear fellow, are those the drawings? Come, let us lock them away at once in my safe! If you had brought me diamonds I should not be one quarter so concerned about thieves. And did you have a comfortable journey? I have had you put in the orange room; it is next to mine. There is no one else staying here, but there are a few people coming to dinner to meet you.'

There was only just time to dress for dinner, so that Lawrence did not get an opportunity to study his host until he saw him seated at the head of the table. Then he was immediately struck by the fact that he looked curiously ill. His face – ordinarily by no means attenuated – seemed to have fallen in, there were dark circles under his eyes, and the perturbed Lawrence, observing him as the meal progressed, thought that his manner too seemed strange and once or twice quite absent-minded. And there was one moment when, though the lady on his right was

addressing him, he sharply turned his head away and looked down at
the side of his chair just as if he saw something on the floor. Then he
apologized, saying that he had a horror of cats, and that sometimes the
tiresome animal from the stables ... But after that he continued to
entertain his guests in his own inimitable way, and, even to the shy
Lawrence, the evening proved very pleasant.

The ensuing three days were wonderful and exciting to the young
artist – days of uninterrupted contact with a master mind which
acknowledged, as the poet himself admitted, none of the petty barriers
which man, for his own convenience, had set up between alleged right
and wrong. Lawrence had learned why his host did not look well; it
was loss of sleep, the price exacted by inspiration. He had a new poetic
drama shaping in his mind which would scale heights that he had not
yet attempted.

There was almost a touch of fever in the young man's dreams tonight
– his last night but one. He had several. First he was standing by the edge
of a sort of mere, inexpressibly desolate and unfriendly, a place he had
never seen in his life, which yet seemed in some way familiar; and something said to him, 'You will never go away from here!' He was alarmed,
and woke, but went to sleep again almost immediately, and this time
was back, oddly enough, in the church where in his earliest years he had
been taken to service by the aunt who had brought him up – a large
church full of pitch-pine pews with narrow ledges for hymn-books,
which ledges he used surreptitiously to lick during the long dull periods
of occultation upon his knees. But most of all he remembered the
window with Adam and Eve in the Garden of Eden, on either side of
an apple tree round whose trunk was coiled a monstrous snake with a
semi-human head. Lawrence had hated and dreaded that window,
and because of it he would never go near an orchard and had no
temptation to steal apples ... Now he was back in that church again,
staring at the window, lit up with some infernal glow from behind. He
woke again, little short of terrified – he, a grown man! But again he went
to sleep quite quickly.

His third dream had for background, as sometimes happens in
nightmares, the very room in which he lay. He dreamed that a door
opened in the wall, and in the doorway, quite plain against the light
from another room behind him, stood Augustine Marchant in his
dressing-gown. He was looking down at something on the ground which
Lawrence did not see, but his hand was pointing at Lawrence in the
bed, and he was saying in a voice of command, 'Go to him, do you
hear? Go to him! Go to *him*! Am I not your master?'

And Lawrence, who could neither move nor utter a syllable,
wondered uneasily what this could be which was thus commanded, but
his attention was chiefly focused on Augustine Marchant's face. After he

had said these words several times, and apparently without result, a dreadful change came upon it, a look of the most unutterable despair. It seemed visibly to age and wither; he said, in a loud, penetrating whisper, 'Is there no escape then?' covered his ravaged face a moment with his hands, and then went back and softly closed the door. At that Lawrence woke; but in the morning he had forgotten all three dreams.

The *tête-à-tête* dinner on the last night of his stay would have lingered in a gourmet's memory, so that it was a pity the young man did not know in the least what he was eating. At last there was happening what he had scarcely dared hope for; the great poet of the sensuous was revealing to him some of the unimaginably strange and secret sources of his inspiration. In the shaded rosy candlelight, his elbows on the table among trails of flowers he, who was not even a neophyte, listened like a man learning for the first time of some spell or spring which will make him more than mortal.

'Yes,' said Augustine Marchant, after a long pause, 'yes, it was a marvellous, an undying experience – one that is not given to many. It opened doors, it – but I despair of doing it justice in mere words.' His look was transfigured, almost dreamy.

'But she – the woman – how did you——?' asked Lawrence Storey in a hushed voice.

'Oh, the woman?' said Augustine, suddenly finishing off his wine. 'The woman was only a common streetwalker.'

A moment or two later Lawrence was looking at his host wonderingly and wistfully. 'But this was in Prague. Prague is a long way off.'

'One does not need to go so far, in reality. Even in Paris——'

'One could – have that experience in Paris?'

'If you knew where to go. And of course, it is necessary to have credentials. I mean that – like all such enlightenments – it has to be kept secret, most secret, from the vulgar minds who lay their restrictions on the finer. That is self-evident.'

'Of course,' said the young man, and sighed deeply.

His host looked at him affectionately. 'You, my dear Lawrence – I may call you Lawrence? – want just that touch of – what shall I call them – *les choses cachées* – to liberate your immense artistic gifts from the shackles which still bind them. Through that gateway you would find the possibility of their full fruition! It would fertilize your genius to a still finer blossoming ... But you would have scruples – and you are very young.'

'You know,' said Lawrence in a low and trembling tone, 'what I feel about your poetry. You know how I ache to lay the best that is in me at your feet. If only I could make my drawings for the Two Queens more worthy – already it is an honour which overwhelms me that you should have selected me to do them – but they are not what they should be. I am *not* sufficiently liberated ...'

Augustine leaned forward on the flower-decked table. His eyes were glowing. 'Do you truly desire to be?'

The young man nodded, too full of emotion to find his voice.

The poet got up, went over to a cabinet in a corner and unlocked it. Lawrence watched his fine figure in a sort of trance. Then he half rose with an exclamation.

'What is it?' asked Augustine very sharply, facing round.

'Oh, nothing, sir – only I believe you hate cats, and I thought I saw one, or rather its tail, disappearing into that corner.'

'There's no cat here,' said Augustine quickly. His face had become all shiny and mottled, but Lawrence did not notice it. The poet stood a moment looking at the carpet; one might almost have thought that he was gathering resolution to cross it; then he came swiftly back to the table.

'Sit down again,' he commanded. 'Have you a pocket-book with you, a pocket-book which you never leave about? Good! Then write *this* in one place; and *this* on another page – write it small – among other entries is best – not on a blank page – write it in Greek characters if you know them ...'

'What – what is it?' asked Lawrence, all at once intolerably excited, his eyes fixed on the piece of paper in Augustine's hand.

'The two halves of the address in Paris.'

*   *   *

Augustine Marchant kept a diary in those days, a locked diary, written in cipher. And for more than a month after Lawrence Storey's visit the tenor of the entries there was almost identical:

No change ... always with me ... How much longer can I endure it? The alteration in my looks is being remarked upon to my face. I shall have to get rid of Thornton [his man] *on some pretext or other, for I begin to think that he has seen It. No wonder, since It follows me about like a dog. When It is visible to everyone it will be the end ... I found It in bed with me this morning, pressed up against me as if for warmth ...*

But there was a different class of entry also, appearing at intervals with an ever-increasing note of impatience:

Will L.S. go there? ... When shall I hear from L.S.? ... Will the experiment do what I think? It is my last hope.

Then, suddenly, after five weeks had elapsed, an entry in a trembling hand:

For twenty-four hours I have seen no sign of It! Can it be possible?

And next day:

Still nothing. I begin to live again. – This evening has just come an ecstatic letter from L.S., from Paris, telling me that he had 'presented his credentials' and was to have the experience next day. He has had it by now – by yesterday, in fact. Have I really freed myself? It looks like it!

In one week from the date of that last entry it was remarked in Abbot's Medding how much better Mr Marchant was looking again. Of late he had not seemed at all himself; his cheeks had fallen in, his clothes seemed to hang loosely upon him, who had generally filled them so well, and he appeared nervous. Now he was as before, cheery, courtly, debonair. And last Sunday, will you believe it, he went to church! The rector was so astonished when he first became aware of him from the pulpit that he nearly forgot to give out his text. And the poet joined in the hymns, too! Several observed this amazing phenomenon.

It was the day after this unwonted appearance at St Peter's. Augustine was strolling in his garden. The air had a new savour, the sun a new light; he could look again with pleasure at Thetis and her nymphs of the fountain, could work undisturbed in the summerhouse. Free, free! All the world was good to the senses once again, and the hues and scents of early autumn better, in truth, than the brilliance of that summer month which had seen his curse descend upon him.

The butler brought him out a letter with a French stamp. From Lawrence Storey, of course; to tell him – what? Where had he caught his first glimpse of it? In one of those oppressively furnished French bedrooms? And how had he taken it?

At first, however, Augustine was not sure that the letter was from Storey. The writing was very different, cramped instead of flowing, and, in places, spluttering, the pen having dug into the paper as if the hand which held it had not been entirely under control – almost, thought Augustine, his eyes shining with excitement, almost as though something had been twined, liana-like, round the wrist. (He had a sudden sick recollection of a day when that had happened to him, quickly submerged in a gush of eager anticipation.) Sitting down upon the edge of the fountain he read – not quite what he had looked for:

I don't know what is happening to me, began the letter without other opening. *Yesterday I was in a café by myself, and had just ordered some absinthe – though I do not like it. And quite suddenly, although I knew that I was in the café, I realized that I was also back in that room. I could see every feature of it, but I could see the café too, with all the people in it; the one was, as it were, superimposed upon the other, the room, which was a good deal smaller than the café, being inside the latter, as a box may be within a larger box. And all the while the room was growing clearer, the café fading. I saw the glass of absinthe suddenly standing on nothing, as it were. All the furniture of the room, all the accessories you know of, were mixed up with the chairs and tables of the café. I do not know how I managed to find my way back to the* comptoir, *pay and get out. I took a fiacre back to my hotel. By the time I arrived there I was all right. I suppose that it was only the after-effects of a very strange and violent emotional experience. But I hope to God that it will not recur!*

'How interesting!' said Augustine Marchant, dabbling his hand in the swirling water where he had once drowned a piece of dark fluff. 'And why indeed should I have expected that It would couch at his door in the same form as at mine?'

Four days more of new-found peace and he was reading this:

In God's name – or the Devil's – come over and help me! I have hardly an hour now by night or day when I am sure of my whereabouts. I could not risk the journey back to England alone. It is like being imprisoned in some kind of infernal half-transparent box, always growing a little smaller. Whereever I go now I carry it about with me; when I am in the street I hardly know which is the pavement and which is the roadway, because I am always treading on that black carpet with the cabalistic designs; if I speak to anyone they may suddenly disappear from sight. To attempt to work is naturally useless. I would consult a doctor, but that would mean telling him everything ...

'I hope to God he won't do that!' muttered Augustine uneasily. 'He can't – he swore to absolute secrecy. I hadn't bargained, however, for his ceasing work. Suppose he finds himself unable to complete the designs for *Theodora and Marozia!* That would be serious ... However, to have freed myself is worth *any* sacrifice ... But Storey cannot, obviously, go on living indefinitely on two planes at once ... Artistically, though, it might inspire him to something quite unprecedented. I'll write to him and point that out; it might encourage him. But go near him in person – is it likely!'

The next day was one of great literary activity. Augustine was so deeply immersed in his new poetical drama that he neglected his correspondence and almost his meals – except his dinner, which seemed that evening to be shared most agreeably and excitingly by these new creations of his brain. Such, in fact, was his preoccupation with them that it was not until he had finished the savoury and poured out a glass of his superlative port that he remembered a telegram which had been handed to him as he came in to dinner. It still lay unopened by his plate. Now, tearing apart the envelope, he read with growing bewilderment these words above his publishers' names:

Please inform us immediately what steps to take are prepared send to France recover drawings if possible what suggestions can you make as to successor Rossell and Ward.

Augustine was more than bewildered; he was stupefied. Had some accident befallen Lawrence Storey of which he knew nothing? But he had opened all his letters this morning though he had not answered any. A prey to a sudden very nasty anxiety he got up and rang the bell.

'Burrows, bring me *The Times* from the library.'

The newspaper came, unopened. Augustine, now in a frenzy of uneasiness, scanned the pages rapidly. But it was some seconds before he came upon the headline: TRAGIC DEATH OF A YOUNG ENGLISH ARTIST, and read the following, furnished by the Paris correspondent:

Connoisseurs who were looking forward to the appearance of the superb illustrated edition of Mr Augustine Marchant's Queen Theodora and Queen Marozia *will learn with great regret of the death by drowning of the gifted young artist, Mr Lawrence Storey, who was engaged upon the designs for it. Mr Storey had recently been staying in Paris, but left one day last week for a remote spot in Brittany, it was supposed in pursuance of his work. On Friday last his body was discovered floating in a lonely pool near Carhaix. It is hard to see how Mr Storey could have fallen in, since this piece of water – the Mare de Plougouven – has a completely level shore surrounded by reeds, and is not in itself very deep, nor is there any boat upon it. It is said the unfortunate young Englishman had been somewhat strange in his manner recently and complained of hallucinations; it is therefore possible that under their influence he deliberately waded out into the Mare de Plougouven. A strange feature of the case is that he had fastened round him under his coat the finished drawings for Mr Marchant's book, which were of course completely spoiled by the water before the body was found. It is to be hoped that they were not the only——*

Augustine threw *The Times* furiously from him and struck the dinner table with his clenched fist.

'Upon my soul, that is too much! It is criminal! My property – and I who had done so much for him! Fastened them round himself – he must have been crazy!'

But had he been so crazy? When his wrath had subsided a little Augustine could not but ask himself whether the young artist had not in some awful moment of insight guessed the truth, or part of it – that his patron had deliberately corrupted him? It looked almost like it. But, if he had really taken all the finished drawings with him to this place in Brittany, what an unspeakably mean trick of revenge thus to destroy them! ... yet, even if it were so, he must regard their loss as the price of his own deliverance, since, from his point of view, the desperate expedient of passing on his 'familiar' had been a complete success. By getting someone else to plunge even deeper than he had done into the unlawful (for he had seen to it that Lawrence Storey should do that) he had proved, as that verse in Genesis said, that he *had* ruled over – what had pursued him in tangible form as a consequence of his own night in Prague. He could not be too thankful. The literary world might well be thankful too. For his own art was of infinitely more importance than the subservient, the parasitic art of an illustrator. He could with a little search find half a dozen just as gifted as that poor hallucination-ridden Storey to finish *Theodora and Marozia* – even, if necessary, to begin an entirely fresh set of drawings. And meanwhile, in the new lease of creative energy which this unfortunate but necessary sacrifice had made possible for him, he would begin to put on paper the masterpiece which was now taking brilliant shape in his liberated mind. A final glass, and then an evening in the workshop!

Augustine poured out some port, and was raising the glass, prepared to drink to his own success, when he thought he heard a sound near the door. He looked over his shoulder. Next instant the stem of the wine-glass had snapped in his hand and he had sprung back to the farthest limit of the room.

Reared up for quite five feet against the door, huge, dark, sleeked with wet and flecked with bits of green waterweed, was something half python, half gigantic cobra, its head drawn back as if to strike – its head, for in its former featureless tapering end were now two reddish eyes, such as furriers put into the heads of stuffed creatures. And they were fixed in an unwavering and malevolent glare upon him, as he cowered there clutching the bowl of the broken wineglass, the crumpled copy of *The Times* lying at his feet.

Don't You Dare
John Burke

She had always prophesied contemptuously that he would die before she did. He wouldn't reach fifty, she said. She would be young enough and attractive enough to marry again, and next time it would be someone she could respect. A real man, next time.

Once he tried to stem the flow of her derision by asking what she wanted him to do if she should happen to go first. She might be involved in an accident. It was only practical to make plans for the children. Michael showed signs of being able to take pretty good care of himself but Candida, at twelve, was sly and difficult, pruriently addicted to reading dubious American thrillers from the public library or even more dubious paperbacks which she bought with her pocket money in spite of being forbidden to do so. It was her father who had forbidden this. Her mother laughed and told him not to be so stuffy.

'I used to read them by the dozen when I was her age,' she said. 'Everything I could get my hands on. It did me good.'

'Did it?' he rashly said. It was the excuse for her to launch another of her scathing attacks on him.

Candida read half surreptitiously, half defiantly. She thought strange thoughts. She came out with outrageous remarks and then had long spells of mysterious silence. Her mother alternately doted on her and raged at her. She would goad Candida into a tantrum and then hit her across the side of the head and scream at her; and then, just as Robert was sickening with the savagery of it, the two of them would be crying and wrapping their arms round each other. Laura was a great believer in the richness of impetuous swings from one emotion to another, declaring that children loved you more this way than if you were nasty and cold and rational; that everyone, in fact, loved you more this way.

But if there was a sudden end to it, if she was no longer there to sneer and rage and coo, to run things her way because there was no other conceivable way – what then?

'I'd be the one who'd have to marry again,' he said, trying to keep it casual and light-hearted.

'You think anyone would have you?'

'Wouldn't be surprised.'

'You're trying to tell me you've already got someone lined up?'

She would have loved such an excuse to pile even further abuse on him. He was perversely tempted to give her this opportunity: the insults would at any rate be in a different vein from the usual ones. But the whole thing was absurd. He said:

'Of course not. There's nobody.'

'I didn't really imagine there would be.'

'But if I *were* left with the kids . . .'

'Don't you dare,' she said. 'Marry again? Don't you dare.'

He ought to have known that such a discussion would get nowhere. None of their arguments ever did. And, after all, it was stupid to talk about dying. You didn't plan for death when you were still only in your late thirties.

'In any case,' Laura summed up, 'it won't happen.' Again she trotted out her happy prediction: 'You'll die before I do.'

Yet she was the first to go. On her fortieth birthday she was dead and he was left with Michael and Candida.

Don't you dare . . .

But he dared.

He married Janet within the year. The quivering tension which Laura had maintained in the house was followed, after her death, by numbness. Now there came warmth and relaxation, a gradual stretching of the limbs and the mind.

Laura had been tall and fair. No matter what the current fashion, she kept her hair long – a beautiful silky mane of which she was swaggeringly proud. Between her shoulder blades she had a streak of faint golden down. She talked about it to friends and even to strangers, and lost no opportunity of exhibiting it. In a swimming costume she would turn her back to the sun and writhe gently so that the light could play on this glimmering fur. She implied that there was something very specially, madly sexy about it.

'Robert' – she would wave her hand at her husband with tolerant despair – 'has hardly any hair anywhere. But *anywhere*, my dears.'

She had married Robert in order to escape from a plump, slack, pathetically ignorant mother whom she despised; but after her mother's death she began to talk of her with growing affection. In no time at all she persuaded herself that they had been an ideal mother and daughter and that she ought to have listened more attentively to her mother's shrewd advice.

'I married too young, of course. Not that I blame Robert for that.

But I didn't have the chance of doing any of the things I really ought to have done.'

She ought to have been taken up by an international playboy, ought to have gone round the world, ought to have taken up skiing and surfing. She would have been so good: she could sense just how good she would have been. She could have become a tennis champion if Robert hadn't come along and penned her in physically and emotionally, and given her two children. They had nothing in common: it was tragic that she should have discovered this too late.

Next time it would be a real man.

'Given my time over again,' she would laugh to her friends, not finishing the sentence but promising them and Robert and herself that she would, before it was too late, somehow have her time over again.

Her interests waxed and waned. Some were taken up merely to spite Robert and in due course were dropped. Others became obsessions. Whatever Laura discovered was indeed a discovery: nobody had ever known it as she knew it, nobody could understand it as she immediately, intuitively understood it.

Swimming was her greatest passion. It was because of this that Robert slaved to buy the house on the river. Then there was more expense because Laura wanted to have people dropping in from the other houses and from the island and from the plushy cabin cruisers, and they all needed drinks and lots of drinks; and she wanted new clothes so that they could go over and drop in on the houses and the island and the cabin cruisers for drinks and lots of drinks. She nagged him about buying a boat. While he worked, she lounged in a bikini on the lawn which sloped down into the river, or swam across to say hello to her friends who weren't ever his friends or swam along the river and communed with herself and came back reinvigorated, ready to sneer at him yet again.

The river became her personal property. No matter how many boats came and went, no matter how many other people plunged into the water, it was her river. She had used it, so it was hers. She loved it – loved to succumb to it and then to dominate it. She flouted the current by surrendering herself and allowing herself to be pulled towards the weir, knowing the exact moment when she could beat it and escape.

Some evenings in moonlight or pitch darkness she walked down the lawn and into the water and swam across to the lawn on the far side. The Major who lived alone across there was always glad to offer her a drink. Between them she and Robert never referred to him as anything other than the Major. At first it had been a joke. Then Laura started to talk less jokingly about him and to indicate that he was nice, a sweetie, rather a pet. A real man.

She went over to the Major naked but for those two strips of nylon and invariably stayed for a long time and came back dripping and laughing.

Sometimes Robert knew, but never dared to raise it as a matter of discipline, that Candida was watching from an upper window. Long after she ought to have been asleep she would watch, wide-eyed and attentive until her mother came out of the water and shook herself and walked arrogantly up the lawn with her hands playing a gentle little tattoo on her scarcely veiled breasts.

On one occasion Laura was prosecuted under some complex waterways by-law. She paid the fine and laughed and made her friends laugh with her. The friends said that one day she would take too big a risk and be swept over the weir on to the harsh, jutting stakes of the breakwater below; but they said it adoringly and didn't really believe it.

Until she went over.

Dead and gone. It was impossible to believe that her vicious, humiliating voice had at last been drowned in the roar of the weir.

'I suppose all marriages go this way.' Robert could not forget it, resonant and repetitive, chattering so lightly and yet so purposefully to as large an audience as she could muster. 'Men! First they leap on you with a glad cry – and then it sort of softens off to a reluctant groan. I suppose it's the same for everyone.'

But she didn't really suppose any such thing. She was sure that somewhere there was a man who could satisfy her. Her hatred was reserved for Robert only, directed tirelessly against Robert.

She was dead. Her hatred must have died with her.

Disconcertingly it didn't feel like that. She had lived on her resentments and it was inconceivable that their power should have ebbed so swiftly. Her vindictiveness had become a living, physical force stronger than herself. Robert had braced himself against it, his head bowed against it, like a man learning to live with a remorseless prevailing wind. He was not ready to adjust to the fact that the wind had dropped.

If he had died before she did, would she have found it possible to fulfil all those threats she had made to him, all the promises she had made to herself? Without the goad of his presence would she have found any of it worth while?

Robert found it easier now to be sympathetic towards her. He could afford to be detached and tolerant. It was easier to assess, to find psychological phrases, to nod understandingly over her disappointments and her knotted agonies. She had made his life hell, but even without him there to storm against could she ever have been happy?

She was gone. He kept telling himself that she was gone.

Janet was small and dark and softly spoken. She could not have been more different from Laura. Robert had not consciously chosen her because of this but he wryly admitted to himself that it would not have worked out so rightly and inevitably if she had not been such a complete contrast. He could not help making comparisons; but he did not pass these onto Janet.

She was more interested in her home than Laura had ever been. She found reasons for liking things rather than for disliking them. Ashtrays were emptied, the place was cleaned, towels were not thrown in a heap on the bathroom floor, lights weren't left on and doors weren't left banging. She was tidy without being fussy. The place had a new smell about it, a new glow, a new comfort.

Janet was thirty-five and had not been married before because of a chain of circumstances not one of which was significant in itself but which, one after the other, had somehow prevented her from settling down. Her parents had gone through various emotional upsets and had both relied on her. Then her father had had a long illness. A job in Wales had been interrupted by the need to look after her brother when he was badly injured in an accident. She spent an unsatisfactory year in Canada. For three years she was involved with a married man and then quietly, resolutely walked out on the situation. If she had been hurt she did not scratch the scars.

After so many years of independence she might well have been diffident and awkward in marriage. Instead, she was graceful and appreciative. Pleasure came to them without having to be desperately pursued.

Laura's body had been magnificent. At forty she had been as sleek and glossy and splendid as a girl of eighteen. In spite of her repeated lamentations she had not suffered from the bearing of two children. Yet for all that flawless beauty she had been cold and brittle and somehow unrewarding.

Janet was ... oh, he had to say it: Janet was cuddly. Ludicrous word. He thought how Laura would have shrieked with laughter. *Cuddly!* but why not? What was so wrong with that? He didn't have to worry ever again about what Laura would say, because Laura could say nothing.

Still it was hard not to listen, not to wait for that harsh laugh. The echoes were taking a long time to die.

One evening he was late leaving the office and was stuck for twenty minutes in a traffic jam. He began to frame excuses. He would be as reasonable as possible until the row started; then he would have to have a few phrases ready, a few parries.

'Nobody's asking you to apologize' – he could hear Laura saying it – 'for not wanting to come home to me. If you want to stop for a drink, at least have the guts to say so.'

'I didn't stop for a drink. I had a call from Paris.'

'As if it matters. Though you *might* have remembered that Harry and Josie were coming in for a chat. I had to let them go, of course.'

'They could have waited.'

'Until you condescended to arrive? A phone call wouldn't have hurt. A little courtesy ...'

'I rang before I left but you must have been out.'

'Liar.'

'I tell you ...'

'I don't want you to tell me anything. It's really not worth the fuss. I don't know why you have to make such a pathetic fuss. Do grow up, Robert, dear.'

He rehearsed it, lived through it before it was even begun. And then, as he swung the car down the slope and saw the river curling below him, he realized that he didn't have to practise the scene, didn't have to anticipate every snarled word and impatient twitch of the shoulders: Laura wasn't there; it was Janet now, and Janet wouldn't want to start a petty argument.

He had thought Janet might be intimidated by the children but she was perfectly at ease. She treated Michael as an equal and was wary yet decisive with Candida.

Michael was in his first year at Sussex University. He had acquired some odd mannerisms but Janet took them as they came and did not make exaggerated faces as Laura would have done, or grow sweetly patronizing as Laura would have done. Michael let it be known that he would eventually become something in television. It was a phrase much used by his friends. He was not sure, any more than they were, of quite what that something was to be; but he wore a pink shirt and a sandy beard in readiness for the day when he was discovered. He spent a holiday in Greece and discovered an island which could be fully appreciated only by himself and two chosen friends. His favourite word during the first few weeks of this Easter vacation, when he and Janet got to know each other, was 'plasticity'. Last year it had been 'conceptual'. Robert felt that he was a nice healthy boy at heart.

Candida, at the local school, was a heavier responsibility. She lived at home and sulked, brooded, sniggered and grew ecstatic or despairing as she had always done, though with added emphasis, as though to challenge Janet and learn how far she dared go.

Janet coped. She was not domineering and she was not prissy. She did not spy, but she contrived to keep the wrong sort of book out of Candida's hands. She didn't force the pace: she was steady, humorous and unfaltering.

'I don't believe it,' said Robert one Sunday.

'Don't believe what?'

'The ... well ...' Again he was thinking something naïve – and enjoying it. 'The happiness,' he said. 'That's all – just happiness, just like that.'

She blushed and gave a little pout, shyly repudiating the idea yet loving it.

She said: 'You're so sweet.'

Every word they said to each other was true and uncomplicated. *Don't you dare ...*

He had dared and he was happy.

'You're looking well,' his business acquaintances said.

The weeks of summer rolled past and at last he began to accept – really to accept – that Laura was dead. He didn't have to keep saying it to himself any more: it was all right and it didn't need repeating.

For some time he had kept neighbours at arm's length. Then Janet got to know one or two of them. Characteristically, he thought, she picked on the nicer ones and somehow just didn't get round to meeting the rowdier ones.

One Saturday afternoon the Major came over for a drink.

'You're looking pretty fit, old boy,' he observed.

He did not gloat over Janet as he had shamelessly gloated over Laura. He spoke to her with genuine warmth and respect, and for the first time began to treat Robert also with respect.

Lulled into ease and near-complacency, Robert was taken off guard when Laura once again smiled her old, evil smile at him.

He should have been ready. He should have known that the contentment wouldn't last.

Laura was back. Laura was smiling.

It was a hot afternoon. In slacks and a white shirt Janet sat in the shade of the cherry tree, reading desultorily. Michael sprawled on the grass a few feet away. Every now and then he murmured something to himself or to Janet – from where Robert was working at the water's edge, clearing away some flotsam which had piled up against the bank, it was difficult to tell which. A small aeroplane buzzed drowsily overhead. The weir roared a faint, undisturbing roar.

Suddenly Michael and Janet began to laugh. Michael pushed himself up on to his knees and leaned towards Janet. He said something quickly, and they laughed again. Their heads turned momentarily towards Robert and then turned away again.

He straightened up and sauntered along the lawn up the slope to the shade of the tree.

'What are you two plotting?' he asked affectionately.

And there was Laura, gleaming her malice at him. Just one swift, savage gleam of a smile. It took his breath away. He stopped where he was, swaying. He closed his eyes and opened them again. Laura's face had disappeared. It could never have been there; couldn't possibly have been there.

Michael had Laura's eyes. Just for a moment, just in a trick of the light and the dappled shade, Michael's eyes and mouth must have fooled him.

But it hadn't been like that. He knew it hadn't. The brief glimpse had not been of Michael's face. Laura had looked at him and jeered at him not out of her son but out of Janet.

'What's the matter, Robert?'

Janet's voice was soft and concerned. She began to get up from her chair. As she emerged into the full blaze of the sun she was his dark, sweet Janet.

An illusion. Nothing more than that. It wouldn't happen again.

Two days later he walked past the open door of Candida's bedroom and saw her sprawled on the bed, reading. He went casually in.

'Not swotting for next term already?'

She drew the edge of the coverlet slowly over the book. The gesture was languid and almost indifferent. She couldn't really be bothered to hide it from him.

'Candida,' he said reproachfully.

She rolled to one side so that he could pull the coverlet back and see the gaudy cover of the book.

It was a paperback showing the photographed back view of a girl wearing only a bra. A man bent over her with a whip in his hand, and there was a streak of blood across her right shoulder. It was crude, yet not as crude as paperbacks had once been: it was too glossy and looked photographically, colourfully real.

'What's wrong?'

Janet had come along the passage and was standing in the open doorway. Robert prodded the book. 'I thought we'd got over this kind of thing. Honestly, Candida, it's stupid – can't you tell that when you read it?'

'I wouldn't know how stupid it was till I'd had a chance of reading it, would I?' she said pertly.

Robert picked it up.

Janet said: 'Do we have to make a big scene about it?'

He froze. There was a crackle in her voice which he recognized. And he saw that this time it wasn't just his imagination. Candida recognized it, too. Candida stared past him, incredulous, and then began to smile, almost hugging herself with glee.

Very carefully he said: 'I thought we'd agreed there would be no more of this nonsense. Janet ...'

'It's nonsense,' she agreed crisply, 'and what harm can it possibly do her?'

'I suppose you used to read them by the dozen when you were her age?'

'Why do you say that?'

'Oh ... never mind. Never mind.'

Janet shrugged. 'Let her get it out of her system.'

Candida went on staring at her and now held out her hand. Janet took the book from Robert and tossed it back onto the bed.

He wanted to talk to Janet. It was imperative that he should talk to her. This whole thing had to be settled today, before trouble overtook them. Yet he found he could not speak. He watched her walk off ahead of him and he couldn't make a move. He wanted to go after her and put his arm round her shoulders and start talking reasonably, as they had always talked until now. But he was afraid. In his fingertips he could already feel how she would shrug him off.

By evening he began to feel safe again. They sat by the open window in companionable silence. The haze from the river made a silvery dusk, softening the outlines of trees and houses on the far bank. Candida was with friends whose parents would drive her home about half an hour from now. Michael was out on one of his meditative rambles. There was peace.

Robert said: 'Darling ...'

'Mm?'

'About Candida.'

'Yes. That business earlier today.' Janet put her head on one side as though to catch a puzzling echo. 'You know, I don't quite ...'

There was the slam of the front door. Michael came in. He flapped a hand amiably at his father and went towards an armchair in the shadows at the end of the room.

Janet said: 'Don't I get a kiss?'

Michael slowly approached the window. Robert tried not to look. He fixed his gaze resolutely on his hands, clasped on his knees. But such resolution could not be sustained. He looked up, looked across at Janet's profile as she turned towards Michael. The silvery twilight blurred even her dark hair. For one dazzling fraction of a second he saw her face and hands and hair bleached fairer and whiter than death.

Michael bent and kissed her.

'Mm,' said Janet throatily. 'It *is* nice to have a man about the house.'

Robert got up and reached for the nearest switch. Light flooded from the squat, wide-shaded lamp by the hearth.

'Since you're up,' said Janet, 'you could pour me a drink. Pour us all a drink.'

Robert's hand shook as he got out the glasses. He poured slowly so that there would be time for everything to become normal again. And on the face of it, when they drank, things were normal enough. Janet asked Michael where he had been and Michael muttered in his usual vague way. But there was a strange sense of communication between them: odd references and unfinished sentences which meant nothing to Robert somehow made sense to Janet; a brief little conspiratorial smile flickered to and fro.

Candida was late getting home. The man who brought her apologized, explaining that there had been difficulty getting the car started and that he had stupidly taken a wrong turning and gone miles out of his way. He accepted a drink and left.

Janet swung round upon Candida with her hand raised.

'I told you what time to be back. I told you to make them bring you back in good time.'

'But it wasn't my fault. He's just told you ...'

'He's covering up for you. I know your little game. You spin things out as long as you can, and then blame other people.'

She struck Candida full across the face. Before Robert could protest, Candida ran from the room. Janet went after her as though to strike her again.

'Janet – stop!'

Robert followed. Janet caught up with the girl at the foot of the stairs and seized her arm. Each of them had a foot on the lowest step. Candida suddenly sagged against Janet. They put their arms round each other and laughed and sobbed weakly.

Above Candida's head, Janet said: 'Let's not have one of your nasty, cold, rational lectures, Robert. You just don't understand girls at all. Girls of any age.'

That night he tried to make love to her. He simply had to restore things to what they had so recently been. But her body had an unyielding softness – a contradiction in terms, an impossibility that was nevertheless a humiliating reality. In the darkness she chuckled. When he fell despairingly away from her she said mockingly: 'Never mind, Robert, dear. Never mind.'

He was glad of the hours he could spend in his office. With staff away on summer holidays, there was a pile-up of work. He welcomed it. It kept him late and he was not sorry to be late. It was not until he was driving home that he began to face up to what lay in wait for him.

Arguments shaped up in his head. He had to work for their living, didn't he? If he stayed late and got home late it was because there was a lot to be done and someone had to do it and he was that someone.

No. No need for arguments. Of course not. Janet was there. Janet would be Janet and nobody else. She would meet him at the door and she would be Janet again.

The arguments seethed over one another, tumbling and twisting.

She would be waiting for him. He kept telling himself that. The old Janet. The only Janet.

When he went into the house there was silence. It was a hot evening, and down here in the river valley it was even more difficult to breathe than it had been in the city.

'Janet?' he called.

There was no reply.

The windows were open on to the garden. Robert went out on to the lawn.

The Major was stretched out in a deck-chair on the other side of the river. He waved. And Laura came swimming back across the river as she had so often done. Robert watched, terrified. How could he stop her coming up out of the water, on to the lawn, savage and vengeful?

But it wasn't Laura. It was Janet. She swam noisily and badly. She was floundering as she reached the bank, having to fight the last few yards of the way against the treacherous snatching of the current.

Robert ran to meet her.

'What are you up to? Don't you know how close we are to the weir?'

She stood up, trim and self-possessed in her one-piece black costume. She was breathing hard but she managed to say:

'Pity to have the river here and not use it.'

'But you oughtn't to risk it. You're not a good swimmer – are you?'

'I will be.'

'But ...'

'Nobody's asking you to come in with me,' Janet snapped. She looked him up and down, then put her hands behind her head and swung languidly round in the evening sunshine. The Major waved as she spun to face him. When she had made the full circuit she appraised Robert again. 'The water too cold for you?' she said, and walked past him and into the house.

The house was haunted. The house ... or perhaps the family. Now he knew it. Haunted not by a separate ghost, an entity, a wandering phantom apart from them, but by a creature indistinguishable from Janet, from Candida, from Michael. They were possessed. This was no mournful shadow waiting in dark corners: it was with them and in them in broad daylight, growing stronger as it fed on them.

Janet took fiercely and repeatedly to the river. One night when Michael and Candida had gone to bed and Robert was yawning, about to comment that it was gone eleven o'clock, Janet abruptly said that she wanted to go out. Just for a little while, to clear her head. Before he could question her, she went up to their room. When she came down she was wearing a wispy bikini. It did not suit her as it had suited Laura: she was an inch or two wrong, slightly too plump, not quite tall enough. But she walked as Laura walked. When she went out down the garden to the darkness of the water, she was Laura.

Robert hurried after her down the lawn.

'You can't. It's mad. At this time of night ...'

'You can stand by with a lifebelt if it worries you.'

Janet plunged in.

He stood there, helpless. Across the river, lights burned in the windows of the Major's house and made a glowing, rippling pool below the bank. Janet swam strongly though clumsily towards it.

Robert turned and looked back at his own house.

Michael's bedroom was at one end, Candida's at the other. Their curtains were drawn back. In each window there was a pale, watching face.

Janet was away for over an hour. When she came back she was breathing hard but laughing at the same time. She cupped her hands over her breasts and her fingers beat out a joyful tattoo on her wet flesh.

She said: 'I've invited the Major over to our party next Wednesday.'

'I didn't know we were having a party next Wednesday.'

'Well, we are. I've just decided.'

Among the people she invited were several Robert had not seen for some months. He hadn't known that Janet had even met them. There were the two alcoholics from the island who had always squealed ecstatically over Laura's jokes and then quarrelled at the end of every evening and had to be taken home. There was the old harpy from one of the boats, and a limp young man whom Michael had once claimed to despise but whom he now greeted as a long-lost friend. And there was the couple who lived in sin on the seediest of the nearby boats and made a point of letting everyone know that they were living in sin as though to proclaim their superiority over duller mortals.

Janet had been to have her hair done for the occasion. She had had it dyed blonde. The black softness of it had been converted to a harsh golden helmet.

Robert stared. She did not bother to ask him what he thought about it.

When the Major arrived, he, too, stared.

'Like it?' said Janet.

He studied the hair again, then looked her up and down and smacked his lips with exaggerated relish.

'Robert,' said Janet in a tone of patient suffering, 'do keep an eye on the drinks, won't you? Do pretend to be a perfect host.'

It was a long time since he had heard this range and volume of voices. It was the first time for months that glass was trodden into the carpet once more. And the Major was touching Janet's arm and gloating, and the couple from the boat were pawing each other and making sure that everyone saw it.

'It's love,' said Janet suddenly. She swayed above them with her glass slopping gin over the side. 'I mean, don't you think it's so pretty to watch?' She waved her free arm towards Robert. 'You know, Robert, perhaps we ought never to have got married. Don't you think marriage spoils things?' Now she addressed the assembly, raising her voice and talking them all down. 'You don't get the same kick when it's all been legalized, do you? At least, men don't seem to. Bags of enthusiasm at first, and then all they want is food and someone to sweep the place up. In no time at all they've given up leaping on you with a glad cry and ...'

'No,' said Robert. 'Don't say it.'

Janet's eyes widened. They looked at him as they had looked at him year after year, year after terrible year. 'Goodness me, we're on edge this evening, aren't we?'

He tried to get close to her and make a last appeal. But she brushed past him and stood above the Major. His arm lay along the arm of his chair. Hair on his wrist was tangled under his watch strap. Janet meditatively stroked the hair up and then smoothed it down again.

She looked at Robert. 'Funny, isn't it? Now, Robert hasn't ...'

'Stop it.'

'Stop what, Robert, dear.'

The way in which the word 'dear' was wrenched out of her mouth was all too familiar. Her eyes were pools of poison. 'Given my time over again ...' Laura had said it but never completed the sentence. She had been given her time over again; and she was just the same, she could do no better than before.

She must not be allowed to do worse.

He said: 'Remember what happened last time.'

Janet said: 'Don't you dare.'

In front of them all he went through it again. They didn't know what he was going to do, so they made no move to stop him; Laura knew, but she wasn't fast enough.

He grabbed the heavy marble ashtray, scattering ash as he swung it. The gilded head ducked and someone screamed – Laura or Janet, he couldn't tell which. Then he slammed the stone edge into the side of that head. The force almost carried him over, but he staggered, gripped the edge of the ashtray, and brought it down again as the head sagged and the body crumpled at his feet. Twice and then three times he was able to lift it and smack it down. Then they were dragging him back.

They didn't let him finish. They couldn't act in time to stop him killing her, but they could stop him carrying her down the darkened lawn and tipping her quietly into the river. This time she would not be carried away down her beloved river. This time she wouldn't suffer the disgrace of being defeated at last by the current and carried over the weir.

Janet did not finish up as Laura had finished up – her beautiful hair tangled, her beautiful body battered and wrenched and beautifully, bloodily pulped against the stakes of the breakwater.

The Hollow Man
Thomas Burke

He came up one of the narrow streets which lead from the docks, and turned into a road whose farther end was gay with the light of London. At the end of this road he went deep into the lights of London, and sometimes into its shadows, farther and farther away from the river, and did not pause until he had reached a poor quarter near the centre.

He was a tall, spare figure, wearing a black mackintosh. Below this could be seen brown dungaree trousers. A peaked cap hid most of his face; the little that was exposed was white and sharp. In the autumn mist that filled the lighted streets as well as the dark he seemed a wraith, and some of those who passed him looked again, not sure whether they had indeed seen a living man. One or two of them moved their shoulders, as though shrinking from something.

His legs were long, but he walked with the short deliberate steps of a blind man, though he was not blind. His eyes were open, and he stared straight ahead; but he seemed to see nothing and hear nothing.

Neither the mournful hooting of sirens across the black water of the river, nor the genial windows of the shops in the big streets near the centre drew his head to right or left. He walked as though he had no destination in mind, yet constantly, at this corner or that, he turned. It seemed that an unseen hand was guiding him to a given point of whose location he was himself ignorant.

He was searching for a friend of fifteen years ago, and the unseen hand, or some dog-instinct, had led him from Africa to London, and was now leading him, along the last mile of his search, to a certain little eating-house. He did not know that he was going to the eating-house of his friend Nameless, but he did know, from the time he left Africa, that he was journeying towards Nameless, and now knew that he was very near to Nameless.

Nameless didn't know that his old friend was anywhere near *him*, though, had he observed conditions that evening, he might have wondered why he was sitting up an hour later than usual. He was seated in one of the pews of his prosperous little workmen's dining-rooms – a little gold-mine his wife's relations called it – and he was smoking and looking at nothing.

He had added up the till and written the copies of the bill of fare for next day, and there was nothing to keep him out of bed after his fifteen hours' attention to business. Had he been asked why he was sitting up later than usual, he would first have answered that he didn't know that he was, and would then have explained, in default of any other explanation, that it was for the purpose of having a last pipe. He was quite unaware that he was sitting up and keeping the door unlatched because a long-parted friend from Africa was seeking him and slowly approaching him, and needed his services.

He was quite unaware that he had left the door unlatched at that late hour – half past eleven – to admit pain and woe.

But even as many bells sent dolefully across the night from their steeples their disagreement as to the point of half past eleven, pain and woe were but two streets away from him. The mackintosh and dungarees and the sharp white face were coming nearer every moment.

There was silence in the house and in the streets; a heavy silence broken, or sometimes stressed, by the occasional night-noises – motor horns, back-firing of lorries, shunting at a distant terminus. That silence seemed to envelop the house, but he did not notice it. He did not notice the bells, and he did not even notice the lagging step that approached his shop, and passed – and returned – and passed again – and halted. He was aware of nothing save that he was smoking a last pipe and he was sitting in that state of hazy reverie which he called thinking, deaf and blind to anything not in his immediate neighbourhood.

But when a hand was laid on the latch, and the latch was lifted, he did hear that, and he looked up. And he saw the door open, and got up and went to it. And there, just within the door, he came face to face with the thin figure of pain and woe.

*   *   *

To kill a fellow creature is a frightful thing. At the time the act is committed the murderer may have sound and convincing reasons (to him) for his act. But time and reflection may bring regret; even remorse; and this may live with him for many years. Examined in wakeful hours of the night or early morning, the reasons for the act may shed their cold logic, and may cease to be reasons and become mere excuses.

And these naked excuses may strip the murderer and show him to himself as he is. They may begin to hunt his soul, and to run into every little corner of his mind and every little nerve, in search of it.

And if to kill a fellow creature and to suffer the recurrent regret for an act of heated blood is a frightful thing, it is still more frightful to kill a fellow creature and bury his body deep in an African jungle, and then, fifteen years later, at about midnight, to see that latch of your door lifted by the hand you had stilled and to see the man, looking much as he did fifteen years ago, walk into your home and claim your hospitality.

*　　*　　*

When the man in mackintosh and dungarees walked into the dining-rooms Nameless stood still; stared; staggered against a table; supported himself by a hand, and said, 'Oh!'

The other man said, 'Nameless!'

Then they looked at each other; Nameless with head thrust forward, mouth dropped, eyes wide; the visitor with a dull, glazed expression. If Nameless had not been the man he was – thick, bovine and costive – he would have flung up his arms and screamed. At that moment he felt the need of some such outlet, but did not know how to find it. The only dramatic expression he gave to the situation was to whisper instead of speak.

Twenty emotions came to life in his head and spine, and wrestled there. But they showed themselves only in his staring eyes and his whisper. His first thought, or rather, spasm, was Ghosts-Indigestion-Nervous Breakdown. His second, when he saw that the figure was substantial and real, was Impersonation. But a slight movement on the part of the visitor dismissed that.

It was a little habitual movement which belonged only to that man; an unconscious twitching of the third finger of the left hand. He knew then that it was Gopak. Gopak, a little changed, but still, miraculously, thirty-two. Gopak, alive, breathing and real. No ghost. No phantom of the stomach. He was as certain of that as he was that fifteen years ago he had killed Gopak stone-dead and buried him.

The blackness of the moment was lightened by Gopak. In thin, flat tones he asked, 'May I sit down? I'm tired.' He sat down, and said: 'So tired. So tired.'

Nameless still held the table. He whispered: 'Gopak ... Gopak ... But I – I *killed* you. I killed you in the jungle. You were dead. I know you were.'

Gopak passed his hand across his face. He seemed about to cry. 'I know you did. I know. That's all I can remember – about this earth. You killed me.' The voice became thinner and flatter. 'And I was so comfortable. So comfortable. It was – such a rest. Such a rest as you don't know. And then they came and – disturbed me. They woke me up. And brought me back.' He sat with shoulders sagged, arms drooping, hands hanging between knees. After the first recognition he did not look at Nameless; he looked at the floor.

'Came and disturbed you?' Nameless leaned forward and whispered the words. 'Woke you up? Who?'

'The Leopard Men.'

'The what?'

'The Leopard Men.' The watery voice said it as casually as if it were saying 'the night watchman'.

'The Leopard Men?' Nameless stared, and his fat face crinkled in an effort to take in the situation of a midnight visitation from a dead man, and the dead man talking nonsense. He felt his blood moving out of its course. He looked at his own hand to see if it was his own hand. He looked at the table to see if it was his table. The hand and the table were facts, and if the dead man was a fact – and he was – his story might be a fact. It seemed anyway as sensible as the dead man's presence. He gave a heavy sigh from the stomach. 'A-ah ... The Leopard Men ... Yes, I heard about them out there. Tales!'

Gopak slowly wagged his head. 'Not tales. They're real. If they weren't real – I wouldn't be here. Would I? I'd be at rest.'

Nameless had to admit this. He had heard many tales 'out there' about the Leopard Men, and had dismissed them as jungle yarns. But now, it seemed, jungle yarns had become commonplace fact in a little London shop.

The watery voice went on. 'They do it. I saw them. I came back in the middle of a circle of them. They killed a nigger to put his life into me. They wanted a white man – for their farm. So they brought me back. You may not believe it. You wouldn't *want* to believe it. You wouldn't want to – see or know anything like them. And I wouldn't want any man to. But it's true. That's how I'm here.'

'But I left you absolutely dead. I made every test. It was three days before I buried you. And I buried you deep.'

'I know. But that wouldn't make any difference to them. It was a long time after when they came and brought me back. And I'm still dead, you know. It's only my body they brought back.' The voice trailed into a thread. 'And I'm so tired. So tired. I want to go back – to rest.'

Sitting in his prosperous eating-house, Nameless was in the presence of an achieved miracle, but the everyday, solid appointments of the eating-house wouldn't let him fully comprehend it. Foolishly, as he realized when he had spoken, he asked Gopak to explain what had happened. Asked a man who couldn't really be alive to explain how he came to be alive. It was like asking Nothing to explain Everything.

Constantly, as he talked, he felt his grasp on his own mind slipping. The surprise of a sudden visitor at a late hour; the shock of the arrival of a long-dead man; and the realization that this long-dead man was not a wraith, were too much for him.

During the next half hour he found himself talking to Gopak as to the Gopak he had know seventeen years ago when they were partners. Then he would be halted by the freezing knowledge that he was talking to a dead man, and that a dead man was faintly answering him. He felt that the thing couldn't really have happened, but in the interchange of talk he kept forgetting the improbable side of it, and accepting it. With each recollection of the truth, his mind would clear and settle in one thought – 'I've got to get rid of him. How am I going to get rid of him?'

'But how did you get here?'

'I escaped.' The words came slowly and thinly, and out of the body rather than the mouth.

'How?'

'I don't – know. I don't remember anything – except our quarrel. And being at rest.'

'But why come all the way here? Why didn't you stay on the coast?'

'I don't – know. But you're the only man I know. The only man I can remember.'

'But how did you find me?'

'I don't know. But I had to – find you. You're the only man – who can help me.'

'But how can I help you?'

The head turned weakly from side to side. 'I don't – know. But nobody else – can.'

Nameless stared through the window, looking onto the lamplit street and seeing nothing of it. The everyday being which had been his half an hour ago had been annihilated; the everyday beliefs and disbeliefs shattered and mixed together. But some shred of his old sense and his old standard remained. He must handle this situation. 'Well – what do you want to do? What are you going to do? I don't see how I can help you. And you can't stay here, obviously.' A demon of perversity sent a facetious notion into his head – introducing Gopak to his wife – 'This is my dead friend.'

But on his last spoken remark Gopak made the effort of raising his head and staring with the glazed eyes at Nameless. 'But I *must* stay here. There's nowhere else I can stay. I must stay here. That's why I came. You've got to help me.'

'But you can't stay here. I've got no room. All occupied. Nowhere for you to sleep.'

The wan voice said: 'That doesn't matter. I *don't* sleep.'

'Eh?'

'I *don't* sleep. I haven't slept since they brought me back. I can sit here – till you can think of some way of helping me.'

'But how *can* I?'

He again forgot the background of the situation, and began to get angry at the vision of a dead man sitting about the place waiting for him to think of something. 'How *can* I if you don't tell me how?'

'I don't – know. But you've got to. You killed me. And I was dead –

and comfortable. As it all came from you – killing me – you're responsible for me being – like this. So, you've got to – help me. That's why I – came to you.'

'But what do you want me to do?'

'I don't – know. I can't – think. But nobody but you can help me. I had to come to you. Something brought me – straight to you. That means that you're the one – that can help me. Now I'm with you, something will – happen to help me. I feel it will. In time you'll – think of something.'

Nameless found his legs suddenly weak. He sat down and stared with a sick scowl at the hideous and the incomprehensible. Here was a dead man in his house – a man he had murdered in a moment of black temper – and he knew in his heart that he couldn't turn the man out. For one thing, he would have been afraid to touch him; he couldn't see himself touching him. For another, faced with the miracle of the presence of a fifteen-years-dead man, he doubted whether physical force or any material agency would be effectual in moving the man.

His sould shivered, as all men's souls shiver at the demonstration of forces outside their mental or spiritual horizon. He had murdered this man, and often, in fifteen years, he had repented the act. If the man's appalling story were true, then he had some sort of right to turn to Nameless. Nameless recognized that, and knew that whatever happened he couldn't turn him out. His hot-tempered sin had literally come home to him.

The wan voice broke into his nightmare. 'You go to rest, Nameless. I'll sit here. You go to rest.' He put his fact down to his hands and uttered a little moan. 'Oh, why can't I rest? Why can't I go back to my beautiful rest?'

*   *   *

Nameless came down early next morning with a half hope that Gopak would not be there. But he was there, seated where Nameless had left him last night. Nameless made some tea, and showed him where he might wash. He washed listlessly, and crawled back to his seat, and listlessly drank the tea which Nameless brought to him.

To his wife and the kitchen helpers Nameless mentioned him as an old friend who had had a bit of a shock. 'Shipwrecked and knocked on the head. But quite harmless, and he won't be staying long. He's waiting for admission to a home. A good pal to me in the past, and it's the least I can do to let him stay here a few days. Suffers from sleeplessness and prefers to sit up at night. Quite harmless.'

But Gopak stayed more than a few days. He outstayed everybody. Even when the customers had gone Gopak was still there.

On the first morning of his visit when the regular customers came in at midday, they looked at the odd, white figure sitting vacantly in the first pew, then stared, then moved away.

All avoided the pew in which he sat. Nameless explained him to them, but his explanation did not seem to relieve the slight tension which settled on the dining-room. The atmosphere was not so brisk and chatty as usual. Even those who had their backs to the stranger seemed to be affected by his presence.

At the end of the first day Nameless, noticing this, told him that he had arranged a nicer corner of the front room upstairs, where he could sit by the window, and took his arm to take him upstairs. But Gopak feebly shook the hand away, and sat where he was. 'No. I don't want to go. I'll stay here. I'll stay here. I don't want to move.'

And he wouldn't move. After a few more pleadings Nameless realized with dismay that his refusal was definite; that it would be futile to press him or force him; that he was going to sit in that dining-room for ever. He was as weak as a child and as firm as a rock.

He continued to sit in that first pew, and the customers continued to avoid it, and to give queer glances at it. It seemed that they half recognized that he was something more than a fellow who had had a shock.

During the second week of his stay three of the regular customers were missing, and more than one of those that remained made acidly facetious suggestions to Nameless that he park his lively friend somewhere else. He made things too exciting for them; all that whoopee took them off their work, and interfered with digestion. Nameless told them he would be staying only a day or so longer, but they found that this was untrue, and at the end of the second week eight of the regulars had found another place.

Each day, when the dinner-hour came, Nameless tried to get him to take a little walk, but always he refused.

He would go out only at night, and then never more than two hundred yards from the shop. For the rest, he sat in his pew, sometimes dozing in the afternoon, at other times staring at the floor. He took his food abstractedly, and never knew whether he had had food or not. He spoke only when questioned, and the burden of his talk was 'I'm so tired. So tired.'

One thing only seemed to arouse any light of interest in him; one thing only drew his eyes from the floor. That was the seventeen-year-old daughter of his host, who was known as Bubbles, and who helped with the waiting. And Bubbles seemed to be the only member of the shop and its customers who did not shrink from him.

She knew nothing of the truth about him, but she seemed to understand him, and the only response he ever gave to anything was to her childish sympathy. She sat and chatted foolish chatter to him –

'bringing him out of himself' she called it – and sometimes he would be brought out to the extent of a watery smile. He came to recognize her step, and would look up before she entered the room. Once or twice in the evening, when the shop was empty, and Nameless was sitting miserably with him, he would ask, without lifting his eyes, 'Where's Bubbles?' and would be told that Bubbles had gone to the pictures or was out at a dance, and would relapse into deeper vacancy.

Nameless didn't like this. He was already visited by a curse which, in four weeks, had destroyed most of his business. Regular customers had dropped off two by two, and no new customers came to take their place. Strangers who dropped in once for a meal did not come agan; they could not keep their eyes or their minds off the forbidding, white-faced figure sitting motionless in the first pew. At midday, when the place had been crowded and late-comers had to wait for a seat, it was now two-thirds empty; only a few of the most thick-skinned remained faithful.

And on top of this there was the interest of the dead man in his daughter, an interest which seemed to be having an unpleasant effect. Nameless hadn't noticed it, but his wife had. 'Bubbles don't seem as bright and lively as she was. You noticed it lately? She's getting quiet – and a bit slack. Sits about a lot. Paler than she used to be.'

'Her age, perhaps.'

'No. She's not one of these thin dark sort. No – it's something else. Just the last week or two I've noticed it. Off her food. Sits about doing nothing. No interest. May be nothing; just out of sorts perhaps ... How much longer's that horrible friend of yours going to stay?'

*   *   *

The horrible friend stayed some weeks longer – ten weeks in all –while Nameless watched his business drop to nothing and his daughter get pale and peevish. He knew the cause of it. There was no home in all England like his: no home that had a dead man sitting in it for ten weeks. A dead man brought, after a long time, from the grave, to sit and disturb his customers and take the vitality from his daughter. He couldn't tell this to anybody. Nobody would believe such nonsense.

But he *knew* that he was entertaining a dead man, and, knowing that a long-dead man was walking the earth, he could believe in any result of that fact. He could believe almost anything that he would have derided ten weeks ago. His customers had abandoned his shop, not because of the presence of a silent, white-faced man, but because of the presence of a dead-living man.

Their minds might not know it, but their blood knew it. And, as his business had been destroyed, so, he believed, would his daughter be destroyed. Her blood was not warming her; her blood told her only that this was a long-ago friend of her father's, and she was drawn to him.

It was at this point that Nameless, having no work to do, began to drink. And it was well that he did so. For out of the drink came an idea, and with that idea he freed himself from the curse upon him and his house.

The shop now served scarcely half a dozen customers at midday. It had become ill-kempt and dusty, and the service and the food were bad. Nameless took no trouble to be civil to his few customers. Often, when he was notably under drink, he went to the trouble of being very rude to them. They talked about this. They talked about the decline of his business and the dustiness of the shop and the bad food. They talked about his drinking, and, of course, exaggerated it.

And they talked about the queer fellow who sat there day after day and gave everybody the creeps. A few outsiders, hearing the gossip, came to the dining-rooms to see the queer fellow and the always tight proprietor; but they did not come again, and there were not enough of the curious to keep the place busy. It went down until it served scarcely two customers a day. And Nameless went down with it into drink.

Then, one evening, out of the drink he fished an inspiration.

He took it downstairs to Gopak, who was sitting in his usual seat, hands hanging, eyes on the floor. 'Gopak – listen. You came here because I was the only man who could help you in your trouble. You listening?'

A faint 'Yes' was his answer.

'Well, now. You told me I'd got to think of something. I've thought of something ... Listen. You say I'm responsible for your condition and have got to get you out of it, because I killed you. I did. We had a row. You made me wild. You dared me. And what with that sun and the jungle and the insects, I wasn't myself. I killed you. The moment it was done I could a-cut me right hand off. Because you and me were pals. I could a-cut me right hand off.'

'I knew. I felt that directly it was over. I knew you were suffering.'

'Ah! ... I have suffered. And I'm suffering now. Well, this is what I've thought. All your present trouble comes from me killing you in that jungle and burying you. An idea came to me. Do you think it would help you – do you think it would put you back to rest if I – if I – if I – killed you again?'

For some seconds Gopak continued to stare at the floor. Then his shoulders moved. Then, while Nameless watched every little response to his idea, the watery voice began. 'Yes. Yes. That's it. That's what I was waiting for. That's why I came here. I can see now. That's why I had to get here. Nobody else could kill me. Only you. I've got to be killed again. Yes, I see. But nobody else – would be able – to kill me. Only the man who first killed me ... Yes, you've found – what we're both – waiting for.

Anybody else could shoot me – stab me – hang me – but they couldn't kill me. Only you. That's why I managed to get here and find you.'

The watery voice rose to a thin strength. 'That's it. And you must do it. Do it now. You don't want to, I know. But you must. You *must*.'

His head dropped and he stared at the floor. Nameless, too, stared at the floor. He was seeing things. He had murdered a man and had escaped all punishment save that of his own mind, which had been terrible enough. But now he was going to murder him again – not in a jungle but in a city; and he saw the slow points of the result.

He saw the arrest. He saw the first hearing. He saw the trial. He saw the cell. He saw the rope. He shuddered.

Then he saw the alternative – the breakdown of his life – a ruined business, poverty, the poorhouse, a daughter robbed of her health and perhaps dying, and always the curse of the dead-living man, who might follow him to the poorhouse. Better to end it all, he thought. Rid himself of the curse which Gopak had brought upon him and his family, and then rid his family of himself with a revolver. Better to follow up his idea.

He got stiffly to his feet. The hour was late evening – half past ten – and the streets were quiet. He had pulled down the shop-blinds and locked the door. The room was lit by one light at the farther end. He moved about uncertainly and looked at Gopak. 'Er – how would you – how shall I——'

Gopak said, 'You did it with a knife. Just under the heart. You must do it that way again.'

Nameless stood and looked at him for some seconds. Then, with an air of resolve, he shook himself. He walked quickly to the kitchen.

Three minutes later his wife and daughter heard a crash, as though a table had been overturned. They called but got no answer. When they came down they found him sitting in one of the pews, wiping sweat from his forehead. He was white and shaking, and appeared to be recovering from a faint.

'Whatever's the matter? You all right?'

He waved them away. 'Yes, I'm all right. Touch of giddiness. Smoking too much, I think.'

'Mmmm. Or drinking . . . Where's your friend? Out for a walk?'

'No. He's gone off. Said he wouldn't impose any longer, and 'd to go and find an infirmary.' He spoke weakly and found trouble in picking words. 'Didn't you hear that bang – when he shut the door?'

'I thought that was you fell down.'

'No. It was him when he went. I couldn't stop him.'

'Mmmm. Just as well, I think.' She looked about her. 'Things seem to a-gone wrong since he's been here.'

There was a general air of dustiness about the place. The table-cloths were dirty, not from use but from disuse. The windows were dim. A long knife, very dusty, was lying on the table under the window. In a corner by the door leading to the kitchen, unseen by her, lay a dusty mackintosh and dungaree, which appeared to have been tossed there. But it was over by the main door, near the first pew, that the dust was thickest – a long trail of it – greyish-white dust.

'Reely this place gets more and more slapdash. Why can't you attend to business? You didn't use to be like this. No wonder it's gone down, letting the place get into this state. Why don't you pull yourself together? Just *look* at that dust by the door. Looks as though somebody's been spilling ashes all over the place.'

Nameless looked at it, and his hands shook a little. But he answered, more firmly than before. 'Yes, I know. I'll have a proper clean-up tomorrow. I'll put it all to rights tomorrow. I been getting a bit slack.'

For the first time in ten weeks he smiled at them; a thin, haggard smile, but a smile.

Browdean Farm

A. M. Burrage

Most people with limited vocabularies such as mine would describe the house loosely and comprehensively as picturesque. But it was more than beautiful in its venerable age. It had certain subtle qualities which are called Atmosphere. It invited you, as you approached it along the rough and narrow road which is ignored by those maps which are sold for the use of motorists. In the language of very old houses it said plainly: 'Come in. Come in.'

It said 'Come in' to Rudge Jefferson and me. In one of the front windows there was a notice, inscribed in an illiterate hand, to the effect that the house was to be let, and that the keys were to be obtained at the first cottage down the road. We went and got them. The woman who handed them over to us remarked that plenty of people looked over the house, but nobody ever took it. It had been empty for years.

'Damp and falling to pieces, I suppose,' said Rudge as we returned. 'There's always a snag about these old places.'

The house – 'Browdean Farm' it was called – stood some thirty yards back from the road, at the end of a strip of garden not much wider than its façade. Most of the building was plainly Tudor, but part of it was even earlier. Time was when it had been the property of prosperous yeomen, but now its acres had been added to those of another farm, and it stood shorn of all its land save the small untended gardens in front and behind, and half an acre of apple orchard.

As in most houses of that description the kitchen was the largest room. It was long and lofty and its arched roof was supported by mighty beams which stretched across its breadth. There was a huge range with a noble oven. One could fancy, in the old days of plenty, a score of harvesters supping there after their work, and beer and cider flowing as freely as spring brooks.

To our surprise the place showed few signs of damp, considering the length of time it had been untenanted, and it needed little in the way of repairs. There was not a stick of furniture in the house, but we could tell that its last occupants had been people of refinement and taste. The wallpapers upstairs, the colours of the faded paints and distempers, the presence of a bathroom – that great rarity in old farmhouses – all pointed to the probability of its having been last in the hands of an amateur of country cottages.

Jefferson told me that he knew in his bones – and for once I agreed with his bones – that Nina would love the farm. He was engaged to my sister, and they were waiting until he had saved sufficient money to give them a reasonable material start in matrimony. Like most painstaking writers of no particular reputation Jefferson had to take care of the pence and the shillings, but, like Nina's, his tastes were inexpensive, and it was an understood thing that they were to live quietly together in the country.

We enquired about the rent. It was astonishingly low. Jefferson had to live somewhere while he finished a book, and he was already paying storage for the furniture which he had bought. I could look forward to some months of idleness before returning to India. There was a trout stream in the neighbourhood which would keep me occupied and out of mischief. We laid our heads together.

Jefferson did not want a house immediately, but bargains of that sort are not everyday affairs in these hard times. Besides, with me to share expenses for the next six months, the cost of living at Browdean Farm would be very low, and it seemed a profitable speculation to take the house then and there on a seven years' lease. This is just what Jefferson did – or rather, the agreement was signed by both parties within a week.

Rudge Jefferson and I were old enough friends to understand each other thoroughly, and make allowances for each other's temperaments. We were neither of us morose but often one or both of us would be anxious to talk. There were indefinite hours when Rudge felt either impelled or compelled to write. We found no difficulty in coming to a working agreement. We did not feel obliged to converse at meals. We could bring books to the table if we so wished. Rudge could go to his work when he chose, and I could go off fishing or otherwise amuse myself. Only when we were both inclined for companionship need we pay any attention to each other's existence.

And, from the April evening when we arrived half an hour after the men with the furniture, it worked admirably.

We lived practically in one room, the larger of the two front sitting-rooms. There we took our meals, talked and smoked and read. The smaller sitting-room Rudge commandeered for a study. He retired thither when the spirit moved him to invoke the muses and tap at his typewriter. Our only servant was the woman who had lately had charge of the keys. She came in every day to cook our meals and do the housework, and, as for convenience we dined in the middle of the day, we had the place to ourselves immediately after tea. The garden we decided to tend ourselves, but although we began digging and planting with the early enthusiasm of most amateurs we soon tired of the job and let wild nature take its course.

Our first month was ideal and idyllic. The weather was kind, and everything seemed to go in our favour. The trout gave me all the fun I could have hoped for, and Rudge was satisfied with the quality and quantity of his output. I had no difficulty in adapting myself to his little ways, and soon discovered that his best hours for working were in the mornings and the late evenings, so I left him to himself at those times. We took our last meal, a light cold supper, at about half past nine, and very often I stayed out until that hour.

You must not think that we lived like two recluses under the same roof. Sometimes Rudge was not in the mood for work and hinted at a desire for companionship. Then we went out for long walks, or he came to watch me fish. He was himself a ham-handed angler and seldom attempted to throw a fly. Often we went to drink the light ale at the village inn, a mile distant. And always after supper we smoked and talked for an hour or so before turning in.

It was then, while we were sitting quietly, that we discovered that the house, which was mute by day, owned strange voices which gave tongue after dark. They were the noises which, I suppose, one ought to expect to hear in an old house half full of timber when the world around it is hushed and sleeping. They might have been nerve-racking if one of us had been there alone, but as it was we took little notice at first. Mostly they proceeded from the kitchen, whence we heard the creaking of beams, sobbing noises, gasping noises and queer indescribable scufflings.

While neither of us believed in ghosts we laughingly agreed that the house ought to be haunted, and by something a little more sensational than the sounds of timber contracting and the wind in the kitchen chimney. We knew ourselves to be the unwilling hosts of a colony of rats, which was in itself sufficient to account for most nocturnal noises. Rudge said that he wanted to meet the ghost of an eighteenth century miser, who couldn't rest until he had shown where the money was hidden. There was some practical use in that sort of bogy. And although, as time went on, these night noises became louder and more persistent, we put them down to 'natural causes' and made no effort to investigate them. It occurred to us both that some more rats had discovered a good home, and although we talked of trapping them our talk came to nothing.

We had been at the farm about a month before Rudge Jefferson began to show symptoms of 'nerves'. All writers are the same. Neurotic brutes! But I said nothing to him and waited for him to diagnose his own trouble and ease up a little with his work.

It was at about that time that I, walking homewards one morning just about lunch-time, with my rod over my shoulder, encountered the local policeman just outside the village inn. He wished me a good day which was at once hearty and respectful, and at the same time passed the back of his hand over a thirsty-looking moustache. The hint was obvious, and only a heart of stone could have refrained from inviting him inside. Besides, I believe in keeping in with the police.

He was one of those country constables who become fixtures in quiet, out of the way districts, where they live and let live, and often go into pensioned retirement without bringing more than half a dozen cases before the petty sessions. This worthy was named Hicks, and I had already discovered that everybody liked him. He did not look for trouble. He had rabbits from the local poachers, beer from local cyclists who rode after dark without lights, and more beer from the landlord who chose to exercise his own discretion with regard to closing-time.

P.C. Hicks drank a pint of bitter with me and gave me his best respects. He asked me how we were getting on up at the farm. Admirably, I told him; and then he looked at me closely, as if to see if I were sincere, or, rather, to search my eyes for the passing of some afterthought.

Having found me guileless, as it seemed, he went on to tell of his length of service – he had been eighteen years on the one beat – and of how little trouble he had been to anybody. There was something pathetic in the protestations of the middle-aged Bobby that, to all the world, he had been a man and a brother. He seemed tacitly to be asking for reciprocity, and his own vagueness drew me out of my depth.

You know those beautifully vague men, who pride themselves for being diplomatists on the principle that a nod is as good as a wink to a blind horse? The people who will hint and hint and hint, the asses who will wander round and round and round the haystack with hardly a nibble at it? He was one of them. He wanted to tell me something without actually telling me, to exact from me a promise about something he chose not to mention.

I had found myself in dialectical tangles with him, and at last I laughingly gave up the task of trying to follow his labyrinthine thoughts. I ordered two more bitters and then he said:

'Well, sir, if anything 'appens up at the farm, you needn' get talkin' about it. We done our best. What's past is past, and can't be altered. There isn't no sense in settin' people against *us*.'

I knew from his inflection on the word that 'us' was the police. He did not look at me while he spoke. He was staring at something straight across the counter, and I happened by sheer chance to follow the direction of his gaze.

Opposite us, and hanging from a shelf so as to face the customers, was a little tear-off calendar. The date recorded there was the nineteenth of May.

* * *

Two evenings later – which is to say the evening of May 21st – I returned home at half past nine full of suppressed excitement. I had a story to tell Rudge, and I was yet not sure if I should be wise in telling it. His nerves had grown worse during the past two days, but after all there are nerves and nerves, and my tale might interest without harming him.

It was only just dusk and not a tithe of the stars were burning as I walked up the garden path, inhaling the rank scents of those hardy flowers which had sprung up untended in that miniature wilderness. The sitting-room window was dark, but the subdued light of an oil lamp burned behind the curtains of Rudge's study. I found the door unbarred, walked in, and entered the study. You see, it was supper-time, and Rudge might safely be intruded upon.

Rather to my surprise the room was empty, but I surmised that Rudge had gone up to wash. That he had lately been at work was evident from the fact that a sheet of paper, half used, lay in the roller of the typewriter. I sat down in the revolving chair to see what he had written – I was allowed that privilege – and was astonished to see that he had ended in the middle of a sentence. In some respects he was a methodical person, and this was unlike him. The last word he had written was 'the', and the last letter of that word was black and prominent as if he had slammed down the key with unnecessary force.

Two minutes later, while I was still reading, a probable explanation was revealed to me. I heard the gate click and footfalls on the path. Naturally I guessed that Rudge, temperamental as he was, had suddenly tired of his work and gone out for a walk. I heard the footsteps come to within a few yards of the house, when they left the path, fell softer on grass and weeds, and approached the window. The curtain obscured my view, but on the glass I heard the tap of finger-tips and the clink of nails.

I did not pause to reflect that Rudge, if he had gone out, must know that he had left the door on the latch, or that he could have no reason to suppose that I was already in the house. One does not consider these things in so brief a time. I just called out, 'Right ho,' and went round to the front door to let him in.

Having opened the front door I leaned out and saw him – Rudge, I imagined – peering in at the study window. He was no more than a dark, bent shadow in the dusk, crowned by a soft felt hat, such as he generally wore. 'Right ho,' I said again, and, leaving the door wide open for him, I hurried into the kitchen. There was some salad left in soak which had to be shaken and wiped before bringing it to the table. I remember that, as I walked through to the sink, one of the beams over my head creaked noisily.

I washed the salad and returned towards the dining-room. As I turned into the hall a gust of air from the still open door passed like a cool caress across my face. Then, before I had time to enter the dining-room, I heard the gate click at the end of the garden path, and footfalls on the gravel. I waited to see who it was. It was Rudge – and he was bareheaded.

He produced a book at supper, and sat scowling at it over his left arm while he ate. This was permitted by our rules, but I had something to tell him, and after a while I forced my voice upon his attention.

'Rudge,' I said, 'I've made a discovery this evening. I know how you got this place so cheap.'

He sat up with a start, stared at me, and winced.

'How?' he demanded.

'This is Stanley Stryde's old house. Don't you remember Stanley Stryde?'

He was pale already, but I saw him turn paler still.

'I remember the name vaguely,' he said. 'Wasn't he a murderer?'

'He was,' I answered. 'I didn't remember the case very well. But my memory's been refreshed today. Everybody here thought we knew, and the curious delicacy of the bucolic mind forbade mentioning it to us. It was rather a grisly business, and the odd thing is that local opinion is all in favour of Stryde's innocence, although he was hanged.'

Rudge's eyes had grown larger.

'I remember the name,' he said, 'but I forget the case. Tell me.'

'Well, Stanley Stryde was an artist who took this place. He was what we would call in common parlance a dirty dog. He'd got himself entangled with the daughter of a neighbouring farmer – the family has left here since – and then he found himself morally and socially compelled to marry her. At the same time he fell in love with another girl, so he lured the old one here and did her in. Don't you remember now?'

Rudge wrinkled his nose.

'Yes, vaguely,' he said. 'Didn't he bury the body and afterwards try to make out she'd committed suicide? So this is the house, is it? Funny nobody told us before?'

'They thought we knew,' I repeated, 'and nobody liked to mention it. As if it were some disgrace to *us*, you know! Oh, and, of course, the house is haunted.'

Rudge stared at me and frowned.

'I don't know about "haunted",' he said, 'but it's been a damned uncomfortable house to sit in for the past few evenings. I mean at twilight, when I've been waiting for you. My nerves have been pretty raw lately. Tonight I couldn't stand it, so I went out for a stroll.'

'Left in the middle of a sentence,' I remarked.

'Oh, so you noticed that, did you?'

'By the way,' I asked, 'what made you go out a second time?'

'I didn't.'

'But my dear chap, you did! Because the first time you came in you wore a hat, and two minutes later I saw you walking up the garden path without one.'

'That's when I did come back. I haven't wore a hat at all this evening.'

'Then who——' I began.

'And that reminds me,' he continued quickly, 'when *you* come in of an evening you needn't sneak up to the window and tap on it with your fingers. It doesn't frighten me, but it's disconcerting. You can always walk into the room to let me know you've come back.'

I sat and looked at him and laughed.

'But, my dear chap, I haven't done such a thing yet.'

'You old liar!' he exclaimed with an uneasy laugh, 'you've been doing it every evening for the past week – until tonight, when I didn't give you the chance.'

'I swear I haven't, Rudge. But if you thought that, it explains why you did the same thing to me tonight.'

I saw from his face that I had made some queer mistake, and interrupted his denial to ask:

'Then who was the man I saw peering in at the window? I saw him from the door. I thought you'd tapped at the window to be let in, not knowing that the door was open. So I went round and saw – I thought it was you – and called out, "Right ho".'

We looked at each other again and laughed uneasily.

'It seems we've got our ghost after all,' Rudge said half jestingly.

'Or somebody's trying to pull our leg,' I amended.

'I don't know that I should fancy meeting the ghost of a murderer. But, joking apart, the house *has* been getting on my nerves of late. And those noises we've always heard have been getting louder and more mysterious lately.'

As if to corroborate a statement which needed no evidence so far as I was concerned we heard a scuffling sound from the kitchen followed by the loud creaking of timber. We laughed again, puzzled uneasy laughter, for the thing was still half a joke.

'There you are!' said Rudge, and got upon his legs. 'I'm going to investigate this.'

He crossed the room and suddenly halted. I knew why. Then he turned about with an odd, shamed chuckle.

'No,' he said, 'there's no sense in it. I shall find nothing there. Why should I pander to my nerves?'

I had nothing to say. But I knew that in turning back he was pandering to cowardice, because just then I would have done almost anything rather than enter that kitchen. Had anybody asked me then where the murder was done, I could have told them with as much certainty as if I had just been reading about it in the papers.

Rudge sat down again.

'Don't laugh at me,' he said. 'I know this is all rot, but I've got a hideous feeling that things hidden and unseen around us are moving steadily to a crisis.'

'Cheerful brute,' I said, smiling.

'I know. It's only my nerves, of course. I don't want to infect you with them. But the noises we hear, and the fellow who comes and taps at the window – they want some explaining away, don't they?'

'Especially now that we know that somebody was murdered here,' I agreed. 'I'm beginning to wish we didn't know about that.'

Rudge went to bed early that night, but I sat up reading. As often happens to me I fell asleep over my book, and when I woke I was almost in darkness, for the lamp needed filling. The last jagged blue flame swelled and dwindled, fluttering like a moth and tapping against the glass. And as I watched it I became suddenly aware of the cause of my waking. I had heard the latch snap on the garden gate. And in that moment I began to hear them – the footfalls.

I heard the rhythmic crunch of gravel and then the swish of long grass and plantains, and then a shadow nodded on the blind. It loomed up large and suddenly became stationary. A loose pane rattled under the impact of fingers.

Perhaps there was a moon, perhaps not, but there was at least bright starlight in the world outside. The drawn blind looked like dim bluish glass, and the shadow of something outside was cut as cleanly as a silhouette clipped away with scissors. I saw only the head and shoulders of a man, who wore a dented felt hat. His head lolled over on to his left shoulder, just as I had always imagined a man's head would loll if – well, if he had been hanged. And I knew in my blood that he was a Horror and that he wanted me for something.

I felt my hair bristle and suddenly I was streaming with sweat. I don't remember turning and running, but I have a vague recollection of cannoning off the door-post and stumbling in the hall. And when I reached my bed I don't know if I fainted or fell asleep.

No, I didn't tell Rudge next day. His nerves were in a bad enough state already. Besides, in the fresh glory of a May morning it was easy to persuade myself that the episode had been an evil dream. But I did question Mrs Jaines, our charwoman, when she arrived, and I saw a look half stubborn and half guilty cross her face.

Yes, of course, she remembered the murder happening, but she didn't remember much about it. Mr Stryde was quite a nice gentleman, although rather a one of the ladies, and she had worked for him sometimes. Stryde's defence was that the poor girl had committed suicide and that he'd lost his head and buried the body when he found it. Lots of people thought that was true, but they'd hanged Mr Stryde for it all the same. And that was all I could get out of Mrs Jaines.

I smiled grimly to myself. As if the woman didn't remember every detail! As if the neighbourhood had talked of anything else for the two following years! And then I remembered the policeman's strange words and how he had been staring at the calendar while he spoke.

So that morning when I called at the inn for my usual glass of beer, I too looked at the calendar, and asked the landlord if he could tell me the date of the murder.

'Yes, sir,' he said, 'it was May the——' And then he stopped himself. 'Why, it was eight years ago, tonight!' he said.

*   *   *

I went out again that evening and came in at the usual hour. But that evening Rudge came down the path to meet me. He was white and sick-looking.

'He's been here again,' he said, 'half an hour ago.'

'You saw him this time?' I asked jerkily.

'Yes, I did as you did and went round to the door.' He paused and added quite soberly: 'He *is* a ghost, you know.'

'What happened?' I asked, looking uneasily around me.

'Oh! I went round to the door when I heard him tapping at the window, and there he was, as you saw him yesterday evening, trying to look through into the room. He must have heard me, for he turned and stared. His head was dropping all on one side, like a poppy on a broken stem. He came towards me, and I couldn't stand that, so I turned and ran into the house and locked the door.'

He spoke in a tone half weary, half matter of fact, and suddenly I knew that it was all true. I don't mean that I knew that just his story was true. I knew that the house was haunted and that the thing which we had both seen was part of the man who had once been Stanley Stryde.

When once one has accepted the hitherto incredible it is strange how soon one can adapt oneself to the altered point of view.

'This is the anniversary of the – the murder,' I said quietly. 'I should think something – something worse will happen tonight. Shall we see it through or shall we beat it?'

And almost in a whisper Rudge said:

'Poor devil! Oughtn't one to pity? He wants to tell us something, you know.'

'Yes,' I agreed, 'or show us something.'

Together we walked into the house. We were braver in each other's company, and we did not again discuss the problem of going or staying. We stayed.

I can pass over the details of how we spent that evening. They are of no importance to the story. We were left in peace until just after eleven o'clock, when once more we heard the garden gate being opened, and footfalls, which by this time we were able to recognize, came up the path and through the long grass to the window. We could see nothing, for our lamp was alight, but I knew what it looked like – the thing that stood outside and now tapped softly upon the glass. And in spite of having Rudge for company I lost my head and screamed at it.

'Get back to hell! Get back to hell, I tell you!' I heard myself shout.

And it was Rudge, Rudge the sensitive neurotic, who kept his head, for human psychology is past human understanding.

'No,' he called out in a thin quaver, 'come in. Come in, if we can help you.'

And then, as if regretting his courage on the instant, he caught my hand and held it, drawing me towards him.

The front door was locked, but it was no barrier to that which responded to the invitation. We heard slow footfalls shuffling through the hall, the footfalls, it seemed to me, of a man whose head was a burden to him. I died a thousand deaths as they approached the door of our room, but they passed and died away up the passage. And then I heard a whisper from Rudge.

'He's gone through into the kitchen. I think he wants us to follow.'

I shouldn't have gone if Rudge hadn't half dragged me by the hand. And as I went the sweat from the roots of my stiffened hair ran down my cheeks.

The kitchen door was closed, and we halted outside it, both of us breathing as if we had been running hard. Then Rudge held his breath for a moment, lifted the latch, and took a quick step across the threshold. And in that same instant he froze my chilled blood with a scream such as I had heard in war-time from a wounded horse.

He had almost fainted when he fell into my arms, but he had the presence of mind to pull the door after him, so that I saw nothing. I half dragged, half carried him into the dining-room and gave him brandy. And suddenly I became aware that a great peace had settled upon the house. I can only liken it to the freshness and the sweetness of the earth after a storm has passed. Rudge felt it too, for presently he began to talk.

'What was he – doing?' I asked in a whisper.

'He? He wasn't there – not in the kitchen.'

'Not in the kitchen? Then what – who———'

'It was She. Only She. She was kicking and struggling. From the middle beam, you know. And there was an overturned chair at her feet.'

He shuddered convulsively.

'She was worse than he,' he said presently – 'far worse.'

And then later:

'Poor devil! So he didn't do it, you see!'

* * *

Next morning we had it out with Mrs Jaines, and we did not permit her memory to be hazy or defective. She must have known that we had seen something and presently she burst into tears.

'He said he'd found her hanging in the kitchen, poor gentleman, and that he'd buried her because he was afraid people would say he'd done it. But the jury wouldn't believe him, and the doctors all said that it wasn't true, and that the marks on her neck were where he'd strangled her with a rope. I don't believe to this day he did it, I don't! But nothing can't ever bring him back.' She paused at that and added. 'Not back to life, I mean – real life, like you and me, I mean.'

And that was all we heard and all we wished to hear.

Afterwards Rudge said to me:

'For his sake, the truth as we know it ought to be told to everybody. I suppose the police know?'

'Yes,' I said, 'the police know – now. But as Mrs Jaines said, it can't bring him back.'

'Who wants to bring him back?' exclaimed Rudge with a shudder. 'But perhaps if people knew – as we know – it might let him rest. I am sure that was what he wanted – just that people should know.'

He paused and drew a long breath through his lips.

'You write it,' he said jerkily. 'I can't.'

And so I have.

A Vindictive Woman
R. Chetwynd-Hayes

Robert C. Hogg was a sparse, shy little man who ambled through life with lowered head and cautious steps, as though harbouring grave suspicions about the suburban paving stones. He lived at the very top of the house, in a miserable two-roomed flat with sagging ceilings, shrunken window-frames and walls that had long ago shed their cheap wallpaper.

It was difficult to define his age, but he must have been at least sixty-five, as I once saw him in the post office drawing his state pension. Nevertheless, his receding, mouse-coloured hair was only just flecked with silver, his pale, narrow face, save for two deep furrows on either side of the thin-lipped mouth, was unlined, and his small, grey eyes were bright with undiminished intelligence. Nothing other than the bowed shoulders and slow walk suggested that a growing burden of years was gradually taking its toll.

The only mail addressed to him that I ever saw on the hall table was the familiar buff envelope from the football pools, which at least testified that he was not lacking a certain element of optimism. He went for a walk every morning: mainly a slow stroll round the town, which generally terminated in one of the many pubs, where he sat nursing a half-pint glass of brown ale. The rest of his time appeared to be spent in that top-floor flat, doing I knew not what.

It might be as well if I were to stress that, although the house was sub-divided into seven – for want of a better term – living units, in fact Robert C. Hogg and I appeared to be the only people living there. Five other unknown and rarely seen tenants either rented a room as an accommodation address, or used it to spend the odd night whenever business brought them into the area. I, needing space that could be used as a place of work and residence, rented the entire basement, and – a completely unwarranted piece of extravagance – the massive back garden as well.

I worked in the back and front rooms alternately, being of the opinion that a change of scene helps to keep the creative stream flowing, and thus did not always see Robert C. Hogg mount the front steps. But sometimes, when the night was overcast and I had yet to close my curtains, I knew he was in his flat, for a rectangular slab of yellowish light lay across the lawn – an almost perfect facsimile of a lighted window, complete with four black-edged squares that bordered each pane – plus a bowed shadow-figure that kept passing back and forth across this illuminated frame.

I often thought how disconcerting it would be for a permanent occupant in the room below to hear this continuous pacing, and I wondered what troubled line of thought prompted the little man to do it. Perhaps he was beset by some problem which required such deep concentration that it could only be maintained by constant movement. Whatever the reason, I soon became a little disturbed by the spectacle and took to closing my curtains whenever the block of light flashed into being.

One night in early January, when the moon illuminated the thirty or so feet of lawn, transforming the slightly frosted grass into a gleaming silver carpet and obliterating every shadow, save for the dense cluster that lurked under two old elm trees at the far end, I walked two-thirds of the way up the garden, then turned and cast a cursory glance at the uppermost windows. Why I took the trouble to come out on such a cold night, I can't think; idle curiosity, I suspect, prompted by an urge to see if my neighbour still paced in front of his window, even when conditions did not allow his silhouette to be projected onto the lawn.

On this night his lights were out, but, even so, I detected the faint outline of a figure that might have been standing some little way back from the curtainless window, staring down, either at me, or at the two trees that were some way to my rear. Embarrassed by being caught out in an act of blatant nosiness, I swung round and pretended to examine the trees myself. I soon came to the conclusion that they were scarcely worthy of attention. Bleak and naked against the cold, steel-grey sky, their skeletal branches creaked forlornly when disturbed by the gentle easterly wind. Then I lowered my eyes and became uncomfortably aware of the dense block of shadow that seemed to be an extension of the sturdy trunks, a thick splodge of darkness that, if viewed in a certain way, took on the form of a black-clad figure.

I quickly switched my gaze back to Hogg's windows, but now they were gleaming mirrors that reflected the bright moonlight, and there was no way of deciding if an unseen spectator still lurked behind the shining façade. My tiny stock of courage was seeping away when I again faced the two trees and dared to ask a simple question.

'Is there anyone there?'

An answer would have been a precious gift from whatever saint watches over frightened men, while the ensuing silence was surely more terrifying even than the shriek of a doomed soul riding in on the wind.

With my head turned to the far right, my left eye had an oblique view of the furthermost tree, and it seemed as though I could see a dark shape that might have been that of a woman dressed in black and wearing a long head-shawl. An inch either side, and the vision was lost, becoming merely a slab of shadow that merged into the tree trunk.

Without further words or thought, I ran to warmth and transient security, without looking up or back. I locked doors and closed curtains in an endeavour to prove that anything which could not be seen did not exist.

*   *   *

Robert C. Hogg made his first tenuous approach the following evening.

There came a timid tap on my hall door which, when opened, revealed the bent-shouldered little figure standing on the bottom stair. Without raising his head, he said quietly:

'My lights have gone out.'

His voice was unexpectedly cultured, in some inexplicable way adding to the air of oddness that was manifest in every line of his body.

I said: 'I expect your fuse has blown. Have you examined it?'

'I know very little about such things. Where exactly will I find the fuse?'

'Would you like me to look at it for you?' I asked.

'If you would be so kind.'

I collected fuse wire, a pair of pliers, a screwdriver, and, as an afterthought, an electric torch, and followed him up three flights of stairs. A strip-light on the top landing enabled me to see the open door of his flat and part of the tiny kitchen beyond, but I was completely unprepared for the unpleasant smell that seemed to waiting to pounce the moment I set foot over the threshold. It had a sweetish, cloying quality that can only be associated with a rotting corpse, and it was so intense that I only just managed to suppress a snort of disgust.

I turned on the torch and was relieved to see that the main switch and its attendant fuse box were just by the door. I lost no time in removing the cover, pulling out the china fuse and replacing the burnt strip of wire. The entire operation took no more than two minutes, but to me, knowing that a still, silent figure was watching from the shadows, it seemed as if my fumbling fingers would never complete the job. Then I pushed the fuse home and instantly a twenty-five-watt bulb that dangled from the bulging ceiling sprang into dingy life. I got up, brushed my trouser legs and gradually became aware of a bone-numbing coldness that had, so to speak, been demanding recognition for some time.

It seemed to grow more intense by the second, and I heard my voice, loud, shrill with something akin to fear, demand:

'Good God, man, haven't you lit a fire?'

He remained unmoving, silent, and I, motivated by irritation and alarm – and perhaps some slight curiosity – walked into the small bed-sitting-room and looked around with incredulous eyes.

An extremely ancient gas fire spluttered angrily from behind a cracked tiled hearth, but for all the heat it sent out, a solitary candle might have been more effective. However, it was the almost terrifying cleanness of the place which attracted my full attention. He had scrubbed the bare floorboards snow-white, a result that can only be achieved by using boiling water well dosed with soda, a potent mixture that can be very tough on the fingernails, as my early days in the army had taught me. The narrow bed, which lurked against one wall, had been stripped, and the blankets (sheets were conspicuous by their absence) folded into neat squares and placed one on top of the other. He had even taken the trouble to clean the gas tap so that it gleamed like a fragment of burnished gold. Walls and ceiling were covered with a thick coating of whitewash that, when supplemented by a naked electric light bulb, dazzled the eye and created the illusion that the room had been carved out of snow.

I detected no concession to comfort. One plain wooden chair crouched in front of the ineffective fire and gave the impression that it would freeze the backside of anyone who was so foolhardy as to sit on it. The only other item of furniture was a plain deal table with a surface that might have been even more well scrubbed than the floor. I managed to laugh and say:

'You certainly keep the place neat.'

He gave me a strange, part anxious, part sly look.

'There are no stains?'

'None that I can see. But how can you stand this cold? It's enough to freeze the what's-its off the proverbial.'

He looked round at his chilly domain and sighed deeply.

'Cold preserves. But there is still the corruption of the soul.'

I shivered and edged towards the door. 'That's too profound for me. How about a cup of tea? I could most certainly do with one.'

He hesitated and for a moment appeared to be on the point of refusing, then slowly nodded.

'That is very kind of you. Yes, I'd like to very much.'

When we reached my flat I motioned him to an armchair and went into the kitchen where I brewed a large pot of tea, deciding the poor wretch needed well thawing out before again ascending to that ice-box. Determined to demonstrate how civilized people live, I placed teapot, cups and saucers, spoons, sugar-basin and slop bowl on to a rather grand trolley I had just acquired and wheeled it into my sitting-room. I found him seated well forward on the chair, hands outstretched, while he gazed almost reproachfully at my elaborate gas fire. He looked up as I entered and produced a rare smile.

'You really shouldn't have gone to all this trouble. Extraordinarily kind of you.'

'Not at all,' I replied, moving a low table beside his chair. 'I have a cup myself at this time. You take sugar?'

He shook his head violently.

'Oh, dear no! That would never do. She would not ...'

He stopped short and my – perhaps – unfortunate lust for knowledge received a little fillip of encouragement. So there was a woman in the background? It was only to be expected, although I had rather imagined him to be a confirmed bachelor.

'Biscuits?' I enquired. 'I've some passable digestives.'

One might have assumed I had just invited him to accept the united crowns of Great Britain.

'Really, that would be too much.'

'Nonsense,' I replied and went to fetch the tin.

We sat and drank tea and nibbled a vast amount of biscuits (at least, he did) while I tried to light a fire of informative conversation. I have often thought that those urbane interviewers on television would soon be out of a job if all of their questions were answered by a plain yes or no. Mr Hogg almost proved my point.

'I assume,' I murmured, with what I could only hope was an air of polite interest, 'you are not married.'

Mr Hogg waited until he had masticated a biscuit before replying.

'Not now.'

'But you have been?'

'Yes.'

The affirmative could be considered a tiny step forward along the path of enquiry. The fellow was either a widower or divorced. I decided to assume the former.

'I'm sorry. You must be very lonely.'

'Yes.'

It was then that he, with a rather ironic smile, posed his own question.

'And you, Mr ... ?'

'Glynn,' I replied, feeling as if I was parting with a state secret. 'Henry Glynn.'

'And you, Mr Glynn – you, too, are alone?'

I shrugged. 'I've had several trial runs, but have yet to discover a woman who does not bore me after three weeks. I'm willing to concede that this may be the result of a flaw in my character.'

He shook his head and emitted a quaint chuckle of amusement.

'How indeed extraordinary! To think that a woman can bore you. Imagine, Mr Glynn, if the shoe was on the other foot. Suppose you bored them.'

'Not an impossibility,' I replied drily. 'I must have often been the subject of a feminine yawn.'

He began to display more animation than I would have thought possible. So much so that he upset his teacup. He was at once profusely apologetic.

'How careless of me! Really unforgivable. If you will fetch a cloth ...'

'Forget it,' I ordered brusquely, alarmed less this mishap deprive me of much-desired information. 'Tea is good for the carpet. You were about to say?'

He replaced the cup carefully on the side table, then wiped his hands on a spotless handkerchief. He spoke slowly, as though savouring each word.

'Suppose, Mr Glynn, you fell hopelessly in love with a woman much younger than yourself and experienced a kind of unsurpassable delight when she agreed to marry you. Then, having given her your all – house, not insignificant savings, devotion, self-respect – suppose one day she yawns in your face and orders you out of the house. What would you do, Mr Glynn?'

'Reach for the nearest hairbrush,' I replied without hesitation.

It was then that he said something which at the time I assumed to be a joke.

'Not a poker, Mr Glynn?'

I shook my head. 'No. The use of a poker could turn out to be more than corrective – it might even be fatal. Another cup of tea, Mr Hogg.'

'You are indeed very kind.' He waited until I had refilled his cup before continuing. 'I sometimes have a fanciful notion that life is a narrow plank that stretches from the cradle to the grave, and if God is kind to us we cross without serious mishap. But one false step, one moment of inattention – and we spend eternity in a black pit of despair.' He looked up. 'Would you say women are vindictive, Mr Glynn?'

'Some,' I replied warily. 'I've met one or two.'

He took a dainty sip from his cup and gazed thoughtfully into the fire. A full two minutes passed before he spoke again.

'Believe me, a really vindictive woman has much in common with a hungry tiger. She will stalk you to perdition, and no amount of penance will placate her.' His voice sank to a thrilling whisper and, despite the warm room, I shivered. 'At first she keeps her distance, and the victim is only permitted to see her a long way off. At the end of a railway platform, on a bridge, looking down – at the bottom of a garden. Then she moves in for the kill.'

He lapsed into silence, and for the first time I became really alarmed and wished the hell I had never let him into the flat. The memory of that shape under the trees was still fresh. At last I was able to marshal words into a number one question.

'And are you ... you, Mr Hogg, pursued by such a woman?'

This time he dropped the cup and was much too agitated to apologize. I thought for a moment he was going to be sick over my best carpet. Then speech came tumbling over lax lips.

'Why do you ask? Have you seen her?'

I spoke slowly while watching him through narrowed eyes.

'Last night I thought I saw someone under the trees.'

And that was it. He got up, his face a mask of pure terror, and all but ran for the door. I called after him: 'It might have been my imagination,' but he took no notice and left me as near dumbfounded as at any time in my life. But he must have slowed down on reaching the hall, for I heard him creeping up the second flight of stairs as though reluctant to reach the top landing.

No power in this world or the next could stop me going into the bedroom and drawing back the curtains. The lighted shadow-window was back, laid out like an illuminated picture across the grass, with the silhouette of my recent guest passing to and fro, much as the imaginary tiger he had used to define a vindictive woman. But it was the almost imperceptible shape that stood just beyond the lighted square that clothed doubt in the cold raiment of reality.

Now there was no need to adjust the angle of vision, for I could dimly see a slim figure that wore some kind of long evening dress and probably a black lace head-shawl. I might even have caught a brief glimpse of a pale blur of a face, although this was uncertain. The thought slipped unbidden into my brain: 'Oh, my God! She's moved nearer!' just before Hogg turned out his light and complete darkness erased both shadow-window and whatever did – or did not – stand beyond.

Some minutes later I made what was probably the most shrewd observation of my life.

'The coldness is fear ... the stench is death.'

Next morning I tried to dismiss the entire business as the result of auto-suggestion.

*   *   *

An entire week passed before I saw Robert C. Hogg again.

I was seated at my desk in the sitting-room, having developed a distaste for looking out over the back garden, when I saw the little man climbing the front steps, his hat pulled well down over his ears, and gripping the handrail with grim determination. At the same time I was aware that someone else was just behind him and well over to the left, allowing me to catch a glimpse of a bobbing head that wore a black lace shawl. I had the ridiculous feeling that if that unseen person were to move one or two inches to the right, I would probably lose my sanity. Then I heard Hogg insert his key into the Yale lock. The door crashed back against the wall, and this was closely followed by him running along the hall. And I do mean running. A terrifying, foot-stamping, ceiling-shaking gallop that continued up two flights of stairs and was finally terminated by the distant slam of a door.

Presently I went upstairs and found the front door open. Having closed it, I ascended to the first-floor landing – now an expanse of shadow-haunted gloom. I peered up at the one above, toying with the unworthy intention of mounting the third flight and possibly pressing my ear against a closed door. But this piece of nefarious behaviour never came to fruition, for scarcely had I put foot to the first step when the merest suggestion of a black shape looking down over the banisters sent me racing back to my own domain.

It would seem that whoever pursued Robert C. Hogg was now in the house. But not yet in his flat. She was up there on the top landing – waiting.

*   *   *

Mr Hogg paid his second and last visit the following night.

The tapping on my hall door was timid but insistent, and finally I had to draw the bolts and open up. As he entered and walked silently to the fireside chair, I shrank back.

Face as white as snow in moonlight, head well forward, he stared into the fire, his limbs twitching in a most frightful manner. At that moment I hated him, alive to a fearsome possibility that something I did not want to see might come through the closed door after him. I shouted, shook clenched fists and even considered the idea of grabbing his scrawny neck and marching him out of the front door.

'For God's sake go! I can't help you. No one can. We all walk in our own hells.'

His face was a mask of frozen terror, and although his mouth opened and closed, it seemed as if speech was beyond him. I knew he was trying to tell me something that he considered to be of extreme importance, but – God help me – I didn't want to know. I could only decide that he must be very ill and that the right place for him was a hospital, so I turned my back on those bulging eyes and constantly writhing mouth and grabbed the telephone receiver. I was irrationally irritated by the number of questions that I had to answer before being informed that an ambulance would be there in the quickest possible time.

When I again looked at him, his eyes were still watching me, his mouth gaping, one hand outstretched, but now there was no movement of any kind. I thought: 'He's dead!' only he didn't really look dead. Just paralysed by fright. To remain in the same room as that ... that thing, was an impossibility, so I wandered around the flat, even occasionally opening the front door, vainly hoping to hear the approaching sound of a siren that would inform me that the dreadful wait was over. Then, possibly to delay having to return to the sitting-room, I strayed into the bedroom and, without thinking of what I was doing, walked over to the window.

There was no moon, and the rectangular slab of light lay across the lawn: the shadow-edged squares – one might almost say the ghost – of that fearful window. And, oh, most merciful God, a shadow figure was passing back and forth, a shape that wore a shawl on its graceful head. Then it suddenly stopped, and another shadow joined it – and I'd recognize that head anywhere – damn you, I could even make out the receding hair, the bloody thin face – but I must have been mad, for wasn't he seated in the next room? And that woman – the bloody, vindictive woman – was hitting him with something – and it might have been a poker – and I could actually see his mouth opening and closing, screaming ... screaming ... *only the screams were coming from my sitting-room.*

Then the light went out and so did I and mercifully knew no more until the ambulance men kicked my door in.

*   *   *

They had to break Robert C. Hogg's arms and legs, for apparently he was frozen stiff and that was the only way his corpse could be put into the zip-fastened stretcher-bag. Later, the police asked a lot of questions: how long had he lived in the house, did he have any visitors, and so on. I did not tell them about the woman who finally caught up with him.

He was traced back to a nice little house situated on the outskirts of Swindon. In it was discovered the body of his young wife, attired in a black evening dress, with a lace-shawl draped about her lovely, if a trifle dented, head. She was in an excellent state of preservation, as he had folded her, more or less neatly, before stowing her in the freezer.

All of which is, I suppose, as good a reason as any for a woman to become vindictive.

The Ghoul
Hugh Clifford

We had been sitting up late upon the veranda of my bungalow at Kuâla Lîpis, which, from the top of a low hill covered with coarse grass, over-looked the long, narrow reach formed by the combined waters of the Lîpis and the Jĕlai. The moon had risen some hours earlier, and the river ran white between the black masses of forest, which seemed to shut it in on all sides, giving to it the appearance of an isolated tarn. The roughly cleared compound, with the tennis-ground which had never got beyond the stage of being dug over and weeded, and the rank growths beyond the bamboo fence, were flooded by the soft light, every tattered detail of their ugliness standing revealed as relentlessly as though it were noon. The night was very still, but the heavy, scented air was cool after the fierce heat of the day.

I had been holding forth to the handful of men who had been dining with me on the subject of Malay superstitions, while they manfully stifled their yawns. When a man has a working knowledge of anything which is not commonly known to his neighbours, he is apt to presuppose their interest in it when a chance to descant upon it occurs, and in those days it was only at long intervals that I had an opportunity of foregathering with other white men. Therefore, I had made the most of it, and looking back, I fear that I had occupied the rostrum during the greater part of that evening. I had told my audience of the *pĕnanggal* – the 'Undone One' – that horrible wraith of a woman who has died in childbirth, who comes to torment and prey upon small children ·n the guise of a ghastly face and bust, with a comet's tail of blood-stained entrails flying in her wake; of the *mâti-ânak*, the weird little white animal which makes beast noises round the graves of children, and is supposed to have absorbed their souls; and of the *pôlong*, familiar spirits, which men bind to their service by raising up from the corpses of babies that have been still-born, the tips of whose tongues they bite off and swallow after the infant has been brought to life by magic agencies. It was at this point that young Middleton began to pluck up his ears; and I, finding that one of my hearers was at last showing signs of being interested, launched out with renewed vigour, until my sorely tried companions, one by one, went off to bed, each to his own quarters.

Middleton was staying with me at the time, and he and I sat for a while in silence, after the others had gone, looking at the moonlight on the river. Middleton was the first to speak.

'That was a curious myth you were telling us about the *pôlong*,' he said. 'There is an incident connected with it which I have never spoken of before, and have always sworn that I would keep to myself; but I have a good mind to tell you about it, because you are the only man I know who will not write me down a liar if I do.'

'That's all right. Fire away,' I said.

'Well,' said Middleton. 'It was like this. You remember Juggins, of course? He was a naturalist, you know, dead nuts upon becoming an F.R.S. and all that sort of thing, and he came to stay with me during the close season* last year. He was hunting for bugs and orchids and things, and spoke of himself as an anthropologist and a botanist and a zoologist, and heaven knows what besides; and he used to fill his bedroom with all sorts of creeping, crawling things, kept in very indifferent custody, and my veranda with all kinds of trash and rotting green trade that he brought in from the jungle. He stopped with me for about ten days, and when he heard that duty was taking me upriver into the Sâkai country, he asked me to let him come, too. I was rather bored, for the tribesmen are mighty shy of strangers and were only just getting used to me; but he was awfully keen, and a decent beggar enough, in spite of his dirty ways, so I couldn't very well say "No." When we had poled upstream for about a week, and had got well up into the Sâkai country, we had to leave our boats behind at the foot of the big rapids, and leg it for the rest of the time. It was very rough going, wading up and down streams when one wasn't clambering up a hill-side or sliding down the opposite slope – you know the sort of thing – and the leeches were worse that I have ever seen them – thousands of them, swarming up your back, and fastening in clusters onto your neck, even when you had defeated those which made a frontal attack. I had not enough men with me to do more than hump the camp-kit and a few clothes, so we had to live on the country, which doesn't yield much up among the Sâkai except yams and tapioca roots and a little Indian corn, and soft stuff of that sort. It was all new to Juggins, and gave him fits; but he stuck to it like a man.

'Well, one evening when the night was shutting down pretty fast and rain was beginning to fall, Juggins and I struck a fairly large Sâkai camp in the middle of a clearing. As soon as we came out of the jungle, and began tight-roping along the felled timber, the Sâkai sighted us and

* 'Close season', *i.e.* from the beginning of November to the end of February, during which time the rivers on the eastern seaboard of the Malay Peninsula used to be closed to traffic on account of the North-East Monsoon.

bolted for covert *en masse*. By the time we reached the huts it was pelting in earnest, and as my men were pretty well fagged out, I decided to spend the night in the camp, and not to make them put up temporary shelters for us. Sâkai huts are uncleanly places at best, and any port has to do in a storm.

'We went into the largest of the hovels, and there we found a woman lying by the side of her dead child. She had apparently felt too sick to bolt with the rest of her tribe. The kid was as stiff as Herod, and had not been born many hours, I should say. The mother seemed pretty bad, and I went to her, thinking I might be able to do something for her; but she did not seem to see it, and bit and snarled at me like a wounded animal, clutching at the dead child the while, as though she feared I should take it from her. I therefore left her alone; and Juggins and I took up our quarters in a smaller hut near by, which was fairly new and not so filthy dirty as most Sâkai lairs.

'Presently, when the beggars who had run away found out that I was the intruder, they began to come back again. You know their way. First a couple of men came and peeped at us, and vanished as soon as they saw they were observed. Then they came a trifle nearer, bobbed up suddenly, and peeped at us again. I called to them in Sĕ-noi,* which always reassures them, and when they at last summoned up courage to approach, gave them each a handful of tobacco. Then they went back into the jungle and fetched the others, and very soon the place was crawling with Sâkai of both sexes and all ages.

'We got a meal of sorts, and settled down for the night as best we could; but it wasn't a restful business. Juggins swore with eloquence at the uneven flooring, made of very roughly trimmed boughs, which is an infernally uncomfortable thing to lied down upon, and makes one's bones ache as though they were coming out at the joints, and the Sâkai are abominably restless bedfellows as you know. I suppose one ought to realize that they have as yet only partially emerged from the animal, and that, like the beasts, they are still naturally nocturnal. Anyway, they never sleep for long at a stretch, though from time to time they snuggle down and snore among the piles of warm wood ashes round the central fireplace, and whenever you wake, you will always see half a dozen of them squatting near the blazing logs, half hidden by the smoke, and jabbering like monkeys. It is a marvel to me what they find to yarn about: food, or rather the patent impossibility of ever getting enough to eat, and the stony-heartedness of providence and of the neighbouring Malays must furnish the principal topics, I should fancy, with an

---

* *Sĕ-noi* – one of the two main branches into which the Sâkai are divided. The other is called *Té-mi-au* by the *Sĕ-noi*. All the Sâkai dialects are variants of the languages spoken by these two principal tribes, which, though they have many words in common, differ from one another almost as much as, say, Italian from Spanish.

occasional respectful mention of beasts of prey and forest demons. That night they were more than ordinarily restless. The dead baby was enough to make them uneasy, and besides, they had got wet while hiding in the jungle after our arrival, and that always sets the skin disease, with which all Sâkai are smothered, itching like mad. Whenever I woke I could hear their nails going on their dirty hides; but I had had a hard day and was used to my hosts' little ways, so I contrived to sleep fairly sound. Juggins told me next morning that he had had *une nuit blanche*, and he nearly caused another stampede among the Sâkai by trying to get a specimen of the fungus or bacillus, or whatever it is, that occasions the skin disease. I do not know whether he succeeded. For my own part, I think it is probably due to chronic anaemia – the poor devils have never had more than a very occasional full meal for hundreds of generations. I have seen little brats, hardly able to stand, white with it, the skin peeling off in flakes, and I used to frighten Juggins out of his senses by telling him he had contracted it when his nose was flayed by the sun.

'Next morning I woke just in time to see the still-born baby put into a hole in the ground. They fitted its body into a piece of bark, and stuck it in the grave they had dug for it at the edge of the clearing. They buried a flint and steel and a wood-knife and some food, and a few other things with it, though no living baby could have had any use for most of them, let alone a dead one. Then the old medicine man of the tribe recited the ritual over the grave. I took the trouble to translate it once. It goes something like this:

'"O Thou, who hast gone forth from among those who dwell upon the surface of the earth, and hast taken for thy dwelling-place the land which is beneath the earth, flint and steel have we given thee to kindle thy fire, raiment to clothe thy nakedness, food to fill thy belly, and a wood-knife to clear thy path. Go, then, and make unto thyself friends among those who dwell beneath the earth, and come back no more to trouble or molest those who dwell upon the surface of the earth."

'It was short and to the point; and then they trampled down the soil, while the mother, who had got upon her feet by now, whimpered about the place like a cat that had lost its kittens. A mangy, half-starved dog came and smelt hungrily about the grave, until it was sent howling away by kicks from every human animal that could reach it; and a poor little brat, who chanced to set up a piping song a few minutes later, was kicked and cuffed and knocked about by all who could conveniently get at him with foot, hand or missile. Abstinence from song and dance for a period of nine days is the Sâkai way of mourning the dead, and any breach of this is held to give great offence to the spirit of the departed and to bring bad luck upon the tribe. It was considered necessary, therefore, to give the urchin who had done the wrong a fairly bad time of it in order to propitiate the implacable dead baby.

'Next the Sâkai set to work to pack all their household goods – not a very laborious business; and in about half an hour the last of the laden women, who was carrying so many cooking-pots and babies and rattan bags and carved bamboo-boxes and things, that she looked like the outside of a gipsy's cart at home, had filed out of the clearing and disappeared in the forest. The Sâkai always shift camp, like that, when a death occurs, because they think the ghost of the dead haunts the place where the body died. When an epidemic breaks out among them they are so busy changing quarters, building new huts, and planting fresh catch crops that they have not time to procure proper food, and half those who are not used up by the disease die of semi-starvation. They are a queer lot.

'Well, Juggins and I were left alone, but my men needed a rest, so I decided to trek no farther that day, and Juggins and I spent our time trying to get a shot at a *sêlâdang*,* but though we came upon great ploughed-up runs, which the herds had made going down to water, we saw neither hoof nor horn, and returned at night to the deserted Sâkai camp, two of my Malays fairly staggering under the piles of rubbish which Juggins called his botanical specimens. The men we had left behind had contrived to catch some fish, and with that and yams we got a pretty decent meal, and I was lying on my mat reading by the aid of a *dâmar* torch, and thinking how lucky it was that the Sâkai had cleared out, when suddenly old Juggins sat up, with his eyes fairly snapping at me through his gig-lamps in his excitement.

'"I say," he said. "I must have that baby. It would make a unique and invaluable ethnological specimen."

'"Rot," I said. "Go to sleep, old man. I want to read."

'"No, but I'm serious," said Juggins. "You do not realize the unprecedented character of the opportunity. The Sâkai have gone away, so their susceptibilities would not be outraged. The potential gain to science is immense – simply immense. It would be criminal to neglect such a chance. I regard the thing in the light of a duty which I owe to human knowledge. I tell you straight, I mean to have that baby whether you like it or not, and that is flat."

'Juggins was forever talking about human knowledge, as though he and it were partners in a business firm.

'"It is not only the Sâkai one has to consider," I said. "My Malays are sensitive about body-snatching, too. One has to think about the effect upon them."

---

* *Sêlâdang*. The gaur or wild buffalo. It is the same as the Indian variety but in the Malay Peninsula attains to a greater size than in any other part of Asia.

'"I can't help that," said Juggins resolutely. "I am going out to dig it up now."

'He had already put his boots on, and was sorting out his botanical tools in search of a trowel. I saw that there was no holding him.

'"Juggins," I said sharply. "Sit down. You are a lunatic, of course, but I was another when I allowed you to come up here with me, knowing as I did that you are the particular species of crank you are. However, I've done you as well as circumstances permitted, and as a mere matter of gratitude and decency, I think you might do what I wish."

'"I am sorry," said Juggins stiffly. "I am extremely sorry not to be able to oblige you. My duty as a man of science, however, compels me to avail myself of this God-sent opportunity of enlarging our ethnological knowledge of a little-known people."

'"I thought you did not believe in God," I said sourly: for Juggins added a militant agnosticism to his other attractive qualities.

'"I believe in my duty to human knowledge," he replied sententiously. "And if you will not help me to perform it, I must discharge it unaided."

'He had found his trowel, and again rose to his feet.

'"Don't be an ass, Juggins," I said. "Listen to me. I have forgotten more about the people and the country here than you will ever learn. If you go and dig up that dead baby, and my Malays see you, there will be the devil to pay. They do not hold with exhumed corpses, and have no liking for or sympathy with people who go fooling about with such things. They have not yet been educated up to the pitch of interest in the secrets of science which has made of you a potential criminal, and if they could understand our talk, they would be convinced that you needed the kid's body for some devilry or witchcraft business, and ten to one they would clear out and leave us in the lurch. Then who would carry your precious botanical specimens back to boats for you, and just think how the loss of them would knock the bottom out of human knowledge for good and all."

'"The skeleton of the child is more valuable still," repled Juggins. "It is well that you should understand that in this matter – which for me is a question of my duty – I am not to be moved from my purpose either by arguments or threats."

'He was as obstinate as a mule, and I was pretty sick with him; but I saw that if I left him to himself he would do the thing so clumsily that my fellows would get wind of it, and if that happened I was afraid that they might desert us. The tracks in that Sâkai country are abominably confusing, and quite apart from the fear of losing all our camp-kit, which we could not hump for ourselves, I was by no means certain that

I could find my own way back to civilization unaided. Making a virtue of necessity, there, I decided that I would let Juggins have his beastly specimen, provided that he would consent to be guided entirely by me in all details connected with the exhumation.

'"You are a rotter of the first water," I said frankly. "And if I ever get you back to my station, I'll have nothing more to do with you as long as I live. All the same, I am to blame for having brought you up here, and I suppose I must see you through."

'"You're a brick," said Juggins, quite unmoved by my insults. "Come on."

'"Wait," I replied repressively. "This thing cannot be done until my people are all asleep. Lie down on your mat and keep quiet. When it is safe, I'll give you the word."

'Juggins groaned, and tried to persuade me to let him go at once; but I swore that nothing would induce me to move before midnight, and with that I rolled over on my side and lay reading and smoking, while Juggins fumed and fretted as he watched the slow hands of his watch creeping round the dial.

'I always take books with me into the jungle, and the more completely incongruous they are to my immediate surroundings the more refreshing I find them. That evening, I remember, I happened to be re-reading Miss Florence Montgomery's *Misunderstood* with the tears running down my nose; and by the time my Malays were all asleep, this incidental wallowing in sentimentality had made me more sick with Juggins and his disgusting project than ever.

'I never felt so like a criminal as I did that night, as Juggins and I gingerly picked our way out of the hut across the prostrate forms of my sleeping Malays; nor had I realized before what a difficult job it is to walk without noise on an openwork flooring of uneven boughs. We got out of the place and down the crazy stair-ladder at last, without waking any of my fellows, and we then began to creep along the edge of the jungle that hedged the clearing about. Why did we think it necessary to creep? I don't know. Partly we did not want to be seen by the Malays, if any of them happened to wake; and besides that, the long wait and the uncanny sort of work we were after had set our nerves going a bit, I expect.

'The night was as still as most nights are in real, *pukka* jungle. That is to say, that it was as full of noises – little, quiet, half-heard beast and tree noises – as an egg is full of meat; and every occasional louder sound made me jump almost out of my skin. There was not a breath astir in the clearing, but miles up above our heads the clouds were racing across the moon, which looked as though it were scudding through them in the opposite direction at a tremendous rate, like a great white fire balloon. It was pitch dark along the edge of the clearing, for the jungle threw a heavy shadow; and Juggins kept knocking those great clumsy feet of his against the stumps, and swearing softly under his breath.

'Just as we were getting near the child's grave the clouds obscuring the moon became a trifle thinner, and the slightly increased light showed me something that caused me to clutch Juggins by the arm.

'"Hold hard!" I whispered, squatting down instinctively in the shadow, and dragging him after me. "What's that on the grave?"

'Juggins hauled out his six-shooter with a tug, and looking at his face, I saw that he was as pale as death and more than a little shaky. He was pressing up against me, too, as he squatted, a bit closer, I fancied, than he would have thought necessary at any other time, and it seemed to me that he was trembling. I whispered to him, telling him not to shoot; and we sat there for nearly a minute, I should think, peering through the uncertain light, and trying to make out what the creature might be which was crouching above the grave and making a strange scratching noise.

'Then the moon came out suddenly into a patch of open sky, and we could see clearly at last, and what it revealed did not make me, for one, feel any better. The thing we had been looking at was kneeling on the grave, facing us. It, or rather she, was an old, old Sâkai hag. She was stark naked, and in the brilliant light of the moon I could see her long, pendulous breasts swaying about like an ox's dewlap, and the creases and wrinkles with which her withered hide was criss-crossed, and the discoloured patches of foul skin disease. Her hair hung about her face in great matted locks, falling forward as she bent above the grave, and her eyes glinted through the tangle like those of some unclean and shaggy animal. Her long fingers, which had nails like claws, were tearing at the dirt of the grave, and her body was drenched with sweat, so that it glistened in the moonlight.

'"It looks as though someone else wanted your precious baby for a specimen, Juggins," I whispered; and a spirit of emulation set him floundering onto his feet, till I pulled him back. "Keep still, man," I added. "Let us see what the old hag is up to. It isn't the brat's mother, is it?"

'"No," panted Juggins. "This is a much older woman. Great God! What a ghoul it is!"

'Then we were silent again. Where we squatted we were hidden from the hag by a few tufts of rank *lâlang* grass, and the shadow of the jungle also covered us. Even if we had been in the open, however, I question whether the old woman would have seen us, she was so eagerly intent upon her work. For full five minutes, as near as I can guess, we squatted there watching her scrape and tear and scratch at the earth of the grave, with a sort of frenzy of energy; and all the while her lips kept

going like a shivering man's teeth, though no sound that I could hear
came from them.

'At length she got down to the corpse, and I saw her lift the bark
wrapper out of the grave, and draw the baby's body from it. Then she
sat back upon her heels, threw up her head, just like a dog, and bayed at
the moon. She did this three times, and I do not know what there was
about those long-drawn howls that jangled up one's nerves, but each
time the sound became more insistent and intolerable, and as I listened,
my hair fairly lifted. Then, very carefully, she laid the child's body
down in a position that seemed to have some connection with the points
of the compass, for she took a long time, and consulted the moon and the
shadows repeatedly before she was satisfied with the orientation of the
thing's head and feet.

'Then she got up, and began very slowly to dance round and round
the grave. It was not a reassuring sight, out there in the awful loneliness
of the night, miles away from everyone and everything, to watch that
abominable old beldam capering uncleanly in the moonlight, while
those restless lips of hers called noiselessly upon all the devils in hell,
with words that we could not hear. Juggins pressed up against me
harder than ever, and his hand on my arm gripped tighter and tighter.
He was shaking like a leaf, and I do not fancy that I was much steadier.
It does not sound very terrible, as I tell it to you here in comparatively
civilized surroundings; but at the time, the sight of that obscure figure
dancing silently in the moonlight with its ungainly shadow scared me
badly.

'She capered like that for some minutes, setting to the dead baby as
though she were inviting it to join her, and the intent purposefulness of
her made me feel sick. If anybody had told me that morning that I was
capable of being frightened out of my wits by an old woman, I should
have laughed; but I saw nothing outlandish in the idea while that
grotesque dancing lasted.

'Her movements, which had been very slow at first, became
gradually faster and faster, till every atom of her was in violent motion,
and her body and limbs were swaying this way and that, like the boughs
of a tree in a tornado. Then, all of a sudden, she collapsed to the ground,
with her back towards us, and seized the baby's body. She seemed to
nurse it, as a mother might nurse her child, and as she swayed from side
to side, I could see first the curve of the creature's head, resting on her
thin left arm, and then its feet near the crook of her right elbow. And
now she was crooning to it in a cracked falsetto chant that might have
been a lullaby or perhaps some incantation.

'She rocked the child at first, but very rapidly the pace quickened,
until her body was swaying to and fro from the hips, and from side to
side, at such a rate that, to me, she looked as though she was falling all

ways at once. And simultaneously her shrill chanting became faster and faster, and every instant more nerve-sawing.

'Next she suddenly changed the motion. She gripped the thing she was nursing by its arms, and began to dance it up and down, still moving with incredible agility, and crooning more damnably than ever. I could see the small, puckered face of the thing above her head every time she danced it up, and then, as she brought it down again, I lost sight of it for a second, until she danced it up once more. I kept my eyes fixed upon the thing's face every time it came into view, and I swear it was not an optical illusion – *it began to be alive.* Its eyes were open and moving, and its mouth was working, like that of a child which tries to laugh, but is too young to do it properly. Its face ceased to be like that of a new-born baby at all. It was distorted by a horrible animation. It was the most unearthly sight.

'Juggins saw it, too, for I could hear him drawing his breath harder and shorter than a healthy man should.

'Then, all in a moment, the hag did something. I did not see clearly precisely what it was, but it looked to me as though she bent forward and kissed it, and at that very instant a cry went up like the wail of a lost soul. It may have been something in the jungle, but I know my Malayan forests pretty thoroughly, and I have never heard any cry like it before nor since. The next thing we knew was that the old hag had thrown the body back into the grave, and was dumping down the earth and jumping on it, while that strange cry grew fainter and fainter. It all happened so quickly that I had not had time to think or move before I was startled back into full consciousness by the sharp crack of Juggins's revolver fired close to my ear.

'"She's burying it alive!" he cried.

'It was a queer thing for a man to say, who had seen the child lying stark and dead more than thirty hours earlier, but the same thought was in my mind too, as we both started forward on a run. The hag had vanished into the jungle as silently as a shadow. Juggins had missed her, of course. He was always a rotten bad shot. However, we had no thought for her. We just flung ourselves upon the grave, and dug at the earth with our hands, until the baby lay in our arms. It was cold and stiff, and putrefaction had already begun its work. I forced open its mouth, and saw something that I had expected. The tip of its tongue was missing. It looked as though it had been bitten off by a set of shocking bad teeth, for the edge left behind was like a saw.

'"The thing's quite dead," I said to Juggins.

'"But it cried – it cried!" whimpered Juggins. "I can hear it now. To think that we let that horrible creature murder it."

'He sat down with his head in his hands. He was utterly unmanned.

'Now that the fright was over, I was beginning to be quite brave again. It is a way I have.

'"Rot," I said. "The thing's been dead for hours, and anyway, here's your precious specimen if you want it."

'I had put it down, and now pointed at it from a distance. Its proximity was not pleasant. Juggins, however, only shuddered.

'"Bury it, in heaven's name,' he said, his voice broken by sobs. "I would not have it for the world. Besides, it *was* alive. I saw and heard it."

'Well, I put it back in its grave, and next day we left the Sâkai country. Juggins had a whacking dose of fever, and anyway we had had about enough of the Sâkai and all of their engaging habits to last us for a bit.

'We swore one another to secrecy as Juggins, when he got his nerve back, said that the accuracy of our observations was not susceptible of scientific proof, which, I understand, was the rock his religion had gone to pieces on, and I did not fancy being told that I was drunk or that I was lying. You, however, know something of the uncanny things of the East, so tonight I have broken our vow. Now I'm going to turn in. Don't give me away.'

Young Middleton died of fever and dysentery, somewhere up-country, a year or two later. His name was not Middleton, of course; so I am not really 'giving him away', as he called it, even now. As for his companion, though when I last heard of him he was still alive and a shining light in the scientific world, I have named him Juggins, and as the family is a large one, he will run no great risk of being identified.

The Horror Under Penmire
Adrian Cole

Penmire is strewn across the edge of one of the bleakest stretches of Cornish moorland in existence. Though the windswept houses are exposed constantly to the buffets of Atlantic gales, the withdrawn inhabitants live their lives in sheltered seclusion, rarely venturing beyond the proximities of their isolated haven. There are few trees in Penmire, or indeed for miles around on this spectral, misted countryside – the hard outcrops of granite permit only the barest growths of gorse and heather. Any who chance to pass this way would wonder how it is that the villagers live.

Yet it has been thus for years without number. In its long, un-chronicled history, Penmire has tenanted miners, farmers, even smug-glers from the secret coves of the not-too-distant coasts, where even today the caves and blow-holes shelter hidden secrets. There have always been people here in Penmire, perhaps from the dawn of man; sometimes it is whispered abroad on shadowed evenings that men worshipped at strange altars in the marshes behind the village, and some folks hold that Arthur took refuge here at one time, pursued across the moors by some hideous foe.

Only the tors of frowning granite know how long Penmire has stood, but the magic of distant ages still hangs wraith-like over the quaint dwellings, suggesting primal antiquity and forgotten knowledge. What scenes of ancient savagery did the inperturbable moon gaze down upon through ragged, storm-rent clouds? What dark arts were practised, what Neolithic sounds mingled with the roaring winds, to be torn and hurled across miles of barren wasteland?

Now the village seems to slumber, oblivious to the outside world, contemplating, perhaps, its fabled past.

Roy Baxter had long been fascinated by the lure of mystic Penmire. He was a hard-working engineer from Bristol, or 'up-country' as the locals termed it, but his hobby was this deep interest in folklore and mythology. It was a hobby which led him all over England, pottering around on ancient sites, and browsing through musty, faded records.

He was on holiday now, driving fairly aimlessly through the enchanting hamlets of Cornwall, the county that perhaps drew him most, and it was here in the tiny pubs that he first heard muted comments about Penmire. It was just the sort of guarded half-secret that he looked for, but no one was anxious to locate the place for him. His curiosity was fully aroused – he often found the local people non-committal concerning the old legends, despite their talkative natures – but an unnatural barrier of silence would always clamp down the moment he tried to bring Penmire into the conversation. In one little pub he saw a group of farmers down pints and fairly rush out into the night, though he may have imagined their rapid exit.

Baxter's fertile imagination worked further overtime when he tried to pinpoint Penmire on a map. All his efforts failed. There simply weren't any records of the place anywhere, on Ordnance Survey maps or local records.

Despite this disappointment, Baxter was thrilled. He was certain that the village existed and determined all the more to find it. Acting on the assumption from what little he had heard, that Penmire was somewhere on the central moorlands, he tried to cover as much of that foreboding landscape as he could, but it was a fruitless task. Thick fingers of fog obscured the hidden paths and narrow roadways that could have led him there. Infuriated, he came off the moors and drove into Bodmin, where he checked into a small hotel.

That evening he came down the creaking stairs, ducking under a thick beam, and came into the foyer.

'May I use the phone?' he asked his dumpy, rosy-cheeked hostess. She was a cheerful soul, ample-bosomed and bouncy, typical of the loquacious landlady.

''Course you can, Mr Baxter,' she chirped in a high voice, elongating her R's in the curious Cornish fashion.

'Fine. I want to call London, actually.'

'Oh, that's all right. Business, I s'pose?' Mrs Harcott was all smiles. She was already imagining Baxter to be a big-time executive or possibly a TV producer. Her gossip circles would shortly be afire with the news.

'Yes,' Baxter grinned, thinking it would all go on the bill anyway. 'Oh, by the way,' he added, trying to sound casual, 'uh, I noticed a turning on the moor for a place called – what was it? – ah, Penmire. Yes, that was it, Penmire. It seems I've heard of it in local customs and the like. Only I'm rather keen on that sort of thing. Do you know the place at all?' He had lied about that turn-off, but he wanted to see if Mrs Harcott would deny all knowledge of Penmire. Her mouth was slightly open, as though he had taken her by surprise. She began idly flicking through her guest-book, and Baxter knew he had found another peculiar link in the mysterious armour of that moorland village.

'Well, I 'ave 'eard of it, Mr Baxter, but I can't say as I know where 'tis. I 'spect you'd find out in the bar tonight, though. We do 'ave some of the local landowners in 'ere sometimes. But if 'tis on the moors, I'd keep away if I were you, Mr Baxter. 'Tis awful bleak up there, 'specially with the mist.'

'I see. Well, thanks anyway, Mrs Harcott. Perhaps you're right.' That was all he'd get out of her. So the place did exist.

'You're welcome,' she returned, but her air of pleasantness had dissipated. Baxter found the phone tucked away in a convenient niche, and after a series of brief interchanges eventually got through to a London number.

'Hallo, Phil? This is Roy.' There was a pause before he heard the voice of his life-long friend.

'Hallo, there. Long time no see. What have you been doing with yourself? Are you at home?' Philip Dayton's voice was warm, firm, painting a picture of a strong character.

'No, I'm in Cornwall, actually.'

'Ah, the legend-haunted south-west,' Dayton chuckled. He was more than familiar with his friend's obsession with mythology. Himself an expert in the field, he guessed the reason for this call at once. Roy was 'on to something'. Dayton grinned to himself as he thought of some of the ridiculous 'finds' his pal had unearthed in the last few years.

'Yes,' said Baxter. 'I've got a few weeks off to pursue my true calling as usual.'

'Very nice. And what have you dug up from the pixie-infested tin mines this time?'

'Well, nothing as yet. But I've come across an interesting case.'

'Oh?' Dayton was intrigued by his friend's tone, for, despite Baxter's ability to stumble across events of absolutely no importance whatsoever, he did occasionally find something interesting.

'Ever heard of Penmire?'

'Penmire? No, can't place it offhand.'

'It's a small village on Bodmin Moor, but I don't know where. If you can't direct me to it, no one can.' Baxter sounded urgent. He knew Philip Dayton's knowledge of legend and folklore was extensive; Dayton had written several authoritative books on the subject, and had read as much material as he could find.

'Ah, Penmire. It does ring the faintest of bells. Vaguely connected with Arthur, and with a history of Druidic dabbings to boot. Yes, I know of it, though I can't tell you the gory details until I've dredged them up.'

'Well, it's a start,' exclaimed Baxter. 'Where the blue blazes is the place?'

'That I don't know. In fact I think you're in a blind alley, old sport. As far as I remember the place is only legendary anyway. A bit like the evasive Camelot.'

'Oh no!' Baxter groaned. 'Don't tell me it doesn't exist!'

'I'm not sure. I'm not too well up in those channels. Tell you what, though.'

'Uh-huh?'

'Where are you exactly?'

Baxter gave his address and his friend took it down.

'Bodmin, eh? Right. You hang on down there, and perhaps have a scout round for our hidden Penmire. In the meantime I'll see what I can find out about it at this end, then I might just drive down and join you.'

'You needn't do that, Phil, thanks all the same. I don't want to drag you off on a wild-goose chase.'

There was a laugh from the other end of the line. 'Nonsense. I'm hooked. Matter of fact I'm at a loose end at the moment. I've just finished a series of University lectures, and I had thought about going up to the Yorkshire Moors for a spot of research. Witches and all that. But I must admit Bodmin Moor sounds just as enterprising.'

'Working on a new book?'

'Yup. Haven't done a damn thing yet, though. So your little find might furnish me with a few new tidbits. I could do with a break, and I haven't drunk a few jars with you for some time.'

'Great. In that case I'll stick around. When will you be here?'

'Oh, say three days. I should be able to ferret something out by then.'

'Right. Give my love to Annie and the kids.' Baxter rang off.

* * *

Philip Dayton scratched his head irritably and sipped his scotch, his thoughts running back once more to the events of the last few days. Where the hell was Roy? Five days ago he'd phoned him, enthusing about Penmire and its superstitious connotations. Two days ago, he, Dayton, had arrived here in Bodmin with enough information to help find the place, but Roy was nowhere to be found. That just wasn't like him.

Dayton now sat in the cramped bar of his friend's hotel, where he too had checked in. No one had been able to help. Mrs Harcott had seen Roy leave shortly after phoning him, and his few things were still in his room; she hadn't seen him since. Dayton had made several abortive attempts to eke information out of the people who used the bar, but he got the same shrugs from all of them. Hardly anyone had seen him, anyway, as he'd left the hotel shortly after checking in.

Dayton got little sleep that night; he began to get progressively more worried. His eyes turned again and again to the monolith on the hill above Bodmin, which stood out clearly against the purple skies. He turned this way and that in a restless half-slumber, while the brass pixies on the mantelpiece seemed to contort themselves into weird shapes. In the early hours of the morning, Dayton settled on a plan of action: he couldn't hang around lamely any longer. Roy must have found Penmire, otherwise he would have been back.

After a hurried breakfast, Dayton drove up on to Bodmin Moor and began searching the hedgeless side-roads and lesser tracks, from time to time consulting a rough map he had improvised in the records section of a London library. He pulled up at the base of a chain of huge, jutting tors, crowned with bare outcrops of wind-swept rock. According to his information, Penmire should be on the other side. There was an old road somewhere, but the chances were that it would be overgrown and hard to find.

Dayton got out, locking the car, and began the steep climb, his feet sinking slightly into the moss that dotted these lowest slopes. It was a gorgeous day; for once the sky was free of clouds and the sun beat down, giving the usually foreboding landscape a more welcoming quality. It was July, typically hot and windless. He could hear the skylarks twittering incessantly, though they were too high up to be seen against the glare. As he climbed he felt fresh and alive, at one with the land. His doubts about Roy dispersed in the joy of the climb.

As he reached the rock sentinels atop the tor, Dayton let out a deep sigh, mopped his brow and looked back at the clear vista below him. Far off he saw the sun glinting on the metal of speeding cars as they raced down the main road. You're missing it all, he thought. After a moment he turned and clambered through the dark rocks which were splotched here and there with thin patches of lichen. Once he'd crossed the top of the tor, he looked down with a satisfied grunt at the straggling houses below.

Unless I miss my guess, that'll be Penmire – picturesque little spot, he mused. A sparkling stream ran out of the distant village, twisting its way into the limits of his vision, where a dark mass of trees formed a wood at the edge of the moors. Before Penmire lay the marshes, a flattish area, peppered with bogs and mires, which the old records had mentioned, and behind them rose a series of rugged tors, leading off hazily into the heart of the moorland.

Dayton was about to start the descent, when he heard muffled voices somewhere behind him. At least, he thought they had come from behind him. He turned, half expecting to see a basking courting couple, but his gaze encountered only the blank rocks. Damn fool, he said to himself. On a day like this voices carry a long way.

He took off his jacket, slung it unceremoniously over his shoulder and began to climb down into the broad valley. He hadn't noticed it, but the skylarks were no longer audible. Looking down on Penmire, he could see that it was oddly lifeless, as though it had been long abandoned. That was strange, because according to Dayton's information it should be populated. Still, he was some way off yet, though he couldn't see any vehicles or telephone wires. To all intents and purposes the place was dead.

As he pressed on, expecting to see at least a sheep or two, Dayton was suddenly aware of the silence, broken only by his passage through the tufts of reed. He stood still and realized just how absurdly quiet it was. He was reminded of Alice stepping though the looking glass. *So where is the white rabbit?* He felt eyes on him too, though he had to suppress a chuckle at his own nerves. Perhaps the villagers had seen him approach – in a place as remote as this they wouldn't appreciate strangers. But he should have been able to hear the birds or at least the teeming insect life: the grasshoppers and crickets usually made a terrific din.

Behind him, towering up into the sunlight, the rocks seemed to leer down mockingly. Dayton shrugged and moved on. Roy's car should be around somewhere, he told himself. He'd feel a lot easier when he saw it. He heard the faintest suggestions of voices again and cursed himself; he put it down to exertion – after all, he was not a young man. Penmire was still some way off when he noticed a sudden chill in the air. The psychical research boys would love this place. Then he laughed inwardly as he saw the reason for the drop in temperature.

Coming across the brow of a nearby tor was a thick mist, lapping over the rocks and overspilling into the valley. These moor mists can be frightening to those who don't know them – they appear from almost nowhere and literally descend like blankets in a matter of minutes. Dayton had tramped Dartmoor to the east, and knew how quickly he would be enveloped by those swirling, silent tendrils.

He speeded up his descent, certain now that he could hear those indefinable voices. It was uncanny, made even more so by this thickening mist. The stuff seemed to tremble with animation as it reached out and engulfed him. Dayton calculated that he had about a mile to go. He stumbled on, muttering obscenities, through the gathering coils.

There then burst on his ears a chorus of sounds that stopped him dead in his tracks. He was in the heart of the mist when, as if at a given signal, thousands of frogs burst into voice, the sound of their deep croaking coming from all around the valley. Dayton reflected that it was the most chilling sound he had ever heard. He tried to see into the mist, but out of all those countless frogs he could see none. He was scared, no use in pretending otherwise, but he smiled grimly. The mist had probably alarmed them. Sitting at home in an armchair was one thing, but when you were alone in this lot it was a different matter.

Far off he heard a splashing vaguely over the cacophony of frogs. That would be the stream, etching its way through the boulders. But this was too rhythmic for a stream, more as though someone were sloshing their way through water or mud. An inhabitant at last? Dayton thought of shouting, but the sound appeared to recede, and, for some unaccountable reason, he thought it had gone *underground*. But so many odd things had occurred already that he cursed himself and carried on.

Abruptly the frogs were silent, and the abysmal silence supplanted their terrible racket. Dayton barked his shins more than once, now only vaguely certain of the direction in which Penmire lay. His progress had become far more difficult, for he had to skirt sinking clods of peat and slime-covered pools of mire. He was sweating profusely, his face damp with mist. Where was that blasted village? He leant on a huge granite slab and wheezed. *Roy, my son, heads shall roll for this.*

The events of the next few seconds were a total shock to him, and concrete proof that something was very much amiss with this weird valley. The rock on which he was leaning seemed to twitch, as the flank of a horse twitches when irritated by a fly. Dayton drew back in horrified alarm, half expecting something dark and malign to rear up out of the mire. Then the earth heaved, and he pitched forward into the soaking reeds. 'This is ridiculous!' he kept saying, over and over again, but the ground *rippled* as though it were water, and Dayton bit off a scream.

It must be an island of turf, he told himself desperately, for anything else would be far too alien to accept. He struggled to his feet and ran, though it was like standing in a small boat. He stumbled again before the movements stopped, then rushed on as far as the reeds and hidden rocks would allow. This time he could definitely hear voices, though they seemed as much inside of him as out in those sentient mists. The voices laughed, chuckling insanely at his plight: voices which he knew instinctively were not human.

The mist was now as thick as the fogs that he knew in London. God, how far away all that was. On and on he wandered, his shins bruised and bleeding from innumerable bumps on the hard granite that lay obscured everywhere he turned. A rumbling like distant thunder caught his attention, coming from the marsh, and again it seemed to come from *under* the earth. But that was unthinkable.

Dayton's progress had slowed right down, his breath coming in laboured gasps. The mist was playing tricks, though the sound had receded. Now all he could hear was the drip, drip of moisture on the reeds, faint though that sound was. Something dark and suggestive loomed up ahead, and he fell to his knees, heart pounding like a locomotive. *God, this is it.*

But it was only a house. He had reached the sanctuary of Penmire at last.

Painfully he limped between two houses, their eaves overhanging the path, their windows dark and shadowed. As he came into the street, he still had no idea where to start looking for Roy, assuming he was here. It was a relief to get off the marsh. Something stirred in the mist, and he recoiled in surprise. The skulking shape of a cat slunk past, eyes blazing with green hate, eyes that never left his own.

Where is everyone? Still the dense mist showed no signs of lifting. Dayton stumbled on up the badly-kept street, hands thrust deep in his pockets, numb with the cold, jacket pulled tight around him. He was conscious now of other cat-like shapes padding around the edge of his vision, but they were always obscured by the mist. At last he saw a dim light, and, coming upon what appeared to be an old inn, he pushed the thick wooden door and went inside.

Hostile eyes regarded him from at least five places as he closed the door. A bar ran the length of the far wall, while several tables were placed here and there around the little room. The walls were fitted with panelled cubicles, and nailed to the roof beams were brass horse-accoutrements, though Dayton couldn't see any horseshoes. He wasn't surprised.

An old woman sat at one of the tables, arms resting on a gnarled stick, a battered bag on the floor beside her slippered feet. Two weather-beaten men sat in one of the chipped cubicles in the corner, smoking and playing cards. The barman, a huge, shirt-sleeved character with a pink, freckled face and thinning, sandy hair, was talking to what appeared to be a local labourer. There was thick mud on his boots. The barman scowled at Dayton as he came forward.

'We aren't open yet,' he said gruffly in a very strong accent. Dayton noticed a grubby collie lying at the labourer's feet, regarding him disdainfully.

'That's all right. Only I, uh, lost my way in this ruddy mist. It's a bit marshy out there and I don't fancy trying to find my way back to the car until the mist lifts.' The old lady regarded him through her spectacles, but never blinked. She might have been carved from granite for all she moved. No one spoke. Dayton edged nearer the bar, wary of the dog. Its owner had turned to inspect him, his gaze as scathing as his animal's. The card players had stopped.

'I don't suppose you've a phone ...'

'No. There b'ain't none in Penmire,' returned the barman, taking a rag and wiping down the bar slowly and methodically.

'Oh. Well, I'm in a bit of a mess. Is there anywhere I can clean up?' The eyes stared questioningly. Christ, thought Dayton, what are they – zombies?

'From outside, be 'ee?' muttered the old girl beside him.

'Yes, that's right. London. I'm, er, looking for a friend of mine. I believe he's staying in Penmire.'

The woman nodded vaguely.

'I thought 'ee was from outside.'

'Hush, Mrs Dinnock,' muttered the barman. 'I think you're mistaken, sir. No one don't come to stay in Penmire.'

'Oh, but my friend expressly stated that he would be here.' Dayton watched the thick pipe-smoke curling up into the beams from the corner.

'No, I don't think so. No one has come. Only you.' Dayton shifted his gaze to the card players. They sat as though paralysed. What if Roy hadn't come here?

'Perhaps he'll turn up later. In the meantime, have you a gents handy? I must try and clean up a bit.'

'Through there,' grunted the barman reluctantly, pointing to a side door. Dayton nodded his thanks and went through. He found a tiny toilet and closed the flaking door behind him. There was an overpowering smell of fish exuding from the drain. Now what? he asked himself as he cleaned himself up in the battered sink. I was better off in the ruddy marsh.

He returned to the bar to find it empty, save for the inhospitable barman, who tried his damndest to ignore him.

'You get this mist often?'

'Ah.'

Dayton decided it was an affirmative. 'Like pea soup, eh?' he grinned, but it had no effect. Now I know how the lepers used to feel, he mused. 'Any chance of me buying a bite to eat?'

'Don't serve meals, sir. There's a shop down the street.'

'Hm. I'll hang on here till the mist lifts, I think. You, er, don't mind?' You hadn't better, he added to himself.

'May be down for a week. Often stops longer in the warm weather. My advice is to take the road off the moor, sir. You'll be all right. Folks in Penmire is wary of strangers.' The barman was fiddling about with glasses and glimpsing at a paper, anything to avoid being drawn into conversation.

'So I noticed. You, uh, sure about that friend of mine?'

'Positive.'

'O.K.' Dayton went over to one of the booths and sat down,

pretending to study a map that he carried. The barman eyed him coldly and began cleaning glasses again. Outside everything remained silent.

Dayton had been seated for only a short time, when he noticed a book of some description poking up from the back of the seat opposite. Gently he reached over, careful not to be seen by the barman who had for a moment turned to his shelves, and picked it up. It was a paperback entitled *Myths and Folklore of the South West*.

That clinched it! It must be Roy's. Hastily Dayton flicked through the book and found several underlined passages and notations, all in pencil and instantly recognizable as Roy's handwriting. He found a section on Druidic practices and certain other primitive rites said to have been handed down from earlier periods. The name Arthur cropped up here and there, along with the usual references to Tintagel, then Dayton found a very brief passage on Penmire.

'... a very old settlement, believed to be the one-time centre of a very primitive culture, centred around the worship of the Sea ... fantastic theory that the earliest inhabitants were settlers from the sinking of Atlantis ... seems a rather fanciful notion ... possibly the survivors from Lyonesse or counterpart ...' Pencilled beside the passage was the word: DAGON?

'I'm closing now,' boomed a voice above him, and Dayton slammed the book shut with a start.

'Oh. Oh, really? I'll be off then. Always carry some light reading matter, you know.' He knows, Dayton thought. *What are these people hiding?* He forced a grin, reflecting that it was still relatively early.

'Keep on the road, sir. One step off and you're likely to sink for good into the marshes.'

Dayton rose, pocketing the book. 'Uh-huh. I expect it'll brighten up soon. Sorry to be a nuisance.' He left as casually as he could, stepping once more into the dank, oppressive mist. The stench of fish came even more strongly to his nostrils now. Still, he'd resigned himself to expect anything in this eerie place, even pixies. But he *was* being observed, he knew at once, and far more intensely than before. Then he saw the glowing, baleful eyes of the cats, never for a moment averting their gaze.

Dayton watched them as he started down the street, having decided to stop at the shop. To his horror he saw that there were now a number of dogs in the mist, all plodding along quietly, as though waiting the command to attack. This was fast becoming a nightmare. What had Roy meant by the pencilled 'Dagon'? Dayton recognized the name as that of a mythical sea-dwelling creature, though as far as he knew it had only appeared in fiction.

Faintly-defined houses slipped past as he hastily moved on,

conscious now of several cats and dogs lurking at his heels, like a hungry pack. A flapping from above made him duck, to see a crow disappear into the gloom. Another house appeared ahead, but before he had taken another step he saw three pairs of eyes glowing in front of him.

What are they – wolves? He felt panic gripping him. They're trying to surround me! Dayton abruptly turned to his left and sprinted between the houses, anywhere to escape the lurking shadows. A bark behind him told him they were giving chase.

He came to the edge of the marsh, and for a moment he almost forgot the pursuit. He had found concrete proof that Roy had come to Penmire; one wheel and part of the front bumper of his Rover 2000 were sticking up out of the mire. Dayton had no time to speculate. Something heavy crashed into the back of his head and he plummeted into a bottomless well of oblivion.

* * *

Dayton came round with a splitting headache. His arms felt as though they were being torn from their sockets, and his mouth was horribly dry. Total darkness enveloped him; his surroundings swam in a blur as he tried to focus on something tangible. Vague thoughts on what had happened trickled back to him, but he was in no condition to struggle.

The first sound he heard was the plop-plop-plop of water somewhere near his head. He tried to move, only to find that he was chained up, back to a damp wall, somewhere in a cellar or cave. *Chained?* His mind raced as he tugged hopelessly in the chill, earthy air. There were scurrying sounds around his feet in response to his movements; he kicked out wildly, his toe digging into a number of squealing, furry bodies. The place was alive with rats, and as they ran hither and thither the air became permeated with the now familiar stink of rotting fish.

'Phil!' hissed a voice nearby, where more chains rattled in the acrid blackness.

'Roy? Is that you?' Dayton could not believe his ears.

''Fraid so, old pal. I was hoping you wouldn't get to find me.'

'What the devil's going on in this village? I've never encountered anything like it in all my travels.'

'I dread to think.' Baxter sounded very tired.

'The rudeness of the local goons I can stomach, but this is going too damn far.'

'Guess so. But save your strength, Phil. You'll probably need it.'

'I found a book of yours in the inn. I notice you've pencilled in a few notes. Have you any ideas on what's happening? Why the chains, for God's sake?' Rivulets of sweat trickled down Dayton's face despite the cold. His arms ached intolerably.

'Something very old and very evil has got Penmire in its grip, Phil. Whether they practise satanic rites or what, I don't know, but I've been shackled up here for bloody ages. I don't know for how long. I can't feel my arms. Some of the things I've heard ... God, it's incredible!' Baxter gasped with the effort.

'Where exactly are we?'

'Under the chapel. You may have noticed it. Sort of crypt. Judging by some of the chanting that goes on up there——' He broke off.

'What have you done for food? You must have been here for several days.'

'Oh, they keep me alive. Christ knows why, but they feed me. A robed figure in black appears now and again. It would be laughably melodramatic if it wasn't for the fact that I'm scared. Really scared, Phil. We're in a helluva situation.' Dayton admired his friend's strength of character; a lesser man would have cracked up in here. Even *he* might ...

'It's insane,' he growled. 'I know about witchcraft and most of its various cults, but I can't believe these people would do us any serious harm. It must be some sort of hoax – a festival, do you think?' Dayton's nerves were rapidly fraying. He had to keep talking.

'The pain's real enough.'

'They'd never get away with it.'

'Oh no? What's to stop the police finding us in the mire? Or not finding us in the mire? No one is safe on these moors. It's one of the bleakest parts of England. We may as well be on Mars.'

'Cheerful bugger!' They were silent for a moment; the humour soon vanished.

'Well,' grunted Dayton at length, 'what do we do?'

'God knows. We can't break these chains. We just wait.'

So they waited, their minds uselessly trying to fathom a way to escape, but there was absolutely none. The seconds slipped into minutes, marked by the ever-dripping, wet walls, and the minutes turned slowly into hours. There was only the pain and discomfort as the scampering rats kept vigil over the two incarcerated men. At last they heard sounds above them – feet shuffling to and fro in the chapel. Dayton, who had slipped to his knees, cocked an ear. Faintly came the strains of weird, ethereal music, like fluted pipes, drifting out from the old walls into the night.

'Roy. Are you awake?' There was a grunt. 'What's that noise?'

'It's them again. It happens every now and then – nights, I suppose ... Another ... ritual.'

'You OK?'

'I'll do. You know that passage I marked in the book? Did you see my reference to Dagon?'

'Yes, it's in my pocket.'

'Well, there could be something in it. It's a crazy notion, but now and again I've heard the name Dagon mentioned in the chanting. You listen for it once they start. One time I thought I heard something . . . out in the marsh. Like a huge wave breaking. Yes, I know it sounds bloody daft, but there was something.'

'Maybe not so daft, Roy. I came here across that marsh and some of the things I heard were pretty odd.'

'Such as?'

'People splashing about. And frogs. God, I never heard so many. All at once they started up in unison.'

They fell silent again. Baxter broke the lull with a forced snort.

'Humph! We're probably behaving like kids. I know we're in a right mess, but the moor *is* spooky. There are probably the usual scientific explanations for it all.'

'Perhaps. But I'd like a good explanation for this.' Dayton rattled his chains. 'I'll create bloody hell when I get back to civilization.'

'Quiet a sec!' They both listened anew to the strange noises from above. A deep, somehow obscene chanting had begun, the words totally indecipherable, utterly alien.

'There they go again. They'll go on for hours, working themselves up into a frenzy. Just when you think it'll die down, they start up again.'

'Again, this is all new to me. I wish I had a tape-recorder.'

'I'd settle for a wrench,' Baxter replied, but neither of them laughed.

All that night the blasphemous sound swelled until, in the early hours of the morning, it reached a peak. There were sounds from around the prisoners, sounds of slopping footsteps, though nothing could be seen in the dark; the fish odour was overpowering. The climax of the terrible dirge above came in a resounding thunderclap which shook the very foundations of the chapel. Its echoes rolled away into the distance.

'Roy, that sound! It's going away beneath us! I'm sure of it.'

'Eh?' Roy Baxter was exhausted, very drowsy, having only partly registered the boom. He couldn't take much more of this.

'Have you heard anything underground?' persisted Dayton.

'Underground? No. Only from up there,' Baxter said sleepily. Dayton was thinking of the marsh and the rippling motion that he had seen.

'Probably an echo,' Baxter suggested. 'There are lots of caves under the, er, village.'

'Caves?'

'Umm. Well, tunnels. I saw a few when they dragged me here. All man-made, though.'

'But what about the mire?' Caves running under that would be geologically impossible.

'I dunno. They seem to avoid that.' Baxter yawned. 'I expect they all go straight down.'

'Curious.' Somehow the two men lapsed into fitful sleep; time had ceased to exist for them in this rancid pit.

*   *   *

They languished for three days, three days of gruelling anguish which were broken only by the brief appearance of a robed, half-glimpsed figure who fed them. After that the villagers came for their prisoners. Above the cellar, the voices had begun chanting again in mournful unison. From out of the ether came whispered sounds of demonic laughter. Baxter and Dayton were too spent to complain as their chains were unlocked, and they were forced, staggering, through numerous cold puddles of muddy water, pushed along by the sinister robed figures of a score of unseen inhabitants.

They were led almost unconsciously along these subterranean, winding tunnels until they came out eventually into the open. Their bodies were weak and their spirits broken.

It was evening as they emerged; the sun was sinking into an orange sea of clouds, tinting the surrounding tors with gold. Wisps of glistening mist hung in shreds above the marsh, like steam rising from a sulphurous pool. The two men registered little of this. They were some distance from the village, at the edge of the marsh, and here they were thrust forward on to a huge, flat slab of granite. Thin beards of stubble darkened both their jaws, while their eyes were rimmed and bloodshot. Neither had the strength to look up at the diminishing glory of the sunset.

Roy Baxter began to mutter to himself, reciting the Lord's Prayer under his breath. Dayton's head lay against cold rock. He regarded his friend through pain-misted eyes; beside him the reeds trembled in the cool breeze.

'Roy. Roy!' he whispered hoarsely. The other turned to him, still praying. Above them the captors were still.

'We're done. Do you understand?'

'Listen!'

Far out over the marsh there came a gibbering of something nebulous, as though the mire itself were alive. The frogs had begun again that heart-stopping croaking – a hundred thousand throats swelling the chorus. Dayton turned his head, forcing a look back at the village, framed between the arms of two of the gaunt figures in black. There were scores of similarly-garbed people filing out of what he took

to be the chapel, all with arms raised in supplication, all walking like
jerky dolls towards the two outsiders and the marsh.

To whom or what are they praying? Dayton asked himself, unable
to credit his eyes. With a start of revulsion he saw that there were a
number of dogs, cats and even a few sheep staring placidly out at the
marsh. The spell on Penmire gripped even the animals. The chant
swelled and the words became clear, though still incomprehensible.

*'Ngah ohahgn, mnahn, ohahgn mnepn phatagn Dagon.
Ngah opahgan, rhantgna Dagon.
Ssna, ssna, phatagn Dagon.'*

Over and over they repeated it. These were words not written for
human mouths to speak. I must get out now. God knows what they'll
do, thought Dayton.

'Roy!' he whispered. 'Roy!' But his friend had passed out over the
altar-like stone. Dayton feigned the same, one eye on the chanting
crowd. Those around had taken up the chant as well. Bloody mumbo-
jumbo.

All around the valley the sound of the frogs was growing in volume;
louder and louder it came, blending malefically with the ululations of
the oncoming worshippers. From the marshes came a rising cloud of
dense vapour, and with it the unbearable fish stench that Dayton had
smelled so frequently. This time it seemed to pulse out from the marsh
in disgusting waves, and he almost vomited.

Now he could see the frogs. They hopped around the stone as if
mocking him – the marshes were teeming with them. Dayton shook
himself. Beside him his captors were kneeling, arms outstretched in
obeisance to the very heart of the marsh. What did they expect to see?
Dayton craned his neck and gasped. Bubbles were bursting all over the
surface as if it were boiling. He fought to control his sanity as he realized
that the chanting was *attracting* something out in that festering pool of
horror.

A movement beside him drew his attention back to his immediate
dilemma. He turned to see some of these devilish acolytes stretching
Roy, still unconscious, over the altar stone, preparing him for the very
sacrifice he had feared. Dayton was stunned. *No, they can't mean it. Not
today, 1974.* But they paid no attention to his torrent of invective.
Dayton flung himself upon them with last reserves of energy, kicking,
biting, hammering with his fists. But it was useless. He was flung
contemptuously aside to roll pathetically into the reeds.

Stark terror gripped him now. He got up, his movement ignored
by the still-chanting villagers, and fled into the treacherous mire,
desperately trying to find a way through the numerous bogs. He looked
back as he panted on, only to see a curved knife, glittering in the

twilight with scarlet jewels, raised high. This is madness, *madness*. Dayton averted his gaze and felt his stomach heave, refusing to believe the knife would fall. But he heard it sink into Roy Baxter's flesh, and a shuddering satisfied sigh went up from the villagers.

> *'Abaghna pnam pnam Dagon.*
> *Accept our sacrifice, O Dagon.*
> *Ssna ssna, phatagn Dagon.'*

Tears of disbelief coursed in grimy runnels down Dayton's face. He shook his head in utter disgust at what they had done. Blood ran freely over the altar into the mud – Roy had died without a sound. Dayton fled farther into the marsh, hoping against hope to reach the tors before they came for him. But further diabolic events were unfolding. From even the farthest reaches of the marsh the fish smell was at its most foul; a new element of horror was emerging.

Unspeakable shapes were thrusting up out of the oozing mud and green scum, shapes so dreadful, so appalling, that only in the wildest fantasies of a madman could they have been conceived. Dayton bit into his hand to stifle a shriek. The constant chanting was taking its effect, as had the spilling of blood, drawing these vile monstrosities up from the depths like enchanted snakes. They were half human, half fish, or so it looked, for their features were a repulsive blend of both, with fins protruding from each jowl and long, plumed spines stretching right down their backs. There were gills in their man-like trunks, their eyes were the wide, filmy eyes of fish, and their arms were long and thin, tapering to webbed claws.

From these came the hellish smell. Dayton reached a boulder and leapt on to it, heart almost bursting with the effort. The mist was thickening, thankfully obscuring many of the beings, while the sun had set, leaving the world in rapidly gathering darkness. Dayton was surrounded by the fish-men, who still continued to rise from the muck like a legion from hell itself. As he stared in fascination, they began emitting croaking sounds of their own, frog-like and deep, until with a shudder Dayton realized that they were chanting in response to the people of Penmire.

From thick, fleshy lips came the same dread words that the villagers were chanting, spoken, he saw, by the very ones *to whom the language belonged*. Although he was some way out in the marsh, none of the terrible people came near. They just waved and writhed gently from side to side as though drugged, arms raised in ecstasy as were those of the villagers. Frogs jumped everywhere, their croaks adding to the swelling din.

Dayton ached with weariness; there was not a muscle in his body that didn't crave rest, but he knew that he must keep on whilst the horde were preoccupied with their incantations. He sprang from the rock and zigzagged his faltering way through islands of turf, constantly sinking to his knees into clinging mud. He wanted to lie down and sleep, but dare not. The thought of that dripping knife gave him more will to go on. Still the creatures were ignoring him, though he passed within feet of several, shutting everything out of his mind except the tors and escape.

Suddenly the ground heaved, pitching him forward into the gurgling slime, so that for terrifying seconds he crawled with cold, reptilian frogs. Within moments he was knee-deep, jerking himself upright and yanking at his arms to get them free. They came out with great sucking sounds, but his feet were held. He beat frantically at the swarming frogs, feeling them squirming beneath him in multitudes. Dayton struggled in despair. He was trapped. And still the chanting went on, rising in volume, driving him ever-closer to madness. Now the ground began rippling and pulsing like a great heart beating. A note of joy had entered the chanting.

Dayton heard, *felt*, the sound from below. He could not put a name to it, not dared to do so. Excitement spurred the invocations around him, and he tried to twist and see what exactly the villagers were doing: were they pursuing, or had they forgotten him in the midst of their insane revels? But he could not see. He was stuck firmly, sinking inexorably to a gruesome death.

> '*Ngah ohahgn, phatagn Dagon.*
> *Abaghna pnam pnan hnam Dagon.*
> *Accept our second sacrifice, O Dagon.*
> *Ssna ssna, phatagn Dagon.*'

Dayton heard the words of the people behind, and the terrible implication. He had escaped the knife, but the mire would take him. Unless ... With a last, vain effort, he stripped off his jacket, ready to throw it in front of him in one final attempt to heave himself out. Then he stopped, eyes wide in utter disbelief. Before him the marsh was heaving and thrashing like the cauldron of a volcano, sending great plumes of mud high into the mist. Dayton felt more tremors in the rumbling ground.

The chanting had abruptly ceased, together with the croaking of the frogs, as all eyes, all arms, had turned to the source of the disturbance. From out of the unknown depths of the mire, ringed by the evil-smelling fish-creatures, something huge, something unutterably ancient was rising. Dayton screamed now, his whole body shaking uncontrollably, unable to free itself from the fatal clutches of the marsh.

Higher and higher rose the mire-coated colossus, and worse grew the unholy stench of that awesome thing. For this was Dagon, Dagon the ageless, summoned at last from an eternal sleep, summoned from the refuge he had sought untold aeons before, when he and all his kind were cursed upon earth.

Up, up rose the towering horror, a throbbing, glistening mass of scaley, amorphous life. Waves of mud, spilling over with frogs, rippled out from the growing monster. A score of thick, oily, tentacle-like protuberances, coated in contracting suckers, whipped up from beneath the ooze in a welter of steaming filth, as the titanic creature rose higher, exuding an aura of clinging vapours. Dayton coughed as he caught the first whiffs of the poisonous diffusion; he had sunk waist deep before it, his eyes riveted on this thing from before the dawn of men.

All around in the night the servants bowed down, eager to serve, smiting themselves and yelling out in exultation. Dagon of the deeps had come. Come to begin a new reign. The earth shook constantly, hissing with escaping steam, and the mire overspilled its contaminated ooze out into the village. Dayton closed his eyes and prayed fervently, sinking lower, lower. Dagon stretched out his many arms to receive the sacrifice that his people had prepared.

The Upper Berth
F. Marion Crawford

I am an old sailor, said Brisbane, and as I have to cross the Atlantic pretty often, I have my favourites. Most men have their favourites. I have seen a man wait in a Broadway bar for three-quarters of an hour for a particular car which he liked. I believe the bar keeper made at least one-third of his living by that man's preference. I have a habit of waiting for certain ships when I am obliged to cross that duck pond. It may be a prejudice, but I was never cheated out of a good passage but once in my life. I remember it very well; it was a warm morning in June, and the Customs House officials, who were hanging about waiting for a steamer already on her way up from the Quarantine, presented a peculiarly haze and thoughtful appearance. I had not much luggage – I never have. I mingled with the crowd of passengers, porters, and officious individuals in blue coats and brass buttons, who seemed to spring up like mushrooms from the deck of a moored steamer to obtrude their unnecessary services upon the independent passenger. I have often noticed with a certain interest the spontaneous evolution of these fellows. They are not there when you arrive; five minutes after the pilot has called 'Go ahead!' they, or at least their blue coats and brass buttons, have disappeared from deck and gangway as completely as though they had been consigned to that locker which tradition unanimously ascribes to Davy Jones. But, at the moment of starting, they are there, clean shaved, blue coated, and ravenous for fees. I hastened on board. The *Kamtschatka* was one of my favourite ships. I say was, because she emphatically no longer is. I cannot conceive of any inducement which could entice me to take another voyage in her. Yes, I know what you are going to say. She is uncommonly clean in the run aft, she has enough bluffing off in the bows to keep her dry, and the lower berths are most of them double. She has a lot of advantages, but I won't cross in her again. Excuse the digression. I got on board. I hailed a steward, whose red nose and redder whiskers were equally familiar to me.

'One hundred and five, lower berth,' said I, in the business-like tone peculiar to men who think no more of crossing the Atlantic than taking a whisky cocktail at down-town Delmonico's.

The steward took my portmanteau, greatcoat, and rug. I shall never forget the expression of his face. Not that he turned pale. It is maintained by the most eminent divines that even miracles cannot change the course of nature. I have no hesitation in saying that he did not turn pale; but, from his expression, I judged that he was either about to shed tears, to sneeze, or to drop my portmanteau. As the latter contained two bottles of particularly fine old sherry presented to me for my voyage by my old friend Snigginson van Pickyns, I felt extremely nervous. But the steward did none of these things.

'Well, I'm d——d!' he said in a low voice, and led the way.

I suppose my Hermes, as he led me to the lower regions, had had a little grog, but I said nothing, and followed him. 105 was on the port side, well aft. There was nothing remarkable about the state-room. The lower berth, like most of those upon the *Kamtschatka*, was double. There was plenty of room; there was the usual washing apparatus, calculated to convey an idea of luxury to the mind of a North American Indian; there was the usual inefficient racks of brown wood, in which it is more easy to hang a large-sized umbrella than the common tooth-brush of commerce. Upon the uninviting mattresses were carefully folded together those blankets which a great modern humorist has aptly compared to cold buckwheat cakes. The question of towels was left entirely to the imagination. The glass decanters were filled with a transparent liquid faintly tinged with brown, but from which an odour less faint, but not more pleasing, ascended to the nostrils, like a far off sea-sick reminiscence of oily machinery. Sand-coloured curtains half closed the upper berth. The hazy June daylight shed a faint illumination upon the desolate little scene. Ugh! How I hated that state-room!

The steward deposited my traps and looked at me, as though he wanted to get away – probably in search of more passengers and more fees. It is always a good plan to start in favour with those functionaries, and I accordingly gave him certain coins there and then.

'I'll try and make yer comfortable all I can,' he remarked, as he put the coins in his pocket. Nevertheless, there was a doubtful intonation in his voice which surprised me. Possibly his scale of fees had gone up, and he was not satisfied; but on the whole I was inclined to think that, as he himself would have expressed it, he was 'the better for a glass'. I was wrong, however, and did the man injustice.

*　　*　　*

Nothing especially worthy of mention occurred during that day. We left the pier punctually, and it was very pleasant to be fairly under way, for the weather was warm and sultry, and the motion of the steamer produced a refreshing breeze. Everybody knows what the first day at sea is like. People pace the decks and stare at each other, and occasionally meet acquaintances whom they did not know to be on board. There is the usual uncertainty as to whether the food will be good, bad, or indifferent, until the first two meals have put the matter beyond a doubt; there is the usual uncertainty about the weather, until the ship is fairly off Fire Island. The tables are crowded at first, and then suddenly thinned. Pale-faced people spring from their seats and precipitate themselves towards the door, and each old sailor breathes more freely as his sea-sick neighbour rushes from his side, leaving him plenty of elbow-room and an unlimited command over the mustard.

One passage across the Atlantic is very much like another, and we who cross very often do not make the voyage for the sake of novelty. Whales and icebergs are indeed always objects of interest, but, after all, one whale is very much like another whale, and one rarely sees an iceberg at close quarters. To the majority of us the most delightful moment of the day on board an ocean steamer is when we have taken our last turn on deck, have smoked our last cigar, and having succeeded in tiring ourselves, feel at liberty to turn in with a clear conscience. On that first night of the voyage I felt particularly lazy, and went to bed in 105 rather earlier than I usually do. As I turned in, I was amazed to see that I was to have a companion. A portmanteau, very like my own, lay in the opposite corner, and in the upper berth had been deposited a neatly folded rug, with a stick and umbrella. I had hoped to be alone, and I was disappointed; but I wondered who my room-mate was to be, and I determined to have a look at him.

Before I had been long in bed he entered. He was, as far as I could see, a very tall man, very thin, very pale, with sandy hair and whiskers and colourless grey eyes. He had about him, I thought, an air of rather dubious fashion; the sort of man you might see in Wall Street, without being able precisely to say what he was doing there – the sort of man who frequents the Café Anglais, who always seems to be alone and who drinks champagne; you might meet him on a racecourse, but he would never appear to be doing anything there either. A little over-dressed – a little odd. There are three or four of his kind on every ocean steamer. I made up my mind that I did not care to make his acquaintance, and I went to sleep saying to myself that I would study his habits in order to avoid him. If he rose early, I would rise late; if he went to bed late, I would go to bed early. I did not care to know him. If you once know people of that kind they are always turning up. Poor fellow! I need not have taken the trouble to come to so many decisions about him, for I never saw him again after that first night in 105.

I was sleeping soundly when I was suddenly waked by a loud noise.

To judge from the sound, my room-mate must have sprung with a single leap from the upper berth to the floor. I heard him fumbling with the latch and bolt of the door, which opened almost immediately, and then I heard his footsteps as he ran at full speed down the passage, leaving the door open behind him. The ship was rolling a little, and I expected to hear him stumble or fall, but he ran as though he were running for his life. The door swung on its hinges with the motion of the vessel, and the sound annoyed me. I got up and shut it, and groped my way back to my berth in the darkness. I went to sleep again; but I had no idea how long I slept.

When I awoke it was still quite dark, but I felt a disagreeable sensation of cold, and it seemed to me that the air was damp. You know the peculiar smell of a cabin which has been wet with sea-water. I covered myself up as well as I could and dozed off again, framing complaints to be made the next day, and selecting the most powerful epithets in the language. I could hear my room-mate turn over in the upper berth. He had probably returned while I was asleep. Once I thought I heard him groan, and I argued that he was sea-sick. That is particularly unpleasant when one is below. Nevertheless, I dozed off and slept till early daylight.

The ship was rolling heavily, much more than on the previous evening, and the grey light which came in through the porthole changed in tint with every movement according as the angle of the vessel's side turned the glass seawards or skywards. It was very cold – unaccountably so for the month of June. I turned my head and looked at the porthole, and I saw to my surprise that it was wide open and hooked back. I believe I swore audibly. Then I got up and shut it. As I turned back I glanced at the upper berth. The curtains were drawn close together; my companion had probably felt cold as well as I. It struck me that I had slept enough. The state-room was uncomfortable, though, strange to say, I could not smell the dampness which had annoyed me in the night. My room-mate was still asleep – excellent opportunity for avoiding him, so I dressed at once and went on deck. The day was warm and cloudy, with an oily smell on the water. It was seven o'clock as I came out – much later than I had imagined. I came across the doctor, who was taking his first sniff of the morning air. He was a young man from the west of Ireland – a tremendous fellow, with black hair and blue eyes, already inclined to be stout; he had a happy-go-lucky, healthy look about him which was rather attractive.

'Fine morning,' I remarked, by way of introduction.

'Well,' said he, eyeing me with an air of ready interest, 'it's a fine morning and it's not a fine morning. I don't think it's much of a morning.'

'Well, no – it is not so very fine,' said I.

'It's just what I call fuggly weather,' replied the doctor.

'It was very cold last night, I thought,' I remarked. 'However, when I looked about I found that the porthole was wide open. I had not noticed it when I went to bed. And the state-room was damp, too.'

'Damp!' said he. 'Whereabouts are you?'

'One hundred and five——'

To my surprise the doctor started visibly, and stared at me.

'What is the matter?' I asked.

'Oh – nothing,' he answered; 'only everybody has complained of that state-room for the last three trips.'

'I shall complain, too,' I said. 'It has certainly not been properly aired. It is a shame!'

'I don't believe it can be helped,' answered the doctor. 'I believe there is something – well, it is not my business to frighten passengers.'

'You need not be afraid of frightening me,' I replied. 'I can stand any amount of damp. If I should get a bad cold I will come to you.'

I offered the doctor a cigar, which he took and examined very critically.

'It is not so much the damp,' he remarked. 'However, I dare say you will get on very well. Have you a room-mate?'

'Yes; a deuce of a fellow, who bolts out in the middle of the night, and leaves the door open.'

Again the doctor glanced curiously at me. Then he lit the cigar and looked grave.

'Did he come back?' he asked presently.

'Yes. I was asleep, but I waked up and heard him moving. Then I felt cold and went to sleep again. This morning I found the porthole open.'

'Look here,' said the doctor quietly, 'I don't care much for this ship. I don't care a rap for her reputation. I tell you what I will do. I have a good-sized place up here. I will share it with you, though I don't know you from Adam.'

I was very much surprised at the proposition. I could not imagine why he should take such a sudden interest in my welfare. However, his manner as he spoke of the ship was peculiar.

'You are very good, Doctor,' I said. 'But, really, I believe even now the cabin could be aired, or cleaned out, or something. Why do you not care for the ship?'

'We are not superstitious in our profession, sir,' replied the doctor, 'but the sea makes people so. I don't want to prejudice you, and I don't want to frighten you, but if you will take my advice you will move in here. I would as soon see you overboard,' he added earnestly, 'as know that you or any other man was to sleep in 105.'

'Good gracious! Why?' I asked.

'Just because on the three last trips the people who have slept there actually have gone overboard,' he answered gravely.

The intelligence was startling and exceedingly unpleasant, I confess. I looked hard at the doctor to see whether he was making game of me, but he looked perfectly serious. I thanked him warmly for his offer, but told him I intended to be the exception to the rule by which everybody who slept in that particular state-room went overboard. He did not say much, but looked grave as ever, and hinted that, before we got across, I should probably reconsider his proposal. In the course of time we went to breakfast, at which only an inconsiderable number of passengers assembled. I noticed that one or two of the officers who breakfasted with us looked grave. After breakfast I went into by state-room in order to get a book. The curtains of the upper berth were still closely drawn. Not a word was to be heard. My room-mate was probably still asleep.

As I came out I heard the steward whose business it was to look after me. He whispered that the captain wanted to see me, and then scuttled away down the passage as if very anxious to avoid any questions. I went towards the captain's cabin, and found him waiting for me.

'Sir,' said he, 'I want to ask a favour of you.'

I answered that I would do anything to oblige him.

'Your room-mate has disappeared,' he said. 'He is known to have turned in early last night. Did you notice anything extraordinary in his manner?'

The question, coming as it did, in exact confirmation of the fears the doctor had expressed half an hour earlier, staggered me.

'You don't mean to say he has gone overboard?' I asked.

'I fear he has,' answered the captain.

'This is the most extraordinary thing——' I began.

'Why?' he asked.

'He is the fourth, then,' I explained. In answer to another question from the captain, I explained, without mentioning the doctor, that I had heard the story concerning 105. He seemed very much annoyed at hearing that I knew of it. I told him what had occurred in the night.

'What you say,' he replied, 'coincides almost exactly with what was told to me by the room-mates of two of the other three. They bolt out of bed and run down the passage. Two of them were seen to go overboard by the watch; we stopped and lowered boats, but they were not found. Nobody, however, saw or heard the man who was lost last night – if he is really lost. The steward, who is a superstitious fellow, perhaps, and expected something to go wrong, went to look for him this morning, and found his berth empty, but his clothes lying about, just as he had left them. The steward was the only man on board who knew him by sight, and he has been searching everywhere for him. He has disappeared! Now sir, I want to beg you not to mention the circumstance to any of the passengers; I don't want the ship to get a bad name, and nothing hangs about an ocean-goer like stories of suicides. You shall have your choice of any one of the officers' cabins you like, including my own, for the rest of the passage. Is that a fair bargain?'

'Very,' said I; 'and I am much obliged to you. But since I am alone, and have the state-room to myself, I would rather not move. If the steward will take out that unfortunate man's things, I would as lief stay where I am. I will not say anything about the matter, and I think I can promise you that I will not follow my room-mate.'

The captain tried to dissuade me from my intention, but I preferred having a state-room alone to being the chum of any officer on board. I do not know whether I acted foolishly, but if I had taken his advice I should have had nothing more to tell. There would have remained the disagreeable coincidence of several suicides occurring among men who had slept in the same cabin, but that would have been all.

That was not the end of the matter, however, by any means. I obstinately made up my mind that I would not be disturbed by such tales, and I even went so far as to argue the question with the captain. There was nothing wrong about the state-room, I said. It was rather damp. The porthole had been left open last night. My room-mate might have been ill when he came on board, and he might have become delirious after he went to bed. He might even now be hiding somewhere on board, and might be found later. The place ought to be aired and the fastening of the port looked to. If the captain would give me leave, I would see that what I thought necessary was done immediately.

'Of course you have a right to stay where you are if you please,' he replied, rather petulantly, 'but I wish you would turn out and let me lock the place up, and be done with it.'

I did not see it in the same light, and left the captain, after promising to be silent concerning the disappearance of my companion. The latter had had no acquaintances on board, and was not missed in the course of the day. Towards evening I met the doctor again, and he asked me whether I had changed my mind. I told him I had not.

'Then you will before long,' he said, very gravely.

*   *   *

We played whist in the evening, and I went to bed late. I will confess now that I felt a disagreeable sensation when I entered my state-room. I could not help thinking of the tall man I had seen on the previous night, who was now dead, drowned, tossing about in the long swell, two or three hundred miles astern. His face rose very distinctly before me as I undressed, and I even went so far as to draw back the curtains of the upper berth, as though to persuade myself that he was actually gone. I also bolted the door of the state-room. Suddenly I became aware that the porthole was open, and fastened back. This was more than I could stand. I hastily drew on my dressing-gown and went in search of Robert, the steward of my passage. I was very angry, I remember, and when I found him I dragged him roughly to the door of 105, and pushed him towards the open porthole.

'What the deuce do you mean, you scoundrel, by leaving that port open every night? Don't you know it is against the regulations? Don't you know that if the ship heeled and the water began to come in, ten men could not shut it? I will report you to the captain, you blackguard, for endangering the ship!'

I was exceedingly wroth. The man trembled and turned pale, and then began to shut the round glass plate with the heavy brass fittings.

'Why don't you answer me?' I said roughly.

'If you please, sir,' faltered Robert, 'there's nobody on board as can keep this 'ere port shut at night. You can try it yourself, sir, I ain't a-going to stop hany longer on board o' this vessel, sir; I ain't, indeed. But if I was you, sir, I'd just clear out and go and sleep with the surgeon, or something, I would. Look 'ere, sir, is that fastened what you may call securely, or not, sir? Try it, sir; see if it will move a hinch.'

I tried the port, and found it perfectly tight.

'Well, sir,' continued Robert triumphantly, 'I wager my reputation as an A1 steward that in 'arf an hour it will be open again; fastened back, too, sir, that's the horful thing – fastened back!'

I examined the great screw and the looped nut that ran on it.

'If I find it open in the night, Robert, I will give you a sovereign. It is not possible. You may go.'

'Soverin' did you say, sir? Very good, sir. Thank ye, sir. Goodnight, sir. Pleasant reepose, sir, and all manner of hinchantin' dreams, sir.'

Robert scuttled away, delighted at being released. Of course, I thought he was trying to account for his negligence by a silly story, intended to frighten me, and I disbelieved him. The consequence was that he got his sovereign, and I spent a very peculiarly unpleasant night.

I went to bed, and five minutes after I had rolled myself up in my blankets the inexorable Robert extinguished the light that burned steadily behind the ground-glass pane near the door. I lay quite still in the dark trying to go to sleep, but I soon found that impossible. It had been some satisfaction to be angry with the steward, and the diversion had banished that unpleasant sensation I had at first experienced when I thought of the drowned man who had been my chum; but I was no longer sleepy, and I lay awake for some time, occasionally glancing at the porthole, which I could just see from where I lay, and which, in the darkness, looked like a faintly luminous soup-plate suspended in blackness. I believe I must have lain there for an hour, and, as I remember, I was just dozing into sleep when I was roused by a draught of cold air, and by distinctly feeling the spray of the sea blown upon my face. I started to my feet, and not having allowed in the dark for the motion of the ship, I was instantly thrown violently across the state-room upon the couch which was placed beneath the porthole. I recovered myself immediately, however, and climbed upon my knees. The porthole was again wide open and fastened back!

Now these things are facts. I was wide awake when I got up, and I should certainly have been waked by the fall had I still been dozing. Moreover, I bruised my elbows and knees badly, and the bruises were there on the following morning to testify to the fact, if I myself had doubted it. The porthole was wide open and fastened back – a thing so unaccountable that I remember very well feeling astonishment rather than fear when I discovered it. I at once closed the plate again, and screwed down the loop-nut with all my strength. It was very dark in the state-room. I reflected that the port had certainly been opened within an hour after Robert had at first shut it in my presence, and I determined to watch it, and see whether it would open again. Those brass fittings are very heavy and by no means easy to move. I could not believe that the clump had been turned by the shaking of the screw. I stood peering out through the thick glass at the alternate white and grey streaks of the sea that foamed beneath the ship's side. I must have remained there a quarter of an hour.

Suddenly, as I stood, I distinctly heard something moving behind me in one of the berths, and a moment afterwards, just as I turned instinctively to look – though I could, of course, see nothing in the darkness – I heard a very faint groan. I sprang across the state-room, and tore the curtains of the upper berth aside, thrusting in my hands to discover if there were anyone there. There was someone.

I remember that the sensation as I put my hands forward was as though I were plunging them into the air of a damp cellar, and from behind the curtains came a gust of wind that smelled horribly of stagnant sea-water. I laid hold of something that had the shape of a man's arm, but was smooth, and wet, and icy cold. But suddenly, as I pulled, the creature sprang violently forward against me, a clammy, oozy mass, as it seemed to me, heavy and wet, yet endowed with a sort of supernatural strength. I reeled across the state-room, and in an instant the door opened and the thing rushed out. I had not had time to be frightened, and quickly recovered myself, I sprang through the door and gave chase at the top of my speed, but I was too late. Ten yards before me I could see – I am sure I saw it – a dark shadow moving in the dimly lighted passage, quickly as the shadow of a fast horse thrown before a dogcart by the lamp on a dark night. But in a moment it had disappeared, and I found myself holding on to the polished rail that ran along the bulkhead where the passage turned towards the companion. My hair stood on end, and the cold perspiration rolled down my face. I am not ashamed of it in the least: I was very badly frightened.

Still I doubted my senses, and pulled myself together. It was absurd, I thought. The Welsh rarebit I had eaten had disagreed with me. I had been in a nightmare. I made my way back to my state-room, and entered it with an effort. The whole place smelled of stagnant sea-water, as it had when I had waked on the previous evening. It required my utmost strength to go in, and grope among my things for a box of wax lights. As I lighted a railway reading lantern which I always carry in case I want to read after the lamps are out, I perceived that the porthole was again open, and a sort of creeping horror began to take possession of me which I never felt before, nor wish to feel again. But I got a light and proceeded to examine the upper berth, expecting to find it drenched with sea-water.

But I was disappointed. The bed had been slept in, and the smell of the sea was strong; but the bedding was as dry as a bone. I fancied that Robert had not had the courage to make the bed after the accident of the previous night – it had all been a hideous dream. I drew the curtains back as far as I could and examined the place very carefully. It was perfectly dry. But the porthole was open again. With a sort of dull bewilderment of horror I closed it and screwed it down, and thrusting my heavy stick through the brass loop, wrenched it with all my might, till the thick metal began to bend under the pressure. Then I hooked my reading lantern into the red velvet at the head of the couch, and sat down to recover my senses if I could. I sat there all night, unable to think of rest – hardly able to think at all. But the porthole remained closed, and I did not believe it would now open again without the application of a considerable force.

The morning dawned at last, and I dressed myself slowly, thinking over all that had happened in the night. It was a beautiful day and I went on deck, glad to get out into the early, pure sunshine, and to smell the breeze from the blue water, so different from the noisome, stagnant odour of my state-room. Instinctively I turned aft, towards the surgeon's cabin. There he stood, with a pipe in his mouth, taking his morning airing precisely as on the preceding day.

'Good morning,' said he quietly, but looking at me with evident curiosity.

'Doctor, you were quite right,' said I. 'There is something wrong about that place.'

'I thought you would change your mind,' he answered, rather triumphantly. 'You have had a bad night, eh? Shall I make you a pick-me-up? I have a capital recipe.'

'No, thanks,' I cried. 'But I would like to tell you what happened.'

I then tried to explain, as clearly as possible, precisely what had occurred, not omitting to state that I had been scared as I had never been scared in my whole life before. I dwelt particularly on the phenomenon of the porthole, which was a fact to which I could testify, even if the rest had been an illusion. I had closed it twice in the night, and the second time I had actually bent the brass in wrenching it with my stick. I believe I insisted a good deal on this point.

'You seem to think I am likely to doubt your story,' said the doctor, smiling at the detailed account of the state of the porthole. 'I do not doubt it in the least. I renew my invitation to you. Bring your traps here and take half my cabin.'

'Come and take half of mine for one night,' I said. 'Help me to get to the bottom of this thing.'

'You will get to the bottom of something else if you try,' answered the doctor.

'What?' I asked.

'The bottom of the sea. I am going to leave this ship. It is not canny.'

'Then you will not help to find out——'

'Not I,' said the doctor quickly. 'It is my business to keep my wits about me – not to go fiddling about with ghosts and things.'

'Do you really believe it is a ghost?' I enquired, rather contemptuously. But as I spoke I remembered very well the horrible sensation of the supernatural which had got possession of me during the night. The doctor turned sharply on me.

'Have you any reasonable explanation of these things to offer?' he asked. 'No; you have not. Well, you say you will find a explanation. I say that you won't, sir, simply because there is not any.'

'But, my dear sir,' I retorted, 'do you, a man of science, mean to tell me that such things cannot be explained?'

'I do,' he answered stoutly. 'And, if they could, I would not be concerned in the explanation.'

I did not care to spend another night alone in the state-room, and yet I was obstinately determined to get at the root of the disturbances. I do not believe there are many men who would have slept there alone, after passing two such nights. But I made up my mind to try it, if I could not get anyone to share a watch with me. The doctor was evidently not inclined for such an experiment. He said he was a surgeon, and that in case any accident occurred on board he must always be in readiness. He could not afford to have his nerves unsettled. Perhaps he was quite right, but I am inclined to think that his precaution was prompted by his inclination. On enquiry, he informed me that there was no one on board who would be likely to join me in my investigations, and after a little more conversation I left him. A little later I met the captain, and told my story. I said that, if no one would spend the night with me, I would ask leave to have the light burning all night, and would try it alone.

'Look here,' said he, 'I will tell you what I will do. I will share your watch myself, and we will see what happens. It is my belief that we can find out between us. There may be some fellow skulking on board who steals a passage by frightening the passengers. It is just possible that there may be something queer in the carpentering of that berth.'

I suggested taking the ship's carpenter below and examining the place; but I was overjoyed at the captain's offer to spend the night with me. He accordingly sent for the workman and ordered him to do anything I required. We went below at once. I had all the bedding cleared out of the upper berth, and we examined the place thoroughly to see if there was a board loose anywhere, or a panel which could be opened or pushed aside. We tried the planks everywhere, tapped the flooring, unscrewed the fittings of the lower berth and took it to pieces – in short, there was not a square inch of the state-room which was not searched and tested. Everything was in perfect order, and we put everything back in its place. As we were finishing out work, Robert came to the door and looked in.

'Well, sir – find anything, sir?' he asked, with a ghastly grin.

'You were right about the porthole, Robert,' I said, and gave him the promised sovereign. The carpenter did his work silently and skilfully, following my directions. When he had done he spoke.

'I'm a plain man, sir,' he said. 'But it's my belief you had better just turn out your things, and let me run a dozen four-inch screws through the door of this cabin. There's no good ever came o' this cabin yet, sir, and that's all about it. There's been four lives lost out o' here to my own remembrance, and that in four trips. Better give it up, sir – better give it up!'

'I will try it for one night more,' I said.

'Better give it up, sir – better give it up! It's a precious bad job,' repeated the workman, putting his tools in his bag and leaving the cabin.

But my spirits had risen considerably at the prospects of having the captain's company, and I made up my mind not to be prevented from going to the end of the strange business. I abstained from Welsh rarebits and grog that evening, and did not even join in the customary game of whist. I wanted to be quite sure of my nerves, and my vanity made me anxious to make a good figure in the captain's eyes.

*　　*　　*

The captain was one of those spendidly tough and cheerful specimens of seafaring humanity whose combined courage, hardihood, and calmness in difficulty leads them naturally into high positions of trust. He was not the man to be led away by an idle tale, and the mere fact that he was willing to join me in the investigation was proof that he thought there was something seriously wrong, which could not be accounted for on ordinary theories, nor laughed down as a common superstition. To some extent, too, his reputation was at stake, as well as the reputation of the ship. It is no light thing to lose passengers overboard, and he knew it.

About ten o'clock that evening, as I was smoking a last cigar, he came up to me, and drew me aside from the beat of the other passengers who were patrolling the deck in the warm darkness.

'This is a serious matter, Mr Brisbane,' he said. 'We must make up our minds either way – to be disappointed or to have a pretty rough time of it. You see I cannot afford to laugh at the affair, and I will ask you to sign your name to a statement of whatever occurs. If nothing happens tonight we will try it again tomorrow and next day. Are you ready?'

So we went below, and entered the state-room. As we went in I could see Robert the steward, who stood a little farther down the passage, watching us, with his usual grin, as though certain that something dreadful was about to happen. The captain closed the door behind us and bolted it.

'Supposing we put your portmanteau before the door,' he suggested. 'One of us can sit on it. Nothing can get out then. Is the port screwed down?'

I found it as I had left it in the morning. Indeed, without using a lever, as I had done, no one could have opened it. I drew back the curtains of the upper berth so that I could see well into it. By the captain's advice I lighted my reading lantern, and placed it so that it shone upon the white sheets above. He insisted upon sitting on the portmanteau, declaring that he wished to be able to swear that he had sat before the door.

Then he requested me to search the state-room thoroughly, an operation very soon accomplished, as it consisted merely in looking beneath the lower berth and under the couch below the porthole. The spaces were quite empty.

'It is impossible for any human being to get in,' I said, 'or for any human being to open the port.'

'Very good,' said the captain calmly. 'If we see anything now, it must be either imagination of something supernatural.'

I sat down on the edge of the lower berth.

'The first time it happened,' said the captain, crossing his legs and leaning back against the door, 'was in March. The passenger who slept here, in the upper berth, turned out to have been a lunatic – at all events, he was known to have been a little touched, and he had taken his passage without the knowledge of his friends. He rushed out in the middle of the night, and threw himself overboard, before the officer who had the watch could stop him. We stopped and lowered a boat; it was a quiet night, just before that heavy weather came on; but we could not find him. Of course his suicide was afterwards accounted for on the grounds of his insanity.'

'I suppose that often happens?' I remarked rather absently.

'Not often – no,' said the captain; 'never before in my experience, though I have heard of it happening on board other ships. Well, as I was saying, that occurred in March. On the very next trip—— What are you looking at?' he asked, stopping suddenly in his narration.

I believe I gave no answer. My eyes were riveted upon the porthole. It seemed to me that the brass loop-nut was beginning to turn very slowly upon the screw – so slowly, however, that I was not sure it moved at all. I watched it intently, fixing its position in my mind and trying to ascertain whether it changed. Seeing where I was looking, the captain looked, too.

'It moves!' he exclaimed, in a tone of conviction. 'No, it does not,' he added, after a minute.

'If it were the jarring of the screw,' said I, 'it would have opened during the day; but I found it this evening jammed tight as I left it this morning.'

I rose and tried the nut. It was certainly loosened, for by an effort I could move it with my hands.

'The queer thing,' said the captain, 'is that the second man who was lost is supposed to have got through that very port. We had a terrible time over it. It was in the middle of the night, and the weather was very heavy; there was an alarm that one of the ports was open and the sea running in. I came below and found everything flooded, the water pouring in every time she rolled, and the whole port swinging from the top bolts – not the porthole in the middle. Well, we managed to shut it, but the water did some damage. Ever since that the place smells of sea-water from time to time. We supposed the passenger had thrown himself out, though the Lord only knows how he did it. The steward kept telling me that he cannot keep anything shut here. Upon my word – I can smell it now, cannot you?' he enquired, sniffing the air suspiciously.

'Yes – distinctly,' I said, and I shuddered as that same odour of stagnant sea-water grew stronger in the cabin. 'Now, to smell like this, the place must be damp,' I continued, 'and yet when I examined it with the carpenter this morning everything was perfectly dry. It is most extraordinary – hallo!'

My reading lantern, which had been placed in the upper berth, was suddenly extinguished. There was still a good deal of light from the pane of ground glass near the door, behind which loomed the regulation lamp. The ship rolled heavily, and the curtain of the upper berth swung far out into the state-room and back again. I rose quickly from my seat on the edge of the bed, and the captain at the same moment started to his feet with a loud cry of surprise. I had turned with the intention of taking down the lantern to examine it, when I heard his exclamation, and immediately afterwards his call for help. I sprang towards him. He was wrestling with all his might with the brass loop of the port. It seemed to turn against his hands in spite of all his efforts. I caught up my cane, a heavy oak stick I always used to carry, and thrust it through the ring and bore on it with all my strength. But the strong wood snapped suddenly and I fell upon the couch. When I rose again the port was wide open, and the captain was standing with his back against the door, pale to the lips.

'There is something in that berth!' he cried, in a strange voice, his eyes almost starting from his head. 'Hold the door, while I look – it shall not escape us, whatever it is!'

But instead of taking his place, I sprang upon the lower bed, and seized something which lay in the upper berth.

It was something ghastly, horrible beyond words, and it moved in my grip. It was like the body of a man long drowned, and yet it moved, and had the strength of ten men living; but I gripped it with all my might – the slippery, oozy, horrible thing – the dead white eyes seemed to stare at me out of the dusk; the putrid odour of rank sea-water was about it, and its shiny hair hung in foul wet curls over its dead face. I wrestled with the dead thing; it thrust upon me and forced me back and nearly broke my arms; it wound its corpse's arms about my neck, the living death, and overpowered me, so that I, at last, cried aloud and fell, and left my hold.

As I fell the thing sprang across me, and seemed to throw itself upon the captain. When I last saw him on his feet his face was white and his lips set. It seemed to me that he struck a violent blow at the dead being, and then he, too, fell forward upon his face, with an inarticulate cry of horror.

The thing paused an instant, seeming to hover over his prostrate body, and I could have screamed again for very fright, but I had no voice left. The thing vanished suddenly, and it seemed to my disturbed senses that it made its exit through the open port, though how that was possible, considering the smallness of the aperture, is more than anyone can tell. I lay a long time upon the floor, and the captain lay beside me. At last I partially recovered my senses and moved, and instantly knew that my arm was broken – the small bone of the left forearm near the wrist.

I got upon my feet somehow, and with my remaining hand I tried to raise the captain. He groaned and moved, and at last came to himself. He was not hurt, but he seemed badly stunned.

Well, do you want to hear any more? There is nothing more. That is the end of my story. The carpenter carried out his scheme of running half a dozen four-inch screws through the door of 105; and if ever you take a passage in the *Kamtschatka*, you may ask for a berth in that stateroom. You will be told that it is engaged – yes – it is engaged by that dead thing.

I finished the trip in the surgeon's cabin. He doctored my broken arm, and advised me not to 'fiddle about with ghosts and things' any more. The captain was very silent, and never sailed again in that ship, though it is still running. And I will not sail in her either. It was a very disagreeable experience, and I was very badly frightened, which is a thing I do not like. That is all. That is how I saw a ghost – if it was a ghost. It was dead, anyhow.

The Engelmayer Puppets
Mary Danby

'Antiques for the masses. How exhilarating,' drawled Sir William Porter-Grant, pointing across the market place. 'Come along, Gwendoline. We'll see what it's all about.'

Above the entrance to the old Corn Exchange hung a large notice: 'Castle Fenton Annual Antiques Fair. Open daily (Sundays inc.) 10–6 March 30th to April 12th.'

Gwen Porter-Grant followed her son across the square. Weighted down with two full bags of groceries, she would rather have made for the car park, or Fuller's, perhaps, for a cup of tea and a slice of walnut layer cake. But William wanted to see the antiques.

Inside the Corn Exchange, thirty or so stalls were arranged around the sides of the vast inner hall, with a block of a further ten in the centre. There were displays of china and glass, jewellery, bric-à-brac, pictures, books, dolls and fans, along with a few small pieces of furniture. Gwen Porter-Grant saw a rather nice high-backed tapestry chair and wondered if they might buy it for the top landing – at least she could try it out and take the load off her feet for a while – but William was pulling her away, telling her there were some duelling pistols on the next stall, and if she didn't hurry up he'd buy one and shoot her with it. He laughed his noisiest laugh then, and one or two people turned to look. Gwen smiled weakly and pretended to be busy with her shopping bags.

William was tall for sixteen, with freckled skin, a large, heavy-featured face and a mop of pale yellow hair. He was a little like his father had been, only much coarser. Those pale, slightly hooded eyes held none of the twinkling warmth that Gwen had so loved in her late husband. Gerald. Dear, sweet Gerry. He had been her life. But the war had come – a huge, obscuring cloud which stayed six years then moved away. And when the skies were clear again, Gerald Porter-Grant was gone, blown apart like a dandelion clock on Monte Cassino, leaving his young wife with a four-year-old son and a large, bleak mansion on an unfashionable hillside to the west of Doncaster. Marlins, the house was called, but there were those who, romantically connecting it with the Arthurian Legend, insisted it had once been 'Merlin's'. There was, however, no evidence for this, apart from a small section of the surrounding wall, which apparently dated from the seventh century. The rest of the house was about two hundred years old: a severe, granite mausoleum, cold in all seasons.

William had inherited house, property and baronetcy, though the first two were held in trust for him by his mother until he should reach the age of twenty-one. In five years, then, he would have everything, and she nothing, except such bounty as he might generously confer on her. His favourite threat was to cut her off without a penny, leaving her homeless and struggling for survival on her war widow's pension. And he would be quite capable of that, she told herself, wondering where she had gone wrong with his upbringing. Heaven knows, she had tried. It wasn't easy without a father.

He had moved on now to another stall, where he was inspecting a china figurine of a dancer, captured in mid-pirouette. It was a pretty thing, and Gwen would have liked it for her mantelpiece, but William would not want such frippery. Even now, he was just idling with it, turning it around on his hand.

There was a sudden hush as the figurine fell and shattered on the wooden floor. William raised his eyebrows and looked down at the broken dancer. 'A shame. Such a shame,' he said, not looking too unhappy.

The stallkeeper hurried round, tutting. 'It'll have to be paid for,' he said. 'Just like it says.' He indicated a postcard which read: 'Please do not touch. All breakages must be paid for.'

'Oh dear,' said Gwen. 'How much do you want?'

Before the stallkeeper could answer, William had given his mother a sharp kick on the ankle. 'Let's go, Gwendoline, shall we?' he said haughtily.

The stallkeeper caught hold of his sleeve. 'Just a minute,' he said. 'You haven't paid.'

'Paid? What for?' William shook his arm free. 'That coy little knick-knack? Not worth tuppence. Besides, it fell by itself. You must have moved the table.'

'It was Meissen,' argued the stallkeeper. 'And you dropped it. Anyway, what about the notice. "All breakages must be paid for".'

William sniggered. 'I dare say they must. But not by me. Try the Salvation Army – they're usually good for a touch.'

'I don't know who you think you are, young man——' the stallkeeper said sternly.

'I am Sir William Porter-Grant, which is more than you'll ever be,' sneered the boy.

Listening to this exchange was a tall, thin man with a chalk-white face and steel-rimmed spectacles. He moved forward now and introduced himself to William and Gwen.

'You may like to know that I am called Julius von Bick,' he said with a stagily strong Viennese accent.

William, taken off guard, merely stared, his mouth slack with surprise.

'If you would like to step over here,' went on von Bick, 'I will show you something which may be more to your taste, perhaps.'

'That wouldn't be difficult,' said William, recovering himself.

Gwen whispered 'I'm so sorry' to the owner of the figurine, and reached into her handbag for her purse, with the object of slipping him a few pounds, but William saw and tugged her roughly away. 'Oh, really, Gwendoline, you're so wet,' he said under his voice.

Gwen smiled her weak smile. She should stand up to him, of course, tell him when his schoolboy humour went too far, but she was afraid to. He could be so cutting. And she hated the way he called her 'Gwendoline' in that pointedly refined fashion. 'Mother' was so much more pleasant ...

Von Bick led them to a stall in the corner where the light was not too good, and they had to come quite close to see that the items on display were toys. Side by side on a table stood a model fort, a peg top, a wooden engine, a kaleidoscope and a clockwork clown.

'Do look,' said Gwen, picking up a rag doll. 'I used to have one just like this, only with black hair.'

William tested the wheels of a hobby-horse. Its head was made of calico, and it was beginning to split at the seams. He pulled some of the stuffing out, gave von Bick a defiant smirk and lobbed the stuffing into the fort. 'Well?' he said. 'Where's this thing I'm supposed to be so interested in?'

If the man objected to William's behaviour, he gave no sign. With quiet politeness, he said: 'Please wait,' and pushed forward a tall, wooden, box-like structure. It was a puppet theatre.

'Oh, Punch and Judy,' said William in a bored voice.

'Not at all,' replied von Bick. 'What I am showing you is a puppet theatre which once belonged to an Austrian duke. His palace was famous for its entertainments, and his puppeteers second to none. Look, please, at the workmanship.'

The theatre was richly covered with oil paintings depicting clowns and ballerinas, dragons and demons, fairies and sorcerers. On either side of the proscenium arch were columns of acrobatic cherubs, delicately gilded.

'Beautiful,' breathed Gwen. 'It's quite beautiful. But then, the Austrians are marvellous at this sort of thing.' She had spent one summer near Innsbruck, practising her German. She felt something of an expert. 'Beautiful,' she said again.

'Belonged to a duke, eh?' mused William, obviously impressed.

Von Bick disappeared, and a few seconds later emerged from the back of the theatre with a painted box. 'The players,' he explained, opening the box and removing two puppets. 'They have performed before many a king and queen. Haven't you, my little friends – *meine kleinen Freunde?*'

He made the puppets nod their heads. One of them, which von Bick called 'Herr Professor', was not unlike himself, lean and grey, with precariously balanced spectacles. 'He was born in Salzburg,' said von Bick, 'and was educated in the great universities of Europe. A fellow of refinement, of great sensibility.'

'Well, well. Bully for him,' said William.

'And this dear lady is the widow Vogelbauer,' von Bick went on. 'See how she loves her fine clothes. Charming, is she not?'

Frau Vogelbauer was getting on in years, but elegant, with her silver hair drawn back into a large bun. Her dress was made of purple taffeta, which rustled as she moved. Like Herr Professor, she was a rod puppet, a jointed doll held up by a stick attached to her back, her arms moved by thin rods fixed to her wrists. 'She is a *bon viveur*,' said von Bick, 'and her musical evenings, her *salons*, are attended by the most celebrated music-lovers in Vienna.'

William said: 'How quaint.'

Gwen, looking round, saw that the hall was almost empty. A few stallholders were packing away their antiques, the rest had left.

'Six o'clock,' she said to William. 'We ought to be going.'

'Do be quiet, Gwendoline,' he replied.

She felt he, too, would have wanted to leave, if only it hadn't been her who'd suggested it. Now he'd stay till they were thrown out, just to upset her.

'What else have you in there?' William was asking von Bick.

A jolly-looking, gaily-dressed character was introduced next. Rollo the Jester wore the traditional cap and bells costume, and his face was painted with a merry grin. 'A lover of gladness, a friend to the children, the maker of smiles,' they were told. Beneath him in the box were Hedwig, a beautiful blonde peasant girl 'as sweet and pure as the mountain flowers', and Hans, a smart young soldier, upright of bearing and character. 'He loves but one girl, his little Hedwig,' explained von Bick, 'and I place them side by side in the box. So.'

'Why do you make up stories about them?' asked William. 'I mean, they're only puppets.'

Von Bick clutched the box to his waistcoat. '*Only puppets?*' he said slowly, with exaggerated astonishment. 'Oh, no, young man. They are more alive than most of the people you see around you. More alive than you or me, perhaps. You think I am pretending. You think: "This poor old fool, he is in his dotage. He can't tell dolls from human beings." If you were Austrian, I would say: "These puppets were made by the hands of Engelmayer himself, the greatest of all puppet-makers," and you would recognize, and bow the head. But you are an English nobleman, barren in your mind, and you say "pooh" to anything you cannot understand.'

William guffawed. 'Pooh, then,' he said jauntily. 'Pooh, I say. Hear that, Gwendoline? Got a bit of cheek, hasn't he, for someone who's trying to sell something.'

'It does not matter,' said von Bick. 'You will buy.'

'Yeah? Who says? What do I want with a puppet theatre, anyway?'

'You will buy because the price is just one guinea, and you will say to yourself: "My goodness, it must be worth a lot more. I will buy it and sell it again for a big, big profit."'

William frowned. 'One guinea? You have to be crazy. Why so cheap, eh? Stolen, is it?'

Von Bick shook his head. 'One guinea is all we want,' he said softly.

William, chuckling to himself over the possibility of making easy money out of the senile naïvety of an old man, didn't notice the plural, but took a pound from his wallet and a shilling from his pocket and handed them over. Smiling quietly, von Bick folded up the theatre and placed the lid on the box of puppets, murmuring as he did so, as if bidding farewell to his friends.

In a short time, William and Gwen, together with their bargain, were driving away from Castle Fenton in their open-topped Alvis tourer, on the road to Marlins.

*   *   *

Since the war, Gwendoline had been unable to find any live-in staff, and she relied solely on a part-time gardener and a cleaning lady who cycled the four miles from the nearest hamlet twice a week. It was a struggle, and many of the rooms at Marlins were now closed and dust-sheeted. The games room, however, was kept clean and relatively warm, as William spent a great deal of his time there in the school holidays, playing chess with a correspondent in Edinburgh, and cheating against himself at snooker.

The puppet theatre had been erected in one corner. It had not been touched since the day they had brought it home, and the paintings on the sides seemed now to glow less richly, while the gold of the cherubs was dulled by dust.

'A good investment,' William had declared. 'We'll keep it a while, then sell it for an enormous sum. And the Engelmayer puppets seem to be collectors' pieces, too. I looked them up. Perhaps Sotheby's would be interested.'

It was the fifth week of the summer holidays when, at breakfast – a grim, appetite-killing time, with William glowering into his cereal bowl at Gwen's suggestions for the day's activities – the subject of the theatre was raised again.

'What will you do today, dear?' Gwen asked her son. She glanced towards the window, at the wet slates on the stable roof. 'Too wet to go out. What a pity.'

William grunted.

Gwen pleaded with her mind for ideas. She couldn't bear those days when he sat around, nagging her, or criticizing, as she went about her household tasks. He never offered to help, and she never liked to ask him. She suspected she had spoilt him, but there, it would be wrong to add to the burdens of a fatherless child.

'I know,' she said at last, swallowing a mouthful of toast. 'There's that old puppet theatre. Why not have a go with that – see if you can work the puppets. You could put on a little show.'

In reply, William snorted disdainfully, but later she heard him in the games room, talking in funny voices.

Smiling to herself as she imagined him in childlike play, she pushed open the door.

Immediately, William appeared from behind the theatre.

'Why don't you shove off and get lost,' he said nastily. Then a gleam came into his eyes. 'Right. Right then. You've done it now. This time you've really done it.'

She didn't know what he meant, but it was plain something unpleasant was in store for her. And ... 'He may be my son,' she later confided to the cleaning lady as they drank tea together in the kitchen, 'but sometimes I do believe I could throttle him.'

Shortly, she was summoned from the kitchen by a shout from the games room.

'Come on, then, Gwendoline! We haven't got all day. If you want your little show, you'll jolly well have to buck up. I'm starting now.'

With a look that was half apprehension, half resignation, she did as she was told, and made her way to the games room. Inside, she found the curtains drawn and the theatre lit by a bare bulb hanging from the ceiling just above it. She seated herself on the chair provided, and waited.

After a few moments, William's voice came through the front of the theatre, below the stage. 'You are about to see a puppet show. An intimate revue.' He gave a dry laugh. 'Kindly do not utter remarks during the performance.'

Gwen shifted in her seat. She was aware that this would be no

Goody Two-Shoes – but she was quite unprepared for the characters now paraded for her between the gilt cherubs.

An odd little chuckle preceded the appearance of Herr Professor, that dapper intellectual. But he was now a filthy tramp, rolling drunkenly about, spitting curses and obscenities. He looked as if he had been smeared with dirt and trampled on. His spectacles were misshapen and lopsided. At last, with a 'good, bleeding, bye!' he brought the stream of hate to an end.

'Oh dear! Oh, how dreadful!' exclaimed Gwen, as the puppet dipped out of sight.

Immediately, William's voice said: 'Quiet! How can I do the show if you keep talking?'

Poor Frau Vogelbauer came next. Her purple taffeta dress was a mass of tears, and her hair was wild and witchlike. She began to croak out a song in a coarse, Cockney voice. It was about death and putrefaction, disease and defecation. It was completely disgusting. At the end, she cackled loud and long. But it wasn't funny. It was revolting, humiliating.

'Stop it, William!' called out Gwen, in what was almost a shout. 'You mustn't do this. It's wrong. Terribly wrong. She's supposed to be a lady – a fine, elegant person. Mr von Bick said so. You're hurting her!'

''Ark at 'er!' cackled Frau Vogelbauer. 'She ought to shut 'er marf if she knows what's good for 'er. Be left wivout a farthing, else.' Another cackle, and the puppet retired.

The jester was vile: a sneering, sleazy individual, oozing insincerity. William had altered his mouth, somehow, so that it no longer grinned merrily but was set in a loathsome leer. He was made to crack a couple of lewd jokes, which made Gwen wince. What was it von Bick had said? A lover of gladness? A friend to the children? She would no more let this posturing creature near a child than she would a serpent.

Hedwig, the peasant girl, came next, together with her soldier boyfriend, Hans. By this time, William had given up trying to operate them as puppets and simply clutched each around the waist.

'Hi, gorgeous,' he made Hedwig say through pouting, ruby-red lips. 'Wanna see what I got? All things to all men, I call it. You can have ten per cent off, though, seeing as how I'm a sucker for uniforms.'

Hans did a little dance, and his handsome head wobbled from side to side. 'Whoops-a-daisy!' he said. William made him wag a limp wrist as he trilled: 'I've got a someone crazy for me – he's funny that way ...'

'Twenty per cent?' offered Hedwig.

Hans made as if to peer under her skirt, then bobbed up again.

'No thanks, ducky. You ain't got what it takes.'

Gwen felt dizzy and sick. She put her hands over her ears. 'Oh, do stop it!' she begged. 'Do, do stop it!'

The stage curtains were abruptly drawn. Seconds later, they swung back to reveal William's grinning head. 'Had enough, Gwendoline, dear?' he asked.

'Filthy!' Gwen was muttering, unable to look up at him. 'Degrading. Immoral.'

'Nauseating?' suggested William. 'Well, dear, you did ask for it.'

For a puppet show. Not for this. Not for that horrifying performance. It upset her to think that William's head harboured such unpleasantness. Who had put it there? His fashionable public school? Surely not. Not at nearly a hundred pounds a term.

'You've spoilt it,' she said. 'Those wonderful puppets. They were made to be loved and admired, to bring happiness and laughter.'

'Didn't you laugh, then?' said William. 'Oh no, of course not. You've got no sense of humour. Personally, I thought they were hilarious.'

'And you've ruined the puppets,' Gwen went on. 'What will they be worth now, with their clothes all spoiled and horrible muck on their faces?'

William shrugged. 'They look better to me. It gives them a bit of character.'

'That nice Mr von Bick would be so upset if he knew,' said Gwen, shaking her head.

In answer, William made a rude noise, came out from behind the theatre and announced he was going off to shoot rabbits.

Gwen, in a delayed reaction to the assault on her senses, dissolved into tears. She cried for her husband, who had given her this child, this fiend of inhumanity, and left her to its bludgeoning. She wished for death, as a merciful escape, knowing that life for her would never be anything but a vile torment.

*   *   *

Howard Jones nosed his van along the narrow back street by the river.

'There it is,' said his wife, Marilyn.

At the end of the street was a dark little shop, which seemed to grow out of the cobbled pavement, as if it had been there for centuries. Painted in a curve on the window were the words 'J. von Bick. Antiques'.

'Bill was right,' Marilyn said, as Howard parked the van. 'This really is the back of nowhere.'

Bill Middleton was another dealer – a friendly rival, Marilyn called him. Only the friendliness was mostly on Bill's side. Right now, Marilyn was planning a mean little stab in the back.

'Are you sure you should?' Howard was asking. 'It does seem a rotten thing to do.'

'Look,' said Marilyn, pushing a wisp of bleached hair back into its French pleat, 'we haven't driven sixty miles to start having doubts. Anyway, why should I care about Bill? This is business. He'd do the same to me.'

Last night, at a party, Bill Middleton had said: 'I've just heard of a set of Engelmayer puppets, up Doncaster way. Theatre, too. Think I'll take a look at them Thursday.'

Today was Wednesday, a dull, breezy day. Cold for October.

Marilyn made an elegant descent from the van. 'Do you *have* to lock it?' she said petulantly, as Howard made the van secure. 'It's hardly likely to be stolen. And couldn't you have parked it a bit nearer? You know how I hate a cold wind.'

She pulled her jacket tightly around her and strode down the pavement towards the shop.

As Howard caught up with her, and they both stood peering into the dimness behind the window, she clutched his arm.

'Wow!' she exclaimed. 'There it is. At the back, see? That's the theatre, all right.'

She tried the door of the shop, but it was locked. 'Oh, hell!' she said. 'Early closing,' suggested Howard.

They started as a voice behind them said: 'You wish to see my theatre? There are puppets, too, you know. Come and meet them, please.'

They turned to see an old man fishing in his waistcoat pocket for a key. He unlocked the door and, as they followed him inside, he said: 'But excuse me. I must introduce myself. My name is Julius von Bick.' He waved an arm. 'My shop.'

'Very nice,' murmured Howard.

Marilyn was admiring the theatre. 'Cherubs, great!' she was saying. 'Where did it come from?'

Von Bick described the theatre's history, the high life it had known as the plaything of princes. 'It was most recently the property of a young Englishman,' he concluded, 'but, sadly, he was unable to continue his ownership.' Then, ducking behind the theatre, von Bick produced the box of puppets. 'Allow me to introduce my little friends,' he said.

* * *

Foul play was not ruled out, but there was no evidence to connect Gwen with murder, other than the remark she had confided to the cleaning lady on the eve of William's disappearance, that she wished him dead.

Various theories were propounded: about how he had gone for a midnight swim and drowned in the lake. They dragged the lake for days, with no result. About how he might accidentally have shot himself – but no body was ever found. He had run away, some said. With a girl, perhaps, added others. But as the weeks went by, and there was no word, the police became bored with the case and moved on to more spicy investigations. Gwen bought herself some new clothes and attracted the eye of a local historian, who paid a research visit to Marlins while compiling a book on the area. Eventually, the courts agreed that the ownership of Marlins and its contents, and the rest of the family fortune, such as it was, should pass to Gwen. She promptly sold everything she could and removed herself and the historian to a warmer climate.

But though Gwen Porter-Grant thrived in her new life, there was a terrible secret she carried always with her. She never told a single soul, and, if she had, no one would have believed her. Except, perhaps, Julius von Bick.

On the night of William's disappearance, she had awoken very suddenly. It seemed to her that she had just heard a terrible cry. A howl of pure terror. Sitting up in bed, though, her ears and eyes straining in the darkness, she heard something else – the chatter of small, high voices. The noise was coming from below her. From the games room.

She wondered whether she should wake William, but dreaded the fuss he always made if disturbed from his sleep. Instead, she pulled on her dressing-gown and descended the stairs alone, carrying for protection a stiletto-heeled shoe.

The door of the games room was ajar, and she peeped inside.

The rest was not quite real. But it wasn't a dream, either, though none of it seemed to make sense.

What she saw, or thought she saw, was William, completely naked, lying on the floor, with the five puppets cavorting around him, their manipulating rods trailing about them and clattering against each other. William's chest and stomach were split wide open, but there was no blood, not even a trickle. He appeared to be empty – perhaps his insides had been removed, only they were nowhere to be seen – and the puppets were stuffing him with little wads of kapok, which they were pulling out of an old velvet cushion.

William seemed to be paralysed from the neck down, but his eyes were open, and, in obvious agony and horror, he was watching everything that was going on. At one point, his eyes swivelled desperately to the door, where Gwen stood, mesmerized, unable to help him.

The puppets were plainly enjoying themselves. Herr Professor began a sing-song chant, which the others joined in.

'Eins, zwei, drei, und Du bist klein,
Sollst klein wie eine Puppe sein!'

One, two, three, and you'll be small – no taller than a little doll.

Frau Vogelbauer was holding aloft a needle and thread. She advanced on William, whose eyes contracted in fright. As she stabbed at his skin, he opened his mouth in a silent scream, and the others laughed delightedly, their voices tinkling like cowbells.

As Frau Vogelbauer stitched, William, wincing each time the needle entered his bloodless skin, seemed to shrink. Smaller and smaller he became, until, by the time the thread was cut, he was tiny – no bigger than a puppet.

Then Herr Professor knelt over him, obscuring William's face, and Gwen heard him issuing some sort of command. When he arose, William's expression was set firm, as if he had been carved from wood.

The puppets danced a gleeful little dance around him, their rods clattering a macabre accompaniment. '*Willkommen, willkommen,*' they sang in hellish chorus, and their voices jarred and jangled through the night ...

It was a dream. Upset by William's puppet show the previous day, Gwen had had at least three Scotches before dinner. She normally kept to one. She might have known they would give her a nightmare. Please, please could she wake up now, be safe upstairs in her bed? She fainted.

When she woke up, she *was* in her bed, and the sheets were damp with sweat.

William's absence at breakfast was unremarkable, but when Gwen found his bed not slept in, and the empty cover of a velvet cushion left lying on the games room floor, she had to admit to herself that last night had perhaps been no dream.

She took care to avoid the puppet theatre, and no power in hell could have persuaded her to touch the box of puppets. In due course, she found Mr von Bick's address and arranged for the theatre and puppets to be returned to him. She felt it was the least she could do.

*   *   *

'Who's this, then?' asked Marilyn Jones, as von Bick brought Hedwig out of the box.

The little puppet looked demure and fresh. Like the others, she had been restored to her original beauty by the caring, sorrowing hands of von Bick.

'This,' said the old man, 'is little Hedwig. She is a simple peasant girl, as sweet and pure as the mountain flowers. And here is her soldier boyfriend, Hans.'

'Perfect!' declared Marilyn. 'Real Engelmayer, without any doubt at all. Just look how finely their faces have been carved. Not unlike some of the early Czech puppets, don't you think?'

Julius von Bick inclined his head in acknowledgement.

Marilyn went on to describe the puppets she had bought and sold: the Polish marionettes, the *fantoccini* from Italy, Chinese shadow puppets, German glove puppets, Japanese *bunraku* ... Punch and Judy, Hanswurst and Kasperle, Guignol ...

'That is so?' said von Bick, nodding.

'But these ...' Marilyn looked at Howard and laughed unattractively. 'Won't Bill be positively *steaming* when he finds out! How much?' she asked von Bick.

'Just one guinea,' said the old man.

Marilyn gave Howard a sharp nudge. 'He's crackers,' she whispered. Out loud, she said: 'Fine. Yes, very fair. Right, we'll take the whole thing, theatre and all.'

Howard was peering into the puppet box. 'You've forgotten one,' he said.

Von Bick shrugged. 'Oh, he is not an Engelmayer.'

This puppet had none of the charm of the others. Its flabby, pyjama-clad body was topped by a round, scowling face, startled grey eyes and a straggling lump of yellow hair.

'He is a nobleman,' went on von Bick, eyeing the puppet with distaste. 'A joke, yes?'

'We'll have him, too,' said Marilyn. 'He looks a bit stupid, but we could say he is the *Pickelhering*, the little buffoon. Has he a name?'

Von Bick nodded. 'He is called ... Wilhelm.'

As the last puppet was placed in the box, covering William's impassive, wooden face, von Bick murmured: '*Auf Wiedersehn meine kleinen Freunde*. Come back soon,' he whispered.

Marilyn turned to Howard. 'Well, go on, then,' she said. 'Fetch the van.'

The Signal-Man

Charles Dickens

'Halloa! Below there!'

When he heard a voice thus calling to him, he was standing at the door of his box, with a flag in his hand, furled round its short pole. One would have thought, considering the nature of the ground, that he could not have doubted from what quarter the voice came; but, instead of looking up to where I stood on the top of the steep cutting nearly over his head, he turned himself about and looked down the Line. There was something remarkable in his manner of doing so, though I could not have said, for my life, what. But, I know it was remarkable enough to attract my notice, even though his figure was foreshortened and shadowed, down in the deep trench, and mine was high above him, so steeped in the glow of an angry sunset that I had shaded my eyes with my hand before I saw him at all.

'Halloa! Below!'

From looking down the Line, he turned himself about again, and, raising his eyes, saw my figure high above him.

'Is there any path by which I can come down and speak to you?'

He looked up at me without replying, and I looked down at him without pressing him too soon with a repetition of my idle question. Just then, there came a vague vibration in the earth and air, quickly changing into a violent pulsation, and an oncoming rush that caused me to start back, as though it had force to draw me down. When such vapour as rose to my height from this rapid train had passed me and was skimming away over the landscape, I looked down again, and saw him re-furling the flag he had shown while the train went by.

I repeated my enquiry. After a pause, during which he seemed to regard me with fixed attention, he motioned with his rolled-up flag towards a point on my level, some two or three hundred yards distant. I called down to him, 'All right!' and made for that point. There, by dint of looking closely about me, I found a rough zigzag descending path notched out: which I followed.

The cutting was extremely deep, and unusually precipitate. It was made through a clammy stone that became oozier and wetter as I went down. For these reasons, I found the way long enough to give me time to recall a singular air of reluctance or compulsion with which he had pointed out the path.

When I came down low enough upon the zigzag descent, to see him again, I saw that he was standing between the rails on the way by which the train had lately passed, in an attitude as if he were waiting for me to appear. He had his left hand at his chin, and that left elbow rested on his right hand crossed over his breast. His attitude was one of such expectation and watchfulness, that I stopped a moment, wondering at it.

I resumed my downward way, and, stepping out upon the level of the railroad and drawing nearer to him, saw that he was a dark sallow man, with a dark beard and rather heavy eyebrows. His post was in as solitary and dismal a place as ever I saw. On either side, a dripping wet wall of jagged stone, excluding all view but a strip of sky; the perspective one way, only a crooked prolongation of this great dungeon; the shorter perspective in the other direction, terminating in a gloomy red light, and the gloomier entrance to a black tunnel, in whose massive architecture there was a barbarous, depressing and forbidding air. So little sunlight ever found its way to this spot, that it had an earthy, deadly smell; and so much cold wind rushed through it, that it struck chill to me, as if I had left the natural world.

Before he stirred, I was near enough to him to have touched him. Not even then removing his eyes from mine, he stepped back one step, and lifted his hand.

This was a lonesome post to occupy (I said), and it had riveted my attention when I looked down from up yonder. A visitor was a rarity, I should suppose; not an unwelcome rarity, I hoped? In me, he merely saw a man who had been shut up within narrow limits all his life, and who, being at last set free, had a newly awakened interest in these great works. To such purpose I spoke to him; but I am far from sure of the terms I used, for, besides that I am not happy in opening any conversation, there was something in the man that daunted me.

He directed a most curious look towards the red light near the tunnel's mouth, and looked all about it, as if something were missing from it, and then looked at me.

That light was part of his charge? Was it not?

He answered in a low voice: 'Don't you know it is?'

The monstrous thought came into my mind as I perused the fixed eyes and the saturnine face, that this was a spirit, not a man. I have speculated since, whether there may have been infection in his mind.

In my turn, I stepped back. But in making the action, I detected in his eyes some latent fear of me. This put the monstrous thought to flight.

'You look at me,' I said, forcing a smile, 'as if you had a dread of me.'
'I was doubtful,' he returned, 'whether I had seen you before.'
'Where?'
He pointed to the red light he had looked at.
'There?' I said.
Intently watchful of me, he replied (but without sound), 'Yes.'
'My good fellow, what should I do there? However, be that as it may,
I never was there, you may swear.'
'I think I may,' he rejoined. 'Yes. I am sure I may.'

His manner cleared, like my own. He replied to my remarks with
readiness, and in well chosen words. Had he much to do there?
Yes; that was to say, he had enough responsibility to bear; but exact-
ness and watchfulness were what was required of him, and of actual
work – manual labour he had next to none. To change that signal, to
trim those lights, and to turn this iron handle now and then, was
all he had to do under that head. Regarding those many long and
lonely hours of which I seemed to make so much, he could only say that
the routine of his life had shaped itself into that form, and he had grown
used to it. He had taught himself a language down here – if only to know
it by sight, and to have formed his own crude ideas of its pronunciation,
could be called learning it. He had also worked at fractions and
decimals, and tried a little algebra; but he was, and had been as a boy, a
poor hand at figures. Was it necessary for him when on duty, always to
remain in that channel of damp air, and could he never rise into the
sunshine from between those high stone walls? Why, that depended
upon times and circumstances. Under some conditions there would be
less upon the Line than under others, and the same held good as to
certain hours of the day and night. In bright weather, he did choose
occasions for getting a little above these lower shadows; but, being at all
times liable to be called by his electric bell, and at such times listening for
it with redoubled anxiety, the relief was less than I would suppose.

He took me into his box, where there was a fire, a desk for an official
book in which he had to make certain entries, a telegraphic instrument
with its dial face and needles, and the little bell of which he had spoken.
On my trusting that he would excuse the remark that he had been well
educated, and (I hoped I might say without offence), perhaps educated
above that station, he observed that instances of slight incongruity in
such-wise would rarely be found wanting among large bodies of men;
that he had heard it was so in workhouses, in the police force, even in that
last desperate resource, the army; and that he knew it was so, more or
less, in any great railway staff. He had been, when young (if I could
believe it, sitting in that hut; he scarcely could), a student of natural
philosophy, and had attended lectures; but he had run wild, misused his
opportunities, gone down, and never risen again. He had no complaint

to offer about that. He had made his bed, and he lay upon it. It was far too late to make another.

All that I have here condensed, he said in a quiet manner, with his grave dark regards divided between me and the fire. He threw in the word 'Sir' from time to time, and especially when he referred to his youth: as though to request me to understand that he claimed to be nothing but what I found him. He was several times interrupted by the little bell, and had to read off messages, and send replies. Once, he had to stand without the door, and display a flag as a train passed, and make some verbal communication to the driver. In the discharge of his duties I observed him to be remarkably exact and vigilant, breaking off his discourse at a syllable, and remaining silent until what he had to do was done.

In a word, I should have set this man down as one of the safest of men to be employed in that capacity, but for the circumstance that while he was speaking to me he twice broke off with a fallen colour, turned his face towards the little bell when it did *not* ring, opened the door of the hut (which was kept shut to exclude the unhealthy damp), and looked out towards the red light near the mouth of the tunnel. On both those occasions, he came back to the fire with the inexplicable air upon him which I had remarked, without being able to define, when we were so far asunder.

Said I when I rose to leave him: 'You almost make me think that I have met with a contented man.'

(I am afraid I must acknowledge that I said it to lead him on.)

'I believe I used to be so,' he rejoined, in the low voice in which he had first spoken; 'but I am troubled, sir, I am troubled.'

He would have recalled the words if he could. He had said them, however, and I took them up quickly.

'With what? What is your trouble?'

'It is very difficult to impart, sir. It is very, very difficult to speak of. If ever you make me another visit, I will try to tell you.'

'But I expressly intend to make you another visit. Say, when shall it be?'

'I go off early in the morning, and I shall be on again at ten tomorrow night, sir.'

'I will come at eleven.'

He thanked me, and went out at the door with me. 'I'll show my white light, sir,' he said, in his peculiar low voice, 'till you have found the way up. When you have found it, don't call out! And when you are at the top, don't call out!'

His manner seemed to make the place strike colder to me, but I said no more than 'Very well.'

'And when you come down tomorrow night, don't call out! Let me

ask you a parting question. What made you cry "Halloa! Below there!"
tonight?'

'Heaven knows,' said I. 'I cried something to that effect——'

'Not to that effect, sir. Those were the very words. I know them well.'

'Admit those were the very words. I said them, no doubt, because I
saw you below.'

'For no other reason?'

'What other reason could I possibly have?'

'You had no feeling that they were conveyed to you in any
supernatural way?'

'No.'

He wished me goodnight, and held up his light. I walked by the side
of the down Line of rails (with a very disagreeable sensation of a train
coming behind me), until I found the path. It was easier to mount than
to descend, and I got back to my inn without any adventure.

Punctual to my appointment, I placed my foot on the first notch of
the zigzag next night, as the distant clocks were striking eleven. He was
waiting for me at the bottom, with his white light on. 'I have not called
out,' I said, when we came close together; 'may I speak now?' 'By all
means, sir.' 'Goodnight then, and here's my hand.' 'Goodnight, sir, and
here's mine.' With that, we walked side by side to his box, entered it,
closed the door, and sat down by the fire.

'I have made up my mind, sir,' he began, bending forward as soon as
we were seated, and speaking in a tone but a little above a whisper, 'that
you shall not have to ask me twice what troubles me. I took you for
someone else yesterday evening. That troubles me.'

'That mistake?'

'No. That someone else.'

'Who is it?'

'I don't know.'

'Like me?'

'I don't know. I never saw the face. The left arm is across the face,
and the right arm is waved. Violently waved. This way.'

I followed his action with my eyes, and it was the action of an arm
gesticulating with the utmost passion and vehemence: 'For God's sake
clear the way!'

'One moonlit night,' said the man, 'I was sitting here, when I heard a
voice cry "Halloa! Below there!" I stared up, looked from that door, and
saw this someone else standing by the red light near the tunnel, waving
as I just now showed you. The voice seemed hoarse with shouting, and it
cried, "Look out! Look out!" And then again "Halloa! Below there!
Look out!" I caught up my lamp, turned it on red, and ran towards the
figure, calling, "What's wrong? What has happened? Where?" It stood
just outside the blackness of the tunnel. I advanced so close upon it that I

wondered at its keeping the sleeve across its eyes. I ran right up at it, and had my hand stretched out to pull the sleeve away, when it was gone.'

'Into the tunnel,' said I.

'No. I ran on into the tunnel, five hundred yards. I stopped and held my lamp above my head, and saw the figures of the measured distance, and saw the wet stains stealing down the walls and trickling through the arch. I ran out again, faster than I had run in (for I had a mortal abhorrence of the place upon me), and I looked all round the red light with my own red light, and I went up the iron ladder to the gallery atop of it, and I came down again, and ran back here. I telegraphed both ways, "An alarm has been given. Is anything wrong?" The answer came back, both ways: "All well."'

Resisting the slow touch of a frozen finger tracing out my spine, I showed him how that this figure must be a deception of his sense of sight, and how that figures, originating in disease of the delicate nerves that minister to the functions of the eye, were known to have often troubled patients, some of whom had become conscious of the nature of their affliction, and had even proved it by experiments upon themselves. 'As to an imaginary cry,' said I, 'do but listen for a moment to the wind in this unnatural valley while we speak so low, and to the wild harp it makes of the telegraph wires!'

That was all very well, he returned, after we had sat listening for a while, and he ought to know something of the wind and the wires, he who so often passed long winter nights there, alone and watching. But he would beg to remark that he had not finished.

I asked his pardon, and he slowly added these words, touching my arm:

'Within six hours after the appearance, the memorable accident on this Line happened, and within ten hours the dead and wounded were brought along through the tunnel over the spot where the figure had stood.'

A disagreeable shudder crept over me, but I did my best against it. It was not to be denied, I rejoined, that this was a remarkable coincidence, calculated deeply to impress his mind. But it was unquestionable that remarkable coincidences did continually occur, and they must be taken into account in dealing with such a subject. Though to be sure I must admit, I added (for I thought I saw that he was going to bring the objection to bear upon me), men of common sense did not allow much for coincidences in making the ordinary calculations of life.

He again begged to remark that he had not finished.

I again begged his pardon for being betrayed into interruptions.

'This,' he said, again laying his hand upon my arm, and glancing over his shoulder with hollow eyes, 'was just a year ago. Six or seven months passed, and I had recovered from the surprise and shock, when one morning, as the day was breaking, I, standing at that door, looked towards the red light, and saw the spectre again.' He stopped, with a fixed look at me.

'Did it cry out?'

'No. It was silent.'

'Did it wave its arm?'

'No. It leaned against the shaft of the light, with both hands before the face. Like this.'

Once more, I followed his action with my eyes. It was an action of mourning. I have seen such an attitude in stone figures on tombs.

'Did you go up to it?'

'I came in and sat down, partly to collect my thoughts, partly because it had turned me faint. When I went to the door again, daylight was above me, and the ghost was gone.'

'But nothing followed? Nothing came of this?'

He touched me on the arm with his forefinger twice or thrice, giving a ghastly nod each time:

'That very day, as a train came out of the tunnel, I noticed, at a carriage window on my side, what looked like a confusion of hands and heads, and something waved. I saw it, just in time to signal the driver, Stop! He shut off, and put his brake on, but the train drifted past here a hundred and fifty yards or more. I ran after it, and, as I went along, heard terrible screams and cries. A beautiful young lady had died instantaneously in one of the compartments, and was brought in here, and laid down on this floor between us.'

Involuntarily, I pushed my chair back, as I looked from the boards at which he pointed, to himself.

'True, sir. True. Precisely as it happened, so I tell it you.'

I could think of nothing to say, to any purpose, and my mouth was very dry. The wind and the wires took up the story with a long lamenting wail.

He resumed. 'Now, sir, mark this, and judge how my mind is troubled. The spectre came back, a week ago. Ever since, it has been there, now and again, by fits and starts.'

'At the light?'

'At the Danger-light.'

'What does it seem to do?'

He repeated, if possible with increased passion and vehemence, that former gesticulation of 'For God's sake clear the way!'

Then, he went on. 'I have no peace or rest for it. It calls to me for many minutes together, in an agonized manner, "Below there! Look out! Look out!" It stands waving to me. It rings my little bell——'

I caught at that. 'Did it ring your bell yesterday evening when I was here, and you went to the door?'

'Twice.'

'Why, see,' said I, 'how your imagination misleads you. My eyes were on the bell, and my ears were open to the bell, and if I am a living man, it did *not* ring at those times. No, nor at any other time, except when it was rung in the natural course of physical things by the station communicating with you.'

He shook his head. 'I have never made a mistake as to that, yet, sir. I have never confused the spectre's ring with the man's. The ghost's ring is a strange vibration in the bell that it derives from nothing else, and I have not asserted that the bell stirs to the eye. I don't wonder that you failed to hear it. But *I* heard it.'

'And did the spectre seem to be there, when you looked out?'

'It was there.'

'Both times?'

He repeated firmly: 'Both times.'

'Will you come to the door with me, and look for it now?'

He bit his underlip as though he were somewhat unwilling, but arose. I opened the door, and stood on the step, while he stood in the doorway. There, was the Danger-light. There, was the dismal mouth of the tunnel. There, were the high wet stone walls of the cutting. There, were the stars above them.

'Do you see it?' I asked him, taking particular note of his face. His eyes were prominent and strained; but not very much more so, perhaps, than my own had been when I had directed them earnestly towards the same spot.

'No,' he answered. 'It is not there.'

'Agreed,' said I.

We went in again, shut the door, and resumed our seats. I was thinking how best to improve this advantage, if it might be called one, when he took up the conversation in such a matter of course way, so assuming that there could be no serious question of fact between us, that I felt myself placed in the weakest of positions.

'By this time you will fully understand, sir,' he said, 'that what troubles me so dreadfully, is the question, What does the spectre mean?'

I was not sure, I told him, that I did fully understand.

'What is its warning against?' he said, ruminating, with his eyes on the fire, and only by times turning them on me. 'What is the danger? Where is the danger? There is danger overhanging, somewhere on the Line. Some dreadful calamity will happen. It is not to be doubted this third time, after what has gone before. But surely this is a cruel haunting of *me*. What can *I* do?'

He pulled out his handkerchief, and wiped the drops from his heated forehead.

'If I telegraph Danger, on either side of me, or on both, I can give no reason for it,' he went on, wiping the palms of his hands. 'I should get into trouble, and do no good. They would think I was mad. This is the way it would work: Message: "Danger! Take care!" Answer: "What danger? Where?" Message: "Don't know. But for God's sake take care!" They would displace me. What else could they do?'

His pain of mind was most pitiable to see. It was the mental torture of a conscientious man, oppressed beyond endurance by an unintelligible responsibility involving life.

'When it first stood under the Danger-light,' he went on, putting his dark hair back from his head, and drawing his hands outwards across and across his temples in an extremity of feverish distress, 'why not tell me where that accident was to happen – if it must happen? Why not tell me how it could be averted – if it could have been averted? When on its second coming it hid its face, why not tell me instead: "She is going to die. Let them keep her at home"? If it came, on those two occasions, only to show me that its warnings were true, and so to prepare me for the third, why not warn me plainly now? And I, Lord help me! A mere poor signal-man on this solitary station! Why not go to somebody with credit to be believed, and power to act!'

When I saw him in this state, I saw that for the poor man's sake, as well as for the public safety, what I had to do for the time was, to compose his mind. Therefore, setting aside all question of reality or unreality between us, I represented to him that whoever thoroughly discharged his duty, must do well, and that at least it was his comfort that he understood his duty, though he did not understand these confounding appearances. In this effort I succeeded far better than in the attempt to reason him out of his conviction. He became calm; the occupations incidental to his post as the night advanced, began to make larger demands on his attention; and I left him at two in the morning. I had offered to stay through the night, but he would not hear of it.

That I more than once looked back at the red light as I ascended the pathway, that I did not like the red light, and that I should have slept but poorly if my bed had been under it, I see no reason to conceal. Nor did I like the two sequences of the accident and the dead girl. I see no reason to conceal that, either.

But, what ran most in my thoughts was the consideration how ought I to act, having become the recipient of this disclosure? I had proved the man to be intelligent, vigilant, painstaking and exact; but how long might he remain so, in his state of mind? Though in a subordinate position, still he held a most important trust, and would I (for instance) like to stake my own life on the chances of his continuing to execute it with precision?

Unable to overcome a feeling that there would be something treacherous in my communicating what he had told me to his superiors in the company, without first being plain with himself and proposing a middle course to him, I ultimately resolved to offer to accompany him (otherwise keeping his secret for the present) to the wisest medical practitioner we could hear of in those parts, and to take his opinion. A change in his time of duty would come round next night, he had apprised me, and he would be off an hour or two after sunrise, and on again soon after sunset. I had appointed to return accordingly.

Next evening was a lovely evening, and I walked out early to enjoy it. The sun was not yet quite down when I traversed the field-path near the top of the deep cutting. I would extend my walk for an hour, I said to myself, half an hour on and half an hour back, and it would then be time to go to my signal-man's box.

Before pursuing my stroll, I stepped to the brink, and mechanically looked down, from the point from which I had first seen him. I cannot describe the thrill that seized upon me, when, close at the mouth of the tunnel, I saw the appearance of a man, with his left sleeve across his eyes, passionately waving his right arm.

The nameless horror that oppressed me, passed in a moment, for in a moment I saw that this appearance of a man was a man indeed, and that there was a little group of other men standing at a short distance, to whom he seemed to be rehearsing the gesture he made. The Danger-light was not yet lighted. Against its shaft, a little low hut, entirely new to me, had been made of some wooden supports and tarpaulin. It looked no bigger than a bed.

With an irresistible sense that something was wrong – with a flashing self-reproachful fear that fatal mischief had come of my leaving the man there, and causing no one to be sent to overlook or correct what he did – I descended the notched path with all the speed I could make.

'What is the matter?' I asked the men.

'Signal-man killed this morning, sir.'

'Not the man belonging to that box?'

'Yes, sir.'

'Not the man I know?'

'You will recognize him, sir, if you knew him,' said the man who spoke for the others, solemnly uncovering his own head and raising an end of the tarpaulin, 'for his face is quite composed.'

'O! how did this happen, how did this happen?' I asked, turning from one to another as the hut closed in again.

'He was cut down by an engine, sir. No man in England knew his work better. But somehow he was not clear of the outer rail. It was just at broad day. He had struck the light, and had the lamp in his hand. As the engine came out of the tunnel, his back was towards her, and she cut him down. That man drove her, and was showing how it happened. Show the gentleman, Tom.'

The man who wore a rough dark dress, stepped back to his former place at the mouth of the tunnel!

'Coming round the curve in the tunnel, sir,' he said, 'I saw him at the end, like as if I saw him down a perspective-glass. There was no time to check speed, and I knew him to be very careful. As he didn't seem to take heed of the whistle, I shut it off when we were running down upon him, and called to him as loud as I could call.'

'What did you say?'

'I said, Below there! Look out! Look out! For God's sake clear the way!'

I started.

'Ah! it was a dreadful time, sir. I never left off calling to him. I put this arm before my eyes, not to see, and I waved this arm to the last; but it was no use.'

*   *   *

Without prolonging the narrative to dwell on any one of its curious circumstances more than on any other, I may, in closing it, point out the coincidence that the warning of the engine-driver included, not only the words which the unfortunate signal-man had repeated to me as haunting him, but also the words which I myself – not he – had attached, and that only in my own mind, to the gesticulation he had imitated.

The House of Balfother
William Croft Dickinson

'I sometimes wonder about those traditional immortals who live in secret chambers, like Earl Beardie at Glamis. Do they grow older and older? Do the years weary them? Or do they live on and on at exactly the same age? That's the worst of legends,' continued Drummond, addressing the company at large, 'they leave too much to the imagination.'

'Well, if Earl Beardie is growing older and older, his beard must be mighty long by now, after some four hundred years,' put in Sharples, with mock gravity. 'Unless at some point in time, or at some given length, a man's beard ceases to grow.'

'I know nothing about legends. Scottish history is too full of them,' said Petrie, critical as always. 'But, if someone will give me a long drink, I will tell you of one "immortal" who was certainly burdened by the years – so much so that he had declined into something worse than a second childhood. Yet from what I saw and experienced, I shudder to think what "life" would have meant to him had he not suffered an unnatural and terrible end.'

Someone got up to provide the drink.

'It will have to be a long one,' Petrie added quickly, 'for I shall have to tell you how I came to the House of Balfother, before I try to describe what happened there. And, after that, you will still have to hear the end of the tale.'

A very long drink was provided.

*   *   *

It all happened when I was a student at St Andrews – a 'magistrand', in my final year. And when I was also a great walker: which meant something more than the traditional ten-mile walk of St Andrews men, 'out by Cameron, and in by Grange'. To me, walking in those days meant striding across the hills by map and compass – the road to be taken only in times of sheer necessity – and never doing less than twenty miles a day. I can still do my twenty miles, but, in my student days, my long walks also meant trusting to hospitality, and hoping that the lonely farm or shepherd's cottage, marked with a small dot on the map, would somehow or other provide me with shelter for the night. Youth hostels were still unknown. Yet I was seldom turned away – even though, upon occasion, I must have been taken in at great inconvenience. And when I knew that that had been the case, I always strove to show my gratitude by giving any services I could on the following morning before setting out again – for I knew that any offer of payment would certainly be refused.

After the night of my strange experience, however, I left long before the day broke. And I was glad to be gone.

It was the Easter vacation of my final year and, faced with my examinations at the end of the coming summer term, I had decided upon a noble walk. I would take with me a copy of *Kidnapped*, and I would retrace David Balfour's route – partly that of 'the lad with the silver button', and partly that of David Balfour and Alan Breck when they 'took to the heather' after the murder of the 'Red Fox', Glenure. But I would do it in reverse, from North Queensferry to the Ross of Mull. Then back to Oban, and thence to St Andrews by train – to be at my books once more.

I had set out with high heart and, blessed with fine clear days, I was well ahead of my schedule when I reached the few small houses of Kilchonan, on Loch Rannoch-side. From there I walked the mile or so to the Bridge of Ericht and then struck northwards towards Loch Ericht. It was hardly midday, so I planned to go up the valley of the stream, skirt the loch on its western side (for I would find no Cluny's 'gillie' to row me across), and, with luck, find shelter for the night at Ben Alder Cottage. I knew I was giving myself something of a task for, according to the map, it was ten miles and a bit, with no habitation of any kind between Kilchonan and the Cottage. But I was in fine fettle, the day was glorious, and I had every confidence.

And then, for the first time, I found myself in difficulties. The way by the fast-running stream soon proved to be more troublesome than I had expected, so I struck up to the higher ground on the west. There I was beginning to make better progress, with a track to help me when, gradually, the sun paled and the afternoon grew colder. I knew well enough what that meant. I knew that before long I should be running the dangers of a mountain mist.

Wisely, I decided to turn back to Kilchonan. And then came the mist: thin at first, but soon, all too soon, thick and enveloping. I knew that all I had to do was to keep on due south. If I did that, I was bound to strike Loch Rannoch – and Kilchonan – again; or, if I had strayed too far west, I would strike the road that ran from the western end of the loch to Rannoch Station. After all, I had my compass – a fine prismatic one, with a luminous dial, a legacy of my father's service in the First World

War. More than once I had had to rely upon it amid the hills, and more than once it had served me well. But, although I could keep on walking in the right direction, I could not see where I was going; and almost immediately I was reminded of a new danger. Stumbling badly on some rough ground, I twisted my foot. Fortunately I was wearing heavy boots, but there and then I pictured myself, with a sprained ankle, trying painfully to make my way back and perhaps not succeeding, perhaps not being found. I took greater care but, trying to pick my way slowly in thick white mist, over ground that I could barely see ahead of me, meant that before long I was chilled to the bone.

I cannot say that I was alarmed or dispirited. To the best of my recollection, my first feeling was simply one of frustration – partly that I had had to abandon my plan of reaching Ben Alder Cottage that night, and partly at the enforced slowness of my return to Kilchonan. But as the afternoon wore on, and still I had reached neither Loch Rannoch nor the road, I began to feel worried. Also, I was tired out. My slow groping through the mist would have tired anyone. But why had I made such poor progress? I had kept steadily south. Where was I? By now, too, although the mist was beginning to lift, darkness was taking its place.

And then, in the strange light that was half mist and half darkness, a tall square-standing tower suddenly loomed up a few yards ahead of me. Here was luck, indeed. Here I could find shelter for the night. Then came a strange sense of puzzlement, perhaps even of disquiet. What was this tower-house? It was certainly not marked on the map. There was no house of this kind anywhere between Kilchonan and Loch Ericht. But there it stood: a solid pile, much like a Border tower. It was no figment of my imagination.

There was no surrounding wall of any kind, and I walked straight up to the door. Again I was puzzled. The door was of solid oak, studded with iron nails. Surely no house still boasted such a medieval defence? I knocked as loudly as I could, but my knuckles seemed to make no sound that would carry through the thick oak. Wondering what to do, I kicked the door with my heavy boots, and knew that the noise I made was bound to be heard. Standing there, cold and shivering, I kicked again and again. And at last my demand was answered. I heard the drawing of bars, the door opened slowly, and a man stood in the narrow opening as though to contest any entry.

'For why are ye makand sic dunts on the door?' he asked.

'Could I have shelter for the night?' I replied.

'Na stranger enters Balfother. It's weel kent. The king's writ aye has it so,' he answered, and would have closed the door.

But I was in no mood to be put off so easily and, being young and impetuous, I thrust my foot into the gap.

'I'm sorry,' I said firmly, 'but you can't leave me out all night. I will

be no trouble to you. I have food in my pack, and I can sleep on the
kitchen floor, or in an outhouse if you have one. I want only that, and a
fire to dry out my clothes.'

He seemed to hesitate, and then said again, almost as though it were
a set phrase, 'Na stranger enters Balfother. The king's writ has it. It
canna be.'

'But it must be,' I returned and, pushing against the door, I edged
myself in.

'Bide ye there, then,' said the man, seeing that I had indeed entered
Balfother, and apparently not wishing to dispute my entry. He shuffled
away in the darkness of what I assumed to be some kind of entrance
passage, and left me standing there. A minute or two later, however, he
reappeared, carrying a lighted tallow candle on a dish. Beckoning me to
follow him, he led the way up a winding stone stairway, opened a door,
and ushered me into a small room. There he set the candle upon a rough
table and, without a word, left me again.

I looked at my quarters for the night, and again I felt that strange
sense of disquiet. The room was perhaps twelve feet square and
completely empty save for the rough table on which the man had set my
candle, and a bed that was even more roughly made and was completely
devoid of bed-clothes of any kind. The stone walls were cold and bare; as
also was the stone floor. Only a small window, high up in one of the
walls, and a crude fire-place in the wall opposite the bed, broke the
forbidding monotony of stone. More that that, the whole room smelled
dank and musty, as though the one window had never been opened, and
the room had never been used, for countless years.

'A chilly reception, if ever there was one,' I muttered resentfully.
'Surely there's a fire in the house, somewhere.'

But I did my reluctant host an injustice. I had barely muttered my
resentment than he came into the room, bearing an armful of logs. Again
without speaking he laid them in a neat pile in the fire-place and went
out, returning a second time with a log that was still glowing from a fire
elsewhere. He placed the glowing log in the centre of the pile, lay full
length upon the floor and blew until the log broke into flames and began
to set the other logs alight.

At any rate I shall have a fire, I thought, thankfully, as I watched
him at his task. And then once more I was puzzled. What was this house
with an ancient look about everything? Who was this man? And why did
his coarse clothes seem so odd? Had he inherited them from a
grandfather, or a great-grandfather?

As the man rose from his task, I thanked him sincerely for his attention to my wants. But he merely looked at me blankly and moved to the
door. There, however, he turned before leaving.

'God keep ye through the night,' he said and, with that, he was gone.

'And what might that mean?' I wondered. Was it just a benison, or was it a warning? I had virtually commanded shelter for the night, but what sort of shelter had I taken? What sort of a night was I to have?

Dismissing various vague apprehensions which flitted through my mind, I opened my pack and took out the spare socks, shirt and underclothing which I always carried on my long walks. These I laid, like a hearth-rug, on the stone floor in front of the fire, and then stripped to the skin. Standing on my hearth-rug, I rubbed myself hard and long with my towel. Then I began to dry out my soaking clothes, first arranging them in small pyramids before the fire and then holding them up, one at a time, close to the flames. I knew I ran the risk of singeing them, but dry clothes I had to have if I was to sleep without blankets. For perhaps an hour I continued this task until all my clothes were dry. Then I dressed, ate some chocolate and plain biscuits, and felt completely refreshed.

I stress all this to show that I was fully alert and far from likely to 'imagine' things. Sitting on the edge of the bed I was ready to accept the shelter I had demanded and to face whatever the night might bring. Again taking out my map, I looked for a house somewhere in the hills to the south of Loch Ericht. No house was marked. But surely a tower-house like this was bound to be marked. What was this House of Balfother? And what had my queer host meant about 'na stranger', and 'the king's writ'? Well, I was ready for anything.

The fire was now burning low, but there was still life in the tallow candle. And then, just as I was debating whether or not to trust myself to the bed, and its possible vermin, I saw the door slowly opening. I flatter myself I was not in the least afraid. If robbery was intended, I felt in just the right mood to put up a good fight for my few pounds and pence. But it was not my host who entered. I was being visited by a large dog.

The animal, yellowish-white, and strangely devoid of fur, crawled slowly into the room and made straight for the fireplace and the warmth of the glowing embers there. But, instead of lying down, it *sat* down, much as a human would sit on the floor in front of a fire. Startled, I looked more closely at that strange posture. With a sudden feeling of revulsion, I realized that I was looking, not at a dog, but at a man.

He was completely naked. His skin was yellow, loose and wrinkled – much like a piece of faded paper that had been crumpled up and then roughly smoothed out again. Soon, as he sat there, warming himself before the fire, he began to make little noises, similar to those made by a baby before it first begins to talk. After a while, he stopped and, teetering to and fro, began to croon to himself: 'Robbie Norrie, Robbie Norrie canna die. Robbie Norrie wilna die.'

It is impossible to describe my feelings as I witnessed this complete degradation of humanity. And, as I wondered what to do, the man turned, and saw me sitting on the bed. With a gurgle of delight, he got up and crawled towards me. Never had I seen, never shall I see again such an old, old face. It looked as though it had aged through centuries. Now too, as he came close to me, I could smell his body – a horrible, indefinable smell of rank flesh.

'Robbie Norrie,' he gibbered. 'Robbie Norrie.'

I strove to push him away, and his body yielded to my hands like a soft sponge.

'Robbie Norrie. Robbie Norrie,' I heard in a kind of childish sing-song as I feverishly struggled to avoid an approach that sent shivers of horror through every nerve in my frame.

I have no idea how long I struggled with that degenerate lump of human flesh. I was contending with a creature (for that is the only appropriate name) that seemed to have risen in bodily form from an age-old grave; a creature that sought to nestle close to me and that I pushed away again and again.

'Robbie Norrie, Robbie Norrie.' The childish repetition, as the foul creature constantly returned and strove to nestle against me, suddenly snapped my control. I seized him by the throat, and might well have strangled him, had not the door opened, just in time.

I let go my hold as I saw my host enter the room. The creature dropped on all fours at my feet; my host gave a sharp word of command; and the horrible thing, that once had been a man, sidled slowly out. My host, without a word, followed it.

I am not ashamed to say that I was in a state of complete collapse. I was a strong, well-built youngster of twenty-two, and all I had had to do was to repulse a weak and decrepit creature, feeble alike in body and mind. Yet somehow, I felt that I had been struggling with something so unwholesome that I myself had been in danger of corruption. Perhaps people in the middle ages felt like that about contact with a leper. I do not know.

As I gradually became myself again, I decided there was only one course to take. I had had enough of Balfother. I put my things into my pack and, creeping out of the room, felt my way about until I had discovered the stairway. I stole quietly down, found the door, drew back the wooden bars, and literally ran out into the night. It was still dark, but the mist had cleared. Again I struck south by compass, this time not caring whether I sprained my ankle or not. And, to my surprise, I had been walking for barely a quarter of an hour when I reached Loch Rannoch. There I stayed until dawn, resting my back against a tree, pondering over my strange adventure and regaining peace of mind.

My walk was over, save for the few miles to Rannoch Station. I caught a train there, changed at Crianlarich, and journeyed slowly, across country, back to St Andrews.

*   *   *

A week or so after my return, I received a note from John Barnet, my professor of Greek, inviting me to his house for tea. Term had not yet started, and the only other guest at tea was Duncan Mackinnon, the senior lecturer in History. I had told Barnet of my intention to walk from North Queensferry to the Ross of Mull, and naturally his first question was to ask me how I had fared. You can easily understand that my immediate response was to tell the whole story of my night at Balfother. But I was not prepared for what followed.

'Balfother?' interrupted Mackinnon, when I told of my arrival at the house.

'Robert Norrie?' he asked, excitedly, a little later.

But he let me finish.

'You know something about all this?' queried Barnet, turning to Mackinnon, when my tale had ended.

'Wait!' he answered. 'I'll slip over to my house and bring back a document which goes some way towards an explanation – though even then the whole thing is incredible.'

Mackinnon went out, leaving us to await his return impatiently – wondering what his document could be, and what explanation it could possibly give.

About ten minutes later he was back.

'As you know,' he began, taking a folded paper from his pocket, 'I have been working on the Fortingall Papers in the Scottish Record Office. And as soon as Petrie mentioned Balfother I remembered a queer letter under the Privy Seal which I found in the Fortingall Papers and which intrigued me so much that I transcribed it in full.'

He unfolded his sheet of paper, and although I cannot give you the exact words – though I still have a copy of the document at home – what he read out to us ran roughly like this:

A letter made to William Fowler of Balfother, his heirs and assigns, making mention that for the good, true and thankful service done and to be done by the said William, his heirs and assigns, in the keeping and maintaining of Robert Norrie, the man to whom the French leech Damian gave the quintessence in the time of our sovereign Lord's predecessor King James IV, whom God assoil, and the said Robert Norrie being still on life, therefore our sovereign Lord grants to the said William, his heirs and assigns, an annual rent of five hundred shillings to be uptaken yearly of the lands of Dall and Finnart. Providing always that the said William Fowler, his heirs and assigns, shall keep the said Robert Norrie close from all other persons whatsomever that he may be scatheless and harmless in his body, and that our sovereign Lord and, if God wills, our sovereign Lord's successors, may know to what age the said Robert shall live.

'Now you can understand my excitement,' continued Mackinnon. 'The date of that letter is April 3rd 1622. James IV died at Flodden in 1513. So already Robert Norrie had lived to at least the age of 109, and probably several years more – for the quintessence would hardly be given to him in his infancy. That had aroused my interest when I first read the extract; but, if Petrie saw the same Robert Norrie at Balfother, as he seems to have done, the man must now be more than 400 years old.'

For a minute or so we digested this in silence.

'He *was* centuries old,' I said. 'I felt it at the time.'

'And what's all this about the French leech Damian, and the quintessence?' asked Barnet.

'Oh, that part is straightforward enough,' answered Mackinnon. 'We know that James IV encouraged the experiments of a certain Damian who believed he could distil the "quintessence" – not only to turn base metals into gold but also to yield an elixir that would prolong man's life indefinitely. James IV even made him abbot of Tongland; and, if you are interested, you can find the materials which he used in his experiments, and for which the King paid, in the *Accounts of the Lord High Treasurer* from about 1501 to 1513. My extract proves conclusively that Robert Norrie, who had been given the "quintessence", lived to be at least 109. Is he still alive? At 400? What's more, when Petrie knocked at the door of Balfother he was told that no stranger could be admitted, and that the King's writ said so. Doesn't that mean that the same Robert Norrie is still being kept "close"?'

'We'll go to Balfother ourselves,' cried Barnet. 'And we'll ask James Waters to come with us. He takes so much interest in his anatomical reconstructions from the skulls and bones of men who have been dead for centuries that he's sure to be interested in the anatomy of a man who is still alive at the age of at least 400. All that puzzles me is how the affair has been kept secret for so long. Food – and even tallow candles – must be bought; and people are always curious about any queer goings-on in their neighbourhood. Surely the good folk of Kilchonan must know of the strange "creature" kept in Balfother. However, we'll see. I propose we ring up Waters and, if he's free, we'll drive to Kilchonan tomorrow.'

*　　*　　*

Waters was free. And Barnet was a good driver. We arrived at Kilchonan about noon and, after a picnic lunch by the loch-side, the four of us retraced my steps up the high ground to the west of the stream that runs from Loch Ericht into Loch Rannoch. But we found no tower-house. Reaching the point where I thought I had turned back, we spread out, far wider than beaters on a grouse moor, and walked southwards again. We met on the road by the Loch, and again we had failed to find Balfother.

'Are you sure you didn't fall asleep and dream it all?' asked Barnet, turning to me with a twinkle in his eye.

'I'm certain I didn't,' I replied, firmly.

'It can't have been a dream,' confirmed Mackinnon. 'Petrie had never heard of Balfother and Robert Norrie. He knew nothing of a letter under the Privy Seal – a "king's writ" – which banned the entry of strangers.'

'Well,' said the practical Waters, 'I suggest we enquire at Kilchonan. Perhaps we should have done so first of all.'

We enquired. But no one in Kilchonan had heard of a house called Balfother. One encouragement, however, did emerge from our enquiries. It was suggested that we should call on a Mr Alastair MacGregor, in Aberfeldy, who, we were told, was writing a local history, and who, of all people, was the most likely to be of help to us.

We drove to Aberfeldy, and we found Mr MacGregor.

'Balfother?' he repeated. 'Yes, there was certainly a tower-house of that name. It belonged to the Fowlers; but it was destroyed long ago. A grim and tragic affair. Come in, and I'll tell you about it.'

*   *   *

Alastair MacGregor did not live long enough to see his book in print. I can give you no reference to volume and page. But I am not likely to forget his account.

It appears that in 1649 there was a veritable epidemic of witch-huntings, witch-trials and witch-burnings throughout all Scotland from one end of the country to the other. And, in the August of that year, someone denounced William Fowler of Balfother, and Bessie Wilson, his wife, of keeping a 'familiar'. The 'familiar' had been seen. It was in the form of an old and naked man, who could not be clothed, and who ran about on all fours like a dog.

A body of men, headed by a minister, went out to Balfother. Apparently they had difficulty in gaining an entrance, but when, at last, they had broken down the door, had entered the house, and had secured Fowler and his wife, they began a search for the 'familiar'. And, according to the story, they found it – an old and decrepit man, stark naked, who babbled the words of some devilish incantation which put them all in terror until the minister cried out: 'Get thee behind me, Satan,' when they rushed at it and bound it with strong cords.

William Fowler and Bessie Wilson were burned as agents of the devil and, with them, was burned their 'familiar'. It is said that William Fowler produced something which he called 'the king's writ', and which he offered in his defence. But the court refused to look at it, let alone accept it.

As for the house itself, after the burnings, the minister had preached a powerful sermon on the text, 'We will destroy this place ... and the Lord hath sent us to destroy it.' Whereupon all the people had marched out to Balfother and, with crowbars and irons, had pulled down the house, stone by stone, scattering the stones over the land. And yet, apparently, the sight of good cut freestone was too much for the people of a later time. According to MacGregor, many of the stones of Balfother were still to be seen in some of the walls in Kilchonan.

*　　*　　*

We left the knowledgeable MacGregor and we drove from Aberfeldy in silence.

'What a horrible story,' said Barnet, at last.

'Yes,' agreed Mackinnon. 'One of far too many. Horrible. And yet,' he continued with his historian's eye for dates, 'Robert Norrie must have lived to at least the age of 136. Is that possible, Waters?'

'Certainly it's possible,' replied Waters, crisply. 'All the same, I'm glad that modern medicine has not yet discovered the prescription for Damian's quintessence. Old age is already a social problem, without further complications from an elixir of life.'

'But,' I cried impatiently, 'can any of you explain how I came to the House of Balfother when the house was no longer there, and how Robert Norrie came to visit me when Robert Norrie had long been dead.'

No one answered me. And I know that no one ever will.

The Brown Hand
Arthur Conan Doyle

Everyone knows that Sir Dominick Holden, the famous Indian surgeon, made me his heir, and that his death changed me in an hour from a hard-working and impecunious medical man to a well-to-do landed proprietor. Many know also that there were at least five people between the inheritance and me, and that Sir Dominick's selection appeared to be altogether arbitrary and whimsical. I can assure them, however, that they are quite mistaken, and that, although I only knew Sir Dominick in the closing years of his life, there were none the less very real reasons why he should show his goodwill towards me. As a matter of fact, though I say it myself, no man ever did more for another than I did for my Indian uncle. I cannot expect the story to be believed, but it is so singular that I should feel that it was a breach of duty if I did not put it upon record – so here it is, and your belief or incredulity is your own affair.

Sir Dominick Holden, C.B., K.C.S.I., and I don't know what besides, was the most distinguished Indian surgeon of his day. In the Army originally, he afterwards settled down into civil practice in Bombay, and visited as a consultant every part of India. His name is best remembered in connection with the Oriental Hospital, which he founded and supported. The time came, however, when his iron constitution began to show signs of the long strain to which he had subjected it, and his brother practitioners (who were not, perhaps, entirely disinterested upon the point) were unanimous in recommending him to return to England. He held on so long as he could, but at last he developed nervous symptoms of a very pronounced character, and so came back, a broken man, to his native county of Wiltshire. He bought a considerable estate with an ancient manor-house upon the edge of Salisbury Plain, and devoted his old age to the study of Comparative Pathology, which had been his learned hobby all his life, and in which he was a foremost authority.

We of the family were, as may be imagined, much excited by the news of the return of this rich and childless uncle to England. On his part, although by no means exuberant in his hospitality, he showed some sense of his duty to his relations, and each of us in turn had an invitation to visit him. From the accounts of my cousins it appeared to be a melancholy business, and it was with mixed feelings that I at last received my own summons to appear at Rodenhurst. My wife was so carefully excluded in the invitation that my first impulse was to refuse it, but the interests of the children had to be considered, and so, with her consent, I set out one October afternoon upon my visit to Wiltshire, with little thought of what that visit was to entail.

My uncle's estate was situated where the arable land of the plains begins to swell upwards into the rounded chalk hills which are characteristic of the country. As I drove from Dinton Station in the waning light of that autumn day, I was impressed by the weird nature of the scenery. The few scattered cottages of the peasants were so dwarfed by the huge evidences of prehistoric life, that the present appeared to be a dream and the past to be the obtrusive and masterful reality. The road wound through the valleys, formed by a succession of grassy hills, and the summit of each was cut and carved into the most elaborate fortifications, some circular and some square, but all on a scale which has defied the winds and the rains of many centuries. Some call them Roman and some British, but their true origin and the reasons for this particular tract of country being so interlaced with en-trenchments have never been finally made clear. Here and there on the long, smooth, olive-coloured slopes there rose small rounded barrows or tumuli. Beneath them lie the cremated ashes of the race which cut so deeply into the hills, but their graves tell us nothing save that a jar full of dust represents the man who once laboured under the sun.

It was through this weird country that I approached my uncle's residence of Rodenhurst, and the house was, as I found, in due keeping with its surroundings. Two broken and weather-stained pillars, each surmounted by a mutilated heraldic emblem, flanked the entrance to a neglected drive. A cold wind whistled through the elms which lined it, and the air was full of the drifting leaves. At the far end, under the gloomy arch of trees, a single yellow lamp burned steadily. In the dim half-light of the coming night I saw a long, low building stretching out two irregular wings, with deep eaves, a sloping gambrel roof, and walls which were criss-crossed with timber balks in the fashion of the Tudors. The cheery light of a fire flickered in the broad, latticed window to the left of the low-porched door, and this, as it proved, marked the study of my uncle, for it was thither that I was led by his butler in order to make my host's acquaintance.

He was cowering over his fire, for the moist chill of an English autumn had set him shivering. His lamp was unlit, and I only saw the red glow of the embers beating upon a huge, craggy face, with a Red

Indian nose and cheek, and deep furrows and seams from eye to chin, the sinister marks of hidden volcanic fires. He sprang up at my entrance with something of an old-world courtesy and welcomed me warmly to Rodenhurst. At the same time I was conscious, as the lamp was carried in, that it was a very critical pair of light-blue eyes which looked out at me from under shaggy eyebrows, like scouts beneath a bush, and that this outlandish uncle of mine was carefully reading off my character with all the ease of a practised observer and an experienced man of the world.

For my part I looked at him, and looked again, for I had never seen a man whose appearance was more fitted to hold one's attention. His figure was the framework of a giant, but he had fallen away until his coat dangled straight down in a shocking fashion from a pair of broad and bony shoulders. All his limbs were huge and yet emaciated, and I could not take my gaze from his knobby wrists, and long, gnarled hands, But his eyes – those peering light blue eyes – they were the most arrestive of any of his peculiarities. It was not their colour alone, nor was it the ambush of hair in which they lurked; but it was the expression which I read in them. For the appearance and bearing of the man were masterful, and one expected a certain corresponding arrogance in his eyes, but instead of that I read the look which tells of a spirit cowed and crushed, the furtive, expectant look of the dog whose master has taken the whip from the rack. I formed my own medical diagnosis upon one glance at those critical and yet appealing eyes. I believed that he was stricken with some mortal ailment, that he knew himself to be exposed to sudden death, and that he lived in terror of it. Such was my judgement – a false one, as the event showed; but I mention it that it may help you to realize the look which I read in his eyes.

My uncle's welcome was, as I have said, a courteous one, and in an hour or so I found myself seated between him and his wife at a comfortable dinner, with curious pungent delicacies upon the table, and a stealthy, quick-eyed Oriental waiter behind his chair. The old couple had come round to that tragic imitation of the dawn of life when husband and wife, having lost or scattered all those who were their intimates, find themselves face to face and alone once more, their work done, and the end nearing fast. Those who have reached that stage in sweetness and love, who can change their winter into a gentle Indian summer, have come as victors through the ordeal of life. Lady Holden was a small, alert woman, with a kindly eye, and her expression as she glanced at him was a certificate of character to her husband. And yet, though I read a mutual love in their glances, I read also a mutual horror, and recognized in her face some reflection of that stealthy fear which I detected in his. Their talk was sometimes merry and sometimes sad, but there was a forced note in their merriment and a naturalness in their sadness which told me that a heavy heart beat upon either side of me.

We were sitting over our first glass of wine, and the servants had left the room, when the conversation took a turn which produced a remarkable effect upon my host and hostess. I cannot recall what it was which started the topic of the supernatural, but it ended in my showing them that the abnormal in psychical experiences was a subject to which I had, like many neurologists, devoted a great deal of attention. I concluded by narrating my experiences when, as a member of the Psychical Research Society, I had formed one of a committee of three who spent the night in a haunted house. Our adventures were neither exciting nor convincing, but, such as it was, the story appeared to interest my auditors in a remarkable degree. They listened with an eager silence, and I caught a look of intelligence between them which I could not understand. Lady Holden immediately afterwards rose and left the room.

Sir Dominick pushed the cigar box over to me, and we smoked for some little time in silence. That huge bony hand of his was twitching as he raised it with his cheroot to his lips, and I felt that the man's nerves were vibrating like fiddle-strings. My instincts told me that he was on the verge of some intimate confidence, and I feared to speak lest I should interrupt it. At last he turned towards me with a spasmodic gesture like a man who throws his last scruple to the winds.

'From the little that I have seen of you it appears to me, Dr Hardacre,' said he, 'that you are the very man I have wanted to meet.'

'I am delighted to hear it, sir.'

'Your head seems to be cool and steady. You will acquit me of any desire to flatter you, for the circumstances are too serious to permit of insincerities. You have some special knowledge upon these subjects, and you evidently view them from that philosophical standpoint which robs them of all vulgar terror. I presume that the sight of an apparition would not seriously discompose you?'

'I think not, sir.'

'Would even interest you, perhaps?'

'Most intensely.'

'As a psychical observer, you would probably investigate it in as impersonal a fashion as an astronomer investigates a wandering comet?'

'Precisely.'

He gave a heavy sigh.

'Believe me, Dr Hardacre, there was a time when I could have spoken as you do now. My nerve was a by-word in India. Even the Mutiny never shook it for an instant. And yet you see what I am reduced to – the most timorous man, perhaps, in all this country of Wiltshire. Do not speak too bravely upon this subject, or you may find yourself subjected to as long-drawn a test as I am – a test which can only end in the madhouse or the grave.'

I waited patiently until he should see fit to go farther in his confidence. His preamble had, I need not say, filled me with interest and expectation.

'For some years, Dr Hardacre,' he continued, 'my life and that of my wife have been made miserable by a cause which is so grotesque that it borders upon the ludicrous. And yet familiarity has never made it more easy to bear – on the contrary, as time passes my nerves become more worn and shattered by the constant attrition. If you have no physical fears, Dr Hardacre, I should very much value your opinion upon this phenomenon which troubles us so.'

'For what it is worth my opinion is entirely at your service. May I ask the nature of the phenomenon?'

'I think that your experiences will have a higher evidential value if you are not told in advance what you may expect to encounter. You are yourself aware of the quibbles of unconscious cerebration and subjective impressions with which a scientific sceptic may throw a doubt upon your statement. It would be as well to guard against them in advance.'

'What shall I do, then?'

'I will tell you. Would you mind following me this way?' He led me out of the dining-room and down a long passage until we came to a terminal door. Inside there was a large bare room fitted as a laboratory, with numerous scientific instruments and bottles. A shelf ran along one side, upon which there stood a long line of glass jars containing pathological and anatomical specimens.

'You see that I still dabble in some of my old studies,' said Sir Dominick. 'These jars are the remains of what was once a most excellent collection, but unfortunately I lost the greater part of them when my house was burned down in Bombay in '92. It was a most unfortunate affair for me – in more ways than one. I had examples of many rare conditions, and my splenic collection was probably unique. These are the survivors.'

I glanced over them, and saw that they really were of a very great value and rarity from a pathological point of view: bloated organs, gaping cysts, distorted bones, odious parasites – a singular exhibition of the products of India.

'There is, as you see, a small settee here,' said my host. 'It was far from our intention to offer a guest so meagre an accommodation, but since affairs have taken this turn, it would be a great kindness upon your part if you would consent to spend the night in this apartment. I beg that you will not hesitate to let me know if the idea should be at all repugnant to you.'

'On the contrary,' I said, 'it is most acceptable.'

'My own room is the second on the left, so that if you should feel that you are in need of company a call would always bring me to your side.'

'I trust that I shall not be compelled to disturb you.'

'It is unlikely that I shall be asleep. I do not sleep much. Do not hesitate to summon me.'

And so with this agreement we joined Lady Holden in the drawing-room and talked of lighter things.

It was no affectation upon my part to say that the prospect of my night's adventure was an agreeable one. I have no pretence to greater physical courage than my neighbours, but familiarity with a subject robs it of those vague and undefined terrors which are the most appalling to the imaginative mind. The human brain is capable of only one strong emotion at a time, and if it be filled with curiosity or scientific enthusiasm, there is no room for fear. It is true that I had my uncle's assurance that he had himself originally taken this point of view, but I reflected that the breakdown of his nervous system might be due to his forty years in India as much as to any psychical experiences which had befallen him. I at least was sound in nerve and brain, and it was with something of the pleasurable thrill of anticipation with which the sportsman takes his position beside the haunt of his game that I shut the laboratory door behind me, and partially undressing, lay down upon the rug-covered settee.

It was not an ideal atmosphere for a bedroom. The air was heavy with many chemical odours, that of methylated spirit predominating. Nor were the decorations of my chamber very sedative. The odious line of glass jars with their relics of disease and suffering stretched in front of my very eyes. There was no blind to the window, and a three-quarter moon streamed its white light into the room, tracing a silver square with filigree lattices upon the opposite wall. When I had extinguished my candle this one bright patch in the midst of the general gloom had certainly an eerie and discomposing aspect. A rigid and absolute silence reigned throughout the old house, so that the low swish of the branches in the garden came softly and soothingly to my ears. It may have been the hypnotic lullaby of this gentle susurrus, or it may have been the result of my tiring day, but after many dozings and many efforts to regain my clearness of perception, I fell at last into a deep and dreamless sleep.

I was awakened by some sound in the room, and I instantly raised myself upon my elbow on the couch. Some hours had passed, for the square patch upon the wall had slid downwards and sideways until it lay obliquely at the end of my bed. The rest of the room was in deep shadow. At first I could see nothing. Presently, as my eyes became accustomed to the faint light, I was aware, with a thrill which all my scientific absorption could not entirely prevent, that something was moving slowly along the line of the wall. A gentle, shuffling sound, as of soft slippers, came to my ears, and I dimly discerned a human figure walking stealthily from the direction of the door. As it emerged into the patch of moonlight I was very clearly what it was and how it was employed. It was a man, short and squat, dressed in some sort of dark grey gown, which hung straight from his shoulders to his feet. The moon shone upon the side of his face, and I saw that it was chocolate-brown in colour, with a ball of black hair like a woman's at the back of his head. He walked slowly, and his eyes were cast upwards towards the line of bottles which contained those gruesome remnants of humanity. He seemed to examine each jar with attention, and then to pass on to the next. When he had come to the end of the line, immediately opposite my bed, he stopped, faced me, threw up his hands with a gesture of despair, and vanished from my sight.

I have said that he threw up his hands, but I should have said his arms, for at he assumed that attitude of despair I observed a singular peculiarity about his appearance. He had only one hand! As the sleeves drooped down from the up-flung arms I saw the left plainly, but the right ended in a knobby and unsightly stump. In every other way his appearance was so natural, and I had both seen and heard him so clearly, that I could easily have believed that he was an Indian servant of Sir Dominick's who had come into my room in search of something. It was only his sudden disappearance which suggested anything more sinister to me. As it was I sprang from my couch, lit a candle, and examined the whole room carefully. There were no signs of my visitor, and I was forced to conclude that there had really been something outside the normal laws of nature in his appearance. I lay awake for the remainder of the night, but nothing else occurred to disturb me.

I am an early riser, but my uncle was an even earlier one, for I found him pacing up and down the lawn at the side of the house. He ran towards me in his eagerness when he saw me come out from the door.

'Well, well!' he cried. 'Did you see him?'

'An Indian with one hand?'

'Precisely.'

'Yes, I saw him' – and I told him all that occurred. When I had finished, he led the way into his study.

'We have a little time before breakfast,' said he. 'It will suffice to give you an explanation of this extraordinary affair – so far as I can explain that which is essentially inexplicable. In the first place, when I tell you that for four years I have never passed one single night, either in Bombay, aboard ship, or here in England without my sleep being broken by this fellow, you will understand why it is that I am a wreck of my former self. His programme is always the same. He appears by my bedside, shakes me roughly by the shoulder, passes from my room into the laboratory, walks slowly along the line of my bottles, and then vanishes. For more than a thousand times he has gone through the same routine.'

'What does he want?'

'He wants his hand.'

'His hand?'

'Yes, it came about in this way. I was summoned to Peshawur for a consultation some years ago, and while there I was asked to look at the hand of a native who was passing through with an Afghan caravan. The fellow came from some mountain tribe living away at the back of beyond somewhere on the other side of Kaffiristan. He talked a bastard Pushtoo, and it was all I could do to understand him. He was suffering from a soft sarcomatous swelling of one of the metacarpal joints, and I made him realize that it was only by losing his hand that he could hope to save his life. After much persuasion he consented to the operation, and he asked me, when it was over, what fee I demanded. The poor fellow was almost a beggar, so that the idea of a fee was absurd, but I answered in jest that my fee should be his hand, and that I proposed to add it to my pathological collection.

'To my surprise he demurred very much to the suggestion, and he explained that according to his religion it was an all important matter that the body should be reunited after death, and so make a perfect dwelling for the spirit. This belief is, of course, an old one, and the mummies of the Egyptians arose from an analogous superstition. I answered him that his hand was already off, and asked him how he intended to preserve it. He replied that he would pickle it in salt and carry it about with him. I suggested that it might be safer in my keeping than in his, and that I had better means than salt for preserving it. On realizing that I really intended to keep it carefully, his opposition vanished instantly. 'But remember, sahib,' said he, 'I shall want it back when I am dead.' I laughed at the remark, and so the matter ended. I returned to my practice, and he no doubt in the course of time was able to continue his journey to Afghanistan.

'Well, as I told you last night, I had a bad fire in my house at Bombay. Half of it was burned down, and, among other things, my pathological collection was largely destroyed. What you see are the poor remains of it. The hand of the hillman went with the rest, but I gave the matter no particular thought at the time. That was six years ago.

'Four years ago – two years after the fire – I was awakened one night by a furious tugging at my sleeve. I sat up under the impression that my favourite mastiff was trying to arouse me. Instead of this, I saw my Indian patient of long ago, dressed in the long grey gown which was the badge of his people. He was holding up his stump and looking reproachfully at me. He then went over to my bottles, which at that time I kept in my room, and he examined them carefully, after which he gave a gesture of anger and vanished. I realized that he had just died, and that he had come to claim my promise that I should keep his limb in safety for him.

'Well, there you have it all, Dr Hardacre. Every night at the same hour for four years this performance has been repeated. It is a simple thing in itself, but it has worn me out like water dropping on a stone. It has brought a vile insomnia with it, for I cannot sleep now for the expectation of his coming. It has poisoned my old age and that of my wife, who has been the sharer in this great trouble. But there is the breakfast gong, and she will be waiting impatiently to know how it fared with you last night. We are both much indebted to you for your gallantry, for it takes something from the weight of our misfortune when we share it, even for a single night, with a friend, and it reassures us as to our sanity, which we are sometimes driven to question.'

This was the curious narrative which Sir Dominick confided to me – a story which to many would have appeared to be a grotesque impossibility, but which, after my experience of the night before, and my previous knowledge of such things, I was prepared to accept as an absolute fact. I thought deeply over the matter, and brought the whole range of my reading and experience to bear upon it. After breakfast, I surprised my host and hostess by announcing that I was returning to London by the next train.

'My dear doctor,' cried Sir Dominick in great distress, 'you make me feel that I have been guilty of a gross breach of hospitality in intruding this unfortunate matter upon you. I should have borne my own burden.'

'It is, indeed, that matter which is taking me to London,' I answered; 'but you are mistaken, I assure you, if you think that my experience of last night was an unpleasant one to me. On the contrary, I am about to ask your permission to return in the evening and spend one more night in your laboratory. I am very eager to see this visitor once again.'

My uncle was exceedingly anxious to know what I was about to do, but my fears of raising false hopes prevented me from telling him. I was back in my own consulting room a little after luncheon, and was confirming my memory of a passage in a recent book upon occultism which had arrested my attention when I read it.

'In the case of earth-bound spirits,' said my authority, 'some one dominant idea obsessing them at the hour of death is sufficient to hold them to this material world. They are the amphibia of this life and of the next, capable of passing from one to the other as the turtle passes from land to water. The causes which may bind a soul so strongly to a life which its body has abandoned are any violent emotion. Avarice, revenge, anxiety, love, and pity have all been known to have this effect. As a rule it springs from some unfulfilled wish, and when the wish has been fulfilled the material bond relaxes. There are many cases upon record which show the singular persistence of these visitors, and also their disappearance when their wishes have been fulfilled, or in some cases when a reasonable compromise has been effected.'

'*A reasonable compromise effected*' – those were the words which I had brooded over all the morning, and which I now verified in the original. No actual atonement could be made here – but a reasonable compromise! I made my way as fast as a train could take me to the Shadwell Seamen's Hospital, where my old friend Jack Hewett was house-surgeon. Without explaining the situation I made him understand exactly what it was that I wanted.

'A brown man's hand!' said he, in amazement. 'What in the world do you want that for?'

'Never mind. I'll tell you some day. I know that your wards are full of Indians.'

'I should think so. But a hand——' He thought a little and then struck a bell.

'Travers,' said he to a student-dresser, 'what became of the hands of the Lascar which we took off yesterday? I mean the fellow from the East India Dock who got caught in the steam winch.'

'They are in the post-mortem room, sir.'

'Just pack one of them in antiseptics and give it to Dr Hardacre.'

And so I found myself back at Rodenhurst before dinner with this curious outcome of my day in town. I still said nothing to Sir Dominick, but I slept that night in the laboratory, and I placed the Lascar's hand in one of the glass jars at the end of my couch.

So interested was I in the result of my experiment that sleep was out of the question. I sat with a shaded lamp beside me and waited patiently for my visitor. This time I saw him clearly from the first. He appeared beside the door, nebulous for an instant, and then hardening into as distinct an outline as any living man. The slippers beneath his grey gown were red and heelless, which accounted for the low, shuffling sound which he made as he walked. As on the previous night he passed slowly along the line of bottles until he paused before that which contained the hand. He reached up to it, his whole figure quivering with expectation, took it down, examined it eagerly, and then, with a face which was convulsed with fury and disappointment, he hurled it down on the floor. There was a crash which resounded through the house, and when I looked up the mutilated Indian had disappeared. A moment later my door flew open and Sir Dominick rushed in.

'You are not hurt?' he cried.

'No – but deeply disappointed.'

He looked in astonishment at the splinters of glass, and the brown hand lying upon the floor.

'Good God!' he cried. 'What is this?'

I told him my idea and its wretched sequel. He listened intently, but shook his head.

'It was well thought of,' said he, 'but I fear that there is no such easy end to my sufferings. But one thing I now insist upon. It is that you shall never again upon any pretext occupy this room. My fears that something might have happened to you – when I heard that crash – have been the most acute of all the agonies which I have undergone. I will not expose myself to a repetition of it.'

He allowed me, however, to spend the remainder of that night where I was, and I lay there worrying over the problem and lamenting my own failure. With the first light of morning there was the Lascar's hand still lying upon the floor to remind me of my fiasco. I lay looking at it – and as I lay suddenly an idea flew like a bullet through my head and brought me quivering with excitement out of my couch. I raised the grim relic from where it had fallen. Yes, it was indeed so. The hand was the *left* hand of the Lascar.

By the first train I was on my way to town, and hurried at once to the Seamen's Hospital. I remembered that both hands of the Lascar had been amputated, but I was terrified lest the precious organ which I was in search of might have been already consumed in the crematory. My suspense was soon ended. It had still been preserved in the post-mortem room. And so I returned to Rodenhurst in the evening with my mission accomplished and the material for a fresh experiment.

But Sir Dominick Holden would not hear of my occupying the laboratory again. To all my entreaties he turned a deaf ear. It offended his sense of hospitality, and he could no longer permit it. I left the hand, therefore, as I had done its fellow the night before, and I occupied a comfortable bedroom in another portion of the house, some distance from the scene of my adventures.

But in spite of that my sleep was not destined to be uninterrupted. In the dead of night my host burst into my room, a lamp in his hand. His huge gaunt figure was enveloped in a loose dressing-gown, and his whole appearance might certainly have seemed more formidable to a weaknerved man than that of the Indian of the night before. But it was not his entrance so much as his expression which amazed me. He had turned suddenly younger by twenty years at least. His eyes were shining, his features radiant, and he waved one hand in triumph over his head. I sat up astounded, staring sleepily at this extraordinary visitor. But his words soon drove the sleep from my eyes.

'We have done it! We have succeeded!' he shouted. 'My dear Hardacre, how can I ever in this world repay you?'

'You don't mean to say that it is all right?'

'Indeed I do. I was sure that you would not mind being awakened to hear such blessed news.'

'Mind! I should think not indeed. But is it really certain?'

'I have no doubt whatever upon the point. I owe you such a debt, my dear nephew, as I have never owed a man before, and never expected to. What can I possibly do for you that is commensurate? Providence must have sent you to my rescue. You have saved both my reason and my life, for another six months of this must have seen me either in a cell or a coffin. And my wife – it was wearing her out before my eyes. Never could I have believed that any human being could have lifted this burden off me.' He seized my hand and wrung it in his bony grip.

'It was only an experiment – a forlorn hope – but I am delighted from my heart that it has succeeded. But how do you know that it is all right? Have you seen something?'

He seated himself at the foot of my bed.

'I have seen enough,' said he. 'It satisfies me that I shall be troubled no more. What has passed is easily told. You know that at a certain hour this creature always comes to me. Tonight he arrived at the usual time, and aroused me with even more violence than is his custom. I can only surmise that his disappointment of last night increased the bitterness of his anger against me. He looked angrily at me, and then went on his usual round. But in a few minutes I saw him, for the first time since this persecution began, return to my chamber. He was smiling. I saw the gleam of his white teeth through the dim light. He stood facing me at the end of my bed, and three times he made the low Eastern salaam which is their solemn leave-taking. And the third time that he bowed he raised his arms over his head, and I saw his *two* hands outstretched in the air. So he vanished, and, as I believe, for ever.'

* * *

So that is the curious experience which won me the affection and the gratitude of my celebrated uncle, the famous Indian surgeon. His anticipations were realized, and never again was he disturbed by the visits of the restless hillman in search of his lost member. Sir Dominick and Lady Holden spent a very happy old age, unclouded, so far as I know, by any trouble, and they finally died during the great influenza epidemic within a few weeks of each other. In his lifetime he always turned to me for advice in everything which concerned that English life of which he knew so little; and I aided him also in the purchase and development of his estates. It was no great surprise to me, therefore, that

I found myself eventually promoted over the heads of five exasperated cousins, and changed in a single day from a hard-working country doctor into the head of an important Wiltshire family. I at least have reason to bless the memory of the man with the brown hand, and the day when I was fortunate enough to relieve Rodenhurst of his unwelcome presence.

The Phantom Coach
Amelia B. Edwards

The circumstances I am about to relate to you have truth to recommend them. They happened to myself, and my recollection of them is as vivid as if they had taken place only yesterday. Twenty years, however, have gone by since that night. During those twenty years I have told the story to but one other person. I tell it now with a reluctance which I find it difficult to overcome. All I entreat, meanwhile, is that you will abstain from forcing your own conclusions upon me. I want nothing explained away. I desire no arguments. My mind on this subject is quite made up, and, having the testimony of my own senses to rely upon, I prefer to abide by it.

Well! It was just twenty years ago, and within a day or two of the end of the grouse season. I had been out all day with my gun, and had had no sport to speak of. The wind was due east; the month, December; the place, a bleak wide moor in the far north of England. And I had lost my way. It was not a pleasant place in which to lose one's way, with the first feathery flakes of a coming snow-storm just fluttering down upon the heather, and the leaden evening closing in all around. I shaded my eyes with my hand, and stared anxiously into the gathering darkness, where the purple moorland melted into a range of low hills, some ten or twelve miles distant. Not the faintest smoke-wreath, not the tiniest cultivated patch, or fence, or sheep-track, met my eyes in any direction. There was nothing for it but to walk on, and take my chance of finding what shelter I could, by the way. So I shouldered my gun again, and pushed wearily forward; for I had been on foot since an hour after daybreak, and had eaten nothing since breakfast.

Meanwhile, the snow began to come down with ominous steadiness, and the wind fell. After this, the cold became more intense, and the night came rapidly up. As for me, my prospects darkened with the darkening sky, and my heart grew heavy as I thought how my young wife was already watching for me through the window of our little inn parlour, and thought of all the suffering in store for her throughout this weary night. We had been married four months, and, having spent our autumn in the Highlands, were now lodging in a remote little village situated just on the verge of the great English moorlands. We were very much in love, and, of course, very happy. This morning, when we parted, she had implored me to return before dusk, and I had promised her that I would. What would I not have given to have kept my word!

Even now, weary as I was, I felt that with a supper, an hour's rest, and a guide, I might still get back to her before midnight, if only guide and shelter could be found.

And all this time, the snow fell and the night thickened. I stopped and shouted every now and then, but my shouts seemed only to make the silence deeper. Then a vague sense of uneasiness came upon me, and I began to remember stories of travellers who had walked on and on in the falling snow until, wearied out, they were fain to lie down and sleep their lives away. Would it be possible, I asked myself, to keep on thus through all the long dark night? Would there not come a time when my limbs must fail, and my resolution give way? When I, too, must sleep the sleep of death. Death! I shuddered. How hard to die just now, when life lay all so bright before me! How hard for my darling, whose whole loving heart – but that thought was not to be borne! To banish it, I shouted again, louder and longer, and then listened eagerly. Was my shout answered, or did I only fancy that I heard a far-off cry? I hallooed again, and again the echo followed. Then a wavering speck of light came suddenly out of the dark, shifting, disappearing, growing momentarily nearer and brighter. Running towards it at full speed, I found myself, to my great joy, face to face with an old man and a lantern.

'Thank God!' was the exclamation that burst involuntarily from my lips.

Blinking and frowning, he lifted his lantern and peered into my face.

'What for?' growled he, sulkily.

'Well – for you. I began to fear I should be lost in the snow.'

'Eh, then, folks do get cast away hereabouts fra' time to time, an' what's to hinder you from bein' cast away likewise, if the Lord's so minded?'

'If the Lord is so minded that you and I shall be lost together, friend, we must submit,' I replied; 'but I don't mean to be lost without you. How far am I now from Dwolding?'

'A gude twenty mile, more or less.'

'And the nearest village?'

'The nearest village is Wuke, an' that's twelve mile t'other side.'

'Where do you live, then?'

'Out yonder,' said he, with a vague jerk of the lantern.

'You're going home, I presume?'

'Maybe I am.'

'Then I'm going with you.'

The old man shook his head, and rubbed his nose reflectively with the handle of the lantern.

'It ain't o' no use,' growled he. 'He 'ont let you in – not he.'

'We'll see about that,' I replied, briskly. 'Who is He?'

'The master.'

'Who is the master?'

'That's nowt to you,' was the unceremonious reply.

'Well, well; you lead the way, and I'll engage that the master shall give me shelter and a supper tonight.'

'Eh, you can try him!' muttered my reluctant guide; and, still shaking his head, he hobbled, gnome-like, away through the falling snow. A large mass loomed up presently out of the darkness, and a huge dog rushed out, barking furiously.

'Is this the house?' I asked.

'Ay, it's the house. Down, Bey!' And he fumbled in his pocket for the key.

I drew up close behind him, prepared to lose no chance of entrance, and saw in the little circle of light shed by the lantern that the door was heavily studded with iron nails, like the door of a prison. In another minute he had turned the key and I had pushed past him into the house.

Once inside, I looked round with curiosity, and found myself in a great raftered hall, which served, apparently, a variety of uses. One end was piled to the roof with corn, like a barn. The other was stored with flour-sacks, agricultural implements, casks, and all kinds of miscellaneous lumber; while from the beams overhead hung rows of hams, flitches, and bunches of dried herbs for winter use. In the centre of the floor stood some huge object gauntly dressed in a dingy wrapping-cloth, and reaching halfway to the rafters. Lifting a corner of this cloth, I saw, to my surprise, a telescope of very considerable size, mounted on a rude movable platform, with four small wheels. The tube was made of painted wood, bound round with bands of metal rudely fashioned; the speculum, so far as I could estimate its size in the dim light, measured at least fifteen inches in diameter. While I was yet examining the instrument, and asking myself whether it was not the work of some self-taught optician, a bell rang sharply.

'That's for you,' said my guide, with a malicious grin. 'Yonder's his room.'

He pointed to a low black door at the opposite side of the hall. I crossed over, rapped somewhat loudly, and went in, without waiting for an invitation. A huge, white-haired old man rose from a table covered with books and papers, and confronted me sternly.

'Who are you?' said he. 'How came you here? What do you want?'

'James Murray, barrister-at-law. On foot across the moor. Meat, drink and sleep.'

He bent his bushy brows into a portentous frown.

'Mine is not a house of entertainment,' he said, haughtily. 'Jacob, how dared you admit this stranger?'

'I didn't admit him,' grumbled the old man. 'He followed me over the muir, and shouldered his way in before me. I'm no match for six foot two.'

'And pray, sir, by what right have you forced an entrance into my house?'

'The same by which I should have clung to your boat, if I were drowning. The right of self-preservation.'

'Self-preservation?'

'There's an inch of snow on the ground already,' I replied, briefly; 'and it would be deep enough to cover my body before daybreak.'

He strode to the window, pulled aside a heavy black curtain, and looked out.

'It is true,' he said. 'You can stay, if you choose, till morning. Jacob, serve the supper.'

With this he waved me to a seat, resumed his own, and became at once absorbed in the studies from which I had disturbed him.

I placed my gun in a corner, drew a chair to the hearth, and examined my quarters at leisure. Smaller and less incongruous in its arrangements than the hall, this room contained, nevertheless, much to awaken my curiosity. The floor was carpetless. The whitewashed walls were in parts scrawled over with strange diagrams, and in others covered with shelves crowded with philosophical instruments, the uses of many of which were unknown to me. On one side of the fireplace, stood a bookcase filled with dingy folios; on the other, a small organ, fantastically decorated with painted carvings of medieval saints and devils. Through the half-opened door of a cupboard at the further end of the room, I saw a long array of geological specimens, surgical preparations, crucibles, retorts and jars of chemicals; while on the mantelshelf beside me, amid a number of small objects, stood a model of the solar system, a small galvanic battery and a microscope. Every chair had its burden. Every corner was heaped high with books. The very floor was littered over with maps, casts, papers, tracings and learned lumber of all conceivable kinds.

I stared about me with an amazement increased by every fresh object upon which my eyes chanced to rest. So strange a room I had never seen; yet seemed it stranger still, to find such a room in a lone farmhouse amid those wild and solitary moors! Over and over again, I looked from my host to his surroundings, and from his surroundings back to my host, asking myself who and what he could be? His head was singularly fine; but it was more the head of a poet than of a philosopher. Broad in the temples, prominent over the eyes, and clothed with a rough profusion of perfectly white hair, it had all the ideality and much of the ruggedness that characterizes the head of Ludwig van Beethoven. There were the same deep lines about the mouth, and the same stern furrows in the brow. There was the same concentration of expression. While I was yet observing him, the door opened, and Jacob brought in the supper. His master then closed his book, rose and, with more courtesy of manner than he had yet shown, invited me to the table.

A dish of ham and eggs, a loaf of brown bread and a bottle of admirable sherry were placed before me.

'I have but the homeliest farmhouse fare to offer you, sir,' said my entertainer. 'Your appetite, I trust, will make up for the deficiencies of our larder.'

I had already fallen upon the viands, and now protested, with the enthusiasm of a starving sportsman, that I had never eaten anything so delicious.

He bowed stiffly, and sat down to his own supper, which consisted, primitively, of a jug of milk and a basin of porridge. We ate in silence, and, when we had done, Jacob removed the tray. I then drew my chair back to the fireside. My host, somewhat to my surprise, did the same, and turning abruptly towards me, said:

'Sir, I have lived here in strict retirement for three-and-twenty years. During that time, I have not seen as many strange faces, and I have not read a single newspaper. You are the first stranger who has crossed my threshold for more than four years. Will you favour me with a few words of information respecting that outer world from which I have parted company so long?'

'Pray interrogate me,' I replied. 'I am heartily at your service.'

He bent his head in acknowledgement; leaned forward, with his elbows resting on his knees and his chin supported in the palms of his hands; stared fixedly into the fire; and proceeded to question me.

His enquiries related chiefly to scientific matters, with the later progress of which, as applied to the practical purposes of life, he was almost wholly unacquainted. No student of science myself, I replied as well as my slight information permitted; but the task was far from easy, and I was much relieved when, passing from interrogation to discussion, he began pouring forth his own conclusions upon the facts which I had been attempting to place before him. He talked, and I listened spellbound. He talked till I believe he almost forgot my presence, and only thought aloud. I had never heard anything like it then; I have never heard anything like it since. Familiar with all systems of all philosophies, subtle in analysis, bold in generalization, he poured forth his thoughts in an uninterrupted stream, and, still leaning forward in the same moody attitude with his eyes fixed upon the fire, wandered from topic to topic, from speculation to speculation, like an inspired dreamer. From practical science to mental philosophy; from electricity in the wire to electricity in the nerve; from Watts to Mesmer, from Mesmer to Reichenbach, from Reichenbach to Swedenborg, Spinoza, Condillac, Descartes, Berkeley, Aristotle, Plato and the Magi and mystics of the East, were transitions which, however bewildering in their variety and scope, seemed easy and harmonious upon his lips as sequences in music. By and by – I forgot now by what link of conjecture or illustration – he passed on to that field which lies beyond the boundary line of even conjectural philosophy, and reaches no man knows whither. He spoke of the soul and its aspirations; of the spirit and its powers; of second sight; of prophecy; of those phenomena which, under the names of ghosts, spectres and supernatural appearances, have been denied by the sceptics and attested by the credulous, of all ages.

'The world,' he said, 'grows hourly more and more sceptical of all that lies beyond its own narrow radius; and our men of science foster the fatal tendency. They condemn as fable all that resists experiment. They reject as false all that cannot be brought to the test of the laboratory or the dissecting-room. Against what superstition have they waged so long and obstinate a war, as against the belief in apparitions? And yet what superstition has maintained its hold upon the minds of men so long and so firmly? Show me any fact in physics, in history, in archaeology, which is supported by testimony so wide and so various. Attested by all races of men, in all ages and in all climates, by the soberest sages of antiquity, by the rudest savage of today, by the Christian, the Pagan, the Pantheist, the Materialist, this phenomenon is treated as a nursery tale by the philosophers of our century. Circumstantial evidence weighs with them as a feather in the balance. The comparison of causes with effects, however valuable in physical science, is put aside as worthless and unreliable. The evidence of competent witnesses, however conclusive in a court of justice, counts for nothing. He who pauses before he pronounces, is condemned as a trifler. He who believes, is a dreamer or a fool.'

He spoke with bitterness, and, having said thus, relapsed for some minutes into silence. Presently he raised his head from his hands, and added, with an altered voice and manner,

'I, sir, paused, investigated, believed and was not ashamed to state my convictions to the world. I, too, was branded as a visionary, held up to ridicule by my contemporaries, and hooted from that field of science in which I had laboured with honour during all the best years of my life. These things happened just three-and-twenty years ago. Since then, I have lived as you see me living now, and the world has forgotten me, as I have forgotten the world. You have my history.'

'It is a very sad one,' I murmured, scarcely knowing what to answer.

'It is a very common one,' he replied. 'I have only suffered for the truth, as many a better and wiser man has suffered before me.'

He rose, as if desirous of ending the conversation, and went over to the window.

'It has ceased snowing,' he observed, as he dropped the curtain, and came back to the fireside.

'Ceased!' I exclaimed, starting eagerly to my feet. 'Oh, if it were only possible – but no! it is hopeless. Even if I could find my way across the moor, I could not walk twenty miles tonight.'

'Walk twenty miles tonight!' repeated my host. 'What are you thinking of?'

'Of my wife,' I replied, impatiently. 'Of my young wife, who does not know that I have lost my way, and who is at this moment breaking her heart with suspense and terror.'

'Where is she?'

'At Dwolding, twenty miles away.'

'At Dwolding,' he echoed, thoughtfully. 'Yes, the distance, it is true, is twenty miles; but – are you so very anxious to save the next six or eight hours?'

'So very, very anxious, that I would give ten guineas at this moment for a guide and a horse.'

'Your wish can be gratified at a less costly rate,' said he, smiling. 'The night mail from the north, which changes horses at Dwolding, passes within five miles of this spot, and will be due at a certain cross-road in about an hour and a quarter. If Jacob were to go with you across the moor, and put you into the old coach-road, you could find your way, I suppose, to where it joins the new one?'

'Easily – gladly.'

He smiled again, rang the bell, gave the old servant his directions, and, taking a bottle of whisky and a wineglass from the cupboard in which he kept his chemicals, said:

'The snow lies deep, and it will be difficult walking tonight on the moor. A glass of usquebaugh before you start?'

I would have declined the spirit, but he pressed it on me, and I drank it. It went down my throat like liquid flame, and almost took my breath away.

'It is strong,' he said; 'but it will help to keep out the cold. And now you have no moments to spare. Goodnight!'

I thanked him for his hospitality, and would have shaken hands, but that he had turned away before I could finish my sentence. In another minute I had travelled the hall, Jacob had locked the outer door behind me, and we were out on the wide white moor.

Although the wind had fallen, it was still bitterly cold. Not a star glimmered in the black vault overhead. Not a sound, save the rapid crunching of the snow beneath our feet, disturbed the heavy stillness of the night. Jacob, not too well pleased with his mission, shambled on before in sullen silence, his lantern in his hand, and his shadow at his feet. I followed, with my gun over my shoulder, as little inclined for conversation as himself. My thoughts were full of my late host. His voice yet rang in my ears. His eloquence yet held my imagination captive. I remember to this day, with surprise, how my over-excited brain retained whole sentences and parts of sentences, troops of brilliant images, and fragments of splendid reasoning, in the very words in which he had uttered them. Musing thus over what I had heard, and striving to recall a lost link here and there, I strode on at the heels of my guide, absorbed and unobservant. Presently – at the end, as it seemed to me, of only a few minutes – he came to a sudden halt, and said:

'Yon's your road. Keep the stone fence to your right hand, and you can't fail of the way.'

'This, then, is the old coach-road?'

'Ay, 'tis the old coach-road.'

'And how far do I go, before I reach the cross-roads?'

'Nigh upon three mile.'

I pulled out my purse, and he became more communicative.

'The road's a fair road enough,' said he, 'for foot passengers; but 'twas over steep and narrow for the northern traffic. You'll mind where the parapet's broken away, close again the sign-post. It's never been mended since the accident.'

'What accident?'

'Eh, the night mail pitched right over into the valley below – a gude fifty feet an' more – just at the worst bit o' road in the whole county.'

'Horrible! Were many lives lost?'

'All. Four were found dead, and t'other two died next morning.'

'How long is it since this happened?'

'Just nine year.'

'Near the sign-post, you say? I will bear it in mind. Goodnight.'

'Gude night, sir, and thankee.' Jacob pocketed his half-crown, made a faint pretence of touching his hat, and trudged back by the way he had come.

I watched the light of his lantern till it quite disappeared, and then turned to pursue my way alone. This was no longer matter of the slightest difficulty, for, despite the dead darkness overhead, the line of stone fence showed distinctly enough against the pale gleam of the snow. How silent it seemed now, with only my footsteps to listen to; how silent and how solitary! A strange disagreeable sense of loneliness stole over me. I walked faster. I hummed a fragment of a tune. I cast up enormous sums in my head, and accumulated them at compound interest. I did my best, in short, to forget the startling speculations to which I had but just been listening, and, to some extent, I succeeded.

Meanwhile the night air seemed to become colder and colder, and though I walked fast I found it impossible to keep myself warm. My feet were like ice. I lost sensation in my hands, and grasped my gun mechanically. I even breathed with difficulty, as though, instead of traversing a quiet north country highway, I were scaling the uppermost heights of some gigantic Alp. This last symptom became presently so distressing, that I was forced to stop for a few minutes, and lean against the stone fence. As I did so, I chanced to look back up the road, and there, to my infinite relief, I saw a distant point of light, like the gleam of an approaching lantern. I at first concluded that Jacob had retraced his steps and followed me; but even as the conjecture presented itself, a second light flashed into sight – a light evidently parallel with the first, and approaching at the same rate of motion. It needed no second thought to show me that these must be the carriage-lamps of some private vehicle, though it seemed strange that any private vehicle should take a road professedly disused and dangerous.

There could be no doubt, however, of the fact, for the lamps grew larger and brighter every moment, and I even fancied I could already see the dark outline of the carriage between them. It was coming up very fast, and quite noiselessly, the snow being nearly a foot deep under the wheels.

And now the body of the vehicle became distinctly visible behind the lamps. It looked strangely lofty. A sudden suspicion flashed upon me. Was it possible that I had passed the cross-roads in the dark without observing the sign-post, and could this be the very coach which I had come to meet?

No need to ask myself that question a second time, for here it came round the bend of the road, guard and driver, one outside passenger, and four steaming greys, all wrapped in a soft haze of light, through which the lamps blazed out, like a pair of fiery meteors.

I jumped forward, waved my hat, and shouted. The mail came down at full speed, and passed me. For a moment I feared that I had not been seen or heard, but it was only for a moment. The coachman pulled up; the guard, muffled to the eyes in capes and comforters, and apparently sound asleep in the rumble, neither answered my hail nor made the slightest effort to dismount; the outside passenger did not even turn his head. I opened the door for myself, and looked in. There were but three travellers inside, so I stepped in, shut the door, slipped into the vacant corner, and congrualted myself on my good fortune.

The atmosphere of the coach seemed, if possible, colder than that of the outer air, and was pervaded by a singularly damp and disagreeable smell. I looked round at my fellow-passengers. They were all three, men, and all silent. They did not seem to be asleep, but each leaned back in his corner of the vehicle, as if absorbed in his own reflections. I attempted to open a conversation.

'How intensely cold it is tonight,' I said, addressing my opposite neighbour.

He lifted his head, looked at me, but made no reply.

'The winter,' I added, 'seems to have begun in earnest.'

Although the corner in which he sat was so dim that I could distinguish none of his features very clearly, I saw that his eyes were still turned full upon me. And yet he answered never a word.

At any other time I should have felt, and perhaps expressed, some annoyance, but at the moment I felt too ill to do either. The icy coldness of the night air had struck a chill to my very marrow, and the strange smell inside the coach was affecting me with an intolerable nausea. I shivered from head to foot, and, turning to my left-hand neighbour, asked if he had any objection to an open window?

He neither spoke nor stirred.

I repeated the question somewhat more loudly, but with the same result. Then I lost my patience, and let the sash down. As I did so, the leather strap broke in my hand, and I observed that the glass was covered with a thick coat of mildew, the accumulation, apparently, of years. My attention being thus drawn to the condition of the coach, I examined it more narrowly, and saw by the uncertain light of the outer lamps that it was in the last stage of dilapidation. Every part of it was not only out of repair, but in a condition of decay. The sashes splintered at a touch. The leather fittings were crusted over with mould, and literally rotting from the woodwork. The floor was almost breaking away beneath my feet. The whole machine, in short, was foul with damp, and had evidently been dragged from some outhouse in which it had been mouldering away for years, to do another day or two of duty on the road.

I turned to the third passenger, whom I had not yet addressed, and hazarded one more remark.

'This coach,' I said, 'is in a deplorable condition. The regular mail, I suppose, is under repair?'

He moved his head slowly, and looked me in the face, without speaking a word. I shall never forget that look while I live. I turned cold at heart under it. I turn cold at heart even now when I recall it. His eyes glowed with a fiery unnatural lustre. His face was livid as the face of a corpse. His bloodless lips were drawn back as if in the agony of death, and showed the gleaming teeth between.

The words that I was about to utter died upon my lips, and a strange horror – a dreadful horror – came upon me. My sight had by this time become used to the gloom of the coach, and I could see with tolerable distinctness. I turned to my opposite neighbour. He, too, was looking at me, with the same startling pallor in his face, and the same stony glitter in his eyes. I passed my hand across my brow. I turned to the passenger on the seat beside my own, and saw – oh Heaven! how shall I describe what I saw? I saw that he was no living man – that none of them were living men, like myself! A pale phosphorescent light – the light of putrefaction – played upon their awful faces; upon their hair, dank with the dews of the grave; upon their clothes, earth-stained and dropping to pieces; upon their hands, which were as the hands of corpses long buried. Only their eyes, their terrible eyes, were living; and those eyes were all turned menacingly upon me!

A shriek of terror, a wild unintelligible cry for help and mercy, burst from my lips as I flung myself against the door, and strove in vain to open it.

In that single instant, brief and vivid as a landscape beheld in the flash of summer lightning, I saw the moon shining down through a rift of stormy cloud – the ghastly sign-post rearing its warning finger by the wayside – the broken parapet – the plunging horses – the black gulf below. Then, the coach reeled like a ship at sea. Then, came a mighty crash – a sense of crushing pain – and then, darkness.

*   *   *

It seemed as if years had gone by when I awoke one morning from a deep sleep, and found my wife watching by my bedside. I will pass over the scene that ensued, and give you, in half a dozen words, the tale she told me with tears of thanksgiving. I had fallen over a precipice, close against the junction of the old coach-road and the new, and had only been saved from certain death by lighting upon a deep snowdrift that had accumulated at the foot of the rock beneath. In this snowdrift I was discovered at daybreak, by a couple of shepherds, who carried me to the nearest shelter, and brought a surgeon to my aid. The surgeon found me in a state of raving delirium, with a broken arm and a compound fracture of the skull. The letters in my pocket-book showed my name and address; my wife was summoned to nurse me; and, thanks to youth and a fine constitution, I came out of danger at last. The place of my fall, I need scarcely say, was precisely that at which a frightful accident had happened to the north mail nine years before.

I never told my wife the fearful events which I have just related to you. I told the surgeon who attended me; but he treated the whole adventure as a mere dream born of the fever in my brain. We discussed the question over and over again, until we found that we could discuss it with temper no longer, and then we dropped it. Others may form what conclusions they please – I *know* that twenty years ago I was the fourth inside passenger in that Phantom Coach.

Don't Tell Cissie

Celia Fremlin

'Friday, then. The six-ten from Liverpool Street,' said Rosemary, gathering up her gloves and bag. 'And don't tell Cissie!' she added, 'You *will* be careful about that, won't you, Lois?'

I nodded. People are always talking like this about Cissie, she's that kind of person. She was like that at school, and now, when we're all coming up towards retirement, she's like it still.

You know the kind of person I mean? Friendly, good-hearted, and desperately anxious to be in on everything, and yet with this mysterious knack of ruining things – of bringing every project grinding to a halt, simply by being there.

Because it wasn't ever her fault. Not really. 'Let me come! Oh, *please* let me come too!' she'd beg, when three or four of us from the Lower Fourth had schemed up an illicit trip to the shops on Saturday afternoon. And, because she was our friend (well, sort of – anyway, it was *our* set that she hovered on the fringe of all the time, not anyone else's) – because of this, we usually, let her come; and always it ended in disaster. *She'd* be the one to slip on the edge of the kerb outside Woolworth's, and cut her knee so that the blood ran, and a little crowd collected, and a kind lady rang up the school to have us fetched home. *She'd* be the one to get lost ... to miss the bus ... to arrive back at school bedraggled and tear-stained and late for evening preparation, hopelessly giving the game away for all of us.

You'd think, wouldn't you, that after a few such episodes she'd have given up, or at least have learned caution. But no. Her persistence (perhaps one would have called it courage if only it hadn't been so annoying) – well, her persistence, then, was indomitable. Neither school punishments nor the reproaches of her companions ever kept her under for long. 'Oh, *please* let me come!' she'd be pleading again, barely a week after the last débâcle, 'Oh, plee-ee-ease! Oh, don't be so *mean*!'

And so there, once again, she'd inexorably be, back in action once more. Throwing up in the middle of the dormitory feast. Crying with blisters as we trudged back from a ramble out of bounds. Soaked, and shivering, and starting pneumonia from having fallen through the ice of the pond we'd been forbidden to skate on.

So you can understand, can't you, why Rosemary and I didn't want Cissie with us when we went to investigate the ghost at Rosemary's new weekend cottage. Small as our chances might be of pinning down the ghost in any case, Cissie could have been counted on to reduce them to zero. Dropping a tray of tea things just as the rapping began ... Calling out, 'What? *I* can't hear anything!' as we held our breaths trying to locate the ghostly sobbing ... Falling over a tombstone as we tiptoed through the moonlit churchyard ... No, Cissie must at all costs be kept out of our little adventure; and by now, after nearly half a century, we knew that the only way of keeping Cissie out of anything was to make sure that she knew nothing about it, right from the beginning.

*   *   *

But let me get back to Rosemary's new cottage. I say 'new', because Rosemary has only recently bought it – not because the cottage itself is new. Far from it. It is early eighteenth century, and damp, and dark, and built of the local stone, and Rosemary loves it (*did* love it, rather – but let me not get ahead of myself). Anyway, as I was saying, Rosemary loved the place, loved it on sight, and bought it almost on impulse with the best part of her life's savings. *Their* life's savings, I suppose I should say, because she and Norman are still married to each other, and it must have been his money just as much as hers. But Norman never seems to have much to do with these sort of decisions – indeed, he doesn't seem to have much to do with Rosemary's life at all, these days – certainly, he never comes down to the cottage. I think that was part of the idea, really – that they should be able to get away from each other at weekends. During the week, of course, it's all right, as they are both working full-time, and they both bring plenty of work home in the evenings. Rosemary sits in one room correcting history essays, while Norman sits in another working out export quotas, or something; and the mutual non-communication must be almost companionable, in an arid sort of a way. But the crunch will come, of course, when they both retire in a year or so's time. I think Rosemary was thinking of this when she bought the cottage; it would become a real port in a storm then – a bolthole from what she refers to as 'the last and worst lap of married life'.

At one time, we used to be sorry for Cissie, the only one of our set who never married. But now, when the slow revolving of the decades have left me a widow and Rosemary stranded among the flotsam of a dead marriage – now, lately I have begun wondering whether Cissie hasn't done just as well for herself as any of us, in the long run. Certainly, she has had plenty of fun on the fringes of other people's lives, over the years. She wangles invitations to silver-wedding parties; worms her way into other people's family holidays – and even if it ends up with the whole lot of them in quarantine at the airport because of Cissie coming out in spots – well, at least she's usually had a good run for her money first.

And, to be fair to her, it's not just the pleasures and luxuries of our lives that she tries to share; it's the problems and crises, too. I remember she managed to be present at the birth of my younger son, and if only she hadn't dropped the boiling kettle on her foot just as I went into the second stage of labour, her presence would have been a real help. As it was, the doctor and midwife were both busy treating her for shock in the kitchen, and binding up her scalded leg, while upstairs my son arrived unattended, and mercifully without fuss. Perhaps even the unborn are sensitive to atmosphere? Perhaps he sensed, even then, that, with Cissie around, it's just *no use* anyone else making a fuss about anything?

But let me get back to Rosemary's haunted cottage (or not haunted, as the case may be – let me not pre-judge the issue before I have given you all the facts). Of course, to begin with, we were half-playing a game, Rosemary and I. The tension tends to go out of life as you come up towards your sixties. Whatever problems once tore at you, and kept you fighting, and alive, and gasping for breath – they are solved now, or else have died, quietly, while you weren't noticing. Anyway, what with one thing and another, life can become a bit dull and flavourless when you get to our age; and, to be honest, a ghost was just what Rosemary and I were needing. A spice of danger; a spark of the unknown to re-activate these water-logged minds of ours, weighed down as they are by such a lifetime's accumulation of the known.

I am telling you this because I want to be absolutely honest. In evaluating the events I am to describe, you must remember, and allow for, the fact that Rosemary and I *wanted* there to be a ghost. Well, no, perhaps that's putting it too strongly; we wanted there to *might* be a ghost – if you see what I so ungrammatically mean. We wanted our weekend to bring us at least a small tingling of the blood; a tiny prickling of the scalp. We wanted our journey to reach a little way into the delicious outskirts of fear, even if it *did* have to start from Liverpool Street.

We felt marvellously superior, Rosemary and I, as we stood jam-packed in the corridor, rocking through the rainy December night. We glanced with secret pity at all those blank, commuter faces, trundling towards the security of their homes. *We* were different. *We* were travelling into the unknown.

*   *   *

Our first problems, of course, were nothing to do with ghosts. They were to do with milk, and bread, and damp firewood, and why Mrs Thorpe from the village hadn't come in to air the beds as she'd promised. She hadn't filled the lamps, either, or brought in the paraffin ... how did she think Rosemary was going to get it from the shed in all this rain and dark? And where were all those tins she'd stocked up with in the summer? They couldn't *all* have been eaten...?

I'm afraid I left it all to Rosemary. I know visitors are supposed to trot around at the heels of their hostesses, yapping helpfully, like terriers; but I just won't. After all, I know how little help it is to *me*, when I am a hostess, so why should I suppose that everyone else is different? Besides, by this time I was half frozen, what with the black, sodden fields and marsh-lands without, and the damp stone within; and so I decided to concentrate my meagre store of obligingness on getting a fire going.

What a job it was, though! It was as if some demon was working against me, spitting and sighing down the cavernous chimney, whistling wickedly along the icy, stone-flagged floor, blowing out each feeble flicker of flame as fast as I coaxed it from the damp balls of newspaper piled under the damper wood.

Fortunately there were plenty of matches, and gradually, as each of my abortive efforts left the materials a tiny bit drier than before, hope of success came nearer. Or maybe it was that the mischievous demon grew tired of his dance of obstruction – the awful sameness of frustrating me time and time again – anyway, for whatever reason, I at last got a few splinters of wood feebly smouldering. Bending close, and cupping my hands around the precious whorls to protect them from the sudden damp gusts and sputters of rain down the chimney, I watched, enchanted, while first one tiny speck of gold and then another glimmered on the charred wood. Another ... and yet another ... until suddenly, like the very dawn of creation, a flame licked upwards.

It was the first time in years and years that I had had anything to do with an open fire. I have lived in centrally-heated flats for almost all of my adult life, and I had forgotten this apocalyptic moment when fire comes into being under your hands. Like God on the morning of creation, I sat there, all-powerful, tending the spark I had created. A sliver more of wood here ... a knob of coal there ... soon my little fire was bright, and growing, and needing me no more.

But still I tended it – or pretended to – leaning over it, spreading my icy hands to the beginnings of warmth. Vaguely, in the background, I was aware of Rosemary blundering around the place, clutching in her left hand the only oil lamp that worked, peering disconsolately into drawers and cupboards, and muttering under her breath at each new evidence of disorder and depletion.

Honestly, it was no use trying to help. We'd have to manage somehow for tonight, and then tomorrow, with the coming of the blessed daylight, we'd be able to get everything to rights. Fill the lamps. Fetch food from the village. Get the place properly warm...

Warm! I shivered, and huddled closer into the wide chimney alcove. Although the fire was burning up nicely now, it had as yet made little impact on the icy chill of the room. It was cold as only these ancient, little-used cottages *can* be cold. The cold of centuries seems to be stored up in their old stones, and the idea that you can warm it away with a single brisk weekend of paraffin heaters and hastily-lit fires has always seemed to me laughable.

Not to Rosemary, though. She is an impatient sort of person, and it always seems to her that heaters *must* produce heat. That's what the word *means*! So she was first angered, then puzzled, and finally half-scared by the fact that she just *couldn't* get the cottage warm. Even in late August, when the air outside was still soft, and the warmth of summer lingered over the fields and marshes – even then, the cottage was like an ice-box inside. I remember remarking on it during my first visit – 'Marvellously cool!' was how I put it at the time, for we had just returned, hot and exhausted, from a long tramp through the hazy, windless countryside; and that was the first time (I think) that Rosemary mentioned to me that the place was supposed to be haunted.

'One of those tragic, wailing ladies that the past specializes in,' she explained, rather facetiously. 'She's supposed to have drowned herself away on the marsh somewhere – for love, I suppose; it always was, wasn't it? My God, though, what a thing to drown oneself for! – if only she'd *known*...!'

This set us off giggling, of course; and by the time we'd finished our wry reminiscences, and our speculations about the less than ecstatic love-lives of our various friends – by this time, of course, the end of the ghost story had rather got lost. Something about the woman's ghost moaning around the cottage on stormy nights (or was it moonlight ones?), and about the permanent, icy chill that had settled upon the cottage, and particularly upon the upstairs back bedroom, into which they'd carried her body, all dripping wet from the marsh.

'As good a tale as any, for when your tenants start demanding proper heating,' I remember remarking cheerfully (for Rosemary, at that time, had vague and grandiose plans for making a fortune by letting the place for part of the year) and we had both laughed, and that, it had seemed, was the end of it.

But when late summer became autumn, and autumn deepened into winter, and the North-East wind, straight from Siberia, howled in over the marshes, then Rosemary began to get both annoyed and perturbed.

'I just *can't* get the place warm,' she grumbled. 'I can't understand it! And as for that back room – the one that looks out over the marsh – it's uncanny how cold it is! Two oil heaters, burning day and night, and it's *still*...!'

I couldn't pretend to be surprised: as I say, I *expect* my friends' weekend cottages to be like this. But I tried to be sympathetic; and when, late in November, Rosemary confessed, half laughing, that she really *did* think the place was haunted, it was I who suggested that we should go down together and see if we could lay the ghost.

She welcomed the suggestion with both pleasure and relief.

'If it was just the cold, I wouldn't be bothering,' she explained. 'But there seems to be something eerie about the place – there really does, Lois! It's like being in the presence of the dead.' (Rosemary never has been in the presence of the dead, or she'd know it's not like that at all, but I let it pass.) 'I'm getting to hate being there on my own. Sometimes – I know it sounds crazy, but sometimes I really *do* seem to hear voices!' She laughed, uncomfortably. 'I must be in a bad way, mustn't I? *Hearing voices*...! *Me*...!'

To this day, I don't know how much she was really scared, and how much she was just trying to work a bit of drama into her lonely – and probably unexpectedly boring – trips down to her dream cottage. I don't suppose she even knows herself. All I can say for certain is that her mood of slightly factitious trepidation touched exactly on some deep need of my own, and at once we knew that we would go. And that it would be fun. And that Cissie must at all costs be kept out of it. Once *her* deep needs get involved, you've had it.

*   *   *

A little cry from somewhere in the shadows, beyond the circle of firelight, jerked me from my reveries, and for a moment I felt my heart pounding. Then, a moment later, I was laughing, for the cry came again:

'Spaghetti! Spaghetti Bolognese! Four whole tins of it, all stacked up under the sink! Now, *who* could have...?"

And who could care, anyway? Food, real food, was now within our grasp! Unless... Oh dear...!

'I bet you've lost the tin-opener!' I hazarded, with a sinking heart – for at the words 'Spaghetti Bolognese' I had realized just how hungry I was – and it was with corresponding relief that, in the flickering firelight, I saw a smug smile overspreading her face.

'See?' She held up the vital implement; it flickered through the shadows like a shining minnow as she gesticulated her triumph. '*See*? Though of course, if *Cissie* had been here ...!'

We both began to giggle; and later, as we sat over the fire scooping spaghetti bolognese from pottery bowls, and drinking the red wine which Rosemary had managed to unearth – as we sat there, revelling in creature comforts, we amused ourselves by speculating on the disasters which would have befallen us by now had Cissie been one of the party. How she would have dropped the last of the matches into a puddle, looking for a lost glove ... would have left the front door swinging open in the wind, blowing out our only oil lamp. And the tin-opener, of course, would have been a write-off from the word go; if she hadn't lost it in some dark corner, it would certainly have collapsed into two useless pieces under her big, willing hands... By now, we would have been without light, heat or food...

This depressing picture seemed, somehow, to be the funniest thing imaginable as we sat there, with our stomachs comfortably full and with our third helping of red wine gleaming jewel-like in the firelight.

'To absent friends!' we giggled, raising our glasses. 'And let's hope they *remain* absent.' I added, wickedly, thinking of Cissie; and while we were both still laughing over this cynical toast, I saw Rosemary suddenly go rigid, her glass an inch from her lips, and I watched the laughter freeze on her face.

'Listen!' she hissed. 'Listen, Lois! Do you *hear?*'

For long seconds, we sat absolutely still, and the noises of the night impinged, for the first time, on my consciousness. The wind, rising now, was groaning and sighing around the cottage, moaning in the chimney and among the old beams. The rain spattered in little gusts against the windows, which creaked and rattled on their old hinges. Beyond them, in the dark, overgrown garden, you could hear the stir and rustle of bare twigs and sodden leaves ... and beyond that again there was the faint, endless sighing of the marsh, mile upon mile of it, half-hidden under the dry, winter reeds.

'No...' I began, in a whisper; but Rosemary made a sharp little movement, commanding silence. '*Listen!*' she whispered once more; and this time – or was it my imagination? – I did begin to hear something.

'Ee ... ee ... ee ...!' came the sound, faint and weird upon the wind. 'Ee ... ee ... ee ...!' – and for a moment it sounded so human, and so imploring, that I, too, caught my breath. It must be a trick of the wind, of course; it *must* – and as we sat there, tensed almost beyond bearing by the intentness of our listening, another sound impinged upon our preternaturally sharpened senses – a sound just as faint, and just as far away, but this time very far from ghostly.

'Pr-rr-rr! Ch-ch-ch......!' – the sound grew nearer ... unmistakable... The prosaic sound of a car, bouncing and crunching up the rough track to the cottage.

Rosemary and I looked at each other.

'Norman?' she hazarded, scrambling worriedly to her feet. 'But it *can't* be Norman, he *never* comes! And at this time of night, too! Oh dear, I wonder what can have happened...?' By this time she had reached the window, and she parted the curtains just as the mysterious vehicle screeched to a halt outside the gate. All I could see, from where I sat, was the triangle of darkness between the parted curtains, and Rosemary's broad back, rigid with disbelief and dismay.

Then, she turned on me.

'Lois!' she hissed. 'How *could* you...!'

I didn't ask her what she meant. Not after all these years.

'I didn't! Of course I didn't! What do you take me for?' I retorted, and I don't doubt that by now my face was almost as white as hers.

For, of course, she did not need to tell me who it was who had arrived. Not after nearly half a century of this sort of thing. Besides, who else was there who slammed a car door as if slapping down an invasion from Mars? Who else would announce her arrival by yelling 'Yoo-hoo!' into the midnight air, and bashing open the garden gate with a hat-box, so that latch and socket hurtled together into the night?

'Oops – sorry!' said Cissie, for perhaps the fifty-thousandth time in our joint lives; and she blundered forward towards the light, like an untidy grey moth. For by now we had got the front door open, and lamplight was pouring down the garden path, lighting up her round, radiant face and her halo of wild grey curls, all a-glitter with drops of rain.

'You naughty things! Fancy not *telling* me!' she reproached us, as she surged through the lighted doorway, dumping her luggage to left and right. It was, as always, like a one-man army of occupation. Always, she manages to fill any situation so totally with herself, and her belongings, and her eagerness, that there simply isn't *room* for anyone else's point of view. It's not selfishness, exactly; it's more like being a walking take-over bid, with no control over one's operations.

'A real, live ghost! Isn't it thrilling!' she babbled, as we edged her into the firelit room. 'Oh, but you *should* have told me! You *know* how I love this sort of thing ...!'

On and on she chattered, in her loud, eager, unstoppable voice ... and this, too, we recognized as part of her technique of infiltration. By the time her victims have managed to get a word in edgeways, their first fine fury has already began to wilt ... the cutting edge of their protests has been blunted ... their sense of outrage has become blurred. And anyway, by that time she is *there*. Inescapably, irreversibly, *there*!

Well, what can you do? By the time Rosemary and I got a chance to put a word in, Cissie already had her coat off, her luggage spilling on to the floor, and a glass of red wine in her hand. There she was, reclining in the big easychair (mine), the firelight playing on her face, exactly as if she had lived in the place for years.

'But, Cissie, how did you find *out*?' was the nearest, somehow, that we could get to a reproof; and she laughed her big, merry laugh, and the bright wine sloshed perilously in her raised glass.

'Simple, you poor Watsons!' she declared. 'You see, I happened to be phoning Josie, and Josie happened to mention that Mary had said that Phyllis had told her that she'd heard from Ruth, and...'

See what I mean? You can't win. You might as well try to dodge the Recording Angel himself.

'And when I heard about the ghost, then of course I just *had* to come!' she went on. 'It sounded just *too* fascinating! You see, it just happens that at the moment I know a good deal about ghosts, because...'

Well, of course she did. It was her knowing a good deal about Classical Greek architecture last spring that had kept her arguing with the guide on the Parthenon for so long that the coach went off without us. And it was precisely because she'd boned up so assiduously on rare Alpine plants that she'd broken her leg trying to reach one of them a couple of years ago, and we had to call out the Mountain Rescue for her. The rest of us had thought it was just a daisy.

'Yes, well, we don't even know yet that there *is* a ghost,' said Rosemary, dampingly; but not dampingly enough, evidently, for we spent the rest of the evening – and indeed far into the small hours – trying to dissuade Cissie from putting into practice, then and there, various uncomfortable and hazardous methods of ghost-hunting of which she had recently informed herself – methods which ranged from fixing a tape-recorder on the thatched roof, to ourselves lying all night in the churchyard, keeping our minds a blank.

By two o'clock, our minds were blank anyway – well, Rosemary's and mine were – and we could think about nothing but bed. Here, though, there were new obstacles to be overcome, for not only was Cissie's arrival unexpected and unprepared-for, but she insisted on being put in the haunted room. If it *was* haunted – anyway, the room that was coldest, dampest, and most uncomfortable, and therefore entitled her (well, what can you do?) to the only functioning oil-heater, and more than her share of the blankets.

'Of course, I shan't *sleep!*' she promised (as if this was some sort of special treat for me and Rosemary). 'I shall be keeping vigil all night long! And tomorrow night, darlings, as soon as the moon rises, we must each take a white willow twig, and pace in silent procession through the garden...'

We nodded, simply because we were too sleepy to argue; but beyond the circle of lamplight, Rosemary and I exchanged glances of undiluted negativism. I mean, apart from anything else, you'd have to be crazy to embark on any project which depended for its success on Cissie's not falling over something.

But we did agree, without too much reluctance, to her further suggestion that tomorrow morning we should call on the vicar and ask him if we might look through the parish archives. Even Cissie, we guardedly surmised, could hardly wreck a call on a vicar.

But the next morning, guess what? Cissie was laid up with lumbago, stiff as a board, and unable even to get out of bed, let alone go visiting.

'Oh dear – Oh, please don't bother!' she kept saying, as we ran around with hot water bottles and extra pillows. 'Oh dear, I do so hate to be a nuisance!'

We hated her to be a nuisance, too, but we just managed not to say so; and after a bit our efforts, combined with her own determination not to miss the fun (yes, she was still counting it fun) – after a bit, all this succeeded in loosening her up sufficiently to let her get out of bed and on to her feet; and at once her spirits rocketed sky-high. She decided, gleefully, that her affliction was a supernatural one, consequent on sleeping in the haunted room.

'Damp sheets, more likely!' said Rosemary, witheringly. 'If people *will* turn up unexpectedly like this...'

But Cissie is unsquashable. *Damp sheets?* When the alternative was the ghost of a lady who'd died two hundred years ago? Cissie has never been one to rest content with a likely explanation if there is an *un*likely one to hand.

'I know what I'm talking about!' she retorted. 'I know more about this sort of thing than either of you. I'm a sensitive, you see. I only discovered it just recently, but it seems I'm one of those people with a sort of sixth sense when it comes to the supernatural. It makes me more *vulnerable*, of course, to this sort of thing – look at my bad back – but it also makes me more *aware*. I can *sense* things. Do you know, the moment I walked into this room last night, I could tell that it was haunted! I could feel the ... Ouch!'

Her back had caught her again; all that gesticulating while she talked had been a mistake. However, between us we got her straightened up once more, and even managed to help her down the stairs – though I must say it wasn't long before we were both wishing we'd left well alone – if I may put it so uncharitably. For Cissie, up, was far, far more nuisance than Cissie in bed. In bed, her good intentions could harm no one; but once up and about, there seemed no limit to the trouble she could cause in the name of 'helping'. Trying to lift pans from shelves above her head; trying to rake out cinders without bending, and setting the hearth brush on fire in the process; trying to fetch paraffin in cans too heavy for her to lift, and slopping it all over the floor. Rosemary and I seemed to be forever clearing up after her, or trying to un-crick her from some position she'd got stuck in for some maddening, altruistic reason.

*   *   *

Disturbingly, she seemed to get worse as the day went on, not better. The stiffness increased, and by afternoon she looked blue with cold, and was scarcely able to move. But nothing would induce her to let us call a doctor, or put her to bed.

'What, and miss all the fun?' she protested, through numbed lips. 'Don't you realize that this freezing cold is *significant?* It's the chilling of the air that you always get before the coming of an apparition...!'

By now, it was quite hard to make out what she was saying, so hoarse had her voice become, and so stiff her lips; but you could still hear the excitement and triumph in her croaked exhortations:

'Isn't it thrilling! This is the chill of death, you know, darlings! It's the warning that the dead person is now about to appear! Oh, I'm so thrilled! Any moment now, and we're going to know the truth...!

*   *   *

We did, too. A loud knocking sounded on the cottage door, and Rosemary ran to answer it. From where I stood, in the living-room doorway, I could see her framed against the winter twilight – already the short December afternoon was nearly at an end. Beyond her, I glimpsed the uniforms of policemen, heard their solemn voices.

'"Miss Cecily Curtis"? – Cissie? Yes, of course we know her!' I heard Rosemary saying, in a frightened voice; and then came the two deeper voices, grave and sympathetic.

I could hardly hear their words from where I was standing, yet somehow the story wasn't difficult to follow. It was almost as if, in some queer way, I'd known it all along. How last night, at about 10.30 p.m., a Miss Cecily Curtis had skidded while driving – too fast – along the dyke road, and had plunged, car and all, into deep water. The body had only been recovered and identified this morning.

As I say, I did not really need to hear the men's actual words. Already the picture was in my mind, the picture which has never left it: the picture of Cissie, all lit up with curiosity and excitement, belting through the rain and dark to be in on the fun. Nothing would keep her away, not even death itself...

A little sound in the room behind me roused me from my state of shock, and I turned to see Cissie smiling that annoying smile of hers, for the very last time. It's maddened us for years, the plucky way she smiles in the face of whatever adversity she's got us all into.

'You see?' she said, a trifle smugly, 'I've been dead ever since last night – it's no wonder I've been feeling so awful!' – and with a triumphant little toss of her head she turned, fell over her dressing-gown cord, and was gone.

Yes, gone. We never saw her again. The object they carried in, wet and dripping from the marsh, seemed to be nothing to do with her at all.

*   *   *

We never discovered whether the cottage had been haunted all along; but it's haunted now, all right. I don't suppose Rosemary will go down there much any more – certainly, we will never go ghost-hunting there again. Apart from anything else, we are too scared. There is so much that might go wrong. It was different in the old days, when we could plan just any wild escapade we liked, confident that whatever went wrong would merely be the fault of our idiotic, infuriating, impossible, irreplaceable friend.

The Horsehair Trunk
Davis Grubb

To Marius the fever was like a cloud of warm river fog around him. Or like the blissful vacuum that he had always imagined death would be. He had lain for nearly a week like this in the big corner room while the typhoid raged and boiled inside him. Mary Ann was a dutiful wife. She came and fed him his medicine and stood at the foot of the brass bed when the doctor was there, clasping and unclasping her thin hands; and sometimes from between hot, heavy lids Marius could glimpse her face, dimly pale and working slowly in prayer. Such a fool she was, a praying, stupid fool that he had married five years ago. He could remember thinking that even in the deep, troubled delirium of the fever.

'You want me to die,' he said to her one morning when she came with his medicine. 'You want me to die, don't you?'

'Marius! Don't say such a thing! Don't ever——'

'It's true, though,' he went on, hearing his voice miles above him at the edge of the quilt. 'You want me to die. But I'm not going to. I'm going to get well, Mary Ann. I'm not going to die. Aren't you disappointed?'

'No! No! It's not true! It's not!'

Now, though he could not see her face through the hot blur of fever, he could hear her crying; sobbing and shaking with her fist pressed tight against her teeth. Such a fool.

*   *   *

On the eighth morning Marius woke full of a strange, fiery brilliance as if all his flesh were glass not yet cool from the furnace. He knew the fever was worse, close to its crisis, and yet it no longer had the quality of darkness and mists. Everything was sharp and clear. The red of his necktie hanging in the corner of the bureau mirror was a flame. And he could hear the minutest stirrings down in the kitchen, the breaking of a match stick in Mary Ann's fingers as clear as pistol shots outside his bedroom window. It was a joy.

Marius wondered for a moment if he might have died. But if it was death it was certainly more pleasant than he had ever imagined death would be. He could rise from the bed without any sense of weakness and he could stretch his arms and he could even walk out through the solid door into the upstairs hall. He thought it might be fun to tiptoe downstairs and give Mary Ann a fright, but when he was in the parlour he remembered suddenly that she would be unable to see him. Then when he heard her coming from the kitchen with his medicine he thought of an even better joke. With the speed of thought Marius was back in his body under the quilt again, and Mary Ann was coming into the bedroom with her large eyes wide and worried.

'Marius,' she whispered, leaning over him and stroking his hot forehead with her cold, thin fingers. 'Marius, are you better?'

He opened his eyes as if he had been asleep.

'I see,' he said, 'that you've moved the pianola over to the north end of the parlour.'

Mary Ann's eyes widened and the glass of amber liquid rattled against the dish.

'Marius!' she whispered. 'You haven't been out of bed! You'll kill yourself! With a fever like——'

'No,' said Marius faintly, listening to his own voice as if it were in another room. 'I haven't been out of bed, Mary Ann.'

His eyelids flickered weakly up at her face, round and ghostlike, incredulous. She quickly set the tinkling glass of medicine on the little table.

'Then how——?' she said. 'Marius, how could you know?'

Marius smiled weakly up at her and closed his eyes, saying nothing, leaving the terrible question unanswered, leaving her to tremble and ponder over it for ever if need be. She was such a fool.

It had begun that way, and it had been so easy he wondered why he had never discovered it before. Within a few hours the fever broke in great rivers of sweat, and by Wednesday, Marius was able to sit up in the chair by the window and watch the starlings hopping on the front lawn. By the end of the month he was back at work as editor of the *Daily Argus*. But even those who knew him least were able to detect in the manner of Marius Lindsay that he was a changed man – and a worse one. And those who knew him best wondered how so malignant a citizen, such a confirmed and studied misanthrope as Marius, could possibly change into anything worse than he was. Some said that typhoid always burned the temper from the toughest steel and that Marius's mind had been left a dark and twisted thing. At prayer meeting on Wednesday nights the wives used to watch Marius's young

wife and wonder how she endured her cross. She was such a pretty
thing.

*   *   *

One afternoon in September, as he dozed on the bulging leather couch
of his office, Marius decided to try it again. The secret, he knew, lay
somewhere on the brink of sleep. If a man knew that – any man – he
would know what Marius did. It wasn't more than a minute later that
Marius knew that all he would have to do to leave his body was to get
up from the couch. Presently he was standing there, staring down at his
heavy, middle-aged figure sunk deep into the cracked leather of the
couch, the jowls of the face under the close-cropped moustache sagging
deep in sleep, the heart above his heavy gold watch chain beating
solidly in its breast.

I'm not dead, he thought, delighted. But here is my soul – my
damned, immortal soul standing looking at its body!

It was as simple as shedding a shoe. Marius smiled to himself,
remembering his old partner Charlie Cunningham and how they had
used to spend long hours in the office, in this very room, arguing about
death and atheism and the whither of the soul. If Charlie were still
alive, Marius thought, I would win from him a quart of the best
Kentucky bourbon in the county. As it was, no one would ever know.
He would keep his secret even from Mary Ann, especially from Mary
Ann, who would go to her grave with the superstitious belief that Marius
had died for a moment, that for an instant fate had favoured her; that
she had been so close to happiness, to freedom from him for ever. She
would never know. Still, it would be fun to use as a trick, a practical
joke to set fools like his wife at their wits' edge. If only he could *move*
things. If only the filmy substance of his soul could grasp a tumbler and
send it shattering at Mary Ann's feet on the kitchen floor some morning.
Or tweak a copy boy's nose. Or snatch a cigar from the teeth of Judge
John Robert Gants as he strolled home some quiet evening from the fall
session of the district court.

Well, it was, after all, a matter of will, Marius decided. It was his
own powerful and indomitable will that had made the trick possible in
the first place. He walked to the edge of his desk and grasped at the
letter opener on the dirty, ancient blotter. His fingers were like wisps of
fog that blew through a screen door. He tried again, willing it with all
his power, grasping again and again at the small brass dagger until at
last it moved a fraction of an inch. A little more. On the next try it
lifted four inches in the air and hung for a second on its point before it
dropped. Marius spent the rest of the afternoon practising until at last
he could lift the letter opener in his fist, fingers tight around the haft,

the thumb pressing the cold blade tightly, and drive it through the blotter so deeply that it bit into the wood of the desk beneath.

Marius giggled in spite of himself and hurried around the office picking things up like a pleased child. He lifted a tumbler off the dusty water cooler and stared laughing at it, hanging there in the middle of nothing. At that moment he heard the copy boy coming for the proofs of the morning editorials and Marius flitted quickly back into the cloak of his flesh. Nor was he a moment too soon. Just as he opened his eyes, the door opened and he heard the glass shatter on the floor.

'I'm going to take a nap before supper, Mary Ann,' Marius said that evening, hanging his black hat carefully on the elk-horn hatrack.

'Very well,' said Mary Ann. He watched her young, unhappy figure disappearing into the gloom of the kitchen and he smiled to himself again, thinking what a fool she was, his wife. He could scarcely wait to get to the davenport and stretch out in the cool, dark parlour with his head on the beaded pillow.

Now, thought Marius. Now.

And in a moment he had risen from his body and hurried out into the hallway, struggling to suppress the laughter that would tell her he was coming. He could already anticipate her white, stricken face when the pepper pot pulled firmly from between her fingers cut a clean figure eight in the air before it crashed against the ceiling.

He heard her voice and was puzzled.

'You must go,' she was murmuring. 'You musn't ever come here when he's home. I've told you that before, Jim. What would you do if he woke up and found you here!'

Then Marius, as he rushed into the kitchen, saw her bending through the doorway into the dusk with the saucepan of greens clutched in her white knuckles.

'What would you do? You must go!'

Marius rushed to her side; careful not to touch her, careful not to let either of them know he was there, listening, looking, flaming hatred growing slowly inside him.

*   *   *

The man was young and dark and well built and clean-looking. He leaned against the half-open screen door, holding Mary Ann's free hand between his own. His round, dark face bent to hers, and she smiled with a tenderness and passion that Marius had never seen before.

'I know,' the man said. 'I know all that. But I just can't stand it no more, Mary Ann. I just can't stand it thinking about him beating you up that time. He might do it again, Mary Ann. He might! He's worse, they say, since he had the fever. Crazy, I think. I've heard them say he's crazy.'

'Yes. Yes. You must go away now, though,' she was whispering frantically, looking back over her shoulder through Marius's dark face. 'We'll have time to talk it all over again, Jim. I – I know I'm going to leave him but—— Don't rush me into things, Jim dear. Don't make me do it till I'm clear with myself.'

'Why not now?' came the whisper. 'Why not tonight? We can take a steamboat to Lou'ville and you'll never have to put up with him again. You'll be shed of him for ever, honey. Look! I've got two tickets for Lou'ville right here in my pocket on the *Nancy B. Turner*. My God, Mary Ann, don't make me suffer like this – lyin' abed nights dreaming about him comin' at you with his cane and beatin' you – maybe killin' you!'

The woman grew silent and her face softened as she watched the fireflies dart their zigzags of cold light under the low trees along the street. She opened her mouth, closed it, and stood biting her lip hard. Then she reached up and pulled his face down to hers, seeking his mouth.

'All right,' she whispered then. 'All right. I'll do it! Now go! Quick!'

'Meet me at the wharf at nine,' he said. 'Tell him that you're going to prayer meeting. He'll never suspicion anything. Then we can be together without all this sneakin' around. Oh, honey, if you ever knew how much I——'

The words were smeared in her kiss as he pulled her down through the half-open door and held her.

'All right. All right,' she gasped. 'Now go! Please!'

And he walked away, his heels ringing boldly on the bricks, lighting a cigarette, the match arching like a shooting star into the darkness of the shrubs. Mary Ann stood stiff for a moment in the shadow of the porch vines, her large eyes full of tears, and the saucepan of greens grown cold in her hands. Marius drew back to let her pass. He stood then and watched her for a moment before he hurried back into the parlour and lay down again within his flesh and bone in time to be called for supper.

*　　*　　*

Captain Joe Alexander of the *Nancy B. Turner* was not curious that Marius should want a ticket for Louisville. He remembered years later that he had thought nothing strange about it at the time. It was less than two months till the elections and there was a big Democratic convention there.

Everyone had heard of Marius Lindsay and the power he and his *Daily Argus* held over the choices of the people. But Captain Alexander did remember thinking it strange that Marius should insist on seeing the passenger list of the *Nancy B.* that night and that he should ask particularly after a man named Jim. Smith, Marius had said, but there was no Smith. There was a Jim though, a furniture salesman from Wheeling: Jim O'Toole, who had reserved two staterooms, No. 3 and No. 4.

'What do you think of the Presidential chances this term, Mr Lindsay?' Captain Alexander had said. And Marius had looked absent for a moment (the captain had never failed to recount that detail) and then said that it would be Cleveland, that the Republicans were done for ever.

Captain Alexander had remembered that conversation and the manner of its delivery years later and it had become part of the tale that rivermen told in wharf boats and water-street saloons from Pittsburgh to Cairo long after that night had woven itself into legend.

Then Marius had asked for Stateroom No. 5, and that had been part of the legend, too, for it was next to the room that was to be occupied by Jim O'Toole, the furniture salesman from Wheeling.

'Say nothing,' said Marius, before he disappeared down the stairway from the captain's cabin, 'to anyone about my being aboard this boat tonight. My trip to Louisville is connected with the approaching election and is, of necessity, confidential.'

'Certainly, sir,' said the captain, and he listened as Marius made his way awkwardly down the gilded staircase, lugging his small horsehair trunk under his arm. Presently the door to Marius's stateroom snapped shut and the bolt fell to.

At nine o'clock sharp, two rockaway buggies rattled down the brick pavement of Water Street and met at the wharf. A man jumped from one, and a woman from the other.

'You say he wasn't home when you left,' the man was whispering as he helped the woman down the rocky cobbles, the two carpetbags tucked under his arms.

'No. But it's all right,' Mary Ann said. 'He always goes down to the office this time of night to help set up the morning edition.'

'You reckon he suspicions anything?'

The woman laughed, a low, sad laugh.

'He always suspicions everybody,' she said. 'Marius has the kind of a mind that always suspicions; and the kind of life he leads, I guess he has to. But I don't think he knows about us – tonight. I don't think he ever *knew* about us – ever.'

They hurried up the gangplank together. The water lapped and gurgled against the wharf, and off over the river, lightning scratched the dark rim of mountains like the sudden flare of a kitchen match.

'I'm Jim O'Toole,' Jim said to Captain Alexander, handing him the tickets. 'This is my wife——'

Mary Ann bit her lip and clutched the strap of her carpet-bag till her knuckles showed through the flesh.

'——she has the stateroom next to mine. Is everything in order?'

'Right, sir,' said Captain Alexander, wondering in what strange ways the destinies of this furniture salesman and his wife were meshed with the life of Marius Lindsay.

They tiptoed down the worn carpet of the narrow, white hallway, counting the numbers on the long, monotonous row of doors to either side.

'Goodnight, dear,' said Jim, glancing unhappily at the Negro porter dozing on the split-bottom chair under the swinging oil lantern by the door. 'Goodnight, Mary Ann. Tomorrow we'll be on our way. Tomorrow you'll be shed of Marius for ever.'

* * *

Marius lay in his bunk, listening as the deep-throated whistle shook the quiet valley three times. Then he lay smiling and relaxed as the great drive shafts tensed and plunged once forward and backward, gathering into their dark, heavy rhythm as the paddles bit the black water. The *Nancy B. Turner* moved heavily away into the thick current and headed downstream for the Devil's elbow and the open river. Marius was stiff. He had lain for nearly four hours waiting to hear the voices. Every sound had been as clear to him as the tick of his heavy watch in his vest pocket. He had heard the dry, rasping racket of the green frogs along the shore and the low, occasional words of boys fishing in their skiffs down the shore under the willows.

Then he had stiffened as he heard Mary Ann's excited murmur suddenly just outside his stateroom door and the voice of the man answering her, comforting her. Lightning flashed and flickered out again over the Ohio hills and lit the river for one clear moment. Marius saw all of his stateroom etched suddenly in silver from the open porthole. The mirror, washstand, bowl and pitcher. The horsehair trunk beside him on the floor. Thunder rumbled in the dark and Marius smiled to himself, secure again in the secret darkness, thinking how easy it would be, wondering why no one had thought of such a thing before. Except for the heavy pounding rhythm of the drive shafts and the chatter of the drinking glass against the washbowl as the boat shuddered through the water, everything was still. The Negro porter dozed in his chair under the lantern by the stateroom door. Once Marius thought he heard the lovers' voices in the next room, but he knew then that it was the laughter of the cooks down in the galley.

Softly he rose and slipped past the sleeping porter, making his way for the white-painted handrail at the head of the stairway. Once Marius laughed aloud to himself as he realized that there was no need to tiptoe with no earthly substance there to make a sound. He crept down the narrow stairway to the galley. The Negro cooks bent around the long wooden table eating their supper. Marius slid his long shadow along the wall towards the row of kitchen knives lying, freshly washed and honed, on the zinc table by the pump. For a moment, he hovered over them, dallying, with his finger in his mouth, like a child before an assortment of equally tempting sweets, before he chose the longest of them all, and the sharpest, a knife that would sheer the ham clean from a hog with one quick upward sweep. There was, he realized suddenly, the problem of getting the knife past human eyes even if he himself was invisible. The cooks laughed then at some joke one of them had made and all of them bent forward, their heads in a dark circle of merriment over their plates.

In that instant Marius swept the knife soundlessly from the zinc table and darted into the gloomy companionway. The Negro porter was asleep still, and Marius laughed to himself to imagine the man's horror at seeing the butcher's knife, its razor edge flashing bright in the dull light, inching itself along the wall. But it was a joke he could not afford. He bent at last and slipped the knife cautiously along the thread-bare rug under the little ventilation space beneath the stateroom door; and then, rising, so full of hate that he was half afraid he might shine forth in the darkness, Marius passed through the door and picked the knife up quickly again in his hand.

Off down the Ohio the thunder throbbed again. Marius stepped carefully across the worn rug towards the sleeping body on the bunk. He felt so gay and light he almost laughed aloud. In a moment it would be over and there would be one full-throated cry, and Mary Ann would come beating on the locked door. And when she saw her lover ...

*   *   *

With an impatient gesture, Marius lifted the knife and felt quickly for the sleeping, pulsing throat. The flesh was warm and living under his fingers as he held it taut for the one quick stroke. His arm flashed. It was done. Marius, fainting with excitement, leaned in the darkness to brace himself. His hand came to rest on the harsh, rough surface of the horsehair trunk.

'My God!' screamed Marius. 'My God!'

And at his cry the laughing murmur in the galley grew still and there was a sharp scrape of a chair outside the stateroom door.

'The wrong room!' screamed Marius. 'The wrong room!' And he clawed with fingers of smoke at the jetting fountain of his own blood.

Bobby
John Halkin

Down there, it was, on that stretch of motorway where they'd never had an accident before. So they told me afterwards, when they came with their questions and tried to discover what'd gone wrong. I think at first they imagined I'd done it deliberately – twisted the wheel, slewed across three lanes of traffic, skidded along the hard shoulder . . . well, you know what an accident's like. Wonder I wasn't killed, that's what they said.

Would've been, too, if I'd been wearing a seat belt. That, and the fact I had the hood down. The impact of the car when it smashed through those two fences just lifted me right out of my seat and I flew through the air like I'd been thrown by a horse. The car was a write-off.

I was a goner the moment I lost control. Have you ever been in an accident? Well, you know what it's like, then. Oh, it was all there, all clear in my head. I took decisions, I battled with the wheel, but I knew this was it, this was the one with my number on it. It's like that. Every nerve end tingling, every instinct functioning *click-click-click-click*, but *you know* inside: *Christ, this is it. I've bought it this time.*

Then, when the car threw me and I was in the air flying over that fence – it can't've been more than three or four yards, but, oh God, that was a lifetime – no coherent thought, oh, no, nothing like that. It was no longer a matter of: *What can I do? Do something, quick!* but just a question mark, a big question mark, surprise, why, why . . . ? Then the thump.

I wasn't dead, of course, that's obvious, or I wouldn't be here now. I wasn't even unconscious, not what you'd call unconscious, lying there in cow shit and thistles. *Aware* I suppose is the right word. I was aware of what was going on, though I couldn't do much about it. I remember I tried moving my head, but the clear blue sky burned into my eyes, so I let it slump back again. I made no effort to get up or anything.

Eventually, of course, they came for me, two men with a stretcher. It seemed no more than a couple of minutes, though afterwards they said I was in that field getting on for three-quarters of an hour. Apparently the ambulance had come from ten miles away. They put me on the stretcher, these two men, with me trying to catch what they were saying, thinking I should answer. Maybe I did mumble something. I don't know. It was like the sort of uneasy sleep when you think you're lying awake but really you're dreaming and your mind's in that limbo between the two, so you're not sure what's real any more.

But the pain was real, I can tell you that. The moment they started moving me I felt it jaggedly shooting through my body, first when they lifted me on the stretcher, then when they carried me across the field. They had me strapped down, of course, but I still rolled a bit to this side, a bit to that, as they took me over the uneven ground. I bit my teeth against each other to try and stop myself screaming. I still didn't know whether I screamed aloud. Inside I did, yes, I certainly screamed inside, but they didn't seem to hear. *Just put me down and leave me,* I wanted to shout. *Down on the ground. What the hell are you doing, lugging me around when I'm not in a fit state?* Then I must've passed out completely, because I don't remember the ambulance. That part of it's just blank.

We've all got gaps in our lives, haven't we? We imagine things go on, con ourselves into thinking life's a long stream of experiences, sensations, some shit or other, but there must be blanks, moments of unconsciousness. We go to bed at night and long for them to come. I know I do.

They asked me what caused the accident. Came to the hospital, two of them. One sat on the chair and took notes; the other stood at the foot of the bed. The sheets were white and very clean. The one sitting down had a grease stain on his uniform – on the tunic, or jacket, or whatever they call it – which began to worry me. I couldn't take my eyes off it in case he got too close and dirtied the bed-clothes. They had to remain spotless, that was important to me. I was still pretty dopey, I suppose. I'd a broken collar-bone, ribs, arm, and fractures in both legs. Not too serious, they said, the nurses. Soon have you patched up. And there was this young doctor in a white coat and glasses who came round twice a day, regular as clockwork: 'You'll be all right. Lucky escape. Anyone else, they'd've been dead.'

Too true, mate. Six months later, about three miles up the road. A little green VX, crushed between a pantechnicon and an articulated lorry. No Persil-white bedsheets for him.

I was telling you about the fuzz – no, these weren't fuzz, these were ordinary blokes doing a job, country police, with wives and kids, the whole domestic bit. You could see it in their eyes. Digging their gardens on their days off, ducking under the washing line ... I've nothing against them.

'Then how d'you explain the accident, Mr Brack?' Very official, the questioning. Kind and considerate, yes; after all, the bloke's flat on his back in bed with multiple bruises, broken bones, so go gently. But keep it official, we might have to book him. It's the uniform asking the questions, not the man. Right?

'How d'you explain the accident? You're driving along, good weather conditions, not too much traffic' – would I be here now if there had been? – 'no other car involved . . . And we've had a look at your vehicle. No obvious sign of any mechanical defect before the impact.'

'A blow-out,' I said.

'Hm.'

I could see what they were thinking, but I wasn't going to tell them the truth. I didn't believe the truth myself, so why should I expect them to?

'You were well clear of the bridge when it happened?'

That's this bridge where we are now. I said I was, which is true. Otherwise I might've driven straight into the . . . well, you know, the legs, the supports, whatever you call them, the things the bridge is standing on.

'Have you been in any sort of trouble lately?'

'Trouble?'

'Money trouble, perhaps? You're not married?'

'Divorced.'

'Recently?'

'Three years now. And I'm not upset about it. Didn't even bother me at the time, not all that much.'

'It hasn't been preying on your mind, then?'

'Look,' I told him, 'even if it had, that's not going to burst a front tyre for me, is it?'

You could see him working on it as he sat there, adding up two and two and getting the wrong answer because I hadn't given him everything, not the half of it. Yet what if I'd admitted I'd seen in the windscreen . . . suddenly . . . there, in the windscreen, staring at me, a big, silly face, terrified? What if I told him I'd heard a voice, a small, thin, baby voice like a two-year-old child's: 'Mama, Mama'? Ridiculous. So I played along with him.

'D'you have any difficulty paying your wife the maintenance money?'

'What maintenance money? Look, she went straight from my bed into this other guy's. There's no maintenance.'

'And you're bitter about it?'

'She's moved on from him since. A dozen times. She's that sort of girl. You don't get bitter about that sort of girl. You just take her while you can and when she goes . . . you regret it . . . but . . .'

The one who was sitting down closed his notebook, put it in his pocket, returned the chair to its proper place and then stood there looking down at me. I stared up at him the way you do when you're lying in bed unable to move. Then he told me what was on his mind.

'All four tyres on your car were flat,' he said, taking his time over it, 'but from the skid marks on the road I'd estimate that happened when you hit the fence, not before. I'm not saying you didn't have a blow-out, but the evidence isn't as clear as it might be.'

'Are you sure,' – this was the other one at the foot of the bed – 'are you sure you weren't attempting to take your own life, sir?'

If there's one thing I'm sure of, it's that. Not that I haven't thought of suicide, everybody does from time to time, but just look at that stretch of road. It's clear, unencumbered, with just a fence down the side and a flat field. Cows. You could do it on this motorway in some places, but not here. Nobody in his senses would choose this spot, would they, now? I mean, would you? You must've worked it out for yourself some time or other: *That's where I'd go if* . . . And it wouldn't be here.

So what actually happened?

It was exactly as I told you. I was driving along turning things over in my mind. Nothing serious: I produce documentary films, that's my job, and I'd been down to this sewing-machine factory to set up a week's shooting. So I was thinking about it, and other things too . . . you know . . . it's the advantage of motorways, no hidden corners to surprise you, you're free to think . . . then out of the blue, through the windscreen, I saw this face. A man's face. A young man, almost sitting on the bonnet. I've never known such terror in anybody's eyes as in that face. It was sort of oval and fleshy, not very bright, not intelligent, but scared, like he'd wandered on the road in front of me and I was about to hit him.

I swerved. I didn't stop to think the whole thing was impossible. If he'd really been on the road his face wouldn't have been so close to the windscreen, and if he'd been a grown man, solid flesh and blood, he wouldn't have spoken in that child's voice. 'Mama,' he said. 'Mama.' Like a small child.

I suppose somewhere in my mind I worked it out even while I was struggling to get the car straight again, but by that time it was too late. I ended up in hospital for a month.

I never told the police. I don't know if you can understand that. For one thing I was convinced they wouldn't believe me, and I think I was right there. At best I'd've been sent to the psychiatric ward. I hadn't been drinking either, so don't get that idea. If I'd told the police a story like that, their reaction would've been exactly like yours – he's either pulling our legs or he's round the twist. Well, I'm neither.

Because there was one other thing in the back of my mind. Not at first, but in hospital while I was lying there in that white bed with nothing else to do but stare at the ceiling. I'd read about something like this. In a newspaper. And not all that long ago. I couldn't remember the details, of course, and to tell you the truth I wasn't a hundred per cent convinced I hadn't made it all up. A hospital can do odd things to you.

Those echoing noises somewhere out of reach; the brisk nurses, friendly, sulky; the doctors who may speak to you, or may not, according to which side they got out of bed that morning. It's an odd atmosphere. Then if you haven't got the use of your limbs either, you're held there like some biological specimen, with only your mind free to wander. Which it does, too.

But when I got out I followed it up. The press cuttings library didn't seem to have all that much on road accidents, apart from the big multiple crashes and heavy stuff – statistical analyses, Government policy statements, and so on. I suppose there are just too many ordinary smashes to make it worthwhile filing every one. So I tried a different tack, this time going for the ESP angle. I'd heard stories of police being called to pile-ups which'd never happened, and always on the same spot, so I got on to one of the societies that investigate this sort of thing and, sure enough, they had the cutting.

It'd been not two miles away from where I work, which explains how I'd remembered it. I must've seen it in the local paper, not in one of the nationals. A young woman'd been crossing the road when a car'd suddenly swerved and hit her. She was killed and the driver was charged. As it happens, he got off, because all the witnesses agreed they'd seen the woman unexpectedly run forward shouting something, and he couldn't possibly have avoided her. But why did he swerve in the first place?

This is where his story matched mine. He told the court a man'd stepped right in front of the car, just not looking where he was going. The driver'd braked hard, trying to avoid him – and hit the woman. Yes, he'd also heard her shout a warning. The only trouble was, none of the witnesses remembered this man; according to them, the road'd been clear. 'I stopped the car and thought I heard a child calling "Mama",' he said, 'but I couldn't see any children.'

I didn't tell the ESP people about my own little hallucination, but I did ask them if they'd any other cases of this kind on record. That child's voice worried me. A figure through the windscreen ... well, that could've been anything. A reflection, even. Or maybe the driver'd nodded off for a moment. Maybe I had, too. But why the child's voice? They hunted about a bit in their index of odd happenings but didn't come up with anything, though they were able to give me the names and addresses of the dead woman and the driver.

I went to see him. He was a sensitive sort of man in his fifties. Thin, nervous, and constantly twitching behind those big round glasses he was wearing. I think he was some sort of clerk. Anyway, he said he'd sold the car and hadn't driven since. It takes some people that way. After a lot of persuasion, really working hard on him, I got him to describe what he'd seen. 'A big, round, smooth face, it was,' he told me. 'What you might call a "baby-face". I thought it was a child at first, before I saw he was a fully grown man.'

'What would you say if I told you I'd seen exactly the same person just before my accident?'

He flinched, stepped back and started to close the front door. 'I don't want anything more to do with it. I was cleared by the court. You've no right coming here questioning me like this.'

I wasn't going to be put off so easily. 'The woman shouted a warning. What was it? What did she say?' I'd wedged my foot firmly in the door.

'Bobby. That's all. Just the name, Bobby. Now will you please go away?'

Nothing more to be got out of him, I thought, so I went round to the address where the young woman had lived, thinking maybe someone would remember her. I wasn't too hopeful, though, because of the press cutting which had described her as 'Sarah Snow, 28, a lonely sort of girl who didn't get on with people'.

The street had new council flats down one side and a row of decaying Edwardian villas along the other. I was looking for number 17, which I spotted immediately because it was so much more neglected than the rest. Its grimy windows were heavily curtained, every one of them closed, and dirty milk bottles were clustered on the unwashed step. One of the two bell-pushes had a name by it, so I pressed it.

After a moment I heard someone shuffling inside and the sound of bolts being pulled back. The door opened and a short, thin-faced woman squinted at me. She was about sixty-odd, wearing a frayed, wrap-around apron and with her swollen feet stuck into old slippers.

'Yes?'

'Mrs Robinson?' I asked, that being the name on the bell-push.

She looked at me suspiciously for a moment and then nodded. 'Oh, it's about the flat, is it?' I didn't contradict. 'You'd better come in, then.'

Well, it was as good a way as any to get her talking, so I played along with it and stepped past her into the stale air of that dark hallway. It was hard to see in the gloom, and I almost collided with a pram at the foot of the stairs as I stood aside to let her go up first.

'It's on the top floor,' she explained in a long-suffering voice as though she were doing me some great favour. 'You'll find it a bit on the cold side because it's been empty for some time, but it's not damp. Miss Snow would've complained if it'd been damp.'

'Miss Snow?' I played dumb.

'Had the flat before you.'

She climbed the stairs slowly and painfully, holding on to the shaky banisters. The lino was worn and treacherous. A real death-trap, those stairs. I followed, thinking the flat could hardly be colder than the rest of the house. Outside, it was a mild winter day with pale sunshine; inside, the chill seemed to ooze out of the very plaster and brickwork. And the accumulated smells of decades hung lifelessly in the air.

At last we reached the shabby little three-roomed flat at the top. The old woman was right: it *was* several degrees colder. She pulled back one of the curtains and let in just enough light for me to be able to see the faded brown wallpaper and junk-shop furniture.

'It's a nice flat,' she said. 'Miss Snow always commented what a nice flat it was.'

Through the door I felt I could almost reach out and touch the memory of her, it was so intense.

'Killed in a motor accident. Oh, a lovely girl she was, really lovely, though she had her queer ways, I'll admit that. She was crossing the road, shopping. They never stop for you, these drivers.'

The old woman's squinting eye followed me as I walked through the flat, peering into cupboards and behind doors. In the wardrobe I found a couple of Sarah's dresses, straight and decent. A thick skirt, sort of tweedy. A pair of sensible shoes. And on the bedside table, paperbacks. Heart-throb stories. And a photograph.

'This her? Yes, she's nice-looking.'

Pale lips pulled into a nervous smile. Carefully set hair artificially waved. Glasses.

'The agency send you, did they?'

'That's right,' I lied.

'I usually insist on a girl, but I told them I don't mind a man this time. It's been empty, you see, since the accident. Meant to get rid of all that stuff, but somehow I don't like to.' She sat down on the lumpy sofa. 'And, of course, there's Bobby.'

'Bobby?'

A momentary fear twisted my stomach. You know, when you've had an accident it leaves a mark. You keep telling yourself it won't happen again, events don't repeat themselves, not like that, but who are you kidding?

'She called him Bobby.' The old woman began to laugh, just sat there laughing with her hands folded in her lap. 'She got *me* talking to him as well. I quite slipped into the habit of it. But when I'm here by myself . . . well, it's company, isn't it?'

'Who was he?'

'Bobby? That depends.'

Depends on what? I wanted to scream at her but I let it pass and waited for her to go on in her own time.

'She came home crying one night. I asked her what was the matter, made her a cup of tea, and she told me she was going to have a baby. Real upset, she was. Thought I was going to turn her out – as if I'd do a thing like that! I mean, as long as she could afford the extra rent she could stay here till Doomsday for all I cared. I'm not one to cast a stone. Not that I wasn't surprised, I mean, she wasn't the sort to go with men, but she'd got to know someone who'd kissed her and ... put his arm around her, maybe ... nothing more, I'd swear to that. And there was she imagining the worst had happened!

'Anyway, the upshot was she went to the doctor and he said she wasn't expecting at all, but she wouldn't believe him. Stubborn? Once she'd got an idea into her head there was no talking to her. And she swelled up as well – it really looked like she was going to have this baby. The doctor did tests, examined her, had her at the hospital, but he still said she wasn't. So she stopped going to him.

'A false pregnancy, he called it, but Miss Snow would never accept that. She'd started it, she was going through with it. Came home with that pram one day, and bit by bit she got all the things together. Then when it was due she called me up here ... and ...'

'You delivered the baby?'

She squinted at me, smiling and shaking her head, 'I said you'd call me a silly old woman. Well, I've been through a lot in my time; getting on for seventy, I am. Of course I helped her. I couldn't exactly see the baby, not what you'd call *see* it, but when she took it in her arms and her face lit up with that big, happy smile, I *had* to tell her it was lovely. I didn't have the heart to do otherwise.'

He was still there in that squalid little flat, I knew it in my bones as Mrs Robinson talked on. But in what form? Sarah Snow'd brought him into the world as a baby, fed him, bathed him, put him out in the pram, done all the things any woman does. Then she became afraid he might be stolen from the pram when she left it outside the supermarket, so it wasn't long before she imagined him old enough to walk and play. That way she could take him in with her. And one afternoon a week or so later she came back from the pictures flushed with pleasure and excitement, explaining to Mrs Robinson how nice it was to go out with her grown-up son and how she was able to talk to him now he was so big.

She believed in his existence so strongly, and the power of her imagination was so great, Mrs Robinson also began to feel his warm presence in that cold morgue of a house. And welcome it. Baby, toddler, little boy, grown-up son: Bobby took on whatever shape was needed at the moment. He was all of them simultaneously.

I can only make a guess at what happened on the day of the accident. There's no hard evidence. Thinking over everything Mrs Robinson told me, I've arrived at a possible reconstruction. It frightened me a bit at first, though I've learned to accept it now.

Sarah Snow'd gone out to the shops, taking Bobby with her. He was probably a small boy, trotting along happily at her side and perhaps playing with a ball. The ball rolled into the road, and Bobby ran after it.

Then his mother saw the oncoming car and dashed forward to try and save him. 'Bobby!' She was killed, as we know, but Bobby survived. He was deprived, isolated, bewildered – a new-born baby, a child, a man . . . which?

Can you imagine what it must've been like for him, cut off from his mother by that monster machine? Perhaps he was only a projection, however intense, of Sarah Snow's mind. Yet that mind was no longer there.

I was probably lost in thought working all this out and hadn't noticed Mrs Robinson was standing up again. 'That's given you something to think about,' she was saying, and she seemed amused. 'You haven't spoken a word for the last five minutes.'

I didn't know what to say. 'I'm sorry, I . . .'

'I'll go downstairs and put the kettle on. You'd like a cup of tea, I expect, and we can talk about the rent. Take your time looking round the flat.'

I hardly saw her go. Somewhere, I felt, he was waiting. I went into the bedroom. Quietly. I didn't want to alarm him. 'Bobby . . . ?'

There was no longer much coating on the back of the wardrobe mirror and the glass was scratched, so his face wasn't too clear. But I recognized it all the same as the one I'd seen in the windscreen before my accident: the lovechild whose love had changed to hatred.

*   *   *

I often come up here to this bridge over the motorway where I can watch the traffic. I like motorways. They cut straight through the countryside in good clear lines. No mystery, nothing complicated.

See that petrol tanker down there? The gradient's slowing him down. And the white Rolls-Royce . . . sleek, isn't it. Rich.

Should we, Bobby? The Rolls, eh?

Oh, beautiful! Right across the lanes of traffic and under the wheels of the tanker! Hear the crunch? And the van that ran into them from behind? There's more, look – those two Minis! A multiple crash! Bobby, it's a work of art this time, a real work of art! It's beautiful!

Eh, Bobby?

Ghost of Honour
Pamela Hansford-Johnson

'Of course, it isn't as it should be,' said Mrs St Pancreas, as she showed Robertson into the Great Hall; 'I mean, restoring's a lost art these days, isn't it? The Dennistouns' place is much more picturesque than this; but then theirs was in better repair and didn't have to be pulled down and shored up. Anyway, we have got a ghost.'

'No!' said Robertson.

'But we have! We see him very often.'

'And do you,' he enquired, 'like that?'

'Well,' she answered, rather apologetically, 'it isn't as if he does any harm – sometimes, in fact, he's quite entertaining – so we have to like it. I don't imagine that he'd go if we didn't. Still, I expect you'll hear him before dinner.'

'Hear him?' Robertson turned a little sick.

'Yes. You see—— Oh, here's Henry.'

Mr St Pancreas shook hands with Robertson. 'Nice to meet you again. Have any difficulty finding the way here? How do you like the house? Cost me a bit, but I do like atmosphere.'

'You must get it from what your wife was telling me.'

Mrs St Pancreas gazed into her velvet lap. 'I had to mention the ghost to him, Harry, or he'd wonder who was playing the organ.'

'Not an organ!' Robertson wished he were dead.

'Yes. You see, he always likes to amuse himself for half an hour or so before dinner by playing little tunes, and people think it odd if we don't explain beforehand.'

'Why does he behave like this, and who is he? Is there a legend?'

'Oh, of sorts,' Mr St Pancreas answered deprecatingly. 'The Dunbow family weren't aristocrats, or anything like that, so it isn't a very exciting one.'

'Please tell me about it,' Robertson bowed his head, for he wished to learn the worst. Mr St Pancreas looked at his wife. She looked back at her husband, her eyes troubled. 'Shall we tell him, Harry?'

'Go ahead.'

'Well, you see, the Dunbows were all successful actors on the comedy stage, and they appear to have been very popular in their day. We have quite a lot of old theatre programmes in the library, mouldering old things, you know, with their names printed on them and the parts they played.'

'Shakespeare?'

'Not exactly. As far as I can gather, they played in farce and sung crude comic songs. You know what they were at that time. Well, as I was telling you, they were all actors. The best of the lot, apparently, was Jeremiah, who is going to play the organ to us before dinner. He was a jolly man, but he had, unfortunately, a very bad temper. He used to dramatize every situation; I believe his wife and children had to put up with the most appalling scenes, all about nothing. If he hadn't dramatized his own death, we shouldn't ...'

'... Have to endure him now,' Mr St Pancras put in, forgetting himself.

'Sh-sh-h!' His wife glanced up at the minstrels' gallery. 'Do be careful, dear. I'd hate to put him out of temper. As I was saying, Mr Robertson, he dramatized his death. You see, he was a martyr to indigestion. This gave him a very red face – his contemporaries used to call him "Beefy" Dunbow, which sounds like somebody in the society papers today, doesn't it? – and if he wasn't very careful with his diet, he got heartburn. You can trace all that in the letters we've found relating to the family. Well, this made a good deal of trouble for his wife. She had to buy him the most delicate foods which cost a great deal – I believe, incidentally, that they were up to their ears in debt – and he had a special leaning towards expensive fish. This had to be personally selected and boned by his wife before he would touch it.'

'To cut a long story short,' said Mr St Pancras, who seemed to be listening for something, 'one day Mistress Dunbow had the misfortune to leave quite a large bone in a sole which she had fried for her husband. She might have done it purposely; if she did, more power to her elbow, but that's all by the way. Of course Jeremiah, who, at I always suspect, ate far too quickly, had to get it stuck in his throat. He started choking and choking, and his face grew so red and blue that they were all scared our of their wits. Staggering away from the table, he managed to gasp out – what exactly was it that he managed to gasp out, Agatha?'

She fumbled in her evening bag. 'Wait a minute, dear; I've got it down. I always keep it scribbled on an envelope, Mr Robertson, because people do like to have things accurate, and my memory is so poor. Here we are. He said: "Mistress, you have taken my life away. My blood be on this roof-tree for evermore. Until the fall of this house I will walk within it, and when the last brick crumbles to dust I will walk the site of it. Only one grain of mercy will I leave with you: never shall living soul behold my face"; and as far as I know,' she added, 'nobody ever has.'

'Seems a great deal for a choking man to say, doesn't it?' said Robertson, with a light laugh. He hoped that they would remember and admire, in after years, his courageous acceptance of the legend of Jeremiah.

Mr St Pancreas moistened his lips. 'His descendants probably elaborated the story. Anyway, there it is for what it's worth. Personally, I rather like the fellow. He gives no trouble, except that I'm not keen on organs, and it does add to the atmosphere, don't you agree?'

Robertson agreed. 'Oh, quite. And has he got a special room to haunt?'

'Certainly not,' said Mrs St Pancreas cheerfully. 'He just goes wherever he likes, bless him!'

'What does he play, hellish fugues?'

'Oh no, nothing like that. Quite jolly pieces sometimes, aren't they, Agatha? He's got a sense of humour, too. He's progressive, anyway – wants to learn, if you know what I mean. For instance, I went into the library last night, and there he was, with his back to me, of course, reading my bound volume of *Punch!* Can't dislike a fellow who does that, can you? By the way, do you mind ghosts? Perhaps I should have asked you before.'

'No,' answered Robertson, in a little voice.

'That's fine, because I expect you'll see a good bit of him during the weekend. We'd miss old Jerry if he went, wouldn't we, dear?'

'We would,' she answered vaguely, because she, too, was listening.

'What's that?' cried Robertson. He had heard the rushing of a great wind.

'Oh, that.' Mr St Pancreas smiled. 'He's blowing up the pipes, or whatever you call it. You can't see him; he's just round the corner of the gallery. Ah, here we go!'

The music swelled up, filling every corner of the hall.

'Pretty little thing,' Robertson said carelessly, bracing himself against the back of his chair; 'song by Lawes, I think. He plays very well. Good technique, if a trifle *rubato*.'

'He tried to play some modern stuff last week. Agatha and I left some Gershwin on the organ just to see what he'd do, but he can't sight-read very well. He soon stopped trying, and went back to his "Up-the-Middle-and-Down-Again" tunes.'

'Would you like to have a look at him?' asked Mrs St Pancreas diffidently. 'He won't mind a bit, and you may as well meet him now as later. He never turns round, of course, so there's nothing to be afraid of.'

'Not a bit,' agreed her husband. 'Come along up.'

'Perhaps he won't like a stranger to stare at him,' Robertson mumbled.

'Silly!' said Mrs St Pancreas, slapping him playfully, with a wink to her husband that he might not be jealous.

Robertson arose. 'All right,' he said, 'lead on.'

'We'll go up the stairs to the gallery and round the corner,' Mr St Pancreas smiled. 'Careful of the steps, old man; they're slippery.'

They went up. Robertson hung back a little. 'Perhaps he's sensitive. You go. I shouldn't like to make things awkward for you.'

'You'd like to meet our friend, wouldn't you, Jerry?' Mr St Pancreas called out.

The music stopped for a second.

'Someone laughed,' Robertson said.

'He did, I expect. That means it's okay. Come on. No need to be scared. Just round this corner and there we are.'

But when they had rounded the bend and the music was deafening in their ears, Robertson shut his eyes.

'Go on, look,' said Mrs St Pancreas. 'It's nearly dinner-time, and he'll be off again before we know where we are. I haven't the least idea where he goes to, but it's quite amusing to watch him disappear.'

Robertson looked. He saw, seated on the long stool before the instrument, a fattish bundle of grave clothes. There was an old cape on the shoulders and a nightcap on the head. Of the actual body only the feet were visible, soft white feet on the pedals, a little dirty between the toes as if mould still clung to them. The figure rocked and swayed in an ecstasy of abandonment, pressing the keys joyfully with its swaddled fingers.

'Aren't you afraid he'll turn round?' Robertson whispered. Then he felt a terrible dropping in his belly for the ghost had stopped playing.

'Not he,' said Mr St Pancreas bluffly, 'he's a man of his word,' and Robertson fancied that his voice was conciliatory. Then Jeremiah started again, playing with unusual relish a fughetta by John Blow. 'Nearly dinner-time,' Mrs St Pancreas murmured; 'this will be the last item.'

And so it was. The ghost took his hands from the keyboard. Again there came the sound of a tearing wind, as if a quantity of excess air in the instrument were seeking release. The cape on Jeremiah's shoulders arose to whirl round his head in a cloud of grey dust. Robertson sneezed so violently that his head was jerked down. When he raised it again, the ghost had gone.

'That's that,' said Mrs St Pancreas. She stopped to examine the pedals. 'How I do wish he wouldn't leave his nasty mould about; it makes such a lot of work for the maids! Never mind. I suppose we mustn't complain. He's very nice in all other respects.'

The dinner-gong rang.

'Good!' said Mr St Pancreas, his face creased with contentment. 'I'm hungry, and I haven't got indigestion like Jerry. Come along, Robertson, and I hope you like duck.'

They spent a pleasant enough evening. Mr St Pancreas told Robertson how he had made all his money, which was very useful to know, and Mrs St Pancreas turned the wireless on and off, discovering several strange new stations uncharted in any radio news. Robertson drank a great deal of very excellent Dunbow port, which his host had acquired with the property. After the meal he told a good many humorous stories and related some lengthy reminiscences, for he was not eager to go to bed, but kind Mrs St Pancreas, perceiving his reluctance, hastened to reassure him. He might have no fear, she said, because she had seen the ghost in his room the previous night, and Jeremiah seldom visited the same place twice in succession. Mr St Pancreas, who was an understanding man, gave Robertson a bottle of port to take to bed with him. 'Perhaps we shouldn't have asked you to come here really, old man, but we've got so used to Jerry Dunbow that we never imagine anybody being scared.'

'I'm not scared,' Robertson said. 'After all, one can get used to anything, and I'm having a new experience at least.' The port was mellow within him. 'Don't you imagine I'm scared of you, Massa Dunbow!' he roared, hardily cupping his hands to his mouth that Jeremiah, if he were still in the gallery, might hear him plainly.

'I shouldn't do that if I were you, old boy,' murmured Mr St Pancreas nervously. 'According to the legends he's a bit touchy. Well, cheerio, and sleep well. Don't forget your medicine.'

Robertson said goodnight to Mrs St Pancreas and went upstairs with his host. 'Oh, by the by,' said the latter, as they turned into the left wing, 'you can see Jerry's face even if he won't show it. Here's his picture.' He held up a candle. He had refused to have the house electrified, for he liked the atmosphere.

'Oh, this is he, is it?' remarked Robertson, staring up at the portrait of a jolly gentleman in a lemon-coloured periwig. 'Looks rather fun, doesn't he? Fat, too. Can't see his eyes for cheeks. I'll bet he hit the bottle in his day.'

Mr St Pancreas pushed him gently into his room. 'Goodnight,' he said. 'See you tomorrow.'

So mellow was the port that Robertson did not even say, 'I hope you will.'

He shut the door. His allotted room was pleasant by night, colourfully furnished by Mrs St Pancreas with regard to no particular period and lavishly candle-lit. He was relieved to see that there was no four-poster but a low divan bed, and that there were no portraits on the walls. He examined the few bad water-colours to reassure himself that none of them had any sinister intent, and got into bed. He remembered to his annoyance that he had not blown out the candles. 'Let them burn out,' he thought, and he covered his head with the quilt.

He slept very beautifully until three o'clock in the morning, when Jeremiah came in and stood by the bed.

Robertson, waking out of a deep sleep, knew that he was there, but he made no sign. He lay under the sheets, his fists clenched, his legs stretched stiffly to the bedrail, that he might feel himself strong. 'He will go,' he thought. 'He must. He'll be certain to disappear when he thinks he has no power to wake me.'

Then he heard a sound in the room. Jeremiah was whistling a merry catch. 'I won't stir,' Robertson whispered to himself, feeling the sweat on his cheeks. 'When he's gone through all his tricks he'll leave me alone.'

Jeremiah sang. He sang a song about Clarinda and False Chloe. It was a dubious song, well suited to the fat voice. If he were a little flat, it was no more than might be expected, seeing that the ghost had had no practice for nearly three hundred years.

Jeremiah began to get angry. He had been a popular figure on the stage in his day, and now he was getting no appreciation at all. Also, he disliked the way Robertson had addressed him. He recited a lewd little poem. Robertson knew that his cheeks were so blown out by annoyance that the small eyes were almost invisible.

Jeremiah pulled at the quilt. Robertson cried out. His heart dropped through his stomach, his flesh froze. Then he was suddenly calm, no longer afraid. There was a long silence. He heard the click of the door. After a time the wind rose in the organ, and the drone of a cold *pavan* filled the halls and the winding galleries. Mr and Mrs St Pancreas, lying in the west bedrooms, heard nothing.

Jeremiah came back. Robertson raised the quilt. As he opened his eyes, his lashes brushed the folds of the dusty cerements. He got out of the other side of the bed and stood at the foot of it. The candles still burned brightly, spiralling up to the moulded ceiling. He looked at Jeremiah, at his fat red face, at his small, sunken mouth. A streak of yellowish hair blew from under the night-cap to flutter in the draught of the open door.

Master of himself, Robertson bowed. 'Mr Dunbow,' he said calmly, triumphantly, 'you are not, I fear, a man of your word. I think you promised that never should living soul behold your face. I have you, as I believe they said somewhere around your day or a little before, on the hip.'

Walking to the dressing-table, he searched there for cigarettes and matches. He wondered if Jeremiah had been addicted, at any time, to tobacco. If so, he would hand him a pipe and there would be a pretty story to tell his hosts in the morning. He fumbled under the bed for his slippers, for his feet were very cold.

Then Jeremiah spoke. 'So I did,' he said, and he smiled happily, for he was dramatizing the moment. 'So I did, in truth,' he lisped, offering his arm, 'and I have not broken it. You died of fright – let me see, some fifteen minutes ago. Shall we proceed, sir?'

Monkshood Manor

L. P. Hartley

'He's a strange man,' said Nesta.

'Strange in what way?' I asked.

'Oh, just neurotic. He has a fire-complex or something of the kind. He lies awake at night thinking that a spark may have jumped through the fireguard and set the carpets alight. Then he has to get up and go down to look. Sometimes he does this several times a night, even after the fire has gone out.'

'Does he keep an open fire in his own house?' I asked.

'Yes, he does, because it's healthier, and other people like it, and he doesn't want to give way to himself about it.'

'He sounds a man of principle,' I observed.

'He is,' my hostess said. 'I think that's half the trouble with Victor. If he would let himself go more he wouldn't have these fancies. They are his sub-conscious mind punishing him, he says, by making him do what he doesn't want to. But somebody has told him that if he could embrace his neurosis and really enjoy it——'

I laughed.

'I don't mean in that way,' said Nesta severely. 'What a mind you have, Hugo! And he conscientiously tries to. As if anyone could enjoy leaving a nice warm bed and creeping down cold passages to look after a fire that you pretty well know is out!'

'Are you sure that it *is* a fire he looks at?' I asked. 'I can think of another reason for creeping down a cold passage and embracing what lies at the end of it.'

Nesta ignored this.

'It's not only fires,' she said, 'it's gas taps, electric light switches, anything that he thinks might start a blaze.'

'But seriously, Nesta,' I said, 'there might be some method in his madness. It gives him an alibi for all sorts of things besides love-making: theft, for instance, or murder.'

'You say that because you don't know Victor,' Nesta said. 'He's almost a Buddhist – he wouldn't hurt a fly.'

'Does he want people to know about his peculiarity?' I asked. 'I know he's told you——'

'He does and he doesn't,' Nesta answered.

'It's obvious why he doesn't. It isn't so obvious why he does,' I observed.

'It's rather complicated,' Nesta said. 'I doubt if your *terre-à-terre* mind would understand it. The whole thing is mixed up in his mind with guilt——'

'There you are!' I exclaimed.

'Yes, but not real guilt. And he thinks that if someone caught him prowling about at night they might——'

'I should jolly well think they would!'

'And besides, he doesn't want to keep it a secret, festering. He would rather people laughed at him.'

'Laugh!' I repeated. 'I can't see that it's a laughing matter.'

'No, it isn't really. It all goes back to old Oedipus, I expect. Most men suffer from that, more or less. I expect you do, Hugo.'

'Me?' I protested. 'My father died before I was born. How could I have killed him?'

'You don't understand,' said Nesta, pityingly. 'But what I wanted to say was, if you should hear an unusual noise at night——'

'Yes?'

'Or happen to see somebody walking about——'

'Yes?'

'You'll know it's nothing to be alarmed at. It's just Victor, taking what he calls his safety precautions.'

'I'll count three before I fire,' I said.

*   *   *

Nesta and I had been taking a walk before the other weekend guests arrived.

The house came into sight, long and low with mullioned windows, crouching beyond the lawn. This was my first visit to Nesta's comparatively new home. She was always changing houses. Leaving the subject of Victor we talked of the other guests, of their matrimonial intentions, prospects or entanglements. Our conversation had the pre-war air which Nesta could always command.

'Is Walter here?' I asked. Walter was her husband.

'No, he's away shooting. He doesn't come here very much, as you know. He never cared for Monkshood, I don't know why. Oh, by the way, Hugo,' she went on, 'I've an apology to make to you. I never put any books in your room. I know you're a great reader, but——'

'I'm not,' I said. 'I go to bed to sleep.'

She smiled. 'Then that's all right. Would you like to see the room?'

I said I would.

'It's called the Blue Bachelor's room, and it's on the ground floor.'
We joked a bit about the name.

'Bachelors are always in a slight funk,' I said, 'because of the design-
ing females stalking them. But why didn't you give the room to Victor?
It might have saved him several journeys up and down stairs.'

'It's rather isolated,' she said. 'I know you don't mind that, but he
does.'

'Was that the real reason?' I asked, but she refused to answer.

I didn't meet Victor Chisholm until we assembled for drinks before
dinner. He was a nondescript looking man, neither dark nor fair, tall nor
short, fat nor thin, young nor old. I didn't have much conversation with
him, but he seemed to slide off any subject one brought up – he didn't
drop it like a hot coal, but after a little blowing on it, for politeness' sake,
he quietly extinguished it. At least that was the impression I got. He
smiled quite a lot, as though to prove he was not unsociable, and then
retired into himself. He seemed to be saving himself up for something – a
struggle with his neurosis, perhaps. After dinner we played bridge, and
Victor followed us into the library, half meaning to play, I think; but
when he found there was a four without him he went back into the
drawing-room to join the three non-bridge-playing members of the
party. We sat up late trying to finish the last rubber, and I didn't see him
again before we went to bed. The library had a large open fireplace in
which a few logs were smouldering over a heap of wood-ash. The room
had a shut-in feeling, largely because the door was lined with book-
bindings to make it look like shelves, so that when it was closed you
couldn't tell where it was. Towards midnight I asked Nesta if I should
put another log on and she said carelessly, 'No. I shouldn't bother –
we're bound to get finished sometime, if you'll promise not to overbid,
Hugo,' which reminded me of Victor and his complex. So when at last
we did retire I said meaningly, 'Would you like me to take a look at the
drawing-room fire, Nesta?'

'Well, you might, but it'll be out by this time,' she said.

'And the dining-room?' I pursued, glancing at the others, to see if
there was any reaction, which there was not. She frowned slightly and
said, 'The dining-room's electric. We only run to two real fires,' and
then we separated.

*   *   *

In spite of my boasting, for some reason I couldn't get to sleep. I tossed to
and fro, every now and then turning the light on to see what time it was.
My bedroom walls were painted dark blue, but by artificial light they
looked almost black. They were so shiny and translucent that when I sat
up in bed I could see my reflection in them, or at any rate my shadow. I

grew tired of this and then it occurred to me that if I had a book I might read myself to sleep – it was one of the recognized remedies for insomnia. But I hadn't: there were two book-ends – soap-stone elephants, I remember, facing each other across an empty space. I gave myself till half past two, then I got up, put on my dressing-gown and opened my bedroom door. All was in darkness. The library lay at the other end of the long house and to reach it I had to cross the hall. I had no torch and didn't know where the switches were, so my progress was slow. I tried to make as little noise as possible, then I remembered that if Nesta heard me she would think I was Victor Chisholm going his nightly rounds. After this I grew bolder and almost at once found the central switch panel at the foot of the staircase. This lit up the passage to the library. The library door was open and in I went, automatically fumbling for the switch. But no sooner had my hand touched the wall than it fell to my side, for I had a feeling that I was not alone in the room. I don't know what it was based on, but something was already implicit in my vision before it became physically clear to me; a figure at the far end of the room, in the deep alcove of the fireplace, bending, almost crouching over the fire. The figure had its back to me and was so near to the fire as to be almost in it. Whether it made a movement or not I couldn't tell, but a spurt of flame started up against which the figure showed darker than before. I knew it must be Victor Chisholm and I stifled an impulse to say 'Hallo!' – from a confused feeling that like a sleep-walker he ought not to be disturbed; it would startle and humiliate him. But I wanted a book, and my groping fingers found one. I withdrew it from the shelf, but not quite noiselessly, for with the tail of my eye I saw the figure move.

Back in my room I wondered if I ought to have left the hall lights on for Victor's return journey, but at once concluded that as he hadn't turned them on himself, he knew his way well enough not to need them. A sense of achievement possessed me: I had caught my fellow guest out, and I had got my book. It turned out to be the fourth volume of John Evelyn's *Diary*; but I hadn't read more than a few sentences before I fell asleep.

*　　*　　*

When I met Victor Chisholm at breakfast I meant to ask him how he had slept. It was an innocent, conventional enquiry, but somehow I couldn't bring myself to put it. Instead, we congratulated each other on the bright, frosty, late October morning, almost as if we had been responsible for it. Presently the two other men joined us, but none of the ladies of the party, and lacking their conversational stimulus we relapsed into silence over our newspapers.

But I didn't want to keep my adventure to myself, and later in the morning, when I judged that Nesta would not be preoccupied with household management, I waylaid her.

'Your friend Victor Chisholm has been on the tiles again,' I began, and before she could get a word in I told her the story of last night's encounter. Half-way through I was afraid it might fall flat, for, after all, her guest's peculiarities were no news to her; but it didn't. She looked surprised and faintly worried.

'I oughtn't to have told you,' I said with assumed contrition, 'but I thought it would amuse you.'

She made an effort to smile.

'Oh well, it does,' she said, and then her serious look came back. 'But there's one thing that puzzles me.'

'What's that?'

'He told me he had had a very good night.'

'Oh well, he would say that. It's only civil if you're staying in someone's house. I should have said the same if you had asked me, only I thought you would want to hear about Victor.'

Nesta didn't take this up.

'But we know each other much too well,' she said, arguing with herself. 'Victor comes down here – well, he comes pretty often, and he *always* tells me if he's been taking his security measures. I can't understand it.'

Why does she seem so upset? I asked myself. Does she care more for Victor than she admits? Is she distressed by the thought that he should lie to her? Does she suspect him of infidelity?

'Oh, I expect he thought that for once he wouldn't bother you,' I said.

'You're quite sure it was Victor?' she asked, with an effort.

I opened my eyes.

'Who else could it have been?'

'Well, somebody else looking for a book.'

I said I thought this most unlikely. 'Besides, he wasn't looking for a book. He was looking at the fire – I think he stirred it with his foot.'

'Stirred it with his foot?'

'Well, something made a flame jump up.'

Nesta said nothing, but looked more anxious than before.

Hoping to make her say something that would enlighten me, I observed jokingly:

'But he's come to the right place. I saw a row of buckets in the hall and one of those patent fire-extinguishers——'

'Oh, Walter insisted on having them,' said Nesta, hurriedly. 'This is a very old house, you know, and we have to take reasonable precautions. Having a fire-complex doesn't mean there isn't such a thing as having a fire, any more than having persecution mania means there isn't such a thing as persecution.'

Then I remembered something.

'If he doesn't want to be taken for a burglar,' I said, 'why doesn't he turn on the lights?'

'But he does turn them on,' said Nesta, 'just for that reason.'

I shook my head.

'He didn't turn them on last night.'

*   *   *

The problem of Victor's nocturnal ramblings exercised me and made me unsociable. I never enjoy desultory conversation, and our pre-luncheon chit-chat seemed to me unusually insipid. So when the meal was over I excused myself from playing golf, though I had brought my clubs with me, and announced that I was going to have a siesta as I had slept badly. There was a murmur of sympathy, but Nesta made no comment and no one, least of all Victor, betrayed uneasiness.

In the middle of the afternoon I woke up and had an idea. I strode down to the village to search out the oldest inhabitant. To my surprise I found him, or his equivalent, digging in his front garden. Leaning over the wall I engaged him in conversation; and very soon he told me what I had somehow expected to hear, like so many pieces of knowledge that one picks up, it was difficult to act upon, and I rather wished I had never heard it. What chiefly intrigued me was the question: did Victor know what I knew? It was clear, I thought, that Nesta did. But had she told him?

I did not think that I could ask her, it would seem too like prying; besides if she had wanted to tell me, she would have told me. What I had heard could be held to explain a good many things.

My secret gnawed at me and made the social contacts of the party seem unreal, as though I were a Communist in a Government office, my only accomplice being the head of the Department.

Suddenly, after tea I think it was, the conversation turned my way.

'Is the house haunted, Nesta?' asked one of the visitors, a woman, who like myself was a stranger to the house. 'It ought to be – it wouldn't be complete without a ghost!'

I watched Nesta as she answered carefully, 'No, I'm afraid I must disappoint you – it isn't.' And I watched Victor Chisholm, but he kept what might have been called his poker face – if it had been sinister, which it was not. The speaker wasn't to be satisfied; she returned to the charge more than once, suggesting various phantoms suitable to Monkshood Manor; but Nesta disowned them all, finally suppressing them with a yawn. One by one, on various pretexts, the company disbanded, and Victor Chisholm and I were left alone.

'I once stayed in a country house that was said to be haunted,' I remarked chattily.

'Oh, did you?' he said, with his air of being politely pleased to listen, while he was saving himself up for something in which one had no concern: 'was it fun?'

'Well, not exactly fun,' I said, 'I'll tell you about it if you can bear to hear. The house was an old one, like this, and the land on which it stood had belonged to the Church. Well, after the Dissolution of the Monasteries they pulled the Abbey, or whatever it was, down, and used some of the stones for building this house I'm telling you about. Nobody could stop them. But one of the old monks who had fallen into poverty, as a result of being dissolved, and who remembered the bygone days when they feasted and sang and wassailed and got fat and clapped each other on the back in the way you see in the pictures – he felt sore about it, and on his deathbed he laid a curse on the place and swore that four hundred years later he would come back from wherever he was and set fire to it.'

I watched Victor Chisholm for some sign of uneasiness but he showed none and all he said was:

'Do you think a ghost could do that? I've always understood that it wasn't very easy to set a house on fire. It isn't very easy to light a fire, is it, when it's been laid for the purpose, with paper and sticks and so on.'

This, I thought – and I congratulated myself upon my subtlety – is the voice of reassurance speaking: this is what well-meaning people tell him, and what he tells himself, hoping to calm his fears.

'I'm not up in the subject of ghosts,' I said, 'but they can clank chains and presumably some of them come from a hot place and wouldn't mind handling a burning brand or two. Or kicking one. That fire in the library, for instance——'

'Oh, but surely,' he said – and I saw that I had scared him – 'the library fire is absolutely safe? I – I'm sometimes nervous about fires myself, but I should never bother about that one. There's so much stone flagging around it. Do you really think——'

'I've no idea,' I said, feeling I had the answer to one of my questions. 'But my hostess at the time was certainly apprehensive. I had to worm the story out of her. It's a very usual one, of course, almost the regulation legend, very boring, really.'

'And was the house ever burnt down?' asked Victor.

'I never heard,' I said.

Of course Victor might have been dissembling. He might have known the legend of Monkshood Manor, he might have been afraid of the library fire: neurotic people are notoriously given to lying. But I didn't think so. Yet the alternative was too fantastic. I couldn't believe in it either, and gradually (for logic can sometimes be bluffed) I succeeded in disbelieving both alternatives at once.

*   *   *

Before nightfall I took the precaution of furnishing my blue room with books more interesting than Evelyn's *Diary*. But I didn't need them. I slept excellently, and so, to judge from discreet inquiries I made in the morning, did the rest of the party.

I couldn't get much out of Nesta. She rather avoided me, and for the first time in my life I felt like a policeman who must be treated with reserve in case he finds out too much. I still persuaded myself that Victor Chisholm had been and had not been in the library in the early hours of Saturday morning: if pressed, I should have said he had been. The third possibility, put forward by Nesta, that another guest had been searching for a book, I dismissed. My theory was that Nesta had a superstitious dread of a fire breaking out at Monkshood Manor and was keeping Victor in ignorance while she availed herself of his services as a night-watchman without warning him of the risk he ran.

Risk? There was no risk: yet I vaguely felt that I ought to do something about it, so I tried to make my social prevail over my private conscience and throw myself into the collective life of a week-end party. I thought about the form my coming Collins would take, and wondered if I ought to apologize for being a dull guest. In the meantime I could search Nesta out and make amends for something that I felt had been slightly critical in my attitude towards her.

My quest took me to the library. Nesta was not there but someone was – a housemaid on her hands and knees working vigorously at the carpet with a dust-pan and brush.

'Good heavens!' I exclaimed, surprised into speech by the sight of such antiquated cleaning methods; 'haven't you got a vacuum-cleaner?'

The maid, who was pretty, looked up and said:

'Yes, but it won't bring these marks out.'

'Really?' I said. 'What sort of marks are they?'

'I don't know,' said the maid. 'But they look like footmarks.'

I bent down: they did look like footmarks, but they had another peculiarity which for some reason I refrained from commenting on. Instead I said, glancing at the fireplace:

'It looks as though someone had been paddling in the ashes.'

'That's what I think,' she said, leaning back to study the marks on the carpet.

'Well, it's clean dirt,' I observed, 'and should come off all right.'

'Yes, it should,' she agreed. 'But it doesn't. It's my belief that it's been *burnt* in.'

'Oh no!' I assured her, but curiosity overcame me, and I, too, got down on my hands and knees, and buried my nose in the carpet.

'Hugo, what are you doing?' said Nesta's voice behind me.

I jumped up guiltily.

'What were you doing?' she repeated almost sternly.

I had an inspiration.

'To tell you the truth,' I said, 'I wanted to know whether this lovely Persian carpet had been dyed with an aniline dye. There's only one way to tell, you know – by licking it. Aniline tastes sour.'

'And does it?' asked Nesta.

'Not in the least.'

'I'm glad of that,' said Nesta, and leading me from the room she began to tell me the history of the carpet. This gave me an opportunity to praise the house and all its appointments.

'What treasures you have, Nesta,' I wound up, 'I hope they are fully insured.'

'Yes, they are,' she answered, rather dryly. 'But I didn't know you were an expert on carpets, Hugo.'

As soon as I could I returned to the library. The maid had done her work well: hardly a trace of the footmarks remained, and the smell of burning, which I thought I had detected, clinging to them, had quite worn off. You could still see the track they made, away from the fireplace towards the door: but they didn't reach the door or go in a direct line for it; they stopped at a point half-way between, against the inner wall, which was sheathed in books. There was nothing surprising in that: after a few steps the ashes would have been all rubbed off.

And there was another thing I couldn't see, and almost wondered if I had seen it – the mark of the big toe, which showed that the feet had been bare. Victor might have come down in his bare feet, to avoid making a noise; but it was odd, all the same, if not as odd as I had first thought it.

*   *   *

In the afternoon we went a long motor drive in two cars to have tea with a neighbour. As soon as Monkshood Manor was out of sight its problems began to fade, and in the confusion of the two parties joining forces round the tea-table they seemed quite unreal. And even when the house came into view again, stretched cat-like beyond the lawn, I only felt a twinge of my former uneasiness. By Sunday evening a week-end visit seems almost over; the threads with one's temporary residence are snapping; mentally one is already in next week. Before I got into bed I took out my diary and checked up my engagements. They were quite ordinary engagements for luncheon and dinner and so on, but suddenly they seemed extraordinarily desirable. I fixed my mind on them and went to sleep thinking about them.

I even dreamed about them, or one of them. It started as an ordinary dinner party but one of the guests was late and we had to wait for him. 'Who is he?' someone asked, and our host answered, 'I don't know, he will tell us when he comes.' Everyone seemed to accept this answer as reasonable and satisfactory, and we hung about talking and sipping cocktails until our host said, 'I don't think he can be coming after all. We won't wait any longer.' But just as we were sitting down to dinner there was a knock at the door and a voice said, 'May I come in?' And then I saw that we weren't at my friend's house in London, but back again at Monkshood, and the door that was opening was the library door, which was lined with bindings to make it look like bookshelves. For some reason it wasn't at the end of the wall but in the middle; and I said, 'Why is he coming in by that door?' 'Because it's the door he used to use,' somebody answered. The door was a long time opening, and seemed to be opening by itself with nobody behind it; then came a hand and a sleeve – and a figure wearing a monk's cowl.

I woke with a start and was at once aware of a strong smell. For a moment I thought it was the smell of cooking, and wondered if it could be breakfast-time. If so, the cook had burnt something, for there was a smell of burning too. But it couldn't be breakfast time for not a glimmer of light showed round the window curtains. Actually, as I discovered when I turned on my bedside lamp, it was half past two – the same hour that I had chosen for my sortie two nights before.

The smell seemed to be growing fainter, and I wondered if it could be an illusion, an effect of auto-suggestion. I opened the door and put my head into the passage and as quickly withdrew it. Not only because the smell was stronger there, but for another reason. The passage was not in darkness, as it had been the other night, for the hall lights had been turned on.

Well, let Victor see to it, I thought, whatever it is; no doubt he's on the prowl: let his be the glory. But curiosity overcame me and I changed my mind.

In the hall the smell was stronger. It seemed to come in waves, but where did it come from? My steps took me to the library. The door was open. A flickering light came through, and a smell strong enough to make my throat smart and my eyes water. I lingered, putting off the moment of going in: then I remembered the fire buckets in the hall and ran back for one. The water had a thick film of dust over it and I had an irrational feeling that it would be less effective so, and that I ought to change it. I did not do so, however, but hurried back and somehow forced myself to go into the room.

There were shadows, of course, and there was smoke, drifting about as smoke does. The two together make a shape that is almost opaque. And the shape was opaque that I saw before I saw anything else, a shape that seemed to rise from its knees beside the fireplace and glide slantwise across my vision towards the inner wall of the library. I might not have noticed it so particularly had it not recalled to me the shape of the latecomer in my dream. Before I could ask myself what it was, or meant, it had disappeared, chased perhaps from my attention by the obligation to act. I had the bucket: where should I begin? The dark mass of the big round library table was between me and the fireplace; beyond it should have been the card-table, but that I could not see. Except on the hearth no flames were visible.

Relief struggling with misgiving, I turned the light on and advanced towards the fireplace, but I stopped half-way, for lying in front of it, beside the overturned card-table, lay a body – Victor's. He was lying face downwards, curiously humped like a snail, under his brown Jaeger dressing-gown, which covered him and the floor around him. And it was from his dressing-gown, which was smouldering in patches, and stuck all over with playing cards, some of which were also alight, that the smell of burning came. Yes, and from Victor himself; for when I tried to lift him up I found beneath him a half-charred log, a couple of feet long, which the pressure of his body had almost extinguished, but not quite, and from which I could not at once release him, so deeply had it burnt into his flesh.

But the Persian carpet, being on the unburnt, underside of the log, was hardly scorched.

Afterwards, the explanation given was that the log had toppled off the fireplace and rolled on to the carpet; and Victor, coming down on a tour of inspection, had tripped over it and died of shock before being burnt. The evidence of shock was very strong, the doctor said. I don't know whether Nesta believed this: shortly afterwards she sold the house. I have since come to believe it, but I didn't at the time. At the time I believed that Victor had met his death defending the house against a fire-raising intruder, who, though defeated in his main object, had got the better of Victor in some peculiarly horrible way; for though one of Victor's felt slippers had caught fire, and was nearly burnt through, the other was intact, while the footprints leading to the wall – though they were fainter than they had been the other time – both showed the mark of a great toe. I pointed this out to the police who shrugged their shoulders. He might have taken his slippers off and put them on again, they said. One thing was certain: Victor had literally embraced his neurosis, and by doing so had rid himself of it for ever.

The Ankardyne Pew
W. F. Harvey

The following narrative of the occurrences that took place at
Ankardyne House in February 1890, is made up chiefly of extracts from
letters written by my friend, the Rev. Thomas Prendergast, to his wife,
immediately before taking up residence at the vicarage, together with
transcripts from the diary which I kept at the time. The names
throughout are, of course, fictitious.

February 9th. I am sorry that I had no opportunity yesterday of
getting over to the vicarage, so your questions – I have not lost the list –
must remain unanswered. It is almost a quarter of a mile away from the
church, in the village. You see, the church, unfortunately, is in the
grounds of the park, and there is a flagged passage, cold and horribly
draughty, that leads from Ankardyne House to the great loose box of
the Ankardyne pew. The squires in the old days could come in late and
go out early, or even stay away altogether, without anyone being the
wiser. The whole situation of the church is bad and typically English –
the House of God in the squire's pocket. Why should he have right of
secret access? I haven't had time to examine the interior – early
eighteenth century, I should guess – but as we drove up last evening in
the dusk, the tall gloomy façade of Ankardyne House, with the elegant
little church – a Wren's nest – adjoining it, made me think of a wicked
uncle, setting off for a walk in the woods with one of the babes. The
picture is really rather apt, as you will agree, when you see the place. It's
partly a question of the height of the two buildings, partly a question of
the shape of the windows, those of the one square, deep-set, and grim; of
the other round – the raised eyebrows of startled innocence.

We were quite wrong about Miss Ankardyne. She is a charming
little lady, not a trace of Lady Catherine de Bourgh, and is really
looking forward to having you as her nearest neighbour. I will write
more of her tomorrow, but the stable clock has struck eleven and my
candle is burning low.

February 10th. I measured the rooms as you asked me to. They are, of course, larger than ours at Garvington, and will swallow all our furniture and carpets. But you will like the vicarage. It, at least, is a cheerful house; faces south, and isn't, like this place, surrounded by woods. I suppose familiarity with the skies and wide horizons of the fens accounts for the shut-in feeling one gets here. But I have never seen such cedars!

And now to describe Miss Ankardyne. She is perhaps seventy-five, *petite* and bird-like, with the graceful, alert poise of a bird. I should say that sight and hearing are abnormally acute and have helped to keep her young. She is a good talker, well read, and interested in affairs, and a still better listener. Parson's pride! you will exclaim; since we are only two, and if she listens, I must talk. But I mean what I say. All that the archdeacon told us is true; you are conscious in her presence of a living spirit of peace. By the way, she is an interesting example of your theory that there are some people for whom animals have an instinctive dislike – indeed, the best example I have met. For Miss Ankardyne tells me that, though since childhood she has had a fondness for all living creatures, especially for birds, it is one which is not at first reciprocated. She can, after assiduous, continuous persevering, win their affection; her spaniel, her parrot, and Karkar, the tortoiseshell cat, are obviously attached to her. But strange dogs snarl, if she attempts to fondle them; and she tells me that, when she goes to the farm to feed the fowls, the birds seem to sense her coming and *run from the scattered corn*. I have heard of cows showing this antipathy to individuals, but never before of birds. There is an excellent library here, that badly needs cataloguing. The old vicar had, I believe, begun the task at the time of his fatal seizure.

I have been inside the church. Anything less like dear old Garvington it would be impossible to find. Architecturally, it has its points, but the unity of design, on which everything here depends, is broken by the Ankardyne pew. Its privacy is an abomination. Even from the pulpit it is impossible to see inside, and I can well believe the stories of the dicing squires and their Sunday play. Miss Ankardyne refuses to use it. The glass is crude and uninteresting; but there is an uncommon chancel screen of Spanish workmanship, which somehow seems in keeping with the place. I wish it didn't.

We shall miss the old familiar monuments. There is no snub-nosed crusader here, no worthy Elizabethan knight, like our Sir John Parkington, kneeling in supplication, with those nicely balanced families on right and left. The tombs are nearly all Ankardyne tombs – urns, weeping charities, disconsolate relicts, and all the cold Christian virtues. You know the sort. The Ten Commandments are painted on oak panels on either side of the altar. From the Ankardyne pew I doubt if you can see them.

February 11th. You ask about my neuritis. It is better, despite the fact that I have been sleeping badly. I wake up in the morning, sometimes during the night, with a burning headache and a curious tingling feeling about the tongue, which I can only attribute to indigestion. I am trying the effect of a glass of hot water before retiring. When we move into the vicarage, we shall at least be spared the attention of the owls, which make the nights so dismal here. The place is far too shut in by trees, and I suppose, too, that the disused outbuildings give them shelter. Cats are bad enough, but I prefer the sound of night-walkers to night-fliers. It won't be long now before we meet. They are getting on splendidly with the vicarage. The painters have already started work; the new kitchen range has come, and is only waiting for the plumbers to put it in. Miss Ankardyne is leaving for a visit to friends in a few days' time. It seems that she always goes away about this season of the year – wise woman! – so I shall be alone next week. She said Dr Hulse would be glad to put me up, if I find the solitude oppressive, but I shan't trouble him. You would like the old butler. His name is Mason, and his wife – a Scotchwoman – acts as housekeeper. The three maids are sisters. They have been with Miss Akardyne for thirty years, and are everything that maids should be. They belong to the Peculiar People. I cannot desire that they should be orthodox. If I could be sure that Dr Hulse was as well served ...

February 13th. I had an experience last night which moved me strangely. I hardly know what to make of it. I went to bed at half past ten after a quiet evening with Miss Ankardyne. I thought she seemed in rather poor spirits, and tried to cheer her by reading aloud. She chose a chapter from *The Vicar of Wakefield.* I awoke soon after one with an intolerable feeling of oppression, almost of dread. I was conscious, too – and in some way my alarm was associated with this – of a burning, tingling, piercing pain in my tongue. I got up from bed and was about to pour myself out a glass of water, when I heard the sound of someone speaking. The voice was low and continuous, and seemed to come from an adjoining room. I slipped on my dressing-gown and, candle in hand, went out into the corridor. For a moment I stood in silence. Frankly, I was afraid. The voice proceeded from a room two doors away from mine. As I listened, I recognized it as Miss Ankardyne's. She was repeating the Benedicite.

There were such depths of sadness, so much of the weariness of defeat in this song of triumph of the Three Children saved from the furnace of fire, that I felt I could not leave her. I should have spoken before knocking, for I could almost feel that gasp of fear. 'Oh, no!' she said, 'Oh, no! Not now!' and then, as if bracing herself for a great effort: 'Who is it?'

I told her and she bade me enter. The poor little woman had risen from her knees and was trembling from head to foot. I spent about an hour with her and left her sleeping peacefully. I did not wish to rouse the house, but I managed to find the Masons' room and arranged for Mrs Mason to sit by the old lady.

I can't say what happened in that hour we spent together in talk and in prayer. There is something very horrible about this house, that Miss Ankardyne is dimly aware of. Something connected with pain and fire and a bird, and something that was human too. I was shaken to the very depths of my being. I don't think I ever felt the need for prayer and the power of prayer as I did last night. The stable clock has just struck five.

February 14th. I have arranged for Miss Ankardyne to go away tomorrow. She is fit to travel, and is hardly fit to stay. I had a long talk with her this morning. I think she is the most courageous woman I know. All her life she has felt that the house is haunted, and all her life she has felt pity for that which haunts it. She says that she is sure that she is living it down; that the house is better than it was; but that at this season of the year it is almost too much for her. She is anxious that I should stay with Dr Hulse. I feel, however, that I must see this business through. She then suggested that I should invite a friend to stay with me. I thought of Pellow. You remember how we were obliged to postpone his visit last September. I had a letter from him only last Friday. He is living on this part of the world and could probably run over for a day or two.

*   *   *

The extracts from Mr Prendergast's letters end here. The following are excerpts from my diary:

February 16th. Arrived at Andardyne House at midday. Prendergast had meant to meet me at the station, but had been suddenly called away to visit a dying parishioner. I had in consequence a couple of hours by myself in which to form an impression of the place. The house dates from the early eighteenth century. It is dignified though sombre, and is closely surrounded on three sides by shrubberies of rhododendrons and laurel, that merge into thick woods. The cedars in the park must be older than any of the buildings. Miss Ankardyne, I gather, has lived here all her life, and the house gives you the impression of having been lived in, a slightly sinister mansion, well aired by a kindly soul. There is a library that should be well worth exploring. The family portraits are in the dining-room. None are of outstanding interest. The most unusual feature of the house is its connection with the church, which has many of the characteristics of a private chapel. It does not actually abut on the building, but is joined to it by a low, curved façade, unpierced by windows. A corridor, lighted from above, runs behind the façade and gives a private entry from the house to the church. The door into this corridor opens into the spacious hall of Ankardyne House; but there is a second mode of access (of which Prendergast seemed unaware) from Miss Ankardyne's bed-chamber down a narrow stair. This door is kept locked and has never been opened, as far as Mason, the butler, can recollect. The church, with the curved façade connecting it to the house, is balanced on the other side by the coach-house and stables, which can be approached in a similar manner from the kitchens. The architect has certainly succeeded in conveying the idea that religion and horseflesh can be made elegant adjuncts to the life of a country gentleman. Prendergast came in just before luncheon. He does not look well, and was obviously glad to see me and to unburden himself. In the afternoon I had a long talk with Mason, the butler, a very level-headed man.

From what Prendergast tells me I gather that Miss Ankardyne's experiences have been both auditory and visual. They are certainly vague.

Auditory. The cry of a bird – sometimes she thinks it is an owl, sometimes a cock – sometimes a human cry with something bird-like in it. This she has heard almost as long as she can remember, both outside the house and inside her room, but most frequently in the direction of the corridor that leads to the church. The cry is chiefly heard at night, hardly ever before dusk. (This would point to an owl.) It has become less frequent of recent years, but at this particular season is most persistent. Mason confirms this. He doesn't like the sound, and doesn't know what to make of it. The maids believe that it is an evil spirit; but, as it can have no power over them – they belong to the Peculiar People – they take no notice of it.

Visual and Sensory. From time to time – less frequently, again, of recent years – Miss Ankardyne wakes up 'with her eyes balls of fire.' She can distinguish nothing clearly for several minutes. Then the red spheres slowly contract to pin-pricks; there is a moment of sharp pain; and normal vision is restored. At other times she is aroused from sleep by a sharp, piercing pain in her tongue. She has consulted several oculists, who find that her sight is perfectly normal. I believe she has never known a day's illness. Prendergast seems to have had a similar, though less vivid, experience; he used the term 'burning' headache.

I have elicited from Mason the statement that animals dislike the house, with the exception of Karkar, Miss Ankardyne's cat, who seems entirely unaffected. The spaniel refuses to sleep in Miss Ankardyne's bedroom; and on one occasion, when the parrot's cage was brought up there, the bird 'fell into such a screaming fit, that it nearly brought the house down.' This I believe, for I tried the experiment myself with the reluctant consent of Mrs Mason. The feathers of the bird lay back flat on its head and neck with rage, and then it began to shriek in a really horrible way.

All this, of course, is very vague. We have no real evidence of anything supernatural. What impresses me most is the influence of the house on a woman of Miss Ankardyne's high character and courage.

February 18th. Certainly an interesting night. After a long walk with Prendergast in the afternoon I went to bed early with a volume of Trollope and a long candle. I did what I have never done before – fell asleep with the candle burning. When I awoke, it was within an inch of the socket; the fire had settled into a dull glow. Close to the candlestick on the table by my bedside stood a carafe of water. As I lay in bed, too sleepy to move, I was conscious of the hypnotic effect induced by gazing into a crystal. Slowly the surface of the glass grew dim and then gradually cleared from the centre. I was looking into the interior of a building, which I at once recognized as Ankardyne church. I could make out the screen and the Ankardyne pew. It seemed to be night, though I could see more clearly than if it had been night – the monuments in the aisle, for example. There were not as many as there are now. Presently the door of the Ankardyne pew opened and a man stepped out. He was dressed in black coat and knee-breeches, such as a clergyman might have worn a century or more ago. In one hand he held a lighted candle, the flame of which he sheltered with the other. I judged him to be of middle age. His face wore an expression of extreme apprehension. He crossed the church, casting backward glances as he went, and stopped before one of the mural monuments in the south aisle. Then, placing his candle on the ground, he drew from his pocket a hammer and some tools and, kneeling on the ground, began to work feverishly at the base of the inscription. When he had finished, and the task was not long, he seemed to moisten a finger and, running it along the floor, rubbed the dust into the newly cut stone. He then picked up his tools and began to retrace his steps. But the wind seemed to have risen; he had difficulty in shielding the flame of the candle, and just before he regained the door of the Ankardyne pew, it went out.

That was all that I saw in the crystal. I was now wide awake. I got out of bed, put fresh fuel on the fire, and wrote this account in my diary, while the picture was still vivid.

February 19th. Slept splendidly, despite the fact that I was prepared to spend a wakeful night. After a late breakfast I went with Prendergast into the church and had no difficulty in identifying the monument. It is in the east end of the south aisle, immediately opposite the Ankardyne pew and partly hidden by the American organ. The inscription reads:

IN MEMORY OF
FRANCIS ANKARDYNE, ESQUIRE,
of Ankardyne Hall, in the County of Worcester,
late Captain in His Majesty's 42nd Regiment of
Foot.
He departed this life 27th February 1781.
Rev. xiv. 12, 13.

I brought the Bible from the lectern. 'Here are lives,' said Prendergast, 'which can fitly be commemorated by such verses: "here is the patience of the saints; here are they that keep the commandments of God." Miss Ankardyne's is one. And I suppose,' he added, 'that there may be some of whom the eleventh verse is true.' He read it out to me: 'And the smoke of their torment ascendeth for ever and ever; and they have no rest day nor night, who worship the beast and his image, and whosoever receiveth the mark of his name.'

I thought at first that he was right; that the 12 might originally have been engraved as 11. But closer scrutiny showed that, though some of the figures had certainly been tampered with, it was not either the 2 or the 3. Prendergast hit on what I believe is the right solution. 'The R,' he said, 'has been superimposed on an L, and the 1 was originally 5. The reference is to Leviticus xiv. 52, 53.' If he is correct, we have still far to go. I have read and re-read those verses so often during the day, that I can write them down from memory:

'And he shall cleanse the house with the blood of the bird, and with the running water, and with the living bird, and with the cedar wood, and with the hyssop, and with the scarlet:

'But he shall let go the living bird out of the city into the open fields, and make an atonement for the house; and it shall be clean.'

Miss Ankardyne told Prendergast that she was dimly aware of something connected with pain and fire and a bird. It is at least a curious coincidence.

Mason knows nothing about Francis Ankardyne except his name. He tells me that the Ankardyne squires of a hundred years ago had a reputation for evil living; in that, of course, they were not peculiar.

Spent the afternoon in the library in a rather fruitless search for clues. I found two books with the name 'Francis Ankardyne' written on the fly-leaf. It was perhaps just as well that they should be tucked away on one of the upper shelves. One was inscribed as the gift of his cousin, Cotter Crawley. Query: Who is Crawley, and can he be identified with my man in black?

I tried to reproduce the crystal-gazing under conditions similar to those of the other night, but without success. I have twice heard the bird. It might be either an owl or a cock. The sound seemed to come from outside the house, and was not pleasant.

February 19th. Tomorrow Prendergast moves into the vicarage and I return home. Miss Ankardyne prolongs her stay at Malvern for another fortnight, and is then to visit friends on the south coast. I should like to have seen and questioned her, and so have discovered something more of the family history. Both Prendergast and I are disappointed. It seemed as if we were on the point of solving the mystery, and now it is as dark as ever. This new society in which Myers is interested should investigate the place.

So ends my diary, but not the story. Some four months after the events narrated I managed to secure through a secondhand book dealer four bound volumes of the *Gentleman's Magazine.* They had belonged to a Rev. Charles Phipson, once Fellow of Brasenose College and incumbent of Norton-on-the-Wolds. One evening, as I was glancing through them at my leisure, I came upon the following passage, under the date April 1789:

At Tottenham, John Ardenoif, Esq., a young man of large fortune and in the splendour of his carriages and horses rivalled by few country gentlemen. His table was that of hospitality, where, it may be said, he sacrificed too much to conviviality; but, if he had his foibles, he had his merits also, that far outweighed them. Mr. A. was very fond of cock-fighting and had a favourite cock upon which he won many profitable matches. The last bet he laid upon this cock he lost, which so enraged him that he had the bird tied to a spit and roasted alive before a large fire. The screams of the miserable bird were so affecting, that some gentlemen who were present attempted to interfere, which so enraged Mr. A. that he seized a poker and with the most furious vehemence declared that he would kill the first man who interposed; but, in the midst of his passionate asseverations, he fell down dead upon the spot. Such, we are assured, were the circumstances which attended the death of this great pillar of humanity.

Beneath was written:

See also the narrative of Mr. C—— at the end of this volume.

I give the story as I found it, inscribed in minute handwriting on the terminal fly-leaves:

During his last illness the Rev. Mr. C—— gave me the following account of a similar instance of Divine Judgment. Mr. A—— of A——

House, in the county of W——, was notorious for his open practice of infidelity. He was an ardent votary of the chase, a reckless gamester, and was an enthusiast in his love of cockfighting. After carousing one evening with a boon companion, he proposed that they should then and there match the birds which they had entered for a contest on the morrow. His friend declaring that his bird should fight only in a cockpit, Mr. A—— announced that he had one adjoining the very room in which they were. The birds were brought, lights called for, and Mr. A——, opening the door, led his guest down a flight of stairs and along a corridor to what he at first supposed were the stables. It was only after the match had begun, that he realized to his horror that they were in the family pew of A—— church, to which A—— House had private access. His expostulations only enraged his host, who commenced to blaspheme, wagering his very soul on the success of his bird, the victor of fifty fights. On this occasion the cock was defeated. Beside himself with frenzy, Mr. A—— rushed back to his bed-chamber and, declaring that the Judgment Day had come and that the bird should never crow again, thrust a wire into the embers, burned out its eyes, and bored through its tongue. He then fell down in some form of apoplectic fit. He recovered and continued his frenzied course of living for some years. It was noticed, however, that he had an impediment in his speech, especially remarkable when he was enraged, the effect of which was to make him utter a sound like the crowing of a cock. It became a cant phrase in the neighbourhood: 'When A—— crows, honest men must move.' Two years after this awful occurrence, his sight began to fail. He was killed in the hunting field. His horse took fright and, bolting, carried him for over a mile across bad country to break his neck in an attempt to leap a ten-foot wall. At each obstacle they encountered, Mr. A—— called out, but the noise that came from his throat only seemed to terrify his horse the more. Mr. C—— vouches for the truth of the story, having had personal acquaintance with both the parties.

The supposition that the Rev. Mr C—— was none other than the boon companion of Francis Ankardyne did not seem to occur to the mind of the worthy Mr Phipson. That such was the case, I have no doubt. I saw him once in a glass darkly; and I saw later at Ankardyne House a silhouette of Cotter Crawley in an old album, and recognized the weak, foolish profile.

Who it was who drew up the wording of the monument in Ankardyne church, I do not know. Probably the trustees of the heir, a distant kinsman and a mere boy. Perhaps the mason mistook the R for an L, the 1 for a 5. Perhaps he was a grim jester; perhaps the dead man guided the chisel. But I can picture the horror of Cotter Crawley in being confronted with those suggestive verses. I see him stealing from the house, which after years of absence he has brought himself to revisit, at night. I see him at work, cold, yet feverish, on the tell-tale stone. I see him stricken by remorse and praying, as the publican prayed, without in the shadow.

Part of this story Prendergast and I told to Miss Ankardyne. The family pew is pulled down, and of the passage that connected the church with the house, only the façade is left. The house itself is quieter than it has been for years. A nephew of Miss Ankardyne from India is coming to live there soon. He has children, but I do not think there is anything of which they need be afraid. As I wrote before, it has been well aired by a kindly soul.

Those Lights and Violins
Dorothy K. Haynes

September 16th

Aunt Rachel has just invited me to St Mervyn's for an extended, off-peak holiday. Funny, in all the years she and Mum have written to each other, I've never met her. You'd think, living at the seaside, she'd have asked us down occasionally, but people who keep boarding-houses don't invite relations. They're too busy letting their rooms at a profit.

The reason she's asked me is that I'm at a loose end after finishing university. I haven't got a job yet, and neither have quite a few of my equally well-qualified friends. Aunt Rachel's getting on a bit, and ought to be retiring soon, and Mum thinks, reading between the lines as usual, that she's got some idea of leaving the boarding-house to me. I can't imagine myself running a seaside boarding-house. Still, it would be churlish not to go. A change wouldn't do me any harm.

September 18th

Today I went to the travel agent's to get a brochure about St Mervyn's. It looks a wonderful place, built around a little bay, golden sand cupping the water, with high cliffs at one end, and, in the middle of the bay, a romantic-looking rock with what looks like a castle on top. The whole town seems to sparkle, the houses clustered bright round the bay like a tiara on corn-blonde hair.

I've written to Aunt Rachel, accepting her invitation.

September 25th

The view from The Haven is the view on the brochure – the curved bay, and the rock with its castle right in front. It is quiet, though, so quiet that footsteps echo on the promenade, and the view is empty most of the time. Only the moving waves and the seagulls give it life.

Aunt Rachel isn't at all like my mother. She wears her hair in an old-fashioned bun, she has the beginnings of a dowager's hump, her hands are mottled with brown, and she stumps about restlessly, at a loose end now that the guests have gone. Actually, there are still two left, Mr

Anderson and Mr Haley, but they are not so much guests as regulars, staying on through the winter at a reduced rate.

I met them today at lunch. Mr Anderson is grey-haired, quite distinguished-looking, and wears a Harris tweed jacket. 'He's writing a book about St Mervyn's,' Aunt Rachel whispered to me. 'Used to lecture in history.' Mr Haley is tall and bald, with a clever face disfigured by what seem to be acne scars. I feel edgy in his company, as if he's ill at ease, and it rubs off on me, but both of them are very gallant and eager to please. Maybe they're bored, alone with Aunt Rachel. It's on the cards I'm going to be bored too.

However, I'll give it a try. Aunt Rachel's doing her best. She treats her boarders like the family she's never had, scolding them, cossetting them and, now that she's growing old, being cossetted in turn. We all eat together in the kitchen, and Messrs Haley and Anderson defer to her, and yet humour her. The fact that she doesn't realize this makes her seem older still.

September 26th

I went for my first walk this afternoon. The streets were as quiet as Sunday. Far out, the tide winked across the damp sand, so far away that it was nothing but a luminous line. I started to walk across the sand, making long detours to avoid the lanes of water that the tide had left, and, at last, with the sea in my face and a darkness of rain coming over, I found myself almost at the huge rock I could see from The Haven.

Somehow, the nearness terrified me. On top of the rearing rock was this grey building, a bleak and frightening place, its site shared with the seagulls, the windows salt-caked, sea-spattered, buried deep in stone. There was something frightening, too, in the dangerous steps cut in the rock, and the iron handrails guarding deep drops to the sea.

And yet I had to go on. Surely, with the tide so low, it should be possible to walk right up to the rock, to clamber over weed-streaked ledges and stand triumphantly looking over to St Mervyn's, curved like a sickle around the bay.

But the rock was cut off, after all. A moat of water swilled restlessly, sucking and pounding at the steps, and an iron ring plopped and chinked with the lift of the tide. I was afraid of the dwarfing height of the rock, and the water inching higher as I watched. Suddenly I began to run, in a panic between the sand and the sky, because I was too far out, too small, cut off between the running rivers and the tide beginning to turn. My footsteps dented dry and filled up again, and when I reached the promenade the white waves were already thundering nearer.

Tonight, at teatime, I tried to find out something about the castle, or whatever it is. I meant the question for Mr Anderson, but before it registered Aunt Rachel came in with the answer.

'Oh, that's the Mount Hotel. St Mervyn's Mount, you know. You get a lot of Americans going there.'

'It's shut though, isn't it? It seemed pretty dead-looking to me.'

'Oh yes. They couldn't keep a place like that going all year. It's just a daft notion, anyway. They go because it's almost an island. They lay on a motor boat at high tide to bring the guests over to the town, but – I dunno. They don't mix much. They just come and go, and keep to themselves.'

'I tried to walk over,' I said, 'but there was this deep channel.'

'You don't want to go over there.' Mr Haley removed a kipper bone, and frowned. 'It could be very dangerous.'

'You could be cut off, easy as that,' butted in Aunt Rachel, snapping her fingers. 'The tide ... you want to be careful.'

Mr Haley looked annoyed at the interruption. For a second I had the feeling that he was going to say, 'That's not what I meant,' but Aunt Rachel went on rabbitting happily, '... very exclusive. They bring their own staff, and they say that the staff never leave the Mount all summer. Of course, they'll be well paid for it, but ... I dunno. It must be like living in a lighthouse.'

I was going to say that a lighthouse is always neat and trim, whereas the hotel was neglected, to say the least, but suddenly I noticed that Mr Haley looked anything but well. He pushed back his chair and went striding out of the room, and Mr Anderson cleared his throat and changed the subject. When Haley came back, he didn't join in the conversation.

October 1st

There is absolutely nothing to do in St Mervyn's. I've been to church with Aunt Rachel, but it was a dreigh and dreary experience, a choir of tired landladies and a cold, salty draught making the sermon drier. Tonight I slipped out desperately and tried the pub. I fancied an orange-lit bar with soft music and deep carpets, but all that was open was the Harbour Light, a men's pub; old men, mostly, drinking morosely with their feet in the sawdust. I didn't know you still got sawdust on floors! I slipped out again, guiltily, but not before I had seen Mr Haley knocking back a whisky, and looking as if it wasn't his first. I wonder what Aunt Rachel would say to that?

October 2nd

Had a chat with Mr Anderson. Aunt Rachel had gone to bed early, and I promised to make the supper. There were just the two of us. Mr Haley was out, and I remarked that he seemed to like a drink.

Mr Anderson appears to know all about it. I gathered that he tried to cover up for him so that Aunt Rachel wouldn't know. Luckily, Haley was a quiet drunk. He just got moody and depressed, and usually it was quite easy to get him to bed without causing any disturbance.

'What does he do?' I asked.

Mr Anderson puffed at his pipe, and told me through his clenched smoker's teeth, 'He's a sort of preacher.'

'A preacher?'

'Yes. He's an entertainer as well. He's quite good, actually; that lean, lugubrious type often are. He does a one-man show, with a one-man band – ridiculous, but it needs quite a lot of skill, and it attracts the crowds. He only operates in the summer, of course. He's a great success with the kids, Splitter Haley. He just – slightly – frightens them, and that's an attraction.'

'Is that his real name? Splitter?'

'Seems to be. Unless it's a stage name. I gather his father was a conjuror or something. Splitter decided not to follow in his father's footsteps, but to take Holy Orders; or else the father wanted him to "better himself" . . . And then something happened – I don't know what – and he more or less cracked up. Now he does this minstrel business, with a bit of seaside mission thrown in.'

'Queer mixture. And he doesn't do anything at all in the off season?'

'No. He must have a bit of money. I've never worked out how much he makes in the summer. He does well enough. The kids follow him like the Pied Piper. As I said, they like to be frightened.'

'What does he do to them?'

'Nothing. It's just that they sense that *he's* frightened.'

'But what's he frightened *of* ?'

Mr Anderson just shrugged his shoulders and went on puffing at his pipe.

October 10th

This may be a swinging resort in the summer, but right now it's a dump. The only thing that interests me is St Mervyn's Mount, and that fascinates me. The colour of the rock changes as the sun shifts and shadows the ledges, and sometimes, when the tide is high, and waves break over it, it seems to shiver under a shower of silver needles. One of these days I'll have another go at reaching it.

October 16th

It's all fixed! I'm going over to the Mount! I mentioned at dinner-time, casually, that I was going to walk over at low tide, and Splitter Haley's face went sort of gaunt and guarded. I kept on talking, to cover up, and all of a sudden he seemed to pull himself together, and blurted out that he had the use of the hotel rowing boat and would I like him to row me over?

Eyebrows raised. Eating stopped. 'How come *you* can use the boat?' asked Mr Anderson, rather enviously.

'I used to work there a while back. A sort of chaplain to the guests.'

'You never!' This, obviously, was a revelation to Aunt Rachel. 'And you never told me! What was it like? Was it as posh as——?'

I wasn't bothered about that. All I knew was that I didn't want to go; not with him. I don't know what I was afraid of, but I *was* afraid, and I didn't know how to get out of it.

'Isn't it private?' I asked.

'It doesn't matter. It's empty. It's been empty for years.'

'Oh, no!' Aunt Rachel stopped gouging bits out of an apple dumpling and looked up, surprised. 'It's always well booked. You can see the crowds going backwards and forwards. Will I give you some custard, dear?'

'It *used* to be busy,' said Splitter, so vehemently that I wondered if he was drunk already. But he wasn't. He looked sick. His clever, scarred face was whitish, and he shivered. 'But no one's been there for years. Not a soul.'

'I beg your pardon, Mr Haley.' Aunt Rachel put down the custard jug, to give all her attention to the argument. 'I may be getting old, and I know I lose my knitting, or my glasses, but I'm not as bad as all that. Everyone knows the Mount Hotel's busy every summer. They must make a packet out of all those rich Americans.'

'Well, it's empty now,' I said, to keep the argument from going any further, 'and if Mr Haley wants to take me over . . .' I had made up my mind. I was going to go.

'I hope it's safe. I don't know if your mother would like it.'

'I'll go along too, if it's all right,' said Mr Anderson. 'Keep an eye on her.' And he winked.

Aunt Rachel relaxed immediately. Haley, evidently, was the one she had reservations about. 'What I'd like,' she said dreamily, 'would be to go over one night, for dinner. It's so lovely, all lit up, and you can hear the music, sometimes, over the water. But there's never time . . .'

October 17th

It's been foggy all week, just as we've made our plans for going to the Mount. Sometimes the fog shifts, and the wet sands come into view, the sluggish sea, the whole lost curve of the bay, with the Mount looming hazily like an ogre's castle. Colour leeches into the landscape, muted marine colour, all dripping; then the mist comes up again, like steam, and the foghorns go moan, moan, moan, and condensation blooms the walls and trickles down the paint. Aunt Rachel grumbles a lot. The cold gets into her bones.

November 1st

The wind freshened yesterday, and today we're going over.

November 8th

I haven't been able to write about the visit until today. I still haven't got it all sorted out in my mind. It was so . . . unbelievable, so absolutely terrifying!

We went over at high tide, the water choppy, splashing my trousers, and Mr Anderson sitting with his pipe clenched in his mouth and his anorak hood tight round his face. Splitter Haley reeked of whisky. If I'd had to go with him on my own I'd have called the whole thing off.

If he was drunk, he'd rowed himself sober by the time we got to the Mount. The boat bobbed, tethered to its iron ring, and we scrambled on to the zigzag steps of the rock. Water heaved and receded, and there was so much sea, so much noise and turmoil that I felt my stomach turning over. Splitter Haley led the way, hanging on to the iron handrail, and I clambered after him, glad to get away from the waves.

The steps were treacherous, uneven in size, and slimy with littered seaweed. All around the gulls cried, a sad, mewing screech, and I felt that if I watched them I would lose my balance. The Mount was higher than I expected. When I reached the top I turned and looked backwards, over Mr Anderson's ridiculous hooded head, and there was St Mervyn's, clean and snug and compact, with its sickle of sand, and the cliff sweeping up at one end.

'Note the impressive entrance,' said Splitter, acting the courier. 'The guests were always tickled to death by the entrance.'

'Were,' he said. I noticed that.

It was certainly impressive. The door was iron-studded, the guns pointed landward with a blunt, black menace, and there was an iron lantern swinging on a bracket. 'We'll go round here,' he said. 'You'll be all right. Just don't look down.'

I looked, of course, as soon as he said it, leading me round the side of the rock. We were crossing a bridge over a deep chasm, and through the pattern of the ironwork I could see green water swilling and slapping against black walls. I stood clutching the rail, afraid to move. 'Give me your hand,' said Splitter, looking back at me. 'There you are. I've got you. You're all right now.'

But the back of the rock was even worse. Here we were shut off from St Mervyn's, and there was nothing in front of us but waves, thrusting and curling over in angry fringes of white. The sky was grey, the waves were grey, and there was no way of measuring the horizon. Over the grey, tossing water was America – nothing but sea, all the way to America, except perhaps for an odd, lonely rock like this.

The bleakness got hold of me like horror. 'Two feet thick,' Splitter was saying with dismal pride, pointing to the walls. 'And the glass is thick, too. It has to be. The spray hits the windows like bullets.'

And then he produced a key.

'You're not going *in*?' I yelled at him, over the noise of the waves.

He didn't answer. He turned the huge key in the lock. Surely when he gave up his job he should have given up the key as well?

'I'll show you the kitchens first,' he said, leading the way downstairs. 'The place used to be a fort, and these were the dungeons. It dates back to Cromwell's time.'

I was beginning to feel stifled. There were shafts and pipes, and a smell of stale fat, and too much glossy green paint all streaked with condensation. No windows at all. Fancy being shut up here all summer, no windows, and the boom and thud of the waves...

'I don't think much of it,' I said candidly. 'I thought it would be more modern than this.'

Haley didn't answer. I turned for confirmation to Mr Anderson, and caught my breath at the look on his face. He was a sickly yellow colour, and he was swallowing hard. 'Are you all right?' I asked, thinking he was suffering from the journey over, and remembering that we had the return trip in front of us; but he said nothing, and I didn't want to embarrass him, so I left it at that for the moment.

'The place stinks,' I said. 'It would turn your stomach.'

'Well, what do you expect? It's been a long time...' Haley sounded aggressive now. He hurried us out, over the thick grey linoleum, blotched with grease and spillage; but at the door Anderson put a hand on his arm, and Haley jumped. It was like touching a nervous cat.

'Wasn't there a bottle dungeon? I remember reading——'

'No. Not that I know of. This is deep into the rock already.' He held the door open, pointedly, and we filed out.

I was glad to go upstairs again, to the daylight. The light was grey and muted, like the light that comes through frosted glass; but it wasn't frosting that dimmed the windows, it was salt. It was better here, though, warmer, richer. Money can insulate stone passages, dank walls, and a lot of money had been spent here. I was beginning to feel more comfortable. The air was growing warmer every minute, as if the sleek gold radiators in the passage were turned on. They *were* turned on! I laid my hand on one, and drew it away quickly. So the hotel *was* still in use, then? But how could it be, with no cooking facilities? Unless, of course, they had installed new, modern kitchens. Of course.

But why had Splitter Haley insisted that it was empty? He was forging along now, with the pride of one who knows his way about. He opened a door, and stood aside.

Music. Soft music, soft deep carpets, warm lamps on the wall. There was wine on the tables, and people talking, rich people, dressed for the evening. In one corner a couple danced slowly, holding each other up, and I could smell cigar smoke . . .

It was all just as Aunt Rachel had pictured it, except that, surely, Splitter Haley had no right to usher us in, in our damp and scruffy clothes, to stare and envy. But no one paid any attention. They went on with what they were doing, smiling and dancing and drinking; but slowly, more and more drearily, dragged out like a record running down, the smiles stretched and dreadful, the dancers turning in a dream, the drinks poised above the black parted mouths . . . in a moment they would all be frozen forever. I screamed and screamed, and they were gone – flick! – like that. It was cold, and there was damp everywhere, mould and cobwebs, and all the furniture stained and damp . . . and then we were in the boat, rowing away, and I don't remember crossing the dreadful bridge, or going down the steep steps, or anything except us rowing away as quickly as possible.

We went to the pub. I couldn't have gone to Aunt Rachel's just then. We all had a stiff dram, and then we sat around the smokey little fire while they tried to talk me out of my terror.

'It was the way they *did* everything,' I sobbed. 'Slower and slower, and that music running down, and the dreamy way they turned their heads——'

'Who?' asked Mr Anderson.

'The guests!' I snapped at him. I couldn't understand why he was asking. 'I thought the place was shut up, but they were all there, all those posh people——'

'There wasn't anybody,' said Splitter Haley. 'I thought it was the way the place looks, all those spiders' webs . . . some girls don't like spiders. I thought that's what it was.'

'It was like that afterwards.' I blew my nose, and tried to explain. 'At first, it was all bright and lovely, but the people . . . began running down, and moving like ghosts . . . and then, when I screamed, they vanished. And *then* it was like you said, as if it had stood empty for years.'

'It has,' said Haley suddenly, and, very slowly, Mr Anderson nodded.

'And *you* didn't see the people?' I asked.

'No. Not . . . what you said.'

'Nor me,' said Haley. 'But you're right. That's how it was, all dying one by one . . .'

I was more frightened than ever. If there's one thing worse than seeing a ghost, it's knowing that you're the only one who's seen it. Splitter Haley filled his glass again, but he was sober, dead sober. I was sure of it.

'There's been nobody at that hotel since I was there, and that was, oh – eight years ago. Something happened – I may as well tell you now.

It was plague. Bubonic plague. One of the new guests had been in North Africa, and by the time we discovered what was wrong, it was too late. It was beginning to spread among the others.'

He paused for a while, and we waited.

'The staff walked out; fair enough, they weren't engaged to nurse that sort of thing. We didn't tell them exactly what was wrong, but they sensed it was something serious, something they didn't want to catch. We let them go; we even paid them for the rest of their term on condition they kept their mouths shut, and I suppose it worked out all right. There was no comeback, and we never heard of any other cases being reported. Thank heaven for that.'

After another long silence, he went on again.

'You maybe wonder why we didn't inform the authorities. They could have helped us. But think of the owner's point of view, the talk and the scandal. It wouldn't bring back the dead, would it, and we were sealing off the infection. There was a resident doctor, and he stayed, and made it as easy as he could; but it was hard work, just the owner, the doctor and me, looking after the patients, trying to bathe their sores and keep their beds clean – it was too much. And then the owner took ill and died, and I got a touch of it myself . . .' He fingered his scarred face, and I tried not to look at him.

'I did what I had to do. I prayed with them, I administered the last rites . . .'

'I've never heard of a hotel chaplain,' I said dubiously.

'No, but this wasn't an ordinary hotel. It——'

'How many died?' interrupted Mr Anderson brusquely.

'Well . . . it was near the end of the season, you see, and we were tailing off. There weren't many left, though. Only one or two.' He looked at us pathetically, willing us to understand.

'How do you mean? What happened to them?'

'Well, we decided, the doctor and I – we saw that the others didn't – didn't live. They might have said something, you see, if we'd let them go. But it was done kindly. We were always kind to them. We had hoped, you see, to keep the hotel going. After all, once this lot were gone, there would be others who would need——'

'You mean you let people die, you killed them, just because——'

'All *I* did,' pleaded Haley, 'was to give them a Christian burial. A funeral service. None of them went without a blessing.'

'But where . . .?'

'There *was* a bottle dungeon!' Mr Anderson struck the table with his hand. 'Under that ship's linoleum . . .'

I closed my eyes as horror piled upon already unbearable horror. Once, at St Andrew's, I had seen a bottle dungeon; deep, pitch-black, no ventilation, no way of getting in or out except by a rope ladder. The guide lowered a light down the neck of the bottle to show smooth walls, curved and cold, and then put out the light for a moment of dead silence and blackness. A woman screamed ...

'It's sealed off now,' said Splitter. 'There would be nothing to see. It was all done according to the prayer book. "We commit their bodies to the deep ... in sure and certain hope ..."'

'The deep?'

'The sea comes in, at high tide. The crabs would eat them. It's part of God's plan; like vultures. People condemn vultures, but——'

'If that's true,' said Mr Anderson – and I could see that he believed it; he had seen his own ghosts, the rotting dead being swilled about by the waves – 'if that's true, how did you get away with it? People can't disappear like that. What about their families, their relations?'

'What you don't realize,' said Splitter, dragging himself back from the nightmare, 'what nobody realizes is that these people were not quite ... acceptable. They were all a bit ... queer, one way or another. Nothing outrageous, but just enough to be an embarrassment to their families. That's what the hotel was *for*. They were all rich, see, nearly all American. It was worth a good deal of money to their relations to have daft Aunt Rebecca or eccentric Uncle Silas out of the way for a while, some place where they would be looked after and supervised – why else do you think they always came across by boat? It looked like a gimmick; it was really because you couldn't have them wandering about on their own.

'So no questions were asked; and we were quite honest about it. We wrote to the next of kin, and broke the news of their death, and said we'd attended to the burial, and it was a load off their minds. There wouldn't even be a question of legacies. It was the relations who had the money. So, up till now, no questions have been asked; and who's going to say it ought to be stirred up again?'

Neither of us felt ready to answer; but another idea had struck me.

'Aunt Rachel insists the hotel's full every summer. She just takes it for granted. I mean, she lives just opposite, and she *sees*——'

'Well, that's the funny thing.' Haley took another gulp, and thought for a moment. 'Nobody has ever realized that the hotel was closed. All sorts of people saw the hotel car calling at the station, and the guests being ferried backwards and forwards, but – how many of our lot actually spoke to them? Ask any shopkeeper if they ever bought anything on their shopping expeditions. They'll all say no, they went next door, or round the corner – never to them.'

('They don't mix much,' Aunt Rachel had said. And no wonder.)

We sat gloomily, staring at the fire. How could I tell her – how could I tell anyone – that for years they had been seeing ghosts in broad daylight?

Mr Anderson got out his pipe and began the preliminaries to a comforting smoke.

'If this is true,' he said again, as his match flame was sucked into the bowl, 'and I'm inclined to believe what you say' – he blew out a rich, grey cloud – 'what made you stay on? Obviously the place won't open again. I would have thought you'd have gone as far away as possible.'

Haley's ruined face was intolerably sad as he lifted his glass again.

'I couldn't leave. I daren't forget. Children come here, innocent children, and the least I can do . . . you see, there's something evil about that place. Not a temporary thing, not an isolated incident like the one we've been discussing, but away back, right through the centuries. You, sir, you noticed it——'

'I know.' Anderson's colour drained again, and he laid down his pipe. 'I went rather further back than you. Some dreadful things went on in those dungeons——'

'Don't tell me,' I said quickly.

*　　*　　*

That is where the matter stands. At the moment, none of us want to say any more about it. All I can think of is getting away from St Mervyn's as soon as possible.

There's Aunt Rachel to think about, of course, I couldn't possibly give her my real reasons for leaving. She was talking tonight about retiring, and saying she'd celebrate by having dinner at the Mount, 'with all those lights and violins.'

'It's over-rated,' we told her. 'Far too bleak and blustery. We're far more comfortable here.'

Pray God she never goes to find out for herself.

The Furnished Room
O. Henry

Restless, shifting, fugacious as time itself is a certain vast bulk of the population of the red brick district of the lower West Side. Homeless, they have a hundred homes. They flit from furnished room to furnished room, transients forever – transients in abode, transients in heart and mind. They sing 'Home, Sweet Home' in ragtime; they carry their *lares et penates* in a bandbox; their vine is entwined about a picture hat; a rubber plant is their fig tree.

Hence the houses of this district, having had a thousand dwellers, should have a thousand tales to tell, mostly dull ones, no doubt; but it would be strange if there could not be found a ghost or two in the wake of all these vagrant guests.

One evening after dark a young man prowled among these crumbling red mansions, ringing their bells. At the twelfth he rested his lean hand-baggage upon the step and wiped the dust from his hat-band and forehead. The bell sounded faint and far away in some remote, hollow depths.

To the door of this, the twelfth house whose bell he had rung, came a housekeeper who made him think of an unwholesome, surfeited worm that had eaten its nut to a hollow shell and now sought to fill the vacancy with edible lodgers.

He asked if there was a room to let.

'Come in,' said the housekeeper. Her voice came from her throat; her throat seemed lined with fur. 'I have the third-floor back, vacant since a week back. Should you wish to look at it?'

The young man followed her up the stairs. A faint light from no particular source mitigated the shadows of the halls. They trod noiselessly upon a stair carpet that its own loom would have forsworn. It seemed to have become vegetable; to have degenerated in that rank, sunless air to lush lichen or spreading moss that grew in patches to the staircase and was viscid under the foot like organic matter. At each turn of the stairs were vacant niches in the wall. Perhaps plants had once been set within them. If so they had died in that foul and tainted air. It may be that statues of the saints had stood there, but it was not difficult to conceive that imps and devils had dragged them forth in the darkness and down to the unholy depths of some furnished pit below.

'This is the room,' said the housekeeper, from her furry throat. 'It's a nice room. It ain't often vacant. I had some most elegant people in it last summer – no trouble at all, and paid in advance to the minute. The water's at the end of the hall. Sprowls and Mooney kept it three months. They done a vaudeville sketch. Miss B'retta Sprowls – you may have heard of her – Oh, that was just the stage names – right there over the dresser is where the marriage certificate hung, framed. The gas is here, and you see there is plenty of closet room. It's a room everybody likes. It never stays idle long.'

'Do you have many theatrical people rooming here?' asked the young man.

'They comes and goes. A good proportion of my lodgers is connected with the theatres. Yes, sir, this is the theatrical district. Actor people never stays long anywhere. I get my share. Yes, they comes and they goes.'

He engaged the room, paying for a week in advance. He was tired, he said, and would take possession at once. He counted out the money. The room had been made ready, she said, even to towels and water. As the housekeeper moved away he put, for the thousandth time, the question that he carried at the end of his tongue.

'A young girl – Miss Vashner – Miss Eloise Vashner – do you remember such a one among your lodgers? She would be singing on the stage, most likely. A fair girl, of medium height, and slender, with reddish, gold hair and a dark mole near her left eyebrow.'

'No, I don't remember the name. Them stage people has names they change as often as their rooms. They comes and they goes. No, I don't call that one to mind.'

No. Always no. Five months of ceaseless interrogation and the inevitable negative. So much time spent by day in questioning managers, agents, schools and choruses; by night among the audiences of theatres from all-star casts down to music halls so low that he dreaded to find what he most hoped for. He who had loved her best had tried to find her. He was sure that since her disappearance from home this great, water-girt city held her somewhere, but it was like a monstrous quicksand, shifting its particles constantly, with no foundation, its upper granules of today buried tomorrow in ooze and slime.

The furnished room received its latest guest with a first glow of pseudo-hospitality, a hectic, haggard, perfunctory welcome like the specious smile of a demi-rep. The sophistical comfort came in reflected gleams from the decayed furniture, the ragged brocade upholstery of a couch and two chairs, a foot-wide cheap pier glass between the two

windows, from one or two gilt picture frames and a brass bedstead in a
corner.

The guest reclined, inert, upon a chair, while the room, confused in
speech as though it were an apartment in Babel, tried to discourse to him
of its divers tenantry.

A polychromatic rug like some brilliant-flowered, rectangular
tropical islet lay surrounded by a billowy sea of soiled matting. Upon the
gay-papered wall were those pictures that pursue the homeless one from
house to house – *The Huguenot Lovers, The First Quarrel, The Wedding
Breakfast, Psyche at the Fountain.* The mantel's chastely severe outline was
ingloriously veiled behind some pert drapery drawn rakishly askew like
the sashes of the Amazonian ballet. Upon it was some desolate flotsam
cast aside by the room's marooned when a lucky sail had borne them to a
fresh port – a trifling vase or two, pictures of actresses, a medicine bottle,
some stray cards out of a deck.

One by one, as the characters of a cryptograph become explicit, the
little signs left by the furnished room's procession of guests developed a
significance. The threadbare space in the rug in front of the dresser told
that lovely women had marched in the throng. Tiny finger prints on the
wall spoke of little prisoners trying to feel their way to sun and air. A
splattered stain, raying like a shadow of a bursting bomb, witnessed
where a hurled glass or bottle had splintered with its contents against the
wall. Across the pier glass had been scrawled with a diamond in
staggering letters the name 'Marie'. It seemed that the succession of
dwellers in the furnished room had turned in fury – perhaps tempted
beyond forbearance by its garish coldness – and wreaked upon it their
passions. The furniture was chipped and bruised; the couch, distorted by
bursting springs, seemed a horrible monster that had been slain during
the stress of some grotesque convulsion. Some more potent upheaval had
cloven a great slice from the marble mantel. Each plank in the floor
owned its particular cant and shriek as from a separate and individual
agony. It seemed incredible that all this malice and injury had been
wrought upon the room by those who had called it for a time their home;
and yet it may have been the cheated home instinct surviving blindly,
the resentful rage at false household gods that had kindled their wrath. A
hut that is our own we can sweep and adorn and cherish.

The young tenant in the chair allowed these thoughts to file, soft-
shod, through his mind, while there drifted into the room furnished
sounds and furnished scents. He heard in one room a tittering and
incontinent, slack laughter; in others the monologue of a scold, the
rattling of dice, a lullaby, and one crying dully; above him a banjo
tinkled with spirit. Doors banged somewhere, the elevated trains roared
intermittently; a cat yowled miserably upon a back fence. And he
breathed the breath of the house – a dank savour rather than a smell – a

cold, musty effluvium as from underground vaults mingled with the
reeking exhalations of linoleum and mildewed and rotten woodwork.

Then, suddenly, as he rested there, the room was filled with the
strong, sweet odour of mignonette. It came as upon a single buffet of
wind with such sureness and fragrance and emphasis that it almost
seemed a living visitant. And the man cried aloud: 'What, dear?' as if he
had been called, and sprang up and faced about. The rich odour clung
to him and wrapped him around. He reached out his arms for it, all his
senses for the time confused and commingled. How could one be
peremptorily called by an odour? Surely it must have been a sound. But,
was it not the sound that had touched, that had caressed him?

'She has been in the room,' he cried, and he sprang to wrest from it a
token, for he knew he would recognize the smallest thing that had
belonged to her or that she had touched. This enveloping scent of
mignonette, the odour that she had loved and made her own – whence
came it?

The room had been but carelessly set in order. Scattered upon the
flimsy dresser scarf were half a dozen hairpins – those discreet,
indistinguishable friends of womankind, feminine of gender, infinite of
mood and uncommunicative of tense. These he ignored, conscious of
their triumphant lack of identity. Ransacking the drawers of the dresser
he came upon a discarded, tiny, ragged handkerchief. He pressed it to his
face. It was racy and insolent with heliotrope; he hurled it to the floor. In
another drawer he found odd buttons, a theatre programme, a
pawnbroker's card, two lost marshmallows, a book on the divination of
dreams. In the last was a woman's black satin hair-bow, which halted
him, poised between ice and fire. But the black satin hair-bow also is
femininity's demure, impersonal, common ornament, and tells no tales.

And then he traversed the room like a hound on the scent, skimming
the walls, considering the corners of the bulging matting on his hands
and knees, rummaging mantel and tables, the curtains and hangings,
the drunken cabinet in the corner, for a visible sign, unable to perceive
that she was there beside, around, against, within, above him, clinging
to him, wooing him, calling him so poignantly through the finer senses
that even his grosser ones became cognisant of the call. Once again he
answered loudly: 'Yes dear!' and turned, wild-eyed, to gaze on vacancy,
for he could not yet discern form and colour and love and outstretched
arms in the odour of mignonette. Oh, God! whence that odour, and since
when have odours had a voice to call? Thus he groped.

He burrowed in crevices and corners, and found corks and cigarettes. These he passed in passive contempt. But once he found in a fold of
the matting a half-smoked cigar, and this he ground beneath his heel
with a green and trenchant oath. He sifted the room from end to end. He
found dreary and ignoble small records of many a peripatetic tenant;

but of her whom he sought, and who may have lodged there, and whose spirit seemed to hover there, he found no trace.

And then he thought of the housekeeper.

He ran from the haunted room downstairs and to a door that showed a crack of light. She came out to his knock. He smothered his excitement as best he could.

'Will you tell me, madam,' he besought her, 'who occupied the room I have before I came?'

'Yes, sir. I can tell you again. 'Twas Sprowls and Mooney, as I said. Miss B'retta Sprowls it was in the theatres, but Missis Mooney she was. My house is well known for respectability. The marriage certificate hung, framed, on a nail over——'

'What kind of lady was Miss Sprowls – in looks, I mean?'

'Why, black-haired, sir, short, and stout, with a comical face. They left a week ago Tuesday.'

'And before they occupied it?'

'Why, there was a single gentleman connected with the draying business. He left owing me a week. Before him was Missis Crowder and her two children, they stayed four months; and back of them was old Mr Doyle, whose sons paid for him. He kept the room six months. That goes back a year, sir, and further I do not remember.'

He thanked her and crept back to his room. The room was dead. The essence that had vivified it was gone. The perfume of mignonette had departed. In its place was the old, stale odour of mouldy house furniture, of atmosphere in storage.

The ebbing of his hope drained his faith. He sat staring at the yellow, singing gaslight. Soon he walked to the bed and began to tear the sheets into strips. With the blade of his knife he drove them tightly into every crevice around windows and door. When all was snug and taut he turned out the light, turned the gas full on again and laid himself gratefully upon the bed.

*   *   *

It was Mrs McCool's night to go with the can for beer. So she fetched it and sat with Mrs Purdy in one of those subterranean retreats where housekeepers forgather and the worm dieth seldom.

'I rented out my third floor, back, this evening,' said Mrs Purdy, across a fine circle of foam. 'A young man took it. He went up to bed two hours ago.'

'Now, did ye, Missis Purdy, ma'am?' said Mrs McCool, with intense admiration. 'You do be a wonder for rentin' rooms of that kind. And did ye tell him, then?' she concluded in a husky whisper, laden with mystery.

'Rooms,' said Mrs Purdy, in her furriest tones, 'are furnished for to rent. I did not tell him, Mrs McCool.'

''Tis right ye are, ma'am; 'tis by renting rooms we kape alive. Ye have the rale sense for business, ma'am. There be many people will rayjict the rentin' of a room if they be tould a suicide has been after dyin' in the bed of it.'

'As you say, we has our living to be making,' remarked Mrs Purdy.

'Yis, ma'am, 'tis true. 'Tis just one wake ago this day I helped ye lay out the third floor, back. A pretty slip of a collen she was to be killin' herself wid the gas – a swate little face she had, Mrs Purdy, ma'am.'

'She'd a-been called handsome, as you say,' said Mrs Purdy, assenting but critical, 'but for that mole she had a-growin' by her left eyebrow. Do fill up your glass again, Missis McCool.'

The Whistling Room
William Hope Hodgson

Carnacki shook a friendly fist at me as I entered late. Then he opened
the door into the dining-room, and ushered the four of us – Jessop,
Arkright, Taylor and myself – in to dinner.

We dined well, as usual, and, equally as usual, Carnacki was pretty
silent during the meal. At the end, we took our wine and cigars to our
accustomed positions, and Carnacki – having got himself comfortable in
his big chair – began without any preliminary:

'I have just got back from Ireland again,' he said. 'And I thought
you chaps would be interested to hear my news. Besides, I fancy I shall
see the thing clearer, after I have told it all out straight. I must tell you
this, though, at the beginning – up to the present moment, I have been
utterly and completely "stumped". I have tumbled upon one of the most
peculiar cases of "haunting" – or devilment of some sort – that I have
come against. Now listen.

'I have been spending the last few weeks at Iastrae Castle, about
twenty miles north-east of Galway. I got a letter about a month ago from
a Mr Sid K. Tassoc, who it seemed had bought the place lately, and
moved in, only to find that he had got a very peculiar piece of property.

'When I reached there, he met me at the station, driving a jaunting-
car, and drove me up to the castle, which, by the way, he called a
"house-shanty". I found that he was "pigging it" there with his boy
brother and another American, who seemed to be half servant and half
companion. It appears that all the servants had left the place, in a body,
as you might say; and now they were managing among themselves,
assisted by some day-help.

'The three of them got together a scratch feed, and Tassoc told me all
about the trouble, whilst we were at table. It is most extraordinary, and
different from anything that I have had to do with; though that Buzzing
Case was very queer, too.

'Tassoc began right in the middle of his story. "We've got a room in
this shanty," he said, "which has got a most infernal whistling in it; sort

of haunting it. The thing starts any time: you never know when, and it goes on until it frightens you. All the servants have gone, as I've told you. It's not ordinary whistling, and it isn't the wind. Wait till you hear it."

"'We're all carrying guns," said the boy; and slapped his coat pocket.

"'As bad as that?" I said; and the older brother nodded. "I may be soft," he replied; "but wait till you've heard it. Sometimes I think it's some infernal thing, and the next moment, I'm just as sure that someone's playing a trick on us."

"'Why?" I asked. "What is to be gained?"

"'You mean," he said, "that people usually have some good reason for playing tricks as elaborate as this. Well, I'll tell you. There's a lady in this province, by the name of Miss Donnehue, who's going to be my wife, this day two months. She's more beautiful than they make them, and so far as I can see, I've just stuck my head into an Irish hornet's nest. There's about a score of hot young Irishmen been courting her these two years gone, and now that I've come along and cut them out, they feel raw against me. Do you begin to understand the possibilities?"

"'Yes," I said. "Perhaps I do in a vague sort of way; but I don't see how all this affects the room?"

"'Like this," he said. "When I'd fixed it up with Miss Donnehue, I looked out for a place, and bought this little house-shanty. Afterwards, I told her – one evening during dinner, that I'd decided to tie up here. And then she asked me whether I wasn't afraid of the whistling room. I told her it must have been thrown in gratis, as I'd heard nothing about it. There were some of her men friends present, and I saw a smile go round. I found out, after a bit of questioning, that several people have bought this place during the last twenty odd years. And it was always on the market again, after a trial.

"'Well, the chaps started to bait me a bit, and offered to take bets after dinner that I'd not stay six months in this shanty. I looked once or twice to Miss Donnehue, so as to be sure I was 'getting the note' of the talkee-talkee; but I could see that she didn't take it as a joke, at all. Partly, I think, because there was a bit of a sneer in the way the men were tackling me, and partly because she really believes there is something in this yarn of the whistling room.

"'However, after dinner, I did what I could to even things up with the others. I nailed all their bets, and screwed them down good and safe. I guess some of them are going to be hard hit, unless I lose; which I don't mean to. Well, there you have practically the whole yarn."

"'Not quite," I told him. "All that I know, is that you have bought a castle, with a room in it that is in some way 'queer', and that you've been doing some betting. Also, I know that your servants have got frightened, and run away. Tell me something about the whistling?"

'"Oh, that!" said Tassoc; "that started the second night we were in. I'd had a good look round the room in the daytime, as you can understand; for the talk up at Arlestrae – Miss Donnehue's place – had made me wonder a bit. But it seems just as usual as some of the other rooms in the old wing, only perhaps a bit more lonesome feeling. But that may be only because of the talk about it, you know.

'"The whistling started about ten o'clock, on the second night, as I said. Tom and I were in the library, when we heard an awfully queer whistling, coming along the East Corridor—— The room is in the East Wing, you know.

'"That blessed ghost!" I said to Tom, and we collared the lamps off the table, and went up to have a look. I tell you, even as we dug along the corridor, it took me a bit in the throat, it was so beastly queer. It was a sort of tune, in a way; but more as if a devil or some rotten thing were laughing at you, and going to get round at your back. That's how it makes you feel.

'"When we got to the door, we didn't wait; but rushed it open; and then I tell you the sound of the thing fairly hit me in the face. Tom said he got it the same way – sort of felt stunned and bewildered. We looked all round, and soon got so nervous, we just cleared out, and I locked the door.

'"We came down here, and had a stiff peg each. Then we landed fit again, and began to feel we'd been nicely had. So we took sticks, and went out into the grounds, thinking after all it must be some of these confounded Irishmen working the ghost-trick on us. But there was not a leg stirring.

'"We went back into the house, and walked over it, and then paid another visit to the room. But we simply couldn't stand it. We fairly ran out, and locked the door again. I don't know how to put it into words; but I had a feeling of being up against something that was rottenly dangerous. You know! We've carried our guns ever since.

'"Of course, we had a real turn-out of the room next day, and the whole house-place; and we even hunted the grounds; but there was nothing queer. And now I don't know what to think; except that the sensible part of me tells me that it's some plan of these wild Irishmen to try to take a rise out of me."

'"Done anything since?" I asked him.

'"Yes," he said. "Watched outside of the door of the room at nights, and chased round the grounds, and sounded the walls and floor of the room. We've done everything we could think of; and it's beginning to get on our nerves; so we sent for you."

'By this, we had finished eating. As we rose from the table, Tassoc suddenly called out: "Ssh! Hark!"

'We were instantly silent, listening. Then I heard it, an extraordinary hooning whistle, monstrous and inhuman, coming from far away through corridors to my right.

'"By God!" said Tassoc; "and it's scarcely dark yet! Collar those candles, both of you, and come along."

'In a few moments, we were all out of the door and racing up the stairs. Tassoc turned into a long corridor, and we followed, shielding our candles as we ran. The sound seemed to fill all the passages as we drew near, until I had the feeling that the whole air throbbed under the power of some wanton Immense Force – a sense of an actual taint, as you might say, of monstrosity all about us.

'Tassoc unlocked the door; then, giving it a push with his foot, jumped back, and drew his revolver. As the door flew open, the sound beat out at us, with an effect impossible to explain to one who has not heard it – with a certain, horrible personal note in it; as if in there in the darkness you could picture the room rocking and creaking in a mad, vile glee to its own filthy piping and whistling and hooning; and yet all the time aware of you in particular. To stand there and listen, was to be stunned by Realization. It was as if someone showed you the mouth of a vast pit suddenly, and said: That's Hell. And you *knew* that they had spoken the truth. Do you get it, even a little bit?

'I stepped a pace into the room, and held the candle over my head, and looked quickly around. Tassoc and his brother joined me, and the man came up at the back, and we all held our candles high. I was deafened with the shrill, piping hoon of the whistling; and then, clear in my ear, something seemed to be saying to me: "Get out of here – quick! Quick! Quick!"

'As you chaps know, I never neglect that sort of thing. Sometimes it may be nothing but nerves; but as you will remember, it was just such a warning that saved me in the "Grey Dog" Case, and in the "Yellow Finger" Experiments; as well as other times. Well, I turned sharp round to the others: "Out!" I said. "For God's sake, *out* quick!" And in an instant I had them into the passage.

'There came an extraordinary yelling scream into the hideous whistling, and then, like a clap of thunder, an utter silence. I slammed the door, and locked it. Then, taking the key, I looked round at the others. They were pretty white, and I imagine I must have looked that way too. And there we stood a moment, silent.

'"Come down out of this, and have some whisky," said Tassoc, at last, in a voice he tried to make ordinary; and he led the way. I was the back man, and I knew we all kept looking over our shoulders. When we got downstairs, Tassoc passed the bottle round. He took a drink himself, and slapped his glass onto the table. Then sat down with a thud.

'"That's a lovely thing to have in the house with you, isn't it!" he said. And directly afterwards: "What on earth made you hustle us all out like that, Carnacki?"

'"Something seemed to be telling me to get out, *quick*," I said. "Sounds a bit silly superstitious, I know; but when you are meddling with this sort of thing, you've got to take notice of queer fancies, and risk being laughed at."

'I told him then about the "Grey Dog" business, and he nodded a lot to that. "Of course," I said, "this may be nothing more than those would-be rivals of yours playing some funny game; but, personally, though I'm going to keep an open mind, I feel that there is something beastly and dangerous about this thing."

'We talked for a while longer, and then Tassoc suggested billiards, which we played in a pretty half-hearted fashion, and all the time cocking an ear to the door, as you might say, for sounds; but none came, and later, after coffee, he suggested early bed, and a thorough overhaul of the room on the morrow.

'My bedroom was in the newer part of the castle, and the door opened into the picture gallery. At the east end of the gallery was the entrance to the corridor of the east wing; this was shut off from the gallery by two old and heavy oak doors, which looked rather odd and quaint beside the more modern doors of the various rooms.

'When I reached my room, I did not go to bed; but began to unpack my instrument trunk, of which I had retained the key. I intended to take one or two preliminary steps at once, in my investigation of the extraordinary whistling.

'Presently, when the castle had settled into quietness, I slipped out of my room, and across to the entrance of the great corridor. I opened one of the low, squat doors, and threw the beam of my pocket searchlight down the passage. It was empty, and I went through the doorway, and pushed-to the oak behind me. Then along the great passageway, throwing my light before and behind, and keeping my revolver handy.

'I had hung a "protection belt" of garlic round my neck, and the smell of it seemed to fill the corridor and give me assurance; for, as you all know, it is a wonderful "protection" against the more usual Aeiirii forms of semi-materialization, by which I supposed the whistling might be produced; though, at that period of my investigation, I was still quite prepared to find it due to some perfectly natural cause; for it is astonishing the enormous number of cases that prove to have nothing abnormal in them.

'In addition to wearing the necklet, I had plugged my ears loosely with garlic, and as I did not intend to stay more than a few minutes in the room, I hoped to be safe.

'When I reached the door, and put my hand into my pocket for the key, I had a sudden feeling of sickening funk. But I was not going to back out, if I could help it. I unlocked the door and turned the handle. Then I gave the door a sharp push with my foot, as Tassoc had done, and drew my revolver, though I did not expect to have any use for it, really.

'I shone the searchlight all round the room, and then stepped inside, with a disgustingly horrible feeling of walking slap into a waiting danger. I stood a few seconds, expectant, and nothing happened, and the empty room showed bare from corner to corner. And then, you know, I realized that the room was full of an abominable silence; can you understand that? A sort of purposeful silence, just as sickening as any of the filthy noises the Things have power to make. Do you remember what I told you about that "Silent Garden" business? Well, this room had just that same *malevolent* silence – the beastly quietness of a thing that is looking at you and not seeable itself, and thinks that it has got you. Oh, I recognized it instantly, and I whipped the top off my lantern, so as to have light over the *whole* room.

'Then I set to, working like fury, and keeping my glance all about me. I sealed the two windows with lengths of human hair, right across, and sealed them at every frame. As I worked, a queer, scarcely perceptible tenseness stole into the air of the place, and the silence seemed, if you can understand me, to grow more solid. I knew then that I had no business there without "full protection"; for I was practically certain that this was no mere Aeiirii development; but one of the worst forms, as the Saiitii; like that "Grunting Man" case – you know.

'I finished the window, and hurried over to the great fireplace. This is a huge affair, and has a queer gallows-iron, I think they are called, projecting from back of the arch. I sealed the opening with seven human airs – the seventh crossing the six others.

'Then, just as I was making an end, a low, mocking whistle grew in the room. A cold, nervous prickling went up my spine, and round my forehead from the back. The hideous sound filled all the room with an extraordinary, grotesque parody of human whistling, too gigantic to be human – as if something gargantuan and monstrous made the sounds softly. As I stood there a last moment, pressing down the final seal, I had little doubt but that I had come across one of those rare and horrible cases of the *Inanimate* reproducing the functions of the *Animate*. I made a grab for my lamp and went quickly to the door, looking over my shoulder, and listening for the thing that I expected. It came, just as I got my hand upon the handle – a low squeal of incredible, malevolent anger, piercing through the low hooning of the whistling. I dashed out, slamming the door and locking it.

'I leant a little against the opposite wall of the corridor, feeling rather funny; for it had been a hideously narrow squeak... "Theyr be noe sayfetie to be gained bye gayrds of holieness when the monyster hath pow'r to speak throe woode and stoene." So runs the passage in the

Sigsand MS., and I proved it in that "Nodding Door" business. There is no protection against this particular form of monster, except, possibly, for a fractional period of time; for it can reproduce itself in, or take to its purpose, the very protective material which you may use, and has power to "*forme* wythine the pentycle"; though not immediately. There is, of course, the possibility of the Unknown Last Line of the Saaamaaa Ritual being uttered; but it is too uncertain to count upon, and the danger is too hideous; and even then it has no power to protect for more than "maybee fyve beats of the harte", as the Sigsand has it.

'Inside of the room, there was now a constant, meditative, hooning whistling; but presently this ceased, and the silence seemed worse; for there is such a sense of hidden mischief in a silence.

'After a little, I sealed the door with crossed hairs, and then cleared off down the great passage, and so to bed.

'For a long time I lay awake; but managed eventually to get some sleep. Yet, about two o'clock I was waked by the hooning whistling of the room coming to me, even through the closed doors. The sound was tremendous, and seemed to beat through the whole house with a presiding sense of terror. As if (I remember thinking) some monstrous giant had been holding mad carnival with itself at the end of that great passage.

'I got up and sat on the edge of the bed, wondering whether to go along and have a look at the seal; and suddenly there came a thump on my door, and Tassoc walked in, with his dressing-gown over his pyjamas.

'"I thought it would have waked you, so I came along to have a talk," he said. "*I* can't sleep. Beautiful! Isn't it?"

'"Extraordinary!" I said, and tossed him my case.

'He lit a cigarette, and we sat and talked for about an hour; and all the time that noise went on, down at the end of the big corridor.

'Suddenly Tassoc stood up:

'"Let's take our guns, and go and examine the brute," he said, and turned towards the door.

'"No!" I said. "By Jove – NO! I can't say anything definite yet; but I believe that room is about as dangerous as it well can be."

'"Haunted – *really* haunted?" he asked, keenly and without any of his frequent banter.

'I told him, of course, that I could not say a definite *yes* or *no* to such a question; but that I hoped to be able to make a statement, soon. Then I gave him a little lecture on the False Re-materialization of the Animate Force through the Inanimate Inert. He began then to understand the particular way in which the room might be dangerous, if it were really the subject of a manifestation.

'About an hour later, the whistling ceased quite suddenly and

Tassoc went off again to bed. I went back to mine, also, and eventually got another spell of sleep.

'In the morning, I walked along to the room. I found the seals on the door intact. Then I went in. The window seals and the hair were all right; but the seventh hair across the great fireplace was broken. This set me thinking. I knew that it might, very possibly, have snapped, through my having tensioned it too highly; but then, again, it might have been broken by something else. Yet it was scarcely possible that a man, for instance, could have passed between the six unbroken hairs; for no one would ever have noticed them, entering the room that way, you see; but just walked through them, ignorant of their very existence.

'I removed the other hairs, and the seals. Then I looked up the chimney. It went up straight, and I could see blue sky at the top. It was a big open flue, and free from any suggestion of hiding-places or corners. Yet, of course, I did not trust to any such casual examination, and after breakfast, I put on my overalls, and climbed to the very top, sounding all the way; but I found nothing.

'Then I came down, and went over the whole of the room – floor, ceiling, and walls, mapping them out in six-inch squares, and sounding with both hammer and probe. But there was nothing unusual.

'Afterwards, I made a three-weeks' search of the whole castle, in the same thorough way; but I found nothing. I went even further then; for at night, when the whistling commenced, I made a microphone test. You see, if the whistling were mechanically produced, this test would have made evident to me the working of the machinery, if there were any such concealed within the walls. It certainly was an up to date method of examination, as you must allow.

'Of course, I did not think that any of Tassoc's rivals had fixed up any mechanical contrivance; but I thought it just possible that there had been some such thing for producing the whistling, made away back in the years, perhaps with the intention of giving the room a reputation that would ensure its being free of inquisitive folk. You see what I mean? Well, of course, it was just possible, if this were the case, that someone knew the secret of the machinery, and was utilizing the knowledge to play this devil of a prank on Tassoc. The microphone test of the walls would certainly have made this known to me, as I have said; but there was nothing of the sort in the castle; so that I had practically no doubt at all now, but that it was a genuine case of what is popularly termed "haunting".

'All this time, every night, and sometimes most of each night, the hooning whistling of the room was intolerable. It was as if an Intelligence there knew that steps were being taken against it, and piped and hooned in a sort of mad mocking contempt. I tell you, it was as extraordinary as it was horrible. Time after time I went along –

tiptoeing noiselessly on stockinged feet – to the sealed door (for I always kept the room sealed). I went at all hours of the night, and often the whistling, inside, would seem to change to a brutally jeering note, as though the half-animate monster saw me plainly through the shut door. And all the time, as I would stand watching, the hooning of the whistling would seem to fill the whole corridor, so that I used to feel a precious lonely chap, messing about there with one of Hell's mysteries.

'And every morning I would enter the room, and examine the different hairs and seals. You see, after the first week I had stretched parallel hairs all along the walls of the room, and along the ceiling; but over the floor, which was of polished stone, I had set out little colourless wafers, tacky-side uppermost. Each wafer was numbered, and they were arranged after a definite plan, so that I should be able to trace the exact movements of any living thing that went across.

'You will see that no material being or creature could possibly have entered that room, without leaving many signs to tell me about it. But nothing was ever disturbed, and I began to think that I should have to risk an attempt to stay a night in the room, in the Electric Pentacle. Mind you, I *knew* that it would be a crazy thing to do; but I was getting stumped, and ready to try anything.

'Once, about midnight, I did break the seal on the door and have a quick look in; but, I tell you, the whole room gave one mad yell, and seemed to come towards me in a great belly of shadows, as if the walls had bellied in towards me. Of course, that must have been fancy. Anyway, the yell was sufficient, and I slammed the door, and locked it, feeling a bit weak down my spine. I wonder whether you know the feeling.

'And then, when I had got to that state of readiness for anything, I made what, at first, I thought was something of a discovery.

'It was about one in the morning, and I was walking slowly round the castle, keeping in the soft grass. I had come under the shadow of the east front, and far above me, I could hear the vile hooning whistling of the room, up in the darkness of the unlit wing. Then, suddenly, a little in front of me, I heard a man's voice, speaking low, but evidently in glee:

'"By George! You chaps; but I wouldn't care to bring a wife home to that!" it said, in the tone of the cultured Irish.

'Someone started to reply; but there came a sharp exclamation, and then a rush, and I heard footsteps running in all directions. Evidently, the men had spotted me.

'For a few seconds I stood there, feeling an awful ass. After all, *they* were at the bottom of the haunting! Do you see what a big fool it made me seem? I had no doubt but that they were some of Tassoc's rivals; and here I had been feeling in every bone that I had hit a genuine Case! And then, you know, there came the memory of hundreds of details, that made me just as much in doubt, again. Anyway, whether it was natural, or ab-natural, there was a great deal yet to be cleared up.

'I told Tassoc, next morning, what I had discovered, and through the whole of every night, for five nights, we kept a close watch round the east wing; but there was never a sign of anyone prowling about; and all the time, almost from evening to dawn, that grotesque whistling would hoon incredibly, far above us in the darkness.

'On the morning after the fifth night, I received a wire from here, which brought me home by the next boat. I explained to Tassoc that I was simply bound to come away for a few days; but I told him to keep up the watch round the castle. One thing I was very careful to do, and that was to make him absolutely promise never to go into the Room between sunset and sunrise. I made it clear to him that we knew nothing definite yet, one way or the other; and if the room were what I had first thought it to be, it might be a lot better for him to die first, than enter it after dark.

'When I got here, and had finished my business, I thought you chaps would be interested; and also I wanted to get it all spread out clear in my mind; so I rang you up. I am going over again tomorrow, and when I get back I ought to have something pretty extraordinary to tell you. By the way, there is a curious thing I forgot to tell you. I tried to get a phonographic record of the whistling; but it simply produced no impression on the wax at all. That is one of the things that has made me feel queer.

'Another extraordinary thing is that the microphone will not magnify the sound – will not even transmit it; seems to take no account of it; and acts as if it were non-existent. I am absolutely and utterly stumped, up to the present. I am a wee bit curious to see whether any of your dear clever heads can make daylight of it. *I* cannot – not yet.'

He rose to his feet.

'Goodnight, all,' he said, and began to usher us out abruptly, but without offence, into the night.

* * *

A fortnight later, he dropped us each a card, and you can imagine that I was not late this time. When we arrived, Carnacki took us straight into dinner, and when we had finished, and all made ourselves comfortable, he began again, where he had left off:

'Now just listen quietly; for I have got something very queer to tell you. I got back late at night, and I had to walk up to the castle, as I had not warned them I was coming. It was bright moonlight; so that the walk was rather a pleasure than otherwise. When I got there, the whole place was in darkness, and I thought I would go round outside, to see whether Tassoc or his brother was keeping watch. But I could not find them anywhere, and concluded that they had got tired of it, and gone off to bed.

'As I returned across the lawn that lies below the front of the east wing, I caught the hooning whistling of the room, coming down strangely clear through the stillness of the night. It had a peculiar note in it, I remember – low and constant, queerly meditative. I looked up at the window, bright in the moonlight, and got a sudden thought to bring a ladder from the stable-yard, and try to get a look into the room, from the outside.

'With this notion, I hunted round at the back of the castle, among the straggle of offices, and presently found a long, fairly light ladder; though it was heavy enough for one, goodness knows! I thought at first that I should never get it reared. I managed at last, and let the ends rest very quietly against the wall, a little below the sill of the larger window. Then, going silently, I went up the ladder. Presently, I had my face above the sill, and was looking in, alone with the moonlight.

'Of course, the queer whistling sounded louder up there; but it still conveyed that peculiar sense of something whistling quietly to itself – can you understand? Though, for all the meditative lowness of the note, the horrible, gargantuan quality was distinct – a mighty parody of the human; as if I stood there and listened to the whistling from the lips of a monster with a man's soul.

'And then, you know, I saw something. The floor in the middle of the huge, empty room, was puckered upwards in the centre into a strange, soft-looking mound, parted at the top into an ever-changing hole, that pulsated to that great, gentle hooning. At times, as I watched, I saw the heaving of the indented mound gap across with a queer inward suction, as with the drawing of an enormous breath; then the thing would dilate and pout once more to the incredible melody. And suddenly, as I stared, dumb, it came to me that the thing was living. I was looking at two enormous, blackened lips, blistered and brutal, there in the pale moonlight . . .

'Abruptly, they bulged out to a vast, pouting mound of force and sound, stiffened and swollen, and hugely massive and clean-cut in the moonbeams. And a great sweat lay heavy on the vast upper lip. In the same moment of time, the whistling had burst into a mad screaming note, that seemed to stun me, even where I stood, outside of the window. And then, the following moment, I was staring blankly at the solid, undisturbed floor of the room – smooth, polished stone flooring, from wall to wall. And there was an absolute silence.

'You can imagine me staring into the quiet room, and knowing what I knew. I felt like a sick, frightened child, and I wanted to slide *quietly* down the ladder, and run away. But in that very instant, I heard Tassoc's voice calling to me from within the room, for help, *help*. My

God! but I got such an awful dazed feeling; and I had a vague bewildered notion that, after all, it was the Irishmen who had got him in there, and were taking it out of him. And then the call came again, and I burst the window, and jumped in to help him. I had a confused idea that the call had come from within the shadow of the great fireplace, and I raced across to it; but there was no one there.

'"Tassoc!" I shouted, and my voice went empty-sounding round the great apartment; and then, in a flash, *I knew that Tassoc had never called.* I whirled round, sick with fear, towards the window, and as I did so a frightful, exultant whistling scream burst through the room. On my left, the end wall had bellied in towards me, in a pair of gargantuan lips, black and utterly monstrous, to within a yard of my face. I fumbled for a mad instant at my revolver; not for *it,* but myself; for the danger was a thousand times worse than death. And then, suddenly, the Unknown Last Line of the Saaamaaa Ritual was whispered quite audibly in the room. Instantly, the thing happened that I have known once before. There came a sense as of dust falling continually and monotonously, and I knew that my life hung uncertain and suspended for a flash, in a brief reeling vertigo of unseeable things. Then *that* ended, and I knew that I might live. My soul and body blended again, and life and power came to me. I dashed furiously at the window, and hurled myself out head foremost; for I can tell you that I had stopped being afraid of death. I crashed down on to the ladder, and slithered, grabbing and grabbing; and so came some way or other alive to the bottom. And there I sat in the soft, wet grass, with the moonlight all about me; and far above, through the broken window of the room, there was a low whistling.

'That is the chief of it. I was not hurt, and I went round to the front, and knocked Tassoc up. When they let me in, we had a long yarn, over some good whisky – for I was shaken to pieces – and I explained things as much as I could. I told Tassoc that the room would have to come down, and every fragment of it be burned in a blast-furnace, erected within a pentacle. He nodded. There was nothing to say. Then I went to bed.

'We turned a small army on to the work, and within ten days, that lovely thing had gone up in smoke, and what was left was calcined and clean.

'It was when the workmen were stripping the panelling, that I got hold of a sound notion of the beginnings of that beastly development. Over the great fireplace, after the great oak panels had been torn down, I found that there was let into the masonry a scrollwork of stone, with on it an old inscription, in ancient Celtic, that here in this room was burned Dian Tiansay, Jester of King Alzof, who made the Song of Foolishness upon King Ernore of the Seventh Castle.

'When I got the translation clear, I gave it to Tassoc. He was tremendously excited; for he knew the old tale, and took me down to the library to look at an old parchment that gave the story in detail. Afterwards, I found that the incident was well known about the countryside; but always regarded more as a legend than as history. And no one seemed ever to have dreamt that the old east wing of Iastrae Castle was the remains of the ancient Seventh Castle.

'From the old parchment, I gathered that there had been a pretty dirty job done, away back in the years. It seems that King Alzof and King Ernore had been enemies by birthright, as you might say truly; but that nothing more than a little raiding had occurred on either side for years, until Dian Tiansay made the Song of Foolishness upon King Ernore, and sang it before King Alzof; and so greatly was it appreciated that King Alzof gave the jester one of his ladies to wife.

'Presently, all the people of the land had come to know the song, and so it came at last to King Ernore, who was so angered that he made war upon his old enemy, and took and burned him and his castle; but Dian Tiansay, the jester, he brought with him to his own place, and having torn his tongue out because of the song which he had made and sung he imprisoned him in the room in the east wing (which was evidently used for unpleasant purposes), and the jester's wife he kept for himself, having a fancy for her prettiness.

'But one night Dian Tiansay's wife was not to be found, and in the morning they discovered her lying dead in her husband's arms, and he sitting, whistling the Song of Foolishness, for he had no longer the power to sing it.

'Then they roasted Dian Tiansay in the great fireplace – probably from that selfsame "gallows-iron" which I have already mentioned. And until he died, Dian Tiansay "ceased not to whistle" the Song of Foolishness, which he could no longer sing. But afterwards, "in that room" there was often heard at night the sound of something whistling; and there "grew a power in that room", so that none dared to sleep in it. And presently, it would seem, the King went to another castle; for the whistling troubled him.

'There you have it all. Of course, that is only a rough rendering of the translation from the parchment. It's a bit quaint! Don't you think so?'

*　　*　　*

'Yes,' I said, answering for the lot. 'But how did the thing grow to such a tremendous manifestation?'

'One of those cases of continuity of thought producing a positive action upon the immediate surrounding material,' replied Carnacki. 'The development must have been going forward through centuries, to have produced such a monstrosity. It was a true instance of Saiitii manifestation, which I can best explain by likening it to a living spiritual fungus, which involves the very structure of the aether-fibre itself, and, of course, in so doing, acquires an essential control over the "material-substance" involved in it. It is impossible to make it plainer in a few words.'

'What broke the seventh hair?' asked Taylor.

But Carnacki did not know. He thought it was probably nothing but being too severely tensioned. He also explained that they found out that the men who had run away had not been up to mischief; but had come over secretly merely to hear the whistling, which, indeed, had suddenly become the talk of the whole countryside.

'One other thing,' said Arkright, 'have you any idea what governs the use of the Unknown Last Line of the Saaamaaa Ritual? I know, of course, that it was used by the Ab-human Priests in the Incantation of Raaaee; but what used it on your behalf, and what made it?'

'You had better read Harzam's Monograph, and my Addenda to it, on "Astral and Astarral Co-ordination and Interference", said Carnacki. 'It is an extraordinary subject, and I can only say here that the human vibration may not be insulated from the "astarral" (as is always believed to be the case, in interferences by the Ab-human) without immediate action being taken by those Forces which govern the spinning of the outer circle. In other words, it is being proved, time after time, that there is some inscrutable Protective Force constantly intervening between the human soul (not the body, mind you) and the Outer Monstrosities. Am I clear?'

'Yes, I think so,' I replied. 'And you believe that the room had become the material expression of the ancient jester – that his soul, rotted with hatred, had bred into a monster – eh?' I asked.

'Yes,' said Carnacki, nodding. 'I think you've put my thought rather neatly. It is a queer coincidence that Miss Donnehue is supposed to be descended (so I have heard since) from the same King Ernore. It makes one think some rather curious thoughts, doesn't it? The marriage coming on, and the room waking to fresh life. If she had gone into that room, ever ... eh? IT had waited a long time. Sins of the fathers. Yes, I've thought of that. They're to be married next week, and I am to be best man, which is a thing I hate. And he won his bets, rather! Just think *if* ever she had gone into that room. Pretty horrible, eh?'

He nodded his head grimly, and we four nodded back. Then he rose and took us collectively to the door, and presently thrust us forth in friendly fashion on to the Embankment, and into the fresh night air.

'Goodnight,' we all called back, and went to our various homes.

If she had, eh? If she had? That is what I kept thinking.

Magic Man
Robert Holdstock

Crouched in the mouth of the shrine-cave, One Eye, the painter, shivered as black storm clouds skated overhead and the wind whipped down from the northern ice-wastes to plague the grasslands with its bitter touch.

The tribe should be gathered together before the darkening skies could loose their volleys of rain and lightening; then they would huddle into the cliff wall and wail and moan their misery. When the rains passed the women would come, invading the shrine-cave and screeching at One Eye because he had not stopped their soaking.

He squatted, looking out across the grasslands to the man-high rushes that waved and danced in the biting winds. Stupid women, he thought. Stupid, stupid women. They should understand that his drawings were for the spirit of the hunt, not for their own comfort. They should be pleased when their men brought home bison, deer and, increasingly, the reindeer that strayed from the snows of the north valleys.

'One Eye!' hailed a child's voice. One Eye looked down to where a small boy scrambled up the slopes of the cliff towards the cave.

'Go away, child. Go away!' shouted the old man angrily. But he knew it would be no use. The boy, brown and dusty, crawled into the mouth of the cave and squatted there, breathing heavily. The sight of One Eye's empty eye socket staring at him no longer perturbed the would-be painter as once it had.

'I want to draw.'

One Eye let his grey hair fall over his one good eye, clenched his mouth tight in an obstinate gesture of annoyance and shook his head, 'Go away, child. Wait for the hunters.' Outside the wind howled against the cliff and the dark sky grew perceptibly darker.

'I want to *draw*.' Big eyes stared at the old man, childish features, open, honest. The boy was filthy; his hair was lank and filled with grass from his earlier romping. 'I'm tired of making *these*!' He threw the inaccurately made axe from his hand and it clattered down the slopes to land heavily among the women below. One of them looked up and shouted angrily. She was cleaning a skin and had blood up to her elbows. The fire around which the group squatted burned low, and charred bones and wood poked blackly from the pile of ashes. An adolescent girl, underdeveloped and sulky, prodded the dying embers with a spear. The boy, in the shrine-cave above, was angry. 'I want to draw a bear. One Eye, please! Let me draw a bear, please?'

'Look,' snapped One Eye, pointing. Black shapes against the grey sky, the hunters returned. They walked slowly, spears clutched tightly, animals slung over their shoulders. Leading them came He Who Carries a Red Spear, his scarred face angry, bleeding from gashes on his cheeks. He waved his red-ochred spear at the group and the women stood, shouting their greeting. Red Spear, thought One Eye. How I wish a bison would get *you*. The tall hunter strode into the camp. He had a deer slung over his shoulders. His fur and leather tunic had been torn away and he walked naked, black hair coating his body from neck to toe, acting as a fur in itself. He was unaware of the death-thoughts of the old man above his head. Today he had not killed a bison. Today the hunt, for him, had failed. He was angry.

The men dropped their kills close in to the cliff wall and then dragged the skins and axe baskets from where they had been distributed about the fire. The women crouched against the sloping wall of the overhang and giggled as the hunters covered them with taut skins, making rough and ready tents against the cliff face. They hammered special narrow points through the skins to hold them down, propping them up in the middle with spears. The skies darkened, distant thunder rolled and the grass whispered and sang as it bowed to the groaning winds.

'Go down,' snapped One Eye. 'Into the tents with you. Leave me in peace, brat. Leave me.'

The boy darted back into the cave and laughed as One Eye screeched with surprise. He waited for the painter to come after him, but One Eye had fallen suddenly quiet, watching the slope below him. There was the sound of someone climbing up to the cave. The boy crawled to the entrance and began to shake as he saw his father coming up towards them.

He Who Carries a Red Spear crouched beside One Eye and snarled. 'What happened to your magic today, old man? Why didn't I kill a bison, uh?' Mouth stretched back into a hideous grin, eyes narrowed, Red Spear struck fear into the heart of One Eye. One Eye cowered back, but a hairy and powerful hand reached out and grabbed him by the neck. The hunter snarled, increased the grip until the bone nearly snapped, then released the painter, looking back into the cave.

'Drawings! Paintings!' Hard eyes turned on One Eye. 'Only *spears*
kill animals, you old fool. Spears, stones ... and *these*.' He held up his
bare hands, the fingers curved with the power they possessed. 'I have
killed bison with my bare hands, old man. I have twisted their heads,
their necks twice the thickness of my body. I have twisted them until the
bones snapped and splintered, the muscle tore and the blood spurted
over my body. Drawings! Pah!' He smashed One Eye across the face. 'If
it weren't that *they*, stupid fools, believed this nonsense, I should kill you.
I should break your neck between my thumb and forefinger. I should
snap you in two and throw your useless body to the scavengers. I should
give you to the Grunts to devour.'

'My paintings,' mumbled One Eye, 'show the hunt. They protect
you. They give you power over beasts.'

Red Spear laughed. Behind him a hunter climbed into the cave and
touched the bitter man on his arm. 'Your wife waits, Red Spear. She is
eager.'

He Who Carries a Red Spear grunted. 'Hear that, old man? My
wife waits for me. All the women in this tribe I could have if I so desired.
Because I am the best hunter!' He pounded his naked chest and inched
towards the painter, the stench of his body strong and sickening. 'I hunt
with weapons, not with paintings ...' And as he said it he clutched dirt
in his hand and threw it over the ochred walls. He took his son by the
arm and threw him down the slope before him, sliding down and
disappearing into the tent.

The other hunter looked sympathetically at the old man. 'He killed
no bison today. You must forgive his anger.'

One Eye shook his head. 'He is the sire of a Grunt – that explains
much to me.' Thunder crashed nearby and the black skies flared with
the streaking lightning to the north. 'He sneers at the magic of my
paintings,' One Eye murmured. 'The paintings bring luck, they bring
kills.' He looked at the blood-smeared hunter. 'They don't say *who*
shall make the kills. They bring kills to the tribe. He *must* understand
that ...' He looked away. 'But I fear he never shall – he cannot
understand, just as none of his father's spore can understand, that beasts
and men have spirit.'

The hunter nodded. 'He only understands *kill*. And soon, One Eye,
he will kill *you*. Be careful.' The hunter turned to go. One Eye reached
out a hand and stopped him, 'How many kills today? How many?'

'Ten,' said the hunter. 'More than enough. But we shall go into the
herds again tomorrow.' His eyes flickered beyond One Eye to the cave
walls. 'Paint us luck, old man.'

Then he was gone and the storm broke, rain sheeting down and
drumming off the taut animal hide tents below. The women moaned
and cried and the men laughed and loved. One Eye sat in the darkness

at the back of the cave and thought over and over of the ten dead animals he had drawn the day before.

Always it was the same. The number he drew was the number killed. And yet, he felt he had no real power. But one day *true* power over the paintings would come to one of the tribe, and then, from here to the seas in the south, beasts would be at the mercy of men – and men, perhaps, would no longer be at the mercy of the moving ice-wastes to the north. The tribe must never die, One Eye realized, not with the inherent power it contained, hidden somewhere in the bodies of its hunters.

*   *   *

With the breaking of the sun above the eastern horizon the boy came scrambling up to the shrine-cave. He found One Eye hard at work, drawing the shapes of hunters with a charred wood stick.

'Why don't you draw them full?' asked the boy as he sat, absorbed by the growing picture of a hunt. 'Why so thin? And black?'

'Men are black,' said One Eye mysteriously. Then, pausing to glance at the boy, he lifted his eye to the cave entrance. 'Inside ... we are thin and shallow.' His glance dropped to the boy. 'Beasts kill other beasts in a *natural* way. Man kills beasts with more than his hands. He uses spears and slings, and traps and nets. Man is more than a beast, but he has lost his goodness.' The old man looked at the coloured portraits of his animals. 'They have goodness and they are full and whole. But man is shallow.' He turned to the boy. 'That is why I draw the hunters thin.'

The boy did not understand the old man's talk. But he knew he was right. And when he, too, was a great painter, magicking animals into the traps, on to the spears, of his brothers, he would follow the tradition of One Eye.

'Let me draw. Please. Let me draw.'

One Eye muttered with annoyance but he passed the yellow and red pastes he had made that dawn. The boy dipped his fingers in and smudged the wall with yellow. With his left hand he used a charred stick to draw an outline around the smear. He remembered how the ribs of the bison stood out and he drew them in. He drew the legs and the way the muscles rippled with the power of the beast. One Eye concentrated on his own drawing, but again and again he glanced at the bison taking form at the hands of the boy. Finally he stopped and watched as his small apprentice drew a spear, thrust deep into the neck of the animal.

'It is good,' said One Eye. 'You have skill.' He smiled.

The boy beamed, 'May I draw a bear? Please?'

One Eye shook his head with finality. 'The bear is a hunter of man and he must never be drawn in the shrine-cave – he is beyond our magic.'

'A bear is just a beast,' argued the boy.

'The bear is *more* than a beast. We must only draw animals that *run* from man. Never those that attack him. Do you understand?'

The boy nodded, bitterly disappointed.

'Old man!' He Who Carries a Red Spear crawled into the cave. 'How many kills today, old man?' He sneered. 'You, down!' He looked angrily at his son and the boy left the cave. Red Spear raised a fist at One Eye. 'If I find him here too many more times I shall begin to think you are stopping him from being a great hunter, like me. I shall be forced to kill you ... hear me?'

He was gone before One Eye could answer. The hunters gathered together their spears and furs and walked from the cliff towards the plains where they would find bison and deer, and smaller animals to eat on the way home.

The boy, grinning, scampered back into the cave. One Eye ignored him, staying in the mouth of the cave, watching the distant figures and wishing he was going with them. Behind him he heard charred wood scrape on the wall. He ignored it. The scraping ended and there was silence. Eventually One Eye looked round. 'What do you draw, child?'

The boy said nothing but continued working. One Eye crawled over to him.

What he saw made him gasp with horror. He slapped the boy away from the wall and reached out to try and erase the fully-drawn man from the painting of the hunt.

'No!' cried the boy, but he fell silent. The ochre was too dry; only the arm was erased. One Eye sat and looked at the man with one arm. Then he looked at the bison with the spear in its neck. Then he looked at the boy and his face was white beneath its dusty covering.

When the hunt returned, one of the hunters was dead. They carried him in, stretched on a fur and laid across two poles. His left arm had been severed above the elbow and he had bled to death. One Eye heard the word 'bear' and he knew what had happened. Then his eye wandered to the kills of the day, to the bison still with a spear-head buried deep in its neck.

The women mourned that night. The hunter lay in a shallow pit at the edge of the camp and his wife rubbed ochre into his ice-cold body, groaning and keening with every pass of her hand across her dead husband's strong chest. The fire burned high in the still night and the faces of the children and women who squatted around its warmth were solemn and drawn. Red Spear sat apart from the tribe and time and again his eyes flicked up to the dark cave mouth, where he could see One Eye squatting, watching the gathering.

Suddenly he jumped towards the fire and kicked the burning wood. 'What happened to your magic today, old man?' he screamed up at the figure in the cave. 'Why didn't you save him?' He turned to look at the dead hunter, and there were tears in his eyes, but tears of frustrated anger rather than sorrow. 'He was a *good* hunter. He killed many beasts for the tribe. Nearly as many as me!' Swinging round he raised one clenched fist. 'If you can work magic Old Man, why couldn't you have saved him?'

A hunter jumped up from the ring and caught Red Spear by the shoulders. 'One Eye cannot know the unknowable! He merely spirits the animals into our traps!'

He Who Carries a Red Spear flung the man aside. 'He does *nothing*!' he cried angrily. 'We no longer need One Eye and his stupid paintings.'

As he ran through the circle of seated hunters and their women, a feminine hand reached out and tripped him. Furious, he twisted on the ground and reached for the woman who had insulted him. He stared into the calm face of his wife, brown eyes insolently watching him. 'Leave the old man,' she said softly. 'He does no harm and many here believe him possessed of magical power. Why waste energy and respect on killing the useless?' Her smile was the last straw in the cooling of angry fires in the hunter. He leered up at One Eye and shook his fist. But he spared him.

A wood torch burned in the shrine-cave. A wolf pack howled somewhere on the tundra, and as the night progressed so the sound of their baying moved farther away to the south. One Eye was oblivious to their cries, he was oblivious to the howling wind and the sound of rocks falling outside the cave mouth. He worked on his picture. The boy knelt beside him, watching. He had begged to be allowed to draw, but One Eye had said no, not yet. The anticipation kept the boy silent and now he watched as animals took shape upon the cave wall, overlapped animals that had been drawn in the past, but that did not matter because those animals had been killed and now they were just ochre smears, without meaning, without consequence.

As he worked, One Eye repeatedly glanced at the attentive boy. There was a strange look in the old man's eye, an expression of awe.

Well into the night, when the boy was beginning to yawn, One Eye sat back and handed the charred wood to his apprentice. Wrapped tightly in animals' skins, still One Eye shivered as he began to guide the boy's hand in the drawing of men on the wall scheme. The boy, with small furs round his shoulders, hardly noticed his chill. He was enthralled.

'Draw ... your father, here. That's right,' breathed One Eye as the boy's hand traced the pin shape. 'Arch the back, that's right. Throw the arms up ... no, don't stop ...'

'I don't understand ...' murmured the boy.

'See,' explained the painter, 'see how he scares the bison into the traps – see, they run before him and he has no weapon. Red Spear *needs* no weapon.'

The boy nodded, satisfied, and continued the picture.

'Tomorrow,' said One Eye, 'I shall accompany the hunters. That surprises you?' His whiskered face broke into a smile at the expression on the boy's face. 'I used to be a hunter, long years ago. This hunt ... see how it spreads across the wall. Tomorrow will be a *great* day for the tribe. There will be *many* kills ...' His voice trailed off. 'Many kills. And I wish to join in on such an occasion. Now.' He guided the tiny hand to the wall. 'Draw me, here. See, standing *behind* your father. Draw me a spear. See how I throw it at the bison your father scares ...'

Pin shapes took form upon the grey wall. The boy, excited, creating, drew as the old man instructed him. When it was finished he was beaming. One Eye was satisfied. The boy settled against the cave wall and One Eye looked at the picture of the hunt and dreamt of the kill that would be least expected toworrow. And by the boy's magic hand it had been depicted so! He closed his eyes and slept.

When he was sure One Eye was asleep, the boy crawled to the wall and picked up the charred wood. Carefully he drew more hunters. But he was tired and they didn't form as they should – they were too small, too stooped ... like Grunts. Uncomfortable at what he had done, the boy smudged them away. They remained, shadows on the wall.

*   *   *

A fine mist hung over the grasslands as the hunters, followed by One Eye, moved off towards the grazing herds. There was the feel of snow in the air and the women had wrapped up tightly and insisted that their men put thicker skins around their shoulders, binding them into place with extra thongs. Silently, feet trudging across the cold, dewy grass, the band moved off, away from the cliff, and was swallowed by the mist.

The boy watched them go, and when they were out of sight he scrambled up to the shrine-cave and disappeared inside.

The hunters had moved silently across the mist-covered land for several hours when the first feelings of unease came to them. The fog was dense and they could see only a few paces around them. They grouped together and Red Spear motioned them to silence. One Eye watched him, breath steamy with the cold, as he pricked his ears to the low winds and listened.

There was movement all around them, shuffling, the sound of invisible feet padding across the frozen grass.

A stir went through the hunters. Was it Grunts, was it the squat and ugly men who lived in the shadow of the moving snow walls? Clutching his red-ochred spear, Red Spear motioned for the band to move on. One Eye, his own spear held, ready to stab, followed, but now his eye was wide and watchful, his heart thundering. Grunts were unpredictable. They might pass by or they might attack. There was no way of telling.

The hunters spread out as they neared where they could hear the bison grazing. Still the wall of white separated them from anything that lay ahead or behind. Each hunter was a vague grey shape as he moved through the mist, spear held ready, head turning from side to side. Behind them the sound of creatures grew louder.

'Look!' breathed a hunter close to One Eye. His voice caused them all to stop and turn. What they saw made them howl with fear ...

White shapes, running through the mist. Ghosts, shimmering and flickering in and out of vision. Ghostly spears held high, mouths open in a silent war cry. Grunts, spirits, the spirits of the ugly creatures that had died at the hands of the hunters over the years gone by.

One Eye ran. He ran hard and he ran fast and he was aware of the other hunters running beside him, breathing fast and hard, eyes wide and constantly turned to regard the apparitions that pursued them.

All at once they were among the bison. Their approach, not the most silent, had been muffled by the heavy air, and the animals were taken by surprise. The huge black head of a male bison looked upon One Eye, and the creature stood, for a moment, stunned. Then it snorted and turned, scampering heavily away and out of sight.

From his left there came a scream and the sound of flesh torn. One Eye moved over and saw the shape of a hunter spreadeagled on the ground, being gored by the huge leader of the herd. And beyond the sight of the man threshing against the veil of death, the white ghosts of dead men came running through the fog.

One Eye staggered backwards, his head turning frantically from right to left as he searched for a way out. The silent shapes were all around and now he could see their tiny eyes, black orbs in the white of their spectral faces. Their bodies were naked, squat and heavy, their brows huge and jutting, giving them a peculiarly blind look.

They ran through the fog, and ghostly spears flew from ghostly hands, sailing silently past the hunters and vanishing as they flew from sight. The bison snorted and raged and ran amok among the terrified hunters. One Eye came up to the steaming flank of a small animal, and when it saw him it turned on him. He stabbed at it with his spear and felt the point sink into flesh. The bison roared and thundered away. One Eye stood alone, surrounded by the shifting wall of white. He could see the ghosts moving closer, their bodies swaying as they neared him, mouths open, screaming their silent screams of anger.

Behind him he heard the thunderous approach of a large bison and ran to avoid its maddened gallop. Distantly, a hunter screamed, and the scream was cut off as his life ended at the razor tip of a bison's horn. One Eye ran towards the scream, and as he ran he passed bewildered and terrified hunters who stood still, now, almost ready for the death that was overtaking so many of the tribe.

A bison snorted close by and lumbered out of the mist, its flank catching One Eye and sending him sprawling. As he staggered to his feet a new sound reached his ears. He paused, on his knees, breath coming short and painfully. There was blood on his tightly-wrapped fur breeches, but he felt no pain.

A throaty growl, like no sound he had ever heard in his life. And it was near, very near. A hunter screamed, and it was a scream of terror, not of death. One Eye jumped to his feet and crouched with his spear-point centred unwaveringly on where he could hear something big and cumbersome moving in his direction. The hunter who had screamed so loudly came running out of the mist, face smeared with blood and sweat, eyes open, mouth open. He carried no spear and ran past One Eye as if he hadn't seen him. He disappeared into the mist and a moment later One Eye heard a grunt and a gasp. The hunter reappeared, staggering, a red-ochred spear thrust deep into his belly.

The roar of the animal that approached came again, nearer. One Eye backed away carefully and his eye searched the fog for any sign of what it could be. The ghosts appeared again, dancing towards the lost hunters, and now they seemed almost ... taunting.

Behind One Eye there was the snort of a bison. He swung round but could see nothing. As he walked forward, ears keened for the sound of the beast behind him, he came to He Who Carries a Red Spear, standing with his back to One Eye, crouched and waiting for the bison to charge. One Eye could hear its snorting in the mist and realized that any moment it would tear into sight and Red Spear would either kill or be killed. But that could not be! Remembering how he had drawn the hunt, how he had spirited Red Spear's life into his own hands, One Eye edged forward.

He raised his spear high and threw it with all his strength at the centre of the leader's naked back. Red Spear screamed and arched over backwards, and One Eye saw two feet of spear protruding beyond the other man's chest. Naked, blood pumping down his glistening limbs, Red Spear lay dead at One Eye's feet.

A shadow fell across One Eye and, as he was about to defile the body with his hand axe, he froze. Straightening up, he became aware of the heavy breathing close behind, of the rumbling roar of a wild beast ...

'NO!' he screamed, flinging his body round and staring up at the black creature which towered over him. 'NO!' His hands flew to his face and he staggered backwards, tripping over the body of Red Spear. The monster lumbered forward, rising onto its hindlegs and reaching down with its front paws. Claws as long as a man's forearm glinted and slashed down at the painter, caught him just below his throat and ripped downwards, disembowelling him and throwing him twenty feet across the grass with a last jerk of a bloodstained paw. One Eye had a brief second to assess his killer. It was like a bear, yet so unlike a bear – the muzzle was long and twisted, the teeth too long, too white. The eyes, huge, staring, were the eyes of a dead man, not a living beast. And the fur ... the fur was unlike the fur of any bear that One Eye had ever seen. It was black and red! Black and red!

Then there was only pain for One Eye, intense pain and the sight of his own blood and entrails seeping on to the grass. Followed by the blackness of death.

*   *   *

Crouched in the mouth of the shrine-cave, the boy shivered as black storm clouds skated overhead and icy winds whipped down from the northern ice-wastes, driving the mist before them, clearing the grass-lands to the eyes of the desperate women.

The hunters were late, very late. The women were frightened and they wailed. The fire burned high as a beacon for their men, and soon, tired and bloody, spearless and without a single kill between them, the few hunters that survived returned to the camp.

The boy crawled into the deep of the cave where a small fire burned and illuminated the drawings and paintings on the wall. He reached out a hand and traced the figure of his father, moving his finger to the outline of One Eye poised, ready to throw the spear. Then the boy's fingers traced the great bear that reared up on its hind legs, body finished with red ochre and black charred wood, teeth pearly white with root gum ... It had taken him a long time to draw and he was proud of it. That it was not a realistic likeness of one of the bears which roamed the tundra he was not to know, for he had never seen a bear.

He settled back and regarded the towering shape as it seemed to swoop on the little figure of One Eye, dancing among the smudges of the hunters the boy had drawn earlier.

The boy laughed as he reached out and smudged away the black drawing of his teacher. One Eye would not be coming back. The tribe had a new painter, now.

The Shadow of a Shade
Tom Hood

My sister Lettie has lived with me ever since I had a home of my own. She was my little housekeeper before I married. Now she is my wife's constant companion, and the 'darling auntie' of my children, who go to her for comfort, advice and aid in all their little troubles and perplexities.

But, though she has a comfortable home, and loving hearts around her, she wears a grave, melancholy look on her face, which puzzles acquaintances and grieves friends.

A disappointment! Yes, the old story of a lost lover is the reason for Lettie's looks. She has had good offers often; but since she lost the first love of her heart she has never indulged in the happy dream of loving and being beloved.

George Mason was a cousin of my wife's – a sailor by profession. He and Lettie met one another at our wedding, and fell in love at first sight. George's father had seen service before him on the great mysterious sea, and had been especially known as a good Arctic sailor, having shared in more than one expedition in search of the North Pole and the North-West Passage.

It was not a matter of surprise to me, therefore, when George volunteered to go out in the *Pioneer*, which was being fitted out for a cruise in search of Franklin and his missing expedition. There was a fascination about such an undertaking that I felt I could not have resisted had I been in his place. Of course, Lettie did not like the idea at all, but he silenced her by telling her that men who volunteered for Arctic search were never lost sight of, and that he should not make as much advance in his profession in a dozen years as he would in a year or so of this expedition. I cannot say that Lettie, even after this, was quite satisfied with the notion of his going, but, at all events, she did not argue against it any longer. But the grave look, which is now habitual with her, but was a rare thing in her young and happy days, passed over her face sometimes when she thought no one was looking.

My younger brother, Harry, was at this time an academy student. He was only a beginner then. Now he is pretty well known in the art world, and his pictures command fair prices. Like all beginners in art, he was full of fancies and theories. He would have been a pre-Raphaelite, only pre-Raphaelism had not been invented then. His peculiar craze was for what he styled the Venetian School. Now, it chanced that George had a fine Italian-looking head, and Harry persuaded him to sit for him for his portrait. It was a fair likeness, but a very moderate work of art. The background was so very dark, and George's naval costume so very deep in colour, that the face came out too white and staring. It was a three-quarter picture; but only one hand showed in it, leaning on the hilt of a sword. As George said, he looked much more like the commander of a Venetian galley than a modern mate.

However, the picture pleased Lettie, who did not care much about art provided the resemblance was good. So the picture was duly framed – in a tremendously heavy frame, of Harry's ordering – and hung up in the dining-room.

And now the time for George's departure was growing nearer. The *Pioneer* was nearly ready to sail, and her crew only waited orders. The officers grew acquainted with each other before sailing, which was an adventure. George took up very warmly with the surgeon, Vincent Grieve, and, with my permission, brought him to dinner once or twice.

'Poor chap, he has no friends nearer than the Highlands, and its precious lonely work.'

'Bring him by all means, George! You know that any friends of yours will be welcome here.'

So Vincent Grieve came. I am bound to say I was not favourably impressed by him, and almost wished I had not consented to his coming. He was a tall, pale, fair young man, with a hard Scots face and a cold, grey eye. There was something in his expression, too, that was unpleasant – something cruel or crafty, or both.

I considered that it was very bad taste for him to pay such marked attention to Lettie, coming, as he did, as the friend of her fiancé. He kept by her constantly and anticipated George in all the little attentions which a lover delights to pay. I think George was a little put out about it, though he said nothing, attributing his friend's offence to lack of breeding.

Lettie did not like it at all. She knew that she was not to have George with her much longer, and she was anxious to have him to herself as much as possible. But as Grieve was her lover's friend she bore the infliction with the best possible patience.

The surgeon did not seem to perceive in the least that he was interfering where he had no business. He was quite self-possessed and happy, with one exception. The portrait of George seemed to annoy him. He had uttered a little impatient exclamation when he first saw it which drew my attention to him; and I noticed that he tried to avoid looking at it. At last, when dinner came, he was told to sit exactly facing the picture. He hesitated for an instant and then sat down, but almost immediately rose again.

'It's very childish and that sort of thing,' he stammered, 'but I cannot sit opposite that picture.'

'It is not high art,' I said, 'and may irritate a critical eye.'

'I know nothing about art,' he answered, 'but it is one of those unpleasant pictures whose eyes follow you about the room. I have an inherited horror of such pictures. My mother married against her father's will, and when I was born she was so ill she was hardly expected to live. When she was sufficiently recovered to speak without delirious rambling she implored them to remove a picture of my grandfather that hung in the room, and which she vowed made threatening faces at her. It's superstitious, but constitutional – I have a horror of such paintings!'

I believe George thought this was a ruse of his friend's to get a seat next to Lettie; but I felt sure it was not, for I had seen the alarmed expression of his face.

At night, when George and his friend were leaving, I took an opportunity to ask the former, half in a joke, if he should bring the surgeon to see us again. George made a very hearty assertion to the contrary, adding that he was pleasant enough company among men at an inn, or on board ship, but not where ladies were concerned.

But the mischief was done. Vincent Grieve took advantage of the introduction and did not wait to be invited again. He called the next day, and nearly every day after. He was a more frequent visitor than George now, for George was obliged to attend to his duties, and they kept him on board the *Pioneer* pretty constantly, whereas the surgeon, having seen to the supply of drugs, etc., was pretty well at liberty. Lettie avoided him as much as possible, but he generally brought, or professed to bring, some little message from George to her, so that he had an excuse for asking to see her.

On the occasion of his last visit – the day before the *Pioneer* sailed – Lettie came to me in great distress. The young cub had actually had the audacity to tell her he loved her. He knew, he said, about her engagement to George, but that did not prevent another man from loving her too. A man could no more help falling in love than he could help taking a fever. Lettie stood upon her dignity and rebuked him severely; but he told her he could see no harm in telling her of his passion, though he knew it was a hopeless one.

'A thousand things may happen,' he said at last, 'to bring your engagement with George Mason to an end. Then perhaps you will not forget that another loves you!'

I was very angry, and was forthwith going to give him my opinion on his conduct, when Lettie told me he was gone, that she had bade him go and had forbidden him the house. She only told me in order to protect herself, for she did not intend to say anything to George, for fear it should lead to a duel or some other violence.

That was the last we saw of Vincent Grieve before the *Pioneer* sailed.

George came the same evening, and was with us till daybreak, when he had to tear himself away and join his ship.

After shaking hands with him at the door, in the cold, grey, drizzly dawn, I turned back into the dining-room, where poor Lettie was sobbing on the sofa.

I could not help starting when I looked at George's portrait, which hung above her. The strange light of daybreak could hardly account for the extraordinary pallor of the face. I went close to it and looked hard at it. I saw that it was covered with moisture, and imagined that that possibly made it look so pale. As for the moisture, I supposed poor Lettie had been kissing the beloved's portrait, and that the moisture was caused by her tears.

It was not till a long time after, when I was jestingly telling Harry how his picture had been caressed, that I learnt the error of my conjecture. Lettie assured me most solemnly that I was mistaken in supposing she had kissed it.

'It was the varnish blooming, I expect,' said Harry. And thus the subject was dismissed, for I said no more, though I knew well enough, in spite of my not being an artist, that the bloom of varnish was quite another sort of thing.

The *Pioneer* sailed. We received – or, rather, Lettie received – two letters from George, which he had taken the opportunity of sending by homeward-bound whalers. In the second he said it was hardly likely he should have an opportunity of sending another, as they were sailing into high latitudes – into the solitary sea, to which none but expedition ships ever penetrated. They were all in high spirits, he said, for they had encountered very little ice and hoped to find clear water farther north than usual. Moreover, he added, Grieve had held a sinecure so far, for there had not been a single case of illness on board.

Then came a long silence, and a year crept away very slowly for poor Lettie. Once we heard of the expedition from the papers. They were reported as pushing on and progressing favourably by a wandering tribe of Esquimaux with whom the captain of a Russion vessel fell in. They had laid the ship up for the winter, and were taking the boats on sledges, and believed they had met with traces of the lost crews that seemed to show they were on the right track.

The winter passed again, and spring came. It was a balmy, bright spring such as we get occasionally, even in this changeable and uncertain climate of ours.

One evening we were sitting in the dining-room with the window open, for, although we had long given up fires, the room was so oppressively warm that we were glad of the breath of the cool evening breeze.

Lettie was working. Poor child, though she never murmured, she was evidently pining at George's long absence. Harry was leaning out of the window, studying the evening effect on the fruit blossom, which was wonderfully early and plentiful, the season was so mild. I was sitting at the table, near the lamp, reading the paper.

Suddenly there swept into the room a chill. It was not a gust of cold wind, for the curtain by the open window did not swerve in the least. But the deathly cold pervaded the room – came, and was gone in an instant. Lettie shuddered, as I did, with the intense icy feeling.

She looked up. 'How curiously cold it has got all in a minute,' she said.

'We are having a taste of poor George's Polar weather,' I said with a smile.

At the same moment I instinctively glanced towards his portrait. What I saw struck me dumb. A rush of blood, at fever heat, dispelled the numbing influence of the chill breath that had seemed to freeze me.

I have said the lamp was lighted; but it was only that I might read with comfort, for the violet twilight was still so full of sunset that the room was not dark. But as I looked at the picture I saw it had undergone a strange change. I saw it as plainly as possible. It was no delusion, coined for the eye by the brain.

I saw, in the place of George's head, a grinning skull! I stared at it hard; but it was no trick of fancy. I could see the hollow orbits, the gleaming teeth, the fleshless cheekbones – it was the head of death!

Without saying a word, I rose from my chair and walked straight up to the painting. As I drew nearer a sort of mist seemed to pass before it; and as I stood close to it, I saw only the face of George. The spectral skull had vanished.

'Poor George!' I said unconsciously.

Lettie looked up. The tone of my voice had alarmed her, the expression of my face did not reassure her.

'What do you mean? Have you heard anything? Oh, Robert, in mercy tell me!'

She got up and came over to me and, laying her hands on my arm, looked up into my face imploringly.

'No, my dear; how should I hear? Only I could not help thinking of the privation and discomfort he must have gone through. I was reminded of it by the cold——'

'Cold!' said Harry, who had left the window by this time. 'Cold! what on earth are you talking about? Cold, such an evening as this! You must have had a touch of ague, I should think.'

'Both Lettie and I felt it bitterly cold a minute or two ago. Did you not feel it?'

'Not a bit; and as I was three parts out of the window I ought to have felt it if any one did.'

It was curious, but that strange chill had been felt only in the room. It was not the night wind, but some supernatural breath connected with the dread apparition I had seen. It was, indeed, the chill of polar winter – the icy shadow of the frozen North.

'What is the day of the month, Harry?' I asked.

'Today – the 23rd, I think,' he answered; then added, taking up the newspaper I had been reading: 'Yes, here you are. Tuesday, February 23rd, if the *Daily News* tells truth, which I suppose it does. Newspapers can afford to tell the truth about dates, whatever they may do about art.' Harry had been rather roughly handled by the critic of a morning paper for one of his pictures a few days before, and he was a little angry with journalism generally.

Presently Lettie left the room, and I told Harry what I had felt and seen, and told him to take note of the date, for I feared that some mischance had befallen George.

'I'll put it down in my pocket-book, Bob. But you and Lettie must have had a touch of the cold shivers, and your stomach or fancy misled you – they're the same thing, you know. Besides, as regards the picture, there's nothing in that! There is a skull there, of course. As Tennyson says:

'Any face, however full
padded round with flesh and fat,
Is but modelled on a skull.'

The skull's there – just as in every good figure-subject the nude is there under the costumes. You fancy that is a mere coat of paint. Nothing of the kind! Art lives, sir! That is just as much a real head as yours is with all the muscles and bones, just the same. That's what makes the difference between art and rubbish.'

This was a favourite theory of Harry's, who had not yet developed from the dreamer into the worker. As I did not care to argue with him, I allowed the subject to drop after we had written down the date in our pocket-books. Lettie sent down word presently that she did not feel well and had gone to bed. My wife came down presently and asked what had happened. She had been up with the children and had gone in to see what was the matter with Lettie.

'I think it was very imprudent to sit with the window open, dear. I know the evenings are warm, but the night air strikes cold at times – at any rate, Lettie seems to have caught a violent cold, for she is shivering very much. I am afraid she had got a chill from the open windows.'

I did not say anything to her then, except that both Lettie and I had felt a sudden coldness; for I did not care to enter into an explanation again, for I could see Harry was inclined to laugh at me for being so superstitious.

At night, however, in our room, I told my wife what had occurred, and what my apprehensions were. She was so upset and alarmed that I almost repented having done so.

The next morning Lettie was better again, and as we did not either of us refer to the events of the preceding night the circumstance appeared to be forgotten by us all.

But from that day I was ever inwardly dreading the arrival of bad news. And at last it came, as I expected.

One morning, just as I was coming downstairs to breakfast, there came a knock at the door, and Harry made his appearance. It was a very early visit for him, for he generally used to spend his mornings at the studio, and drop in on his way home at night.

He was looking pale and agitated.

'Lettie's not down, is she, yet?' he asked; and then, before I could answer, added another question: 'What newspaper do you take?'

'The *Daily News*,' I answered. 'Why?'

'She's not down?'

'No.'

'Thank God! Look here!'

He took a paper from his pocket and gave it to me, pointing out a short paragraph at the bottom of one of the columns.

I knew what was coming the moment he spoke about Lettie.

The paragraph was headed, 'Fatal Accident to one of the Officers of the *Pioneer* Expedition Ship.' It stated that news had been received at the Admiralty stating that the expedition had failed to find the missing crews, but had come upon some traces of them. Want of stores and necessaries had compelled them to turn back without following those traces up; but the commander was anxious, as soon as the ship could be refitted, to go out and take up the trail where he left it. An unfortunate accident had deprived him of one of his most promising officers, Lieutenant Mason, who was precipitated from an iceberg and killed while out shooting with the surgeon. He was beloved by all, and his death had flung a gloom over the gallant little troop of explorers.

'It's not in the *News* today, thank goodness, Bob,' said Harry, who

had been searching that paper while I was reading the one he brought –
'but you must keep a sharp look-out for some days and not let Lettie see
it when it appears, as it is certain to do sooner or later.'

Then we both of us looked at each other with tears in our eyes. 'Poor
George! – poor Lettie!' we sighed softly.

'But she must be told at some time or other?' I said despairingly.

'I suppose so,' said Harry; 'but it would kill her to come on it
suddenly like this. Where's your wife?'

She was with the children, but I sent up for her and told her the ill
tidings.

She had a hard struggle to conceal her emotion, for Lettie's sake.
But the tears would flow in spite of her efforts.

'How shall I ever find courage to tell her?' she asked.

'Hush!' said Harry, suddenly grasping her arm and looking towards
the door.

I turned. There stood Lettie, with her face pale as death, with her
lips apart, and with a blind look about her eyes. She had come in
without our hearing her. We never learnt how much of the story she had
overheard; but it was enough to tell her the worst. We all sprang towards
her; but she only waved us away, turned round, and went upstairs again
without saying a word. My wife hastened up after her and found her on
her knees by the bed, insensible.

The doctor was sent for, and restoratives were promptly administered. She came to herself again, but lay dangerously ill for some weeks
from the shock.

It was about a month after she was well enough to come downstairs
again that I saw in the paper an announcement of the arrival of the
Pioneer. The news had no interest for any of us now, so I said nothing
about it. The mere mention of the vessel's name would have caused the
poor girl pain.

One afternoon shortly after this, as I was writing a letter, there came
a loud knock at the front door. I looked up from my writing and
listened; for the voice which enquired if I was in sounded strange, but
yet not altogether unfamiliar. As I looked up, puzzling whose it could
be, my eye rested accidentally upon poor George's portrait. Was I
dreaming or awake?

I have told you that the one hand was resting on a sword. I could see
now distinctly that the forefinger was raised, as if in warning. I looked at
it hard, to assure myself it was no fancy, and then I perceived, standing
out bright and distinct on the pale face, two large drops, as if of
blood.

I walked up to it, expecting the appearance to vanish, as the skull
had done. It did not vanish; but the uplifted finger resolved itself into a
little white moth which had settled on the canvas. The red drops were

fluid, and certainly not blood, though I was at a loss for the time to account for them.

The moth seemed to be in a torpid state, so I took it off the picture and placed it under an inverted wineglass on the mantelpiece. All this took less time to do than to describe. As I turned from the mantelpiece the servant brought in a card, saying the gentleman was waiting in the hall to know if I would see him.

On the card was the name of 'Vincent Grieve, of the exploring vessel *Pioneer.*'

'Thank Heaven, Lettie is out,' thought I; and then added aloud to the servant, 'Show him in here; and Jane, if your mistress and Miss Lettie come in before the gentleman goes, tell them I have someone with me on business and do not wish to be disturbed.'

I went to the door to meet Grieve. As he crossed the threshold, and before he could have seen the portrait, he stopped, shuddered, and turned white, even to his thin lips.

'Cover that picture before I come in,' he said hurriedly, in a low voice. 'You remember the effect it had upon me. Now, with the memory of poor Mason, it would be worse than ever.'

I could understand his feelings better now than at first; for I had come to look on the picture with some awe myself. So I took the cloth off a little round table that stood under the window and hung it over the portrait.

When I had done so Grieve came in. He was greatly altered. He was thinner and paler than ever; hollow-eyed and hollow-cheeked. He had acquired a strange stoop, too, and his eyes had lost the crafty look for a look of terror, like that of a hunted beast. I noticed that he kept glancing sideways every instant, as if unconsciously. It looked as if he heard someone behind him.

I had never liked the man; but now I felt an insurmountable repugnance to him – so great a repugnance that, when I came to think of it, I felt pleased that the incident of covering the picture at his request had led to my not shaking hands with him.

I felt that I could not speak otherwise than coldly to him; indeed, I had to speak with painful plainness.

I told him that, of course, I was glad to see him back, but that I could not ask him to continue to visit us. I should be glad to hear the particulars of poor George's death, but that I could not let him see my sister, and hinted, as delicately as I could, at the impropriety of which he had been guilty when he last visited.

He took it all very quietly, only giving a long, weary sigh when I told him I must beg him not to repeat his visit. He looked so weak and ill that I was obliged to ask him to take a glass of wine – an offer which he seemed to accept with great pleasure.

I got out the sherry and biscuits and placed them on the table between us, and he took a glass and drank it off greedily.

It was not without some difficulty that I could get him to tell me of George's death. He related, with evident reluctance, how they had gone out to shoot a white bear which they had seen on an iceberg stranded along the shore. The top of the berg was ridged like the roof of a house, sloping down on one side to the edge of a tremendous over-hanging precipice. They had scrambled along the ridge in order to get nearer the game, when George incautiously ventured on the sloping side.

'I called out to him,' said Grieve, 'and begged him to come back, but too late. The surface was as smooth and slippery as glass. He tried to turn back, but slipped and fell. And then began a horrible scene. Slowly, slowly, but with ever-increasing motion, he began to slide down towards the edge. There was nothing to grasp at – no irregularity or projection on the smooth face of the ice. I tore off my coat, and hastily attaching it to the stock of my gun, pushed the latter towards him; but it did not reach far enough. Before I could lengthen it, by tying my cravat to it, he had slid yet farther away, and more quickly. I shouted in agony; but there was no one within hearing. He, too, saw his fate was sealed; and he could only tell me to bring his last farewell to you, and – and to her!' – here Grieve's voice broke – 'and it was all over! He clung to the edge of the precipice instinctively for one second, and was gone!'

Just as Grieve uttered the last word, his jaw fell; his eyeballs seemed ready to start from his head; he sprang to his feet, pointed at something behind me, and then flinging up his arms, fell, with a scream, as if he had been shot. He was seized with an epileptic fit.

I instinctively looked behind me as I hurried to raise him from the floor. The cloth had fallen from the picture, where the face of George, made paler than ever by the gouts of red, looked sternly down.

I rang the bell. Luckily, Harry had come in; and, when the servant told him what was the matter, he came in and assisted me in restoring Grieve to consciousness. Of course, I covered the painting up again.

When he was quite himself again, Grieve told me he was subject to fits occasionally.

He seemed very anxious to learn if he had said or done anything extraordinary while he was in the fit, and appeared reassured when I said he had not. He apologized for the trouble he had given, and said as soon as he was strong enough he would take his leave. He was leaning on the mantelpiece as he said this. The little white moth caught his eye.

'So you have had someone else from the *Pioneer* here before me?' he said nervously.

I answered in the negative, asking what made him think so.

'Why, this little white moth is never found in such southern latitudes. It is one of the last signs of life northward. Where did you get it?'

'I caught it here, in this room,' I answered.

'That is very strange. I never heard of such a thing before. We shall hear of showers of blood soon, I should not wonder.'

'What do you mean?' I asked.

'Oh, these little fellows emit little drops of a red-looking fluid at certain seasons, and sometimes so plentifully that the superstitious think it is a shower of blood. I have seen the snow quite stained in places. Take care of it, it is a rarity in the south.'

I noticed, after he left, which he did almost immediately, that there was a drop of red fluid on the marble under the wineglass. The bloodstain on the picture was accounted for; but how came the moth here?

And there was another strange thing about the man, which I had scarcely been able to assure myself of in the room, where there were crosslights, but about which there was no possible mistake, when I saw him walking away up the street.

'Harry, here – quick!' I called to my brother, who at once came to the window. 'You're an artist – tell me, is there anything strange about that man?'

'No; nothing that I can see,' said Harry, but then suddenly, in an altered tone, added, 'Yes, there is. By Jove, *he has a double shadow!*'

That was the explanation of his sidelong glances, of the habitual stoop. There was a something always at his side, which none could see, but which cast a shadow.

He turned presently, and saw us at the window. Instantly, he crossed the road to the shady side of the street. I told Harry all that had passed, and we agreed that it would be as well not to say a word to Lettie.

Two days later, when I returned from a visit to Harry's studio, I found the whole house in confusion.

I learnt from Lettie that while my wife was upstairs, Grieve had called, had not waited for the servant to announce him but had walked straight into the dining-room, where Lettie was sitting. She noticed that he avoided looking at the picture, and, to make sure of not seeing it, had seated himself on the sofa just beneath it. He had then, in spite of Lettie's angry remonstrances, renewed his offer of love, strengthening it finally by assuring her that poor George with his dying breath had implored him to seek her, and watch over her and marry her.

'I was so indignant I hardly knew how to answer him,' said Lettie. 'When, suddenly, just as he uttered the last words, there came a twang like the breaking of a guitar – and – I hardly know how to describe it –

but the portrait had fallen, and the corner of the heavy frame had struck him on the head, cutting it open, and rendering him insensible.'

They had carried him upstairs, by the direction of the doctor, for whom my wife at once sent on hearing what had occurred. He was laid on the couch in my dressing-room, where I went to see him. I intended to reproach him for coming to the house, despite my prohibition, but I found him delirious. The doctor said it was a queer case; for, though the blow was a severe one, it was hardly enough to account for the symptoms of brain fever. When he learnt that Grieve had but just returned in the *Pioneer* from the North, he said it was possible that the privation and hardship had told on his constitution and sown the seeds of the malady.

We sent for a nurse, who was to sit up with him, by the doctor's directions.

The rest of my story is soon told. In the middle of the night I was roused by a loud scream. I slipped on my clothes, and rushed out to find the nurse, with Lettie in her arms, in a faint. We carried her into her room, and then the nurse explained the mystery to us.

It appears that about midnight Grieve sat up in bed, and began to talk. And he said such terrible things that the nurse became alarmed. Nor was she much reassured when she became aware that the light of her single candle flung what seemed to be two shadows of the sick man on the wall.

Terrified beyond measure, she had crept into Lettie's room, and confided her fears to her; and Lettie, who was a courageous and kindly girl, dressed herself, and said she would sit with her. She, too, saw the double shadow – but what she heard was far more terrible.

Grieve was sitting up in bed, gazing at the unseen figure to which the shadow belonged. In a voice that trembled with emotion, he begged the haunting spirit to leave him, and prayed its forgiveness.

'You know the crime was not premeditated. It was a sudden temptation of the devil that made me strike the blow, and fling you over the precipice. It was the devil tempting me with the recollection of her exquisite face – of the tender love that might have been mine, but for you. But she will not listen to me. See, she turns away from me, as if she knew I was your murderer, George Mason!'

It was Lettie who repeated in a horrified whisper this awful confession.

I could see it all now! As I was about to tell Lettie of the many strange things I had concealed from her, the nurse, who had gone to see her patient, came running back in alarm.

Vincent Grieve had disappeared. He had risen in his delirious terror, had opened the window, and leaped out. Two days later his body was found in the river.

A curtain hangs now before poor George's portrait, though it is no longer connected with any supernatural marvels; and never, since the night of Vincent Grieve's death, have we seen aught of that most mysterious haunting presence – the Shadow of a Shade.

A Night at a Cottage
Richard Hughes

On the evening that I am considering, I passed by some ten or twenty cosy barns and sheds without finding one to my liking; for Worcestershire lanes are devious and muddy, and it was nearly dark when I found an empty cottage set back from the road in a little bedraggled garden. There had been heavy rain earlier in the day, and the straggling fruit trees still wept over it.

But the roof looked sound, there seemed no reason why it should not be fairly dry inside – as dry, at any rate, as I was likely to find anywhere.

I decided; and with a long look up the road, and a long look down the road, I drew an iron bar from the lining of my coat and forced the door, which was only held by a padlock and two staples. Inside, the darkness was damp and heavy; I struck a match, and with its haloed light I saw the black mouth of a passage somewhere ahead of me; and then it spluttered out. So I closed the door carefully, though I had little reason to fear passers-by at such a dismal hour and in so remote a lane; and lighting another match, I crept down this passage to a little room at the far end, where the air was a bit clearer, for all that the window was boarded across. Moreover, there was a little rusted stove in this room; and thinking it too dark for any to see the smoke, I ripped up part of the wainscot with my knife, and soon was boiling my tea over a bright, small fire, and drying some of the day's rain out of my steamy clothes. Presently I piled the stove with wood to its top bar, and setting my boots where they would best dry, I stretched my body out to sleep.

I cannot have slept very long, for when I woke the fire was still burning brightly. It is not easy to sleep for long together on the level boards of a floor, for the limbs grow numb, and any movement wakes. I turned over, and was about to go again to sleep when I was startled to hear steps in the passage. As I have said, the window was boarded, and there was no other door from the little room – no cupboard even – in which to hide. It occurred to me rather grimly that there was nothing to do but to sit up and face the music, and that would probably mean being haled back to Worcester Gaol, which I had left two bare days before, and where, for various reasons, I had no anxiety to be seen again.

The stranger did not hurry himself, but presently walked slowly down the passage, attracted by the light of the fire; and when he came in he did not seem to notice me where I lay huddled in a corner, but walked straight over to the stove and warmed his hands at it. He was dripping wet – wetter than I should have thought it possible for a man to get, even on such a rainy night, and his clothes were old and worn. The water dripped from him on to the floor; he wore no hat, and the straight hair over his eyes dripped water that sizzled spitefully on the embers.

It occurred to me at once that he was no lawful citizen, but another wanderer like myself: a gentleman of the road; so I gave him some sort of greeting, and we were presently in conversation. He complained much of the cold and the wet, and huddled himself over the fire, his teeth chattering and his face an ill white.

'No,' I said, 'it is no decent weather for the road, this. But I wonder this cottage isn't more frequented, for it's a tidy little bit of a cottage.'

Outside, the pale dead sunflowers and giant weeds stirred in the rain.

'Time was,' he answered, 'there wasn't a tighter little cot in the co-anty, nor a purtier garden. A regular little parlour, she was. But now no folk'll live in it, and there's very few tramps will stop here either.'

There were none of the rags and tins and broken food about that you find a place where many beggars are used to stay.

'Why's that?' I asked.

He gave a very troubled sigh before answering.

'Gho-asts,' he said; 'gho-asts. Him that lived here. It is a mighty sad tale, and I'll not tell it to you; but the upshot of it was that he drownded hisself, down to the mill-pond. All slimy, he was, and floating, when they pulled him out of it. There are fo-aks have seen un floating on the pond, and fo-aks have seen un set round the corner of the school, waiting for his childer. Seems as if he had forgotten, like how they were all gone dead. and the why he drownded hisself. But there are some say he walks up and down this cottage, up and down; like when the smallpox had 'em, and they couldn't sleep but if they heard his feet going up and down by their do-ars. Drownded hisself down to the pond, he did; and now he *walks*.'

The stranger sighed again, and I could hear the water squelch in his boots as he moved himself.

'But it doesn't do for the like of us to get superstitious,' I answered. 'It wouldn't do for us to get seeing ghosts, or many's the wet night we'd be lying in the roadway.'

'No,' he said; 'no, it wouldn't do at all. I never had belief in *walks* myself.'

I laughed.

'Nor I that,' I said. 'I never see ghosts, whoever may.'

He looked at me again in his queer melancholy fashion.

'No,' he said. ''Spect you don't ever. Some folk do-ant. It's hard enough for poor fellows to have no money to their lodging, apart from gho-asts sceering them.'

'It's the coppers, not spooks, make me sleep uneasy,' said I. 'What with coppers, and meddlesome-minded folk, it isn't easy to get a night's rest nowadays.'

The water was still oozing from his clothes all about the floor, and a dank smell went up from him.

'God, man!' I cried; 'can't you *never* get dry?'

'Dry?' He made a little coughing laughter. 'Dry? I shan't never be dry... 'Tisn't the likes of us that ever get dry, be it wet *or* fine, winter *or* summer. See that!'

He thrust his muddy hands up to the wrist in the fire, glowering over it fiercely and madly. But I caught up my boots and ran crying out into the night.

South Sea Bubble
Hammond Innes

She lay in Kinlochbervie in the north-west of Scotland, so cheap I should have known there was something wrong. I had come by way of Lairg, under the heights of Arkle, and four miles up the road that skirts the north shores of Loch Laxford I turned a corner and there she was a ketch painted black and lying to her own reflection in the evening sun.

Dreams, dreams ... dreams are fine, as an escape, as a means of counteracting the pressures of life in a big office. But when there is no barrier between dream and reality, what then? Draw back, create another dream? But one is enough for any man and this had been mine; that one day I would find the boat of my dream and sail her to the South Seas.

Maybe it was the setting, the loneliness of the loch, the aid of Nordic wildness with the great humped hills of Sutherland as backcloth and the mass of Arkle cloud-capped in splendour. Here the Vikings had settled. From here men only just dead sailed open boats south for the herring. Even her name seemed right – *Samoa*.

I bought her, without a survey, without stopping to think. And then my troubles started.

She was dry when I bought her. Nobody told me the agents had paid a man to pump her out each day. If my wife had been alive I would never have been such a fool. But it was an executor's sale. The agents told me that. Also that she had been taken in tow off Handa Island by a Fraserburgh trawler and was the subject of a salvage claim. With her port of registry Kingston, Jamaica, it explained the low asking price. What they didn't tell me was that the trawler had found her abandoned, drifting water-logged without a soul on board. Nor did they tell me that her copper sheathing was so worn that half her underwater planking was rotten with toredo.

'A wee bit of a mystery,' was the verdict of the crofter who helped me clean her up and pump the water out of her. Nobody seemed to know who had sailed her across the Atlantic, how many had been on board, or what had happened to them.

The first night I spent on board – I shall always remember that; the excitement, the thrill of ownership, of command, of being on board a beautiful ship that was also now my home. The woodwork gleamed in the lamplight (yes, she had oil lamps as well as electric light), and lying in the quarter berth I could look up through the open hatch to the dark shape of the hills black against the stars. I was happy in spite of everything, happier than I had been for a long time, and when I finally went to sleep it was with a picture of coral islands in my mind – white sands and palm trees and proas scudding across the pale green shadows of warm lagoons.

I woke shivering, but not with cold. It was a warm night and the cold was inside me. I was cold to my guts and very frightened. It wasn't the strangeness of my new habitation, for I knew where I was the instant I opened my eyes. And it wasn't fear of the long voyage ahead. It was something else, something I didn't understand.

I shifted to one of the saloon berths, and as I slept soundly the rest of the night I put it down to nerves. It was a nervous breakdown that had led to my early retirement, enabling me to exchange my small suburban house for the thing I had always dreamed of. But I avoided the quarter berth after that, and though I was so tired every night that I fell asleep almost instantly, a sense of uneasiness persisted.

It is difficult to describe, even more difficult to explain. There was no repetition of the waking cold of that first night, but every now and then I had the sense of a presence on board. It was so strong at times that when I came back from telephoning or collecting parts or stores I would find myself looking about me as though expecting somebody to be waiting for me.

There was so much to do, and so little time, that I never got around to making determined enquiries as to whether the previous owner had been on that ill-fated voyage. I did write to his address in Kingston, but with no reply I was left with a sense of mystery and the feeling that whatever it was that had happened, it had become imprinted on the fabric of the boat. How else to explain the sense of somebody, something, trying to communicate?

It was August when I bought her, late September when I sailed out of Kinlochbervie bound for Shetland. It would have been more sensible to have headed south to an English yard, for my deadline to catch the trades across the Atlantic was December. But Scalloway was cheaper. And nearer.

I left with a good forecast, and by nightfall I was motoring north in a flat calm with Cape Wrath light bearing 205° and beginning to dip below the dark line of the horizon. My plan to install larger batteries, an alternator and an automatic pilot had had to be shelved. The money for that was now earmarked for new planking. I stayed on deck, dozing at the helm and watching for trawlers. I was tired before I started and I was tireder now.

A hand touched my shoulder and I woke with a start to complete silence. It was pitch dark, clammily cold. For a moment I couldn't think where I was. Then I saw the shadowy outline of the mainsail above my head. Nothing else – no navigation lights, no compass light, the engine stopped and the boat sluggish. I switched on my torch and the beam shone white on fog. The sails, barely visible, were drawing and we were moving slowly westward, out into the Atlantic.

I pressed the self-starter, but nothing happened, and when I put the wheel over she took a long time to come back on course. I went below then and stepped into a foot or more of water. Fortunately I had installed a powerful, double-action pump. Even so, it took me the better part of four hours to get the water level below the cabin sole. By then it was daylight and the fog had cleared away to the west, a long bank of it looking like a smudge of smoke as the sun glimmered through the damp air.

I tried swinging the engine, but it was no good. Just as well perhaps, because it must have been the prolonged running of the engine that had caused her to take in so much water. Without it the leaks in the planking seemed no worse than when she had been at anchor. I cooked myself a big breakfast on the paraffin stove and it was only when I was sitting over coffee and a cigarette that I remembered how I had woken to the feel of a hand on my shoulder.

I put it out of my mind, not wanting to know about it, and switched to consideration of whether to go on or turn back. But I was already nearly halfway to Shetland and the wind settled the matter by coming from the south-west. I eased sheets and for the next hour we were sailing at almost 6 knots.

*   *   *

The wind held steady all day at Force 3–4, and though there were occasional fog patches I did manage to catch a glimpse of Orkney away to the south-east. Sail trimming and pumping took most of my time, but in the afternoon, when the pump at last sucked dry, I was able to give some thought to navigation.

The tides run strong in the waters between Orkney and Shetland, up to ten knots in the vicinity of the major headlands, and I had an uneasy feeling I was being carried too far to the east. Just before midnight I sighted what looked like the loom of a light almost over the bows, but my eyes were too tired to focus clearly. I pumped until the bilges sucked dry again, checked the compass and the log, then fell into the quarter berth, still with my oilskins on, not caring whether it was a light or a ship, or whether the boat held her course or not.

I was utterly exhausted and I came out of a dead sleep to see the shadowy figure of a man standing over me. He had something in his hand, and as his arm came up, I rolled off the bunk, hit the floorboards and came up crouched, the hair on my neck prickling, my body trembling.

Maybe I dreamèd it; there was nothing there, and the only sound on board the slatting of the sails. But still my body trembled and I was cold with fright. I had a slug of whisky and went up on deck to find the log line hanging inert, the ship drifting in circles; no wind and the fog like a wet shroud.

I stayed on deck until it got light – a ghostly, damp morning, everything dripping. I pumped the bilges dry, cooked breakfast, attended to the navigation. But though I was fully occupied, I couldn't get it out of my head that I wasn't alone on the ship. Now, whatever I was doing, wherever I was on the boat, I was conscious of his presence.

I know I was tired. But why had my reflexes been so instantaneous? How had I known in the instant of waking that the man standing over me was bent on murder?

The day dragged, the wind coming and going, my world enclosed in walls of fog. The circle of sea in which I was imprisoned was never still, enlarging and contracting with the varying density of the fog, and it was cold. Hot tea, exercise, whisky – nothing seemed to dispel that cold. It was deep inside me, a brooding fear.

But of what?

Shetland was getting close now. I knew it would be a tricky landfall, in fog and without an engine. The tidal stream, building up against the long southern finger of the islands, causes one of the worst races in the British Isles. Roost is the local name and the Admiralty Pilot warned particularly of the roost off Sumburgh Head. It would only require a small error of navigation ... And then, dozing at the helm, I though I saw two figures in the bows.

I jerked awake, my vision blurred with moisture, seeing them vaguely. But when I rubbed my eyes they were gone. And just before dusk, when I was at the mainmast checking the halyards, I could have sworn there was somebody standing behind me. The fog, tiredness, hallucinations – it is easy not to rationalize. But the ever-present feeling that I was not alone on the boat, the sense of fear, of something terrible hanging over me – that's not so easy to explain.

*   *   *

Night fell, the breeze died and the damp blanket of fog clamped down. I could feel the wetness of it on my eyeballs, my oilskins clammy with moisture and water dripping off the boom as though it were raining. I pumped the bilges dry and had some food. When I came up on deck again there was the glimmer of a moon low down, the boat's head swinging slowly in an eddy. And then I heard it, to the north of me, the soft mournful note of a diaphone – the fog signal on Sumburgh Head.

The tide had just started its main south-easterly flow and within an hour the roost was running and I was in it. The sea became lumpy, full of unpredictable hollows. Sudden overfalls reared up and broke against the topsides. The movement grew and became indescribable, exhausting, and above the noise of water breaking, the sound of the sails slatting back and forth.

I was afraid of the mast then. I had full main and genoa up. I don't know how long it took me to get the headsail down and lashed, the boat like a mad thing intent on pitching me overboard. An hour maybe. And then the main. I couldn't lash it properly, the movement of the boom was too violent. Blood was dripping from a gash in my head where I had been thrown against a winch, my body a mass of bruises. I left the mainsail heaped on deck and wedged myself into the quarter berth. It was the only safe place, the saloon a shambles of crockery and stores, locker doors swinging, the contents flying.

*　　*　　*

I was scared. The movement was so violent I couldn't pump. I couldn't do anything. I must have passed out from sheer exhaustion when I suddenly saw again the figure standing over the quarter berth, and the thing in his hand was a winch handle. I was seeing it vaguely now, as though from a long way away. I saw the man's arm come up. The metal of the winch handle gleamed. I saw him strike, and as he struck the figure in the bunk moved, rolling out onto the floorboards and coming up in a crouch, his head gashed and blood streaming. There was fear there. I can remember fear then as something solid, a sensation so all-pervading it was utterly crushing, and then the winch handle coming up again and the victim's reaching out to the galley where a knife lay, the fingers grasping for it.

I opened my eyes and a star streaked across the swaying hatch. I was on the floor, in a litter of galley equipment, and I had a knife in my hand. As I held it up, staring at it, dazed, the star streaked back across the hatch, the bottom of the mizzen sail showing suddenly white. The significance of that took a moment to sink in, so appalled was I by my experience. The star came and went again, the sail momentarily illumined; then I was on my feet, clawing my way into the cockpit.

The sky was clear, studded with stars, and to the north the beam of Sumburgh Light swung clear. The fog had gone. There was a breeze from the east now. Somehow I managed to get the genoa hoisted, and inside of half an hour I was sailing in quiet waters clear of the roost.

I went below then and started clearing up the mess. The quarter berth was a tumbled pile of books from the shelf above, and as I was putting them back, a photograph fell to the floor. It showed a man and a woman and two children grouped round the wheel. The man was about forty-five, fair-haired with a fat, jolly face, his eyes squinting against bright sunlight. I have that picture still, my only contact with the man who had owned *Samoa* before me, the man whose ghostly presence haunted the ship.

By nightfall I was in Scalloway, tied up alongside a trawler at the pier. I didn't sell the boat. I couldn't afford to. And I didn't talk about it. Now that I had seen his picture, knew what he looked like, it seemed somehow less disturbing. I made up my mind I would have to live with it, whatever it was.

I never again used the quarter berth – in fact, I ripped it out of her before I left Scalloway. Sailing south I thought a lot about him in the long night watches. But though I speculated on what must have happened, and sometimes felt he was with me, I was never again identified with him.

Maybe I was never quite so tired again. But something I have to add. From the Azores I headed for Jamaica, and as soon as I arrived in Kingston the boat was the focus of considerable interest. She had apparently been stolen. At least, she had disappeared, and her owner with her. Hijacked was the word his solicitors used, for a merchant seaman named O'Sullivan, serving a six-year sentence for armed robbery, had escaped the night before and had never been heard of since. The police now believed he had boarded the boat, hijacked her and her owner and sailed her across the Atlantic, probably with Ireland as his objective.

I didn't attempt to see his wife. My experience – what I thought I now knew – could only add to her grief. I sailed at once for the Canal. But though I have tried to put it out of my mind, there are times when I feel his presence lingering. Maybe writing this will help. Maybe it will exorcise his poor, frightened ghost from my mind – or from the boat – whichever it is.

The Spectre Bridegroom
Washington Irving

'*He that supper for is dight,*
He lyes full cold, I trow, this night!
Yestreen to chamber I him led,
This night Gray-steel has made his bed!'
            —*Sir Eger, Sir Grahame* and *Sir Gray-steel*

On the summit of one of the heights of the Odenwald, a wild and romantic tract of Upper Germany that lies not far from the confluence of the Main and the Rhine, there stood, many, many years since, the Castle of the Baron Von Landshort. It is now quite fallen to decay, and almost buried among beech trees and dark firs; above which, however, its old watch-tower may still be seen struggling, like the former possessor I have mentioned, to carry a high head, and look down upon a neighbouring country.

The Baron was a dry branch of the great family of Katzenellenbogen, and inherited the relics of the property and all the pride of his ancestors. Though the warlike disposition of his predecessors had much impaired the family possessions, yet the Baron still endeavoured to keep up some show of former state. The times were peaceable, and the German nobles, in general, had abandoned their inconvenient old castles, perched like eagles' nests among the mountains, and had built more convenient residences in the valleys; still the Baron remained proudly drawn up in his little fortress, cherishing with hereditary inveteracy all the old family feuds; so that he was on ill terms with some of his nearest neighbours, on account of disputes that had happened between their great-great-grandfathers.

The Baron had but one child, a daughter; but nature, when she grants but one child, always compensates by making it a prodigy; and so it was with the daughter of the Baron. All the nurses, gossips and country cousins, assured her father that she had not her equal for beauty in all Germany; and who should know better than they? She had, moreover, been brought up with great care, under the superintendence of two maiden aunts, who had spent some years of their early life at one of the little German courts, and were skilled in all the branches of knowledge necessary to the education of a fine lady. Under their instructions, she became a miracle of accomplishments. By the time she was eighteen she could embroider to admiration, and had worked whole histories of the saints in tapestry with such strength of expression in their countenances that they looked like so many souls in purgatory. She could read without great difficulty, and had spelled her way through several church legends, and almost all the chivalric wonders of the *Heldenbuch*. She had even made considerable proficiency in writing, could sign her own name without missing a letter, and so legibly that her aunts could read it without spectacles. She excelled in making little good-for-nothing ladylike knick-knacks of all kinds; was versed in the most abstruse dancing of the day; played a number of airs on the harp and guitar; and knew all the tender ballads of the *Minne-lieders* by heart.

Her aunts, too, having been great flirts and coquettes in their younger days, were admirably calculated to be vigilant guardians and strict censors of the conduct of their niece; for there is no duenna so rigidly prudent, and inexorably decorous, as a superannuated coquette. She was rarely suffered out of their sight; never went beyond the domains of the castle, unless well attended, or, rather, well watched; had continual lectures read to her about strict decorum and implicit obedience; and, as to the men – pah! she was taught to hold them at such distance and distrust that, unless properly authorized, she would not have cast a glance upon the handsomest cavalier in the world – no, not if he were even dying at her feet.

The good effects of this system were wonderfully apparent. The young lady was a pattern of docility and correctness. While others were wasting their sweetness in the glare of the world, and liable to be plucked and thrown aside by every hand, she was coyly blooming into fresh and lovely womanhood under the protection of those immaculate spinsters, like a rosebud blushing forth among guardian thorns. Her aunts looked upon her with pride and exultation, and vaunted that though all the other young ladies in the world might go astray, yet, thank Heaven, nothing of the kind could happen to the heiress of Katzenellenbogen.

But however scantily the Baron Von Landshort might be provided with children, his household was by no means a small one, for Providence had enriched him with abundance of poor relations. They, one and all, possessed the affectionate disposition common to humble relatives; were wonderfully attached to the Baron, and took every possible occasion to come in swarms and enliven the castle. All family festivals were commemorated by these good people at the Baron's expense; and when they were filled with good cheer, they would declare that there was nothing on earth so delightful as these family meetings, these jubilees of the heart.

The Baron, though a small man, had a large soul, and it swelled with satisfaction at the consciousness of being the greatest man in the little world about him. He loved to tell long stories about the stark old warriors whose portraits looked grimly down from the walls around, and he found no listeners equal to those who fed at his expense. He was much given to the marvellous, and a firm believer in all those supernatural tales with which every mountain and valley in Germany abounds. The faith of his guests even exceeded his own. They listened to every tale of wonder with open eyes and mouth, and never failed to be astonished, even though repeated for the hundredth time. Thus lived the Baron Von Landshort, the oracle of his table, the absolute monarch of his little territory, and happy, above all things, in the persuasion that he was the wisest man of the age.

At the time of which my story treats there was a great family gathering at the castle, on an affair of the utmost importance: it was to receive the destined bridegroom of the Baron's daughter. A negotiation had been carried on between the father and an old nobleman of Bavaria, to unite the dignity of their houses by the marriage of their children. The preliminaries had been conducted with proper punctilio. The young people were betrothed without seeing each other, and the time was appointed for the marriage ceremony. The young Count Von Altenburg had been recalled from the army for the purpose, and was actually on his way to the Baron's to receive his bride. Missives had even been received from him, from Wurtzburg, where he was accidentally detained, mentioning the day and hour when he might be expected to arrive.

The castle was in a tumult of preparation to give him a suitable welcome. The fair bride had been decked out with uncommon care. The two aunts had superintended her toilet, and quarrelled the whole morning about every article of her dress. The young lady had taken advantage of their contest to follow the bent of her own taste; and fortunately it was a good one. She looked as lovely as a youthful bridegroom could desire; and the flutter of expectation heightened the lustre of her charms.

The suffusions that mantled her face and neck, the gentle heaving of the bosom, the eye now and then lost in reverie, all betrayed the soft tumult that was going on in her little heart. The aunts were continually hovering around her; for maiden aunts are apt to take great interest in affairs of this nature: they were giving her a world of staid counsel, how to deport herself, what to say, and in what manner to receive the expected lover.

The Baron was no less busied in preparations. He had, in truth, nothing exactly to do; but he was naturally a fuming, bustling little man, and could not remain passive when all the world was in a hurry. He worried from top to bottom of the castle, with an air of infinite anxiety; he continually called the servants from their work to exhort them to be diligent, and buzzed about every hall and chamber, as idle, restless and importunate as a bluebottle fly on a warm summer's day.

In the meantime, the fatted calf had been killed; the forests had rung with the clamour of the huntsmen; the kitchen was crowded with good cheer; the cellars had yielded up whole oceans of *Rhein-wein* and *Ferne-wein*, and even the great Heidelberg Tun had been laid under contribution. Everything was ready to receive the distinguished guest with *Saus und Braus* in the true spirit of German hospitality – but the guest delayed to make his appearance. Hour rolled after hour. The sun that had poured his downward rays upon the rich forests of the Odenwald, now just gleamed along the summits of the mountains. The Baron mounted the highest tower, and strained his eyes in hopes of catching a distant sight of the Count and his attendants. Once he thought he beheld them; the sound of horns came floating from the valley, prolonged by the mountain echoes: a number of horsemen were seen far below, slowly advancing along the road; but when they had nearly reached the foot of the mountain they suddenly struck off in a different direction. The last ray of sunshine departed – the bats began to flit by in the twilight – the road grew dimmer and dimmer to the view; and nothing appeared stirring in it but now and then a peasant lagging homeward from his labour.

While the old castle of Landshort was in this state of perplexity, a very interesting scene was transacting in a different part of the Odenwald.

The young Count Von Altenburg was tranquilly pursuing his route in that sober jog-trot way in which a man travels towards matrimony when his friends have taken all the trouble and uncertainty of courtship off his hands, and a bride is waiting for him, as certainly as a dinner, at the end of his journey. He had encountered at Wurtzburg a youthful companion in arms, with whom he had seen some service on the frontiers: Herman Von Starkenfaust, one of the stoutest hands and worthiest hearts of German chivalry, who was now returning from the army. His father's castle was not far distant from the old fortress of Landshort, although a hereditary feud rendered the families hostile and strangers to each other.

In the warm-hearted moment of recognition, the young friends related all their past adventures and fortunes, and the Count gave the whole history of his intended nuptials with a young lady whom he had never seen, but of whose charms he had received the most enrapturing descriptions.

As the route of the friends lay in the same direction, they agreed to perform the rest of their journey together; and, that they might do it more leisurely, set off from Wurtzburg at an early hour, the Count having given directions for his retinue to follow and overtake him.

They beguiled their wayfaring with recollections of their military scenes and adventures; but the Count was apt to be a little tedious, now and then, about the reputed charms of his bride, and the felicity that awaited him.

In this way they had entered among the mountains of the Odenwald, and were traversing one of its most lonely and thickly wooded passes. It is well known that the forests of Germany have always been as much infested with robbers as its castles, by spectres; and, at this time, the former were particularly numerous, from the hordes of disbanded soldiers wandering about the country. It will not appear extraordinary, therefore, that the cavaliers were attacked by a gang of these stragglers in the midst of the forest. They defended themselves with bravery, but were nearly overpowered when the Count's retinue arrived to their assistance. At sight of them the robbers fled, but not until the Count had received a mortal wound. He was slowly and carefully conveyed back to the city of Wurtzburg, and a friar summoned from a neighbouring convent, who was famous for his skill in administering to both soul and body. But half of his skill was superfluous; the moments of the unfortunate Count were numbered.

With his dying breath he entreated his friend to repair instantly to the castle of Landshort, and explain the fatal cause of his not keeping his appointment with his bride. Though not the most ardent of lovers, he was one of the most punctilious of men, and appeared earnestly solicitous that his mission should be speedily and courteously executed. 'Unless this is done,' said he, 'I shall not sleep quietly in my grave!' He repeated these last words with peculiar solemnity. A request, at a moment so impressive, admitted no hesitation. Starkenfaust endeavoured to soothe him to calmness; promised faithfully to execute his wish, and gave him his hand in solemn pledge. The dying man pressed it in acknowledgment, but soon lapsed into delirium – raved about his bride – his engagement – his plighted word; ordered his horse, that he might ride to the castle of Landshort, and expired in the fancied act of vaulting into the saddle.

Starkenfaust bestowed a sigh and a soldier's tear on the untimely fate of his comrade; and then pondered on the awkward mission he had undertaken. His heart was heavy, and his head perplexed; for he was to present himself an unbidden guest among hostile people, and to damp their festivity with tidings fatal to their hopes. Still there was certain whisperings of curiosity in his bosom to see this far-famed beauty of Katzenellenbogen so cautiously shut up from the world; for he was a passionate admirer of the sex, and there was a dash of eccentricity and enterprise in his character that made him fond of all singular adventure.

Previous to his departure, he made all due arrangements with the holy fraternity of the convent for the funeral solemnities of his friend, who was to be buried in the cathedral of Wurtzburg, near some of his illustrious relatives; and the mourning retinue of the Count took charge of his remains.

It is now high time that we should return to the ancient family of Katzenellenbogen, who were impatient for their guest, and still more for their dinner; and to the worthy little Baron, whom we left airing himself on the watch-tower.

Night closed in, but still no guest arrived. The Baron descended from the tower in despair. The banquet, which had been delayed from hour to hour, could no longer be postponed. The meats were already overdone, the cook in an agony, and the whole household had the look of a garrison that had been reduced by famine. The Baron was obliged reluctantly to give orders for the feast without the presence of the guest. All were seated at table, and just on the point of commencing, when the sound of a horn from without the gate gave notice of the approach of a stranger. Another long blast filled the old courts of the castle with its echoes, and was answered by the warder from the walls. The Baron hastened to receive his future son-in-law.

The drawbridge had been let down, and the stranger was before the gate. He was a tall gallant cavalier, mounted on a black steed. His countenance was pale, but he had a beaming, romantic eye, and an air of stately melancholy. The Baron was a little mortified that he should have come in this simple, solitary style. His dignity for a moment was ruffled, and he felt disposed to consider it a want of proper respect for the important occasion, and the important family with which he was to be connected. He pacified himself, however, with the conclusion that it must have been youthful impatience which had induced him thus to spur on sooner than his attendants.

'I am sorry,' said the stranger, 'to break in upon you thus unseasonably——'

Here the Baron interrupted him with a world of compliments and greetings; for, to tell the truth, he prided himself upon his courtesy and his eloquence. The stranger attempted, once or twice, to stem the torrent of words, but in vain; so he bowed his head and suffered it to flow on. By the time the Baron had come to a pause they had reached the inner court of the castle; and the stranger was again about to speak, when he was once more interrupted by the appearance of the female part of the family, leading forth the shrinking and blushing bride. He gazed on her for a moment as one entranced; it seemed as if his whole soul beamed forth in the gaze, and rested upon that lovely form. One of the maiden aunts whispered something in her ear; she made an effort to speak; her moist blue eye was timidly raised, gave a shy glance of enquiry on the stranger, and was cast again to the ground. The words died away; but there was a sweet smile playing about her lips, and a soft dimpling of the cheek, that showed her glance had not been unsatisfactory. It was impossible for a girl of the fond age of eighteen, highly predisposed for love and matrimony, not to be pleased with so gallant a cavalier.

The late hour at which the guest had arrived left no time for parley. The Baron was peremptory, and deferred all particular conversation until the morning, and led the way to the untasted banquet.

It was served up in the great hall of the castle. Around the walls hung the hard-favoured portraits of the heroes of the house of Katzenellenbogen, and the trophies which they had gained in the field and in the chase. Hacked corselets, splintered jousting spears, and tattered banners were mingled with the spoils of sylvan warfare: the jaws of the wolf and the tusks of the boar grinned horribly among crossbows and battleaxes, and a huge pair of antlers branched immediately over the head of the youthful bridegroom.

The cavalier took but little notice of the company or the entertainment. He scarcely tasted the banquet, but seemed absorbed in admiration of his bride. He conversed in a low tone, that could not be overheard – for the language of love is never loud; but where is the female ear so dull that it cannot catch the softest whisper of the lover? There was a mingled tenderness and gravity in his manner that appeared to have a powerful effect upon the young lady. Her colour came and went, as she listened with deep attention. Now and then she made some blushing reply, and when his eye was turned away she would steal a sidelong glance at his romantic countenance, and heave a gentle sigh of tender happiness. It was evident that the young couple were completely enamoured. The aunts, who were deeply versed in the mysteries of the heart, declared that they had fallen in love with each other at first sight.

The feast went on merrily, or at least noisily, for the guests were all blessed with those keen appetites that attend upon light purses and mountain air. The Baron told his best and longest stories, and never had he told them so well, or with such great effect. If there was anything marvellous, his auditors were lost in astonishment; and if anything facetious, they were sure to laugh exactly in the right place. The Baron, it is true, like most great men, was too dignified to utter any joke but a dull one: it was always enforced, however, by a bumper of excellent *Hoch-heimer*; and even a dull joke, at one's own table, served up with jolly old wine, is irresistible. Many good things were said by poorer and keener wits that would not bear repeating, except on similar occasions; many sly speeches whispered in ladies' ears that almost convulsed them with suppressed laughter; and a song or two roared out by a poor, but merry and broad-faced cousin of the Baron, that absolutely made the maiden aunts hold up their fans.

Amid all this revelry, the stranger-guest maintained a most singular and unseasonable gravity. His countenance assumed a deeper cast of dejection as the evening advanced, and, strange as it may appear, even the Baron's jokes seemed only to render him the more melancholy. At times he was lost in thought, and at times there was a perturbed and restless wandering of the eye that bespoke a mind but ill at ease. His conversation with the bride became more and more earnest and mysterious. Lowering clouds began to steal over the fair serenity of her brow, and tremors to run through her tender frame.

All this could not escape the notice of the company. Their gaiety was chilled by the unaccountable gloom of the bridegroom; their spirits were infected; whispers and glances were interchanged, accompanied by shrugs and dubious shakes of the head. The song and the laugh grew less and less frequent, there were dreary pauses in the conversation, which were at length succeeded by wild tales and supernatural legends. One dismal story produced another still more dismal, and the Baron nearly frightened some of the ladies into hysterics with the history of the goblin horseman that carried away the fair Leonora – a dreadful, but true story, which has since been put into excellent verse, and is read and believed by all the world.

The bridegroom listened to this tale with profound attention. He kept his eyes steadily fixed on the Baron and, as the story drew to a close, began gradually to rise from his seat, growing taller and taller, until, in the Baron's entranced eye, he seemed almost to tower into a giant. The moment the tale was finished, he heaved a deep sigh, and took a solemn farewell of the company. They were all amazement. The Baron was perfectly thunderstruck.

'What! going to leave the castle at midnight? Why, everything is prepared for your reception; a chamber is ready for you if you wish to retire.'

The stranger shook his head mournfully and mysteriously: 'I must lay my head in a different chamber tonight!'

There was something in this reply, and the tone in which it was uttered, that made the Baron's heart misgive him; but he rallied his forces, and repeated his hospitable entreaties. The stranger shook his head silently, but positively, at every offer; and, waving his farewell to the company, stalked slowly out of the hall. The maiden aunts were absolutely petrified – the bride hung her head, and a tear stole to her eye.

The Baron followed the stranger to the great court of the castle, where the black charger stood pawing the earth and snorting with impatience. When they had reached the portal, whose deep archway was dimly lighted by a cresset, the stranger paused, and addressed the Baron in a hollow tone of voice, which the vaulted roof rendered still more sepulchral. 'Now that we are alone,' said he, 'I will impart to you the reason of my going. I have a solemn, an indispensable engagement——'

'Why,' said the Baron, 'cannot you send someone in your place?'

'It admits of no substitute – I must attend it in person – I must away to Wurtzburg cathedral——'

'Ay,' said the Baron, plucking up spirit, 'but not until tomorrow – tomorrow you shall take your bride there.'

'No! no!' replied the stranger, with tenfold solemnity, 'my engagement is with no bride – the worms! the worms expect me! I am a dead man – I have been slain by robbers – my body lies at Wurtzburg – at midnight I am to be buried – the grave is waiting for me – I must keep my appointment!'

He sprang on his black charger, dashed over the drawbridge, and the clattering of his horse's hoofs was lost in the whistling of the night-blast.

The Baron returned to the hall in the utmost consternation, and related what had passed. Two ladies fainted outright; others sickened at the idea of having banqueted with a spectre. It was the opinion of some that this might be the wild huntsman famous in German legend. Some talked of mountain sprites, of wood-demons, and of other supernatural beings, with which the good people of Germany have been so grievously harassed since time immemorial. One of the poor relations ventured to suggest that it might be some sportive evasion of the young cavalier, and that the very gloominess of the caprice seemed to accord with so melancholy a personage. This, however, drew on him the indignation of the whole company, and especially of the Baron, who looked upon him as little better than an infidel; so that he was fain to abjure his heresy as speedily as possible, and come into the faith of the true believers.

But, whatever may have been the doubts entertained, they were completely put to an end by the arrival, next day, of regular missives confirming the intelligence of the young Count's murder, and his interment in Wurtzburg cathedral.

The dismay at the castle may well be imagined. The Baron shut himself up in his chamber. The guests who had come to rejoice with him could not think of abandoning him in his distress. They wandered about the courts, or collected in groups in the hall, shaking their heads and shrugging their shoulders at the troubles of so good a man; and sat longer than ever at table, and ate and drank more stoutly than ever, by way of keeping up their spirits. But the situation of the widowed bride was the most pitiable. To have lost a husband before she had even embraced him

– and such a husband! If the very spectre could be so gracious and noble, what must have been the living man? She filled the house with lamentations.

On the night of the second day of her widowhood, she had retired to her chamber, accompanied by one of her aunts, who insisted on sleeping with her. The aunt, who was one of the best tellers of ghost stories in all Germany, had just been recounting one of her longest, and had fallen asleep in the very midst of it. The chamber was remote, and overlooked a small garden. The niece lay pensively gazing at the beams of the rising moon, as they trembled on the leaves of an aspen tree before the lattice. The castle clock had just told midnight, when a soft strain of music stole up from the garden. She rose hastily from her bed and stepped lightly to the window. A tall figure stood among the shadows of the trees. As it raised its head, a beam of moonlight fell upon the countenance. Heaven and earth! She beheld the Spectre Bridegroom! A loud shriek at that moment burst upon her ear, and her aunt, who had been awakened by the music, and had followed her silently to the window, fell into her arms. When she looked again, the spectre had disappeared.

Of the two females, the aunt now required the most soothing, for she was perfectly beside herself with terror. As to the young lady, there was something, even in the spectre of her lover, that seemed endearing. There was still the semblance of manly beauty; and though the shadow of a man is but little calculated to satisfy the affections of a lovesick girl, yet, where the substance is not to be had, even that is consoling. The aunt declared that she would never sleep in that chamber again; the niece, for once, was refractory, and declared as strongly that she would sleep in no other in the castle: the consequence was that she had to sleep in it alone; but she drew a promise from her aunt not to relate the story of the spectre, lest she should be denied the only melancholy pleasure left her on earth – that of inhabiting the chamber over which the guardian shade of her lover kept its nightly vigils.

How long the good old lady would have observed this promise is uncertain, for she dearly loved to talk of the marvellous, and there is a triumph in being the first to tell a frightful story; it is, however, still quoted in the neighbourhood, as a memorable instance of female secrecy, that she kept it to herself for a whole week; when she was suddenly absolved from all further restraint by intelligence brought to the breakfast-table one morning that the young lady was not to be found. Her room was empty – the bed had not been slept in – the window was open – and the bird had flown!

The astonishment and concern with which the intelligence was received can only be imagined by those who have witnessed the agitation which the mishaps of a great man cause among his friends. Even the poor relations paused for a moment from the indefatigable labours of the trencher; when the aunt, who had at first been struck speechless, wrung her hands and shrieked out, 'The goblin! the goblin! She's carried away by the goblin!'

In a few words she related the fearful scene of the garden, and concluded that the spectre must have carried off his bride. Two of the domestics corroborated the opinion, for they had heard the clattering of a horse's hoofs down the mountain about midnight, and had no doubt that it was the spectre on his black charger, bearing her away to the tomb. All present were struck with the direful probability; for events of the kind are extremely common in Germany, as many well-authenticated histories bear witness.

What a lamentable situation was that of the poor Baron! What a heartrending dilemma for a fond father, and a member of the great family of Katzenellenbogen! His only daughter had either been rapt away to the grave, or he was to have some wood-demon for a son-in-law and, perchance, a troop of goblin grandchildren. As usual, he was completely bewildered, and all the castle in an uproar. The men were ordered to take horse and scour every road and path and glen of the Odenwald. The Baron himself had just drawn on his jack-boots, girded on his sword, and was about to mount his steed to sally forth on the doubtful quest, when he was brought to a pause by a new apparition. A lady was seen approaching the castle, mounted on a palfrey attended by a cavalier on horseback. She galloped up to the gate, sprang from her horse, and falling at the Baron's feet, embraced his knees. It was his lost daughter, and her companion – the Spectre Bridegroom! The Baron was astounded. He looked at his daughter, then at the spectre, and almost doubted the evidence of his senses. The latter, too, was wonderfully improved in his appearance, since his visit to the world of spirits. His dress was splendid, and set off a noble figure of manly symmetry. He was no longer pale and melancholy. His fine countenance was flushed with the glow of youth, and joy rioted in his large dark eye.

The mystery was soon cleared up. The cavalier (for, in truth, as you must have known all the while, he was no goblin) announced himself as Sir Herman Von Starkenfaust. He related his adventure with the young Count. He told how he had hastened to the castle to deliver the unwelcome tidings, but that the eloquence of the Baron had interrupted him in every attempt to tell his tale. How the sight of the bride had completely captivated him, and that to pass a few hours near her he had tacitly suffered the mistake to continue. How he had been sorely perplexed in what way to make a decent retreat, until the Baron's goblin stories had suggested his eccentric exit. How, fearing the feudal hostility of the family, he had repeated his visits by stealth – had haunted the garden beneath the young lady's window – had wooed – had won – had borne away in triumph – and, in a word, had wedded, the fair.

Under any other circumstances the Baron would have been inflexible, for he was tenacious of paternal authority and devoutly obstinate in all family feuds; but he loved his daughter; he had lamented her as lost; he rejoiced to find her still alive; and, though her husband was of a hostile house, yet, thank heaven, he was not a goblin. There was something, it must be acknowledged, that did not exactly accord with his notions of strict veracity, in the joke the knight had passed upon him of his being a dead man; but several old friends present, who had served in the wars, assured him that every stratagem was excusable in love, and that the cavalier was entitled to especial privilege, having lately served as a trooper.

Matters, therefore, were happily arranged. The Baron pardoned the young couple on the spot. The revels at the castle were resumed. The poor relations overwhelmed this new member of the family with loving-kindness; he was so gallant, so generous – and so rich. The aunts, it is true, were somewhat scandalized that their system of strict seclusion and passive obedience should be so badly exemplified, but attributed all to their negligence in not having the windows grated. One of them was particularly mortified at having her marvellous story marred, and that the only spectre she had ever seen should turn out a counterfeit; but the niece seemed perfectly happy at having found him substantial flesh and blood – and so the story ends.

The Monkey's Paw
W. W. Jacobs

Without, the night was cold and wet, but in the small parlour of Laburnum Villa the blinds were drawn and the fire burned brightly. Father and son were at chess; the former, who possessed ideas about the game involving radical changes, putting his king into such sharp and unnecessary perils that it even provoked comment from the white-haired old lady knitting placidly by the fire.

'Hark at the wind,' said Mr White, who, having seen a fatal mistake after it was too late, was amiably desirous of preventing his son from seeing it.

'I'm listening,' said the latter, grimly surveying the board as he stretched out his hand. 'Check.'

'I should hardly think that he'd come tonight,' said his father, with his hand poised over the board.

'Mate,' replied the son.

'That's the worst of living far out,' bawled Mr White, with sudden and unlooked-for violence; 'of all the beastly, slushy, out-of-the-way places to live in, this is the worst. Path's a bog, and the road's a torrent. I don't know what people are thinking about. I suppose because only two houses in the road are let, they think it doesn't matter.'

'Never mind, dear,' said his wife soothingly; 'perhaps you'll win the next one.'

Mr White looked up sharply, just in time to intercept a knowing glance between mother and son. The words died away on his lips, and he hid a guilty grin in his thin grey beard.

'There he is,' said Herbert White, as the gate banged to loudly and heavy footsteps came towards the door.

The old man rose with hospitable haste, and opening the door, was heard condoling with the new arrival. The new arrival also condoled with himself, so that Mrs White said, 'Tut, tut!' and coughed gently as her husband entered the room, followed by a tall, burly man, beady of eye and rubicund of visage.

'Sergeant-Major Morris,' he said, introducing him.

The sergeant-major shook hands, and taking the proffered seat by the fire, watched contentedly while his host got out whisky and tumblers and stood a small copper kettle on the fire.

At the third glass his eye got brighter, and he began to talk, the little family circle regarding with eager interest this visitor from distant parts, as he squared his broad shoulders in the chair and spoke of wild scenes and doughty deeds; of wars and plagues and strange peoples.

'Twenty-one years of it,' said Mr White, nodding at his wife and son. 'When he went away he was a slip of a youth in the warehouse. Now look at him.'

'He don't look to have taken much harm,' said Mrs White politely.

'I'd like to go to India myself,' said the old man, 'just to look round a bit, you know.'

'Better where you are,' said the sergeant-major, shaking his head. He put down the empty glass, and sighing softly, shook it again.

'I should like to see these old temples and fakirs and jugglers,' said the old man. 'What was that you started telling me the other day about a monkey's paw or something, Morris?'

'Nothing,' said the soldier hastily. 'Leastways nothing worth hearing.'

'Monkey's paw?' said Mrs White curiously.

'Well, it's just a bit of what you might call magic, perhaps,' said the segeant-major off-handedly.

His three listeners leaned forward eagerly. The visitor absent-mindedly put his empty glass to his lips and then set it down again. His host filled it for him.

'To look at,' said the sergeant-major, fumbling in his pocket, 'it's just an ordinary little paw, dried to a mummy.'

He took something out of his pocket and proffered it. Mrs White drew back with a grimace, but her son taking it, examined it curiously.

'And what is there special about it?' enquired Mr White as he took it from his son, and having examined it, placed it upon the table.

'It had a spell put upon it by an old fakir,' said the sergeant-major, 'a very holy man. He wanted to show that fate ruled people's lives, and that those who interfered with it did so to their sorrow. He put a spell on it so that three separate men could each have three wishes from it.'

His manner was so impressive that his hearers were conscious that their light laughter jarred somewhat.

'Well, why don't you have three, sir?' said Herbert White, cleverly.

The soldier regarded him in the way that middle age is wont to regard presumptuous youth. 'I have,' he said quietly, and his blotchy face whitened.

'And did you really have the three wishes granted?' asked Mrs White.

'I did,' said the sergeant-major, and his glass tapped against his strong teeth.

'And has anybody else wished?' persisted the old lady.

'The first man had his three wishes. Yes,' was the reply; 'I don't know what the first two were, but the third was for death. That's how I got the paw.'

His tones were so grave that a hush fell upon the group.

'If you've had your three wishes, it's no good to you now, then, Morris,' said the old man at last. 'What do you keep it for?'

The soldier shook his head. 'Fancy, I suppose,' he said slowly. 'I did have some idea of selling it, but I don't think I will. It has caused enough mischief already. Besides, people won't buy. They think it's a fairy tale, some of them; and those who do think anything of it want to try it first and pay me afterwards.'

'If you could have another three wishes,' said the old man, eyeing him keenly, 'would you have them?'

'I don't know,' said the other. 'I don't know.'

He took the paw, and dangling it between his forefinger and thumb, suddenly threw it upon the fire. White, with a slight cry, stooped down and snatched it off.

'Better let it burn,' said the soldier solemnly.

'If you don't want it, Morris,' said the other, 'give it to me.'

'I won't,' said his friend doggedly. 'I threw it on the fire. If you keep it, don't blame me for what happens. Pitch it on the fire again like a sensible man.'

The other shook his head and examined his new possession closely. 'How do you do it?' he enquired.

'Hold it up in your right hand and wish aloud,' said the sergeant-major, 'but I warn you of the consequences.'

'Sounds like the *Arabian Nights*,' said Mrs White, as she rose and began to set the supper. "Don't you think you might wish for four pairs of hands for me?'

Her husband drew the talisman from his pocket, and then all three burst into laughter as the sergeant-major, with a look of alarm on his face, caught him by the arm.

'If you must wish,' he said gruffly, 'wish for something sensible.'

Mr White dropped it back in his pocket, and placing chairs, motioned his friend to the table. In the business of supper the talisman was partly forgotten, and afterwards the three sat listening in an enthralled fashion to a second instalment of the soldier's adventures in India.

'If the tale about the monkey's paw is not more truthful than those he has been telling us,' said Herbert, as the door closed behind their guest, just in time to catch the last train, 'we shan't make much out of it.'

'Did you give him anything for it, father?' enquired Mrs White regarding her husband closely.

'A trifle,' said he, colouring slightly. 'He didn't want it, but I made him take it. And he pressed me again to throw it away.'

'Likely,' said Herbert, with pretended horror. 'Why, we're going to be rich, and famous, and happy. Wish to be an emperor, father, to begin with; then you can't be henpecked.'

He darted round the table, pursued by the maligned Mrs White armed with an antimacassar.

Mr White took the paw from his pocket and eyed it dubiously. 'I don't know what to wish for, and that's a fact,' he said slowly. 'It seems to me I've got all I want.'

'If you only cleared the house, you'd be quite happy, wouldn't you!' said Herbert, with his hand on his shoulder. 'Well, wish for two hundred pounds, then; that'll just do it.'

His father, smiling shamefacedly at his own credulity, held up the talisman, as his son, with a solemn face, somewhat marred by the wink at his mother, sat down at the piano and struck a few inpressive chords.

'I wish for two hundred pounds,' said the old man distinctly.

A fine crash from the piano greeted the words, interrupted by a shuddering cry from the old man. His wife and son ran towards him.

'It moved,' he cried, with a glance of disgust at the object as it lay on the floor. 'As I wished, it twisted in my hand like a snake.'

'Well, I don't see the money,' said his son, as he picked it up and placed it on the table, 'and I bet I never shall.'

'It must have been your fancy, father,' said his wife, regarding him anxiously.

He shook his head. 'Never mind, though; there's no harm done, but it gave me a shock all the same.'

They sat down by the fire again while the two men finished their pipes. Outside, the wind was higher than ever, and the old man started nervously at the sound of a door banging upstairs. A silence unusual and depressing settled upon all three, which lasted until the old couple rose to retire for the night.

'I expect you'll find the cash tied up in a big bag in the middle of your bed,' said Herbert, as he bade them goodnight, 'and something horrible squatting up on top of the wardrobe watching you as you pocket your ill-gotten gains.'

He sat alone in the darkness, gazing at the dying fire, and seeing faces in it. The last face was so horrible and so simian that he gazed at it in amazement. It got so vivid that, with a little uneasy laugh, he felt on the table for a glass containing a little water to throw over it. His hand grasped the monkey's paw, and with a little shiver he wiped his hand on his coat and went up to bed.

* * *

In the brightness of the wintry sun next morning as it streamed over the breakfast table he laughed at his fears. There was an air of prosaic wholesomeness about the room which it had lacked on the previous night, and the dirty, shrivelled little paw was pitched on the side-board with a carelessness which betokened no great belief in its virtues.

'I suppose all old soldiers are the same,' said Mrs White. 'The idea of our listening to such nonsense! How could wishes be granted in these days? And if they could, how could two hundred pounds hurt you, father?'

'Might drop on his head from the sky,' said the frivolous Herbert.

'Morris said the things happened so naturally,' said his father, 'that you might if you so wished attribute it to coincidence.'

'Well, don't break into the money before I come back,' said Herbert as he rose from the table. 'I'm afraid it'll turn you into a mean, avaricious man, and we shall have to disown you.'

His mother laughed, and following him to the door, watched him down the road; and returning to the breakfast-table, was very happy at the expense of her husband's credulity. All of which did not prevent her from scurrying to the door at the postman's knock, nor prevent her from referring somewhat shortly to retired sergeant-majors of bibulous habits when she found that the post brought a tailor's bill.

'Herbert will have some more of his funny remarks, I expect, when he comes home,' she said, as they sat at dinner.

'I dare say,' said Mr White, pouring himself out some beer; 'but for all that, the thing moved in my hand; that I'll swear to.'

'You thought it did,' said the old lady soothingly.

'I say it did,' replied the other. 'There was no thought about it; I had just—— What's the matter?'

His wife made no reply. She was watching the mysterious movements of a man outside, who, peering in an undecided fashion at the house, appeared to be trying to make up his mind to enter. In mental connection with the two hundred pounds, she noticed that the stranger was well dressed, and wore a silk hat of glossy newness. Three times he paused at the gate, and then walked on again. The fourth time he stood with his hand upon it, and then with a sudden resolution flung it open and walked up the path. Mrs White at the same moment placed her hands behind her, and hurriedly unfastening the strings of her apron, put that useful article of apparel beneath the cushion of her chair.

She brought the stranger, who seemed ill at ease, into the room. He gazed at her furtively, and listened in a preoccupied fashion as the old lady apologized for the appearance of the room, and her husband's coat, a garment which he usually reserved for the garden. She then waited as patiently as her sex would permit, for him to broach his business, but he was at first strangely silent.

'I – was asked to call,' he said at last, and stooped and picked a piece of cotton from his trousers. 'I come from "Maw and Meggins."'

The old lady started. 'Is anything the matter?' she asked breathlessly. 'Has anything happened to Herbert? What is it? What is it?'

Her husband interposed. 'There, there, mother,' he said hastily. 'Sit down and don't jump to conclusions. You've not brought bad news, I'm sure, sir;' and he eyed the other wistfully.

'I'm sorry——' began the visitor.

'Is he hurt?' demanded the mother wildly.

The visitor bowed in assent. 'Badly hurt,' he said quietly, 'but he is not in any pain.'

'Oh, thank God!' said the old woman, clasping her hands. 'Thank God for that! Thank——'

She broke off suddenly as the sinister meaning of the assurance dawned upon her mind and she saw the awful confirmation of her fears in the other's averted face. She caught her breath, and turning to her slower-witted husband, laid her trembling old hand upon his. There was a long silence.

'He was caught in the machinery,' said the visitor at length in a low voice.

'Caught in the machinery,' repeated Mr White, in a dazed fashion, 'yes.'

He sat staring blankly out at the window, and taking his wife's hand between his own, pressed it as he had been wont to do in their old courting days nearly forty years before.

'He was the only one left to us,' he said, turning gently to the visitor. 'It is hard.'

The other coughed, and rising, walked slowly to the window. 'The firm wished me to convey their sincere sympathy with you in your great loss,' he said, without looking round. 'I beg that you will understand that I am only their servant and merely obeying orders.'

There was no reply; the old woman's face was white, her eyes staring, and her breath inaudible; on the husband's face was a look such as his friend the sergeant might have carried into his first action.

'I was to say that Maw and Meggins disclaim all responsibility,' continued the other. 'They admit no liability at all, but in consideration of your son's services, they wish to present you with a certain sum as compensation.'

Mr White dropped his wife's hand, and rising to his feet, gazed with a look of horror at his visitor. His dry lips shaped the words, 'How much?'

'Two hundred pounds,' was the answer.

Unconscious of his wife's shriek, the old man smiled faintly, put out his hands like a sightless man, and dropped, a senseless heap, to the floor.

*   *   *

In the huge new cemetery, some two miles distant, the old people buried their dead, and came back to the house steeped in shadow and silence. It was all over so quickly that at first they could hardly realize it, and remained in a state of expectation as though of something else to happen – something else which was to lighten this load, too heavy for old hearts to bear.

But the days passed, and expectation gave place to resignation – the hopeless resignation of the old, sometimes called apathy. Sometimes they hardly exchanged a word, for now they had nothing to talk about, and their days were long to weariness.

It was about a week after that the old man, waking suddenly in the night, stretched out his hand and found himself alone. The room was in darkness, and the sound of subdued weeping came from the window. He raised himself in bed and listened.

'Come back,' he said tenderly. 'You will be cold.'

'It is colder for my son,' said the old woman, and wept afresh.

The sound of her sobs died away on his ears. The bed was warm, and his eyes heavy with sleep. He dozed fitfully, and then slept until a sudden wild cry from his wife awoke him with a start.

'*The paw!*' she cried wildly. 'The monkey's paw!'

He started up in alarm. 'Where? Where is it? What's the matter?'

She came stumbling across the room towards him. 'I want it,' she said quietly. 'You've not destroyed it?'

'It's in the parlour, on the bracket,' he replied, marvelling. 'Why?'

She cried and laughed together, and bending over, kissed his cheek.

'I only just thought of it,' she said hysterically. 'Why didn't I think of it before? Why didn't *you* think of it?'

'Think of what?' he questioned.

'The other two wishes,' she replied rapidly. 'We've only had one.'

'Was that not enough?' he demanded fiercely.

'No,' she cried triumphantly: 'we'll have one more. Go down and get it quickly, and wish our boy alive again.'

The man sat up in bed and flung the bedclothes from his quaking limbs. 'Good God, you are mad!' he cried aghast.

'Get it,' she panted; 'get it quickly, and wish—— Oh, my boy, my boy!'

Her husband struck a match and lit the candle, 'Get back to bed,' he said unsteadily. 'You don't know what you are saying.'

'We had the first wish granted,' said the old woman feverishly; 'why not the second?'

'A coincidence,' stammered the old man.

'Go and get it and wish,' cried his wife, quivering with excitement.

The old man turned and regarded her, and his voice shook. 'He has been dead ten days, and besides he – I would not tell you else, but – I could only recognize him by his clothing. If he was too terrible for you to see then, how now?'

'Bring him back,' cried the old woman, and dragged him towards the door. 'Do you think I fear the child I have nursed?'

He went down in the darkness, and felt his way to the parlour, and then to the mantelpiece. The talisman was in its place, and a horrible fear that the unspoken wish might bring his mutilated son before him ere he could escape from the room seized upon him, and he caught his breath as he found that he had lost the direction of the door. His brow cold with sweat, he felt his way round the table, and groped along the wall until he found himself in the small passage with the unwholesome thing in his hand.

Even his wife's face seemed to change as he entered the room. It was white and expectant, and to his fears seemed to have an unnatural look upon it. He was afraid of her.

'*Wish!*' she cried, in a strong voice.

'It is foolish and wicked,' he faltered.

'*Wish!*' repeated his wife.

He raised his hand. 'I wish my son alive again.'

The talisman fell to the floor, and he regarded it fearfully. Then, he sank trembling into a chair as the old woman, with burning eyes, walked to the window and raised the blind.

He sat until he was chilled with the cold, glancing occasionally at the figure of the old woman peering through the window. The candle-end, which had burned below the rim of the china candlestick, was throwing pulsating shadows on the ceiling and walls, until, with a flicker larger than the rest, it expired. The old man, with an unspeakable sense of relief at the failure of the talisman, crept back to his bed, and a minute or two afterwards the old woman came silently and apathetically beside him.

Neither spoke, but lay silently listening to the ticking of the clock. A stair creaked, and a squeaky mouse scurried noisily through the wall. The darkness was oppressive, and after lying for some time screwing up his courage, he took the box of matches, and striking one, went downstairs for a candle.

At the foot of the stairs the match went out, and he paused to strike another; and at the same moment a knock, so quiet and stealthy as to be scarcely audible, sounded on the front door.

The match fell from his hand and spilled in the passage. He stood motionless, his breath suspended until the knock was repeated. Then he turned and fled swiftly back to his room, and closed the door behind him. A third knock sounded through the house.

'*What's that?*' cried the old woman, staring up.

'A rat,' said the old man in shaking tones – 'a rat. It passed me on the stairs.'

His wife sat up in bed listening. A loud knock resounded through the house.

'It's Herbert!' she screamed. 'It's Herbert!'

She ran to the door, but her husband was before her, and catching her by the arm, held her tightly.

'What are you going to do?' he whispered hoarsely.

'It's my boy; it's Herbert!' she cried, struggling mechanically. 'I forgot it was two miles away. What are you holding me for? Let go. I must open the door.'

'For God's sake don't let it in,' cried the old man, trembling.

'You're afraid of your own son,' she cried, struggling. 'Let me go. I'm coming, Herbert; I'm coming.'

There was another knock, and another. The old woman with a sudden wrench broke free and ran from the room. Her husband followed to the landing, and called after her appealingly as she hurried downstairs. He heard the chain rattle back and the bottom bolt drawn slowly and stiffly from the socket. Then the old woman's voice, strained and panting.

'The bolt,' she cried loudly. 'Come down. I can't reach it.'

But her husband was on his hands and knees groping wildly on the floor in search of the paw. If he could only find it before the thing outside got in. A perfect fusillade of knocks reverberated through the house, and he heard the scraping of a chair as his wife put it down in the passage against the door. He heard the creaking of the bolt as it came slowly back, and at the same moment he found the monkey's paw, and frantically breathed his third and last wish.

The knocking ceased suddenly, although the echoes of it were still in the house. He heard the chair drawn back, and the door opened. A cold wind rushed up the staircase and a long loud wail of disappointment and misery from his wife gave him courage to run down to her side, and then to the gate beyond. The street lamp flickering opposite shone on a quiet and deserted road.

Lost Hearts

M. R. James

It was, as far as I can ascertain, in September of the year 1811 that a post-chaise drew up before the door of Aswarby Hall, in the heart of Lincolnshire. The little boy who was the only passenger in the chaise, and who jumped out as soon as it had stopped, looked about him with the keenest curiosity during the short interval that elapsed between the ringing of the bell and the opening of the hall door. He saw a tall, square, red-brick house, built in the reign of Anne; a stone-pillared porch had been added in the purer classical style of 1790; the windows of the house were many, tall and narrow, with small panes and thick white woodwork. A pediment, pierced with a round window, crowned the front. There were wings to right and left, connected by curious glazed galleries, supported by colonnades, with the central block. These wings plainly contained the stables and offices of the house. Each was surmounted by an ornamental cupola with a gilded vane.

An evening light shone on the building, making the window-panes glow like so many fires. Away from the Hall in front stretched a flat park studded with oaks and fringed with firs, which stood out against the sky. The clock in the church tower, buried in trees on the edge of the park, only its golden weather-cock catching the light, was striking six, and the sound came gently beating down the wind. It was altogether a pleasant impression, though tinged with the sort of melancholy appropriate to an evening in early autumn, that was conveyed to the mind of the boy who was standing in the porch waiting for the door to open to him.

The post-chaise had brought him from Warwickshire, where, some six months before, he had been left an orphan. Now, owing to the generous offer of his elderly cousin, Mr Abney, he had come to live at Aswarby. The offer was unexpected, because all who knew anything of Mr Abney looked upon him as a somewhat austere recluse, into whose steady-going household the advent of a small boy would import a new and, it seemed, incongruous element. The truth is that very little was known of Mr Abney's pursuits or temper. The Professor of Greek at

Cambridge had been heard to say that no one knew more of the religious beliefs of the later pagans than did the owner of Aswarby. Certainly his library contained all the then available books bearing on the Mysteries, the Orphic poems, the worship of Mithras, and the Neo-Platonists. In the marble-paved hall stood a fine group of Mithras slaying a bull, which had been inherited from the Levant at great expense by the owner. He had contributed a description of it to the *Gentleman's Magazine*, and he had written a remarkable series of articles in the *Critical Museum* on the superstitions of the Romans of the Lower Empire. He was looked upon, in fine, as a man wrapped up in his books, and it was a matter of great surprise among his neighbours that he should ever have heard of his orphan cousin, Stephen Elliott, much more that he should have volunteered to make him an inmate of Aswarby Hall.

Whatever may have been expected by his neighbours, it is certain that Mr Abney – the tall, the thin, the austere – seemed inclined to give his young cousin a kindly reception. The moment the front door was opened he darted out of his study, rubbing his hands with delight.

'How are you, my boy? – how are you? How old are you?' said he – 'that is, you are not too much tired, I hope, by your journey to eat your supper?'

'No, thank you sir,' said Master Elliott; 'I am pretty well.'

'That's a good lad,' said Mr Abney. 'And how old are you, my boy?'

It seemed a little odd that he should have asked the question twice in the first two minutes of their acquaintance.

'I'm twelve years old next birthday, sir,' said Stephen.

'And when is your birthday, my dear boy? Eleventh of September, eh? That's well – that's very well. Nearly a year hence, isn't it? I like – ha, ha! – I like to get these things down in my book. Sure it's twelve? Certain?'

'Yes, quite sure, sir.'

'Well, well! Take him to Mrs Bunch's room, Parkes, and let him have his tea – supper – whatever it is.'

'Yes, sir,' answered the staid Mr Parkes; and conducted Stephen to the lower regions.

Mrs Bunch was the most comfortable and human person whom Stephen had as yet met in Aswarby. She made him completely at home; they were great friends in a quarter of an hour; and great friends they remained. Mrs Bunch had been born in the neighbourhood some fifty-five years before the date of Stephen's arrival, and her residence at the Hall was of twenty years' standing. Consequently, if anyone knew the ins and outs of the house and the district, Mrs Bunch knew them; and she was by no means disinclined to communicate her information.

Certainly there were plenty of things about the Hall and the Hall gardens which Stephen, who was of an adventurous and enquiring turn, was anxious to have explained to him. 'Who built the temple at the end of the laurel walk? Who was the old man whose picture hung on the staircase, sitting at a table, with a skull under his hand?' These and many similar points were cleared up by the resources of Mrs Bunch's powerful intellect. There were others, however, of which the explanations furnished were less satisfactory.

One November evening Stephen was sitting by the fire in the housekeeper's room reflecting on his surroundings.

'Is Mr Abney a good man, and will he go to heaven?' he suddenly asked, with the peculiar confidence which children possess in the ability of their elders to settle these questions, the decision of which is believed to be reserved for other tribunals.

'Good? – bless the child?' said Mrs Bunch. 'Master's as kind a soul as ever I see! Didn't I never tell you of the little boy as he took in out of the street, as you may say, this seven years back? and the little girl, two years after I first come here?'

'No. Do tell me all about them, Mrs Bunch – now this minute!'

'Well,' said Mrs Bunch, 'the little girl I don't seem to recollect so much about. I know master brought her back with him from his walk one day, and give orders to Mrs Ellis, as was housekeeper then, as she should be took every care with. And the pore child hadn't no one belonging to her – she told me so her own self – and here she lived with us a matter of three weeks it might be; and then, whether she were something of a gypsy in her blood or what not, but one morning she out of her bed afore any of us had opened a eye, and neither track nor yet trace of her have I set eyes on since. Master was wonderful put about, and had all the ponds dragged; but it's my belief she was had away by them gipsies, for there was singing round the house for as much as an hour the night she went, and Parkes, he declare as he heard them a-calling in the woods all that afternoon. Dear, dear! a hodd child she was, so silent in her ways and all, but I was wonderful taken up with her, so domesticated she was – surprising.'

'And what about the little boy?' said Stephen.

'Ah, that pore boy!' sighed Mrs Bunch. 'He were a foreigner – Jevanny he called hisself – and he come a-tweaking his 'urdy-gurdy round and about the drive one winter day, and master 'ad him in that minute, and ast all about where he came from, and how old he was, and how he made his way, and where was his relatives, and all as kind as heart could wish. But it went the same way with him. They're a hunruly lot, them foreign nations, I do suppose, and he was off one fine morning just the same as the girl. Why he went and what he done was our question for as much as a year after; for he never took his 'urdy-gurdy, and there it lays on the shelf.'

The remainder of the evening was spent by Stephen in miscellaneous cross-examination of Mrs Bunch and in efforts to extract a tune from the hurdy-gurdy.

That night he had a curious dream. At the end of the passage at the top of the house, in which his bedroom was situated, there was an old disused bathroom. It was kept locked, but the upper half of the door was glazed, and, since the muslin curtains which used to hang there had long been gone, you could look in and see the lead-lined bath affixed to the wall on the right hand, with its head towards the window.

On the night of which I am speaking, Stephen Elliott found himself, as he thought, looking through the glazed door. The moon was shining through the window, and he was gazing at a figure which lay in the bath.

His description of what he saw reminds me of what I once beheld myself in the famous vaults of St Michan's Church in Dublin, which possesses the horrid property of preserving corpses from decay for centuries. A figure inexpressibly thin and pathetic, of a dusty leaden colour, enveloped in a shroud-like garment, the thin lips crooked into a faint and dreadful smile, the hands pressed tightly over the region of the heart.

As he looked upon it, a distant, almost inaudible moan seemed to issue from its lips, and the arms began to stir. The terror of the sight forced Stephen backwards and he awoke to the fact that he was indeed standing on the cold boarded floor of the passage in the full light of the moon. With a courage which I do not think can be common among boys of his age, he went to the door of the bathroom to ascertain if the figure of his dream were really there. It was not, and he went back to bed.

Mrs Bunch was much impressed next morning by his story, and went so far as to replace the muslin curtain over the glazed door of the bathroom. Mr Abney, moreover, to whom he confided his experiences at breakfast, was greatly interested, and made notes of the matter in what he called 'his book'.

The spring equinox was approaching, as Mr Abney frequently reminded his cousin, adding that this had been always considered by the ancients to be a critical time for the young: that Stephen would do well to take care of himself, and to shut his bedroom window at night; and that Censorinus had some valuable remarks on the subject. Two incidents that occurred about this time made an impression upon Stephen's mind.

The first was after an unusually uneasy and oppressed night that he had passed – though he could not recall any particular dream that he had had.

The following evening Mrs Bunch was occupying herself in mending his nightgown.

'Gracious me, Master Stephen!' she broke forth rather irritably, 'how do you manage to tear your nightdress all to flinders this way? Look here, sir, what trouble you do give to poor servants that have to darn and mend after you!'

There was indeed a most destructive and apparently wanton series of slits or scorings in the garment, which would undoubtedly require a skilful needle to make good. They were confined to the left side of the chest – long, parallel slits, about six inches in length, some of them not quite piercing the texture of the linen. Stephen could only express his entire ignorance of their origin: he was sure they were not there the night before.

'But,' he said, 'Mrs Bunch, they are just the same as the scratches on the outside of my bedroom door: and I'm sure I never had anything to do with making *them.*'

Mrs Bunch gazed at him open-mouthed, then snatched up a candle, departed hastily from the room, and was heard making her way upstairs. In a few minutes she came down.

'Well,' she said, 'Master Stephen, it's a funny thing to me how them marks and scratches can 'a' come there – too high up for any cat or dog to 'ave made 'em, much less a rat: for all the world like a Chinaman's finger-nails, as my uncle in the tea trade used to tell us of when we was girls together. I wouldn't say nothing to master, not if I was you, Master Stephen, my dear; and just turn the key of the door when you go to your bed.'

'I always do, Mrs Bunch, as soon as I've said my prayers.'

'Ah, that's a good child: always say your prayers, and then no one can't hurt you.'

Herewith Mrs Bunch addressed herself to mending the injured nightgown, with intervals of meditation, until bedtime. This was on a Friday night in March 1812.

On the following evening the usual duet of Stephen and Mrs Bunch was augmented by the sudden arrival of Mr Parkes, the butler, who as a rule kept himself rather to himself in his own pantry. He did not see that Stephen was there: he was, moreover, flustered and less slow of speech than was his wont.

'Master may get up his own wine, if he likes, of an evening,' was his first remark. 'Either I do it in the daytime or not at all, Mrs Bunch. I don't know what it may be: very like it's the rats, or the wind got into the cellars; but I'm not so young as I was, and I can't go through with it as I have done.'

'Well, Mr Parkes, you know it is a surprising place for the rats, is the Hall.'

'I'm not denying that, Mrs Bunch; and, to be sure, many a time I've heard the tale from the men in the shipyards about the rat that could speak. I never laid no confidence in that before; but tonight, if I'd demeaned myself to lay my ear to the door of the further bin, I could pretty much have heard what they was saying.'

'Oh, there, Mr Parkes, I've no patience with your fancies! Rats talking in the wine-cellar indeed!'

'Well, Mrs Bunch, I've no wish to argue with you: all I say is, if you choose to go to the far bin, and lay your ear to the door, you may prove my words this minute.'

'What nonsense you do talk, Mr Parkes – not fit for children to listen to! Why, you'll be frightening Master Stephen there out of his wits.'

'What! Master Stephen?' said Parkes, awaking to the consciousness of the boy's presence. 'Master Stephen knows well enough when I'm a-playing a joke with you, Mrs Bunch.'

In fact, Master Stephen knew much too well to suppose that Mr Parkes had in the first instance intended a joke. He was interested, not altogether pleasantly, in the situation; but all his questions were unsuccessful in inducing the butler to give any more detailed account of his experiences in the wine-cellar.

*   *   *

We have now arrived at March 24th 1812. It was a day of curious experiences for Stephen: a windy, noisy day, which filled the house and the gardens with a restless impression. As Stephen stood by the fence of the grounds, and looked out into the park, he felt as if an endless procession of unseen people were sweeping past him on the wind, borne on resistlessly and aimlessly, vainly striving to stop themselves, to catch at something that might arrest their flight and bring them once again into contact with the living world of which they had formed a part. After luncheon that day Mr Abney said:

'Stephen, my boy, do you think you could manage to come to me tonight as late as eleven o'clock in my study? I shall be busy until that time, and I wish to show you something connected with your future life which it is most important that you should know. You are not to mention this matter to Mrs Bunch nor to anyone else in the house; and you had better go to your room at the usual time.'

Here was a new excitement added to life: Stephen eagerly grasped at the opportunity of sitting up till eleven o'clock. He looked in at the library door on his way upstairs that evening, and saw a brazier, which He had often noticed in the corner of the room, moved out before the fire: an old silver-gilt cup stood on the table, filled with red wine, and some written sheets of paper lay near it. Mr Abney was sprinkling some incense on the brazier from a round silver box as Stephen passed, but did not seem to notice his step.

The wind had fallen, and there was a still night and a full moon. At about ten o'clock Stephen was standing at the open window of his bedroom, looking out over the country. Still as the night was, the mysterious population of the distant moon-lit woods was not yet lulled to rest. From time to time strange cries as of lost and despairing wanderers sounded from across the mere. They might be the notes of owls or water-birds, yet they did not quite resemble either sound. Were not they coming nearer? Now they sounded from the nearer side of the water, and in a few moments they seemed to be floating about among the shrubberies. Then they ceased; but just as Stephen was thinking of shutting the window and resuming his reading of *Robinson Crusoe*, he caught sight of two figures standing on the gravelled terrace that ran along the garden side of the Hall – the figures of a boy and a girl, as it seemed; they stood side by side, looking up at the windows. Something in the form of the girl recalled irresistibly his dream of the figure in the bath. The boy inspired him with more acute fear.

Whilst the girl stood still, half smiling, with her hands clasped over her heart, the boy, a thin shape, with black hair and ragged clothing, raised his arms in the air with an appearance of menace and of unappeasable hunger and longing. The moon shone upon his almost transparent hands, and Stephen saw that the nails were fearfully long and that the light shone through them. As he stood with his arms thus raised, he disclosed a terrifying spectacle. On the left side of his chest there opened a black and gaping rent; and there fell upon Stephen's brain, rather than upon his ear, the impression of one of those hungry and desolate cries that he had heard resounding over the woods of Aswarby all that evening. In another moment this dreadful pair had moved swiftly and noiselessly over the dry gravel, and he saw them no more.

Inexpressibly frightened as he was, he determined to take his candle and go down to Mr Abney's study, for the hour appointed for their meeting was near at hand. The study or library opened out of the front hall on one side, and Stephen, urged on by his terrors, did not take long in getting there. To effect an entrance was not so easy. It was not locked, he felt sure, for the key was on the outside of the door as usual. His repeated knocks produced no answer. Mr Abney was engaged: he was speaking. What! why did he try to cry out? and why was the cry choked in his throat? Had he, too, seen the mysterious children? But now everything was quiet, and the door yielded to Stephen's terrified and frantic pushing.

*   *   *

On the table in Mr Abney's study certain papers were found which explained the situation to Stephen Elliott when he was of an age to understand them. The most important sentences were as follows:
'It was a belief very strongly and generally held by the ancients – of

whose wisdom in these matters I have had such experience as induces me to place confidence in their assertions – that by enacting certain processes, which to us moderns have something of a barbaric complexion, a very remarkable enlightenment of the spiritual faculties in man may be attained: that, for example, by absorbing the personalities of a certain number of his fellow creatures, an individual may gain a complete ascendancy over those orders of spiritual beings which control the elemental forces of our universe.

'It is recorded of Simon Magnus that he was able to fly in the air, to become invisible, or to assume any form he pleased, by the agency of the soul of a boy whom, to use the libellous phrase employed by the author of the *Clementine Recognitions*, he had "murdered". I find it set down, moreover, with considerable detail in the writings of Hermes Trismegistus, that similar happy results may be produced by the absorption of the hearts of not less than three human beings below the age of twenty-one years. To the testing of the truth of this receipt I have devoted the greater part of the last twenty years, selecting as the *corpora vilia* of my experiment such persons as could conveniently be removed without occasioning a sensible gap in society. The first step I effected by the removal of one Phoebe Stanley, a girl of gipsy extraction, on March 24th 1792. The second, by the removal of a wandering Italian lad, named Giovanni Paoli, on the night of March 23rd 1805. The final "victim" – to employ a word repugnant in the highest degree to my feelings – must be my cousin, Stephen Elliott. His day must be this March 24th 1812.

'The best means of effecting the required absorption is to remove the heart from the *living* subject, to reduce it to ashes, and to mingle them with about a pint of some red wine, preferably port. The remains of the first two subjects, at least, it will be well to conceal: a disused bathroom or wine-cellar will be found convenient for such a purpose. Some annoyance may be experienced from the psychic portion of the subjects, which the popular language dignifies with the name of ghosts. But the man of philosophic temperament – to whom alone the experiment is appropriate – will be little prone to attach importance to the feeble efforts of these beings to wreak their vengeance on him. I contemplate with the liveliest satisfaction the enlarged and emancipated existence which the experiment, if successful, will confer on me; not only placing me beyond the reach of human justice (so-called), but eliminating to a great extent the prospect of death itself.'

*   *   *

Mr Abney was found in his chair, his head thrown back, his face stamped with an expression of rage, fright, and mortal pain. In his left side was a terrible lacerated wound, exposing the heart. There was no blood on his hands, and a long knife that lay on the table was perfectly clean. A savage wildcat might have inflicted the injuries. The window of the study was open, and it was the opinion of the coroner that Mr Abney had met his death by the agency of some wild creature. But Stephen Elliott's study of the papers I have quoted led him to a very different conclusion.

Carnival on the Downs
Gerald Kersh

We are a queer people: I do not know what to make of us. Whatever anyone says for us is right; whatever anyone says against us is right. A conservative people, we would turn out our pockets for a rebel; and prim as we are, we love an eccentric.

We are an eccentric people. For example: we make a cult of cold baths – and of our lack of plumbing – and a boast of such characters as Dirty Dick of Bishopsgate, and Mr Lagg who is landlord of The White Swan at Wettendene.

Dirty Dick of Bishopsgate had a public house, and was a dandy, once upon a time. But it seems that on the eve of his marriage to a girl with whom he was in love he was jilted, with the wedding breakfast on the table. Thereafter, everything had, by his order, to be left exactly as it was on that fatal morning. The great cake crumbled, the linen mouldered, the silver turned black. The bar became filthy. Spiders spun their webs, which grew heavy and grey with insects and dirt. Dick never changed his wedding suit, nor his linen, either. His house became a byword for dirt and neglect ... whereupon, he did good business there, and died rich.

Mr Lagg, who had a public house in Wettendene, which is in Sussex, seeing The Green Man redecorated and furnished with chromium chairs, capturing carriage trade, was at first discouraged. His house, The White Swan, attracted the local men who drank nothing but beer – on the profit of which, at that time, a publican could scarcely live.

Lagg grew depressed; neglected the house. Spiders spun their webs in the cellar, above and around the empty, mouldering barrels, hogsheads, kilderkins, nipperkins, casks and pins. He set up a bar in this odorous place – and so made his fortune. As the dirtiest place in Sussex, it became a meeting place for people who bathed every day. An American from New Orleans started the practice of pinning visiting cards to the beams. Soon, everybody who had a card pinned it up, so that Lagg's cellar was covered with them.

When he went to town, Lagg always came back with artificial spiders and beetles on springy wires, to hang from the low ceiling; also, old leather jacks, stuffed crocodiles and spiky rays from the Caribbean gulfs, and even a dried human head from the Amazon. Meanwhile, the cards accumulated, and so did the bills advertising local attractions – cattle shows, flower shows, theatricals, and what not.

And the despisers of what they called the 'great Unwashed' congregated there – the flickers-away of specks of dust – the ladies and gentlemen who could see a thumb print on a plate. Why? Homesickness for the gutter, perhaps – it is an occupational disease of people who like strong perfumes.

I visited the White Swan, in passing, on holiday. The people in Wettendene called it – not without affection – The Mucky Duck. There was the usual vociferous gathering of long-toothed women in tight-cut tweeds, and ruddy men with two slits to their jackets howling confidences, while old Lagg, looking like a half-peeled beetroot, brooded under the cobwebs.

He took notice of me when I offered him something to drink, and said: 'Stopping in Wettendene, sir?'

'Overnight,' I said. 'Anything doing?'

He did not care. 'There's the flower show,' he said, flapping about with a loose hand. 'There's the Christian Boys' Sports. All pinned up. Have a dekko. See for yourself.'

So I looked about me.

That gentleman from New Orleans, who had pinned up the first card on the lowest beam, had started a kind of chain reaction. On the beams, the ceiling, and the very barrels, card jostled card, and advertisement advertisement. I saw the card of the Duke of Chelsea overlapped by the large, red-printed trade card of one George Grape, Rat-Catcher; a potato-crisp salesman's card half overlaid by that of the Hon. Iris Greene. The belly of a stuffed trout was covered with cards as an autumn valley with leaves.

But the great hogshead, it seemed, was set aside for the bills advertising local attractions. Many of these were out of date – for example, an advertisement of a Baby Show in 1932, another of a Cricket Match in 1934, and yet another for 'Sports' in 1923. As Mr Lagg had informed me, there were the printed announcements of the Christian Boys' affair and the Flower Show.

Under the Flower Show, which was scheduled for 14 August, was pinned a wretched little bill advertising, for the same date, a 'Grand Carnival' in Wagnall's Barn on Long Meadow, Wettendene. Everything was covered with dust.

It is a wonderful place for dust. It is necessary, in The Mucky Duck cellar, to take your drink fast or clasp your hand over the top of the glass before it accumulates a grey scum or even a dead spider: the nobility and gentry like it that way. The gnarled old four-ale drinkers go to The Green Man: they have no taste for quaintness.

I knew nobody in Wettendene, and am shy of making new acquaintances. The 'Grand Carnival' was to begin at seven o'clock; entrance fee sixpence, children half price. It could not be much of a show, I reflected, at that price and in that place: a showman must be hard up, indeed, to hire a barn for his show in such a place. But I like carnivals and am interested in the people that follow them; so I set off at five o'clock.

Long Meadow is not hard to find: you go to the end of Wettendene High Street, turn sharp right at Scott's Corner where the village ends, and take the winding lane, Wettendene Way. This will lead you, through a green tunnel, to Long Meadow, where the big Wagnall's Barn is.

Long Meadow was rich grazing land in better times, but now it is good for nothing but a pitiful handful of sheep that nibble the coarse grass. There has been no use for the barn these last two generations. It was built to last hundreds of years; but the land died first. This had something to do with water – either a lack or an excess of it. Long Meadow is good for nothing much, at present, but the Barn stands firm and four-square to the capricious rains and insidious fogs of Wettendene Marsh. (If it were not for the engineers who dammed the river, the whole area would, by now, be under water.) However, the place is dry, in dry weather.

Still, Long Meadow has the peculiarly dreary atmosphere of a swamp and Wagnall's Barn is incongruously sturdy in that wasteland. It is a long time since any produce was stocked in Wagnall's Barn. Mr Etheridge, who owns it, rents it for dances, amateur theatrical shows and what not.

That playbill aroused my curiosity. It was boldly printed in red, as follows:

!!! JOLLY JUMBO'S CARNIVAL !!!
!! THE ONE AND ONLY !!
COME AND SEE
!! GORGON, The Man Who Eats Bricks & Swallows Glass !!
!! THE HUMAN SKELETON !!
!! THE INDIA RUBBER BEAUTY –
She Can Put Her Legs Around Her Neck & Walk On
Her Hands !!
!! A LIVE MERMAID !!
!! ALPHA, BETA, AND DOT.
The World-Famous Tumblers
With The Educated Dog!!
! JOLLY JUMBO !
!! JOLLY JUMBO !!

I left early, because I like to look behind the scenes, and have a chat with a wandering freak or two. I remembered a good friend of mine who had been a Human Skeleton – six foot six and weighed a hundred pounds – ate five meals a day, and was as strong as a bull. He told good stories in that coffee-bar that is set up where the Ringling Brothers and Barnum and Bailey Combined Circuses rest in Florida for the winter. I 'tasted sawdust', as the saying goes, and had a yearning to sit on the ground and hear strange stories. Not that I expected much of Wettendene. All the same the strangest people turn up at the unlikeliest places...

Then the rain came down, as it does in an English summer. The sky sagged, rumbled a borborygmic threat of thunderstorms, which seemed to tear open clouds like bags of water.

Knowing our English summer, I had come prepared with a mackintosh, which I put on as I ran for the shelter of the barn.

I was surprised to find it empty. The thunder was loud, now, and there were zigzags of lightning in the east; the pelting rain sounded on the meadow like a maracca. I took off my raincoat and lit a cigarette – and then, in the light of the match flame, I caught a glimpse of two red-and-green eyes watching me, in a far corner, about a foot away from the floor.

It was not yet night, but I felt in that moment such a pang of horror as comes only in the dark; but I am so constituted that, when frightened, I run forward. There was something unholy about Wagnall's Barn, but I should have been ashamed not to face it, whatever it might be. So I advanced, with my walking-stick; but then there came a most melancholy whimper, and I knew that the eyes belonged to a dog.

I made a caressing noise and said: 'Good dog, good doggie! Come on, doggo!' – feeling grateful for his company. By the light of another match, I saw a grey poodle, neatly clipped in the French style. When he saw me, he stood up on his hindlegs and danced.

In the light of that same match I saw, also, a man squatting on his haunches with his head in his hands. He was dressed only in trousers and a tattered shirt. Beside him lay a girl. He had made a bed for her of his clothes and, the rain falling softer, I could hear her breathing, harsh and laborious. The clouds lifted. A little light came into the barn. The dog danced, barking, and the crouching man awoke, raising a haggard face.

'Thank God you've come,' he said. 'She can't breathe. She's got an awful pain in her chest, and a cough. She can't catch her breath, and she's burning. Help her, Doctor – Jolly Jumbo has left us high and dry.'

'What?' I said. 'Went on and left you here, all alone?'

'Quite right, Doctor.'

I said: 'I'm not a doctor.'

'Jumbo promised to send a doctor from the village,' the man said, with a laugh more unhappy than tears. 'Jolly Jumbo promised! I might have known. I did know. Jolly Jumbo never kept his word. Jumbo lives for hisself. But he didn't ought to leave us here in the rain, and Dolores in a bad fever. No, nobody's got the right. No!'

I said: 'You might have run down to Wettendene yourself, and got the doctor.'

'"Might" is a long word, mister. I've broke my ankle and my left wrist. Look at the mud on me, and see if I haven't tried... Third time, working my way on my elbows – and I am an agile man – I fainted with the pain, and half drowned in the mud... But Jumbo swore his Bible oath to send a physician for Dolores. Oh, dear me!'

At this the woman between short, agonized coughs, gasped: '*Alma de mi corazan* – heart of my soul – not leave? So cold, so hot, so cold. Please, not go?'

'I'll see myself damned first,' the man said, 'and so will Dot. Eh, Dot?'

At this the poodle barked and stood on its hindlegs, dancing.

The man said, drearily: 'She's a woman, do you see, sir. But one of the faithful kind. She come out of Mexico. That *alma de mi corazan* – she means it. Actually, it means "soul of my heart". There's nothing much more you can say to somebody you love, if you mean it... So you're not a doctor? More's the pity! I'd hoped you was. But oh, sir, for the sake of Christian charity, perhaps you'll give us a hand.

'She and me, we're not one of that rabble of layabouts, and gyppos, and what not. Believe me, sir, we're artists of our kind. I know that a gentleman like you doesn't regard us, because we live rough. But it would be an act of kindness for you to get a doctor up from Wettendene, because my wife is burning and coughing, and I'm helpless.

'I'll tell you something, guv'nor – poor little Dot, who understands more than the so-called Christians in these parts, she knew, *she* knew! She ran away. I called her: "Dot – Dot – Dot!" – but she run on. I'll swear she went for a doctor, or something.

'And in the meantime Jolly Jumbo has gone and left us high and dry. Low and wet is the better word, sir, and we haven't eaten this last two days.'

The girl, gripping his wrist, sighed: 'Please, not to go, not to leave?'

'Set your heart at ease, sweetheart,' the man said. 'Me and Dot, we are with you. And here's a gentleman who'll get us a physician. Because, to deal plainly with you, my one and only, I've got a bad leg now and a bad arm, and I can't make it through the mud to Wettendene. The dog tried and she come back with a bloody mouth where somebody kicked her...'

I said: 'Come on, my friends, don't lose heart. I'll run down to Wettendene and get an ambulance, or at least a doctor. Meanwhile,' I said, taking off my jacket, 'peel off some of those damp clothes. Put this on her. At least it's dry. Then I'll run down and get you some help.'

He said: 'All alone? It's a dretful thing, to be all alone. Dot'll go with you, if you will, God love you! But it's no use, I'm afraid.'

He said this in a whisper, but the girl heard him, and said, quite clearly: 'No use. Let him not go. Kind voice. Talk' – this between rattling gasps.

He said: 'All right, my sweet, he'll go in a minute.'

The girl said: 'Only a minute. Cold. Lonely——'

'What, Dolores, lonely with me and Dot?'

'Lonely, lonely, lonely.'

So the man forced himself to talk. God grant that no circumstances may compel any of you who read this to talk in such a voice. He was trying to speak evenly; but from time to time, when some word touched his heart, his voice broke like a boy's, and he tried to cover the break with a laugh that went inward, a sobbing laugh.

Holding the girl's hand and talking for her comfort, interrupted from time to time by the whimpering of the poodle Dot, he went on:

They call me Alpha, you see, because my girl's name is Beta. That is her real name – short for Beatrice Dolores. But my real name is Alfred, and I come from Hampshire.

They call us 'tumblers', sir, but Dolores is an artist. I can do the forward rolls and the triple back-somersaults; but Dolores is the genius. Dolores, and that dog, Dot, do you see?

It's a hard life, sir, and it's a rough life. I used to be a Joey – a kind of a clown – until I met Dolores in Southampton, where she'd been abandoned by a dago that run a puppet show, with side-shows, as went broke and left Dolores high and dry. All our lives, from Durham to Land's End, Carlisle to Brighton, north, south, east, west, I've been left high and dry when the rain came down and the money run out. Not an easy life, sir. A hard life, as a matter of fact. You earn your bit of bread, in this game.

Ever since Dolores and me joined Jolly Jumbo's Carnival, there was a run of bad luck. At Immersham, there was a cloudburst; Jumbo had took Grote's Meadow – we was two foot under water. The weather cleared at Athelboro' and they all came to see Pollux, the Strong Man, because, do you see, the blacksmith at Athelboro' could lift an anvil over his head, and there was a fi'-pun prize for anybody who could out-lift Pollux (his name was really Michaels).

Well, as luck would have it, at Athelboro' Pollux sprained his wrist. The blacksmith out-lifted him, and Jolly Jumbo told him to come back next morning for his fiver. We pulled out about midnight: Jumbo will never go to Athelboro' again. Then, in Pettydene, something happened to Gorgon, the man that eats bricks and swallows glass. His act was to bite lumps out of a brick, chew them up, wash them down with a glass of water, and crunch up and swallow the glass. We took the Drill Hall at Pettydene, and had a good house. And what happens, but Gorgon breaks a tooth!

I tell you, sir, we had no luck. After that, at Firestone, something went wrong with the Mermaid. She was my property, you know – an animal they call a manatee – I bought her for a round sum from a man who caught her in South America. A kind of seal, but with breasts like a woman, and almost a human voice. She got a cough, and passed away.

There was never such a round. Worst of all, just here, Dolores caught a cold.

I dare say you've heard of my act, Alpha, Beta and Dot? . . . Oh, a stranger here; are you sir? I wish you could have seen it. Dolores is the genius – her and Dot. I'm only the under-stander. I would come rolling and somersaulting in, and stand. Then Dolores'd come dancing in and take what looked like a standing jump – I gave her a hand-up – on to my shoulders, so we stood balanced. Then, in comes poor little Dot, and jumps; first on to my shoulder, then on to Dolores' shoulder from mine, and so on to Dolores' head where Dot stands on her hind legs and dances . . .

The rain comes down, sir. Dolores has got a cold in the chest. I beg her: 'Don't go on, Dolores – don't do it!' But nothing will satisfy her, bless her heart: the show must go on. And when we come on, she was burning like a fire. Couldn't do the jump. I twist sidewise to take the weight, but her weight is kind of a deadweight, poor girl! My ankle snaps, and we tumbles.

Tried to make it part of my act – making funny business, carrying the girl in my arms, hopping on one foot, with good old Dot dancing after us.

That was the end of us in Wettendene. Jolly Jumbo says to us: 'Never was such luck. The brick-eater's bust a tooth. The mermaid's good and dead. The strong-man has strained hisself . . . and I'm not sure but that blacksmith won't be on my trail, with a few pals, for that fi'pun note. I've got to leave you to it, Alph, old feller. I'm off to Portsmouth.'

I said: 'And what about my girl? I've only got one hand and one foot, and she's got a fever.'

He said: 'Wait a bit, Alph, just wait a bit. My word of honour, and my Bible oath, I'll send a sawbones up from Wettendene.'

'And what about our pay?' I ask.

Jolly Jumbo says: 'I swear on my mother's grave, Alph, I haven't got it. But I'll have it in Portsmouth, on my Bible oath. You know me. Sacred word of honour! I'll be at The Hope and Anchor for a matter of weeks, and you'll be paid in full. And I'll send you a doctor, by my father's life I will. Honour bright! In the meantime, Alph, I'll look after Dot for you.'

And so he picked up the dog – I hadn't the strength to prevent him – and went out, and I heard the whips cracking and the vans squelching in the mud.

But little Dot got away and came back...

I've been talking too much, sir. I thought you was the doctor. Get one for the girl, if you've a heart in you – and a bit of meat for the dog. I've got a few shillings on me.

I said: 'Keep still. I'll be right back.' And I ran in the rain, closely followed by the dog Dot, down through that dripping green tunnel into Wettendene, and rang long and loud at a black door to which was affixed the brass plate, well worn, of one Dr MacVitie, M.R.C.S., L.R.C.P.

The old doctor came out, brushing crumbs from his waistcoat. There was an air of decrepitude about him. He led me into his surgery. I saw a dusty old volume of *Gray's Anatomy*, two fishing rods, four volumes of the Badminton Library – all unused these past twenty years. There were also some glass-stoppered bottles that seemed to contain nothing but sediment; a spirit lamp without spirit; some cracked test-tubes; and an ancient case-book into the cover of which was stuck a rusty scalpel.

He was one of the cantankerous old Scotch school of doctors that seem incapable of graciousness, and grudging even of a civil word. He growled: 'I'm in luck this evening. It's six months since I sat down to my bit of dinner without the bell going before I had the first spoonful of soup half-way to my mouth. Well, you've let me finish my evening meal. Thank ye.'

He was ponderously ironic, this side of offensiveness. 'Well, out with it. What ails ye? Nothing, I'll wager. Nothing ever ails 'em hereabouts that a dose of castor oil or an aspirin tablet will not cure – excepting always rheumatism. Speak up, man!'

I said: 'There's nothing wrong with me at all. I've come to fetch you to treat two other people up at Wagnall's Barn. There's a man with a broken ankle and a girl with a congestion of the lungs. So get your bag and come along.'

He snapped at me like a turtle, and said: 'And since when, may I ask, were you a diagnostician? And who are you to be giving a name to symptoms? In any case, young fellow, I'm not practising. I'm retired. My son runs the practice, and he's out on a child-bed case . . . Damn that dog – he's barking again!'

The poodle, Dot, was indeed barking hysterically and scratching at the front door.

I said: 'Doctor, these poor people are in desperate straits.'

'Aye, poor people always are. And who's to pay the bill?'

'I'll pay,' I said, taking out my wallet.

'Put it up, man, put it up! Put your hand in your pocket for all the riff-raff that lie about in barns and ye'll end in the workhouse.'

He got up laboriously, sighing: 'Alex is over Iddlesworth way with the car. God give us strength to bear it. I swore my oath and so I'm bound to come, Lord preserve us!'

'If——' I said, 'if you happen to have a bit of meat in the house for the dog, I'd be glad to pay for it——'

'– And what do you take this surgery for? A butcher's shop?' Then he paused. 'What sort of a dog, as a matter of curiosity would ye say it was?'

'A little grey French poodle.'

'Oh, aye? Very odd. Ah well, there's a bit of meat on the chop bones, so I'll put 'em in my pocket for the dog, if you like . . . Wagnall's Barn, did ye say? A man and a girl, is that it? They'll be some kind of vagrant romanies, or gyppos, no doubt?'

I said: 'I believe they are some kind of travelling performers. They are desperately in need of help. Please hurry, Doctor.'

His face was sour and his voice harsh, but his eyes were bewildered, as he said: 'Aye, no doubt. I dare say, very likely. A congestion of the lungs, ye said? And a fractured ankle, is that it? Very well.' He was throwing drugs and bandages into his disreputable-looking black bag. I helped him into his immense black mackintosh.

He said: 'As for hurrying, young man, I'm seventy-seven years old, my arteries are hard, and I could not hurry myself for the crack of doom. Here, carry the bag. Hand me my hat and my stick, and we'll walk up to Wagnall's Barn on this fool's errand of yours. Because a fool's errand it is, I fancy. Come on.'

The little dog, Dot, looking like a bit of the mud made animate, only half distinguishable in the half dark, barked with joy, running a little way backwards and a long way forwards, leading us back to the Barn through that darkened green tunnel.

The doctor had a flash-lamp. We made our way to the barn, he grumbling and panting and cursing the weather. We went in. He swung the beam of his lamp from corner to corner, until it came to rest on my jacket. It lay as I had wrapped it over poor Dolores, but it was empty.

I shouted: 'Alpha, Beta! Here's the doctor!'

The echo answered: '*Octor!*'

I could only pick up my jacket and say: 'They must have gone away.'

Dr MacVitie said, drily: 'Very likely, if they were here at all.'

'Here's my jacket, damp on the inside and dry on the outside,' I said. 'And I have the evidence of my own eyes——'

'No doubt. Very likely. In a lifetime of practice I have learned, sir, to discredit the evidence of my eyes, and my other four senses, besides. Let's away. Come!'

'But where have they gone?'

'Ah, I wonder!'

'And the dog, where's the dog?' I cried.

He said, in his dour way: 'For that, I recommend you consult Mr Lindsay, the vet.'

So we walked down again, without exchanging a word until we reached Dr MacVitie's door. Then he said: 'Where did you spend your evening?'

I said: 'I came straight to the Barn from The White Swan.'

'Well, then,' he said, 'I recommend ye go back, and take a whisky and water, warm; and get ye to bed in a dry night-shirt. And this time take a little more water with it. Goodnight to ye——' and slammed the door in my face.

I walked the half mile to The White Swan, which was still open. The landlord, Mr Lagg, looked me up and down, taking notice of my soaking wet clothes and muddy boots. 'Been out?' he asked.

In Sussex they have a way of asking unnecessary, seemingly innocent questions of this nature which lead to an exchange of witticisms – for which, that night, I was not in the mood.

I said: 'I went up to Wagnall's Barn for Jolly Jumbo's Carnival. but he pulled out, it seems, and left a man, a woman, and a dog——'

'You hear that, George?' said Mr Lagg to a very old farmer whose knobbed ash walking-stick seemed to have grown out of the knobbed root of his earthy, arthritic hand, and who was smoking a pipe mended in three places with insulating tape.

'I heerd,' said old George, with a chuckle. 'Dat gen'lemen'll been a liddle bit late for dat carnival, like.'

At this they both laughed. But then Mr Lagg said, soothingly, as to a cash customer: 'Didn't you look at the notice on the bill, sir? Jolly Jumbo was here all right, and flitted in a hurry too. And he did leave a man and a girl (not lawfully married, I heerd) and one o' them liddle shaved French dogs.

'I say, you'm a liddle late for Jolly Jumbo's Carnival, sir. 'Cause if you look again at Jolly Jumbo's bill, you'll see – I think the programme for the Cricket Match covers up the corner – you'll see the date on it is August the fourteenth, 1904. I was a boy at the time; wasn't I, George?'

'Thirteen-year-old,' old George said, 'making you sixty-three to my seventy-two. Dat were a sad business, but as ye sow, so shall ye reap, they says. Live a vagabond, die a vagabond. Live in sin, die in sin——'

'All right, George,' said Mr Lagg, 'you're not in chapel now ... I don't know how you got at it, sir, but Jolly Jumbo (as he called hisself) lef' two people and a dog behind. Hauled out his vans, eleven o'clock at night, and left word with Dr MacVitie (the old one, that was) to go up to Wagnall's Barn.

'But he was in the middle o' dinner, and wouldn't go. Then he was called out to the Squire's place, and didn't get home till twelve o'clock next night. And there was a liddle dog that kep' barking and barking, and trying to pull him up the path by the trousis-leg. But Dr Mac-Vitie——'

'Dat were a mean man, dat one, sure enough!'

'You be quiet, George. Dr MacVitie kicked the liddle dog into the ditch, and unhooked the bell, and tied up the knocker, and went to bed. Couple o' days later, Wagnall, going over his land, has a look at that barn, and he sees a young girl stone dead, a young fellow dying, and a poor liddle dog crying fit to break your heart. Oh, he got old Dr MacVitie up to the barn then all right, but t'was too late. The fellow, he died in the Cottage Hospital.

'They tried to catch the dog, but nobody could. It stood off and on, like, until that pair was buried by the parish. Then it run off into the woods, and nobody saw it again——'

'Oh, but didn't they, though?' said old George.

Mr Lagg said: 'It's an old wives' tale, sir. They *do* say that this here liddle grey French dog comes back every year on August the fourteenth to scrat and bark at the doctor's door, and lead him to Wagnall's Barn. And be he in the middle of his supper or be he full, be he weary or rested, wet or dry, sick or well, go he must ... *He* died in 1924, so you see it's nothing but an old wives' tale——'

'Dey did used to git light-headed, like, here on the marshes,' said old George, 'but dey do say old Dr MacVitie mustn't rest. He mus' pay dat call to dat empty barn, every year, because of his hard heart. Tomorrow, by daylight, look and see if doctor's door be'nt all scratted up, like.'

'George, you're an old woman in your old age,' said Mr Lagg. 'We take no stock of such things in these parts, sir. Would you like to come up to the lounge and look at the television until closing time?'

The Mark of the Beast
Rudyard Kipling

Your Gods and my Gods – do you or I know which are the stronger?
Native Proverb

East of Suez, some hold, the direct control of providence ceases; man being there handed over to the power of the gods and devils of Asia, and the Church of England providence only exercising an occasional and modified supervision in the case of Englishmen.

This theory accounts for some of the more unnecessary horrors of life in India: it may be stretched to explain my story.

My friend Strickland of the police who knows as much of natives of India as is good for any man, can bear witness to the facts of the case. Dumiose, our doctor, also saw what Strickland and I saw. The inference which he drew from the evidence was entirely incorrect. He is dead now; he died in a rather dubious manner, which has been elsewhere described.

When Fleete came to India he owned a little money and some land in the Himalayas, near a place called Dharmsala. Both properties had been left him by an uncle, and he came out to finance them. He was a big, heavy, genial and inoffensive man. His knowledge of natives was, of course, limited, and he complained of the difficulties of the language.

He rode in from his place in the hills to spend New Year in the station, and he stayed with Strickland. On New Year's Eve there was a big dinner at the club, and the night was excusably wet. When men foregather from the uttermost ends of the Empire, they have a right to be riotous. The Frontier had sent down a contingent of 'Catch-'em-Alive-O's' who had not seen twenty white faces for a year, and were used to riding fifteen miles to dinner at the next fort at the risk of a Khyberee bullet where their drink should lie. They profited by their new security, for they tried to play pool with a curled up hedgehog found in the garden, and one of them carried the marker round the room in his teeth. Half a dozen planters had come in from the south and were talking 'horse' to the biggest liar in Asia, who was trying to cap all their stories at once. Everybody was there, and there was a general closing up of ranks and taking stock of our losses in dead or disabled that had fallen during the past year. It was a very wet night, and I remember that we sang 'Auld Lang Syne' with our feet in the Polo Championship Cup, and our heads among the stars, and swore that we were all dear friends. Then some of us went away and annexed Burma, and some tried to open up the Soudan and were opened up by Fuzzies in that cruel scrub outside Suakim, and some found stars and medals, and some were married, which was bad, and some did other things which were worse, and the others of us stayed in our chains and strove to make money on insufficient experiences.

Fleete began the night with sherry and bitters, drank champagne steadily up to dessert, then raw, rasping Capri with all the strength of whisky, took Benedictine with his coffee, four or five whiskys and sodas to improve his pool strokes, beer and bones at half past two, winding up with old brandy. Consequently, when he came out, at half past three in the morning, into fourteen degrees of frost, he was very angry with his horse for coughing, and tried to leapfrog into the saddle. The horse broke away and went to his stables; so Strickland and I formed a guard of dishonour to take Fleete home.

Our road lay through the bazaar, close to a little temple of Hanuman, the monkey-god, who is a leading divinity worthy of respect. All gods have good points, just as have all priests. Personally I attach much importance to Hanuman, and am kind to his people – the great grey apes of the hills. One never knows when one may want a friend.

There was a light in the temple, and as we passed we could hear voices of men chanting hymns. In a native temple the priests rise at all hours of the night to do honour to their god. Before we could stop him, Fleete dashed up the steps, patted two priests on the back, and was gravely grinding the ashes of his cigar butt into the forehead of the red stone image of Hanuman. Strickland tried to drag him out, but he sat down and said solemnly:

'Shee that? Mark of the B-beasht! *I* made it. Ishn't it fine?'

In half a minute the temple was alive and noisy, and Strickland, who knew what came of polluting gods, said that things might occur. He, by virtue of his official position, long residence in the country, and weakness for going among the natives, was known to the priests, and he felt unhappy. Fleete sat on the ground and refused to move. He said that 'good old Hanuman' made a very soft pillow.

Then, without any warning, a silver man came out of a recess behind the image of the god. He was perfectly naked in that bitter, bitter cold, and his body shone like frosted silver, for he was what the

Bible calls 'a leper as white as snow'. Also he had no face, because he was a leper of some years' standing, and his disease was heavy upon him. We two stooped to haul Fleete up, and the temple was filling and filling with folk who seemed to spring from the earth, when the silver man ran in under our arms, making a noise exactly like the mewing of an otter, caught Fleete round the body and dropped his head on Fleete's breast before we could wrench him away. Then he retired to a corner and sat mewing while the crowd blocked all the doors.

The priests were very angry until the silver man touched Fleete. That nuzzling seemed to sober them.

At the end of a few minutes' silence one of the priests came to Strickland and said, in perfect English, 'Take your friend away. He has done with Hanuman, but Hanuman has not done with him.' The crowd gave room and we carried Fleete into the road.

Strickland was very angry. He said that we might all three have been knifed, and that Fleete should thank his stars that he had escaped without injury.

Fleete thanked no one. He said that he wanted to go to bed. He was gorgeously drunk.

We moved on, Strickland silent and wrathful, until Fleete was taken with violent shivering fits and sweating. He said that the smells of the bazaar were overpowering, and he wondered why slaughter-houses were permitted so near English residences. 'Can't you smell the blood?' said Fleete.

We put him to bed at last, just as the dawn was breaking, and Strickland invited me to have another whisky and soda. While we were drinking he talked of the trouble at the temple, and admitted that it baffled him completely. Strickland hates being mystified by natives, because his business in life is to overmatch them with their own weapons. He has not yet succeeded in doing this, but in fifteen or twenty years he will have made some small progress.

'They should have mauled us,' he said, 'instead of mewing at us. I wonder what they meant. I don't like it one little bit.'

I said that the managing committee of the temple would in all probability bring a criminal action against us for insulting their religion. There was a section of the Indian Penal Code which exactly met Fleete's offence. Strickland said he only hoped and prayed that they would do this. Before I left I looked into Fleete's room, and saw him lying on his right side, scratching his left breast. Then I went to bed, cold, depressed, and unhappy, at seven o'clock in the morning.

At one o'clock I rode over to Strickland's house to enquire after Fleete's head. I imagined it would be a sore one. Fleete was breakfasting and seemed unwell. His temper was gone, for he was abusing the cook for not supplying him with an underdone chop. A man who can eat raw meat after a wet night is a curiosity. I told Fleete this, and he laughed.

'You breed queer mosquitoes in these parts,' he said. 'I've been bitten to pieces, but only in one place.'

'Let's have a look at the bite,' said Strickland. 'It may have gone down since this morning.'

While the chops were being cooked, Fleete opened his shirt and showed us, just over his left breast, a mark, the perfect double of the black rosettes – the five or six irregular blotches arranged in a circle – on a leopard's hide. Strickland looked and said, 'It was only pink this morning. It's gone black now.'

Fleete ran to a glass.

'By Jove!' he said, 'this is nasty. What is it?'

We could not answer. Here the chops came in, all red and juicy, and Fleete bolted three in a most offensive manner. He ate on his right grinders only, and threw his head over his right shoulder as he snapped the meat. When he had finished, it struck him that he had been behaving strangely, for he said apologetically, 'I don't think I ever felt so hungry in my life. I've bolted like an ostrich.'

After breakfast Strickland said to me, 'Don't go. Stay here, and stay for the night.'

Seeing that my house was not three miles from Strickland's, this request was absurd. But Strickland insisted, and was going to say something when Fleete interrupted by declaring in a shamefaced way that he felt hungry again. Strickland sent a man to my house to fetch over my bedding and a horse, and we three went down to Strickland's stables to pass the hours until it was time to go out for a ride. The man who has a weakness for horses never wearies of inspecting them; and when two men are killing time in this way they gather knowledge and lies, the one from the other.

There were five horses in the stables, and I shall never forget the scene as we tried to look them over. They seemed to have gone mad. They reared and screamed and nearly tore up their pickets; they sweated and shivered and lathered and were distraught with fear. Strickland's horses used to know him as well as his dogs; which made the matter more curious. We left the stables for fear of the brutes throwing themselves in their panic. Then Strickland turned back and called me. The horses were still frightened, but they let us 'gentle' and make much of them, and put their heads in our bosoms.

'They aren't afraid of *us*,' said Strickland. 'D'you know, I'd give three months' pay if Outrage here could talk.'

But Outrage was dumb, and could only cuddle up to his master and blow out his nostrils, as is the custom of horses when they wish to explain things but can't. Fleete came up when we were in the stalls, and as soon as the horses saw him their fright broke out afresh. It was all we could do to escape from the place unkicked. Strickland said, 'They don't seem to love you, Fleete.'

'Nonsense,' said Fleete; 'my mare will follow me like a dog.' He went to her; she was in a loose box; but as he slipped the bars she plunged, knocked him down, and broke away into the garden. I laughed, but Strickland was not amused. He took his moustache in both fists, and pulled at it till it nearly came out. Fleete, instead of going off to chase his property, yawned, saying that he felt sleepy. He went to the house to lie down, which was a foolish way of spending New Year's Day.

Strickland sat with me in the stables and asked if I had noticed anything peculiar in Fleete's manner. I said that he ate his food like a beast; but that this might have been the result of living alone in the hills out of the reach of society as refined and elevating as ours, for instance. Strickland was not amused. I do not think that he listened to me, for his next sentence referred to the mark on Fleete's breast, and I said that it might have been caused by blister flies, or that it was possibly a birth-mark newly born and now visible for the first time. We both agreed that it was unpleasant to look at, and Strickland found occasion to say that I was a fool.

'I can't tell you what I think now,' said he, 'because you would call me a madman; but you must stay with me for the next few days, if you can. I want you to watch Fleete, but don't tell me what you think till I have made up my mind.'

'But I am dining out tonight,' I said.

'So am I,' said Strickland, 'and so is Fleete. At least if he doesn't change his mind.'

We walked about the garden smoking, but saying nothing – because we were friends, and talking spoils good tobacco – till our pipes were out. Then we went to wake up Fleete. He was wide awake and fidgeting about his room.

'I say, I want some more chops,' he said. 'Can I get them?'

We laughed and said, 'Go and change. The ponies will be round in a minute.'

'All right,' said Fleete. 'I'll go when I get the chops – underdone ones, mind.'

He seemed to be quite in earnest. It was four o'clock, and we had breakfast at one; still, for a long time, he demanded those underdone chops. Then he changed into riding clothes and went out onto the verandah. His pony – the mare had not been caught – would not let him come near. All three horses were unmanageable – mad with fear – and finally Fleete said that he would stay at home and get something to eat. Strickland and I rode out wondering. As we passed the temple of Hanuman, the silver man came out and mewed at us.

'He is not one of the regular priests of the temple,' said Strickland. 'I think I should peculiarly like to lay my hands on him.'

There was no spring in our gallop on the race course that evening. The horses were stale, and moved as though they had been ridden out.

'The fright after breakfast has been too much for them,' said Strickland.

That was the only remark he made through the remainder of the ride. Once or twice I think he swore to himself; but that did not count.

We came back in the dark at seven o'clock, and saw that there were no lights in the bungalow. 'Careless ruffians my servants are!' said Strickland.

My horse reared at something on the carriage-drive and Fleete stood up under its nose.

'What are you doing, grovelling about the garden?' said Strickland.

But both horses bolted and nearly threw us. We dismounted by the stables and returned to Fleete, who was on his hands and knees under the orange-bushes.

'What the devil's wrong with you?' said Strickland.

'Nothing, nothing in the world,' said Fleete, speaking very quickly and thickly. 'I've been gardening – botanizing, you know. The smell of the earth is delightful. I think I'm going for a walk – long walk – all night.'

Then I saw that there was something excessively out of order somewhere, and I said to Strickland, 'I am not dining out.'

'Bless you!' said Strickland. 'Here, Fleete, get up. You'll catch fever there. Come in to dinner and let's have the lamps lit. We'll all dine at home.'

Fleete stood up unwillingly, and said, 'No lamps – no lamps. It's much nicer here. Let's dine outside and have some more chops – lots of 'em and underdone – bloody ones with gristle.'

Now a December evening in Northern India is bitterly cold, and Fleete's suggestion was that of a maniac.

'Come in,' said Strickland sternly. 'Come in at once.'

Fleete came, and when the lamps were brought, we saw that he was literally plastered with dirt from head to foot. He must have been rolling in the garden. He shrank from the light and went to his room. His eyes were horrible to look at. There was a green light behind them, not in them, if you understand, and the man's lower lip hung down.

Strickland said, 'There is going to be trouble – big trouble – tonight. Don't you change your riding things.'

We waited and waited for Fleete's reappearance, and ordered dinner in the meantime. We could hear him moving about his own room, but there was no light there. Presently from the room came the long-drawn howl of a wolf.

People write and talk lightly of blood running cold and hair standing up and things of that kind. Both sensations are too horrible to be trifled with. My heart stopped as though a knife had been driven through it, and Strickland turned as white as the table-cloth.

The howl was repeated and was answered by another howl far across the fields.

That set the gilded roof on the horror. Strickland dashed into Fleete's room. I followed, and we saw Fleete getting out of the window. He made beast noises in the back of his throat. He could not answer us when we shouted at him. He spat.

I don't quite remember what followed, but I think that Strickland must have stunned him with the long boot-jack or else I should never have been able to sit on his chest. Fleete could not speak, he could only snarl, and his snarls were those of a wolf, not of a man. The human spirit must have been giving way all day and have died out with the twilight. We were dealing with a beast that had once been Fleete.

The affair was beyond any human and rational experience. I tried to say 'Hydrophobia', but the word wouldn't come, because I knew I was lying.

We bound this beast with leather thongs of the punkah-rope, and tied its thumbs and big toes together, and gagged it with a shoe horn, which makes a very efficient gag if you know how to arrange it. Then we carried it into the dining-room and sent a man to Dumoise, the doctor, telling him to come over at once. After we had despatched the messenger and were drawing breath, Strickland said, 'It's no good. This isn't any doctor's work.' I, also, knew that he spoke the truth.

The beast's head was free, and it threw it about from side to side. Anyone entering the room would have believed that we were curing a wolf's pelt. That was the most loathsome accessory of all.

Strickland sat with his chin in the heel of his fist, watching the beast as it wriggled on the ground, but saying nothing. The shirt had been torn open in the scuffle and showed the black rosette mark on the left breast. It stood out like a blister.

In the silence of the watching we heard something without, mewing like a she-otter. We both rose to our feet, and, I answer for myself, not Strickland, felt sick – actually and physically sick. We told each other, as did the men in 'Pingafore', that it was the cat.

Dumoise arrived, and I never saw a little man so unprofessionally shocked. He said that it was a heartrending case of hydrophobia and that nothing could be done. At least any palliative measures would only prolong the agony. The beast was foaming at the mouth. Fleete, as we told Dumoise, had been bitten by dogs once or twice. Any man who keeps half a dozen terriers must expect a nip now and again. Dumoise could offer no help. He could only certify that Fleete was dying of hydrophobia. The beast was then howling, for it had managed to spit out the shoe horn. Dumoise said that he would be ready to certify to the cause of death, and that the end was certain. He was a good little man, and he offered to remain with us; but Strickland refused the kindness. He did not wish to poison Dumoise's New Year. He would only ask him not to give the real cause of Fleete's death to the public.

So Dumoise left, deeply agitated; and as soon as the noise of the cart-wheels had died away, Strickland told me, in a whisper, his suspicions. They were so wildly improbable that he dared not say them aloud; and I, who entertained all Strickland's beliefs, was so ashamed of owning to them that I pretended to disbelieve.

'Even if the silver man had bewitched Fleete for polluting the image of Hanuman, the punishment could not have fallen so quickly.'

As I was whispering this the cry outside the house rose again, and the beast fell into a fresh paroxysm of struggling till we were afraid that the thongs that held it would give way.

'Watch!' said Strickland. 'If this happens six times I shall take the law into my own hands. I order you to help me.'

He went into his room and came out in a few minutes with the barrels of an old shotgun, a piece of fishing-line, some thick cord, and his heavy wooden bedstead. I reported that the convulsions had followed the cry by two seconds in each case, and the beast seemed perceptibly weaker.

Strickland muttered, 'But he can't take away the life! He can't take away the life!'

I said, though I knew that I was arguing against myself, 'It may be a cat. It must be a cat. If the silver man is responsible, why does he dare to come here?'

Strickland arranged the wood on the hearth, put the gun-barrels into the glow of the fire, spread the twine on the table, and broke a walking-stick in two. There was one yard of fishing-line, gut, lapped with wire, such as is used for *mahseer*-fishing, and he tied the two ends together in a loop.

Then he said, 'How can we catch him? He must be taken alive and unhurt.'

I said that we must trust in Providence, and go out softly with polo-sticks into the shrubbery at the front of the house. The man or animal that made the cry was evidently moving round the house as regularly as a night-watchman. We could wait in the bushes till he came by, and knock him over.

Strickland accepted this suggestion, and we slipped out from a bathroom window onto the front verandah and then across the carriage-drive into the bushes.

In the moonlight we could see the leper coming round the corner of the house. He was perfectly naked, and from time to time he mewed and stopped to dance with his shadow. It was an unattractive sight, and thinking of poor Fleete, brought to such degradation by so foul a creature, I put away all my doubts and resolved to help Strickland from the heated gun-barrels to the loop of twine – from the loins to the head and back again – with all tortures that might be needful.

The leper halted in the front porch for a moment and we jumped out on him with the sticks. He was wonderfully strong, and we were afraid that he might escape or be fatally injured before we caught him. We had an idea that lepers were frail creatures, but this proved to be incorrect. Strickland knocked his legs from under him, and I put my foot on his neck. He mewed hideously, and even through my riding-boots I could feel that his flesh was not the flesh of a clean man.

He struck at us with his hand and feet stumps. We looped the lash of a dog-whip round him, under the armpits, and dragged him backwards into the hall and so into the dining-room where the beast lay. There we tied him with trunk-straps. He made no attempt to escape, but mewed.

When we confronted him with the beast the scene was beyond description. The beast doubled backwards into a bow, as though he had been poisoned with strychnine, and moaned in the most pitiable fashion. Several other things happened also, but they cannot be put down here.

'I think I was right,' said Strickland. 'Now we will ask him to cure this case.'

But the leper only mewed. Strickland wrapped a towel round his hand and took the gun-barrels out of the fire. I put the half of the broken walking-stick through the loop of fishing-line and buckled the leper comfortably to Strickland's bedstead. I understood then how men and women and little children can endure to see a witch burnt alive; for the beast was moaning on the floor, and though the silver man had no face, you could see horrible feelings passing through the slab that took its place, exactly as waves of heat play across red-hot iron gun-barrels for instance.

Strickland shaded his eyes with his hands for a moment, and we got to work. This part is not to be printed.

The dawn was beginning to break when the leper spoke. His mewings had not been satisfactory up to that point. The beast had fainted from exhaustion, and the house was very still. We unstrapped the leper and told him to take away the evil spirit. He crawled to the beast and laid his hand upon the left breast. That was all. Then he fell face down and whined, drawing in his breath as he did so.

We watched the face of the beast, and saw the soul of Fleete coming back into the eyes. Then a sweat broke out on the forehead, and the eyes

– they were human eyes – closed. We waited for an hour, but Fleete still slept. We carried him to his room and bade the leper go, giving him the bedstead, and the sheet on the bedstead to cover his nakedness, the gloves and the towels with which we had touched him, and the whip that had been hooked round his body. He put the sheet about him and went out into the early morning without speaking or mewing.

Strickland wiped his face and sat down. A night-gong, far away in the city, made seven o'clock.

'Exactly four-and-twenty hours!' said Strickland. 'And I've done enough to ensure my dismissal from the service, besides permanent quarters in a lunatic asylum. Do you believe that we are awake?'

The red-hot gun-barrel had fallen on the floor and was singeing the carpet. The smell was entirely real.

That morning at eleven we two together went to wake up Fleete. We looked and saw that the black leopard-rosette on his chest had disappeared. He was very drowsy and tired, but as soon as he saw us, he said, 'Oh! Confound you fellows. Happy New Year to you. Never mix your liquors. I'm nearly dead.'

'Thanks for your kindness, but you're over time,' said Strickland. 'Today is the morning of the second. You've slept the clock round with a vengeance.'

The door opened, and little Dumoise put his head in. He had come on foot, and fancied that we were laying out Fleete.

'I've brought a nurse,' said Dumoise. 'I suppose that she can come in for ... what is necessary.'

'By all means,' said Fleete cheerily, sitting up in bed. 'Bring on your nurses.'

Dumoise was dumb. Strickland led him out and explained that there must have been a mistake in the diagnosis. Dumoise remained dumb and left the house hastily. He considered that his professional reputation had been injured, and was inclined to make a personal matter of the recovery. Strickland went out too. When he came back, he said that he had been to call on the temple of Hanuman to offer redress for the pollution of the god, and had been solemnly assured that no white man had ever touched the idol, and that he was an incarnation of all the virtues labouring under a delusion. 'What do you think?' said Strickland.

I said, 'There are more things ...'

But Strickland hates that quotation. He says that I have worn it threadbare.

One other curious thing happened which frightened me as much as anything in all the night's work. When Fleete was dressed he came into the dining-room and sniffed. He had a quaint trick of moving his nose when he sniffed. 'Horrid doggy smell, here,' said he. 'You should really keep those terriers of yours in better order. Try sulphur, Strick.'

But Strickland did not answer. He caught hold of the back of a chair, and, without warning, went into an amazing fit of hysterics. It is terrible to see a strong man overtaken with hysteria. Then it struck me that we had fought for Fleete's soul with the silver man in that room, and that we had disgraced ourselves as Englishmen for ever, and I laughed and gasped and gurgled just as shamefully as Strickland, while Fleete thought that we had both gone mad. We never told him what we had done.

Some years later, when Strickland had married and was a church-going member of society for his wife's sake, we reviewed the incident dispassionately, and Strickland suggested that I should put it before the public.

I cannot myself see that this step is likely to clear up the mystery; because, in the first place, no one will believe a rather unpleasant story, and, in the second, it is well known to every right-minded man that the gods of the heathen are stone and brass, and any attempt to deal with them otherwise is justly condemned.

Minuke
Nigel Kneale

The estate agent kept an uncomfortable silence until we had reached his car. 'Frankly, I wish you hadn't got wind of that,' he said. 'Don't know how you did: I thought I had the whole thing carefully disposed of. Oh, please get in.'

He pulled his door shut and frowned. 'It puts me in a rather awkward spot. I suppose I'd better tell you all I know about that case, or you'd be suspecting me of heaven-knows-what kinds of chicanery in your own.'

As we set off to see the property I was interested in, he shifted the cigarette to the side of his mouth.

'It's quite a distance, so I can tell you on the way there,' he said. 'We'll pass the very spot, as a matter of fact, and you can see it for yourself. Such as there is to see.'

*   *   *

It was away back before the war (said the estate agent). At the height of the building boom. You remember how it was: ribbon development in full blast everywhere; speculative builders sticking things up almost overnight. Though at least you could get a house when you wanted it in those days.

I've always been careful in what I handle – I want you to understand that. Then one day I was handed a packet of coast-road bungalows, for letting. Put up by one of these gone tomorrow firms, and bought by a local man. I can't say I exactly jumped for joy, but for once the things looked all right, and – business is inclined to be business.

The desirable residence you heard about stood at the end of the row. Actually, it seemed to have the best site. On a sort of natural platform, as it were, raised above road level and looking straight out over the sea. Like all the rest, it had a simple two-bedroom, lounge, living-room, kitchen, bathroom layout. Red-tiled roof, roughcast walls. Ornamental portico, garden strip all round. Sufficiently far from town, but with all conveniences.

It was taken by a man named Pritchard. Cinema projectionist, I think he was. Wife, a boy of ten or so, and a rather younger daughter. Oh – and dog, one of those black, lop-eared animals. They christened the place 'Minuke', M-I-N-U-K-E. My Nook. Yes, that's what I said too. And not even the miserable excuse of its being phonetically correct. Still, hardly worse than most.

Well, at the start everything seemed quite jolly. The Pritchards settled in and busied themselves with rearing a privet hedge and shoving flowers in. They'd paid the first quarter in advance, and as far as I was concerned, were out of the picture for a bit.

Then, about a fortnight after they'd moved in, I had a telephone call from Mrs P to say there was something odd about the kitchen tap. Apparently the thing had happened twice. The first time was when her sister was visiting them, and tried to fill the kettle: no water would come through for a long time, then suddenly squirted violently and almost soaked the woman. I gather the Pritchards hadn't really believed this – thought she was trying to find fault with their little nest – it had never happened before, and she couldn't make it happen again. Then, about a week later, it did: with Mrs Pritchard this time. After her husband had examined the tap and could find nothing wrong with it, he decided that the water supply must be faulty; so they got on to me.

I went round personally, as it was the first complaint from any of these bungalows. The tap seemed normal, and I remember asking if the schoolboy son could have been experimenting with their main stop, when Mrs Pritchard, who had been fiddling with the tap, suddenly said, 'Quick, look at this! It's off now!' They were quite cocky about its happening when I was there.

It really was odd. I turned the tap to the limit, but – not a drop! Not even the sort of gasping gurgle you hear when the supply is turned off at the main. After a couple of minutes, though, it came on. Water shot out, I should say, with about ten times' normal force, as if it had been held under pressure. Then gradually it died down and ran steadily.

Both children were in the room with us until we all dodged out of the door to escape a soaking – it had splashed all over the ceiling – so they couldn't have been up to any tricks. I promised the Pritchards to have the pipes checked. Before returning to town, I called at the next two bungalows in the row: neither of the tenants had had any trouble at all with the water. I thought, well, that localized it at least.

When I reached my office there was a telephone message waiting from Pritchard. I rang him back and he was obviously annoyed. 'Look here,' he said, 'not ten minutes after you left, we've had something else happen! The wall of the large bedroom's cracked from top to bottom.

Big pieces of plaster fell, and the bed's in a terrible mess.' And then he said, 'You wouldn't have got me in a jerry-built place like this if I'd known!'

I had plasterers on the job next morning, and the whole water supply to 'Minuke' under examination. For about three days there was peace. The tap behaved itself, and absolutely nothing was found to be wrong. I was annoyed at what seemed to have been unnecessary expenditure. It looked as if the Pritchards were going to be difficult – and I've had my share of that type: fault-finding cranks occasionally carry eccentricity to the extent of a little private destruction, to prove their points. I was on the watch from now on.

Then it came again.

Pritchard rang me at my home, before nine in the morning. His voice sounded a bit off. Shaky.

'For God's sake can you come round here right away,' he said. 'Tell you about it when you get here.' And then he said, almost fiercely, but quietly and close to the mouthpiece, 'There's something damned queer about this place!' Dramatizing is a typical feature of all cranks, I thought, but particularly the little mousy kind, like Pritchard.

I went to 'Minuke' and found that Mrs Pritchard was in bed, in a state of collapse. The doctor had given her a sleeping dose.

Pritchard told me a tale that was chiefly remarkable for the expression on his face as he told it.

I don't know if you're familiar with the layout of that type of bungalow? The living-room is in the front of the house, with the kitchen behind it. To get from one to the other you have to use the little hallway, through two doors. But for convenience at meal times, there's a serving hatch in the wall between these rooms. A small wooden door slides up and down over the hatch-opening.

'The wife was just passing a big plate of bacon and eggs through from the kitchen,' Pritchard told me, 'when the hatch door came down on her wrists. I saw it and I heard her yell. I thought the cord must've snapped, so I said, "All right, all right!" and went to pull it up because it's only a light wooden frame.'

Pritchard was a funny colour and as far as I could judge, it was genuine.

'Do you know, it wouldn't come! I got my fingers under it and heaved, but it might have weighed two hundredweight. Once it gave an inch or so, and then pressed harder. I said, "Hold on!" and nipped round through the hall. When I got into the kitchen she was on the floor, fainted. And the hatch-door was hitched up as right as ninepence. That gave me a turn!' He sat down, quite deflated; it didn't appear to be put on. Still, ordinary neurotics can be almost as troublesome as out-and-out cranks.

I tested the hatch, gingerly; and, of course, the cords were sound and it ran easily.

'Possibly a bit stiff at times, being new,' I said. 'They're apt to jam if you're rough with them.' And then, 'By the way, just what were you hinting on the phone?'

He looked at me. It was warm sunlight outside, with a bus passing. Normal enough to take the mike out of Frankenstein's monster. 'Never mind,' he said, and gave a sheepish half-grin. 'Bit of – well, funny construction in this house, though, eh?'

I'm afraid I was rather outspoken with him.

Let alone any twaddle about a month-old bungalow being haunted, I was determined to clamp down on this 'jerry-building' talk. Perhaps I was beginning to have doubts myself.

I wrote straight off to the building company when I'd managed to trace them, busy developing an arterial road about three counties away. I dare say my letter was in the insinuating side: I think I asked if they had any record of difficulties in the construction of this bungalow. At any rate I got a sniffy reply by return, stating that the matter was out of their hands; in addition, their records were not available for discussion. Blind alley.

In the meantime, things at 'Minuke' had worsened to a really frightening degree. I dreaded the phone ringing. One morning the two Pritchards senior awoke to find that nearly all the furniture in their bedroom had been moved about, including the bed they had been sleeping in: they had felt absolutely nothing. Food became suddenly and revoltingly decomposed. All the chimney pots had come down, not just into the garden, but to the far side of the high road, except one which appeared, pulverized, on the living-room floor. The obvious attempts of the Pritchards to keep a rational outlook had put paid to most of my suspicions by this time.

I managed to locate a local man who have been employed during the erection of the bungalows, as an extra hand. He had worked only on the foundations of 'Minuke', but what he had to say was interesting.

They had found the going slow because of striking a layer of enormous flat stones, apparently trimmed slate, but as the site was otherwise excellent, they pressed on, using the stone as foundation where it fitted in with the plan, and laying down rubble where it didn't. The concrete skin over the rubble – my ears burned when I heard about that, I can tell you – this wretched so-called concrete had cracked, or shattered, several times. Which wasn't entirely surprising, if it had been laid as he described. The flat stones, he said had not been seriously disturbed. A workmate had referred to them as a 'giant's grave', so it was possibly an old burial mound. Norse, perhaps – those are fairly common along this coast – or even very much older.

Apart from this – I'm no diehard sceptic, I may as well confess – I was beginning to admit modest theories about a poltergeist, in spite of a lack of corroborative knockings and ornament-throwing. There were two young children in the house, and the lore has it that kids are often unconsciously connected with phenomena of that sort, though usually adolescents. Still, in the real-estate profession you have to be careful, and if I could see the Pritchards safely off the premises without airing these possibilities, it might be kindest to the bungalow's future.

I went to 'Minuke' the same afternoon.

It was certainly turning out an odd nook. I found a departing police-man on the doorstep. That morning the back door had been burst in by a hundredweight or so of soil, and Mrs Pritchard was trying to convince herself that a practical joker had it in for them. The policeman had taken some notes, and was giving vague advice about 'civil action' which showed that he was out of his depth.

Pritchard looked very tired, almost ill. 'I've got leave from my job, to look after them,' he said, when we were alone. I thought he was wise. He had given his wife's illness as the reason, and I was glad of that.

'I don't believe in – unnatural happenings,' he said.

I agreed with him, non-committally.

'But I'm afraid of what ideas the kids might get. They're both at impressionable ages, y'know.'

I recognized the symptoms without disappointment. 'You mean, you'd rather move elsewhere,' I said.

He nodded. 'I like the district, mind you. But what I——'

There was a report like a gun in the very room.

I found myself with both arms up to cover my face. There were tiny splinters everywhere, and a dust of fibre in the air. The door had exploded. Literally.

To hark back to constructional details, it was one of those light, hollow frame-and-plywood jobs. As you'll know, it takes considerable force to splinter plywood: well this was in tiny fragments. And the oddest thing was that we had felt no blast effect.

In the next room I heard their dog howling. Pritchard was as stiff as a poker.

'I felt it!' he said. 'I felt this lot coming. I've got to knowing when something's likely to happen. It's all round!' Of course I began to imagine I'd sensed something too, but I doubt if I had really; my shock came with the crash. Mrs Pritchard was in the doorway by this time with the kids behind her. He motioned them out and grabbed my arm.

'The thing is,' he whispered, 'that I can still feel it! Stronger than ever, by God! Look, will you stay at home tonight, in case I need – well, in case things get worse? I can phone you.'

On my way back I called at the town library and managed to get hold of a volume on supernatural possession and whatnot. Yes, I was committed now. But the library didn't specialize in that line, and when I opened the book at home, I found it was very little help. 'Vampires of south-eastern Europe' type of stuff. I came across references to something the jargon called an 'elemental' which I took to be a good deal more vicious and destructive than any poltergeist. A thoroughly nasty form of manifestation, if it existed. Those Norse gravestones were fitting into the picture uncomfortably well; it was fashionable in those days to be buried with all the trimmings, human sacrifice and even more unmentionable attractions.

But I read on. After half a chapter on zombies and Rumanian werewolves, the whole thing began to seem so fantastic that I turned seriously to working out methods of exploding somebody's door as a practical joke. Even a totally certifiable joker would be likelier than vampires. In no time I'd settled down with a whisky, doodling wiring diagrams and only occasionally – like twinges of conscience – speculating on contacting the psychic investigation people.

When the phone rang I was hardly prepared for it.

It was a confused, distant voice, gabbling desperately, but I recognized it as Pritchard. 'For God's sake, don't lose a second! Get here – it's all hell on earth! Can't you hear it? My God, I'm going crazy!' And in the background I thought I was able to hear something. A sort of bubbling, shushing 'wah-wah' noise. Indescribable. But you hear some odd sounds on telephones at any time.

'Yes,' I said, 'I'll come immediately. Why don't you all leave——' But the line had gone dead.

Probably I've never moved faster. I scrambled out to the car with untied shoes, though I remembered to grab a heavy stick in the hall – whatever use it was to be. I drove like fury, heart belting, straight to 'Minuke', expecting to see heaven knows what.

But everything looked still and normal there. The moon was up and I could see the whole place clearly. Curtained lights in the windows. Not a sound.

I rang. After a moment Pritchard opened the door. He was quiet and seemed almost surprised to see me.

I pushed inside. 'Well?' I said. 'What happened?'

'Not a thing, so far,' he said. 'That's why I didn't expect——'

I felt suddenly angry. 'Look here,' I said, 'what are you playing at? Seems to me that any hoaxing round here begins a lot nearer home than you'd have me believe!' Then the penny dropped. I saw by the fright in his face that he knew something had gone wrong. That was the most horrible, sickening moment of the whole affair for me.

'Didn't you ring?' I said.

And he shook his head.

I've been in some tight spots. But there was always some concrete actual business in hand to screw the mind safely down to. I suppose panic is when the subconscious breaks loose and everything in your head dashes screaming out. It was only just in time that I found a touch of the concrete and actual. A kiddie's paintbox on the floor, very watery.

'The children,' I said. 'Where are they?'

'Wife's just putting the little 'un to bed. She's been restless tonight; just wouldn't go, crying and difficult. Arthur's in the bathroom. Look here, what's happened?'

I told him, making it as short and matter of fact as I could. He turned ghastly.

'Better get them dressed and out of here right away,' I said. 'Make some excuse, not to alarm them.'

He'd gone before I finished speaking.

I smoked hard, trying to build up the idea of 'Hoax! Hoax!' in my mind. After all, it could have been. But I knew it wasn't.

Everything looked cosy and normal. Clock ticking. Fire red and mellow. Half-empty cocoa mug on the table. The sound of the sea from beyond the road. I went through to the kitchen. The dog was there, looking up from its sleeping-basket under the sink. 'Good dog,' I said, and it wriggled its tail.

Pritchard came in from the hall. He jumped when he saw me.

'Getting nervy!' he said. 'They won't be long. I don't know where we can go if we – well, if we have to – to leave tonight——'

'My car's outside,' I told him. 'I'll fix you up. Look here, did you ever "hear things"? Odd noises?' I hadn't told him that part of the telephone call.

He looked at me so oddly, I thought he was going to collapse.

'I don't know,' he said. 'Can you?'

'At this moment?'

I listened.

'No,' I said. 'The clock on the shelf. The sea. Nothing else. No.'

'The sea,' he said, barely whispering. 'But you can't hear the sea in this kitchen!'

He was close to me in an instant. Absolutely terrified. 'Yes, I have heard this before! I think we all have. I said it was the sea: so as not to frighten them. But it isn't! And I recognized it when I came in here just now. That's what made me start. It's getting louder: it does that.'

He was right. Like slow breathing. It seemed to emanate from inside the walls, not at a particular spot, but everywhere. We went into the hall, then the front room; it was the same there. Mixed with it now was a sort of thin crying.

'That's Nellie,' Pritchard said. 'The dog: she always whimpers when it is on – too scared to howl. My God. I've never heard it as loud as this before.'

'Hurry them up, will you!' I almost shouted. He went.

The 'breathing' was ghastly. Slobbering. Stertorous. I think the term is. And faster. Oh, yes, I recognized it. The background music to the phone message. My skin was pure ice.

'Come along!' I yelled. I switched on the little radio to drown the noise. The old National Programme, as it was in those days, for late dance music. Believe it or not, what came through that loud-speaker was the same vile sighing noise, at double the volume. And when I tried to switch it off, it stayed the same.

The whole bungalow was trembling. The Pritchards came running in, she carrying the little girl. 'Get them into the car,' I shouted. We heard glass smashing somewhere.

Above our heads there was an almighty thump. Plaster showered down.

Half-way out of the door the little girl screamed, 'Nellie! Where's Nellie? Nellie, Nellie!'

'The dog,' Pritchard moaned. 'Oh, curse it!' He dragged them outside. I dived for the kitchen where I'd seen the animal, feeling a lunatic for doing it. Plaster was springing out of the walls in painful showers.

In the kitchen I found water everywhere. One tap was squirting like a fire-hose. The other was missing, water belching across the window from a torn end of pipe.

'Nellie!' I called.

Then I saw the dog. It was lying near the oven, quite stiff. Round its neck was twisted a piece of painted piping with the other tap on the end.

Sheer funk got me then. The ground was moving under me. I bolted down the hall, nearly bumped into Pritchard. I yelled and shoved. I could actually feel the house at my back.

We got outside. The noise was like a dreadful snoring, with rumbles and crashes thrown in. One of the lights went out. 'Nellie's run away,' I said, and we all got in the car, the kids bawling. I started up. People were coming out of the other bungalows – they're pretty far apart and the din was just beginning to make itself felt. Pritchard grumbled, 'We can stop now. Think it'd be safe to go back and grab some of the furniture?' As if he was at a fire; but I don't think he knew what he was doing.

'Daddy – look!' screeched the boy.

We saw it. The chimney of 'Minuke' was going up in a horrible way. In the moonlight it seemed to grow quite slowly, to about sixty feet, like a giant crooked finger. And then – burst. I heard bricks thumping down. Somewhere somebody screamed.

There was a glare like an ungodly great lightning flash. It lasted for a second or so.

Of course, we were dazzled, but I thought I saw the whole of 'Minuke' fall suddenly and instantaneously flat, like a swatted fly. I probably did, because that's what happened, anyway.

There isn't much more to tell.

Nobody was really hurt, and we were able to put down the whole thing to a serious electrical fault. Main fuses had blown throughout the whole district, which helped this theory out. Perhaps it was unfortunate in another respect, because a lot of people changed over to gas.

There wasn't much recognizably left of 'Minuke'. But some of the bits were rather unusual. Knots in pipes for instance – I buried what was left of the dog myself. Wood and brick cleanly sliced. Small quantities of completely powdered metal. The bath had been squashed flat, like tinfoil. In fact, Pritchard was lucky to land the insurance money for his furniture.

My professional problem, of course, remained. The plot where the wretched place had stood. I managed to persuade the owner it wasn't ideal for building on. Incidentally, lifting those stones might reveal something to somebody some day – but not to me, thank you!

I think my eventual solution showed a touch of wit: I let it very cheaply as a scrap-metal dump.

Well? I know I've never been able to make any sense out of it. I hate telling you all this stuff, because it must make me seem either a simpleton or a charlatan. In so far as there's any circumstantial evidence in looking at the place, you can see it in a moment or two. Here's the coast road——

*　　*　　*

The car pulled up at a bare spot beyond a sparse line of bungalows. The space was marked by a straggling, tufty square of privet bushes. Inside I could see a tangle of rusty iron; springs, a car chassis, oil drums.

'The hedge keeps it from being too unsightly,' said the estate agent, as we crossed to see it. 'See – the remains of the gate.'

A few half-rotten slats dangled from an upright. One still bore part of a chrome-plated name. 'MI——' and, a little farther on, 'K'.

'Nothing worth seeing now,' he said. I peered inside. 'Not that there ever was much—— Look out!' I felt a violent push. In the same instant something zipped past my head and crashed against the car behind. 'My God!'

'Went right at you!' gasped the agent.

It had shattered a window of the car and gone through the open door opposite. We found it in the road beyond, sizzling on the tarmac. A heavy steel nut, white-hot.

'I don't know about you,' the estate agent said, 'but I'm rather in favour of getting out of here.'

And we did. Quickly.

An Account of Some Strange Disturbances in Aungier Street

J. Sheridan Le Fanu

It is not worth telling, this story of mine – at least, not worth writing. Told, indeed, as I have sometimes been called upon to tell it, to a circle of intelligent and eager faces, lighted up by a good after-dinner fire on a winter's evening, with a cold wind rising and wailing outside, and all snug and cosy within, it has gone off – though I say it, who should not – indifferent well. But it is a venture to do as you would have me. Pen, ink and paper are cold vehicles for the marvellous, and a 'reader' decidedly a more critical animal than a 'listener'. If, however, you can induce your friends to read it after nightfall, and when the fireside talk has run for a while on thrilling tales of shapeless terror; in short, if you will secure me the *mollia tempora fandi*, I will go to my work, and say my say, with better heart. Well, then, these conditions presupposed, I shall waste no more words, but tell you simply how it all happened.

My cousin (Tom Ludlow) and I studied medicine together. I think he would have succeeded, had he stuck to the profession; but he preferred the Church, poor fellow, and died early, a sacrifice to contagion, contracted in the noble discharge of his duties. For my present purpose, I say enough of his character when I mention that he was of a sedate but frank and cheerful nature; very exact in his observance of truth, and not by any means like myself – of an excitable or nervous temperament.

My Uncle Ludlow – Tom's father – while we were attending lectures, purchased three or four old houses in Aungier Street, one of which was unoccupied. *He* resided in the country, and Tom proposed that we should take up our abode in the untenanted house, so long as it should continue unlet; a move which would accomplish the double end of settling us nearer alike to our lecture-rooms and to our amusements, and of relieving us from the weekly charge of rent for our lodgings.

Our furniture was very scant – our whole equipage remarkably modest and primitive; and, in short, our arrangements pretty nearly as simple as those of a bivouac. Our new plan was, therefore, executed almost as soon as conceived. The front drawing-room was our sitting-room. I had the bedroom over it, and Tom the back bedroom on the same floor, which nothing could have induced me to occupy.

The house, to begin with, was a very old one. It had been, I believe, newly fronted about fifty years before; but with this exception, it had nothing modern about it. The agent who bought it and looked into the titles for my uncle, told me that it was sold, along with much other forfeited property, at Chichester House, I think, in 1702; and had belonged to Sir Thomas Hacket, who was Lord Mayor of Dublin in James II's time. How old it was *then*, I can't say; but, at all events, it had seen years and changes enough to have contracted all that mysterious and saddened air, at once exciting and depressing, which belongs to most old mansions.

There had been very little done in the way of modernizing details; and, perhaps, it was better so; for there was something queer and bygone in the very walls and ceilings – in the shape of doors and windows – in the odd diagonal site of the chimney-pieces – in the beams and ponderous cornices – not to mention the singular solidity of all the woodwork, from the banisters to the window-frames, which hopelessly defied disguise, and would have emphatically proclaimed their antiquity through any conceivable amount of modern finery and varnish.

An effort had, indeed, been made, to the extent of papering the drawing-rooms; but, somehow, the paper looked raw and out of keeping; and the old woman, who kept a little dirt-pie of a shop in the lane, and whose daughter – a girl of two-and-fifty – was our solitary handmaid, coming in at sunrise, and chastely receding again as soon as she had made all ready for tea in our state apartment – this woman, I say, remembered it, when old Judge Horrocks (who, having earned the reputation of a particularly 'hanging judge', ended by hanging himself, as the coroner's jury found, under an impulse of 'temporary insanity', with a child's skipping-rope, over the massive old banisters) resided there, entertaining good company, with fine venison and rare old port. In those halcyon days, the drawing-rooms were hung with gilded leather, and, I dare say, cut a good figure, for they were really spacious rooms.

The bedrooms were wainscoted, but the front one was not gloomy; and in it the cosiness of antiquity quite overcame its sombre associations. But the back bedroom, with its two queerly placed melancholy windows, staring vacantly at the foot of the bed, and with the shadowy recess to be found in most old houses in Dublin, like a large ghostly closet, which, from congeniality of temperament, had amalgamated with the bedchamber, and dissolved the partition. At night-time, this 'alcove' – as our 'maid' was wont to call it – had, in my eyes, a specially sinister and suggestive character. Tom's distant and solitary candle glimmered vainly into its darkness. *There* it was always overlooking him

– always itself impenetrable. But this was only part of the effect. The whole room was, I can't tell how, repulsive to me. There was, I suppose, in its proportions and features, a latent discord – a certain mysterious and indescribable relation, which jarred indistinctly upon some secret sense of the fitting and the safe, and raised indefinable suspicions and apprehensions of the imagination. On the whole, as I began by saying, nothing could have induced me to pass a night alone in it.

I had never pretended to conceal from poor Tom my superstitious weakness; and he, on the other hand, most unaffectedly ridiculed my tremors. The sceptic was, however, destined to receive a lesson as you shall hear.

We had not been very long in occupation of our respective dormitories when I began to complain of uneasy nights and disturbed sleep. I was, I suppose, the more impatient under this annoyance, as I was usually a sound sleeper, and by no means prone to nightmares. It was now, however, my destiny, instead of enjoying my customary repose, every night to 'sup full of horrors'. After a preliminary course of disagreeable and frightful dreams, my troubles took a definite form, and the same vision, without an appreciable variation in a single detail, visited me at least (on an average) every second night in the week.

Now, this dream, nightmare or infernal illusion – which you please – of which I was the miserable sport, was on this wise:

I saw or thought I saw, with the most abominable distinctness, although at the time in profound darkness, every article of furniture and accidental arrangement of the chamber in which I lay. This, as you know, is incidental to ordinary nightmare. Well, while in this clair-voyant condition, which seemed but the lighting up of the theatre in which was to be exhibited the monotonous tableau of horror, which made my nights insupportable, my attention invariably became, I know not why, fixed upon the windows opposite the foot of my bed; and, uniformly with the same effect, a sense of dreadful anticipation always took slow but sure possession of me. I became somehow conscious of a sort of horrid but undefined preparation going forward in some unknown quarter, and by some unknown agency, for my torment; and, after an interval, which always seemed to me of the same length, a picture suddenly flew up to the window, where it remained fixed, as if by an electrical attraction, and my discipline of horror then commenced, to last perhaps for hours. The picture thus mysteriously glued to the window-panes, was the portrait of an old man, in a crimson flowered silk dressing-gown, the folds of which I could now describe, with a countenance embodying a strange mixture of intellect, sen-suality, and power, but withal sinister and full of malignant omen. His nose was hooked, like the beak of a vulture; his eyes large, grey, and prominent, and lighted up with a more than mortal cruelty and coldness. These features were surmounted by a crimson velvet cap, the hair that peeped from under which was white with age, while the eyebrows retained their original blackness. Well I remember every line, hue and shadow of the stony countenance, and well I may! The gaze of this hellish visage was fixed upon me, and mine returned it with the inexplicable fascination of nightmare, for what appeared to me to be hours of agony. At last

'The cock he crew, away then flew'

the fiend who had enslaved me through the awful watches of the night; and, harassed and nervous, I rose to the duties of the day.

I had – I can't say exactly why, but it may have been from the exquisite anguish and profound impressions of unearthly horror, with which this strange phatasmagoria was associated – an insurmountable antipathy to describing the exact nature of my nightly troubles to my friend and comrade. Generally, however, I told him that I was haunted by abominable dreams; and, true to the imputed materialism of medicine, we put our heads together to dispel my horrors, not by exorcism, but by a tonic.

I will do this tonic justice, and frankly admit that the accursed portrait began to intermit its visits under its influence. What of that? Was this singular apparition – as full of character as of terror – therefore the creature of my fancy, or the invention of my poor stomach? Was it, in short, *subjective* (to borrow the technical slang of the day) and not the palpable aggression and intrusion of an external agent? That, good friend, as we will both admit, by no means follows. The evil spirit, who enthralled my senses in the shape of that portrait, may have been just as near me, just as energetic, just as malignant, though I saw him not. What means the whole moral code of revealed religion regarding the due keeping of our own bodies, soberness, temperance, etc.? Here is an obvious connection between the material and the invisible; the healthy tone of the system, and its unimpaired energy, may, for aught we can tell, guard us against influences which would otherwise render life itself terrific. The mesmerist and the electro-biologist will fail upon an average with nine patients out of ten – so may the evil spirit. Special conditions of the corporeal system are indispensable to the production of certain spiritual phenomena. The operation succeeds sometimes – sometimes fails – that is all.

I found afterwards that my would-be sceptical companion had his troubles too. But of these I knew nothing yet. One night, for a wonder, I was sleeping soundly, when I was roused by a step on the lobby outside my room, followed by the loud clang of what turned out to be a large brass candlestick, flung with all his force by poor Tom Ludlow over the banisters, and rattling with a rebound down the second flight of stairs; and almost concurrently with this, Tom burst open my door and bounced into my room backwards, in a state of extraordinary agitation.

I had jumped out of bed and clutched him by the arm before I had any distinct idea of my own whereabouts. There we were – in our shirts – standing before the open door – staring through the great old banister opposite, at the lobby window, through which the sickly light of a clouded moon was gleaming.

'What's the matter, Tom? What's the matter with you? What the devil's the matter with you, Tom?' I demanded, shaking him with nervous impatience.

He took a long breath before he answered me, and then it was not very coherently.

'It's nothing, nothing at all – did I speak? – what did I say? – where's the candle, Richard? It's dark; I – I had a candle!'

'Yes, dark enough,' I said; 'but what's the matter? – what *is* it? – why don't you speak, Tom? – have you lost your wits? – what is the matter?'

'The matter? – oh, it is all over. It must have been a dream – nothing at all but a dream – don't you think so? It could not be anything more than a dream.'

'Of *course*,' said I, feeling uncommonly nervous, 'it *was* a dream.'

'I thought,' he said, 'there was a man in my room, and – and I jumped out of bed; and – and – where's the candle?'

'In your room, most likely,' I said. 'Shall I go and bring it?'

'No; stay here – don't go; it's no matter – don't, I tell you; it was all a dream. Bolt the door, Dick; I'll stay here with you – I feel nervous. So, Dick, like a good fellow, light your candle and open the window – I am in a *shocking state*.'

I did as he asked me, and robing himself like Granuaile in one of my blankets, he seated himself close beside my bed.

Everybody knows how contagious is fear of all sorts, but more especially that particular kind of fear under which poor Tom was at that moment labouring. I would not have heard, nor I believe would he have recapitulated, just at that moment, for half the world, the details of the hideous vision which had so unmanned him.

'Don't mind telling me anything about your nonsensical dream, Tom,' said I, affecting contempt, really in a panic; 'let us talk about something else; but it is quite plain that this dirty old house disagrees with us both, and hang me if I stay here any longer, to be pestered with indigestion and – and – bad nights, so we may as well look out for lodgings – don't you think so? – at once.'

Tom agreed, and, after an interval, said:

'I have been thinking, Richard, that it is a long time since I saw my father, and I have made up my mind to go down tomorrow and return in a day or two, and you can take rooms for us in the meantime.'

I fancied that this resolution, obviously the result of the vision which had so profoundly scared him, would probably vanish next morning with the damps and shadows of night. But I was mistaken. Off went Tom at peep of day to the country, having agreed that so soon as I had secured suitable lodgings, I was to recall him by letter from his visit to my Uncle Ludlow.

Now, anxious as I was to change my quarters, it so happened, owing to a series of petty procrastinations and accidents, that nearly a week elapsed before my bargain was made and my letter of recall on the wing to Tom; and, in the meantime, a trifling adventure or two had occurred to your humble servant, which, absurd as they now appear, diminished by distance, did certainly at the time serve to whet my appetite for change considerably.

A night or two after the departure of my comrade, I was sitting by my bedroom fire, the door locked, and the ingredients of a tumbler of hot whiskey-punch upon the spider-table; for, as the best mode of keeping the

> '*Black spirits and white,*
> *Blue spirits and grey,*'

with which I was environed, at bay, I had adopted the practice recommended by the wisdom of my ancestors, and 'kept my spirits up by pouring spirits down'. I had thrown aside my volume of Anatomy, and was treating myself by way of a tonic, preparatory to my punch and bed, to half a dozen pages of the *Spectator*, when I heard a step on the flight of stairs descending from the attics. It was two o'clock, and the streets were as silent as a churchyard – the sounds were, therefore, perfectly distinct. There was a slow, heavy tread, characterized by the emphasis and deliberation of age, descending by the narrow staircase from above; and, what made the sound more singular, it was plain that the feet which produced it were perfectly bare, measuring the descent with something between a pound and flop, very ugly to hear.

I knew quite well that my attendant had gone away many hours before, and that nobody but myself had any business in the house. It was quite plain also that the person who was coming downstairs had no intention whatever of concealing his movements; but, on the contrary, appeared disposed to make even more noise, and proceed more deliberately, than was at all necessary. When the step reached the foot of the stairs outside my room, it seemed to stop; and I expected every moment to see my door open spontaneously and give admission to the original of my detested portrait. I was, however, relieved in a few seconds by hearing the descent renewed, just in the same manner, upon the staircase leading down to the drawing-rooms, and thence, after another pause, down the next flight, and so on to the hall, whence I heard no more.

Now, by the time the sound had ceased, I was wound up, as they say, to a very unpleasant pitch of excitement. I listened, but there was not a stir. I screwed up my courage to a decisive experiment – opened my door, and in a stentorian voice bawled over the banisters, 'Who's there?' There was no answer, but the ringing of my own voice through the empty old house – no renewal of the movement; nothing, in short, to give my unpleasant sensations a definite direction. There is, I think, something most disagreeably disenchanting in the sound of one's own voice under such circumstances, exerted in solitude and in vain. I redoubled my sense of isolation, and my misgivings increased on perceiving that the door, which I certainly thought I had left open, was closed behind me; in a vague alarm, lest my retreat should be cut off, I got again into my room as quickly as I could, where I remained in a state of imaginary blockade, and very uncomfortable indeed, till morning.

Next night brought no return of my barefooted fellow-lodger; but the night following, being in my bed, and in the dark – somewhere, I suppose, about the same hour as before, I distinctly heard the old fellow again descending from the garrets.

This time I had my punch, and the *morale* of the garrison was consequently excellent. I jumped out of bed, clutched the poker as I passed the expiring fire, and in a moment was upon the lobby. The sound had ceased by this time – the dark and chill were discouraging; and, guess my horror when I saw, or thought I saw, a black monster, whether in the shape of a man or a bear I could not say, standing with its back to the wall, on the lobby, facing me, with a pair of great greenish eyes shining dimly out. Now, I must be frank, and confess that the cupboard which displayed our plates and cups stood just there, though at the moment I did not recollect it. At the same time I must honestly say, that making every allowance for an excited imagination, I never could satisfy myself that I was made the dupe of my own fancy in this matter; for this apparition, after one or two shiftings of shape, as if in the act of incipient transformation, began, as it seemed on second thoughts, to advance upon me in its original form. From an instinct of terror rather than of courage, I hurled the poker, with all my force, at its head; and to the music of a horrid crash made my way into my room, and double-locked the door. Then, in a minute more, I heard the horrid bare feet walk down the stairs, till the sound ceased in the hall, as on the former occasion.

If the apparition of the night before was an ocular delusion of my fancy sporting with the dark outlines of our cupboard, and if its horrid eyes were nothing but a pair of inverted teacups, I had, at all events, the satisfaction of having launched the poker with admirable effect, and in true 'fancy' phrase, 'knocked its two daylights into one', as the commingled fragments of my tea-service testified. I did my best to gather comfort and courage from these evidences; but it would not do. And then what could I say of those horrid bare feet, and the regular tramp, tramp, tramp, which measured the distance of the entire staircase through the solitude of my haunted dwelling, and at an hour when no good influence was stirring? Confound it! – the whole affair was abominable. I was out of spirits, and dreaded the approach of night.

It came, ushered ominously in with a thunderstorm and dull torrents of depressing rain. Earlier than usual the streets grew silent; and by twelve o'clock nothing but the comfortless pattering of the rain was to be heard.

I made myself as snug as I could. I lighted *two* candles instead of one. I forswore bed, and held myself in readiness for a sally, candle in hand; for, *coûte que coûte*, I was resolved to *see* the being, if visible at all, who troubled the nightly stillness of my mansion. I was fidgety and nervous, and tried in vain to interest myself with my books. I walked up and down my room, whistling in turn martial and hilarious music, and listening ever and anon for the dreaded noise. I sat down and stared at the square label on the solemn and reserved-looking black bottle, until 'FLANAGAN & CO.'s BEST OLD MALT WHISKEY' grew into a sort of subdued accompaniment to all the fantastic and horrible speculations which chased one another through my brain.

Silence, meanwhile, grew more silent, and darkness darker. I listened in vain for the rumble of a vehicle, or the dull clamour of a distant row. There was nothing but the sound of a rising wind, which had succeeded the thunderstorm that had travelled over the Dublin mountains quite out of hearing. In the middle of this great city I began to feel myself alone with nature, and Heaven knows what beside. My courage was ebbing. Punch, however, which makes beasts of so many, made a man of me again – just in time to hear with tolerable nerve and firmness the lumpy, flabby, naked feet deliberately descending the stairs again.

I took a candle, not without a tremor. As I crossed the floor I tried to extemporize a prayer, but stopped short to listen, and never finished it. The steps continued. I confess I hesitated for some seconds at the door before I took heart of grace and opened it. When I peeped out the lobby was perfectly empty – there was no monster standing on the staircase; and as the detested sound ceased, I was reassured enough to venture forward nearly to the banisters. Horror of horrors! within a stair or two beneath the spot where I stood the unearthly tread smote the floor. My eye caught something in motion; it was about the size of Goliath's foot – it was grey, heavy and flapped with a dead weight from one step to another. As I am alive, it was the most monstrous grey rat I ever beheld or imagined.

Shakespeare says: 'Some men there are cannot abide a gaping pig, and some that are mad if they behold a cat.' I went well-nigh out of my wits when I beheld this *rat*; for, laugh at me as you may, it fixed upon me, I thought, a perfectly human expression of malice; and, as it shuffled about and looked up into my face almost from between my feet, I saw, I could swear it – I felt it then, and know it now, the infernal gaze and the accursed countenance of my old friend in the portrait, transfused into the visage of the bloated vermin before me.

I bounced into my room again with a feeling of loathing and horror I cannot describe, and locked and bolted my door as if a lion had been at the other side. D——n him or *it*; curse the portrait and its original! I felt in my soul that the rat – yes, the *rat*, the RAT I had just seen, was that evil being in masquerade, and rambling through the house upon some infernal night lark.

Next morning I was early trudging through the miry streets; and, among other transactions, posted a peremptory note recalling Tom. On my return, however, I found a note from my absent 'chum', announcing his intended return next day. I was doubly rejoiced at this, because I had succeeded in getting rooms; and because the change of scene and return of my comrade were rendered specially pleasant by the last night's half ridiculous half horrible adventure.

I slept extemporaneously in my new quarters in Digges' Street that night, and next morning returned for breakfast to the haunted mansion, where I was certain Tom would call immediately on his arrival.

I was quite right – he came; and almost his first question referred to the primary object of our change of residence.

'Thank God,' he said with genuine fervour, on hearing that all was arranged. 'On *your* account I am delighted. As to myself, I assure you that no earthly consideration could have induced me ever again to pass a night in this disastrous old house.'

'Confound the house!' I ejaculated, with a genuine mixture of fear and detestation, 'we have not had a pleasant hour since we came to live here'; and so I went on, and related incidentally my adventure with the plethoric old rat.

'Well, if that were *all*,' said my cousin, affecting to make light of the matter, 'I don't think I should have minded it very much.'

'Ay, but its eye – its countenance, my dear Tom,' urged I; 'if you had seen *that*, you would have felt it might be *anything* but what it seemed.'

'I am inclined to think the best conjurer in such a case would be an able-bodied cat,' he said, with a provoking chuckle.

'But let us hear your own adventure,' I said tartly.

At this challenge he looked uneasily round him. I had poked up a very unpleasant recollection.

'You shall hear it, Dick; I'll tell it to you,' he said. 'Begad, sir, I should feel quite queer, though, telling it *here*, though we are too strong a body for ghosts to meddle with just now.'

Though he spoke this like a joke, I think it was serious calculation. Our Hebe was in a corner of the room, packing our cracked Delf tea-and dinner-services in a basket. She soon suspended operations, and with mouth and eyes wide open became an absorbed listener. Tom's experiences were told nearly in these words:

'I saw it three times. Dick – three distinct times; and I am perfectly certain it meant me some infernal harm. I was, I say, in danger – in *extreme* danger; for, if nothing else had happened, my reason would most certainly have failed me, uless I had escaped so soon. Thank God. I *did* escape.

'The first night of this hateful disturbance, I was lying in the attitude of sleep, in that lumbering old bed. I hate to think of it. I was really wide awake, though I had put out my candle, and was lying as quietly as if I had been asleep; and although accidentally restless, my thoughts were running in a cheerful and agreeable channel.

'I think it must have been two o'clock at least when I thought I heard a sound in that – that odious dark recess at the far end of the bedroom. It was as if someone was drawing a piece of cord slowly along the floor, lifting it up, and dropping it softly down again in coils. I sat up once or twice in my bed, but could see nothing so I concluded it must be mice in the wainscot. I felt no emotion graver than curiosity, and after a few minutes ceased to observe it.

'While lying in this state, strange to say, without at first a suspicion of anything supernatural, on a sudden I saw an old man, rather stout and square, in a sort of roan-red dressing-gown, and with a black cap on his head, moving stiffly and slowly in a diagonal direction, from the recess, across the floor of the bedroom, passing my bed at the foot, and entering the lumber-closet at the left. He had something under his arm; his head hung a little at one side; and merciful God! when I saw his face.'

Tom stopped for a while, and then said:

'That awful countenance, which living or dying I never can forget, disclosed what he was. Without turning to the right or left, he passed beside me, and entered the closet by the bed's head.

'While this fearful and indescribable type of death and guilt was passing, I felt that I had no more power to speak or stir than if I had been myself a corpse. For hours after it had disappeared I was too terrified and weak to move. As soon as daylight came, I took courage and examined the room, and especially the course which the frightful intruder had seemed to take, but there was not a vestige to indicate anybody's having passed there; no sign of any disturbing agency visible among the lumber that strewed the floor of the closet.

'I now began to recover a little. I was fagged and exhausted, and at last, overpowered by a feverish sleep, I came down late; and finding you out of spirits on account of your dreams about the portrait, whose *original* I am now certain disclosed himself to me, I did not care to talk about the infernal vision. In fact, I was trying to persuade myself that the whole thing was an illusion, and I did not like to revive in their intensity the hated impressions of the past night – or to risk the constancy of my scepticism by recounting the tale of my sufferings.

'It required some nerve, I can tell you, to go to my haunted chamber next night, and lie down quietly in the same bed,' continued Tom. 'I did so with a degree of trepidation, which, I am not ashamed to say, a very little matter would have sufficed to stimulate to downright panic. This night, however, passed off quietly enough, as also the next; and so too did two or three more. I grew more confident and began to fancy that I believed in the theories of spectral illusions, with which I had at first vainly tried to impose upon my convictions.

'The apparition had been, indeed, altogether anomalous. It had crossed the room without any recognition of my presence: I had not disturbed *it*, and *it* had no mission to *me*. What, then, was the imaginable use of its crossing the room in a visible shape at all? Of course it might have *been* in the closet instead of *going* there, as easily as it introduced itself into the recess without entering the chamber in a shape discernible by the senses. Besides, how the deuce *had* I seen it? It was a dark night; I had no candle; there was no fire; and yet I saw it as distinctly, in colouring and outline, as ever I beheld human form! A cataleptic dream would explain it all; and I was determined that a dream it should be.

'One of the most remarkable phenomena connected with the practice of mendacity is the vast number of deliberate lies we tell ourselves, whom, of all persons, we can least expect to deceive. In all this, I need hardly tell you, Dick, I was simply lying to myself, and did not believe one word of the wretched humbug. Yet I went on, as men will do, like persevering charlatans and impostors, who tire people into credulity by the mere force of reiteration; so I hoped to win myself over at last to a comfortable scepticism about the ghost.

'He had not appeared a second time – that certainly was a comfort; and what, after all, did I care for him and his queer old toggery and strange looks? Not a fig! I was nothing the worse for having seen him, and a good story the better. So I tumbled into bed, put out my candle, and, cheered by a loud drunken quarrel in the back lane, went fast asleep.

'From this deep slumber I awoke with a start. I knew I had had a horrible dream; but what it was I could not remember. My heart was thumping furiously; I felt bewildered and feverish; I sat up in the bed and looked about the room. A broad flood of moonlight came in through the curtainless window; everything was as I had last seen it; and though the domestic squabble in the back lane was, unhappily for me, allayed, I yet could hear a pleasant fellow singing, on his way home, the then popular comic ditty called "Murphy Delany". Taking advantage of this diversion, I lay down again, with my face towards the fireplace and, closing my eyes, did my best to think of nothing else but the song, which was every moment growing fainter in the distance:

> "'Twas Murphy Delany, so funny and frisky,
>   Stept into a shebeen shop to get his skin full;
> He reeled out again pretty well lined with whiskey,
>   As fresh as a shamrock, as blind as a bull."

'The singer, whose condition I dare say resembled that of his hero, was soon too far off to regale my ears any more; and as his music died away, I myself sank into a doze, neither sound nor refreshing. Somehow the song had got into my head, and I went meandering on through the adventures of my respectable fellow-countryman, who, on emerging from the "shebeen shop", fell into a river, from which he was fished up to be "sat upon" by a coroner's jury, who having learned from a "horse-doctor" that he was "dead as a door-nail, so there was an end", returned their verdict accordingly, just as he returned to his senses, when an angry altercation and a pitched battle between the body and the coroner winds up the lay with due spirit and pleasantry.

'Through this ballad I continued with a weary monotony to plod, down to the very last line, and then *da capo*, and so on, in my uncomfortable half-sleep, for how long, I can't conjecture. I found myself at last, however, muttering, "*dead* as a door-nail, so there was an end"; and something like another voice within me, seemed to say, very faintly, but sharply, "dead! dead! *dead!* and may the Lord have mercy on your soul!" and instantaneously I was wide awake, and staring right before me from the pillow.

'Now – will you believe it, Dick? – I saw the same accursed figure standing full front, and gazing at me with its stony and fiendish countenance, not two yards from the bedside.'

Tom stopped here and wiped the perspiration from his face. I felt very queer. The girl was as pale as Tom; and, assembled as we were in the very scene of these adventures, we were all, I dare say, equally grateful for the clear daylight and the resuming bustle out of doors.

'For about three seconds only I saw it plainly; then it grew indistinct; but for a long time there was something like a column of dark vapour where it had been standing between me and the wall; and I felt sure that he was still there. After a good while, this appearance went too. I took my clothes downstairs to the hall, and dressed there, with the door half open; then went out into the street, and walked about town till morning, when I came back, in a miserable state of nervousness and exhaustion. I was such a fool, Dick, as to be ashamed to tell you how I came to be so upset. I thought you would laugh at me; especially as I had always talked philosophy, and treated *your* ghosts with contempt. I concluded you would give me no quarter; and so kept my tale of horror to myself.

'Now, Dick, you will hardly believe me when I assure you that for many nights after this last experience I did not go to my room at all. I used to sit up for a while in the drawing-room after you had gone up to your bed; and then steal down softly to the hall-door, let myself out, and sit in the "Robin Hood" tavern until the last guest went off; and then I got through the night like a sentry, pacing the streets till morning.

'For more than a week I never slept in bed. I sometimes had a snooze on a form in the "Robin Hood", and sometimes a nap in a chair during the day; but regular sleep I had absolutely none.

'I was quite resolved that we should get into another house; but I could not bring myself to tell you the reason, and I somehow put it off from day to day, although my life was, during every hour of this procrastination, rendered as miserable as that of a felon with the constables on his track. I was growing absolutely ill from this wretched mode of life.

'One afternoon I determined to enjoy an hour's sleep upon your bed. I hated mine; so that I had never, except in a stealthy visit every day to unmake it, lest Martha should discover the secret of my nightly absence, entered the ill-omened chamber.

'As ill luck would have it, you had locked your bedroom and taken away the key. I went into my own to unsettle the bed-clothes, as usual, and give the bed the appearance of having been slept in. Now, a variety of circumstances concurred to bring about the dreadful scene through which I was that night to pass. In the first place, I was literally overpowered with fatigue and longing for sleep; in the next place, the effect of this extreme exhaustion upon my nerves resembled that of a narcotic and rendered me less susceptible than, perhaps, I should in any other condition have been of the exciting fears which had become habitual to me. Then again, a little bit of the window was open, a pleasant freshness pervaded the room and, to crown all, the cheerful sun of day was making the room quite pleasant. What was to prevent my enjoying an hour's nap *here*? The whole air was resonant with the cheerful hum of life, and the broad matter-of-fact light of day filled every corner of the room.

'I yielded – stifling my qualms – to the almost overpowering temptation; and merely throwing off my coat and loosening my cravat, I lay down, limiting myself to *half* an hour's doze in the unwonted enjoyment of a feather bed, a coverlet, and a bolster.

'It was horribly insidious; and the demon, no doubt, marked my infatuated preparations. Dolt that I was, I fancied, with mind and body worn out for want of sleep, and an arrear of a full week's rest to my credit, that such measure as *half* an hour's sleep, in such a situation, was possible. My sleep was death-like, long and dreamless.

'Without a start or fearful sensation of any kind, I waked gently, but completely. It was, as you have good reason to remember, long past midnight – I believe, about two o'clock. When sleep has been deep and long enough to satisfy nature thoroughly, one often wakens in this way, suddenly, tranquilly and completely.

'There was a figure seated in that lumbering, old sofa-chair, near the fireplace. Its back was rather towards me, but I could not be mistaken; it turned slowly round, and, merciful heavens! there was the stony face, with its infernal lineaments of malignity and despair, gloating on me. There was now no doubt as to its consciousness of my presence, and the hellish malice with which it was animated, for it arose and drew close to the bedside. There was a rope about its neck, and the other end, coiled up, it held stiffly in its hand.

'My good angel nerved me for this horrible crisis. I remained for some seconds transfixed by the gaze of this tremendous phantom. He came close to the bed and appeared on the point of mounting upon it. The next instant I was upon the floor at the far side, and in a moment more was, I don't know how, upon the lobby.

'But the spell was not yet broken; the valley of the shadow of death was not yet traversed. The abhorred phantom was before me there; it was standing near the banisters, stooping a little, and with one end of the rope round its own neck, was poising a noose at the other, as if to throw over mine; and while engaged in this baleful pantomime, it wore a smile so sensual, so unspeakably dreadful, that my senses were nearly overpowered. I saw and remember nothing more until I found myself in your room.

'I had a wonderful escape, Dick – there is no disputing *that* – an escape for which, while I live, I shall bless the mercy of heaven. No one can conceive or imagine what it is for flesh and blood to stand in the presence of such a thing, but one who has had the terrific experience. Dick, Dick, a shadow has passed over me – a chill has crossed my blood and marrow, and I will never be the same again – never, Dick – never!'

Our handmaid, a mature girl of two-and-fifty, as I have said, stayed her hand, as Tom's story proceeded, and by little and little drew near to us, with open mouth, and her brows contracted over her little, beady black eyes, till, stealing a glance over her shoulder now and then, she established herself close behind us. During the relation, she had made various earnest comments, in an undertone; but these and her ejaculations, for the sake of brevity and simplicity, I have omitted in my narration.

'It's often I heard tell of it,' she now said, 'but I never believed it right till now – though, indeed, why should not I? Does not my mother, down there in the lane, know quare stories, God bless us, beyant telling about it? But you ought not to have slept in the back bedroom. She was loath to let me be going in and out of that room even in the daytime, let alone for any Christian to spend the night in it; for sure she says it was his own bedroom.'

'Whose own bedroom?' we asked, in a breath.

'Why, *his* – the ould Judge's – Judge Horrocks', to be sure, God rest his sowl'; and she looked fearfully round.

'Amen!' I muttered. 'But did he die there?'

'Die there! No, not quite *there*,' she said. 'Shure, was not it over the banisters he hung himself, the ould sinner, God be merciful to us all? and was not it in the alcove they found the handles of the skipping-rope cut off, and the knife where he was settling the cord, God bless us, to hang himself with? It was his housekeeper's daughter owned the rope, my mother often told me, and the child never throve after, and used to be starting up out of her sleep, and screeching in the night-time, wid dhrames and frights than cum an her; and they said how it was the speerit of the ould Judge that was tormentin' her; and she used to be roaring and yelling out to hould back the big ould fellow with the crooked neck; and then she'd screech "Oh, the master! the master! he's stampin' at me and beckoning to me! Mother, darling, don't let me go!" And so the poor crathure died at last, and the docthers said it was wather on the brain, for it was all they could say.'

'How long ago was all this?' I asked.

'Oh, then, how would I know?' she answered. 'But it must be a wondherful long time ago, for the housekeeper was an ould woman, with a pipe in her mouth, and not a tooth left, and better nor eighty years ould when my mother was first married; and they said she was a rale buxom, fine-dressed woman when the ould Judge come to his end; an', indeed, my mother's not far from eighty years ould herself this day; and what made it worse for the unnatural ould villain, God rest his soul, to frighten the little girl out of the world the way he did, was what was mostly thought and believed by everyone. My mother says how the poor little crathure was his own child; for he was by all accounts an ould villain every way, an' the hangin'est judge that ever was known in Ireland's ground.'

'From what you said about the danger of sleeping in that bedroom,' said I, 'I suppose there were stories about the ghost having appeared there to others.'

'Well, there *was* things said – quare things, surely,' she answered, as it seemed, with some reluctance. 'And why would not there? Sure was it not up in that same room he slept for more than twenty years? and was it not in the *alcove* he got the rope ready that done his own business at last, the way he done many a betther man's in his lifetime? – and was not the body lying in the same bed after death, and put in the coffin there, too, and carried out to his grave from it in Pether's churchyard, after the coroner was done? But there was quare stories – my mother has them all – about how one Nicholas Spaight got into trouble on the head of it.'

'And what did they say of this Nicholas Spaight?' I asked.

'Oh, for that matther, it's soon told,' she answered.

And she certainly did relate a very strange story, which so piqued my curiosity that I took occasion to visit the ancient lady, her mother, from whom I learned many very curious particulars. Indeed, I am tempted to tell the tale, but my fingers are weary, and I must defer it. But if you wish to hear it another time, I shall do my best.

When we heard the strange tale I have *not* told you, we put one or two further questions to her about the alleged spectral visitations, to which the house had, ever since the death of the wicked old Judge, been subjected.

'No one ever had luck in it,' she told us. 'There was always cross accidents, sudden deaths, and short times in it. The first that tuck it was family – I forget their name – but at any rate there was two young ladies and their papa. He was about sixty, and a stout, healthy gentleman as you'd wish to see at that age. Well, he slept in that unlucky back bedroom; and, God between us an' harm! sure enough he was found dead one morning, half out of the bed, with his head as black as a sloe, and swelled like a puddin', hanging down near the floor. It was a fit, they said. He was as dead as a mackerel, and so *he* could not say what it was; but the ould people was all sure that it was nothing at all but the ould Judge, God bless us! that frightened him out of his senses and his life together.

'Some time after there was a rich old maiden lady took the house. I don't know which room *she* slept in, but she lived alone; and at any rate, one morning, the servants going down early to their work, found her sitting on the passage-stairs, shivering and talkin' to herself, quite mad;

and never a word more could any of *them* or her friends get from her ever afterwards but "Don't ask me to go, for I promised to wait for him". They never made out from her who it was she meant by *him*, but of course those that knew all about the ould house were at no loss for the meaning of all that happened to her.

'Then afterwards, when the house was let out in lodgings, there was Micky Byrne that took the same room, with his wife and three little children; and sure I heard Mrs Byrne telling how the children used to be lifted up in the bed at night, she could not see by what mains; and how they were starting and screeching every hour, just all as one as the housekeeper's little girl that died, till at last one night poor Micky had a dhrop in him, the way he used now and again; and what do you think in the middle of the night he thought he heard a noise on the stairs, and being in liquor, nothing less id do him but out he must go himself to see what was wrong. Well, after that, all she ever heard of him was himself sayin', "Oh, God!" and a tumble that shook the very house; and there, sure enough, he was lying on the lower stairs, under the lobby, with his neck smashed double undher him, where he was flung over the banisters.'

Then the handmaiden added:

'I'll go down to the lane and send up Joe Gavvey to pack up the rest of the taythings, and bring all the things across to your new lodgings.'

And so we all sallied out together, each of us breathing more freely, I have no doubt, as we crossed that ill-omened threshold for the last time.

Now, I may add thus much, in compliance with the immemorial usage of the realm of fiction, which sees the hero not only through his adventures, but fairly out of the world. You must have perceived that what the flesh, blood and bone hero of romance proper is to the regular compounder of fiction, this old house of brick, wood and mortar is to the humble recorder of this true tale. I therefore relate, as in duty bound, the catastrophe which ultimately befell it, which was simply this – that about two years ago subsequently to my story it was taken by a quack doctor, who called himself Baron Duhlestoerf, and filled the parlour windows with bottles of indescribable horrors preserved in brandy, and the newspapers with the usual grandiloquent and mendacious advertisements. This gentleman among his virtues did not reckon sobriety, and one night, being overcome with much wine, he set fire to his bed curtains, partially burned himself, and totally consumed the house. It was afterwards rebuilt, and for a time an undertaker established himself in the premises.

I have now told you my own and Tom's adventures, together with some valuable collateral particulars; and having acquitted myself of my engagement, I wish you a very goodnight, and pleasant dreams.

For the Love of Pamela
Kay Leith

Once, in my weary search for the right place, an estate agent said: 'There's a buyer for every house, no matter how odd.' It was in connection with a remark I had made about one peculiar place that seemed all front – no back nor middle, just front. The agent said: 'One day somebody will walk in and say, "This is for me."'

When Pamela and I first saw 12, Drayfield Grove we felt that, for us, it was that house and no other. Built around the turn of the century, it had a clean stone front and gracious bow windows – a house of character.

I didn't know then, naturally, that I would rue the day I ever clapped eyes on the place.

But *then* it meant that, once the contracts had been exchanged, we could name the day. Everything went without a hitch. Decoratively, it was a bit of a mess, which was why the price was within our range, but we intended to take care of that ourselves.

Pamela and I believed that pleasures deferred are sweeter; therefore we had not anticipated marriage, and didn't mind being labelled old-fashioned.

The first intimation of something sinister came when I was at the house myself one morning, checking electric points and making a rough list of what we needed for each room.

The place seemed to purr like a cat as I wandered from room to room, forming my plans. It was on the half-landing, at the heart, so to speak, of the two-storey house, that something seemed to beckon me.

Without thinking why, I went into the sun-filled room that faced the back garden, looking on to the spears of lilac blooms. It was beautifully proportioned, with a carved, marble-topped fireplace, too fine to rip out. This, I thought, will make a superb sitting-room-cum-work-room for Pamela.

I stood gazing out at the lilacs and, quite distinctly, the floorboards under my feet quivered slightly – so quickly and so briefly that I doubted that it had happened at all. The house was too solidly built to tremble at the passing of heavy traffic.

The front door bell rang. Pamela had brought the makings of the light lunch we'd decided to have there in the house that day. Her eyes, warm hazel, danced in her beautiful face with happiness and conspiracy.

'I bought a bottle of wine!'

'Bang goes a yard of curtain,' I said, pretending dismay. 'It'll be sackcloth instead of brocade, at this rate.'

'Oh, isn't it lovely!' Her long, luxuriant black hair swung gaily as she looked about. Her slim, white fingers caressed the walls.

Just watching her face, as she skipped in and out of the rooms, gave me more pleasure than I'd known for years. She had a tremendous capacity for the enjoyment of simple things.

She doted on the house, thrilled by the promise of the future. I made mental notes of her suggestions. It would be as she wished it to be.

'Gosh, I'm suddenly chilly!' she said, her bare arms goose-pimpled, as we reached the half-landing.

Quickly, she turned to go down for her coat. I was ahead of her on the landing and in no position to catch her when she seemed to trip and went tumbling down the wooden stairs.

'Pam!' I yelled, leaping down two at a time, beside myself with fright.

Dazedly, she looked up at me, hurt disbelief on her face. 'Joe, oh, Joe,' she gasped. 'What happened?'

'Are you hurt?' I ascertained that nothing was broken.

'No, no.' She tried laughing it off, blaming her fashionable shoes, but the incident, oddly enough, made her jittery and uneasy.

She followed me around as though unwilling to let me out of her sight. At three-thirty I suggested that we should stop for the day, but she insisted that, although shaken, she was all right and that I should stay on to finish the measuring up.

When she had gone, the atmosphere became warmer. It was quite definite and distinct, but I attributed that to my exertions.

The following Sunday, it being Easter, we planned to camp there and work through the weekend and Bank Holiday. Pamela brought along a couple of her brother's sleeping-bags and enough food for our needs.

By Saturday at lunchtime I'd finished stripping the old paper off the walls of the room on the half-landing.

It is difficult – no, impossible – to describe this adequately, but the walls seemed to co-operate in some peculiar way, as though they were shedding the strips of paper like constricting garments.

When I finished and looked around at the results of my labours, it seemed that – lewdly almost, coyly certainly – the room seemed to enjoy being looked at in its nudity of bare plaster.

'You're having hallucinations,' I accused myself wryly, sitting on the floor and lighting a cigarette.

I tried to find something funny in the idea of a sexually aware room. For some reason, which defied analysis, it didn't seem funny at all. My mind switched off; I was attuned to purely sensual things.

There was a barely perceptible throbbing coming from somewhere. It seemed to travel up through the floor and invade my body. Involuntarily, I lay back and closed my eyes.

The reverberations lulled, soothing and exciting at the same time. I was sinking, drifting, succumbing.

'Joe?'

Reluctantly, I opened my eyes, dragging my consciousness back. What now? Why didn't Pam let me lie there, undisturbed?

'Joe? What are you doing?'

The door opened, the throbbing receded, and I felt exposed, as though I'd been caught in some forbidden act. Utterly enervated, I staggered to my feet.

'Lunch is ready,' said Pamela, looking at me curiously.

Vaguely resentful, I balked at any explanation. I wanted only to be left alone.

'All right. I'll be down in a minute, when I've finished my cigarette.'

'Don't be long. It's hot.'

Over lunch I managed to shove the experience into the back of my mind. I shied away from examining it.

Before the shops closed finally for two whole days, I dashed out to buy the white spirit I'd forgotten earlier. I left Pamela in the kitchen, washing the paintwork and singing to the music from her transistor.

When I returned half an hour later she was sitting on the stairs, shaking like a leaf and as pale as death.

'Joe!' She wrapped me in a wiry, demanding grip. 'Something spoke to me!'

It was like trying to extricate myself from a coiled spring. 'Take it easy,' I said, putting my arms round her shivering shoulders. 'What spoke to you?'

'I don't know.' She shuddered. 'I was in the kitchen and it seemed to come up behind me.'

I stared my disbelief. 'The house is empty but for us.'

'I know that. Nevertheless, somebody whispered at me.'

'A man?'

'I don't know.' Her eyes were wide, fearful, staring in the direction of the kitchen.

'What did it say?'

'Oh, Joe! It was – it was horrible!' She hid her face in her trembling hands.'

I prised her hands away. 'What did the whisper say?'

She looked away, avoiding my eyes. 'Peculiar, weird, disgusting things, Joe.'

Nonplussed, I led her into the lower front room where our camp table and chairs were. 'Look, you've had some sort of delusion. Sit down and I'll go and search the place.'

'Delusion?' She looked at me indignantly. 'Do you think that I'm imagining things?'

I knelt before her. 'Of course not, but if you were working with your arms over your head, you may have had a blackout. Stay here. I'll go and make sure there's nobody in the house. I'll make a cup of coffee as well.'

She clutched my hand. 'Joe, there's something weird here. Don't leave me.'

'I'm only going around the house. You'll be all right.'

I went along the passage to the kitchen, catlike, examining every shadow. The basin and sponge were as she had left them on the draining board, the place empty. I filled the kettle and plugged it in, leaning against the table.

Just at my right ear, a caressing, breathless voice whispered: 'Darling lover ...'

My heart and guts turned to cold stone, the blood in my veins congealed to ice. But above all, I felt inexpressibly unclean.

'Come!' the voice urged.

Without having to be told, I knew where it was. In a daze, I left the kitchen.

'Joe?' came Pam's voice.

'All right. Just going to check upstairs.' My tones were normal so as not to cause her alarm ... but at the same time I didn't want any interference, any diversion from my exciting purpose.

When I opened the door on the half-landing a fetid warmth met me, and the throbbing came up through the soles of my shoes. Invisible hands reached out to me. I tottered forward, one step, two.

The throbbing increased; my ears sang with salacious suggestions. I was drowning in a hot bath of sensation.

Afraid suddenly, I hissed, 'No! Leave me alone!'

The phantom hands loosened, the throbbing eased, the flood receded.

With a great effort of will I closed the door, and stood sweating, shaking, wondering where I'd found the strength to break the spell.

Pamela was standing at the foot of the stairs, gazing up at me, and I knew where my strength to break free had come from. The antithesis of the evil thing that inhabited the house, she, in her goodness, was the best equipped to fight it.

She saw the look on my face, which must have confirmed any conclusions she'd reached herself.

'There's something very odd here,' I admitted when I could speak. 'There's no point in denying it – it's too dangerous to ignore.'

It was fairly obvious to me that, whatever it was, it was antipathetic to – probably jealous of – Pamela.

'Yes – and I don't think it likes me,' she said. 'The other day – on the stairs – I didn't trip. It was as if the stairs disappeared into blackness.'

'Well, what do we do, Pam? I vote that we go home. We don't know how powerful this thing is.'

She shook her head. 'I don't like the idea that we are being driven out by something as evil as that, Joe.'

'Better safe than sorry.'

We argued. I was all for prudence, frankly scared for her safety. Pamela grew more indignant by the minute that anything, mortal or otherwise, should force us to alter our plans and deprive us of the enjoyment of our home.

Over a drink at the local that night, we were still undecided, but away from the house we felt braver. Surrounded by bibulous holiday-makers, it was inconceivable that we could be threatened by anything so ethereal.

'We planned to do so much,' reasoned Pam. 'The entire weekend will be wasted.'

'It's risky.'

'If we stay together all the time, it will be quite safe,' she assured me. 'Then, next week, we can get someone from the psychic phenomena people to come to examine the place.'

I gave in, unwilling to be less brave than she was. We crawled into our sleeping-bags downstairs at about midnight, a trifle tipsy, certainly quite cheerful. We even called out rude suggestions up the gloomy stairs, collapsing in merriment at our audacity.

I slept only fitfully, forever waking to check, in the light of my torch, that Pamela's dark head still lay on her pillow and that the shiny cover of her sleeping-bag moved to her gentle breathing.

As dawn broke I fell into a deeper sleep.

Warning bells clanged in my brain. The sun touched my face, and my eyes snapped wide open. What had I been thinking of! It was criminal to have slept! I shot up into a sitting position.

I needn't have whipped myself into such a panic. There she was. Safe enough, lying with her eyes open, smiling at me.

I grinned back.

There was the clink of bottles from a passing milk-float which made me conscious of my thirst. 'How about some coffee?'

Pamela yawned and stretched her bare arms luxuriously above her head. The sun bathed her satin skin and flowing hair. She looked amazingly refreshed and rested.

I rose, went over, and knelt beside her. She stretched her arms again, and I realized she was nude. Then she lowered her arms, letting them circle down around my neck.

She was pulling me down to her, and I was drowning in a hot, throbbing sensation.

'Darling lover . . .' the filthy thing said out of the purity of Pamela's mouth.

The Moon-Bog
H. P. Lovecraft

Somewhere, to what remote and fearsome region I know not, Denys Barry has gone. I was with him the last night he lived among men, and heard his screams when the thing came to him; but all the peasants and police in County Meath could never find him, or the others, though they searched long and far. And now I shudder when I hear the frogs piping in swamps, or see the moon in lonely places.

I had known Denys Barry well in America, where he had grown rich, and had congratulated him when he bought back the old castle by the bog at sleepy Kilderry. It was from Kilderry that his father had come, and it was there that he wished to enjoy his wealth among ancestral scenes. Men of his blood had once ruled over Kilderry and built and dwelt in the castle, but those days were very remote, so that for generations the castle had been empty and decaying. After he went to Ireland Barry wrote to me often, and told me how under his care the grey castle was rising tower by tower to its ancient splendour, how the ivy was climbing slowly over the restored walls as it had climbed so many centuries ago, and how the peasants blessed him for bringing back the old days with his gold from over the sea. But in time there came troubles, and the peasants ceased to bless him, and fled away instead as from a doom. And then he sent a letter and asked me to visit him, for he was lonely in the castle with no one to speak to save the new servants and labourers he had brought from the North.

The bog was the cause of all these troubles, as Barry told me the night I came to the castle. I had reached Kilderry in the summer sunset, as the gold of the sky lighted the green of the hills and groves and the blue of the bog, where on a far islet a strange olden ruin glistened spectrally. The sunset was very beautiful, but the peasants at Ballylough had warned me against it and said that Kilderry had become accursed, so that I almost shuddered to see the high turrets of the castle gilded with fire. Barry's motor had met me at the Ballylough station, for Kilderry is off the railway. The villagers had shunned the car and the driver from the

North, but had whispered to me with pale faces when they saw I was going to Kilderry. And that night, after our reunion, Barry told me why.

The peasants had gone from Kilderry because Denys Barry was to drain the great bog. For all his love of Ireland, America had not left him untouched, and he hated the beautiful wasted space where peat might be cut and land opened up. The legends and superstitions of Kilderry did not move him, and he laughed when the peasants first refused to help, and then cursed him and went away to Ballylough with their few belongings as they saw his determination. In their place he sent for labourers from the North, and when the servants left he replaced them likewise. But it was lonely among strangers, so Barry had asked me to come.

When I heard the fears which had driven the people from Kilderry I laughed as loudly as my friend had laughed, for these fears were of the vaguest, wildest and most absurd character. They had to do with some preposterous legend of the bog, and of a grim guardian spirit that dwelt in the strange olden ruin on the far islet I had seen in the sunset. There were tales of dancing lights in the dark of the moon, and of chill winds when the night was warm; of wraiths in white hovering over the waters, and of an imagined city of stone deep down below the swampy surface. But hovering over the waters, and of an imagined absolute unanimity, was that of the curse awaiting him who should dare to touch or drain the vast reddish morass. There were secrets, said the peasants, which must not be uncovered; secrets that had lain hidden since the plague came to the children of Partholan in the fabulous years beyond history. In the *Book of Invaders* it is told that these sons of the Greeks were all buried at Tallaght, but old men in Kilderry said that one city was overlooked save by its patron moon-goddess; so that only the wooded hills buried it when the men of Nemed swept down from Scythia in their thirty ships.

Such were the idle tales which had made the villagers leave Kilderry, and when I heard them I did not wonder that Denys Barry had refused to listen. He had, however, a great interest in antiquities, and proposed to explore the bog thoroughly when it was drained. The white ruins on the islet he had often visited, but though their age was plainly great, and their contour very little like that of most ruins in Ireland, they were too dilapidated to tell the days of their glory. Now the work of drainage was ready to begin, and the labourers from the North were soon ready to strip the forbidden bog of its green moss and red heather, and kill the tiny shell-paved streamlets and quiet blue pools fringed with rushes.

After Barry had told me these things I was very drowsy, for the travels of the day had been wearying and my host had talked late into the night. A manservant showed me to my room, which was in a remote tower overlooking the village, and the plain at the edge of the bog, and the bog itself; so that I could see from my windows in the moonlight the silent roofs from which the peasants had fled and which now sheltered the labourers from the North, and too, the parish church with its antique spire and far out across the brooding bog the remote olden ruin on the islet gleaming white and spectral. Just as I dropped to sleep I fancied I heard faint sounds from the distance; sounds that were wild and half musical, and stirred me with a weird excitement which coloured my dreams. But when I awakened next morning I felt it had all been a dream, for the visions I had seen were more wonderful than any sounds of wild pipes in the night. Influenced by the legends that Barry had related, my mind had in slumber hovered around a stately city in a green valley, where marble streets and statues, villas and temples, carvings and inscriptions, all spoke in certain tones the glory that was Greece. When I told this dream to Barry we both laughed; but I laughed the louder, because he was perplexed about his labourers from the North. For the sixth time they had all overslept, waking very slowly and dazedly, and acting as if they had not rested, although they were known to have gone early to bed the night before.

That morning and afternoon I wandered alone through the sun-gilded village and talked now and then with idle labourers, for Barry was busy with the final plans for beginning his work of drainage. The labourers were not as happy as they might have been, for most of them seemed uneasy over some dream which they had had, yet which they tried in vain to remember. I told them of my dream, but they were not interested till I spoke of the weird sounds I thought I had heard. Then they looked oddly at me, and said that they seemed to remember weird sounds, too.

In the evening Barry dined with me and announced that he would begin the drainage in two days. I was glad, for although I disliked to see the moss and the heather and the little streams and lakes depart, I had a growing wish to discern the ancient secrets the deep-matted peat might hide. And that night my dreams of piping flutes and marble peristyle came to a sudden and disquieting end; for upon the city in the valley I saw a pestilence descend, and then a frightful avalanche of wooded slopes that covered the dead bodies in the streets and left unburied only the temples of Artemis on the high peak, where the aged moon-priestess Cleis lay cold and silent with a crown of ivory on her silver head.

I had said that I awakened suddenly and in alarm. For some time I could not tell whether I was waking or sleeping, for the sound of flutes still rang shrilly in my ears; but when I saw on the floor the icy moonbeams and the outlines of a latticed Gothic window I decided I must be awake and in the castle of Kilderry. Then I heard a clock from some remote landing below strike the hour of two, and knew I was awake. Yet still there came that monotonous piping from afar; wild, weird airs that made me think of some dance of fauns on distant

Maenalus. It would not let me sleep, and in impatience I sprang up and paced the floor. Only by chance did I go to the north window and look out upon the silent village and the plain at the edge of the bog. I had no wish to gaze abroad, for I wanted to sleep; but the flutes tormented me, and I had to do or see something. How could I have suspected the thing I was to behold?

There in the moonlight that flooded the spacious plain was a spectacle which no mortal, having seen it, could ever forget. To the sound of reedy pipes that echoed over the bog there glided silently and eerily a mixed throng of swaying figures, reeling through such a revel as the Sicilians may have danced to Demeter in the old days under the harvest moon beside the Cyane. The wide plain, the golden moonlight, the shadowy moving forms, and above all the shrill monotonous piping, produced an effect which almost paralysed me; yet I noted amidst my fear that half of these tireless, mechanical dancers were the labourers whom I had thought asleep, whilst the other half were strange airy beings in white, half-indeterminate in nature, but suggesting pale wistful naiads from the haunted fountains of the bog. I do not know how long I gazed at this sight from the lonely turret window before I dropped suddenly in a dreamless swoon, out of which the high sun of morning aroused me.

My first impulse on awaking was to communicate all my fears and observations to Denys Barry, but as I saw the sunlight glowing through the latticed east window I became sure that there was no reality in what I thought I had seen. I am given to strange phantasms, yet am never weak enough to believe in them; so on this occasion contented myself with questioning the labourers, who slept very late and recalled nothing of the previous night save misty dreams of shrill sounds. This matter of the spectral piping harassed me greatly, and I wondered if the crickets of autumn had come before their time to vex the night and haunt the visions of men. Later in the day I watched Barry in the library pouring over his plans for the great work which was to begin on the morrow, and for the first time felt a touch of the same kind of fear that had driven the peasants away. For some unknown reason I dreaded the thought of disturbing the ancient bog and its sunless secrets, and pictured terrible sights lying black under the unmeasured depth of age-old peat. That these secrets should be brought to light seemed injudicious, and I began to wish for an excuse to leave the castle and the village. I went so far as to talk casually to Barry on the subject, but did not dare continue after he gave his resounding laugh. So I was silent when the sun set fulgently over the far hills, and Kilderry blazed all red and gold in a flame that seemed a portent.

Whether the events of that night were reality or illusion I shall never ascertain. Certainly they transcend anything we dream of in nature and the universe; yet in no normal fashion can I explain those disappearances which were known to all men after it was over. I retired early and full of dread, and for a long time could not sleep in the uncanny silence of the tower. It was very dark, for although the sky was clear the moon was now well on the wane, and would not rise till the small hours. I thought as I lay there of Denys Barry, and of what would befall that bog when the day came, and found myself almost frantic with an impulse to rush out into the night, take Barry's car, and drive madly to Ballylough out of the menaced lands. But before my fears could crystallize into action, I had fallen asleep, and gazed in dreams upon the city in the valley, cold and dead under a shroud of hideous shadow.

Probably it was the shrill piping that awaked me, yet that piping was not what I noticed first when I opened my eyes. I was lying with my back to the east window overlooking the bog, where the waning moon would rise, and therefore expected to see light cast on the opposite wall before me; but I had not looked for such a sight as now appeared. Light indeed glowed on the panels ahead, but it was not any light that the moon gives. Terrible and piercing was the shaft of ruddy refulgence that streamed through the Gothic window, and the whole chamber was brilliant with a splendour intense and unearthly. My immediate actions were peculiar for such a situation, but it is only in tales that a man does the dramatic and foreseen thing. Instead of looking out across the bog, towards the source of the new light. I kept my eyes from the window in panic and fear, and clumsily drew on my clothing with some dazed idea of escape. I remember seizing my revolver and hat, but before it was over I had lost them both without firing the one or donning the other. After a time the fascination of the red radiance overcame my fright, and I crept to the east window and looked out whilst the maddening, incessant piping whined and reverberated through the castle and over all the village.

Over the bog was a deluge of flaring light, scarlet and sinister, and pouring from the strange olden ruin on the far islet. The aspect of that ruin I cannot describe – I must have been mad, for it seemed to rise majestic and undecayed, splendid and column-cinctured, the flame-reflecting marble of its entablature piercing the sky like the apex of a temple on a mountain-top. Flutes shrieked and drums began to beat, and as I watched in awe and terror I thought I saw dark saltant forms silhouetted grotesquely against the vision of marble and effulgence. The effect was titanic – altogether unthinkable – and I might have stared indefinitely had not the sound of the piping seemed to grow stronger at my left. Trembling with a terror oddly mixed with ecstasy I crossed the circular room to the north window from which I could see the village and the plain at the edge of the bog. There my eyes dilated again with a wild wonder as great as if I had not just turned from a scene beyond the pale of nature, for on the ghastly red-lit plain was moving a procession of beings in such a manner as none ever saw before save in night-mares.

Half-gliding, half-floating in the air, the white-clad bog-wraiths were slowly retreating towards the still waters and the island ruin in fantastic formations suggesting some ancient and solemn ceremonial dance. Their waving translucent arms, guided by the detestable piping of those unseen flutes, beckoned in uncanny rhythm of a throng of lurching labourers who followed doglike with blind, brainless, flounder-ing steps as if dragged by a clumsy but resistless demon-will. As the naiads neared the bog, without altering their course, a new line of stumbling stragglers zigzagged drunkenly out of the castle from some door far below my window, groped sightlessly across the courtyard and through the intervening bit of village, and joined the floundering column of labourers on the plain. Despite their distance below me I at once knew they were the servants brought from the North, for I recognized the ugly and unwieldy form of the cook, whose very absurdness had now become unutterably tragic. The flutes piped horribly, and again I heard the beating of the drums from the direction of the island ruin. Then silently and gracefully the naiads reached the water and melted one by one into the ancient bog; while the line of followers, never checking their speed, splashed awkwardly after them and vanished amidst a tiny vortex of unwholesome bubbles which I could barely see in the scarlet light. And as the last pathetic straggler, the fat cook, sank heavily out of sight in that sullen pool, the flutes and the drums grew silent, and the blinding red rays from the ruins snapped instantaneously out, leaving the village of doom lone and desolate in the wan beams of a new-risen moon.

My condition was now one of indescribable chaos. Not knowing whether I was mad or sane, sleeping or waking, I was saved only by a merciful numbness. I believe I did ridiculous things such as offering prayers to Artemis, Latona, Demeter, Persephone and Plouton. All that I recalled of a classical youth came to my lips as the horrors of the situation roused my deepest superstitions. I felt that I had witnessed the death of a whole village, and knew I was alone in the castle with Denys Barry, whose boldness had brought down a doom. As I thought of him new terrors convulsed me, and I fell to the floor, not fainting, but physically helpless. Then I felt the icy blast from the east window where the moon had risen, and began to hear the shrieks in the castle far below me. Soon these shrieks had attained a magnitude and quality which cannot be written of, and which make me faint as I think of them. All I can say is that they came from something I had known as a friend.

At some time during this shocking period the cold wind and the screaming must have roused me, for my next impression is of racing madly through inky rooms and corridors and out across the courtyard into the hideous night. They found me at dawn wandering mindless near Ballylough, but what unhinged me utterly was not any of the horrors I had seen or heard before. What I muttered about as I came slowly out of the shadows was a pair of fantastic incidents which occurred in my flight: incidents of no significance, yet which haunt me unceasingly when I am alone in certain marshy places or in the moonlight.

As I fled from that accursed castle along the bog's edge I heard a new sound: common, yet unlike any I had heard before at Kilderry. The stagnant waters, lately quite devoid of animal life, now teemed with a horde of enormous, slimy frogs which piped shrilly and incessantly in tones strangely out of keeping with their size. They glistened bloated and green in the moonbeams, and seemed to gaze up at the fount of light. I followed the gaze of one very fat and ugly frog, and saw the second of the things which drove my senses away.

Stretching directly from the strange olden ruin on the far islet to the waning moon, my eyes seemed to trace a beam of faint quivering radiance having no reflection in the waters of the bog. And upward along that pallid path my fevered fancy pictured a thin shadow slowly writhing, a vague contorted shadow struggling as if drawn by unseen demons. Crazed as I was, I saw in that awful shadow a monstrous resemblance – a nauseous, unbelievable caricature – a blasphemous effigy of him who had been Denys Barry.

A Fair Lady
Roger Malisson

The sight of her made his day.

She had long blonde hair and long brown legs, the tall slim girl dressed in brief denim shorts and what looked like a liberty bodice. She also had a bulging rucksack, a cheap camera slung round her neck, and a cross expression.

''Morning, miss,' said Jack, getting an eyeful as he wheeled his bike towards her over the grass verge.

'How far is it to Seachester, Officer?' she demanded, pushing her hair away from her face impatiently.

'Ten miles or so, straight down the road,' he answered.

'Is there much traffic later in the day?'

'Not a lot, but you may be lucky.'

'Bloody hell.' She shaded her eyes and scowled at the sea, sparkling peacefully in the July sun, then turned abruptly and jerked her head at the rolling countryside opposite.

'Not much point in going that way, then? Only bloody tractors and things, I suppose.' Her voice was faintly Cockney.

''Fraid so,' he said, smiling slightly. Her sulking, vapid stare reminded him of a model's in a glossy magazine; she had to be all of sixteen.

'If you don't mind my mentioning it, miss,' he said, recalling his duty, 'it's a bit dangerous for attractive girls to go hitch-hiking on their own. There's a bus goes from Hobston to Seachester every hour, and——'

'Hobston? Where's that?'

'The village just down the road. You can get a cup of tea, and the buses ...'

She was already striding away.

'I can take care of myself,' she snapped over her shoulder.

Suppressing a sarcastic retort, Jack watched her neat figure until she disappeared round a bend in the road. She couldn't help being rude. To kids like her he was just 'the fuzz', a hated symbol of a world they despised, criticized and coveted. She also made him feel quite piqued and old.

It was too bright a day for depressing thoughts. Jack remounted his bicycle and set off along the road on his rounds. The sun beat down on his shoulders; the heat would be fierce later on. They'd said on the radio it was the warmest summer since nineteen-something.

His route took him past a couple of farms and a trendy pub. A farm worker waved at him from a field. He exchanged a pleasantry with the trendy pub's landlord and set off back down the same road towards Hobston. Sometimes he felt as if he'd wandered into a soap opera, cast as Mr Plod; it was that blasted girl who'd disturbed him, he decided. She reminded him of city life – and 'life' was the word – London especially, before his return home to Hobston as the village bobby. Cycling along the smooth road with the shimmering sea lapping the beach below on his right and the rich green pastures spreading to the horizon on his left, Jack Merril, thirty-four and healthy, being the envy of his mates on the force as one who had unquestionably got it made, surrendered to wistful reminiscences.

He remembered the dingy, smoky offices and the city slums, the degradation, corruption, ingenuity and, above all, the vast quantity of crime there. He'd seen everything in the last ten years from high-life vice to sordid murder: the blackmailers and the cat-burglars, the tarts and the freaks, that spy case where the Specials had turned nasty, the nutcase with the hamner ... How glad and relieved he'd been when he had landed this job at Hobston, where the last felony had been a breaking and entering at the off-licence two years ago, and that had been down to some drunken tourist. He'd been nine when his parents had moved away from the village; it was only because he'd been born here that he was accepted back, along with Sheila and the kids.

Cycling round a bend in the road, his musings were scattered by a terrible shock. It wasn't the sort of horrific fright that makes the hair prickle and the mouth open in an involuntary scream, but that spasm of tension experienced by every animal when suddenly confronted by a long-dreaded, potentially threatening, stronger animal. And so Jack's stomach contracted, his head jerked upright, his shoulders squared themselves – not easy on a bike – his pulse and heart rate accelerated as the adrenalin flowed, and he glanced down surreptitiously to see whether his shoes were polished. The creature which had caused these atavistic reactions advanced with an air of regal authority; it was his old headmistress. She stopped as he approached, her keen eyes undimmed with sixty years of clean living, and her memory circuits snapped into action.

'Jack Merril.'

Jack dismounted and straightened his tie. 'Miss Brophy.'

'Well, Jack, you've returned to Hobston, I see.'

Jack smiled foolishly and nodded, recalling her undeniable gift for making unanswerable statements.

'I hear you've done well in the Force. Inspector, aren't you?'

'No, sergeant.' Due for promotion soon, he nearly added, but checked himself in time. She wouldn't be interested in possibilities.

''H'm. You're married, aren't you?'

'Yes, they've given us one of the workers' cottages at the north end. A bit small, but it's rent-free.'

'Good. I hope you settle in.' Nodding curtly, she continued on her way, leaving him with the clear impression that she'd never thought he would ever amount to much, and by God she'd been right. Pedalling humbly down the road, Jack marvelled at the fact that the teacher, with her short grey hair and neat tweeds, hadn't altered a day in twenty years. By some alchemy, Miss Brophy seemed to have discovered the secret of eternal middle-age.

Funny old life, as Sid Fletcher would say. He was heading towards Sid's farm now, a mile or so past the spot where he'd met the hitch-hiker earlier. 'Fletcher's Farm' was a euphemism really. Sid owned a decrepit cottage and an acre or so on which he raised a few vegetables, a cow and some chickens – a smallholding by means of which Sid scraped a living. He also sold watery lemonade and rather dry biscuits to the tourists who wandered down from Seachester in the summer. Jack grinned to himself as he caught sight of the stone wall which surrounded Sid's place. Old Sid never could build a wall properly, and he was too stubborn to get professional help. Every winter, without fail, the searing North Yorkshire storms smashed his barrier, and the wind-lashed seas flooded his land. Every spring, Sid was to be seen painstakingly cementing his wall again and cursing his ill-luck. Sid wasn't very bright, in fact he was something of a local joke.

'Hey up, lad. Fancy a cuppa?'

'Nay, Sid, I s'll have to get back to t' station.'

The exchange was becoming a morning ritual. Jack waved and rode on towards Hobston, grinning to himself. It was easy to slip back into the dialect, and he did it half-ironically.

One of the Hobston job's perks was getting home for a decent lunch while John Duncan, the village's junior guardian of the law, minded the shop. Farewell to the curling cellophane-wrapped sandwich, hello to homemade steak and kidney pie. Hello to a spreading waistline, come to that.

'I took the kids to school this morning,' chattered Sheila as she shovelled an omelette onto a plate. 'Jamie was fretful, – just first-day nerves, I think – but Sally will look after him. She's good that way.'

'How about you? Do you think you're going to like it here?' Jack asked. His wife was cheerful, strong and capable, but Hobston didn't readily take to strangers.

'Oh, I think so.' Sheila turned from the cooking and shook her hair from her eyes, a mannerism that reminded him for a moment of the girl he'd met that morning.

'They're a bit old-fashioned, though, aren't they? Eccentric, almost. I saw a dark-haired man on a horse when I was doing the shopping, and one of the farm workers all but touched his cap as he passed.'

'That would be Dick Hobston,' answered Jack. 'I went to primary school with him. His family owned the whole area a hundred years ago. Then his father sold off most of the land and went into plastics. The people round here still look up to the Hobstons.'

'Sounds feudal,' commented Sheila, busy at the stove.

Jack stretched in his chair and yawned. 'Look 'ee, there be young Squire Hobston, a-gallopin' off on his foam-flecked mare. A devil for the ladies be young Squire. Ar.'

Sheila laughed dutifully and served his lunch before broaching her favourite topic of the moment.

'This house is rather small, isn't it, Jack? And there's no proper garden. I could save a fortune if we grew our own vegetables. Do you think we could buy a place of our own, maybe next year?'

Jack blanched at the thought of cutting into their savings.

'I like small houses,' he said petulantly, then, seeing Sheila's crest-fallen face, he added: 'Oh, we'll see.'

But Jack's domestic plans were abruptly forgotten when news came of the hitch-hiker's disappearance. The girl never reached her destination; Jack was the last person known to have seen her alive. During the weary days and weeks of questioning and search – the Seachester C.I.D. combing the area like rabbits – he was profoundly grateful for the villagers' silent support. Never once was a whisper of gossip or glance of suspicion directed against him, though the grilling he had from his superiors left him feeling like a criminal. Eventually the police decamped, the case unsolved. The locals were glad to see the back of them; nobody born and bred outside of Hobston could possibly be up to any good, ran their philosophy.

Jack wasn't sorry to see them go, either. He took the family for a pre-lunch drink to the Hobston Arms the following Sunday, slipping easily into the village custom.

'This is the life, Sheila,' he said, stretching luxuriously in his wicker chair.

She smiled, adjusting her sunglasses. 'It's the first time I've seen you relaxed in weeks.'

Jamie, who was only six, began to fidget.

'I want to play at Droos, Sally! Let's play at Droos!'

'Druids, he means,' explained his sister. 'We learned about them in History.'

Jack ruffled his son's hair. 'I'll bet you don't want to be a fireman any more. I bet you're going to be a Druid when you leave school, right?'

Sally shrieked with laughter. 'Don't be silly, Daddy, it takes *years*!'

'Well, whatever do they teach you kids these days?' Jack teased her. 'Turning you into a right couple of little pagans, by the sound of – oh, ah – hello, Miss Brophy.'

He smiled weakly as the teacher settled herself and her dry sherry primly at a nearby table.

'Good morning to you. Lovely day. I see James and Sarah are looking much healthier than when they arrived, Mrs Merril.'

'Yes, they love it here,' Sheila agreed as the children ran off to their game. 'Talking of health, how's old Sid Fletcher now?'

'He'll be better soon.' Miss Brophy sniffed. 'The man's a weakling. Always was.'

Bet she's never been ill in her life, thought Jack, and marvelled again at the ease with which his wife had settled into this tight little community. She was a clever girl, and Sally was 'promising fair' to grow up just like her.

'See this, Jack?' Arthur Bell, the landlord, handed him a tabloid as he served their drinks.

MY DESPAIR, shouted the headline. *Heartbroken Mother in Police Row Drama. Mrs Cynthia Brown, 40, wept yesterday as she told of her agony over 'police delays and cover-ups' in the case of her missing daughter. 'I have now given up hope of seeing her again. Lynda and I were very close. I know in my heart she will never be found alive.'*

Attractive 16-year-old Lynda Brown, who vanished while hitch-hiking from London to Darlington, was last seen in the Hobston area of Seachester. Harrassed Chief Inspector Lewis, who led the search for Lynda, said last night, 'This is a very worrying case. We are doing everything possible to trace the missing girl.'

Jack threw down the paper. He knew what the woman was getting at, of course; she'd decided the moment she saw him that Jack was implicated, and that his colleagues were concealing the facts. Two and two make sixty-four, don't they, Mrs Brown?

'She might have got amnesia,' he muttered aloud. 'She might just have taken off – some bloke she met on the road ...'

'She's dead,' said Sheila calmly, and with such conviction that he started, suddenly aware of the rapt and sympathetic attention of every person there.

'Oh yes? Sure of that, are you?'

Sheila bent her blonde head over her glass. 'It's obvious,' she said slowly. 'A good-looking girl like that, *dressed* like that, hitch-hiking alone. Surely——'

'You're quite right, Mrs Merril.' Miss Brophy's brittle voice broke in. 'These modern young people! No discipline, no religion. They think the old ways are foolish, but they learn, they learn.'

During the totally predictable murmur of agreement from the rest of them, Jack rose to his feet and called the kids.

'Well – time to go, Sheila. 'Bye, all.' See you next week, he thought bitterly. See all of you next week, same time, same bloody place.

'Don't worry, old chap,' said Dick Hobston as they walked together out of the gate. 'Bound to be upsetting, but it'll blow over soon. These things always do, you know.'

He was right, of course. The summer weeks stretched on with sunny monotony and Hobston thrived. For a hobby, Sheila began to study ancient history at Miss Brophy's evening class and nagged gently for a place of their own. The children, apple-cheeked and tanned, did well at school. Dick Hobston wrote off his racing car and walked unscathed from the wreck. The dairyfarming Dobsons turned down an enormous offer for some of their land from a man who wanted to build a hotel. Mrs Dobson reported the theft of her purse, which was later found intact by the postman in the field where she had dropped it, and Sid Fletcher grew a little more potty every day. Jack worried about his chances of promotion, and occasionally wondered whether Lynda Brown was raving it up on the Continent or rotting quietly in some makeshift grave.

Autumn arrived with wind and rain. The children chattered constantly of the Harvest Festival, an important date in Hobston's calendar. It was always held in the village hall, or on the green in fine weather, as the nearest church was a couple of miles away. Jack missed it. He was called to Seachester that day for a meeting with his superiors. The meeting turned out to be a waste of time for him, and he came home tired, cold and dispirited. Sheila hadn't had time to cook anything hot, and he started a row over the meal before slamming out to the pub. It was all very well for her and the kids – they loved the village – but he was sick of the same faces and routine, and the clannishness of the place was beginning to get on his nerves.

There was a mood of celebration in the Hobston Arms that evening, and Jack was quick to catch it.

'Here's to prosperity,' he said, raising his glass.

'Oh, we'll prosper all right,' said the landlord jubilantly. 'All the proper rites have been observed today, so there's no reason why we shouldn't.'

Jack laughed. 'Rites? You can't be serious, Arthur. What have you all been doing, sacrificing white cockerels? I never took you for a superstitious bloke.'

Arthur reddened. 'Look, Jack, you can't argue with bloody——'

'"There are more things in heaven and earth, Horatio,"' drawled Dick Hobston. 'Isn't that right, Arthur?'

Miss Brophy put her oar in. 'I'm surprised at your scoffing, Jack Merril. You know we've always valued our traditions in Hobston, and with the world in the state it is today we are all in favour of a return to the old ways. It's just ignorance that——'

Her harangue was left unfinished as the door crashed open and a shabby, dishevelled man stumbled into the room, his face so distorted with fear that it took Jack some moments to recognize Sid Fletcher. He stood swaying, with pleading desperation in his bloodshot eyes, then collapsed into a chair and covered his face, keening quietly to himself.

'What's up, Sid? What's happened?' Jack broke the silence.

'He's drunk again,' said someone contemptuously.

'Come on, Sid. Tell us what's the matter.'

The old man clutched his arm, staring inwards.

'It's coming closer,' he whispered. 'Every day, a bit closer. And I can't stop it. It's horrible, Jack.'

'Take a grip on yourself, man!' snapped Miss Brophy. 'Nothing's going to harm you as long as you keep some control!'

'It's too late,' mourned Sid. 'I should never have listened. You don't know what it's like . . .'

'Look, will someone start talking sense?' said Jack in exasperation. 'What's going on?'

'Quite simple, old lad,' Dick Hobston replied smoothly. 'Poor old Sid's taken to the bottle and he's seeing things. Ghosts, isn't it, Sid? Sad, really.'

'You're a feeble-minded old fool, Sid Fletcher!' said Miss Brophy brutally. 'Get home to your bed – it's all you're fit for.'

'Just a minute.' Jack looked at the woman with real loathing. 'Arthur, give me a double brandy. Right . . . Get that down you, Sid, and I'll take you home.'

Ignoring the disapproving glances and mutterings all around him, he sat while Sid gulped his drink, then steered him out of the door and down the coast road that led to the farm. Sid was drunk, and kept up a low, desultory monologue all the way to his gate, but he'd stopped shaking and could walk reasonably steadily.

'You should see a doctor, Sid.'

'What for? All right, I am. Just keep going. It'll work, lad. Very angry, see – and that's good . . . only I can't take it, Jack . . . shouldn't have been me, no, it shouldn't. I'm sick, and too old . . .'

'What's angry, Sid?' Jack interrupted gently. 'You, or this ghost you think you're seeing?'

Sid stared at him, and his eyes in the moonlight were crafty and mad.

'No more!' he shouted suddenly. 'Not much longer now. The old ways! The old ways!'

With a curious, tattered dignity, he walked the last few yards to his door.

Jack watched him with mingled pity and irritation. The village idiot, he thought, but what had happened to turn his brain like this? Idly, he turned his steps towards the beach. He didn't feel like going home yet. The glint of the moon on the dark waves reminded him for a moment of the sunlight's gleam on the girl's bright hair, that summer day ... Poor Sid ...

He turned sharply, staring at the cottage. Suppose the old fool had murdered that girl? What if guilt feelings were responsible for the illusion of her ghost? No, that was nonsense; no motive. There wasn't any money involved, and if she'd been rude her insults would have been met with bewilderment, not fury. And he couldn't figure old Sid for a sex murderer. Still, he decided on the way home to mention Sid's strange behaviour to Inspector Lewis next time they met. Opening the door of his own silent house, he walked inside and made a bed of the sofa.

Three days later Sid was found dead in his fireside chair. His heart had given out, and he must have died in some anguish, for the look on his face was far from peaceful. He was scarcely cold when Sheila began to talk of buying the farm, improving the cottage and cultivating a vegetable garden. Jack's opposition was confounded with relentless logic. The house was going cheap because it was so decrepit, a unique chance to make a worthwhile investment, good for the kids ...

'What about the flooding?' argued Jack. 'Your precious vegetables will be ruined every time that wall gives way.'

'It won't,' said Sheila.

'Oh?'

Sheila just smiled.

'Of course, dear, you know best, as always,' Jack said sarcastically. 'I suppose you'll be selling lemonade to the tourists, as well.'

'Why not?' said Sheila happily, and before he knew it Jack was stripping walls and putting up shelves in his spare time, while she scrubbed the place clean and made trips to Seachester for carpets and extra furniture.

They moved in on a Friday morning, only two months after Sid Fletcher's death. The conveyancing had gone smoothly, and the cottage, newly-decorated and shining, was waiting for them. Some essential renovating had been done; the rest could wait till they had more cash. The children were thrilled and ran about the house and garden with noisy delight. Sheila was all sunshine and surveyed her home with the expression of a woman whose nest-building instincts had found fulfilment.

Jack, on the other hand, couldn't care less. The atmosphere of the cottage, laden with old associations, was as cold to him as the bitter winter outside. He remembered sneaking into the place as a kid, tears streaking his dirty face and his hands tingling from Miss Brophy's strap. Sid had always been kind, and wasn't in the least concerned with things like talking in class or getting homework sums wrong. Jack remembered Sid's harmless swearing when his wall was knocked down during the storms, in the years before his stubborn habits had hardened into eccentricity. But he was gone now. Jack shivered suddenly at the thought of the old man's lonely, frightened death, here in this very room. He stared out through the window at Sid's wall, thick and solid, which was braving a savage wind from the east. Blow down, you fool, he thought angrily. Prove to Sheila that she was wrong about you at least.

Sally ran in from the garden.

'Daddy!' she cried, 'we're going to the shops with Mummy to buy things for the housewarming party tomorrow. Are you coming with us?'

'You realize all this could be a waste of time.' Jack ignored Sally and spoke directly to his wife. 'I might get promoted soon and we'd have to move out of the area.'

'Commute, then,' Sheila snapped. 'I'm staying.' Taking the children by the hand she walked out of the house, leaving Jack to his gloomy contemplation of the weather and his marriage.

Despite an uneasy truce with Sheila – no quarrelling when the kids were present – Jack had trouble sleeping that first night. After his third semi-nightmare he gave up and went downstairs for a drink. He stood at the window with his coffee and cigarette, staring moodily at the moonlit front garden, the stone wall and the sheet of grey sea beyond.

He shivered, and rubbed his eyes. Must be still half-asleep, because that white, nebulous thing moving slowly across the wall was surely pure imagination ... old Sid and his ghosts ... It's moving to and fro before the wall now – helpless, agitated, such a waste, such a pity ... catching at his thoughts ... And now it had stopped, and turned, as if it saw him, and he was the sole focus of its inimicable will. A silent roaring filled his brain, and his numbed limbs began to shake with shock and terror. The thin, luminous shape was moving towards him, a demonic embodiment of hatred, rage and destruction, and he thought he saw the eyes alight with all the fury and torment of hell, eager to rend his soul. It was getting closer, advancing across the garden towards the window. Brick walls would not stop it. Not this confused thought, but a mortal dread of encountering the face that might belong to that sinister being overcame the paralysis of fear. He ran from the room like a hunted hare and up the stairs to his bedroom. It was empty; Sheila had gone.

As in moments of physical danger, Jack thrust the panic from his mind and waited for the hammering of his heart to subside. Then, gathering all his courage, he forced himself to walk along the landing to the children's room, which faced on to the front of the house. Opening the door quietly, he stepped inside. A low, unintelligible sing-song met his ears, like plain chant. By the window stood a woman, ghostly in the moonlight. Keeping a firm hold of his consciousness Jack walked towards her, melting in wordless relief as he saw it was Sheila. But his wife had become a stranger in this weird, midnight world. She was staring into the garden and murmuring in a foreign tongue. From where he stood he thought he could see the malignant spirit recoil, and go back, leave them alone – at least, he thought he could ... Out of here, kids still sleeping, thank God, back along the landing and here was his bed ... mustn't pass out ...

'Are you all right, Jack? I just went to see if the kids were OK. Couldn't you sleep?' Sheila's voice was soothing as she climbed into bed.

'Sheila, you saw it, didn't you? The thing in the garden?'

'What? You've been having nightmares. Poor old Jack, never mind. Sure you're all right? You sound drunk. Try to get some sleep.'

Jack laughed mirthlessly. 'I only drank coffee,' he said. Turning his back upon the stranger in the bed, he fell asleep.

It was a relief the next day to be out of the house and alone at the station. His constable, John Duncan, had been requested yet again to help out in Seachester, much to John's disgust. But Inspector Lewis's word was, of course, law. Jack concentrated fiercely on overdue reports and tried to convince himself that he had dreamed all last night's events. He didn't succeed, but managed to keep his mind off any of the implications, real or imaginary. He had no evidence that anything untoward had occurred; he wasn't trained to deal with irrational hocus-pocus and old-fashioned superstition. He must wait for developments. That was right, wasn't it? He lunched off a chocolate bar and a packet of crisps and continued working.

But the evening brought a different mood. At six o'clock, he locked the filing cabinet, dragged on his overcoat and made straight for the Hobston Arms.

'Bit empty tonight, aren't you, Arthur?' he asked, nursing his pint. The landlord gave him a strange look.

'Not surprising. They're all over at your place for the house-warming. Hope to be looking in myself later on.'

'Good God. I'd forgotten the bloody party.'

Arthur winced – perhaps he disapproved of swearing – as Jack knocked back his drink and hurried home, bent against the cutting wind that howled inland from the sea.

Jamie came running up the pathway to meet him.

'The party, Daddy! The party!'

'Cheers,' he said gloomily, allowing himself to be dragged into the house. And everyone was there, of course: Sheila, looking dishy, amazingly grown-up Sally, Miss Brophy, John Duncan, Dick Hobston, Harry Dobson, old Uncle Tom Cobley and all ...

'You're late, Jack,' Sheila remarked.

'Acutely observed, my dear.'

Sheila smiled winningly and dragged him to one side.

'Look, if you're in *that* mood – well, just don't show me up in front of the guests, do you hear? What's the matter with you, anyway? Have you been drinking?'

'Not really, but we'll soon remedy that, as they say.'

It was a fair-to-horrible party, but Jack was determined to struggle through it with the aid of several large scotches. One good thing, he thought, if that ghost comes again tonight I won't see it, I'll be dead to the world after all this booze. What ghost? Just imagination. More to the point, what booze? His glass was empty again. Only eight o'clock; two or three hours to go yet, at the least. Hold on, lad. Smile and chat to them all, from Dick Hobston to his stable lad, play the host. Good harvest, wasn't it? Rotten weather, isn't it? Quite.

What were they really thinking?

Nothing, from the look of it. A normal crowd of provincial people enjoying themselves at a well-organized party. You had to hand it to Sheila.

Sally and the older children were singing in a corner of the room, watched with approval by a group of adults.

'*Build it up with wood and clay* ...'

What's this? Can't have people bunched up like that at a party.

'*Wood and clay will wash away, wash away, wash away.*'

Other kids of her age are singing pop songs.

'*Set a watchman at the gate* ...'

'You're a bit old for nursery rhymes, Sally,' he said loudly.

There was a painful silence, and Sally blushed scarlet.

'Oh, Daddy! It's not really a nursery rhyme, it's part of a very old ballad, and——'

'Rubbish,' he said loftily. 'If you must sing, pick something cheerful and modern, for Heaven's sake. Ballad, my foot! It's a baby song.'

But adolescent dignity was affronted, and Sally was determined to carry her point.

'It *is* an old ballad, Daddy, truly – no one knows how old.' She was

almost sobbing now, battling against the easy tears of childhood. 'You
must know about it. I wish you wouldn't tease!'

'Tell me,' said Jack softly.

'Well, the people always knew that the water spirits would be
offended if they built bridges and things on their stretch of water. So
They had to offer human sacrifices to propitiate them, and the
people who were sacrificed had to be young and, you know, untouched,
so they'd be really angry at all they'd missed, their whole life, really,
and they would guard their territory against the water gods, so the
bridge or whatever it was would keep standing. Like Stonehenge. They
found skulls and things there, and that's still standing, and – don't look
like that, Daddy, please!'

'But this is all – this is nonsense.'

'No, dear,' said Sheila. 'There's a castle in Brittany where they found
the skeleton of a four-year-old bricked into the wall with a candle in
one hand and a piece of bread in the other, to keep him awake and
nourished ... It happened all over Europe. Don't you think this sort of
thing is worth investigating?'

Jack was cold, suddenly freezing cold. He gazed around the room,
seeing his neighbours as if from another plane, as though he were looking
at them down the centuries. Sickened, his mind recoiled from the
primeval, reptilian cruelty in their ageless eyes as they stared back at
him, their set smiles seeming to mock him while he turned from one
familiar face to another. The atmosphere was stagnant, rancid, suffocating. He broke the spell by moving, first like a sleepwalker, then breaking
into a run as he left the house.

Sheila made to follow him; Miss Brophy laid a restraining hand on
her arm.

'Let him go, dear. He has to know sooner or later.'

Jack found his spade in the shed. He hurried to the wall that kept
out the sea and began to dig like someone demented, jabbing hard at the
stiff, frosty soil.

His family and friends watched with concern, then, smiling,
shrugging, resumed their party. Dick, as usual, got a little drunk;
Arthur, when he arrived, told them some funny stories. Sally, recovering, handed round cold snacks, and everyone complimented Sheila on
her cooking.

Outside, Jack dug and dug into the hard, sandy soil, and the cold
spade rubbed his palms raw. He had to pause often, to fight off waves
of nausea and to chafe his freezing arms. He finally stopped, just as the
moon was beginning to rise, at the moment when his spade struck something hard and rebounded, a matted hank of blonde hair clinging to
its edge.

As he stood spent and motionless in the moonlight, there came the high, clear, timeless sound of children's voices, drifting across the garden:

'*London Bridge is falling down,*
Falling down, falling down ...

A gurgling laugh broke from his lips, and hoarsely, discordantly, he raised his voice.

'*Who will build it up again?*
My fair lady.'

The Master of Blas Gwynedd
Joyce Marsh

The first person to notice the huge, emaciated dog as it slunk in through the kitchen doorway was the cook, and her instant reaction was to command her minion to remove it at once before its great muddy feet should mar the hygienic cleanliness of her floor.

The lad told to perform this task looked up from his lethargic scrubbing of the already pristine white hearth with an expression of ill-concealed insolence. There was not very much that young Glyn enjoyed about his work in the hotel kitchen, but the thing he most disliked was the cook's habit of vacillating – of setting him to one chore and then, half-way through its performance, switching him to another. He shot her a baleful glance, but one did not argue with Cookie, so, wiping his hands on his apron, he got up and advanced upon the dog.

Glyn had been born and raised on a farm and was well used to dogs. Small dogs, large dogs, working dogs and useless pets, they had all marched in a never-ending procession through his childhood years. But this great brute was a queer'n, he thought. Got something of an Irish wolfhound in him.

The dog stood quite still in the doorway, head and tail drooping, its back leg quivering slightly as if too weak to support the tall, bony frame. The poor beast was thin – hideously thin. Every bone in its body was clearly visible through the rough grey coat, which was matted and plastered with a wet, slimy mud.

'Here, Cookie, I wonder where he got s'wet – we've had no rain to speak of in weeks.'

The boy, advancing closer, wrinkled his nose distastefully and answered his own question.

'I reckon he's bin in the bottom pond. He stinks like a sewer.'

'Just get him out of here, young Glyn, and be quick about it.'

Glyn clapped his hands. 'Go'rn, get-off-out-of-it!' he shouted authoritatively. The dog lifted his long, heavy head and looked at the boy full in the face. Glyn would no more have feared a dog than he would fear one of the fat cabbages awaiting attention on the cook's well-scrubbed table, but such a glittering malevolence shone in this dog's yellow-green eyes that now he drew back.

The eyes, surprisingly bright, sparkled out from behind a fringe of tangled, matted hair, and they never wavered, never left the boy's face. The hand he had put out to scuff the dog away dropped limply to his side.

'I don't think he wants to go, Cookie, and, look you, he is a dirty great brute.' The gentle sing-song of the boy's Welsh tongue so easily became a pleading whine.

'He looks half starved. There's a bit of a bone in the larder – chuck that out and he'll soon go out after it.'

The cook was not an unkindly soul. Indeed, on the completion of yet another successful meal she could become positively benevolent.

Glyn waved the bone temptingly before the dog's nose, but the expression never changed and the eyes never lost their evil glare. The lad looked back pleadingly. It was plain to him that no scraggy old bone was going to tempt this dog to do something he did not want to, and the lad had no mind to use force.

Cook was busying herself at the oven with her back turned. Swiftly, the boy opened the door of the boiler room.

'Go on then – get you in there in the warm.'

As an added inducement, he threw the bone down the cellar steps. To his enormous relief, the weary stray slunk off into the boiler room. It was a compromise, but it saved the kitchen lad, at least for the time being, from the lash of Cookie's tongue.

The warmth of the boiler room dried out the dog's coat, and, somehow, by his own unaided efforts, he cleaned himself and emerged looking considerably more presentable. The dog had the good sense to know that his presence in the kitchen would never be acceptable, so, at the first opportunity, he slipped through the swing doors and into the main part of the hotel. Thus, practically unnoticed, the stray dog took up his residence at Blas Gwynedd.

He was a quiet dog, interfering with nobody as he padded with ungainly grace along the dark passages or in and out of the rooms, where he seemed to seek no more than the comfort of stretching full length before a wide, blazing fire. His only really offensive habit was to disappear occasionally, to return dripping slimy mud, having apparently taken a fancy to a dip in the foulness of the Bottom Pond. Even on these occasions, however, he had the good sense to go and clean himself in the boiler room before reappearing.

Even at the peak of prime condition, it is doubtful if the dog could ever have been described as handsome, but his enormous size, his rough, grey, shaggy coat, heavy head and even the sharp angularity of his protruding bones gave him a kind of bizarre attraction. Old Ap Evans, the proprietor, was quick to realize the dog's ornamental value.

'Gives the place a touch of atmosphere,' he said, and he was right.

Somewhere in the distant past, Blas Gwynedd had been a private house, a gentleman's country residence, and it had survived the years magnificently. Even the transformation into a hotel had been achieved without much visible change. The great hound-dog could himself have been an inheritance from the past: he blended to perfection with the heavy, carved panelling and the wide stone fireplaces.

But if he interfered with nobody, then the dog himself made it plain that in return he expected no interference. He maintained an air of detached dignity. Occasionally, new arrivals tried to curry favour with him, but he refused their attempted caresses with a purposeful movement of his head. A few visitors were irritated by his unfriendliness, a few feared him, but eventually all came to accept him with the same disregard that they gave to the ornamental furnishings.

There was one, however, who never came to accept the dog – young Glyn. He hated that dog. He did not trust the eyes, which could turn like a cat's from green to yellow, he did not trust the insular detachment and, above all, he did not trust the dog's refusal of all food.

'You mark my words,' Glyn would mutter darkly. 'It's gone wild, and a dog like that only eats live meat. I've seen it happen before. I reckon some poor farmer's chickens and lambs are going to feed that great brute.'

If Glyn was right, the dog must have been a singularly unsuccessful hunter, for he never seemed to gain an extra ounce of flesh.

As the hot, profitable summer passed away, the stream of holiday-makers became a trickle, then died away, but the late days of glorious autumn brought back the 'regulars'.

There were about a dozen of these, and they came back to Blas Gwynedd year after year when the noisy, boisterous 'casuals' had gone and they could enjoy what they no doubt considered a more sophisticated type of holiday. They liked to have the hotel to themselves, to relax in the rich rooms so heavy with the atmosphere of bygone luxury. During the days they went their separate ways, to walk or motor through the autumn countryside, but each evening they met together in what was once a sort of baronial hall, but was now known as the 'Resident's Lounge'. It was the part of the day they enjoyed most of all, as they sat in the cosy shadows with a log fire throwing dancing patterns on the panelled walls, and the great, grey hound, stretched at full length on the hearth-rug, could only add to the romantic nobility of their surroundings.

Over the years, they had come to know each other very well, and several times each evening they promised themselves that they would not let another year pass before they met again. Arrangements must be made for a dinner or a luncheon reunion. The fact that these plans never came to fruition was neither here nor there; the making of them was most enjoyable to all – all, that is, save the one youngster of the party, a girl who would rather have been holiday-making on the Costa Brava. *She* spent her evenings promising herself that, as soon as her eighteenth birthday released her from parental dictatorship, that was exactly what she would do.

These pleasant evenings always ended at precisely ten o'clock, when Ap Evans knocked discreetly on the door and brought in the supper. It was his habit to join his guests for a few minutes, politely enquiring into their day's doings whilst they enjoyed hot, milky coffee and deliciously savoury sandwiches.

It was a ritual, a strict, unalterable routine. It was, therefore, more than surprising when, one evening, his knock came very loudly, imperiously and unexpectedly. All eyes turned to the clock, and all eyebrows were raised. It was some ten minutes, still, before official supper-time. There was a long pause; the ladies fidgeted restlessly, moving things to make space for the coffee cups. The dog lifted his head.

A paunchy, middle-aged man, who almost qualified for the description of elderly, turned his head irritably.

'Well, come in then, man, come in.'

The ladies stilled their trivial movements, the silence thickened. Then the knock came again more loudly, more imperiously, shattering the tense quietness into a thousand vibrant fragments.

The dog struggled to his feet. The hairs along the ridge of his back bristled and the green eyes stared fixedly at the door. A thin-faced, nervous bank clerk leaned forward to peer around the winged sides of his chair, following the direction of the dog's eyes. Slowly, rhythmically at first, the door handle began to rattle, then faster and more violently, until the whole door shook against its hinges.

'Oh, poor old Mr Evans. The handle's stuck again. He can't get in.'

The girl's fresh young voice and her mundane explanation instantly washed away the tension. As she left her chair to cross to the door the ladies resumed their fiddling and the men visibly sank deeper into their chairs. But the dog did not move – did not relax.

The girl opened the door. 'Come on in, then, Mr Evans,' she said. But the passage outside was empty, the dark shadows so thick that they seemed to form an impenetrable barrier against the glowing warmth of the cosy room. For a long moment she stood there, her face showing the foolish, self-conscious expression that the young sometimes wear.

There came a tiny sound, a very soft, low whimper. The dog left the hearth-rug and, walking with slow, controlled eagerness, he came to the centre of the room and lifted his long, heavy head. His eyes stared upwards, and now they were a melting, golden yellow – inexpressably gentle and loving. He lowered his head, stretching it forward, and slowly, ecstatically, arched his back. The scrawny tail fanned from side to side.

The group before the fire watched the dog in silence as he moved in a curious little semi-circle around the floor before padding back to the fireplace. He walked now with his head bowed respectfully, but without humility, and he sat down facing the chair the girl had just vacated. His liquid, golden eyes stared fixedly upwards to one spot in empty space.

'I suppose old Evans forgot something and nipped back to the kitchen.'

The older people relaxed again and did not notice that the girl had shuddered slightly before she spoke and the movement had carried on in a little tremor of her voice.

The dog barred the girl's way to her chair, so she gently prodded his shoulder with her knee. He turned his head, and the glittering warning in his eyes was so malevolent that she drew back. She pushed him again, but this time he reinforced his warning with a curling of the lip, baring one long, yellow fang. The girl capitulated and sat down on a low footstool. The dog accepted his victory with dignity as he lowered his head on to the seat of the chair.

Evans came in with supper at precisely ten o'clock and, oddly enough, no one thought to ask him why, or even if, he had knocked earlier and so loudly upon the door.

From that evening the dog changed. He was no longer content to slink unobtrusively about the hotel. Now he stalked the rooms and passages with an air of arrogant proprietorship, whilst his glittering eyes and curling lip flashed an awesome warning to any who dared bar his way.

Sometimes he would pad quietly, with soft golden eyes and head lowered, but even these moments of comparative meekness could turn, on an instant, to vicious malevolence, if anyone approached too close. He took to stretching at full length, belly down, across a door sill or at the foot of the stairs, defying anyone to pass. Thus guests and staff alike were prevented, often for hours at a time, from moving freely about the hotel.

The great hound was a nuisance. The young female staff were the first to surrender and give up their places. Then the guests began to complain.

'Evans, old man, you want to do something about that dog,' the paunchy man counselled, using that tone of bluff heartiness which one man often uses when giving unasked for advice to another.

'Indeed, yes, sir,' Evans agreed pleasantly, although he had already come to that same conclusion for himself. He had, in fact, tried once –

and failed – to rid his hotel of its unwanted watch-dog. He had waited until the hound had slipped outside, then he had heaved half a brick after it and slammed shut the door. Contemptuously, the dog had not whined or scratched for re-entry. He had merely exerted his bony strength against the door, and the ancient lock had proved unequal to the strain. Now Evans had another and, hopefully, more successful plan. He intended to catch the dog in an unwary moment, tie a rope around its neck and haul it off to the police station. After all, he reasoned, the dog was a stray, and if it was not the constable's duty to take charge of strays then he would like to know whose it was.

The only snag in this excellent plan was finding the dog in an unguarded moment, and then finding someone willing to take advantage of it. The dubious honour fell to young Glyn.

'You can do it, boy. Indeed, with your father being a breeder an' all, there's not a lad in the country better at handlin' dogs.'

The command was given with a nice touch of flattery, and Glyn accepted the task with mixed feelings, partly of fear and partly of elation – fear of the dog, and elation at the thought that he was to be the one to defeat the animal he had come to look upon as his own personal enemy.

Fortune favoured the lad, or appeared to do so, for he soon came upon the dog sleeping before a fire. He had ready his rope as he crept cautiously closer with the loop held open over stretched fingers. The noose dangled inches from the animal's nose – one quick movement and the slip-knot would pull tight; then, the more the brute struggled, the closer he would come to strangling himself.

But the lad triumphed too soon, and the dog sensed it. With a jerk, the head came up, yellow fangs instantly bared. Glyn was no coward. He pressed forward, lunging with his rope, but the dog thrust it aside and, in the same movement, sprang. His fore-paws hit the boy full on the chest, carrying him backwards to the floor. Wide open jaws, dripping strings of saliva, were inches from the boy's throat, and there came from the dog an overpowering stench – a stench of utter foulness. It filled the lad's nose, mouth and lungs; it suffocated him. He closed his eyes and waited for the final agony of those fangs ripping into his throat.

'LEAVE!'

In after years, Glyn never knew whether he had heard that shouted word or whether it had sprung from somewhere within his own mind. Albeit, on an instant, the dog left him, to lie down staring evilly but motionless. Glyn scrambled up and ran. He was the first and the last person who ever tried to trap the hound of Blas Gwynedd.

For more than a year, Ap Evans struggled against the dog. He tried poisoned meat that was never touched, shotguns that missed their target, even spring traps, but the cruel steel jaws yawned fruitlessly wide and forever empty.

He endured one disastrous summer season when no visitors stayed more than one night, then he capitulated. He was getting on and he had made his pile, as they say, so he moved out – left Blas Gwynedd to the dog and the inevitable, creeping dereliction.

I have set down the foregoing events exactly as they occurred, neither adding nor omitting one detail, for I remember it all as if it were ... well, I was going to say 'yesterday', but I am an old lady now, and yesterday's events are not as clear in my mind as that last holiday I spent with my parents at Blas Gwynedd.

It is sixty years since I last saw the old hotel, but now, un-accountably, I have an urge to go there once more, and for the last time. I can sit here upon a hillock and look down on to what was once the kitchen yard. The house has all but gone; tall bracken, brambles and wild, creeping things have smothered the tumbled bricks. Only a few timbers stand out starkly to show the place where doors and windows once were.

A grey, lithe shape steals out from the ruins of the kitchen and pads across the yard. I see a long, heavy head lifted to sniff the breeze, and I know that if I had the sight to conquer the distance I would see the glitter of evil green eyes.

There is another, newer hotel now – The Gwynedd Arms. The proprietor is an old man, but I know him, not by his face and figure, so changed by the years, but by the tale he tells to his guests of an evening.

Glyn has remembered; he has remembered it all as well as I, but he can speak of something I did not know, for he can tell of a long-dead owner of Blas Gwynedd who drowned in his own pond, and who now lies buried in the churchyard, with the great wolfhound, who died trying to save him, lying forever at his feet.

But then I could tell Glyn whose hand, so long ago, had opened the door, and whose voice it was that invited in the real master of Blas Gwynedd.

Who Knows?

Guy de Maupassant
Translated by H. N. P. Sloman

Merciful heaven! At last I've made up my mind to put on record what I've been through! But shall I ever be able to do it, shall I have the courage? It's all so mysterious, so inexplicable, so unintelligible, so crazy!

If I were not sure of what I've seen, certain that there has been no flaw in my reasoning, no mistake in my facts, no gap in the strict sequence of my observations, I should consider myself merely the victim of a hallucination, the sport of some strange optical delusion.

After all, who knows?

Today I am in a mental home, but I went there of my own free will, as a precaution, because I was afraid. Only one man knows my story, the House Doctor. Now I'm going to put it on paper, I really don't quite know why. Perhaps in order to shake off the obsession, which haunts me like some ghastly nightmare.

Anyhow, here it is:

I have always been a lonely man, a dreamer, a kind of solitary: good-natured, easily satisfied, harbouring no bitterness against mankind and no grudge against heaven. I have always lived alone, because of a sort of uneasiness, which the presence of others sets up in me. How can I explain it? I can't. It's not that I shun society; I enjoy conversation, and dining with my friends, but when I am conscious of them near me, even the most intimate, for any length of time, I feel tired, exhausted, on edge, and I am aware of a growing and distressing desire to see them go away or to go away myself and be alone.

This desire is more than a mere craving, it is an imperative necessity. And if I had to remain in their company, if I had to go on, I do not say listening to, but merely hearing their conversation, I am sure something dreadful would happen. What? Who knows? Possibly, yes, probably, I should simply collapse.

I am so fond of being alone that I cannot even endure the proximity of other human beings sleeping under the same roof; I cannot live in Paris; it is a long, drawn-out fight for life to me. It is spiritual death: this huge, swarming crowd living all round me, even in its sleep, causes me physical and nervous torture. Indeed, other people's sleep is even more painful to me than their conversation. And I can never rest, when I know or feel that there are living beings, on the other side of the wall, suffering this nightly suspension of consciousness.

Why do I feel like this? Who knows? Perhaps the reason is quite simple: I get tired very quickly of anything outside myself. And there are many people like me.

There are two kinds of human beings. Those who need others, who are distracted, amused, soothed by company, while loneliness, such as the ascent of some forbidding glacier or the crossing of a desert, worries them, exhausts them, wears them out: and those whom, on the contrary, the society of their fellows wearies, bores, irritates, cramps, while solitude gives them peace and rest in the unshackled world of their phantasy.

It is, in fact, a recognized psychological phenomenon. The former are equipped to lead the life of the extrovert, the latter that of the introvert. In my own case my ability to concentrate on things outside myself is limited and quickly exhausted, and as soon as this limit is reached I am conscious of unbearable physical and mental discomfort. The result of this has been that I am, or rather I was, very much attached to inanimate objects, which take on for me the importance of human beings, and that my house has, or rather had, become a world in which I led a lonely but purposeful life, surrounded by things, pieces of furniture and ornaments that I knew and loved like friends. I had gradually filled my home and decorated it with them, and in it I felt at peace, contented, completely happy as in the arms of a loving wife, the familiar touch of whose caressing hand has become a comforting, restful necessity.

I had had this house built in a beautiful garden, standing back from the road, not far from a town, where I could enjoy the social amenities, of which I felt the need from time to time. All my servants slept in a building at the far end of a walled kitchen-garden. In the silence of my home, deep hidden from sight beneath the foliage of tall trees, the enveloping darkness of the nights was so restful and so welcome that every evening I put off going to bed for several hours in order to prolong my enjoyment of it.

That evening there had been a performance of *Sigurd* at the local theatre. It was the first time I had heard this beautiful fairy play with music and I had thoroughly enjoyed it.

I was walking home briskly, with scraps of melody running in my head and the entrancing scenes still vivid in my memory. It was dark, pitch dark, and when I say that, I mean I could hardly see the road, and several times I nearly fell headlong into the ditch. From the toll-gate to my house is a little more than half a mile, or about twenty minutes' slow walking. It was one o'clock in the morning, one o'clock or half past one; suddenly the sky showed slightly luminous in front of me, and the crescent moon rose, the melancholy crescent of the waning moon. The moon in its first quarter, when it rises at four or five o'clock in the evening, is bright, cheerful, silvery; but in the last quarter, when it rises after midnight, it is copper-coloured, gloomy and foreboding, a real Witches' Sabbath moon. Anyone given to going out much at night must have noticed this. The first quarter's crescent, even when slender as a thread, sheds a faint but cheering gleam, at which the heart lifts, and throws clearly defined shadows on the ground: the last quarter's crescent gives a feeble, fitful light, so dim that it casts almost no shadow.

The dark outline of my garden loomed ahead, and for some reason I felt an odd disinclination to go in. I slackened my pace. The night was very mild. The great mass of trees looked like a tomb, in which my house lay buried.

I opened the garden gate and entered the long sycamore drive leading to the house with the trees meeting overhead; it stretched before me like a lofty tunnel through the black mass of the trees and past lawns, on which the flower-beds showed up in the less intense darkness as oval patches of no particular colour.

As I approached the house an unaccountable uneasiness gripped me. I paused. There was not a sound, not a breath of air stirring in the leaves. 'What has come over me?' I thought. For ten years I had been coming home like this without the least feeling of nervousness. I was not afraid. I have never been afraid in the dark. The sight of a man, a thief or a burglar, would merely have thrown me into a rage, and I should have closed with him, unhesitatingly. Moreover, I was armed; I had my revolver. But I did not put my hand on it, for I wanted to resist this feeling of fear stirring within me.

What was it? A presentiment? That unaccountable presentiment which grips a man's mind at the approach of the supernatural? Perhaps. Who knows?

As I went on, I felt shivers running down my spine, and when I was close to the wall of my great shuttered house, I felt I must pause for a few moments before opening the door and going in. Then I sat down on a garden seat under my drawing-room windows. I stayed there, my heart thumping, leaning my head against the wall, staring into the blackness of the foliage. For the first few minutes I noticed nothing unusual. I *was* aware of a kind of rumbling in my ears, but that often happens to me. I sometimes think I can hear trains passing, bells ringing, or the tramp of a crowd.

But soon the rumbling became more distinct, more definite, more unmistakable. I had been wrong. It was not the normal throbbing of my arteries which was causing this buzzing in my ears, but a quite definite though confused noise, coming, without any question, from inside my house. I could hear it through the wall, a continuous noise, a rustling rather than a noise, a faint stirring, as of many objects being moved about, as if someone were shifting all my furniture from its usual place and dragging it about gently.

Naturally, for some time I did not trust my hearing. But after putting my ear close to the shutters in order to hear the strange noises in the house more clearly, I remained quite firmly convinced that something abnormal and inexplicable was going on inside. I was not afraid, but – how can I express it? – startled by the sheer surprise of the thing. I did not slip the safety-catch of my revolver, somehow feeling certain it would be of no use. I waited.

I waited a long while, unable to come to any decision, with my mind perfectly clear but deeply disturbed. I waited motionless, listening all the time to the growing noise, which swelled at times to a violent crescendo, and then seemed to turn to an impatient, angry rumble, which made one feel that some outburst might follow at any minute.

Then, suddenly, ashamed of my cowardice, I seized my bunch of keys, picked out the one I wanted, thrust it into the lock, turned it twice, and pushing the door with all my force, hurled it back against the inside wall.

The bang echoed like a gunshot, and immediately the crash was answered by a terrific uproar from cellar to attic. It was so sudden, so terrifying, so deafening, that I stepped back a few paces and, though I realized it was useless, I drew my revolver from its holster.

I waited again, but not for long. I could now distinguish an extraordinary sound of trampling on the stairs, parquet floors and carpets, a trampling, not of human feet or boot soles, but of crutches, wooden crutches and iron crutches, that rang with the metallic insistence of cymbals. And then, suddenly, on the threshold of the front door, I saw an armchair, my big reading chair, come waddling out; it moved off down the drive. It was followed by others from the drawing-room, then came the sofas, low on the ground and crawling along like crocodiles on their stumpy legs, then all the rest of my chairs, leaping like goats, and the little stools loping along like rabbits.

Imagine my feelings! I slipped into a clump of shrubs, where I crouched, my legs glued all the time to the procession of my furniture, for it was all on the way out, one piece after the other, quickly or slowly, according to its shape and weight. My piano, my concert grand, galloped past like a runaway horse, with a faint jangle of wires inside; the smaller objects, brushes, cut glass and goblets, slid over the gravel like ants, gleaming like glow-worms in the moonlight. The carpets and hangings crawled away, sprawling pools of living matter, for all the world like devil-fish. I saw my writing-desk appear, a rare eighteenth century collector's piece, containing all my letters, the whole record of anguished passion long since spent. And in it were also my photographs.

Suddenly all fear left me; I threw myself upon it, and grappled with it, as one grapples with a burglar; but it went on its way irresistibly and, in spite of my furious efforts, I could not even slow it up. As I wrestled like a madman against this terrible strength, I fell to the ground in the struggle. Then it rolled me over and over, and dragged me along the gravel, and already the pieces of furniture behind were beginning to tread on me, trampling and bruising my legs; then, when I let go, the others swept over me, like a cavalry charge over an unhorsed soldier.

At last, mad with terror, I managed to drag myself off the main drive and hide again among the trees, watching the disappearance of the smallest, tiniest, humblest pieces that I had ever owned, whose very existence I had forgotten.

Then I heard, in the distance, inside the house, which was full of echoes like an empty building, a terrific din of doors being shut. They banged from attic to basement, and last of all the hall door slammed, which I had foolishly opened myself to allow the exodus.

Then I fled and ran towards the town, and I didn't recover myself till I got to the streets, and met people going home late. I went and rang at the door of a hotel where I was known. I had beaten my clothes with my hands to shake the dust out of them, and I made up a story that I had lost my bunch of keys with the key of the kitchen-garden, where my servants slept in a house by itself, behind the garden wall which protected my fruit and vegetables from thieves.

I pulled the bed-clothes up to my eyes in the bed they gave me; but I couldn't sleep, and I waited for dawn, listening to the violent beating of my heart. I had given orders for my servants to be informed as soon as it was light, and my valet knocked at my door at seven o'clock in the morning. His face showed how upset he was.

'An awful thing has happened during the night, sir,' he said.

'What is it?'

'All your furniture has been stolen, sir, absolutely everything, down to the smallest objects.'

Somehow I was relieved to hear this. Why? I don't know. I had complete control of myself; I knew I could conceal my feelings, tell no one what I had seen, hide it, bury it in my breast like some ghastly secret. I replied:

'Then they are the same people who stole my keys. The police must be informed at once. I'm getting up, and I'll be with you in a few minutes at the police station.'

The enquiry lasted five months. Nothing was brought to light.

Neither the smallest of my ornaments nor the slightest trace of the thieves was ever found. Good heavens! If I had told them what I knew ... If I had told ... they would have shut up, not the thieves, but me, the man who could have seen such a thing.

Of course, I knew how to keep my mouth shut. But I never furnished my house again. It was no good. The same thing would have happened. I never wanted to go back to it again. I never did go back. I never saw it again. I went to a hotel in Paris, and consulted doctors about the state of my nerves, which had been causing me considerable anxiety since that dreadful night.

They prescribed travel and I took their advice.

*   *   *

I began with a trip to Italy. The sun did me good. For six months I wandered from Genoa to Venice, from Venice to Florence, from Florence to Rome, from Rome to Naples. Then I toured Sicily, an attractive country, from the point of view of both scenery and monuments, the remains left by the Greeks and the Normans. I crossed to Africa, and travelled at my leisure through the great sandy, peaceful desert, where camels, gazelles and nomad Arabs roam, and where, in the clear, dry air, no obsession can persist either by day or by night.

I returned to France via Marseilles, and, in spite of the Provençal gaiety, the diminished intensity of the sunlight depressed me. On my return to Europe I had the old feeling of a patient who thinks he is cured, but is suddenly warned, by a dull pain, that the seat of the trouble is still active.

Then I went back to Paris. After a month I got bored. It was autumn, and I decided to take a trip, before the winter, through Normandy, which was new ground to me.

I began with Rouen, of course, and for a week I wandered about, intrigued, charmed, thrilled, in this medieval town, this amazing museum of rare specimens of Gothic art.

Then one evening, about four o'clock, as I was entering a street that seemed too good to be true, along which flows an inky-black stream called the Eau de Robec, my attention, previously centred on the unusual, old-fashioned aspect of the houses, was suddenly arrested by a number of second-hand furniture shops next door to one another.

They had, indeed, chosen their haunt well, these seedy junk dealers, in this fantastic alley along this sinister stream, under pointed roofs of tile or slate, on which the weather-vanes of a vanished age still creaked.

Stacked in the depths of the cavernous shops could be seen carved chests, china from Rouen, Nevers and Moustiers, statues, some painted, some in plain oak, crucifixes, Madonnas, Saints, church ornaments, chasubles, copes, even chalices, and an old tabernacle of gilded wood, now vacated by its Almighty tenant. What astonishing caverns there were in these great, lofty houses, packed from cellar to attic with pieces of every kind, whose usefulness seemed finished, and which had outlived their natural owners, their century, their period, their fashion, to be bought as curios by later generations!

My passion for old things was reviving in this collector's paradise. I went from shop to shop, crossing in two strides the bridges made of four rotten planks thrown over the stinking water of the Eau de Robec. And then – Mother of God! My heart leapt to my mouth. I caught sight of one of my finest cabinets at the edge of a vault crammed with junk, that looked like the entrance to the catacombs of some cemetery of old furniture. I went towards it trembling all over, trembling to such an extent that I did not dare touch it. I stretched out my hand, then I hesitated. It *was* mine, there was no question about it, a unique Louis XIII cabinet, unmistakable to anyone who had ever seen it. Suddenly, peering farther into the sombre depths of this gallery, I noticed three of my arm-chairs covered with *petit point* embroidery, then farther off my two Henry II tables, which were so rare that people came specially from Paris to see them.

Imagine, just imagine my feelings!

Then I went forward, dazed and faint with excitement, but I went in, for I am no coward, I went in like a knight in the dark ages entering a witches' kitchen. As I advanced, I found all my belongings, my chandeliers, my books, my pictures, my hangings and carpets, my weapons, everything except the writing-desk containing my letters, which I could not discover anywhere.

I went on, downstairs, along dark passages, and then up again to the floors above. I was alone. I called, but there was no answer. I was quite alone; there was no one in this huge, winding labyrinth of a house.

Night came on, and I had to sit down in the dark on one of my own chairs, for I wouldn't go away. At intervals I shouted: 'Hullo! Hullo! Anybody there?'

I had been there, I am sure, more than an hour, when I heard footsteps, light, slow steps: I could not tell where they came from. I nearly ran away, but, bracing myself, I called again, and I saw a light in the next room.

'Who's there?' said a voice.

I answered:

'A customer.'

The answer came:

'It's very late, we're really closed.'

I retorted:

'I've been waiting for you an hour.'

'You could have come back tomorrow.'

'Tomorrow I shall have left Rouen.'

I did not dare to move, and he did not come to me. All this time I saw the reflection of his light shining on a tapestry, in which two angels were flying above the dead on a battlefield. That, too, belonged to me.

I said:

'Well, are you coming?'

He replied:

'I'm waiting for you.'

I got up and went towards him.

In the centre of a large room stood a very short man, very short and very fat, like the fat man at a show, and hideous into the bargain. He had a sparse, straggling, ill-kept, dirty-yellow beard, and not a hair on his head, not a single one. As he held his candle raised at arm's length in order to see me, the dome of his bald head looked like a miniature moon in this huge room stacked with old furniture. His face was wrinkled and bloated, his eyes mere slits.

After some bargaining I bought three chairs that were really mine, and paid a large sum in cash, merely giving the number of my room at the hotel. They were to be delivered next morning before nine o'clock. Then I left the shop. He showed me to the door most politely. I went straight to the Head Police Station, where I told the story of the theft of my furniture and the discovery I had just made.

The Inspector telegraphed, on the spot, for instructions, the Public Prosecutor's Office, where the investigation into the theft had been held, asking me to wait for the answer. An hour later it was received, completely confirming my story.

'I'll have this man arrested and questioned at once,' he said, 'for he may have become suspicious, and he might move your belongings. I suggest you go and dine, and come back in two hours' time: I'll have him here, and I'll put him through a second examination in your presence.'

'Excellent, Inspector! I'm more than grateful to you.'

I went and dined at my hotel, and my appetite was better than I should have thought possible. But I was pretty well satisfied. They had got him.

Two hours later I was back at the police station, where the officer was waiting for me.

'Well, sir,' he said, when he saw me, 'we haven't got your friend. My men haven't been able to lay hands on him.'

'Do you mean . . .?'

A feeling of faintness came over me.

'But . . . you *have* found the house?' I asked.

'Oh yes! And it will, of course, be watched and guarded till he comes back. But he has disappeared.'

'Disappeared?'

'Yes, disappeared. He usually spends the evening with his next-door neighbour, a queer old hag, a widow called Mrs Bidoin, a second-hand dealer like himself. She hasn't seen him this evening and can't give any information about him. We shall have to wait till tomorrow.'

I went away. The streets of Rouen now seemed sinister, disturbing, haunted.

I slept badly, with nightmares every time I dropped off.

As I didn't want to seem unduly anxious, or in too much of a hurry, I waited next morning till ten o'clock before going round to the police station.

The dealer had not reappeared: his shop was still closed.

The Inspector said to me:

'I've taken all the necessary steps. The Public Prosecutor's Department has been informed; we'll go together to the shop and have it opened: you can show me what belongs to you.'

We drove to the place. Policemen were on duty, with a locksmith, in front of the door, which had been opened.

When I went in, I saw neither my cabinet nor my armchairs, nor my tables, not a single one of all the contents of my house, though the evening before I could not take a step without running into something of mine.

The Chief Inspector, in surprise, at first looked at me suspiciously.

'Well, I must say, Inspector, the disappearance of this furniture coincides oddly with that of the dealer,' I said.

He smiled:

'You're right! You made a mistake buying and paying for your pieces yesterday. It was that gave him the tip.'

I replied:

'What I can't understand is that all the space occupied by my furniture is now filled with other pieces.'

'Oh well,' answered the Inspector, 'he had the whole night before him, and accomplices too, no doubt. There are sure to be means of communication with the houses on either side. Don't be alarmed, sir, I shall leave no stone unturned. The thief won't evade us for long, now we've got his hide-out.'

My heart was beating so violently that I thought it would burst.

*   *   *

I stayed on in Rouen for a fortnight. The man did not come back. God knows, nobody could outwit or trap a man like that.

Then on the following morning I got this strange letter from my gardener, who was acting as caretaker of my house, which had been left unoccupied since the robbery:

Dear Sir,
I beg to inform you that something happened last night, which we can't explain, nor the police neither. All the furniture has come back, absolutely everything, down to the smallest bits. The house is now just as it was the evening before the burglary. It's fit to send you off your head. It all happened on the night between Friday and Saturday. The paths are cut up, as if everything had been dragged from the garden gate to the front door. It was just the same the day it all disappeared.

I await your return and remain,
Yours respectfully,
PHILIP RAUDIN.

No! No! No! I will *not* return there!

I took the letter to the Chief Inspector of Rouen.

'It's a very neat restitution,' he said. 'We'll lie doggo, and we'll nab the fellow one of these days.'

*   *   *

But he has not been nabbed. No! They've never got him, and now I'm afraid of him, as if a wild animal were loose on my track.

He can't be found! He'll never be found, this monster with the bald head like a full moon. They'll never catch him. He'll never go back to his shop. Why should he? Nobody but me *can* meet him, and I won't. I won't! I won't! I won't!

And if he does go back, if he returns to his shop, who will be able to prove that my furniture was ever there? There's only my evidence, and I've a feeling that that is becoming suspect.

No! My life was getting impossible. And I couldn't keep the secret of what I had seen. I couldn't go on living like everyone else, with the fear that this sort of thing might begin again at any moment.

I went and consulted the doctor who keeps this mental home, and told him the whole story.

After putting me through a lengthy examination, he said:

'My dear sir, would you be willing to stay here for a time?'

'I should be very glad to.'

'You're not short of money?'

'No, Doctor.'

'Would you like a bungalow to yourself?'

'Yes, I should.'

'Would you like your friends to come and see you?'

'No, Doctor, no one. The man from Rouen might venture to follow me here to get even with me.'

*   *   *

And I have been here alone for three months, absolutely alone. I have practically no anxieties. I am only afraid of one thing ... Supposing the second-hand dealer went mad ... and suppose he was brought to this home ...? Even prisons are not absolutely safe...

The Apple Tree
Daphne du Maurier

It was three months after she died that he first noticed the apple tree. He had known of its existence, of course, with the others, standing upon the lawn in front of the house, sloping upwards to the field beyond. Never before, though, had he been aware of this particular tree looking in any way different from its fellows, except that it was the third one on the left, a little apart from the rest and leaning more closely to the terrace.

It was a fine clear morning in early spring, and he was shaving by the open window. As he leant out to sniff the air, the lather on his face, the razor in his hand, his eye fell upon the apple tree. It was a trick of light, perhaps, something to do with the sun coming up over the woods, that happened to catch the tree at this particular moment; but the likeness was unmistakable.

He put his razor down on the window-ledge and stared. The tree was scraggy and of a depressing thinness, possessing none of the gnarled solidity of its companions. Its few branches, growing high up on the trunk like narrow shoulders on a tall body, spread themselves in martyred resignation, as though chilled by the fresh morning air. The roll of wire circling the tree, and reaching to about halfway up the trunk from the base, looked like a grey tweed skirt covering lean limbs; while the topmost branch, sticking up into the air above the ones below, yet sagging slightly, could have been a drooping head poked forward in an attitude of weariness.

How often he had seen Midge stand like this, dejected. No matter where it was, whether in the garden, or in the house, or even shopping in the town, she would take upon herself this same stooping posture, suggesting that life treated her hardly, that she had been singled out from her fellows to carry some impossible burden, but in spite of it would endure to the end without complaint. 'Midge, you look worn out, for heaven's sake sit down and take a rest!' But the words would be received with the inevitable shrug of the shoulder, the inevitable sigh, 'Someone has got to keep things going,' and straightening herself she would embark upon the dreary routine of unnecessary tasks she forced herself to do, day in, day out, through the interminable changeless years.

He went on staring at the apple tree. That martyred bent position, the stooping top, the weary branches, the few withered leaves that had not blown away with the wind and rain of the past winter and now shivered in the spring breeze like wispy hair; all of it protested soundlessly to the owner of the garden looking upon it, 'I am like this because of you, because of your neglect.'

He turned away from the window and went on shaving. It would not do to let his imagination run away with him and start building fancies in his mind just when he was settling at long last to freedom. He bathed and dressed and went down to breakfast. Egg and bacon were waiting for him on the hot-plate, and he carried the dish to the single place laid for him at the dining-table. *The Times,* folded smooth and new, was ready for him to read. When Midge was alive he had handed it to her first, from long custom, and when she gave it back to him after breakfast, to take with him to the study, the pages were always in the wrong order and folded crookedly, so that part of the pleasure of reading it was spoilt. The news, too, would be stale to him after she had read the worst of it aloud, which was a morning habit she used to take upon herself, always adding some derogatory remark of her own about what she read. The birth of a daughter to mutual friends would bring a click of the tongue, a little jerk of the head, 'Poor things, another girl,' or if a son, 'A boy can't be much fun to educate these days.' He used to think it psychological, because they themselves were childless, that she should so grudge the entry of new life into the world; but as time passed it became thus with all bright or joyous things, as though there was some fundamental blight upon good cheer.

'It says here that more people went on holiday this year than ever before. Let's hope they enjoyed themselves, that's all.' But no hope lay in her words, only disparagement. Then, having finished breakfast, she would push back her chair and sigh and say, 'Oh well ...', leaving the sentence unfinished; but the sigh, the shrug of the shoulders, the slope of her long, thin back as she stooped to clear the dishes from the serving-table – thus sparing work for the daily maid – was all part of her long term reproach, directed at him, that had marred their existence over a span of years.

Silent, punctilious, he would open the door for her to pass through to the kitchen quarters, and she would labour past him, stooping under the weight of the laden tray that there was no need for her to carry, and presently, through the half-open door, he would hear the swish of the running water from the pantry tap. He would return to his chair and sit down again, the crumpled *Times,* a smear of marmalade upon it, lying against the toast-rack; and once again, with monotonous insistence, the question hammered at his mind, 'What have I done?'

It was not as though she nagged. Nagging wives, like mothers-in-law, were chestnut jokes for music halls. He could not remember Midge ever losing her temper or quarrelling. It was just that the undercurrent of reproach, mingled with suffering nobly borne, spoilt the atmosphere of his home and drove him to a sense of furtiveness and guilt.

Perhaps it would be raining and he, seeking sanctuary within his study, electric fire aglow, his after-breakfast pipe filling the small room with smoke, would settle down before his desk in a pretence of writing letters, but in reality to hide, to feel the snug security of four safe walls that were his alone. Then the door would open and Midge, struggling into a raincoat, her wide-brimmed felt hat pulled low over her brow, would pause and wrinkle her nose in distaste.

'Phew! What a fug.'

He said nothing, but moved slightly in his chair, covering with his arm the novel he had chosen from a shelf in idleness.

'Aren't you going into the town?' she asked him.

'I had not thought of doing so.'

'Oh! Oh, well, it doesn't matter.' She turned away again towards the door.

'Why, is there anything you want done?'

'It's only the fish for lunch. They don't deliver on Wednesdays. Still, I can go myself if you are busy. I only thought ...'

She was out of the room without finishing her sentence.

'It's all right, Midge,' he called, 'I'll get the car and go and fetch it presently. No sense in getting wet.'

Thinking she had not heard he went out into the hall. She was standing by the open front door, the mizzling rain driving in upon her. She had a long flat basket over her arm and was drawing on a pair of gardening gloves.

'I'm bound to get wet in any case,' she said, 'so it doesn't make much odds. Look at those flowers, they all need staking. I'll go for the fish when I've finished seeing to them.'

Argument was useless. She had made up her mind. He shut the front door after her and sat down again in the study. Somehow the room no longer felt so snug, and a little later, raising his head to the window, he saw her hurry past, her raincoat not buttoned properly and flapping, little drips of water forming on the brim of her hat and the garden basket filled with limp michaelmas daisies already dead. His conscience pricking him, he bent down and turned out one bar of the electric fire.

Or yet again it would be spring, it would be summer. Strolling out hatless into the garden, his hands in his pockets, with no other purpose in his mind but to feel the sun upon his back and stare out upon the woods and fields and the slow winding river, he would hear, from the bedrooms above, the high-pitched whine of the Hoover slow down suddenly, gasp, and die. Midge called down to him as he stood there on the terrace.

'Were you going to do anything?' she said.

He was not. It was the smell of spring, of early summer, that had driven him out into the garden. It was the delicious knowledge that being retired now, no longer working in the City, time was a thing of no account, he could waste it as he pleased.

'No,' he said, 'not on such a lovely day. Why?'

'Oh, never mind,' she answered, 'it's only that the wretched drain under the kitchen window has gone wrong again. Completely plugged up and choked. No one ever sees to it, that's why. I'll have a go at it myself this afternoon.'

Her face vanished from the window. Once more there was a gasp, a rising groan of sound, and the Hoover warmed to its task again. What foolishness that such an interruption could damp the brightness of the day. Not the demand, nor the task itself – clearing a drain was in its own way a schoolboy piece of folly, playing with mud – but that wan face of hers looking out upon the sunlit terrace, the hand that went up wearily to push back a strand of falling hair, and the inevitable sigh before she turned from the window, the unspoken, 'I wish I had the time to stand and do nothing in the sun. Oh, well . . .'

He had ventured to ask once why so much cleaning of the house was necessary. Why there must be the incessant turning out of rooms. Why chairs must be lifted to stand upon other chairs, rugs rolled up and ornaments huddled together on a sheet of newspaper. And why, in particular, the sides of the upstairs corridor, on which no one ever trod, must be polished laboriously by hand, Midge and the daily woman taking it in turns to crawl upon their knees the whole endless length of it, like slaves of bygone days.

Midge stared at him, not understanding.

'You'd be the first to complain,' she said, 'if the house was like a pigsty. You like your comforts.'

So they lived in different worlds, their minds not meeting. Had it been always so? He did not remember. They had been married nearly twenty-five years and were two people who, from force of habit, lived under the same roof.

When he had been in business, it seemed different. He had not noticed it so much. He came home to eat, to sleep, and to go up by train again in the morning. But when he retired he became aware of her forcibly, and day by day his sense of her resentment, of her disapproval, grew stronger.

Finally, in that last year before she died, he felt himself engulfed in it, so that he was led into every sort of petty deception to get away from her, making a pretence of going up to London to have his hair cut, to see the dentist, to lunch with an old business friend; and in reality he would be sitting by his club window, anonymous, at peace.

It was mercifully swift, the illness that took her from him. Influenza, followed by pneumonia, and she was dead within a week. He hardly knew how it happened, except that as usual she was overtired and caught a cold, and would not stay in bed. One evening, coming home by the late train from London, having sneaked into a cinema during the afternoon, finding release amongst the crowd of warm friendly people enjoying themselves – for it was a bitter December day – he found her bent over the furnace in the cellar, poking and thrusting at the lumps of coke.

She looked up at him, white with fatigue, her face drawn.

'Why, Midge, what on earth are you doing?' he said.

'It's the furnace,' she said, 'we've had trouble with it all day, it won't stay alight. We shall have to get the men to see it tomorrow. I really cannot manage this sort of thing myself.'

There was a streak of coal dust on her cheek. She let the stubby poker fall on the cellar floor. She began to cough, and as she did so winced with pain.

'You ought to be in bed,' he said, 'I never heard of such nonsense. What the dickens does it matter about the furnace?'

'I thought you would be home early,' she said, 'and then you might have known how to deal with it. It's been bitter all day, I can't think what you found to do with yourself in London.'

She climbed the cellar stairs slowly, her back bent, and when she reached the top she stood shivering and half closed her eyes.

'If you don't mind terribly,' she said, 'I'll get your supper right away, to have it done with. I don't want anything myself.'

'To hell with my supper,' he said, 'I can forage for myself. You go up to bed. I'll bring you a hot drink.'

'I tell you, I don't want anything,' she said. 'I can fill my hot-water bottle myself. I only ask one thing of you. And that is to remember to turn out the lights everywhere, before you come up.' She turned into the hall, her shoulders sagging.

'Surely a glass of hot milk?' he began uncertainly, starting to take off his overcoat; and as he did so the torn half of the ten-and-sixpenny seat at the cinema fell from his pocket on to the floor. She saw it. She said nothing. She coughed again and began to drag herself upstairs.

The next morning her temperature was a hundred and three. The doctor came and said she had pneumonia. She asked if she might go to a private ward in the cottage hospital, because having a nurse in the house would make too much work. This was on the Tuesday morning. She went there right away, and they told him on the Friday evening that she was not likely to live through the night. He stood inside the room, after they told him, looking down at her in the high impersonal hospital bed, and his heart was wrung with pity, because surely they had given her too many pillows, she was propped too high, there could be no rest for her that way. He had brought some flowers, but there seemed no purpose now in giving them to the nurse to arrange, because Midge was too ill to look at them. In a sort of delicacy he put them on a table beside the screen, when the nurse was bending down to her.

'Is there anything she needs?' he said. 'I mean, I can easily ...' He did not finish the sentence, he left it in the air, hoping the nurse would understand his intention, that he was ready to go off in the car, drive somewhere, fetch what was required.

The nurse shook her head. 'We will telephone you,' she said, 'if there is any change.'

What possible change could there be, he wondered, as he found himself outside the hospital? The white pinched face upon the pillows would not alter now, it belonged to no one.

Midge died in the early hours of Saturday morning.

He was not a religious man, he had no profound belief in immortality, but when the funeral was over, and Midge was buried, it distressed him to think of her poor body lying in that brand-new coffin with the brass handles: it seemed such a churlish thing to permit. Death should be different. It should be like bidding farewell to someone at a station before a long journey, but without the strain. There was something of indecency in this haste to bury underground the thing that but for ill chance would be a living breathing person. In his distress he fancied he could hear Midge saying with a sigh, 'Oh, well ...' as they lowered the coffin into the open grave.

He hoped with fervour that after all there might be a future in some unseen Paradise and that poor Midge, unaware of what they were doing to her mortal remains, walked somewhere in green fields. But who with, he wondered? Her parents had died in India many years ago; she would not have much in common with them now if they met her at the gates of Heaven. He had a sudden picture of her waiting her turn in a queue, rather far back, as was always her fate in queues, with that large shopping bag of woven straw which she took everywhere, and on her face that patient martyred look. As she passed through the turnstile into Paradise she looked at him, reproachfully.

These pictures, of the coffin and the queue, remained with him for about a week, fading a little day by day. Then he forgot her. Freedom was his, and the sunny empty house, the bright crisp winter. The routine he followed belonged to him alone. He never thought of Midge until the morning he looked out upon the apple tree.

Later that day he was taking a stroll round the garden, and he found himself drawn to the tree through curiosity. It had been stupid fancy after all. There was nothing singular about it. An apple tree like any other apple tree. He remembered then that it had always been a poorer tree than its fellows, was in fact more than half dead, and at one time there had been talk of chopping it down, but the talk came to nothing. Well, it would be something for him to do over the weekend. Axing a tree was healthy exercise, and apple wood smelt good. It would be a treat to have it burning on the fire.

Unfortunately wet weather set in for nearly a week after that day, and he was unable to accomplish the task he had set himself. No sense in pottering out of doors this weather, and getting a chill into the bargain. He still noticed the tree from his bedroom window. It began to irritate him, humped there, straggling and thin, under the rain. The weather was not cold, and the rain that fell upon the garden was soft and gentle. None of the other trees wore this aspect of dejection. There was one young tree – only planted a few years back, he recalled quite well – growing to the right of the old one and standing straight and firm, the lithe young branches lifted to the sky, positively looking as if it enjoyed the rain. He peered through the window at it, and smiled. Now why the devil should he suddenly remember that incident, years back, during the war, with the girl who came to work on the land for a few months at the neighbouring farm? He did not suppose he had thought of her in months. Besides, there was nothing to it. At weekends he had helped them at the farm himself – war work of a sort – and she was always there, cheerful and pretty and smiling; she had dark curling hair, crisp and boyish, and a skin like a very young apple.

He looked forward to seeing her, Saturdays and Sundays; it was an antidote to the inevitable news bulletins put on throughout the day by Midge, and to ceaseless war talk. He liked looking at the child – she was scarcely more than that, nineteen or so – in her slim breeches and gay shirts; and when she smiled it was as though she embraced the world.

He never knew how it happened, and it was such a little thing; but one afternoon he was in the shed doing something to the tractor, bending over the engine, and she was beside him, close to his shoulder, and they were laughing together; and he turned round, to take a bit of waste to clean a plug, and suddenly she was in his arms and he was kissing her. It was a happy thing, spontaneous and free, and the girl so warm and jolly, with her fresh young mouth. Then they went on with the work of the tractor, but united now, in a kind of intimacy that brought gaiety to them both, and peace as well. When it was time for the girl to go and feed the pigs he followed her from the shed, his hand on her shoulder, a careless gesture that meant nothing really, a half caress; and as they came out into the yard he saw Midge standing there, staring at them.

'I've got to go in to a Red Cross meeting,' she said. 'I can't get the car to start. I called you. You didn't seem to hear.'

Her face was frozen. She was looking at the girl. At once guilt covered him. The girl said good evening cheerfully to Midge, and crossed the yard to the pigs.

He went with Midge to the car and managed to start it with the handle. Midge thanked him, her voice without expression. He found himself unable to meet her eyes. This, then, was adultery. This was sin. This was the second page in a Sunday newspaper – 'Husband Intimate with Land Girl in Shed. Wife Witnesses Act.' His hands were shaking when he got back to the house and he had to pour himself a drink. Nothing was ever said. Midge never mentioned the matter. Some craven instinct kept him from the farm the next weekend, and then he heard that the girl's mother had been taken ill and she had been called back home.

He never saw her again. Why, he wondered, should he remember her suddenly, on such a day, watching the rain falling on the apple trees? He must certainly make a point of cutting down the old dead tree, if only for the sake of bringing more sunshine to the little sturdy one; it hadn't a fair chance, growing there so close to the other.

On Friday afternoon he went round to the vegetable garden to find Willis, the jobbing gardener, who came three days a week, to pay him his wages. He wanted, too, to look in the toolshed and see if the axe and saw were in good condition. Willis kept everything neat and tidy there – this was Midge's training – and the axe and saw were hanging in their accustomed place upon the wall.

He paid Willis his money, and was turning away when the man suddenly said to him, 'Funny thing, sir, isn't it, about the old apple tree?'

The remark was so unexpected that it came as a shock. He felt himself change colour.

'Apple tree? What apple tree?' he said.

'Why, the one at the far end, near the terrace,' answered Willis. 'Been barren as long as I've worked here, and that's some years now. Never an apple from her, nor as much as a sprig of blossom. We were going to chop her up that cold winter, if you remember, and we never did. Well, she's taken on a new lease now. Haven't you noticed?' The gardener watched him smiling, a knowing look in his eye.

What did the fellow mean? It was not possible that he had been struck also by that fantastic freak resemblance – no, it was out of the question, indecent, blasphemous; besides, he had put it out of his own mind now, he had not thought of it again.

'I've noticed nothing,' he said, on the defensive.

Willis laughed. 'Come round to the terrace, sir,' he said, 'I'll show you.'

They went together to the sloping lawn, and when they came to the apple tree Willis put his hand up and pulled down a branch within reach. It creaked a little as he did so, as though stiff and unyielding, and Willis brushed away some of the dry lichen and revealed the spiky twigs. 'Look there, sir,' he said, 'she's growing buds. Look at them, feel them for yourself. There's life here yet, and plenty of it. Never known such a thing before. See this branch too.' He released the first, and leant up to reach another.

Willis was right. There were buds in plenty, but so small and brown that it seemed to him they scarcely deserved the name, they were more like blemishes upon the twig, dusty and dry. He put his hands in his pockets. He felt a queer distaste to touch them.

'I don't think they'll amount to much,' he said.

'I don't know, sir,' said Willis, 'I've got hopes. She's stood the winter, and if we get no more bad frosts there's no knowing what we'll see. It would be some joke to watch the old tree blossom. She'll bear fruit yet.' He patted the trunk with his open hand, in a gesture at once familiar and affectionate.

The owner of the apple tree turned away. For some reason he felt irritated with Willis. Anyone would think the damned tree lived. And now his plan to axe the tree, over the weekend, would come to nothing.

'It's taking the light from the young tree,' he said. 'Surely it would be more to the point if we did away with this one, and gave the little one more room?'

He moved across to the young tree and touched a limb. No lichen here. The branches smooth. Buds upon every twig, curling tight. He let go the branch and it sprang away from him, resilient.

'Do away with her, sir,' said Willis, 'while there's still life in her? Oh no, sir, I wouldn't do that. She's doing no harm to the young tree. I'd give the old tree one more chance. If she doesn't bear fruit, we'll have her down next winter.'

'All right, Willis,' he said, and walked swiftly away. Somehow he did not want to discuss the matter any more.

That night, when he went to bed, he opened the window wide as usual and drew back the curtains; he could not bear to wake up in the morning and find the room close. It was full moon, and the light shone down upon the terrace and the lawn above it, ghostly pale and still. No wind blew. A hush upon the place. He leant out, loving the silence. The moon shone full upon the little apple tree, the young one. There was a radiance about it in this light that gave it a fairy-tale quality. Small and lithe and slim, the young tree might have been a dancer, her arms upheld, poised ready on her toes for flight. Such a careless, happy grace about it. Brave young tree. Away to the left stood the other one, half of it in shadow still. Even the moonlight could not give it beauty. What in heaven's name was the matter with the thing that it had to stand there, humped and stooping, instead of looking upwards to the light? It marred the still quiet night, it spoilt the setting. He had been a fool to give way to Willis and agree to spare the tree. Those ridiculous buds would never blossom, and even if they did . . .

His thoughts wandered, and for the second time that week he found himself remembering the land-girl and her joyous smile. He wondered what had happened to her. Married probably, with a young family. Made some chap happy, no doubt. Oh, well . . . He smiled. Was he going to make use of that expression now? Poor Midge! Then he caught his breath and stood quite still, his hand upon the curtain. The apple tree, the one on the left, was no longer in shadow. The moon shone upon the withered branches, and they looked like skeleton's arms raised in supplication. Frozen arms, stiff and numb with pain. There was no wind, and the other trees were motionless; but there, in those topmost branches, something shivered and stirred, a breeze that came from nowhere and died away again. Suddenly a branch fell from the apple tree to the ground below. It was the near branch, with the small dark buds upon it, which he would not touch. No rustle, no breath of movement came from the other trees. He went on staring at the branch as it lay there on the grass, under the moon. It stretched across the shadow of the young tree close to it, pointing as though in accusation.

For the first time in his life that he could remember he drew the curtains over the window to shut out the light of the moon.

*   *   *

Willis was supposed to keep to the vegetable garden. He had never shown his face much round the front when Midge was alive. That was because Midge attended to the flowers. She even used to mow the grass, pushing the wretched machine up and down the slope, her back bent low over the handles.

It had been one of the tasks she set herself, like keeping the bedrooms swept and polished. Now Midge was no longer there to attend to the front garden and to tell him where he should work, Willis was always coming through to the front. The gardener liked the change. It made him feel responsible.

'I can't understand how that branch came to fall, sir,' he said on the Monday.

'What branch?'

'Why, the branch on the apple tree. The one we were looking at before I left.'

'It was rotten, I suppose. I told you the tree was dead.'

'Nothing rotten about it, sir. Why, look at it. Broke clean off.'

Once again the owner was obliged to follow his man up the slope above the terrace. Willis picked up the branch. The lichen upon it was wet, bedraggled looking, like matted hair.

'You didn't come again to test the branch, over the weekend, and loosen it in some fashion, did you, sir?' asked the gardener.

'I most certainly did not,' replied the owner, irritated. 'As a matter of fact I heard the branch fall, during the night. I was opening the bedroom window at the time.'

'Funny. It was a still night too.'

'These things often happen to old trees. Why you bother about this one I can't imagine. Anyone would think ...'

He broke off; he did not know how to finish the sentence.

'Anyone would think that the tree was valuable,' he said.

The gardener shook his head. 'It's not the value,' he said. 'I don't reckon for a moment that this tree is worth any money at all. It's just that after all this time, when we thought her dead, she's alive and kicking, as you might say. Freak of nature, I call it. We'll hope no other branches fall before she blossoms.'

Later, when the owner set off for his afternoon walk, he saw the man cutting away the grass below the tree and placing new wire around the base of the trunk. It was quite ridiculous. He did not pay the fellow a fat wage to tinker about with a half-dead tree. He ought to be in the kitchen garden, growing vegetables. It was too much effort, though, to argue with him.

He returned home about half past five. Tea was a discarded meal since Midge had died, and he was looking forward to his armchair by the fire, his pipe, his whisky and soda, and silence.

The fire had not long been lit and the chimney was smoking. There was a queer, rather sickly smell about the living-room. He threw open the windows and went upstairs to change his heavy shoes. When he came down again the smoke still clung about the room and the smell was as strong as ever. Impossible to name it. Sweetish, strange. He called to the woman out in the kitchen.

'There's a funny smell in the house,' he said. 'What is it?'

The woman came out into the hall from the back.

'What sort of a smell, sir?' she said, on the defensive.

'It's in the living-room,' he said. 'The room was full of smoke just now. Have you been burning something?'

Her face cleared. 'It must be the logs,' she said. 'Willis cut them up specially, sir, he said you would like them.'

'What logs are those?'

'He said it was apple wood, sir, from a branch he had sawed up. Apple wood burns well, I've always heard. Some people fancy it very much. I don't notice any smell myself, but I've got a slight cold.'

Together they looked at the fire. Willis had cut the logs small. The woman, thinking to please him, had piled several on top of one another, to make a good fire to last. There was no great blaze. The smoke that came from them was thin and poor. Greenish in colour. Was it possible she did notice that sickly rancid smell?

'The logs are wet,' he said abruptly. 'Willis should have known better. Look at them. Quite useless on my fire.'

The woman's face took on a set, rather sulky expression. 'I'm very sorry,' she said. 'I didn't notice anything wrong with them when I came to light the fire. They seemed to start well. I've always understood apple wood was very good for burning, and Willis said the same. He told me to be sure and see that you had these on the fire this evening, he had made a special job of cutting them for you. I thought you knew about it and had given orders.'

'Oh, all right,' he answered, abruptly. 'I dare say they'll burn in time. It's not your fault.'

He turned his back on her and poked at the fire, trying to separate the logs. While she remained in the house there was nothing he could do. To remove the damp smouldering logs and throw them somewhere round the back, and then light the fire afresh with dry sticks would arouse comment. He would have to go through the kitchen to the back passage where the kindling wood was kept, and she would stare at him, and come forward and say, 'Let me do it, sir. Has the fire gone out then?' No, he must wait until after supper, when she had cleared away and washed up and gone off for the night. Meanwhile, he would endure the smell of the apple wood as best he could.

He poured out his drink, lit his pipe and stared at the fire. It gave out no heat at all, and with the central heating off in the house the living-room struck chill. Now and again a thin wisp of the greenish smoke puffed from the logs, and with it seemed to come that sweet sickly smell, unlike any sort of wood smoke that he knew. That interfering fool of a gardener ... Why saw up the logs? He must have known they were damp. Riddled with damp. He leant forward, staring more closely. Was it damp, though, that oozed there in a thin trickle from the pale logs? No, it was sap, unpleasant, slimy.

He seized the poker, and in a fit of irritation thrust it between the logs, trying to stir them to flame, to change that green smoke into a normal blaze. The effort was useless. The logs would not burn. And all the while the trickle of sap ran on to the grate and the sweet smell filled the room, turning his stomach. He took his glass and his book and went and turned on the electric fire in the study and sat in there instead.

It was idiotic. It reminded him of the old days, how he would make a pretence of writing letters, and go and sit in the study because of Midge in the living-room. She had a habit of yawning in the evenings, when her day's work was done; a habit of which she was quite unconscious. She would settle herself on the sofa with her knitting, the click-click of the needles going fast and furious; and suddenly they would start, those shattering yawns, rising from the depths of her, a prolonged 'Ah ... Ah ... Hi-Oh!' followed by the inevitable sigh. Then there would be silence except for the knitting needles, but as he sat behind his book, waiting, he knew that within a few minutes another yawn would come, another sigh.

A hopeless sort of anger used to stir within him, a longing to throw down his book and say, 'Look, if you are so tired, wouldn't it be better if you went to bed?'

Instead, he controlled himself, and after a little while, when he could bear it no longer, he would get up and leave the living-room, and take refuge in the study. Now he was doing the same thing, all over again, because of the apple logs. Because of the damned sickly smell of the smouldering wood.

He went on sitting in his chair by the desk, waiting for supper. It was nearly nine o'clock before the daily woman had cleared up, turned down his bed and gone for the night.

He returned to the living-room, which he had not entered since leaving it earlier in the evening. The fire was out. It had made some effort to burn, because the logs were thinner than they had been before, and had sunk low into the basket grate. The ash was meagre, yet the sickly smell clung to the dying embers. He went out into the kitchen and found an empty scuttle and brought it back into the living-room. Then he lifted the logs into it, and the ashes too. There must have been some damp residue in the scuttle, or the logs were still not dry, because as they settled there they seemed to turn darker than before, with a kind of scum upon them. He carried the scuttle down to the cellar, opened the door of the central heating furnace, and threw the lot inside.

He remembered then, too late, that the central heating had been given up now for two or three weeks, owing to the spring weather, and that unless he relit it now the logs would remain there, untouched, until the following winter. He found paper, matches, and a can of paraffin, and setting the whole alight closed the door of the furnace, and listened to the roar of flames. That would settle it. He waited a moment and then went up the steps, back to the kitchen passage, to lay and relight the fire in the living-room. The business took time, he had to find kindling and coal, but with patience he got the new fire started, and finally settled himself down in his arm-chair before it.

He had been reading perhaps for twenty minutes before he became aware of the banging door. He put down his book and listened. Nothing at first. Then, yes, there it was again. A rattle, a slam of an unfastened door in the kitchen quarters. He got up and went along to shut it. It was the door at the top of the cellar stairs. He could have sworn he had fastened it. The catch must have worked loose in some way. He switched on the light at the head of the stairs, and bent to examine the catch. There seemed nothing wrong with it. He was about to close the door firmly when he noticed the smell again. The sweet sickly smell of smouldering apple wood. It was creeping up from the cellar, finding its way to the passage above.

Suddenly, for no reason, he was seized with a kind of fear, a feeling of panic almost. What if the smell filled the whole house through the night, came up from the kitchen quarters to the floor above, and while he slept found its way into his bedroom, choking him, stifling him, so that he could not breathe? The thought was ridiculous, insane – and yet ...

Once more he forced himself to descend the steps into the cellar. No sound came from the furnace, no roar of flames. Wisps of smoke, thin and green, oozed their way from the fastened furnace door; it was this that he had noticed from the passage above.

He went to the furnace and threw open the door. The paper had all burnt away, and the few shavings with them. But the logs, the apple logs, had not burnt at all. They lay there as they had done when he threw them in, one charred limb above another, black and huddled, like the bones of someone darkened and dead by fire. Nausea rose in him. He thrust his handkerchief into his mouth, choking. Then, scarcely knowing what he did, he ran up the steps to find the empty scuttle, and with a shovel and tongs tried to pitch the logs back into it, scraping for them through the narrow door of the furnace. He was retching in his belly all the while. At last the scuttle was filled, and he carried it up the steps and through the kitchen to the back door.

He opened the door. Tonight there was no room and it was raining. Turning up the collar of his coat he peered about him in the darkness, wondering where he should throw the logs. Too wet and dark to stagger all the way to the kitchen garden and chuck them on the rubbish heap, but in the field behind the garage the grass was thick and long and they might lie there hidden. He crunched his way over the gravel drive, and coming to the fence beside the field threw his burden on to the concealing grass. There they could rot and perish, grow sodden with rain, and in the end become part of the mouldy earth; he did not care. The responsibility was his no longer. They were out of his house, and it did not matter what became of them.

He returned to the house, and this time made sure the cellar door was fast. The air was clear again, the smell had gone.

He went back to the living-room to warm himself before the fire, but his hands and feet, wet with the rain, and his stomach, still queasy from the pungent smoke, combined together to chill his whole person, and he sat there, shuddering.

He slept badly when he went to bed that night, and awoke in the morning feeling out of sorts. He had a headache, and an ill-tasting tongue. He stayed indoors. His liver was thoroughly upset. To relieve his feelings he spoke sharply to the daily woman.

'I've caught a bad chill,' he said to her, 'trying to get warm last night. So much for apple wood. The smell of it has affected my inside as well. You can tell Willis, when he comes tomorrow.'

She looked at him in disbelief.

'I'm sure I'm very sorry,' she said. 'I told my sister about the wood last night, when I got home, and that you had not fancied it. She said it was most unusual. Apple wood is considered quite a luxury to burn, and burns well, what's more.'

'This lot didn't, that's all I know,' he said to her, 'and I never want to see any more of it. As for the smell ... I can taste it still, it's completely turned me up.'

Her mouth tightened. 'I'm sorry,' she said. And then, as she left the dining-room, her eye fell on the empty whisky bottle on the sideboard. She hesitated a moment, then put it on her tray.

'You've finished with this, sir?' she said.

Of course he had finished with it. It was obvious. The bottle was empty. He realized the implication, though. She wanted to suggest that the idea of apple-wood smoke upsetting him was all my eye, he had done himself too well. Damned impertinence.

'Yes,' he said, 'you can bring another in its place.'

That would teach her to mind her own business.

He was quite sick for several days, queasy and giddy, and finally rang up the doctor to come and have a look at him. The story of the apple wood sounded nonsense, when he told it, and the doctor, after examining him, appeared unimpressed.

'Just a chill on the liver,' he said, 'damp feet, and possibly something you've eaten combined. I hardly think wood smoke has much to do with it. You ought to take more exercise, if you're inclined to have a liver. Play golf. I don't know how I should keep fit without my weekend golf.' He laughed, packing up his bag. 'I'll make you up some medicine,' he said, 'and once this rain has cleared off I should get out and into the air. It's mild enough, and all we want now is a bit of sunshine to bring everything on. Your garden is farther ahead than mine. Your fruit trees are ready to blossom.' And then, before leaving the room, he added, 'You mustn't forget, you had a bad shock a few months ago. It takes time to get over these things. You're still missing your wife, you know. Best thing is to get out and about and see people. Well, take care of yourself.'

His patient dressed and went downstairs. The fellow meant well, of course, but his visit had been a waste of time. 'You're still missing your wife, you know.' How little the doctor understood. Poor Midge ... At least he himself had the honesty to admit that he did not miss her at all, that now she was gone he could breathe, he was free, and that apart from the upset liver he had not felt so well for years.

During the few days he had spent in bed the daily woman had taken the opportunity to spring-clean the living-room. An unnecessary piece of work, but he supposed it was part of the legacy Midge had left behind her. The room looked scrubbed and straight and much too tidy. His own personal litter cleared, books and papers neatly stacked. It was an infernal nuisance, really, having anyone to do for him at all. It would not take much for him to sack her and fend for himself as best he could. Only the bother, the tie of cooking and washing up, prevented him. The ideal life, of course, was that led by a man out East, or in the South Seas, who took a native wife. No problem there. Silence, good service, perfect waiting, excellent cooking, no need for conversation; and then, if you wanted something more than that, there she was, young, warm, a companion for the dark hours. No criticism ever, the obedience of an animal to its master, and the light-hearted laughter of a child. Yes, they had wisdom all right, those fellows who broke away from convention. Good luck to them.

He strolled over to the window and looked out up the sloping lawn. The rain was stopping and tomorrow it would be fine; he would be able to get out, as the doctor had suggested. The man was right, too, about the fruit trees. The little one near the steps was in flower already, and a blackbird had perched himself on one of the branches, which swayed slightly under his weight.

The raindrops glistened and the opening buds were very curled and pink, but when the sun broke through tomorrow they would turn white and soft against the blue of the sky. He must find his old camera, and put a film in it, and photograph the little tree. The others would be in flower, too, during the week. As for the old one, there on the left, it looked as dead as ever; or else the so-called buds were so brown they did not show up from this distance. Perhaps the shedding of the branch had been its finish. And a good job too.

He turned away from the window and set about rearranging the room to his taste, spreading his things about. He liked pottering, opening drawers, taking things out and putting them back again. There was a red pencil in one of the side tables that must have slipped down behind a pile of books and been found during the turn-out. He sharpened it, gave it a sleek fine point. He found a new film in another drawer, and kept it out to put in his camera in the morning. There were a number of papers and old photographs in the drawer, heaped in a jumble, and snapshots too, dozens of them. Midge used to look after these things at one time and put them in albums; then during the war she must have lost interest, or had too many other things to do.

All this junk could really be cleared away. It would have made a fine fire the other night, and might have got even the apple logs to burn. There was little sense in keeping any of it. This appalling photo of Midge, for instance, taken heaven knows how many years ago, not long after their marriage, judging from the style of it. Did she really wear her hair that way? That fluffy mop, much to thick and bushy for her face, which was long and narrow even then. The low neck, pointing to a V, and the dangling ear-rings, and the smile, too eager, making her mouth seem larger than it was. In the left-hand corner she had written 'To my own darling Buzz, from his loving Midge'. He had completely forgotten his old nickname. It had been dropped years back, and he seemed to remember he had never cared for it: he had found it ridiculous and embarrassing and had chided her for using it in front of people.

He tore the photograph in half and threw it on the fire. He watched it curl up upon itself and burn, and the last to go was that vivid smile. My own darling Buzz . . . Suddenly he remembered the evening dress in the photograph. It was green, not her colour ever, turning her sallow; and she had bought it for some special occasion, some big dinner party with friends who were celebrating their wedding anniversary. The idea of the dinner had been to invite all those friends and neighbours who had been married roughly around the same time, which was the reason Midge and he had gone.

There was a lot of champagne, and one or two speeches, and much conviviality, laughter, and joking – some of the joking rather broad – and he remembered that when the evening was over, and they were climbing into the car to drive away, his host, with a gust of laughter, said, 'Try paying your addresses in a top hat, old boy, they say it never fails!' He had been aware of Midge beside him, in that green evening frock, sitting very straight and still, and on her face that same smile which she had worn in the photograph just destroyed, eager yet uncertain, doubtful of the meaning of the words that her host, slightly intoxicated, had let fall upon the evening air, yet wishing to seem advanced, anxious to please, and more than either of these things desperately anxious to attract.

When he had put the car away in the garage and gone into the house he had found her waiting there, in the living-room, for no reason at all. Her coat was thrown off to show the evening dress, and the smile, rather uncertain, was on her face.

He yawned, and settling himself down in a chair picked up a book. She waited a little while, then slowly took up her coat and went upstairs. It must have been shortly afterwards that she had that photograph taken. 'My own darling Buzz, from his loving Midge.' He threw a great handful of dry sticks on to the fire. They crackled and split and turned the photograph to ashes. No damp green logs tonight . . .

It was fine and warm the following day. The sun shone, and the birds sang. He had a sudden impulse to go to London. It was a day for sauntering along Bond Street, watching the passing crowds. A day for calling in at his tailors, for having a hair-cut, for eating a dozen oysters at his favourite bar. The chill had left him. The pleasant hours stretched before him. He might even look in at a matinée.

The day passed without incident, peaceful, untiring, just as he had planned, making a change from day-by-day country routine. He drove home about seven o'clock, looking forward to his drink and to his dinner. It was so warm he did not need his overcoat, not even now, with the sun gone down. He waved a hand to the farmer, who happened to be passing the gate as he turned into the drive.

'Lovely day,' he shouted.

The man nodded, smiled. 'Can do with plenty of these from now on,' he shouted back. Decent fellow. They had always been very matey since those war days, when he had driven the tractor.

He put away the car and had a drink, and while waiting for supper took a stroll around the garden. What a difference those hours of sunshine had made to everything. Several daffodils were out, narcissi too, and the green hedgerows fresh and sprouting. As for the apple trees, the buds had burst, and they were all of them in flower. He went to his little favourite and touched the blossom. It felt soft to his hand and he gently shook a bough. It was firm, well-set, and would not fall. The scent was scarcely perceptible as yet, but in a day or two, with a little more sun, perhaps a shower or two, it would come from the open flower and softly fill the air, never pungent, never strong, a modest scent. A scent which you would have to find for yourself, as the bees did. Once found it stayed with you, it lingered always, alluring, comforting, and sweet. He patted the little tree, and went down the steps into the house.

Next morning, at breakfast, there came a knock on the dining-room window, and the daily woman said that Willis was outside and wanted to have a word with him. He asked Willis to step in.

The gardener looked aggrieved. Was it trouble, then?

'I'm sorry to bother you, sir,' he said, 'but I had a few words with Mr Jackson this morning. He's been complaining.'

Jackson was the farmer, who owned the neighbouring fields.

'What's he complaining about?'

'Says I've been throwing wood over the fence into his field, and the young foal out there, with the mare, tripped over it and went lame. I've never thrown wood over the fence in my life, sir. Quite nasty he was, sir. Spoke of the value of the foal, and it might spoil his chances to sell it.'

'I hope you told him, then, it wasn't true.'

'I did, sir. But the point is someone has been throwing wood over the fence. He showed me the very spot. Just behind the garage. I went with

Mr Jackson, and there they were. Logs had been tipped there, sir. I thought it best to come to you about it before I spoke in the kitchen, otherwise you know how it is, there would be unpleasantness.'

He felt the gardener's eye upon him. No way out, of course. And it was Willis's fault in the first place.

'No need to say anything in the kitchen, Willis,' he said. 'I threw the logs there myself. You brought them into the house, without my asking you to do so, with the result that they put out my fire, filled the room with smoke, and ruined an evening. I chucked them over the fence in a devil of a temper, and if they have damaged Jackson's foal you can apologize for me, and tell him I'll pay him compensation. All I ask is that you don't bring any more logs like those into the house again.'

'No sir, I understood they had not been a success. I didn't think, though, that you would go so far as to throw them out.'

'Well, I did. And there's an end to it.'

'Yes, sir.' He made as if to go, but before he left the dining-room he paused and said, 'I can't understand about the logs not burning, all the same. I took a small piece back to the wife, and it burnt lovely in our kitchen, bright as anything.'

'It did not burn here.'

'Anyway, the old tree is making up for one spoilt branch, sir. Have you seen her this morning?'

'No.'

'It's yesterday's sun that has done it, sir, and the warm night. Quite a treat she is, with all the blossom. You should go out and take a look at her directly.'

Willis left the room, and he continued his breakfast.

Presently he went on to the terrace. At first he did not go up on to the lawn; he made a pretence of seeing to other things, of getting the heavy garden seat out, now that the weather was set fair. And then, fetching a pair of clippers, he did a bit of pruning to the few roses, under the windows. Yet, finally, something drew him to the tree.

It was just as Willis said. Whether it was the sun, the warmth, the mild still night, he could not tell; but the small brown buds had unfolded themselves, had ripened into flower, and now spread themselves above his head into a fantastic cloud of white, moist blossom. It grew thickest at the top of the tree, the flowers so clustered together that they looked like wad upon wad of soggy cotton wool, and all of it, from the topmost branches to those nearer to the ground, had this same pallid colour of sickly white.

It did not resemble a tree at all; it might have been a flapping tent, left out in the rain by campers who had gone away, or else a mop, a giant mop, whose streaky surface had been caught somehow by the sun, and so turned bleached. The blossom was too thick, too great a burden for the long thin trunk, and the moisture clinging to it made it heavier still. Already, as if the effort had been too much, the lower flowers, those nearest the ground, were turning brown; yet there had been no rain.

Well, there it was. Willis had been proved right. The tree had blossomed. But instead of blossoming to life, to beauty, it had somehow, deep in nature, gone awry and turned a freak. A freak which did not know its texture or its shape, but thought to please. Almost as though it said, self-conscious, with a smirk, 'Look. All this is for you.'

Suddenly he heard a step behind him. It was Willis.

'Fine sight, sir, isn't it?'

'Sorry, I don't admire it. The blossom is far too thick.'

The gardener stared at him and said nothing. It struck him that Willis must think him very difficult, very hard, and possibly eccentric. He would go and discuss him in the kitchen with the daily woman.

He forced himself to smile at Willis.

'Look here,' he said, 'I don't mean to damp you. But all this blossom doesn't interest me. I prefer it small and light and colourful, like the little tree. But you take some of it back home, to your wife. Cut as much of it as you like, I don't mind at all. I'd like you to have it.'

He waved his arm, generously. He wanted Willis to go now, and fetch a ladder, and carry the stuff away.

The man shook his head. He looked quite shocked.

'No, thank you, sir, I wouldn't dream of it. It would spoil the tree. I want to wait for the fruit. That's what I'm banking on, the fruit.'

There was no more to be said.

'All right, Willis. Don't bother, then.'

He went back to the terrace. But when he sat down there in the sun, looking up the sloping lawn, he could not see the little tree at all, standing modest and demure above the steps, her soft flowers lifting to the sky. She was dwarfed and hidden by the freak, with its great cloud of sagging petals, already wilting, dingy white, on to the grass beneath. And whichever way he turned his chair, this way or that upon the terrace, it seemed to him that he could not escape the tree, that it stood there above him, reproachful, anxious, desirous of the admiration that he could not give.

*   *   *

That summer he took a longer holiday than he had done for many years – a bare ten days with his old mother in Norfolk, instead of the customary month that he had been used to spend with Midge, and the rest of August and the whole of September in Switzerland and Italy.

He took his car, and so was free to motor from place to place as the mood inclined. He cared little for sight-seeing or excursions, and was not much of a climber. What he liked most was to come upon a little town in the cool of the evening, pick out a small but comfortable hotel, and then stay there, if it pleased him, for two or three days at a time, doing nothing, mooching.

He liked sitting about in the sun all morning, at some café or restaurant, with a glass of wine in front of him, watching the people; so many gay young creatures seemed to travel nowadays. He enjoyed the chatter of conversation around him, as long as he did not have to join in; and now and again a smile would come his way, a word or two of greeting from some guest in the same hotel, but nothing to commit him, merely a sense of being in the swim, of being a man of leisure on his own, abroad.

The difficulty in the old days, on holiday anywhere with Midge, would be her habit of striking up acquaintance with people, some other couple who struck her as looking 'nice' or, as she put it, 'our sort'. It would start with conversation over coffee, and then pass on to mutual planning of shared days, car drives in foursomes – he could not bear it, the holiday would be ruined.

Now, thank heaven, there was no need for this. He did what he liked, in his own time. There was no Midge to say, 'Well, shall we be moving?' when he was still sitting contentedly over his wine, no Midge to plan a visit to some old church that did not interest him.

He put on weight during his holiday, and he did not mind. There was no one to suggest a good long walk to keep fit after the rich food, thus spoiling the pleasant somnolence that comes with coffee and dessert; no one to glance, surprised, at the sudden wearing of a jaunty shirt, a flamboyant tie.

Strolling through the little towns and villages, hatless, smoking a cigar, receiving smiles from the jolly young folk around him, he felt himself a dog. This was the life, no worries, no cares. No 'We have to be back on the fifteenth because of that committee meeting at the hospital'; no 'We can't possibly leave the house shut up for longer than a fortnight, something might happen'. Instead, the bright lights of a little country fair, in a village whose name he did not even bother to find out; the tinkle of music, boys and girls laughing, and he himself, after a bottle of the local wine, bowing to a young thing with a gay handkerchief round her head and sweeping her off to dance under the hot tent. No matter if her steps did not harmonize with his – it was years since he had danced – this was the thing, this was it. He released her when the music stopped, and off she ran, giggling, back to her young friends, laughing at him no doubt. What of it? He had had his fun.

He left Italy when the weather turned, at the end of September, and was back home the first week in October. No problem to it. A telegram to the daily woman, with the probable date of arrival, and that was all.

Even a brief holiday with Midge and the return meant complications. Written instructions about groceries, milk, and bread; airing of beds, lighting of fires, reminders about the delivery of the morning papers. The whole business turned into a chore.

He turned into the drive on a mellow October evening and there was smoke coming from the chimneys, the front door open, and his pleasant home awaiting him. No rushing through to the back regions to learn of possible plumbing disasters, breakages, water shortages, food difficulties; the daily woman knew better than to bother him with these. Merely, 'Good evening, sir. I hope you had a good holiday. Supper at the usual time?' And then silence. He could have his drink, light his pipe, and relax; the small pile of letters did not matter. No feverish tearing of them open, and then the start of the telephoning, the hearing of those endless one-sided conversations between women friends. 'Well? How are things? Really? My dear ... And what did you say to that? ... She did? ... I can't possibly on Wednesday...'

He stretched himself contentedly, stiff after his drive, and gazed comfortably around the cheerful, empty living-room. He was hungry, after his journey up from Dover, and the chop seemed rather meagre after foreign fare. But there it was, it wouldn't hurt him to return to plainer food. A sardine on toast followed the chop, and then he looked about him for dessert.

There was a plate of apples on the sideboard. He fetched them and put them down in front of him on the dining-room table. Poor-looking things. Small and wizened, dullish brown in colour. He bit into one, but as soon as the taste of it was on his tongue he spat it out. The thing was rotten. He tried another. It was just the same. He looked more closely at the pile of apples. The skins were leathery and rough and hard; you would expect the insides to be sour. On the contrary they were pulpy soft, and the cores were yellow. Filthy-tasting things. A stray piece stuck to his tooth and he pulled it out. Stringy, beastly...

He rang the bell, and the woman came through from the kitchen.

'Have we any other dessert?' he said.

'I am afraid not, sir. I remembered how fond you were of apples, and Willis brought in these from the garden. He said they were especially good, and just ripe for eating.'

'Well, he's quite wrong. They're uneatable.'

'I'm very sorry, sir. I wouldn't have put them through had I known. There's a lot more outside, too. Willis brought in a great basketful.'

'All the same sort?'

'Yes, sir. The small brown ones. No other kind at all.'

'Never mind, it can't be helped. I'll look for myself in the morning.'

He got up from the table and went through to the living-room. He had a glass of port to take away the taste of the apples, but it seemed to make no difference, not even a biscuit with it. The pulpy rotten tang clung to his tongue and the roof of his mouth, and in the end he was obliged to go up to the bathroom and clean his teeth. The maddening thing was that he could have done with a good clean apple, after that rather indifferent supper; something with a smooth clear skin, the inside not too sweet, a little sharp in flavour. He knew the kind. Good biting texture. You had to pick them, of course, at just the right moment.

He dreamt that night he was back again in Italy, dancing under the tent in the little cobbled square. He woke with the tinkling music in his ear, but he could not recall the face of the peasant girl or remember the feel of her, tripping against his feet. He tried to recapture the memory, lying awake, over his morning tea, but it eluded him.

He got up out of bed and went over to the window, to glance at the weather. Fine enough, with a slight nip in the air.

Then he saw the tree. The sight of it came as a shock, it was so unexpected. Now he realized at once where the apples had come from the night before. The tree was laden, bowed down, under the burden of fruit. They clustered, small and brown, on every branch, diminishing in size as they reached the top, so that those on the high boughs, not grown yet to full size, looked like nuts. They weighed heavy on the tree, and because of this it seemed bent and twisted out of shape, the lower branches nearly sweeping the ground; and on the grass, at the foot of the tree, were more and yet more apples, windfalls, the first-grown, pushed off by their clamouring brothers and sisters. The ground was covered with them, many split open and rotting where the wasps had been. Never in his life had he seen a tree so laden with fruit. It was a miracle that it had not fallen under the weight.

He went out before breakfast – curiosity was too great – and stood beside the tree, staring at it. There was no mistake about it, these were the same apples that had been put in the dining-room last night. Hardly bigger than tangerines, and many of them smaller than that, they grew so close together on the branches that to pick one you would be forced to pick a dozen.

There was something monstrous in the sight, something distasteful; yet it was pitiful too that the months had brought this agony upon the tree, for agony it was, there could be no other word for it. The tree was tortured by fruit, groaning under the weight of it, and the frightful part about it was that not one of the fruit was eatable. Every apple was rotten through and through. He trod them underfoot, the windfalls on the grass, there was no escaping them; and in a moment they were mush and slime, clinging about his heels – he had to clean the mess off with wisps of grass.

It would have been far better if the tree had died, stark and bare, before this ever happened. What use was it to him or anyone, this load of rotting fruit, littering up the place, fouling the ground? And the tree itself, humped, as it were, in pain, and yet he could almost swear triumphant, gloating.

Just as in spring, when the mass of fluffy blossom, colourless and sodden, dragged the reluctant eye away from the other trees, so it did now. Impossible to avoid seeing the tree, with its burden of fruit. Every window in the front part of the house looked out upon it. And he knew how it would be. The fruit would cling there until it was picked, staying upon the branches through October and November, and it never would be picked, because nobody could eat it. He could see himself being bothered with the tree throughout the autumn. Whenever he came out onto the terrace there it would be, sagging and loathsome.

It was extraordinary the dislike he had taken to the tree. It was a perpetual reminder of the fact that he ... well, he was blessed if he knew what ... a perpetual reminder of all the things he most detested, and always had, he could not put a name to them. He decided then and there that Willis should pick the fruit and take it away, sell it, get rid of it, anything, as long as he did not have to eat it, and as long as he was not forced to watch the tree drooping there, day after day, throughout the autumn.

He turned his back upon it and was relieved to see that none of the other trees had so degraded themselves to excess. They carried a fair crop, nothing out of the way, and as he might have known the young tree, to the right of the old one, made a brave little show on its own, with a light load of medium-sized, rosy-looking apples, not too dark in colour, but freshly reddened where the sun had ripened them. He would pick one now, and take it in, to eat with breakfast. He made his choice, and the apple fell at the first touch into his hand. It looked so good that he bit into it with appetite. That was it, juicy, sweet-smelling, sharp, the dew upon it still. He did not look back at the old tree. He went indoors, hungry, to breakfast.

It took the gardener nearly a week to strip the tree, and it was plain he did it under protest.

'I don't care what you do with them,' said his employer. 'You can sell them and keep the money, or you can take them home and feed them to your pigs. I can't stand the sight of them, and that's all there is to it. Find a long ladder, and start on the job right away.'

It seemed to him that Willis, from sheer obstinacy, spun out the time. He would watch the man from the windows act as though in slow motion. First the placing of the ladder. Then the laborious climb, and the descent to steady it again. After that the performance of plucking off the fruit, dropping them, one by one, into the basket. Day after day it was the same. Willis was always there on the sloping lawn with his ladder, under the tree, the branches creaking and groaning, and beneath him on the grass baskets, pails, basins, any receptacle that would hold the apples.

At last the job was finished. The ladder was removed, the baskets and pails also, and the tree was stripped bare. He looked out at it, the evening of that day, in satisfaction. No more rotting fruit to offend his eye. Every single apple gone.

Yet the tree, instead of seeming lighter from the loss of its burden, looked, if it were possible, more dejected than ever. The branches still sagged, and the leaves, withering now to the cold autumnal evening, folded upon themselves and shivered. 'Is this my reward?' it seemed to say. 'After all I've done for you?'

As the light faded, the shadow of the tree cast a blight upon the dank night. Winter would soon come. And the short, dull days.

*   *   *

He had never cared much for the fall of the year. In the old days, when he went up to London every day to the office, it had meant that early start by train, on a nippy morning. And then, before three o'clock in the afternoon, the clerks were turning on the lights, and as often as not there would be fog in the air, murky and dismal, and a slow chugging journey home, daily bread-ers like himself sitting five abreast in a carriage, some of them with colds in their heads. Then the long evening followed, with Midge opposite him before the living-room fire, and he listening, or feigning to listen, to the account of her days and the things that had gone wrong.

If she had not shouldered any actual household disaster, she would pick upon some current event to cast a gloom. 'I see fares are going up again, what about your season ticket?', or 'This business in South Africa looks nasty, quite a long bit about it on the six o'clock news', or yet again 'Three more cases of polio over at the isolation hospital. I don't know, I'm sure, what the medical world thinks it's doing ...'

Now, at least, he was spared the role of listener, but the memory of those long evenings was with him still, and when the lights were lit and the curtains were drawn he would be reminded of the click-click of the needles, the aimless chatter, and the 'Heigh-ho' of the yawns. He began to drop in, sometimes before supper, sometimes afterwards, at the Green Man, the old public house a quarter of a mile away on the main road. Nobody bothered him there. He would sit in a corner, having said good evening to genial Mrs Hill, the proprietress, and then, with a cigarette and a whisky and soda, watch the local inhabitants stroll in to have a pint, to throw a dart, to gossip.

In a sense it made a continuation of his summer holiday. It bore resemblance, admittedly slight, to the care-free atmosphere of the cafés and the restaurants; and there was a kind of warmth about the bright smoke-filled bar, crowded with working men who did not bother him, which he found pleasant, comforting. These visits cut into the length of the dark winter evenings, making them more tolerable.

A cold in the head, caught in mid-December, put a stop to this for more than a week. He was obliged to keep to the house. And it was odd, he thought to himself, how much he missed the Green Man, and how sick to death he became of sitting about in the living-room or in the study, with nothing to do but read or listen to the wireless. The cold and the boredom made him morose and irritable, and the enforced inactivity turned his liver sluggish. He needed exercise. Whatever the weather, he decided towards the end of yet another cold grim day, he would go out tomorrow. The sky had been heavy from mid-afternoon and threatened snow, but no matter, he could not stand the house for a further twenty-four hours without a break.

The final edge to his irritation came with the fruit tart at supper. He was in that final stage of a bad cold when the taste is not yet fully returned, appetite is poor, but there is a certain emptiness within that needs ministration of a particular kind. A bird might have done it. Half a partridge, roasted to perfection, followed by a cheese soufflé. As well ask for the moon. The daily woman, not gifted with imagination, produced plaice, of all fish the most tasteless, the most dry. When she had borne the remains of this away – he had left most of it upon his plate – she returned with a tart, and because hunger was far from being satisfied he helped himself to it liberally.

One taste was enough. Choking, spluttering, he spat out the contents of his spoon upon the plate. He got up and rang the bell.

The woman appeared, a query on her face, at the unexpected summons.

'What the devil is this stuff?'

'Jam tart, sir.'

'What sort of jam?'

'Apple jam, sir. Made from my own bottling.'

He threw down his napkin on the table.

'I guessed as much. You've been using some of those apples that I complained to you about months ago. I told you and Willis quite distinctly that I would not have any of those apples in the house.'

The woman's face became tight and drawn.

'You said, sir, not to cook the apples, or to bring them in for dessert. You said nothing about not making jam. I thought they would taste all right as jam. And I made some myself, to try. It was perfectly all right. So I made several bottles of jam from the apples Willis gave me. We always made jam here, madam and myself.'

'Well, I'm sorry for your trouble, but I can't eat it. Those apples disagreed with me in the autumn, and whether they are made into jam or whatever you like they will do so again. Take the tart away, and don't let me see it, or the jam, again. I'll have some coffee in the living-room.'

He went out of the room, trembling. It was fantastic that such a small incident should make him feel so angry. God! What fools people were. She knew, Willis knew, that he disliked the apples, loathed the taste and smell of them, but in their cheese-paring way they decided that it would save money if he was given home-made jam, jam made from the apples he particularly detested.

He swallowed down a stiff whisky and lit a cigarette.

In a moment or two she appeared with the coffee. She did not retire immediately on putting down the tray.

'Could I have a word with you, sir?'

'What is it?'

'I think it would be for the best if I gave in my notice.'

Now this, on top of the other. What a day, what an evening.

'What reason? Because I can't eat apple-tart?'

'It's not just that, sir. Somehow I feel things are very different from what they were. I have meant to speak several times.'

'I don't give much trouble, do I?'

'No, sir. Only in the old days, when madam was alive, I felt my work was appreciated. Now it's as though it didn't matter one way or the other. Nothing's ever said, and although I try to do my best I can't be sure. I think I'd be happier if I went where there was a lady again who took notice of what I did.'

'You are the best judge of that, of course. I'm sorry if you haven't liked it here lately.'

'You were away so much too, sir, this summer. When madam was alive it was never for more than a fortnight. Everything seems so changed. I don't know where I am, or Willis either.'

'So Willis is fed up too?'

'That's not for me to say, of course. I know he was upset about the apples, but that's some time ago. Perhaps he'll be speaking to you himself.'

'Perhaps he will. I had no idea I was causing so much concern to you both. All right, that's quite enough. Goodnight.'

She went out of the room. He stared moodily about him. Good riddance to them both, if that was how they felt. Things aren't the same. Everything so changed. Damned nonsense. As for Willis being upset about the apples, what infernal impudence. Hadn't he a right to do what he liked with his own tree? To hell with his cold and with the weather. He couldn't bear sitting about in front of the fire thinking about Willis and the cook. He would go down to the Green Man and forget the whole thing.

He put on his overcoat and muffler and his old cap and walked briskly down the road, and in twenty minutes he was sitting in his usual corner in the Green Man, with Mrs Hill pouring out his whisky and expressing her delight to see him back. One or two of the habitués smiled at him, asked after his health.

'Had a cold, sir? Same everywhere. Everyone's got one.'

'That's right.'

'Well, it's the time of year, isn't it?'

'Got to expect it. It's when it's on the chest it's nasty.'

'No worse than being stuffed up, like, in the head.'

'That's right. One's as bad as the other. Nothing to it.'

Likeable fellows. Friendly. Not harping at one, not bothering.

'Another whisky, please.'

'There you are, sir. Do you good. Keep out the cold.'

Mrs Hill beamed behind the bar. Large, comfortable old soul. Through a haze of smoke he heard the chatter, the deep laughter, the click of the darts, the jocular roar at a bull's eye.

'... and if it comes on to snow, I don't know how we shall manage,' Mrs Hill was saying, 'them being so late delivering the coal. If we had a load of logs it would help us out, but what do you think they're asking? Two pounds a load. I mean to say ...'

He leant forward and his voice sounded far away, even to himself.

'I'll let you have some logs,' he said.

Mrs Hill turned round. She had not been talking to him.

'Excuse me?' she said.

'I'll let you have some logs,' he repeated. 'Got an old tree, up at home, needed sawing down for months. Do it for you tomorrow.'

He nodded, smiling.

'Oh no, sir. I couldn't think of putting you to the trouble. The coal will turn up, never fear.'

'No trouble at all. A pleasure. Like to do it for you, the exercise, you know, do me good. Putting on weight. You count on me.'

He got down from his seat and reached, rather carefully, for his coat.

'It's apple wood,' he said. 'Do you mind apple wood?'

'Why no,' she answered, 'any wood will do. But can you spare it, sir?'

He nodded, mysteriously. It was a bargain, it was a secret.

'I'll bring it down to you in my trailer tomorrow night,' he said.

'Careful, sir,' she said, 'mind the step ...'

He walked home, through the cold crisp night, smiling to himself. He did not remember undressing or getting into bed, but when he woke the next morning the first thought that came to his mind was the promise he had made about the tree.

It was not one of Willis's days, he realized with satisfaction. There would be no interfering with his plan. The sky was heavy and snow had fallen in the night. More to come. But as yet nothing to worry about, nothing to hamper him.

He went through to the kitchen garden, after breakfast, to the tool shed. He took down the saw, the wedges, and the axe. He might need all of them. He ran his thumb along the edges. They would do. As he shouldered his tools and walked back to the front garden he laughed to himself, thinking that he must resemble an executioner of old days, setting forth to behead some wretched victim in the Tower.

He laid his tools down beneath the apple tree. It would be an act of mercy, really. Never had he seen anything so wretched, so utterly woebegone, as the apple tree. There couldn't be any life left in it. Not a leaf remained. Twisted, ugly, bent, it ruined the appearance of the lawn. Once it was out of the way the whole setting of the garden would change.

A snow-flake fell on to his hand, then another. He glanced down past the terrace to the dining-room window. He could see the woman laying his lunch. He went down the steps and into the house. 'Look,' he said, 'if you like to leave my lunch ready in the oven, I think I'll fend for myself today. I may be busy, and I don't want to be pinned down for time. Also it's going to snow. You had better go off early today and get home, in case it becomes really bad. I can manage perfectly well. And I prefer it.'

Perhaps she thought his decision came through offence at her giving notice the night before. Whatever she thought, he did not mind. He wanted to be alone. He wanted no face peering from the window.

She went off at about twelve-thirty, and as soon as she had gone he went to the oven and got his lunch. He meant to get it over, so that he could give up the whole short afternoon to the felling of the tree.

No more snow had fallen, apart from a few flakes that did not lie. He took off his coat, rolled up his sleeves, and seized the saw. With his left hand he ripped away the wire at the base of the tree. Then he placed the saw about a foot from the bottom and began to work it, backwards, forwards.

For the first dozen strokes all went smoothly. The saw bit into the wood, the teeth took hold. Then after a few moments the saw began to bind. He had been afraid of that.

He tried to work it free, but the opening that he had made was not yet large enough, and the tree gripped upon the saw and held it fast. He drove in the first wedge, with no result. He drove in the second, and the opening gaped a little wider, but still not wide enough to release the saw.

He pulled and tugged at the saw, to no avail. He began to lose his temper. He took up his axe and started hacking at the tree, pieces of the trunk flying outwards, scattering on the grass.

That was more like it. That was the answer.

Up and down went the heavy axe, splitting and tearing at the tree. Off came the peeling bark, the great white strips of underwood, raw and stringy. Hack at it, blast at it, gouge at the tough tissue, throw the axe away, claw at the rubbery flesh with the bare hands. Not far enough yet, go on, go on.

There goes the saw, the wedge, released. Now up with the axe again. Down there, heavy, where the stringy threads cling so steadfast. Now she's groaning, now she's splitting, now she's rocking and swaying, hanging there upon one bleeding strip. Boot her, then. That's it, kick her, kick her again, one final blow, she's over, she's falling . . . she's down . . . damn her, blast her . . . she's down, splitting the air with sound, and all her branches spread about her on the ground.

He stood back, wiping the sweat from his forehead, from his chin. The wreckage surrounded him on either side, and below him, at his feet, gaped the torn, white, jagged stump of the axed tree.

It began snowing.

*   *   *

His first task, after felling the apple tree, was to hack off the branches and the smaller boughs, and so to grade the wood in stacks, which made it easier to drag away.

The small stuff, bundled and roped, would do for kindling; Mrs Hill would no doubt be glad of that as well. He brought the car, with the trailer attached, to the garden gate, hard by the terrace. This chopping up of the branches was simple work; much of it could be done with a hook. The fatigue came with bending and tying the bundles, and then heaving them down past the terrace and through the gate up on to the trailer. The thicker branches he disposed of with the axe, then split them into three or four lengths, which he could also rope and drag, one by one, to the trailer.

He was fighting all the while against time. The light, what there was of it, would be gone by half past four, and the snow went on falling. The ground was already covered, and when he paused for a moment in his work, and wiped the sweat away from his face, the thin frozen flakes fell upon his lips and made their way, insidious and soft, down his collar to his neck and body. If he lifted his eyes to the sky he was blinded at once. The flakes came thicker, faster, swirling about his head, and it was as though the heaven had turned itself into a canopy of snow, ever descending, coming nearer, closer, stifling the earth. The snow fell upon the torn boughs and the hacked branches, hampering his work. If he rested but an instant to draw breath and renew his strength, it seemed to throw a protective cover, soft and white, over the pile of wood.

) He could not wear gloves. If he did so he had no grip upon his hook or his axe, nor could he tie the rope and drag the branches. His fingers were number with cold, soon they would be too stiff to bend. He had a pain now, under the heart, from the strain of dragging the stuff on to the trailer; and the work never seemed to lessen. Whenever he returned to the fallen tree the pile of wood would appear as high as ever, long boughs, short boughs, a heap of kindling there, nearly covered with the snow, which he had forgotten: all must be roped and fastened and carried or pulled away.

It was after half past four, and almost dark, when he had disposed of all the branches, and nothing now remained but to drag the trunk, already hacked into three lengths, over the terrace to the waiting trailer.

He was very nearly at the point of exhaustion. Only his will to be rid of the tree kept him to the task. His breath came slowly, painfully, and all the while the snow fell into his mouth and into his eyes and he could barely see.

He took his rope and slid it under the cold slippery trunk, knotting it fiercely. How hard and unyielding was the naked wood, and the bark was rough, hurting his numb hands.

'That's the end of you,' he muttered, 'that's your finish.'

Staggering to his feet he bore the weight of the heavy trunk over his shoulder, and began to drag it slowly down over the slope to the terrace and to the garden gate. It followed him, bump ... bump ... down the steps of the terrace. Heavy and lifeless, the last bare limbs of the apple tree dragged in his wake through the wet snow.

It was over. His task was done. He stood panting, one hand upon the trailer. Now nothing more remained but to take the stuff down to the Green Man before the snow made the drive impossible. He had chains for the car, he had thought of that already.

He went into the house to change the clothes that were clinging to him and to have a drink. Never mind about his fire, never mind about drawing curtains, seeing what there might be for supper, all the chores the daily woman usually did – that would come later. He must have his drink and get the wood away.

His mind was numb and weary, like his hands and his whole body. For a moment he thought of leaving the job until the following day, flopping down into the armchair, and closing his eyes. No, it would not do. Tomorrow there would be more snow, tomorrow the drive would be two or three feet deep. He knew the signs. And there would be the trailer, stuck outside the garden gate, with the pile of wood inside it, frozen white. He must make the effort and do the job tonight.

He finished his drink, changed, and went out to start the car. It was still snowing, but now that darkness had fallen a colder, cleaner feeling had come into the air, and it was freezing. The dizzy, swirling flakes came more slowly now, with precision.

The engine started and he began to drive downhill, the trailer in tow. He drove slowly, and very carefully, because of the heavy load. And it was an added strain, after the hard work of the afternoon, peering

through the falling snow, wiping the windscreen. Never had the lights of
the Green Man shone more cheerfully as he pulled up into the little yard.

He blinked as he stood within the doorway, smiling to himself.

'Well, I've brought your wood,' he said.

Mrs Hill stared at him from behind the bar, one or two fellows
turned and looked at him, and a hush fell upon the dart-players.

'You never . . .' began Mrs Hill, but he jerked his head at the door
and laughed at her.

'Go and see,' he said, 'but don't ask me to unload it tonight.'

He moved to his favourite corner, chuckling to himself, and there
they all were, exclaiming and talking and laughing by the door, and he
was quite a hero, the fellows crowding round with questions, and Mrs
Hill pouring out his whisky and thanking him and laughing and shaking
her head. 'You'll drink on the house tonight,' she said.

'Not a bit of it,' he said, 'this is my party. Rounds one and two on me.
Come on, you chaps.'

It was festive, warm, jolly, and good luck to them all, he kept saying,
good luck to Mrs Hill, and to himself, and to the whole world. When was
Christmas? Next week, the week after? Well, here's to it, and a merry
Christmas. Never mind the snow, never mind the weather. For the first
time he was one of them, not isolated in his corner. For the first time he
drank with them, he laughed with them, he even threw a dart with
them, and there they all were in that warm stuffy smoke-filled bar, and
he felt they liked him, he belonged, he was no longer 'the gentleman'
from the house up the road.

The hours passed, and some of them went home, and others took
their place, and he was still sitting there, hazy, comfortable, the warmth
and the smoke blending together. Nothing of what he heard or saw
made very much sense but somehow it did not seem to matter, for there
was jolly, fat, easy-going Mrs Hill to minister to his needs, her face
glowing at him over the bar.

Another face swung into his view, that of one of the labourers from
the farm, with whom, in the old war days, he had shared the driving of
the tractor. He leant forward, touching the fellow on the shoulder.

'What happened to the little girl?' he said.

The man lowered his tankard. 'Beg pardon, sir?' he said.

'You remember. The little land-girl. She used to milk the cows, feed
the pigs, up at the farm. Pretty girl, dark curly hair, always smiling.'

Mrs Hill turned round from serving another customer.

'Does the gentleman mean May, I wonder?' she asked.

'Yes, that's it, that was the name, young May,' he said.

'Why, didn't you ever hear about it, sir?' said Mrs Hill, filling up his
glass. 'We were all very much shocked at the time, everyone was talking
of it, weren't they, Fred?'

'That's right, Mrs Hill.'

The man wiped his mouth with the back of his hand.

'Killed,' he said, 'thrown from the back of some chap's motorbike. Going to be married very shortly. About four years ago, now. Dreadful thing, eh? Nice kid too.'

'We all sent a wreath, from just around,' said Mrs Hill. 'Her mother wrote back, very touched, and sent a cutting from the local paper, didn't she, Fred? Quite a big funeral they had, ever so many floral tributes. Poor May. We were all fond of May.'

'That's right,' said Fred.

'And fancy you never hearing about it, sir!' said Mrs Hill.

'No,' he said, 'no, nobody ever told me. I'm sorry about it. Very sorry.'

He stared in front of him at his half-filled glass.

The conversation went on around him but he was no longer part of the company. He was on his own again, silent, in his corner. Dead. That poor, pretty girl was dead. Thrown off a motor-bike. Been dead for three or four years. Some careless, bloody fellow, taking a corner too fast, the girl behind him, clinging on to his belt, laughing probably in his ear, and then crash ... finish. No more curling hair, blowing about her face, no more laughter.

May, that was the name; he remembered clearly now. He could see her smiling over her shoulder, when they called to her. 'Coming,' she sang out, and put a clattering pail down in the yard and went off, whistling, with big clumping boots. He had put his arm about her and kissed her for one brief, fleeting moment. May, the land-girl, with the laughing eyes.

'Going, sir?' said Mrs Hill.

'Yes. Yes, I think I'll be going now.'

He stumbled to the entrance and opened the door. It had frozen hard during the past hour and it was no longer snowing. The heavy pall had gone from the sky and the stars shone.

'Want a hand with the car, sir?' said someone.

'No, thank you,' he said, 'I can manage.'

He unhitched the trailer and let it fall. Some of the wood lurched forward heavily. That would do tomorrow. Tomorrow, if he felt like it, he would come down again and help to unload the wood. Not tonight. He had done enough. Now he was really tired; now he was spent.

It took him some time to start the car, and before he was halfway up the side road leading to his house he realized that he had made a mistake by bringing it at all. The snow was heavy all about him, and the track he had made earlier in the evening was now covered. The car lurched and slithered, and suddenly the right wheel dipped and the whole body plunged sideways. He had got into a drift.

He climbed out and looked about him. The car was deep in the drift, impossible to move without two or three men to help him, and even then, if he went for assistance, what hope was there of trying to continue further, with the snow just as thick ahead? Better leave it. Try again in the morning, when he was fresh. No sense in hanging about now, spending half the night pushing and shoving at the car, all to no purpose. No harm would come to it, here on the side road; nobody else would be coming this way tonight.

He started walking up the road towards his own drive. It was bad luck that he had got the car into the drift. In the centre of the road the going was not bad and the snow did not come above his ankles. He thrust his hands deep in the pockets of his overcoat and ploughed on, up the hill, the countryside a great white waste on either side of him.

He remembered that he had sent the daily woman home at midday and that the house would strike cheerless and cold on his return. The fire would have gone out, and in all probability the furnace too. The windows, uncurtained, would stare bleakly down at him, letting in the night. Supper to get into the bargain. Well, it was his own fault. No one to blame but himself. This was the moment when there should be someone waiting, someone to come running through from the living-room to the hall, opening the front-door, flooding the hall with light. 'Are you all right, darling? I was getting anxious.'

He paused for breath at the top of the hill and saw his home, shrouded by trees, at the end of the short drive. It looked dark and forbidding, without a light in any window. There was more friendliness in the open, under the bright stars, standing on the crisp white snow, than in the sombre house.

He had left the side gate open, and he went through that way to the terrace, shutting the gate behind him. What a hush had fallen upon the garden – there was no sound at all. It was as though some spirit had come and put a spell upon the place, leaving it white and still.

He walked softly over the snow towards the apple trees.

Now the young one stood alone, above the steps, dwarfed no longer; and with her branches spread, glistening white, she belonged to the spirit world, a world of fantasy and ghosts. He wanted to stand beside the little tree and touch the branches, to make certain she was still alive, that the snow had not harmed her, so that in the spring she would blossom once again.

She was almost within his reach when he stumbled and fell, his foot twisted underneath him, caught in some obstacle hidden by the snow. He tried to move his foot but it was jammed, and he knew suddenly, by the sharpness of the pain biting his ankle, that what had trapped him was the jagged split stump of the old apple tree he had felled that afternoon.

He leant forward on his elbows, in an attempt to drag himself along the ground, but such was his position, in falling, that his leg was bent backwards, away from his foot, and every effort that he made only succeeded in imprisoning the foot still more firmly in the grip of the trunk. He felt for the ground, under the snow, but where he felt his hands touched the small broken twigs from the apple tree that had scattered there, when the tree fell, and then were covered by the falling snow. He shouted for help, knowing in his heart no one could hear.

'Let me go,' he shouted, 'let me go,' as though the thing that held him there in its mercy had the power to release him, and as he shouted tears of frustration and of fear ran down his face. He would have to lie there all night, held fast in the clutch of the old apple tree. There was no hope, no escape, until they came to find him in the morning, and supposing it was then too late, that when they came he was dead, lying stiffly in the frozen snow?

Once more he struggled to release his foot, swearing and sobbing as he did so. It was no use. He could not move. Exhausted, he laid his head upon his arms, and wept. He sank deeper, ever deeper into the snow, and when a stray piece of brushwood, cold and wet, touched his lips, it was like a hand, hesitant and timid, feeling its way towards him in the darkness.

John Charrington's Wedding
E. Nesbit

No one ever thought that May Forster would marry John Charrington; but he thought differently, and things which John Charrington intended had a queer way of coming to pass. He asked her to marry him before he went up to Oxford. She laughed and refused him. He asked her again next time he came home. Again she laughed, tossed her dainty blonde head and again refused. A third time he asked her; she said it was becoming a confirmed bad habit, and laughed at him more than ever.

John was not the only man who wanted to marry her: she was the belle of our village coterie, and we were all in love with her more or less; it was a sort of fashion, like heliotrope ties or Inverness capes. Therefore we were as much annoyed as surprised when John Charrington walked into our little local Club – we held it in a loft over the saddler's, I remember – and invited us all to his wedding.

'Your wedding?'

'You don't mean it?'

'Who's the happy pair? When's it to be?'

John Charrington filled his pipe and lighted it before he replied. Then he said:

'I'm sorry to deprive you fellows of your only joke – but Miss Forster and I are to be married in September.'

'You don't mean it?'

'He's got the mitten again, and it's turned his head.'

'No,' I said, rising, 'I see it's true. Lend me a pistol someone – or a first-class fare to the other end of Nowhere. Charrington has bewitched the only pretty girl in our twenty-mile radius. Was it mesmerism, or a love-potion, Jack?'

'Neither, sir, but a gift you'll never have – perseverance – and the best luck a man ever had in this world.'

There was something in his voice that silenced me, and all chaff of the other fellows failed to draw him further.

The queer thing about it was that when we congratulated Miss

Forster, she blushed and smiled and dimpled, for all the world as though she were in love with him, and had been in love with him all the time. Upon my word, I think she had. Women are strange creatures.

We were all asked to the wedding. In Brixham everyone who was anybody knew everybody else who was anyone. My sisters were, I truly believe, more interested in the *trousseau* than the bride herself, and I was to be best man. The coming marriage was much canvassed at afternoon tea-tables, and at our little Club over the saddler's, and the question was always asked, 'Does she care for him?'

I used to ask that question myself in the early days of their engagement, but after a certain evening in August I never asked it again. I was coming home from the Club through the churchyard. Our church is on a thyme-grown hill, and the turf about it is so thick and soft that one's footsteps are noiseless.

I made no sound as I vaulted the low lichened wall, and threaded my way between the tombstones. It was at the same instant that I heard John Charrington's voice, and saw her. May was sitting on a low flat gravestone, her face turned towards the full splendour of the western sun. Its expression ended, at once and for ever, any question of love for him; it was transfigured to a beauty I should not have believed possible, even to that beautiful little face.

John lay at her feet, and it was his voice that broke the stillness of the golden August evening.

'My dear, my dear, I believe I should come back from the dead if you wanted me!'

I coughed at once to indicate my presence, and passed on into the shadow fully enlightened.

The wedding was to be early in September. Two days before I had to run up to town on business. The train was late, of course, for we are on the South-Eastern, and as I stood grumbling with my watch in my hand, whom should I see but John Charrington and May Forster. They were walking up and down the unfrequented end of the platform, arm in arm, looking into each other's eyes, careless of the sympathetic interest of the porters.

Of course I knew better than to hesitate a moment before burying myself in the booking-office, and it was not till the train drew up at the platform, that I obtrusively passed the pair with my Gladstone, and took the corner in a first-class smoking-carriage. I did this with as good an air of not seeing them as I could assume. I pride myself on my discretion, but if John were travelling alone I wanted his company. I had it.

'Hullo, old man,' came his cheery voice as he swung his bag into my carriage; 'here's luck; I was expecting a dull journey!'

'Where are you off to?' I asked, discretion still bidding me turn my eyes away, though I saw, without looking, that hers were red-rimmed.

'To old Branbridge's,' he answered, shutting the door and leaning out for a last word with his sweetheart.

'Oh, I wish you wouldn't go, John,' she was saying in a low, earnest voice. 'I feel certain something will happen.'

'Do you think I should let anything happen to keep me, and the day after tomorrow our wedding day?'

'Don't go,' she answered, with a pleading intensity which would have sent my Gladstone on to the platform and me after it. But she wasn't speaking to me. John Charrington was made differently: he rarely changed his opinions, never his resolutions.

He only stroked the little ungloved hands that lay on the carriage door.

'I must, May. The old boy's been awfully good to me, and now he's dying I must go and see him, but I shall come home in time for——' the rest of the parting was lost in a whisper and in the rattling lurch of the starting train.

'You're sure to come?' she spoke as the train moved.

'Nothing shall keep me,' he answered; and we steamed out. After he had seen the last of the little figure on the platform he leaned back in his corner and kept silence for a minute.

When he spoke it was to explain to me that his godfather, whose heir he was, lay dying at Peasmarsh Place, some fifty miles away, and had sent for John, and John had felt bound to go.

'I shall be surely back tomorrow,' he said, 'or, if not, the day after, in heaps of time. Thank heaven, one hasn't to get up in the middle of the night to get married nowadays!'

'And suppose Mr Branbridge dies?'

'Alive or dead I mean to be married on Thursday!' John answered, lighting a cigar and unfolding *The Times*.

At Peasmarsh station we said 'goodbye', and he got out, and I saw him ride off; I went on to London, where I stayed the night.

When I got home the next afternoon, a very wet one, by the way, my sister greeted me with:

'Where's Mr Charrington?'

'Goodness knows,' I answered testily. Every man, since Cain, has resented that kind of question.

'I thought you might have heard from him,' she went on, 'as you're to give him away tomorrow.'

'Isn't he back?' I asked, for I had confidently expected to find him at home.

'No, Geoffrey,' my sister Fanny always had a way of jumping to conclusions, especially such conclusions as were least favourable to her fellow-creatures – 'he has not returned, and, what is more, you may depend upon it he won't. You mark my words, there'll be no wedding tomorrow.'

My sister Fanny has a power of annoying me which no other human being possesses.

'You mark my words,' I retorted with asperity, 'you had better give up making such a thundering idiot of yourself. There'll be more wedding tomorrow than ever you'll take the first part in.' A prophecy which, by the way, came true.

But though I could snarl confidently to my sister, I did not feel so comfortable when late that night, I, standing on the doorstep of John's house, heard that he had not returned. I went home gloomily through the rain. Next morning brought a brilliant blue sky, gold sun, and all such softness of air and beauty of cloud as go to make up a perfect day. I woke with a vague feeling of having gone to bed anxious, and of being rather averse to facing that anxiety in the light of full wakefulness.

But with my shaving-water came a note from John which relieved my mind and sent me up to the Forsters with a light heart.

May was in the garden. I saw her blue gown through the hollyhocks as the lodge gates swung to behind me. So I did not go up to the house, but turned aside down the turfed path.

'He's written to you too,' she said, without preliminary greeting, when I reached her side.

'Yes, I'm to meet him at the station at three, and come straight on to the church.'

Her face looked pale, but there was a brightness in her eyes, and a tender quiver about the mouth that spoke of renewed happiness.

'Mr Branbridge begged him so to stay another night that he had not the heart to refuse,' she went on. 'He is so kind, but I wish he hadn't stayed.'

I was at the station at half past two. I felt rather annoyed with John. It seemed a sort of slight to the beautiful girl who loved him, that he should come as it were out of breath, and with the dust of travel upon him, to take her hand, which some of us would have given the best years of our lives to take.

But when the three o'clock train glided in, and glided out again having brought no passengers to our little station, I was more than annoyed. There was no other train for thirty-five minutes; I calculated that, with much hurry, we might just get to the church in time for the ceremony; but, oh, what a fool to miss that first train! What other man could have done it?

That thirty-five minutes seemed a year, as I wandered round the station reading the advertisements and the timetables, and the company's bye-laws, and getting more and more angry with John Charrington. This confidence in his own power of getting everything he wanted the minute he wanted it was leading him too far. I hate waiting. Everyone does, but I believe I hate it more than anyone else. The three thirty-five was late, of course.

I ground my pipe between my teeth and stamped with impatience as I watched the signals. Click. The signal went down. Five minutes later I flung myself into the carriage that I had brought for John.

'Drive to the church!' I said, as someone shut the door. 'Mr Charrington hasn't come by this train.'

Anxiety now replaced anger. What had become of the man? Could he have been taken suddenly ill? I had never known him have a day's illness in his life. And even so he might have telegraphed. Some awful accident must have happened to him. The thought that he had played her false never – no, not for a moment – entered my head. Yes, something terrible had happened to him, and on me lay the task of telling his bride. I almost wished the carriage would upset and break my head so that someone else might tell her, not I, who – but that's nothing to do with this story.

It was five minutes to four as we drew up at the churchyard gate. A double row of eager onlookers lined the path from lychgate to porch. I sprang from the carriage and passed up between them. Our gardener had a good front place near the door. I stopped.

'Are they waiting still, Byles?' I asked, simply to gain time, for of course I knew they were by the waiting crowd's attentive attitude.

'Waiting, sir? No, no, sir; why, it must be over by now.'

'Over! Then Mr Charrington's come?'

'To the minute, sir; must have missed you somehow, and I say, sir,' lowering his voice, 'I never see Mr John the least bit so afore, but my opinion is he's been drinking pretty free. His clothes was all dusty and his face like a sheet. I tell you I didn't like the looks of him at all, and the folks inside are saying all sorts of things. You'll see, something's gone very wrong with Mr John, and he's tried liquor. He looked like a ghost, and in he went with his eyes straight before him, with never a look or a word for none of us: him that was always such a gentleman!'

I had never heard Byles make so long a speech. The crowd in the churchyard were talking in whispers and getting ready rice and slippers to throw at the bride and bridegroom. The ringers were ready with their hands on the ropes to ring out the merry peal as the bride and bridegroom should come out.

A murmur from the church announced them; out they came. Byles was right. John Charrington did not look himself. There was dust on his coat, his hair was disarranged. He seemed to have been in some row, for there was a black mark above his eyebrow. He was deathly pale. But his pallor was not greater than that of the bride, who might have been carved in ivory – dress, veil, orange blossoms, face and all.

As they passed out the ringers stooped – there were six of them – and then, on the ears expecting the gay wedding peal, came the slow tolling of the passing bell.

A thrill of horror at so foolish a jest from the ringers passed through us all. But the ringers themselves dropped the ropes and fled like rabbits out into the sunlight. The bride shuddered, and grey shadows came about her mouth, but the bridegroom led her on down the path where the people stood with the handfuls of rice; but the handfuls were never thrown, and the wedding bells never rang. In vain the ringers were urged to remedy their mistake: they protested with many whispered expletives that they would see themselves further first.

In a hush like the hush in the chamber of death the bridal pair passed into their carriage and its door slammed behind them.

Then the tongues were loosed. A babel of anger, wonder, conjecture from the guests and the spectators.

'If I'd seen his condition, sir,' said old Forster to me as we drove off, 'I would have stretched him on the floor of the church, sir, by heaven I would, before I'd have let him marry my daughter!'

Then he put his head out of the window.

'Drive like hell,' he cried to the coachman; 'don't spare the horses.'

He was obeyed. We passed the bride's carriage. I forbore to look at it, and old Forster turned his head away and swore. We reached home before it.

We stood in the doorway, in the blazing afternoon sun, and in about half a minute we heard wheels crunching the gravel. When the carriage stopped in front of the steps old Forster and I ran down.

'Great heaven, the carriage is empty! And yet——'

I had the door open in a minute, and this is what I saw ...

No sign of John Charrington; and of May, his wife, only a huddled heap of white satin lying half on the floor of the carriage and half on the seat.

'I drove straight here, sir,' said the coachman, as the bride's father lifted her out; 'and I'll swear no one got out of the carriage.'

We carried her into the house in her bridal dress and drew back her veil. I saw her face. Shall I ever forget it? White, white and drawn with agony and horror, bearing such a look of terror as I have never seen since except in dreams. And her hair, her radiant blonde hair, I tell you it was white like snow.

As we stood, her father and I, half mad with the horror and mystery of it, a boy came up the avenue – a telegraph boy. They brought the orange envelope to me. I tore it open.

Mr Charrington was thrown from the dogcart on his way to the station at half past one. Killed on the spot!

And he was married to May Forster in our parish church at *half past three*, in presence of half the parish.

'*I shall be married, dead or alive!*'

What had passed in that carriage on the homeward drive? No one knows – no one will ever know. Oh, May! oh, my dear!

Before a week was over they laid her beside her husband in our little churchyard on the thyme-covered hill – the churchyard where they had kept their love-trysts.

Thus was accomplished John Charrington's wedding.

Midnight Express
Alfred Noyes

It was a battered old book, bound in red buckram. He found it, when he was twelve years old, on an upper shelf in his father's library; and, against all the rules, he took it to his bedroom to read by candlelight, when the rest of the rambling old Elizabethan house was flooded with darkness. That was how young Mortimer always thought of it. His own room was a little isolated cell, in which, with stolen candle ends, he could keep the surrounding darkness at bay, while everyone else had surrendered to sleep and allowed the outer night to come flooding in. By contrast with those unconscious ones, his elders, it made him feel intensely alive in every nerve and fibre of his young brain. The ticking of the grandfather clock in the hall below; the beating of his own heart; the longdrawn rhythmical 'ah' of the sea on the distant coast, all filled him with a sense of overwhelming mystery; and, as he read, the soft thud of a blinded moth, striking the wall above the candle, would make him start and listen like a creature of the woods at the sound of a cracking twig.

The battered old book had the strangest fascination for him, though he never quite grasped the thread of the story. It was called *The Midnight Express*, and there was one illustration, on the fiftieth page, at which he could never bear to look. It frightened him.

Young Mortimer never understood the effect of that picture on him. He was an imaginative, but not neurotic youngster; and he avoided that fiftieth page as he might have hurried past a dark corner on the stairs when he was six years old, or as the grown man on the lonely road, in the *Ancient Mariner*, who, having once looked round, walks on, and turns no more his head. There was nothing in the picture – apparently – to account for this haunting dread. Darkness, indeed, was almost its chief characteristic. It showed an empty railway platform – at night – lit by a single dreary lamp; an empty railway platform that suggested a deserted and lonely junction in some remote part of the country. There was only one figure on the platform: the dark figure of a man, standing almost directly under the lamp, with his face turned away towards the black mouth of a tunnel, which – for some strange reason – plunged the imagination of the child into a pit of horror. The man seemed to be listening. His attitude was tense, expectant, as though he were awaiting some fearful tragedy. There was nothing in the text, so far as the child read, and could understand, to account for this waking nightmare. He could neither resist the fascination of the book, nor face that picture in the stillness and loneliness of the night. He pinned it down to the page facing it, with two long pins, so that he should not come upon it by accident. Then he determined to read the whole story through. But, always, before he came to page fifty, he fell asleep; and the outlines of what he had read were blurred; and the next night he had to begin again; and again, before he came to the fiftieth page, he fell asleep.

He grew up, and forgot all about the book and the picture. But halfway through his life, at that strange and critical time when Dante entered the dark wood, leaving the direct path behind him, he found himself, a little before midnight, waiting for a train at a lonely junction; and, as the station clock began to strike twelve, he remembered; remembered like a man awaking from a long dream——

*　　*　　*

There, under the single dreary lamp, on the long glimmering platform, was the dark and solitary figure that he knew. Its face was turned away from him towards the black mouth of the tunnel. It seemed be listening, tense, expectant, just as it had been thirty-eight years ago.

But he was not frightened now, as he had been in childhood. He would go up to that solitary figure, confront it, and see the face that had so long been hidden, so long averted from him. He would walk up quietly, and make some excuse for speaking to it: he would ask it, for instance, if the train was going to be late. It should be easy for a grown man to do this; but his hands were clenched, when he took the first step, as if he, too, were tense and expectant. Quietly, but the old vague instincts awaking, he went towards the dark figure under the lamp, passed it, swung round abruptly to speak to it; and saw – without speaking, without being able to speak——

It was himself – staring back at himself – as in some mocking mirror, his own eyes alive in his own white face, looking into his own eyes, alive——

The nerves of his heart tingled as though their own electric currents would paralyse it. A wave of panic went through him. He turned, gasped, stumbled, broke into a blind run, out through the deserted and echoing ticket office, on to the long moonlight road behind the station. The whole countryside seemed to be utterly deserted. The moonbeams flooded it with the loneliness of their own deserted satellite.

He paused for a moment, and heard, like the echo of his own footsteps, the stumbling run of something that followed over the wooden floor within the ticket office. Then he abandoned himself shamelessly to his fear; and ran, sweating like a terrified beast, down the long white road between the two endless lines of ghostly poplars each answering another, into what seemed an infinite distance. On one side of the road there was a long straight canal, in which one of the lines of poplars was again endlessly reflected. He heard the footsteps echoing behind him. They seemed to be slowly, but steadily, gaining upon him. A quarter of a mile away, he saw a small white cottage by the roadside, a white cottage with two dark windows and a door that somehow suggested a human face. He thought to himself that, if he could reach it in time, he might find shelter and security – escape.

The thin implacable footsteps, echoing his own, were still some way off when he lurched, gasping, into the little porch; rattled the latch, thrust at the door, and found it locked against him. There was no bell or knocker. He pounded on the wood with his fists until his knuckles bled. The response was horribly slow. At last, he heard heavier footsteps within the cottage. Slowly they descended the creaking stair. Slowly the door was unlocked. A tall shadowy figure stood before him, holding a lighted candle, in such a way that he could see little either of the holder's face or form; but to his dumb horror there seemed to be a cerecloth wrapped round the face. No words passed between them. The figure beckoned him in; and, as he obeyed, it locked the door behind him. Then, beckoning him again, without a word, the figure went before him up the crooked stair with the ghostly candle casting huge and grotesque shadows on the whitewashed walls and ceiling.

They entered an upper room, in which there was a bright fire burning, with an armchair on either side of it, and a small oak table, on which there lay a battered old book, bound in dark red buckram. It seemed as though the guest had been long expected and all things were prepared.

The figure pointed to one of the armchairs, placed the candlestick on the table by the book (for there was no other light but that of the fire) and withdrew without a word, locking the door behind him.

Mortimer looked at the candlestick. It seemed familiar. The smell of the guttering wax brought back the little room in the old Elizabethan house. He picked up the book with trembling fingers. He recognized it at once, though he had long forgotten everything about the story. He remembered the inkstain on the title page; and then, with a shock of recollection, he came on the fiftieth page, which he had pinned down in childhood. The pins were still there. He touched them again – the very pins which his trembling childish fingers had used so long ago.

He turned to the beginning. He was determined to read it to the end now, and discover what it all was about. He felt that it must all be set down there, in print; and, though in childhood he could not understand it, he would be able to fathom it now.

It was called *The Midnight Express*; and, as he read the first paragraph, it began to dawn upon him slowly, fearfully, inevitably –

It was the story of a man who, in childhood, long ago, had chanced upon a book, in which there was a picture that frightened him. He had grown up and forgotten it, and one night, upon a lonely railway platform, he had found himself in the remembered scene of that picture; he had confronted the solitary figure under the lamp; recognized it, and fled in panic. He had taken shelter in a wayside cottage; had been led to an upper room, found the book awaiting him and had begun to read it right through, to the very end, at last. And this book, too, was called *The Midnight Express*. And it was the story of a man who, in childhood – it would go on thus, forever and forever, and forever. There was no escape.

But when the story came to the wayside cottage, for the third time, a deeper suspicion began to dawn upon him, slowly, fearfully, inevitably – although there was no escape, he could at least try to grasp more clearly the details of the strange circle, the fearful wheel, in which he was moving.

There was nothing new about the details. They had been there all the time; but he had not grasped their significance. That was all. The strange and dreadful being that had led him up the crooked stair – who and what was That?

The story mentioned something that had escaped him. The strange host, who had given him shelter, was about his own height. Could it be that he also – and was this why the face was hidden?

At the very moment when he asked himself that question, he heard the click of the key in the locked door.

The strange host was entering – moving towards him from behind – casting a grotesque shadow, larger than human, on the white walls in the guttering candlelight.

It was there, seated on the other side of the fire, facing him. With a horrible nonchalance, as a woman might prepare to remove a veil, it raised its hands to unwind the cerecloth from its face. He knew to whom it would belong. But would it be dead or living?

There was no way but one. As Mortimer plunged forward and seized the tormentor by the throat, his own throat was gripped with the same brutal force. The echoes of their strangled cry were indistinguishable; and when the last confused sounds died out together, the stillness of the room was so deep that you might have heard – the ticking of the old grandfather clock, and the longdrawn rhythmical 'ah' of the sea, on a distant coast, thirty-eight years ago.

But Mortimer had escaped at last. Perhaps, after all, he had caught the midnight express.

It was a battered old book, bound in red buckram ...

Mary

Roger B. Pile

'Jennie, what's this you've written?'
'That? Oh, that's nothing.'
'Who's this Martin?'
'Martin's nice. He plays with me.'
'Not Martin Wills? But he's twenty-three!'

I could still remember it clearly: Helen, smiling as she spoke, reading something Jennie had scribbled inside the cover of a pink, dog-eared book; and Jennie – Jennie looking up, puzzled, from where she was sitting on the rug, saying repetitively:

'Martin's nice. He plays games with me.'
'What sort of games, Jennie?' I'd said.

But that was a month ago, and London was a hundred miles away. I stopped the car in front of the house.

Jennie climbed out straight away, dragging her shoes in the gravel and staring about with the natural inquisitiveness of a child half her age. Repeatedly, she brushed back strands of the light sandy hair that fringed her slightly too prominent forehead. She had Helen's wide, startling blue eyes.

'Jennie, your *shoes!*' Helen's voice was strained, overloud in the confined space of the car. It had been a long drive from the city, and she was tired. Jennie didn't seem to hear, or, if she did, took no notice.

'She's all right,' I said. 'They're only her old ones.'

'You're always sticking up for her, Paul. How's she ever going to learn?' Annoyed, Helen got out of the car, slamming the door harder than was necessary.

It had been years – I forget how many now – before I learned to come to terms with Jennie's condition; before I could accept that she would never grow beyond the mental age of a ten-year-old. Too many years, that was all I was certain of. But Helen had been different. After the initial shock, she had accepted Jennie's mongolism with almost disconcerting calmness, and it was only later, as Jennie entered puberty, that I finally understood. Other children grew up, married, left home.

But always, even if subconsciously, Helen had known Jennie would never leave home. Helen would always be a mother to her child.

'Well, if we're *going* in ...'

Helen was standing at the top of the steps, framed in the open doorway. Jennie had already disappeared inside. I followed them into the house.

Inside, the house was no more inviting than its exterior suggested it would be. The rooms smelled musty, unlived in for too long. High, small windows, thick with dust, admitted only a thin grey light. The first door leading off the entrance hall opened on to a big, high-ceilinged lounge.

'Don't they ever clean this place?' Helen said, running her fingers disapprovingly over the top of a massive old table.

'Doubt it. Probably rent a penthouse suite and only visit here once or twice a year.'

'Make sure the peasants are behaving themselves, not making off with the silver, you mean.'

In the owners' place, I thought, I'd do the same. This big grey box in the middle of nowhere was hardly my idea of a country retreat.

Quiet and seclusion, I reminded myself. It's a big, ugly house, but it's quiet and very secluded, and that's what Jennie needs: quiet and seclusion.

Despite the peculiarity of her forehead, Jennie was an attractive girl, and a cheerful one. She'd made plenty of friends among the children of the neighbourhood we lived in, and sometimes it was easy to forget that she wasn't a normal, healthy child herself. At least, until recently it had been, but then – almost overnight, it seemed – Jennie had 'grown up'. Suddenly she was no longer 'cute' but just an embarrassment to other girls her own age; while her disastrous attempts to befriend younger children, whose intelligence more closely approximated her own, were met with suspicion and, in some cases, outright hostility.

And the others – the older ones – I guessed it hadn't taken some of them long to discover her backwardness, and take advantage of it.

'*What* sort *of games, Jennie?*'

Then: 'Daddy! Mummy!'

The tips of my fingers were smudged with dirt, and I realized I'd been daydreaming, absently drawing on the dusty table top. I studied the lines I'd traced in the dust, then obliterated them with a quick sweep of my hand. I was alone in the room.

'Come and see the garden, it's lovely!'

*   *   *

I stepped from the back porch on to a broad strip of concrete which bordered the back of the house. The concrete had subsided and cracked slightly in places. A short flight of steps, also cracked, led onto a gravel path. Jennie was at the bottom of the garden, probing a small pond with a stick.

It was a big garden. Surrounded by a high laurel hedge, it sloped gently away from the house. The path wound aimlessly through the garden, forking madly and looping back on itself, disappearing here and there beneath overhanging clumps of shrubbery. At the bottom of the garden was a single tree: an elm, I thought, though I wasn't sure. Beneath the tree was a small red summer-house.

'Jennie, come away from there, you'll fall in!'

Helen had emerged from a door at the far end of the house. She looked around, then walked towards me along the concrete paving, being careful not to trip over any of the larger cracks.

'I've just been looking over the kitchen,' she said.

'Oh, any good then?'

Helen nodded, pleased. 'I was expecting to find a big kettle hanging in the fireplace, and a dirty porcelain sink, things like that.'

'It's not?'

'No, all very modern, actually. Stainless steel as far as the eye can see, deep-freeze, the lot. All a bit dusty, of course, but that's nothing.'

'The garden's not bad, either,' I said.

'No. I suppose.'

There was a trace of reluctance in her voice, but she'd spoken without taking her eyes off Jennie, and had probably only half heard me. Impulsively, she started down the steps.

'Let's take a look at the summer-house.'

The only sound as we walked through the garden was the crunching of gravel under our feet. The sky, which had been overcast, threatening rain, had cleared a little since we'd arrived, and a pale, warmthless sun appeared. The path led through some bushes, taking us out of sight of Jennie, and by the time we reached her she'd lost interest in the pond and turned her attention to the summer-house, standing on tip-toe to peer in through one of the windows.

The place was larger than I'd suspected, and I wondered if it was, indeed, a summer-house at all, or if in better days it might have served as a gardener's lodge. It was solidly built: the walls were red brick; the cornerstones and surrounds to door and windows, granite; the door had lost most of its paintwork but looked sturdy enough; the step was a single, massive block of slate. It was difficult to distinguish much through the windows for the dirt behind the glass, but the room appeared to be stripped bare of any furnishings.

'It's locked,' Jennie said when I tried the door.

It was a depressing spot, there at the bottom of the garden. The laurels were highest behind the summer-house, rising almost to the roof, and the tree threw a shadow over all: the summer-house with its blank, dark windows, the pond thinly filmed with weed. Even the air was stagnant and heavy. I tried telling myself that it would be pleasant to sit here on a hot day, in the shade of the tree, but it made no difference, and I was relieved when Helen had satisfied herself that the pond wasn't deep enough to present any threat to Jennie, and we went back to the house.

* * *

There were six bedrooms, and we wasted some time arguing over which to use, but eventually, Helen and I agreed on one of the front rooms: a bright, spacious room decorated in pale blue, while Jennie had her heart set on the smaller bedroom just across the hall.

Also upstairs was a big room that must once have been a study or library. I needed a room to work in, and it seemed ideal. There were half a dozen leather armchairs, carelessly arranged, a rosewood coffee table and, in one corner, a desk. But it was the window that decided me in favour of the room. Unlike the other windows of the house, this was a great bay window. Overlooking the garden, it took up almost the entire length of one wall, the recess it formed creating, in effect, a room within a room. There would be light to work by and more than enough room to set up my drawing-board and anything else I might need.

The walls of the room were lined with shelves holding weighty, dull-looking volumes with worn spines. Idly, I took down one of the books. It was a travelogue of the sort popular a century or more ago. The book felt oddly swollen, and the covers lay not quite flush against the pages. I opened the book and a shower of faded pressed flowers fell out onto the carpet.

* * *

I'd become so absorbed in the complicated business of setting up the drawing-board, and arranging papers and equipment handily on the coffee table, that I hadn't noticed how quickly the time had gone by.

'Mummy says tea's ready, and you're not to let it go cold.'

Jennie had entered the room silently, and I hadn't noticed her standing there. It was an annoying habit that she had, and one that I'd told her off for several times before.

'Jennie, are you deaf as well as stupid? I've told you before: one day you'll give someone a heart attack, creeping up on them like that!' Immediately I'd spoken the words, I regretted them. But I needn't have worried. She hadn't even heard me.

'What are these?' she said, kneeling beside the flowers on the carpet.

'They're flowers.'

'But they're all dead.'

'That's because they've been pressed. You'll have to ask your mother about it. She'll tell you how it's done.'

It was an old ploy, and once I'd have been annoyed at myself for using it: *Ask your mother. She'll know.*

Now it was just another habit.

*   *   *

Helen had been busy transforming the lounge. A standard lamp with a red shade – I couldn't remember seeing it there before – lit the room, and the warm glow reflected everywhere in freshly polished wood. A log fire burned brightly in the grate, and above, on the mantelpiece, she'd arranged photos: a recently taken one of Jennie, and another: a group photo of the three of us, taken on some long-ago holiday abroad. There were one or two of Helen's favourite ornaments that she'd brought with her, and, between these, a solidly-ticking marble clock.

'The finishing touch.' Helen indicated the clock proudly. 'I found it tucked away in the back of a kitchen cupboard; can you imagine?'

There were also some paintings: pleasant enough, if indifferent landscapes.

'Those? Oh, I found them in a cupboard under the stairs.'

After tea, I settled in an armchair, wishing I'd thought to bring along some cigars. Helen squatted on the rug in front of the fire, looking even prettier in the light of the flames. At the table, Jennie was engrossed in piecing together a jig-saw puzzle. She had a natural aptitude for putting together the coloured pieces of card, and at home had literally dozens of puzzles, but on wet afternoons she would sometimes spend hours tirelessly fitting, taking apart and re-fitting the same one. I nudged Helen with my foot.

'Let's send her to bed early.'

'Certainly not!' she said, primly. 'You're getting spoilt.' Then she grinned. 'Later.'

*   *   *

Helen was in the kitchen, sorting jars and packets and arranging them neatly on the shelves, when I came downstairs the next morning.

'Jennie tells me she's made a new friend,' she said as I mixed myself a cereal.

'Already? That's quick work.'

'They're out in the garden now. Seem to be getting along fine. At least, I can't hear any squabbling noises.'

When I'd finished eating, I took my coffee out on to the step. Helen didn't smoke and complained of the smell, so to keep the peace I usually smoked outdoors or in my own room. It was a pleasant enough morning: the sun, not long risen, had just begun to warm the air, the grass and bushes were fresh and dripping, and for the first time I noticed the sea, just visible over a dip in the surrounding hills. Down in the garden, I could see Jennie playing with another girl. The girl wore a yellow dress and had long dark hair; she seemed about the same age as Jennie, though, as they were both quite a distance away, kneeling by the pond, it was impossible to be certain.

Finishing the coffee, I decided to take a walk through the garden before starting work. At the back of my mind, I suppose I was fearing a recurrence of the circumstances that had brought about this vacation in the first place, though as Helen didn't seem concerned it was probably all right.

The path forked, and when I came out on the other side of the laurels, Jennie was sitting alone by the pond. She'd cleared a space in the gravel and was playing fivestones with coloured pebbles.

'All alone, then.'

Jennie tossed the pebbles, frowning as the round stones rolled and fell from the back of her hand.

'They're too round. You need flat ones,' I said.

She shrugged. 'These are pretty.'

'Where did your friend go?'

Again the shrug. 'She saw you coming and said she had to go.'

I laughed. 'Do I look that frightening, then?'

Jennie didn't answer, concentrating on her game.

'What's her name – your friend?'

'Mary.'

I left Jennie with her stones and went back up the path. Just past the laurel clump I almost stepped on a sparrow. It was still alive, its breast pumping fiercely; one wing was crumpled under its body. I knelt and picked it up. A crimson trickle ran through my fingers, and when I turned the bird over to examine it, the wing came off in my hand. The next moment it was dead, and I pushed it into the bushes, out of sight.

I went into the kitchen to wash my hands.

'Cut yourself?' Helen said, looking over my shoulder as I ran the tap. 'There's plasters in the top drawer.'

'No. I found a bird on the path. Think a cat must have got it.'

In my room, I settled to work at the drawing-board, but found it difficult to concentrate. Repeatedly, my thoughts wandered, and I found myself staring blankly out through the window. I began to think it was a mistake, setting up the board in this room: the garden was beautiful, but also a distraction. Annoyed at myself for wasting time, I took a pencil and began to work. By the end of the day the wastebasket was overflowing, but there were a number of rough layouts pinned to the workboard.

I should have been tired, but couldn't sleep. I lay staring into the darkness, trying to make sense of the jumbled images that crowded my mind: a bird with a torn wing, dead flowers tumbling from the pages of an old book, two children playing by a pond, a quiet garden, where the only sound was the crunching of gravel beneath my feet.

I awoke with light blazing painfully in my eyes, and must have lain there for over a minute before realizing that it wasn't yet morning; that someone had switched on the light.

'Helen?'

She moaned softly, turning over in her sleep.

I sat up, careful not to wake her. It was the main light; the small lamp at Helen's side of the bed was out. I tried to make sense of this, but found I was too tired. I got out of bed.

When I pressed the switch, a thin yellow bar outlined the edge of the door. The hall light was on. Puzzled, I crossed the hall and looked into Jennie's bedroom. She'd thrown most of the clothes off the bed, and her breathing was slightly uneven, but otherwise she seemed soundly enough asleep. I covered her up and closed the door quietly behind me.

The light switch was at the head of the stairs. It was a double switch: one for the hall, the other for the lower landing. And the landing light was on too. Genuinely uneasy by now, I began descending the stairs.

Reaching the landing, I was able to look down into the entrance hall. The lights were on, all of them, and the lounge door was open, though I was certain I remembered closing it. There was a faint, not unpleasant smell that I couldn't quite identify. As I descended, the smell grew stronger, intensifying with each step I took. It reminded me vaguely of the scent of a garden on a warm day, or of walking into a room occupied moments before by a woman wearing strong perfume.

At the foot of the stairs, I stopped. Someone was moving about in the lounge.

I walked quietly to the door. The noises were slight but quite distinct: a faint shuffling and, now and again, a more puzzling, rustling sound. I reached out my hand to swing the door further open, and, as I did so, something moved across the room with frightening suddenness.

'Who's there? Who is that?'

The stench hit me.

It was vile. It rushed through the open door in suffocating waves: fetid, stale, putrid. I swayed giddily against the wall, retching, trying to block my ears against the insanely high-pitched giggling that seemed to come from all around, then was only a steady, monotonous shrieking from the other side of the wall by the door, then was silent. I fought off the nausea, knowing that I had to make it back to the stairs, that at the top of the stairs lay safety. I opened my eyes, but the lights were out, and there was someone behind me. I felt my body turning slowly, automatically, as if against its will. My mind seemed elsewhere: escaped. Then I was running across the hall, blind in the darkness, but my foot caught against something and I sprawled headlong. There was a sound in the darkness, so close that it might have been the rattling of breath in my own throat. But wasn't.

*   *   *

I woke and again it was light, but this time it was soft light, sunlight. It was morning. Dressing quickly, I went downstairs.

In the hall I hesitated, undecided, then, making up my mind, stepped into the lounge. What I'd expected to find, I wasn't sure, but in any case I was disappointed. Not as much as a cushion was out of place.

A place for everything, and everything in its place. Helen was fond of saying that, usually when Jennie left one of her puzzles lying around. The sun was on the other side of the house, and the room was dim and chilly. Shivering slightly, I turned to leave, then noticed the flower lying on the rug by the fireplace.

I went to pick it up, thinking to tease Helen about the state she was letting the house get into. The flower was dry and brittle between my fingers: it had been pressed. Probably, I thought, Jennie had brought it down from my room, or it might even have stuck to my own clothing, and I could have dropped it there myself, unknowingly.

There was the sound of breaking china, and along the hall I heard Helen swearing to herself. Dropping the dead flower into the grate, I went into the kitchen, where she'd just finished sweeping the remains of a plate into a dustpan.

'Well, if it isn't Mr Universe.'

Glimpsing my reflection in the mirror, I said: 'I didn't sleep too well, last night.'

She pointed with the brush at the oven. 'Your breakfast's keeping warm.'

I ate slowly, noticing that, as usual, she'd managed to break the yolks of both eggs: something that I found stupidly reassuring.

'Jennie's sulking because she can't go out to play,' she said.

'Oh?' I glanced out of the window and was surprised to see that though the garden was bright with sunlight, a strong wind was blowing, tossing the boughs of the tree by the summer-house, whipping leaves from the laurel hedges: a fierce, strangely silent wind. It was oddly disturbing.

'Why doesn't she invite one of her friends over for the day?'

'She's only got one – you know that; and I don't think Jennie knows where she lives.'

'Not far, surely. And there can't be more than three houses within a mile of this place. She must live in one of them.'

Helen shrugged. 'All right, I'll ask her.'

Later, it started to rain. A dull, persistent drizzle: the sort that might keep up all day, or clear away in the next half hour. I sat at the drawing-board, watching the mist trickle in rivulets down the window. It was the stub of the cigarette burning my fingers that brought me back to reality. I pushed aside the cold remains of the coffee, and reached for a pencil, then realized I was already holding one – in my left hand, though I was right-handed. And there were words: odd, backward-slanting words, almost, but not quite illegible, scrawled on the paper in front of me. I remembered other, similar words, traced in dust on an old table. I stared at the writing for a long time, feeling slightly uneasy. When I next looked out of the window, it had stopped raining.

*   *   *

Over lunch, Helen cross-examined Jennie, but, as usual, without much success.

'You seem to be getting along well with your friend – Mary, that's what you said her name was, didn't you?'

'Uh, huh.' Jennie was attempting determinedly to load her fork with peas, and didn't look up.

'That's not the way to use your fork. I'm always telling you.' Helen paused. 'She seems a nice, quiet girl. Why don't you invite her in for tea some time?'

Jennie gave up her attempts with the fork. 'I'll ask her,' she said, then: 'Can I go out now?'

The door slammed behind her, and Helen glared at me. 'What are you grinning about?'

I laughed. 'Nothing,' I said. 'Nothing at all.'

Within an hour, the sun was beating down too strongly to be pleasant, and I was forced to open the window of my room. I could hear Helen using the vacuum cleaner downstairs and, at the bottom of the garden, Jennie and her friend were playing some mysterious game. I watched them for a while before returning to work. Ten minutes later, I found I'd drawn the same line half a dozen times. I put down the pencil and called to Helen. The sound of the vacuum died away and she walked in, obviously annoyed.

'It's all very well for some people, sitting in the sun all day!'

'Sorry, love, but I was just wondering——' I hesitated, choosing my words carefully. 'Jennie's friend ... Does she come to the house when she calls on her?'

Helen shook her head. 'No, I haven't really met her to speak to yet. She always meets Jennie in the garden.'

'That's what's puzzling me. There's no gate. How does she get in?'

'Must be a gap in the hedge, I suppose. You know what kids are like.' The annoyed expression returned to her face. 'Anyway, I can't stand around chatting all day. Some people have work to do.'

Huffily, she left the room, and shortly the vacuum was humming again; then there were screams, Helen's, ringing through the house. By the time I reached the door of the lounge, she'd stopped screaming and was standing, white-faced, trembling, by the fireplace, the vacuum humming unattended by her feet. She was staring fixedly at one of the photos on the mantelpiece.

'Jennie,' she said when I reached her. 'Look at Jennie!'

I reached out and was about to pick up the photo, but stopped, my hand just inches away.

'What's happened to Jennie? My Jennie isn't like that. Why is she looking like that?'

Her voice was small and broken like a frightened child's. The photograph had been changed, obscenely, defaced with a dreadful ingenuity that transcended spite. I was unable to tell quite how it was different. But it wasn't Jennie any more.

Helen shivered uncontrollably. 'I feel sick,' she said.

When she'd gone, I removed the picture from the frame and dropped it into the grate, setting light to it. As it burned, an odd smell filled the room: sweet and cloying, like a woman wearing too much scent, or a garden on a warm day.

When I found Helen, she was standing by the door that led out on to the garden. She was still shivering, and when I came up and touched her on the shoulder, she started, turning quickly to stare at me.

'Did you see?' she said. 'The eyes – they weren't hers.'

*   *   *

The next two days passed quietly and uneventfully. The sun shone without a break, and Helen seemed to forget the incident with the photograph. Once, we drove down to the coast. There was a small, deserted cove, surrounded by high grey cliffs, and Helen and I sunbathed while Jennie paddled in the rock pools, collecting odd bits of seaweed and pebbles, which she kept in jam jars filled with water. On the third day, it rained.

*   *   *

The drawings were already behind schedule, but I knew that if I worked any longer on them today, I'd begin finding imaginary faults and have to begin all over again. I pinned the drawings to the layout board and went downstairs, into the kitchen.

Jennie was pressing flowers. I remembered her coming into my room earlier in the day to borrow some sheets of blotting-paper, and that she'd spent some time lugging several enormous books off the shelves, but I hadn't paid much attention at the time.

Helen had shown her how to fold the flowers in the blotting-paper, and Jennie was meticulously trimming the stems with a pair of nail scissors before consigning them to the leaves of a Greek lexicon.

'Careful you don't go pressing any weeds by mistake,' I said, ruffling her hair.

'There aren't any.'

Helen turned from the sink. 'No weeds? You mean you can't tell them from the flowers.'

Jennie shook her head stubbornly and persisted until Helen gave in. 'All right, we've got the only garden in the whole world without a single weed.'

*   *   *

That night the wind howled around the house, shrieking beneath the eaves and rattling the windows and doors, until it seemed that the whole massive building groaned and rocked madly in its foundations. I lay in bed, listening to the gale outside, and Helen's steady breathing beside me. Sometimes I reached over and touched her in the darkness, needing reassurance, without knowing why. I lit a cigarette, watching the red glow as it burned down towards my fingers, waiting for the morning.

*   *   *

I awoke early, and after breakfast went out on to the step. The air was clear after the storm of the previous night, and the garden seemed to have suffered little damage from the wind. From my seat on the step I cound see a web stretched across a nearby fuchsia bush. The web was huge – at least eighteen inches across – and, curious to see the monster that had built it, I flicked a tiny piece of twig into its centre. The web quivered, spraying tiny glistening droplets as it caught the twig on its sticky threads. Warning signals vibrated along a dozen primary strands, but though I watched for several minutes, no spider emerged to investigate the twig.

As I climbed the stairs to my room, it occurred to me that, despite the humidity of the weather lately, we were troubled very little by flies or insects. Even the spider's web had held nothing but the twig that I'd flicked into it myself. The garden was like a beautiful three-dimensional picture, in which the artist had neglected to paint any form of life other than the flowers and bushes themselves.

But no, that was wrong. I stopped at the door of my room. There *had* been something else. Something alive. There had been a bird ... I opened the door.

The room was a shambles.

Chairs had been overturned, and the drawing-board had been flung half-way across the room, where it lay buried in a wreckage of books and torn paper. Everywhere, books had been tumbled from the shelves. They lay in mountainous heaps all over the floor and, spilling from their open pages in a livid carpet were thousands of dead flowers. The flowers rustled, shifting slightly in the draught from the open window. The room stank.

I was sifting through the debris, hoping that a few at least of my drawings had been spared, when Helen appeared in the doorway. She stared blankly, uncomprehending, and stupidly I tried to make a joke of it.

'Jennie needs her hobbies, I know,' I said, 'but you really will have to have a word with her about this.'

Helen looked puzzled. 'Jennie? – Jennie did this?' Then realization dawned and she flushed.

'My God, Paul, you may not have a very high opinion of my intelligence, but at least you don't have to treat me like a child!'

She walked into the room, the brittle flowers snapping beneath her feet.

'I've known something's been wrong, ever since – since Jennie's photograph. I know you've been keeping things from me, but I thought you'd tell me in time. Jesus Christ, I'm not just a bloody machine to take to bed and wash your dirty underwear. Or *is* that what you think?'

Confused and hurt, she ran out and left me standing in the middle of the wrecked library, one half of a torn drawing in my hand. Cursing myself for my own stupidity, I screwed the paper into a ball and threw it away. Later, I found her in the kitchen, and I began to tell her about the nightmare I'd had, and about the garden, and a bird with a torn wing. When I'd finished, she stood up and began walking nervously around the kitchen, picking things up, putting them down.

'I read this book once: one of those occult books. There was a chapter on poltergeists.' She stared at me, defying ridicule.

'Go on,' I said.

'They're supposed to emanate ... centre on mentally disturbed people: children, especially.'

The same thought had already occurred to me. I said: 'I've never heard of them actually taking on physical shape.'

'Sometimes, children see things older people don't.' She hesitated, embarrassed now. 'When I was small – I don't remember this, but they told me – I used to have an invisible friend.'

Then suddenly the frightened look was back in her eyes.

'Jennie! – Jennie's in the garden with Mary!'

I didn't bother to follow her, but, from the step, watched her running down the path to the bottom of the garden. They were too far away for me to make out their expressions or hear what they were saying, but I could imagine Helen, worried and questioning, and Jennie, staring up, puzzled, with wide blue eyes that were like reflections of Helen's own.

I walked back into the kitchen and saw the pen and notepad Helen used to list groceries. It had been lying on the table in front of me while Helen had been talking, and now there were words, odd, backward-slanting words, just as before, scrawled on it. I didn't have to study them to know what was written there.

'Mary, Mary, quite contrary, how——' I tore the page out just as Helen entered the door. She didn't say anything but began clattering dishes and preparing the vegetables for lunch. When she finally spoke, the frightened look was gone from her eyes, replaced by a hardness I'd never seen there before.

'Who *is* Mary?' she said.

*   *   *

Who was Mary?

The question whispered and echoed from the dark corners of the room. But, more to the point, *what* was Mary? Did Mary press flowers? Did Mary tear off sparrows' wings? Did Mary throw books from shelves? Did Mary turn on lights in the middle of the night?

The light was on.

I sat up to find Helen already sitting on the edge of the bed, pulling on her dressing-gown.

'This is the way it happened before, isn't it?' she said.

I nodded.

'I'm going to see if Jennie's all right.' She got up from the bed and walked deliberately to the door.

'Wait,' I said. 'I'll come with you.'

The hall light was on, and the door of Jennie's room was open. Jennie was gone. She'd gone without any fuss, neatly pulling back the covers of her bed and taking her dressing-gown and slippers with her.

'Where?' Helen stared desperately around the room, as if expecting to find Jennie hiding in a corner, or behind the door. Then her expression lightened slightly. 'She must have woken up and felt hungry. She's gone downstairs for something to eat; that must be it.'

Yes, and turned on all the lights behind her, I thought. But I said nothing and followed Helen out of the room and along the hallway. As we descended the stairs, the smell rose to meet us, stronger, if anything, than before. But this time the door of the lounge was tightly shut. The lights stayed on.

The kitchen was cold, glacial-looking under the strip lighting that

ran its length, gleaming off polished chrome surfaces. Cold and empty.
Jennie wasn't here, either.

I went over to the door that led out to the garden and it swung open
at my touch. I stepped through. It was freezing outside, and the light
that spilled from every window of the great house streamed over the
bushes, accentuating the blackness beyond. I felt Helen's hand touch
my arm, and when I turned she pointed down to the bottom of the
garden, where a single yellow shaft split the darkness under the tree. I
remembered then – Jennie always met Mary in the garden.

I'd forgotten to put on my shoes, and the gravel cut into my feet as
we stumbled down the path, tripping over borders in the dark. Once,
Helen fell. I helped her to her feet, and after that we clutched each
other's hands in case we became separated. Leaves caught at our faces
as we hurried through the laurels, but then we were past them, and
there was the pond, glinting dully in the light that shafted through the
open door of the summer-house.

The slate step was cold as ice, and the door moved silently as we
stepped inside. Helen coughed and held the corner of her gown to her
face against the disgusting smell. We stood in a tiny hall lit by a single
unshaded bulb – obviously the summer-house was linked to the house's
electricity supply. Leading off the hall were three doors. The first two,
at either side, stood open, and the rooms beyond were dark and empty.
The last, directly facing us, was closed, and from behind it came voices,
one of them Jennie's.

Before I could move, Helen had stepped ahead of me and opened
the door. The room we entered was large and brightly lit, utterly
filthy. On the floor of the room, two figures squatted, one with its back to
us. Long, matted hair trailed on the floor behind it, and the hand it
reached out to stroke Jennie's cheek was black, with curling, broken
nails. At the sound of the door opening, it stood and turned, facing us. It
had the physique of a man: broad-shouldered and deep-chested, but it
wore women's clothes. Its dress had probably once been yellow or
white, but was now filthy, streaked with grime and fecal matter. It stood
even shorter than Jennie. It looked at me and smiled, stretching out its
hand. The hand was open, and resting in the palm were five brightly-
coloured stones. Its eyes were almost shockingly wide, totally imbecilic.

Impossibly, then, Helen walked straight past the figure, seeming
unaware of it, though she almost brushed its skirts. She picked Jennie up
off the floor.

'This is Mary,' Jennie said, smiling happily.

'Yes, darling,' Helen said. 'Of course it is.'

She carried Jennie back across the room, making soothing noises.
Mary grinned idiotically, her head hanging to one side like a doll's.

'Mary says she wants to stay,' Jennie said, drowsily.

Helen turned hopelessly to me. 'She's almost asleep,' she said. 'Let's save the scolding for tomorrow.'

I wanted to open my mouth and scream, and point at the idiot smiling thing with us in the room. I wanted her to see it too. But then she carried Jennie out, and I was alone in the summer-house with Mary – her lipless slit of a mouth still stretched in a smile, her hand still insistently thrust forward, offering the pebbles.

Mary says she wants to stay. The words spun around in my head as if on an endless loop of tape. I stood, paralysed, knowing that the alternative was to leave the summer-house and walk back up the path, afraid that I wouldn't walk it alone, that she would be there beside me. Or had she always been with us: lonely, hiding, waiting for just this moment?

I looked into Mary's blue eyes and her terrible smile, and it was like looking into an abyss: gaping, empty. But, too, there was awareness, a dreadful understanding there. Appalled, I turned away.

Then I was on the path leading back to the house.

The windows were still lighted, the bushes in the garden outlined clearly in their glow, but now as I watched, one by one, the lighted squares vanished. I thought of Helen walking through the hallways of the great house, opening doors, snapping switches. Soon the house would be dark again.

I walked on through the quiet garden, listening to the sound my feet made on the path, keeping my eyes fixed on the windows still lighted, determined not to look aside, where other feet stepped in a horrid pantomime of my own.

The Facts in the Case of M. Valdemar
Edgar Allan Poe

Of course I shall not pretend to consider it any matter for wonder, that the extraordinary case of M. Valdemar has excited discussion. It would have been a miracle had it not – especially under the circumstances. Through the desire of all parties concerned, to keep the affair from the public, at least for the present, or until we had further opportunities for investigation – through our endeavours to effect this – a garbled or exaggerated account made its way into society, and became the source of many unpleasant misrepresentations, and, very naturally, of a great deal of disbelief.

It is now rendered necessary that I give the *facts* – as far as I comprehend them myself. They are, succinctly, these:

My attention, for the last three years, had been repeatedly drawn to the subject of Mesmerism; and, about nine months ago, it occurred to me, quite suddenly, that in the series of experiments made hitherto, there had been a very remarkable and most unaccountable omission – no person had as yet been mesmerised *in articulo mortis*. It remained to be seen, first, whether, in such condition, there existed in the patient any susceptibility to the magnetic influence; secondly, whether, if any existed, it was impaired or increased by the condition; thirdly, to what extent, or for how long a period, the encroachments of death might be arrested by the process. There were other points to be ascertained, but these most excited my curiosity – the last in especial, from the immensely important character of its consequences.

In looking around me for some subject by whose means I might test these particulars, I was brought to think of my friend, M. Ernest Valdemar, the well-known compiler of the *Bibliotheca Forensica*, and author (under the *nom de plume* of Issachar Marx) of the Polish versions of *Wallenstein* and *Gargantua*. M. Valdemar, who has resided principally at Harlem, N.Y., since the year 1839, is (or was) particularly noticeable for the extreme spareness of his person – his lower limbs much resembling those of John Randolph; and, also, for the whiteness of his whiskers, in violent contrast to the blackness of his hair. His temperament was markedly nervous, and rendered him a good subject for mesmeric experiment. On two or three occasions I had put him to sleep with little difficulty, but was disappointed in other results which his peculiar constitution had naturally led me to anticipate. His will was at no period positively, or thoroughly, under my control, and in regard to *clairvoyance*, I could accomplish with him nothing to be relied upon. I always attributed my failure at these points to the disordered state of his health. For some months previous to my becoming acquainted with him, his physicians had declared him in a confirmed phthisis. It was his custom, indeed, to speak calmly of his approaching dissolution, as of a matter neither to be avoided nor regretted.

When the ideas to which I have alluded first occurred to me, it was of course very natural that I should think of M. Valdemar. I knew the steady philosophy of the man too well to apprehend any scruples from *him*; and he had no relatives in America who would be likely to interfere. I spoke to him frankly upon the subject; and, to my surprise, his interest seemed vividly excited. I say to my surprise; for, although he had always yielded his person freely to my experiments, he had never before given me any tokens of sympathy with what I did. His disease was of that character which would admit of exact calculation in respect to the epoch of its termination in death; and it was finally arranged between us that he would send for me about twenty-four hours before the period announced his physicians as that of his decease.

It is now rather more than seven months since I received, from M. Valdemar himself, the subjoined note:

> My Dear P——,
> You may as well come *now*. D—— and F—— are agreed that I cannot hold out beyond to-morrow midnight; and I think they have hit the time very nearly.
>
> > Valdemar.

I received this note within half an hour after it was written, and in fifteen minutes more I was in the dying man's chambers. I had not seen him for ten days, and was appalled by the fearful alteration which the brief interval had wrought in him. His face wore a leaden hue; the eyes were utterly lustreless; and the emaciation was so extreme that the skin had been broken through by the cheek bones. His expectoration was excessive. The pulse was barely perceptible. He retained, nevertheless, in a very remarkable manner, both his mental power and a certain degree of physical strength. He spoke with distinctness – took some palliative medicines without aid – and, when I entered the room, was occupied in pencilling memoranda in a pocket-book. He was propped up in the bed by pillows. Doctors D—— and F—— were in attendance.

After pressing Valdemar's hand, I took these gentlemen aside, and obtained from them a minute account of the patient's condition. The left lung had been for eighteen months in a semi-osseous or cartilaginous state, and was, of course, entirely useless for all purposes of vitality. The right, in its upper portion, was also partially, if not thoroughly, ossified, while the lower region was merely a mass of purulent tubercles, running one into another. Several extensive perforations existed; and, at one point, permanent adhesion to the ribs had taken place. These appearances in the right lobe were of comparatively recent date. The ossification had proceeded with very unusual rapidity; no sign of it had been discovered a month before, and the adhesion had only been observed during the three previous days. Independently of the phthisis, the patient was suspected of aneurism of the aorta; but on this point the osseous symptoms rendered an exact diagnosis impossible. It was the opinion of both physicians that M. Valdemar would die about midnight on the morrow (Sunday). It was then seven o'clock on Saturday evening.

On quitting the invalid's bedside to hold conversation with myself, Doctors D—— and F—— had bidden him a final farewell. It had not been their intention to return; but, at my request, they agreed to look in upon the patient about ten the next night.

When they had gone, I spoke freely with M. Valdemar on the subject of his approaching dissolution, as well as, more particularly, of the experiment proposed. He still professed himself quite willing and even anxious to have it made, and urged me to commence it at once. A male and female nurse were in attendance; but I did not feel myself altogether at liberty to engage in a task of this character with no more reliable witnesses than these people, in case of sudden accident, might prove. I therefore postponed operations until about eight the next night, when the arrival of a medical student with whom I had some acquaintance (Mr Theodore L——l), relieved me from further embarrassment. It had been my design, originally, to wait for the physicians; but I was induced to proceed, first, by the urgent entreaties of M. Valdemar, and secondly, by my conviction that I had not a moment to lose, as he was evidently sinking fast.

Mr L——l was so kind as to accede to my desire that he would take notes of all that occurred; and it is from his memoranda that what I now have to relate is, for the most part, either condensed or copied *verbatim*.

It wanted about five minutes of eight when, taking the patient's hand, I begged him to state, as distinctly as he could, to Mr L——l, whether he (M. Valdemar) was entirely willing that I should make the experiment of mesmerizing him in his then condition.

He replied feebly, yet quite audibly, 'Yes, I wish to be mesmerized' – adding immediately afterwards, 'I fear you have deferred it too long.'

While he spoke thus, I commenced the passes which I had already found most effectual in subduing him. He was evidently influenced with the first lateral stroke of my hand across his forehead; but although I exerted all my powers, no further perceptible effect was induced until some minutes after ten o'clock, when Doctors D—— and F—— called, according to appointment. I explained to them, in a few words, what I designed, and as they opposed no objection, saying that the patient was already in the death agony, I proceeded without hesitation – exchanging, however, the lateral passes for downward ones, and directing my gaze entirely into the right eye of the sufferer.

By this time his pulse was imperceptible and his breathing was stertorous, and at intervals of half a minute.

This condition was nearly unaltered for a quarter of an hour. At the expiration of this period, however, a natural although a very deep sigh escaped the bosom of the dying man, and the stertorous breathing ceased – that is to say, its stertorousness was no longer apparent; the intervals were undiminished. The patient's extremities were of an icy coldness.

At five minutes before eleven I perceived unequivocal signs of the mesmeric influence. The glassy roll of the eye was changed for that expression of uneasy *inward* examination which is never seen except in cases of sleep-walking, and which it is quite impossible to mistake. With a few rapid lateral passes I made the lids quiver, as in incipient sleep, and with a few more I closed them altogether. I was not satisfied, however, with this, but continued the manipulations vigorously, and with the fullest exertion of the will, until I had completely stiffened the limbs of the slumberer, after placing them in a seemingly easy position. The legs were at full length; the arms were nearly so, and reposed on the bed at a moderate distance from the loins. The head was very slightly elevated.

When I had accomplished this, it was fully midnight, and I requested the gentlemen present to examine M. Valdemar's condition. After a few experiments, they admitted him to be in an unusually perfect state of mesmeric trance. The curiosity of both the physicians was greatly excited. Dr D—— resolved at once to remain with the patient all night, while Dr F—— took leave with a promise to return at daybreak. Mr L——l and the nurses remained.

We left M. Valdemar entirely undisturbed until about three o'clock in the morning, when I approached him and found him in precisely the same condition as when Dr F—— went away – that is to say, he lay in the same position; the pulse was imperceptible; the breathing was gentle (scarcely noticeable, unless through the application of a mirror to the lips); the eyes were closed naturally; and the limbs were as rigid and as cold as marble. Still, the general appearance was certainly not that of death.

As I approached M. Valdemar I made a kind of half effort to
influence his right arm into pursuit of my own, as I passed the latter
gently to and fro above his person. In such experiments with this patient
I had never perfectly succeeded before, and assuredly I had little
thought of succeeding now; but to my astonishment, his arm very
readily, although feebly, followed every direction I assigned it with
mine. I determined to hazard a few words of conversation.

'M. Valdemar,' I said, 'are you asleep?' He made no answer, but I
perceived a tremor about the lips, and was thus induced to repeat the
question, again and again. At its third repetition, his whole frame was
agitated by a very slight shivering; the eyelids unclosed themselves so far
as to display a white line of the ball; the lips moved sluggishly, and from
between them, in a barely audible whisper, issued the words:

'Yes – asleep now. Do not wake me! – let me die so!'

I here felt the limbs and found them as rigid as ever. The right arm,
as before, obeyed the direction of my hand. I questioned the sleep-
walker again:

'Do you still feel pain in the breast, M. Valdemar?'

The answer now was immediate, but even less audible than before:
'No pain – I am dying.'

I did not think it advisable to disturb him further just then, and
nothing more was said or done until the arrival of Dr F——, who came a
little before sunrise, and expressed unbounded astonishment at finding
the patient still alive. After feeling the pulse and applying a mirror to the
lips, he requested me to speak to the sleep-walker again. I did so, saying:

'M. Valdemar, do you still sleep?'

As before, some minutes elapsed ere a reply was made; and during
the interval the dying man seemed to be collecting his energies to speak.
At my fourth repetition of the question, he said very faintly, almost
inaudibly:

'Yes; still asleep – dying.'

It was now the opinion, or rather the wish, of the physicians, that M.
Valdemar should be suffered to remain undisturbed in his present
apparently tranquil condition, until death should supervene – and this,
it was generally agreed, must now take place within a few minutes. I
concluded, however, to speak to him once more, and merely repeated
my previous question.

While I spoke, there came a marked change over the countenance of
the sleep-waker. The eyes rolled themselves slowly open, the pupils
disappearing upwardly; the skin generally assumed a cadaverous hue,
resembling not so much parchment as white paper; and the circular
hectic spots which, hitherto, had been strongly defined in the centre of
each cheek, went out at once. I use this expression, because the
suddenness of their departure put me in mind of nothing so much as the

extinguishment of a candle by a puff of the breath. The upper lip, at the same time, writhed itself away from the teeth, which it had previously covered completely; while the lower jaw fell with an audible jerk, leaving the mouth widely extended, and disclosing in full view the swollen and blackened tongue. I presume that no member of the party then present had been unaccustomed to death-bed horrors; but so hideous beyond conception was the appearance of M. Valdemar at this moment, that there was a general shrinking back from the region of the bed.

I now feel that I have reached a point of this narrative at which every reader will be startled into positive disbelief. It is my business, however, simply to proceed.

There was no longer the faintest sign of vitality in M. Valdemar; and concluding him to be dead, we were consigning him to the charge of the nurses, when a strong vibratory motion was observable in the tongue. This continued for perhaps a minute. At the expiration of this period, there issued from the distended and motionless jaws a voice – such as it would be madness in me to attempt describing. There are, indeed, two or three epithets which might be considered as applicable to it in parts; I might say for example, that the sound was harsh, and broken, and hollow; but the hideous whole is indescribable, for the simple reason that no similar sounds have ever jarred upon the ear of humanity. There were two particulars, nevertheless, which I thought then, and still think, might fairly be stated as characteristic of the intonation – as well adapted to convey some idea of its unearthly peculiarity. In the first place, the voice seemed to reach our ears – at least mine – from a vast distance, or from some deep cavern within the earth. In the second place, it impressed me (I fear, indeed, that it will be impossible to make myself comprehended) as gelatinous or glutinous matters impress the sense of touch.

I have spoken both of 'sound' and of 'voice.' I mean to say that the sound was one of distinct – of even wonderfully, thrillingly distinct – syllabification. M. Valdemar *spoke* – obviously in reply to the question I had propounded to him a few minutes before. I had asked him, it will be remembered, if he still slept. He now said:

'Yes – no – I *have been* sleeping – and no – now – *I am dead.*'

No person present even affected to deny, or attempted to repress, the unutterable, shuddering horror which these few words, thus uttered, were so well calculated to convey. Mr L——l (the student) swooned. The nurses immediately left the chamber, and could not be induced to return. For nearly an hour, we busied ourselves, silently – without the utterance of a word – in endeavours to revive Mr L——l. When he came to himself, we addressed ourselves again to an investigation of M. Valdemar's condition.

It remained in all respects as I have last described it, with the exception that the mirror no longer afforded evidence of respiration. An attempt to draw blood from the arm failed. I should mention, too, that this limb was no further subject to my will. I endeavoured in vain to make it follow the direction of my hand. The only real indication, indeed, of the mesmeric influence, was now found in the vibratory movement of the tongue, whenever I addressed M. Valdemar a question. He seemed to be making an effort to reply, but had no longer sufficient volition. To queries put to him by any other person than myself he seemed utterly insensible – although I endeavoured to place each member of the company in mesmeric *rapport* with him. I believe that I have now related all that is necessary to an understanding of the sleep-waker's state at this epoch. Other nurses were procured; and at ten o'clock I left the house in company with the two physicians and Mr L——l.

In the afternoon we all called again to see the patient. His condition remained precisely the same. We had now some discussion as to the propriety and feasibility of awakening him; but we had little difficulty in agreeing that no good purpose would be served by so doing. It was evident that, so far, death (or what is usually termed death) had been arrested by the mesmeric process. It seemed clear to us all that to awaken M. Valdemar would be merely to insure his instant, or at least his speedy dissolution.

From this period until the close of last week – *an interval of nearly seven months* – we continued to make daily calls at M. Valdemar's house, accompanied, now and then, by medical and other friends. All this time the sleep-waker remained *exactly* as I have last described him. The nurses' attentions were continual.

It was on Friday last that we finally resolved to make the experiment of awakening, or attempting to awaken him; and it is the (perhaps) unfortunate result of this latter experiment which has given rise to so much discussion in private circles – to so much of what I cannot help thinking unwarranted popular feeling.

For the purpose of relieving M. Valdemar from the mesmeric trance, I made use of the customary passes. These, for a time, were unsuccessful. The first indication of revival was afforded by a partial descent of the iris. It was observed, as especially remarkable, that this lowering of the pupil was accompanied by the profuse out-flowing of a yellowish ichor (from beneath the lids with a pungent and highly offensive odour.

It was now suggested that I should attempt to influence the patient's arm, as heretofore. I made the attempt and failed. Dr F—— then intimated a desire to have me put a question. I did so, as follows:

'M. Valdemar, can you explain to us what are your feelings or wishes now?'

There was an instant return of the hectic circles on the cheeks; the tongue quivered, or rather rolled violently in the mouth (although the jaws and lips remained rigid as before); and at length the same hideous voice which I have already described, broke forth:

'For God's sake – quick! – quick! – put me to sleep – or, quick! – waken me! – quick! – *I say to you that I am dead!*'

I was thoroughly unnerved, and for an instant remained undecided what to do. At first I made an endeavour to recompose the patient; but, failing in this through total abeyance of the will, I retraced my steps and as earnestly struggled to awaken him. In this attempt I soon saw that I should be successful – or at least I soon fancied that my success would be complete – and I am sure that all in the room were prepared to see the patient awaken.

For what really occurred, however, it is quite impossible that any human being could have been prepared.

As I rapidly made the mesmeric passes, amid ejaculations of 'dead! dead!' absolutely *bursting* from the tongue and not from the lips of the sufferer, his whole frame at once – within the space of a single minute, or even less, shrunk – crumbled – absolutely *rotted* away beneath my hands. Upon the bed, before that whole company, there lay a nearly liquid mass of loathsome – of detestable putridity.

A Story of Don Juan
V. S. Pritchett

It is said that on one night of his life Don Juan slept alone, though I think
the point has been disputed. Returning to Seville in the spring he was
held up, some hours' ride from the city, by the floods of the
Quadalquiver, a river as dirty as an old lion after the rains, and was
obliged to stay at the *finca* of the Quintero family. The doorway, the
walls, the windows of the house were hung with the black and violet
draperies of mourning when he arrived there. God rest her soul (the
peasants said), the lady of the house was dead. She had been dead a year.
The young Quintero was a widower. Nevertheless Quintero took him in
and even smiled to see a gallant spattered and drooping in the rain like a
sodden cockerel. There was malice in that smile, for Quintero was mad
with loneliness and grief; the man who had possessed and discarded all
women, was received by a man demented because he had lost only one.

'My house is yours,' said Quintero, speaking the formula. There was
bewilderment in his eyes; those who grieve do not find the world and its
people either real or believable. Irony inflects the voices of mourners,
and there was malice, too, in Quintero's further greetings; for grief
appears to put one at an advantage, the advantage (in Quintero's case)
being the macabre one that he could receive Juan now without that fear,
that terror which Juan brought to the husbands of Seville. It was perfect,
Quintero thought, that for once in his life Juan should have arrived at an
empty house.

There was not even (as Juan quickly ascertained) a maid, for
Quintero was served only by a manservant, being unable any longer to
bear the sight of women. This servant dried Don Juan's clothes and in an
hour or two brought in a bad dinner, food which stamped up and down
in the stomach like people waiting for a coach in the cold. Quintero was
torturing his body as well as his mind, and as the familiar pains arrived
they agonized him and set him off about his wife. Grief had also made
Quintero an actor. His eyes had that hollow, taper-haunted dusk of the
theatre as he spoke of the beautiful girl. He dwelled upon their
courtship, on details of her beauty and temperament, and how he had

rushed her from the church to the marriage bed like a man racing a tray of diamonds through the streets into the safety of a bank vault. The presence of Don Juan turned every man into an artist when he was telling his own love story – one had to tantalize and surpass the great seducer – and Quintero, rolling it all off in the grand manner, could not resist telling that his bride had died on her marriage night.

'Man!' cried Don Juan. He started straight off on stories of his own. But Quintero hardly listened; he had returned to the state of exhaustion and emptiness which is natural to grief. As Juan talked, the madman followed his own thoughts like an actor preparing and mumbling the next entrance; and the thought he had had when Juan had first appeared at his door returned to him: that Juan must be a monster to make a man feel triumphant that his own wife was dead. Half-listening, and indigestion aiding, Quintero felt within himself the total hatred of all the husbands of Seville for this diabolical man. And as Quintero brooded upon this it occurred to him that it was probably not a chance that he had it in his power to effect the most curious revenge on behalf of the husbands of Seville.

The decision was made. The wine being finished Quintero called for his manservant and gave orders to change Don Juan's room.

'For,' said Quintero drily, 'his Excellency's visit is an honour and I cannot allow one who has slept in the most delicately scented room in Spain to pass the night in a chamber which stinks to heaven of goat.'

'The closed room?' said the manservant, astonished that the room which still held the great dynastic marriage bed and which had not been used more than half a dozen times by his master since the lady's death – and then only at the full moon when his frenzy was worst – was to be given to a stranger.

Yet to this room Quintero led his guest and there parted from him with eyes so sparkling with ill-intention that Juan, who was sensitive to this kind of point, understood perfectly that the cat was being let into the cage only because the bird had long ago flown out. The humiliation was unpleasant. Juan saw the night stretching before him like a desert.

What a bed to lie in: so wide, so unutterably vacant, so malignantly inopportune! Juan took off his clothes, snuffed the lamp wick. He lay down conscious that on either side of him lay wastes of sheet, draughty and uninhabited except by the nomadic bug. A desert. To move an arm one inch to the side, to push out a leg, however cautiously, was to enter desolation. For miles and miles the foot might probe, the fingers or the knee explore a friendless Antarctica. Yet to lie rigid and still was to have a foretaste of the grave. And here, too, he was frustrated; for though the wine kept him yawning, that awful food romped in his stomach, jolting him back from the edge of sleep the moment he got there.

There is an art in sleeping alone in a double bed but, naturally, this art was unknown to Juan; he had to learn it. The difficulty is easily solved. If you cannot sleep on one side of the bed, you move over and try the other. Two hours or more must have passed before this occurred to Juan. Sullen-headed he advanced into the desert and the night air lying chill between the sheets flapped, and made him shiver. He stretched out his arm and crawled towards the opposite pillow. Mother of God, the coldness, the more than virgin frigidity of linen! Juan put down his head and, drawing up his knees, he shivered. Soon, he supposed, he would be warm again, but in the meantime, ice could not have been colder. It was unbelievable.

Ice was the word for that pillow and those sheets. Ice. Was he ill? Had the rain chilled him that his teeth must chatter like this and his legs tremble? Far from getting warmer he found the cold growing. Now it was on his forehead and his cheeks, like arms of ice on his body, like legs of ice upon his legs. Suddenly in superstition he got up on his hands and stared down at the pillow in the darkness, threw back the bed-clothes and looked down upon the sheet; his breath was hot, yet blowing against his cheeks was a breath colder than the grave, his shoulders and body were hot, yet limbs of snow were drawing him down; and just as he would have shouted his appalled suspicion, lips like wet ice unfolded upon his own and he sank down to a kiss, unmistakably a kiss, which froze him like a winter.

In his own room Quintero lay listening. His mad eyes were exalted and his ears were waiting. He was waiting for the scream of horror. He knew the apparition. There would be a scream, a tumble, hands fighting for the light, fists knocking at the door. And Quintero had locked the door. But when no scream came, Quintero lay talking to himself, remembering the night the apparition had first come to him and had made him speechless and left him choked and stiff. It would be even better if there were no scream! Quintero lay awake through the night building castle after castle of triumphant revenge and receiving, as he did so, the ovations of the husbands of Seville. 'The stallion is gelded!' At an early hour Quintero unlocked the door and waited downstairs impatiently. He was a wreck after a night like that.

Juan came down at last. He was (Quintero observed) pale. Or was he pale?

'Did you sleep well?' Quintero asked furtively.

'Very well,' Juan replied.

'I do not sleep well in strange beds myself,' Quintero insinuated. Juan smiled and replied that he was more used to strange beds than his own. Quintero scowled.

'I reproach myself: the bed was large,' he said. But the large, Juan said, were necessarily as familiar to him as the strange. Quintero bit his nails. Some noise had been heard in the night – something like a scream, a disturbance. The manservant had noticed it also. Juan answered him that disturbances in the night had indeed bothered him at the beginning of his career, but now he took them in his stride. Quintero dug his nails into the palms of his hands. He brought out the trump.

'I am afraid,' Quintero said, 'it was a cold bed. You must have *frozen.*'

'I am never cold for long,' Juan said, and, unconsciously anticipating the manner of a poem that was to be written in his memory two centuries later, declaimed: 'The blood of Don Juan is hot, for the sun is the blood of Don Juan'.

Quintero watched. His eyes jumped like flies to every movement of his guest. He watched him drink his coffee. He watched him tighten the stirrups of his horse. He watched Juan vault into the saddle. Don Juan was humming and when he went off was singing, was singing in that intolerable tenor of his which was like a cock crow in the olive groves.

Quintero went into the house and rubbed his unshaven chin. Then he went out again to the road where the figure of Don Juan was now only a small smoke of dust between the eucalyptus trees. Quintero went up to the room where Juan had slept and stared at it with accusations and suspicions. He called the manservant.

'I shall sleep here tonight,' Quintero said.

The manservant answered carefully. Quintero was mad again and the moon was still only in its first quarter. The man watched his master during the day looking towards Seville. It was too warm after the rains, the country steamed like a laundry.

And then, when the night came, Quintero laughed at his doubts. He went up to the room and as he undressed he thought of the assurance of those ice-cold lips, those icicle fingers and those icy arms. She had not come last night; oh what fidelity! To think, he would say in his remorse to the ghost, that malice had so disordered him that he had been base and credulous to use the dead for a trick.

Tears were in his eyes as he lay down and for some time he dared not turn on his side and stretch out his hand to touch what, in his disorder, he had been willing to betray. He loathed his heart. He craved – yet how could he hope for it now? – the miracle of recognition and forgiveness. It was this craving which moved him at last. His hands went out. And they were met.

The hands, the arms, the lips moved out of their invisibility and soundlessness towards him. They touched him, they clasped him, they drew him down, but – what was this? He gave a shout, he fought to get away, kicked out and swore; and so the manservant found him wrestling with the sheets, striking out with fists and knees, roaring that he was in hell. Those hands, those lips, those limbs, he screamed, were *burning* him. They were of ice no more. They were of fire.

The Open Window
Saki

'My aunt will be down presently, Mr Nuttel,' said a very self-possessed young lady of fifteen; 'in the meantime you must try and put up with me.'

Framton Nuttel endeavoured to say the correct something which should duly flatter the niece of the moment without unduly discounting the aunt that was to come. Privately he doubted more than ever whether these formal visits on a succession of total strangers would do much towards helping the nerve cure which he was supposed to be undergoing.

'I know how it will be,' his sister had said when he was preparing to migrate to this rural retreat; 'you will bury yourself down there and not speak to a living soul, and your nerves will be worse than ever from moping. I shall just give you letters of introduction to all the people I know there. Some of them, as far as I can remember, were quite nice.'

Framton wondered whether Mrs Sappleton, the lady to whom he was presenting one of the letters of introduction, came into the nice division.

'Do you know many of the people round here?' asked the niece, when she judged that they had had sufficient silent communion.

'Hardly a soul,' said Framton. 'My sister was staying here, at the rectory, you know, some four years ago, and she gave me letters of introduction to some of the people here.'

He made the last statement in a tone of distinct regret.

'Then you know practically nothing about my aunt?' pursued the self-possessed young lady.

'Only her name and address,' admitted the caller. He was wondering whether Mrs Sappleton was in the married or widowed state. An undefinable something about the room seemed to suggest masculine habitation.

'Her great tragedy happened just three years ago,' said the child; 'that would be since your sister's time.'

'Her tragedy?' asked Framton; somehow in this restful country spot tragedies seemed out of place.

'You may wonder why we keep that window wide open on an October afternoon,' said the niece, indicating a large French window that opened on to a lawn.

'It is quite warm for the time of the year,' said Framton; 'but has that window got anything to do with the tragedy?'

'Out through that window, three years ago to a day, her husband and her two young brothers went off for their day's shooting. They never came back. In crossing the moor to their favourite snipe-shooting ground they were all three engulfed by a treacherous piece of bog. It had been that dreadful wet summer, you know, and places that were safe in other years gave way suddenly without warning. Their bodies were never recovered. That was the dreadful part of it.' Here the child's voice lost its self-possessed note and became falteringly human. 'Poor aunt always thinks that they will come back some day, they and the little brown spaniel that was lost with them, and walk in at that window just as they used to do. That is why the window is kept open every evening till it is quite dusk. Poor dear aunt, she has often told me how they went out, her husband with his white waterproof coat over his arm, and Ronnie, her youngest brother, singing "Bertie, why do you bound?" as he always did to tease her, because she said it got on her nerves. Do you know, sometimes on still, quiet evenings like this, I almost get a creepy feeling that they will all walk in through that window——'

She broke off with a little shudder. It was a relief to Framton when the aunt bustled into the room with a whirl of apologies for being late in making her appearance.

'I hope Vera has been amusing you?' she said.

'She has been very interesting,' said Framton.

'I hope you don't mind the open window,' said Mrs Sappleton briskly; 'my husband and brothers will be home directly from shooting, and they always come in this way. They've been out for snipe in the marshes today, so they'll make a fine mess over my poor carpets. So like you men-folk, isn't it?'

She rattled on cheerfully about the shooting and the scarcity of birds, and the prospects for duck in the winter. To Framton it was all purely horrible. He made a desperate but only partially successful effort to turn the talk on to a less ghastly topic; he was conscious that his hostess was giving him only a fragment of her attention, and her eyes were constantly straying past him to the open window and the lawn beyond. It was certainly an unfortunate coincidence that he should have paid his visit on this tragic anniversary.

'The doctors agree in ordering me complete rest, an absence of mental excitement, and avoidance of anything in the nature of violent physical exercise,' announced Framton, who laboured under the tolerably widespread delusion that total strangers and chance acquaintances are hungry for the least detail of one's ailments and infirmities, their cause and cure. 'On the matter of diet they are not so much in agreement,' he continued.

'No?' said Mrs Sappleton, in a voice which only replaced a yawn at the last moment. Then she suddenly brightened into alert attention – but not to what Framton was saying.

'Here they are at last!' she cried. 'Just in time for tea, and don't they look as if they were muddy up to the eyes!'

Framton shivered slightly, and turned towards the niece with a look intended to convey sympathetic comprehension. The child was staring out through the open window with dazed horror in her eyes. In a chill shock of nameless fear Framton swung round in his seat and looked in the same direction.

In the deepening twilight three figures were walking across the lawn towards the window; they all carried guns under their arms, and one of them was additionally burdened with a white coat hung over his shoulders. A tired brown spaniel kept close at their heels. Noiselessly they neared the house, and then a hoarse young voice chanted out of the dusk:

'I said, Bertie, why do you bound?'

Framton grabbed wildly at his stick and hat; the hall door, the gravel drive, and the front gate were dimly-noted stages in his headlong retreat. A cyclist coming along the road had to run into the hedge to avoid imminent collision.

'Here we are, my dear,' said the bearer of the white mackintosh, coming in through the window; 'fairly muddy, but most of it's dry. Who was that who bolted out as we came up?'

'A most extraordinary man, a Mr Nuttel,' said Mrs Sappleton; 'could only talk about his illnesses, and dashed off without a word of goodbye or apology when you arrived. One would think he had seen a ghost.'

'I expect it was the spaniel,' said the niece calmly; 'he told me he had a horror of dogs. He was once hunted into a cemetery somewhere on the banks of the Ganges by a pack of pariah dogs, and had to spend the night in a newly-dug grave with the creatures snarling and grinning and foaming just above him. Enough to make anyone lose their nerve.'

Romance at short notice was her speciality.

A Woman Seldom Found
William Sansom

Once a young man was on a visit to Rome.

It was his first visit; he came from the country – but he was neither on
the one hand so young nor on the other so simple as to imagine that a
great and beautiful capital should hold out finer promises than
anywhere else. He already knew that life was largely illusion, that
though wonderful things could happen, nevertheless as many
disappointments came in compensation: and he knew, too, that life
could offer a quality even worse – the probability that nothing would
happen at all. This was always more possible in a great city intent on its
own business.

Thinking in this way, he stood on the Spanish steps and surveyed the
momentous panorama stretched before him. He listened to the swelling
hum of the evening traffic and watched, as the lights went up against
Rome's golden dusk. Shining automobiles slunk past the fountains and
turned urgently into the bright Via Condotti, neon-red signs stabbed
the shadows with invitation; the yellow windows of buses were packed
with faces intent on going somewhere – everyone in the city seemed
intent on the evening's purpose. He alone had nothing to do.

He felt himself the only person alone of everyone in the city. But
searching for adventure never brought it – rather kept it away. Such a
mood promised nothing. So the young man turned back up the steps,
passed the lovely church, and went on up the cobbled hill towards his
hotel. Wine-bars and food-shops jostled with growing movement in
those narrow streets. But out on the broad pavements of the Vittorio
Veneto, under the trees mounting to the Borghese Gardens, the high
world of Rome would be filling the most elegant cafés in Europe to enjoy
with apéritifs the twilight. That would be the loneliest of all! So the
young man kept to the quieter, older streets on his solitary errand home.

In one such street, a pavementless alley between old yellow houses, a
street that in Rome might suddenly blossom into a secret piazza of
fountain and baroque church, a grave secluded treasure-place – he

noticed that he was alone but for the single figure of a woman walking down the hill towards him.

As she drew nearer, he saw that she was dressed with taste, that in her carriage was a soft Latin fire, that she walked for respect. Her face was veiled, but it was impossible to imagine that she would not be beautiful. Isolated thus with her, passing so near to her, and she symbolizing the adventure of which the evening was so empty – a greater melancholy gripped him. He felt wretched as the gutter, small, sunk, pitiful. So that he rounded his shoulders and lowered his eyes – but not before casting one furtive glance into hers.

He was so shocked at what he saw that he paused, he stared, shocked, into her face. He had made no mistake. She was smiling. Also – she too had hesitated. He thought instantly: 'Whore?' But no – it was not that kind of smile, though as well it was not without affection. And then amazingly she spoke:

'I – I know I shouldn't ask you ... but it is such a beautiful evening – and perhaps you are alone, as alone as I am ...'

She was very beautiful. He could not speak. But a growing elation gave him the power to smile. So that she continued, still hesitant, in no sense soliciting:

'I thought ... perhaps ... we could take a walk, an apéritif ...'

At last the young man achieved himself:

'Nothing, *nothing* would please me more. And the Veneto is only a minute up there.'

She smiled again:

'My home is just here ...'

They walked in silence a few paces down the street, to a turning that young man had already passed. This she indicated. They walked to where the first humble houses ended in a kind of recess. In the recess was set the wall of a garden, and behind it stood a large and elegant mansion. The woman, about whose face shone a curious glitter – something fused of the transparent pallor of fine skin, of grey but brilliant eyes, of dark eyebrows and hair of lucent black – inserted her key in the garden gate.

They were greeted by a servant in velvet livery. In a large and exquisite salon, under chandeliers of fine glass and before a moist green courtyard where water played, they were served with a frothy wine. They talked. The wine – iced in the warm Roman night – filled them with an inner warmth of exhilaration. But from time to time the young man looked at her curiously.

With her glances, with many subtle inflections of teeth and eyes she was inducing an intimacy that suggested much. He felt he must be careful. At length he thought the best thing might be to thank her – somehow thus to root out whatever obligation might be in store. But here she interrupted him, first with a smile, then with a look of some sadness. She begged him to spare himself any perturbation: she knew it was strange, that in such a situation he might suspect some second purpose: but the simple truth remained that she was lonely and – this with a certain deference – something perhaps in him, perhaps in that moment of dusk in the street, had proved to her inescapably attractive. She had not been able to help herself.

The possibility of a perfect encounter – a dream that years of disillusion will never quite kill – decided him. His elation rose beyond control. He believed her. And thereafter the perfections compounded. At her invitation they dined. Servants brought food of great delicacy; shell-fish, fat bird-flesh, soft fruits. And afterwards they sat on a sofa near the courtyard, where it was cool. Liqueurs were brought. The servants retired. A hush fell upon the house. They embraced.

A little later, with no word, she took his arm and led him from the room. How deep a silence had fallen between them! The young man's heart beat fearfully – it might be heard, he felt, echoing in the hall whose marble they now crossed, sensed through his arm to hers. But such excitement rose now from certainty. Certainty that at such a moment, on such a charmed evening – nothing could go wrong. There was no need to speak. Together they mounted the great staircase.

In her bedroom, to the picture of her framed by the bed curtains and dimly naked in a silken shift, he poured out his love; a love that was to be eternal, to be always perfect, as fabulous as this their exquisite meeting.

Softly she spoke the return of his love. Nothing would ever go amiss, nothing would ever come between them. And very gently she drew back the bedclothes for him.

But suddenly, at the moment when at last he lay beside her, when his lips were almost upon hers – he hesitated.

Something was wrong. A flaw could be sensed. He listened, felt – and then saw the fault was his. Shaded, soft-shaded lights by the bed – but he had been so careless as to leave on the bright electric chandelier in the centre of the ceiling. He remembered the switch was by the door. For a fraction, then, he hesitated. She raised her eyelids – saw his glance at the chandelier, understood.

Her eyes glittered. She murmured:

'My beloved, don't worry – don't move...'

And she reached out her hand. Her hand grew larger, her arm grew longer and longer, it stretched out through the bed-curtains, across the long carpet, huge and overshadowing the whole of the long room, until at last its giant fingers were at the door. With a terminal click, she switched out the light.

The Body Snatcher
Robert Louis Stevenson

Every night in the year, four of us sat in the small parlour of the George at Debenham – the undertaker, and the landlord, and Fettes, and myself. Sometimes there would be more; but blow high, blow low, come rain or snow or frost, we four would be each planted in his own particular armchair. Fettes was an old drunken Scotsman, a man of education obviously, and a man of some property, since he lived in idleness. He had come to Debenham years ago, while still young, and by a mere continuance of living and grown to be an adopted townsman. His blue camlet cloak was a local antiquity, like the church-spire. His place in the parlour at the George, his absence from church, his old, crapulous, disreputable vices, were all things of course in Debenham. He had some vague Radical opinions and some fleeting infidelities, which he would now and again set forth and emphasize with tottering slaps upon the table. He drank rum – five glasses regularly every evening; and for the greater portion of his nightly visit to the George sat, with his glass in his right hand, in a state of melancholy alcoholic saturation. We called him the Doctor, for he was supposed to have some special knowledge of medicine and had been known, upon a pinch, to set a fracture or reduce a dislocation; but beyond these slight particulars, we had no knowledge of his character and antecedents.

One dark winter night – it had struck nine some time before the landlord joined us – there was a sick man in the George, a great neighbouring proprietor suddenly struck down with apoplexy on his way to Parliament; and the great man's still greater London doctor had been telegraphed to his bedside. It was the first time that such a thing had happened in Debenham, for the railway was but newly open, and we were all proportionately moved by the occurrence.

'He's come,' said the landlord, after he had filled and lighted his pipe.

'He?' said I. 'Who? – not the doctor?'

'Himself,' replied our host.

'What is his name?'

'Dr Macfarlane,' said the landlord.

Fettes was far through this third tumbler, stupidly fuddled, now nodding over, now staring mazily around him; but at the last word he seemed to awaken and repeated the name 'Macfarlane' twice, quietly enough the first time, but with sudden emotion at the second.

'Yes,' said the landlord, 'that's his name, Doctor Wolfe Macfarlane.'

Fettes became instantly sober; his eyes awoke, his voice became clear, loud and steady, his language forcible and earnest. We were all startled by the transformation, as if a man had risen from the dead.

'I beg your pardon,' he said, 'I am afraid I have not been paying much attention to your talk. Who is this Wolfe Macfarlane?' And then, when he had heard the landlord out, 'It cannot be, it cannot be,' he added; 'and yet I would like well to see him face to face.'

'Do you know him, Doctor?' asked the undertaker, with a gasp.

'God forbid!' was the reply. 'And yet the name is a strange one; it were too much to fancy two. Tell me, landlord, is he old?'

'Well,' said the host, 'he's not a young man, to be sure, and his hair is white; but he looks younger than you.'

'He is older, though; years older. But,' with a slap upon the table, 'it's the rum you see in my face – rum and sin. This man, perhaps, may have an easy conscience and a good digestion. Conscience! Hear me speak. You would think I was some good, old, decent Christian, would you not? But no, not I; I never canted. Voltaire might have canted if he'd stood in my shoes; but the brains' – with a rattling fillip on his bald head – 'the brains were clear and active and I saw and made no deductions.'

'If you know this doctor,' I ventured to remark, after a somewhat awful pause, 'I should gather that you do not share the landlord's good opinion.'

Fettes paid no regard to me.

'Yes,' he said, with sudden decision, 'I must see him face to face.'

There was another pause and then a door was closed rather sharply on the first floor and a step was heard upon the stair.

'That's the doctor,' cried the landlord. 'Look sharp and you can catch him.'

It was but two steps from the small parlour to the door of the old George inn; the wide oak staircase landed almost in the street; there was room for a Turkey rug and nothing more between the threshold and the last round of the descent; but this little space was every evening brilliantly lit up, not only by the light upon the stair and the great signal-lamp below the sign, but by the warm radiance of the bar-room window. The George thus brightly advertised itself to passers-by in the cold street. Fettes walked steadily to the spot and we, who were hanging behind, beheld the two men meet, as one of them had phrased it, face to face. Dr Macfarlane was alert and vigorous. His white hair set off his pale and placid, although energetic, countenance. He was richly dressed in the finest of broadcloth and the whitest of linen, with a great gold watch-chain, and studs and spectacles of the same precious material. He wore a broad-folded tie, white and speckled with lilac, and he carried on his arm a comfortable driving-coat of fur. There was no doubt but he became his years, breathing, as he did, of wealth and consideration; and it was a surprising contrast to see our parlour sot – bald, dirty, pimpled and robed in his old camlet cloak – confront him at the bottom of the stairs.

'Macfarlane!' he said somewhat loudly, more like a herald than a friend.

The great doctor pulled up short on the fourth step, as though the familiarity of the address surprised and somewhat shocked his dignity.

'Toddy Macfarlane!' repeated Fettes.

The London man almost staggered. He stared for the swiftest of seconds at the man before him, glanced behind him with a sort of scare, and then in a startled whisper, 'Fettes!' he said, 'you!'

'Ay,' said the other, 'me! Did you think I was dead too? We are not so easy shut of our acquaintance.'

'Hush, hush!' exclaimed the doctor. 'Hush, hush! this meeting is so unexpected – I can see you are unmanned. I hardly knew you, I confess, at first, but I am overjoyed – overjoyed to have this opportunity. For the present it must be how-d'ye-do and goodbye in one, for my fly is waiting and I must not fail the train; but you shall – let me see – yes – you shall give me your address and you can count on early news of me. We must do something for you, Fettes. I fear you are out at elbows; but we must see to that for auld lang syne, as once we sang at suppers.'

'Money!' cried Fettes; 'money from you! The money that I had from you is lying where I cast it in the rain.'

Dr Macfarlane had talked himself into some measure of superiority and confidence, but the uncommon energy of this refusal cast him back into his first confusion.

A horrible, ugly look came and went across his almost venerable countenance. 'My dear fellow,' he said, 'be it as you please; my last thought is to offend you. I would intrude on none. I will leave you my address, however——'

'I do not wish it – I do not wish to know the roof that shelters you,' interrupted the other. 'I heard your name; I feared it might be you; I wished to know if, after all, there were a God; I know now that there is none. Begone!'

He still stood in the middle of the rug, between the stair and the doorway; and the great London physician, in order to escape, would be forced to step to one side. It was plain that he hesitated before the thought of this humiliation. White as he was, there was a dangerous glitter in his spectacles; but while he still paused uncertain, he became aware that the driver of his fly was peering in from the street at this unusual scene and caught a glimpse at the same time of our little body from the parlour, huddled by the corner of the bar. The presence of so many witnesses decided him at once to flee. He crouched together, brushing on the wainscot, and made a dart like a serpent, striking for the door. But his tribulation was not yet entirely at an end, for even as he was passing Fettes clutched him by the arm and these words came in a whisper, and yet painfully distinct, 'Have you seen it again?'

The great rich London doctor cried out aloud with a sharp, throttling cry; he dashed his questioner across the open space, and, with his hands over his head, fled out of the door like a detected thief. Before it had occurred to one of us to make a movement, the fly was already rattling towards the station. The scene was over like a dream, but the dream had left proofs and traces of its passage. Next day the servant found the fine gold spectacles broken on the threshold, and that very night we were all standing breathless by the bar-room window, and Fettes at our side, sober, pale, and resolute in look.

'God protect us, Mr Fettes!' said the landlord, coming first into possession of his customary senses. 'What in the universe is all this? These are strange things you have been saying.'

Fettes turned towards us; he looked us each in succession in the face. 'See if you can hold your tongues,' said he. 'That man Macfarlane is not safe to cross; those that have done so already have repented it too late.'

And then, without so much as finishing his third glass, far less waiting for the other two, he bade us goodbye and went forth, under the lamp of the hotel, into the black night.

We three turned to our places in the parlour, with the big red fire and four clear candles; and as we recapitulated what had passed the first chill of our surprise soon changed into a glow of curiosity. We sat late; it was the latest session I have known in the old George. Each man, before we parted, had his theory that he was bound to prove; and none of us had any nearer business in this world than to track out the past of our condemned companion, and surprise the secret that he shared with the great London doctor. It was no great boast, but I believe I was a better hand at worming out a story than either of my fellows at the George; and perhaps there is now no other man alive who could narrate to you the following foul and unnatural events.

In his young days Fettes studied medicine in the schools of Edinburgh. He had talent of a kind, the talent that picks up swiftly what it hears and readily retails it for its own. He worked little at home; but he was civil, attentive, and intelligent in the presence of his masters. They soon picked him out as a lad who listened closely and remembered well;

nay, strange as it seemed to me when I first heard it, he was in those days well favoured, and pleased by his exterior. There was, at that period, a certain extramural teacher of anatomy, whom I shall here designate by the letter K. His name was subsequently too well known. The man who bore it skulked through the streets of Edinburgh in disguise, while the mob that applauded at the execution of Burke called loudly for the blood of his employer. But Mr K—— was then at the top of his vogue; he enjoyed a popularity due partly to his own talent and address, partly to the incapacity of his rival, the university professor. The students, at least, swore by his name, and Fettes believed himself, and was believed by others, to have laid the foundations of success when he had acquired the favour of this meteorically famous man. Mr K—— was a *bon vivant* as well as an accomplished teacher; he liked a sly allusion no less than a careful preparation. In both capacities Fettes enjoyed and deserved his notice, and by the second year of his attendance he held the half-regular position of second demonstrator or sub-assistant in his class.

In this capacity, the charge of the theatre and lecture room devolved in particular upon his shoulders. He had to answer for the cleanliness of the premises and the conduct of the other students, and it was a part of his duty to supply, receive, and divide the various subjects. It was with a view to this last – at that time very delicate – affair that he was lodged by Mr K—— in the same wynd, and at last in the same building, with the dissecting rooms. Here, after a night of turbulent pleasures, his hand still tottering, his sight still misty and confused, he would be called out of bed in the black hours before the winter dawn by the unclean and desperate interlopers who supplied the table. He would open the door to these men, since infamous throughout the land. He would help them with their tragic burthen, pay them their sordid price, and remain alone, when they were gone, with the unfriendly relics of humanity. From such a scene he would return to snatch another hour or two of slumber, to repair the abuses of the night, and refresh himself for the labours of the day.

Few lads could have been more insensible to the impressions of a life thus passed among the ensigns of mortality. His mind was closed against all general considerations. He was incapable of interest in the fate and fortunes of another, the slave of his own desires and low ambitions. Cold, light and selfish in the last resort, he had that modicum of prudence, miscalled morality, which keeps a man from inconvenient drunkenness or punishable theft. He coveted, besides, a measure of consideration from his masters and his fellow-pupils, and he had no desire to fail conspicuously in the external parts of life. Thus he made it his pleasure to gain some distinction in his studies, and day after day rendered unimpeachable eye-service to his employer, Mr K——. For his day of work he indemnified himself by nights of roaring, blackguardly enjoyment; and when that balance had been struck, the organ that he called his conscience declared itself content.

The supply of subjects was a continual trouble to him as well as to his master. In that large and busy class, the raw material of the anatomists kept perpetually running out; and the business thus rendered necessary was not only unpleasant in itself, but threatened dangerous consequences to all who were concerned. It was the policy of Mr K—— to ask no questions in his dealings with the trade. 'They bring the body, and we pay the price,' he used to say, dwelling on the alliteration – '*quid pro quo.*' And again, and somewhat profanely, 'Ask no questions,' he would tell his assistants, 'for conscience' sake.' There was no understanding that the subjects were provided by the crime of murder. Had that idea been broached to him in words, he would have recoiled in horror; but the lightness of his speech upon so grave a matter was, in itself, an offence against good manners, and a temptation to the men with whom he dealt. Fettes, for instance, had often remarked to himself upon the singular freshness of the bodies. He had been struck again and again by the hang-dog, abominable looks of the ruffians who came to him before the dawn; and, putting things together clearly in his private thoughts, he perhaps attributed a meaning too immoral and too categorical to the unguarded counsels of his master. He understood his duty, in short, to have three branches: to take what was brought, to pay the price, and to avert the eye from any evidence of crime.

One November morning this policy of silence was put sharply to the test. He had been awake all night with a racking toothache – pacing his room like a caged beast or throwing himself in fury on his bed – and had fallen at last into that profound, uneasy slumber that so often follows on a night of pain, when he was awakened by the third or fourth angry repetition of the concerted signal. There was a thin, bright moonshine: it was bitter cold, windy, and frosty; the town had not yet awakened, but an indefinable stir already preluded the noise and business of the day. The ghouls had come later than usual, and they seemed more than usually eager to be gone. Fettes, sick with sleep, lighted them upstairs. He heard their grumbling Irish voices through a dream; and as they stripped the sack from their sad merchandise he leaned dozing with his shoulder propped against the wall; he had to shake himself to find the men their money. As he did so his eyes lighted on the dead face. He started; he took two steps nearer, with the candle raised.

'God Almighty!' he cried. 'That is Jane Galbraith!'

The men answered nothing, but they shuffled nearer the door.

'I know her, I tell you,' he continued. 'She was alive and hearty yesterday. It's impossible she can be dead; it's impossible you should have got this body fairly.'

'Sure, sir, you're mistaken entirely,' asserted one of the men.

But the other looked Fettes darkly in the eyes, and demanded the money on the spot.

It was impossible to misconceive the threat or to exaggerate the danger. The lad's heart failed him. He stammered some excuses, counted out the sum, and saw his hateful visitors depart. No sooner were they gone than he hastened to confirm his doubts. By a dozen unquestionable marks he identified the girl he had jested with the day before. He saw, with horror, marks upon her body that might well betoken violence. A panic seized him, and he took refuge in his room. There he reflected at length over the discovery that he had made; considered soberly the bearing of Mr K——'s instructions and the danger to himself of interference in so serious a business, and at last, in sore perplexity, determined to wait for the advice of his immediate superior, the class assistant.

This was a young doctor, Wolfe Macfarlane, a high favourite among all the restless students, clever, dissipated, and unscrupulous to the last degree. He had travelled and studied abroad. His manners were agreeable and a little forward. He was an authority on the stage, skilful on the ice or the links with skate or golf-club; he dressed with nice audacity, and, to put the finishing touch upon his glory, he kept a gig and a strong trotting-horse. With Fettes he was on terms of intimacy; indeed their relative positions called for some community of life; and when subjects were scarce the pair would drive far into the country in Macfarlane's gig, visit and desecrate some lonely graveyard, and return before dawn with their booty to the door of the dissecting room.

On that particular morning Macfarlane arrived somewhat earlier than his wont. Fettes heard him, and met him on the stairs, told him his story, and showed him the cause of his alarm. Macfarlane examined the marks on her body.

'Yes,' he said with a nod, 'it looks fishy.'

'Well, what should I do?' asked Fettes.

'Do?' repeated the other. 'Do you want to do anything? Least said soonest mended, I should say.'

'Someone else might recognize her,' objected Fettes. 'She was as well known as the Castle Rock.'

'We'll hope not,' said Macfarlane, 'and if anybody does – well you didn't, don't you see, and there's an end. The fact is, this has been going on too long. Stir up the mud, and you'll get K—— into the most unholy trouble; you'll be in a shocking box yourself. So will I, if you come to that. I should like to know how any one of us would look, or what the devil we should have to say for ourselves, in any Christian witness-box. For me, you know there's one thing certain – that, practically speaking, all our subjects have been murdered.'

'Macfarlane!' cried Fettes.

'Come now!' sneered the other. 'As if you hadn't suspected it yourself!'

'Suspecting is one thing——'

'And proof another. Yes, I know; and I'm as sorry as you are this should have come here,' tapping the body with his cane. 'The next best thing for me is not to recognize it; and,' he added coolly, 'I don't. You may, if you please. I don't dictate, but I think a man of the world would do as I do; and I may add, I fancy that is what K—— would look for at our hands. The question is, why did he choose us two for his assistants? And I answer, because he didn't want old wives.'

This was the tone of all others to affect the mind of a lad like Fettes. He agreed to imitate Macfarlane. The body of the unfortunate girl was duly dissected, and no one remarked or appeared to recognize her.

One afternoon, when his day's work was over, Fettes dropped into a popular tavern and found Macfarlane sitting with a stranger. This was a small man, very pale and dark, with coal-black eyes. The cut of his features gave a promise of intellect and refinement which was but feebly realized in his manners, for he proved, upon a nearer acquaintance, coarse, vulgar, and stupid. He exercised, however, a very remarkable control over Macfarlane; issued orders like the Great Bashaw; became inflamed at the least discussion or delay, and commented rudely on the servility with which he was obeyed. This most offensive person took a fancy to Fettes on the spot, plied him with drinks, and honoured him with unusual confidences on his past career. If a tenth part of what he confessed were true, he was a very loathsome rogue; and the lad's vanity was tickled by the attention of so experienced a man.

'I'm a pretty bad fellow myself,' the stranger remarked, 'but Macfarlane is the boy – Toddy Macfarlane I call him. Toddy, order your friend another glass.' Or it might be, 'Toddy, you jump up and shut the door.' 'Toddy hates me,' he said again. 'Oh, yes, Toddy, you do!'

'Don't call me that confounded name,' growled Macfarlane.

'Hear him! Did you ever see the lads play knife? He would like to do that all over my body,' remarked the stranger.

'We medicals have a better way than that,' said Fettes. 'When we dislike a dead friend of ours, we dissect him.'

Macfarlane looked up sharply, as though this jest was scarcely to his mind.

The afternoon passed. Gray, for that was the stranger's name, invited Fettes to join them at dinner, ordered a feast so sumptuous that the tavern was thrown in commotion, and when all was done commanded Macfarlane to settle the bill. It was late before they separated; the man Gray was incapably drunk. Macfarlane, sobered by his fury, chewed the cud of the money he had been forced to squander and the slights he had been obliged to swallow. Fettes, with various liquors singing in his head, returned home with devious footsteps and a mind entirely in abeyance. Next day Macfarlane was absent from the class, and Fettes smiled to himself as he imagined him still squiring the intolerable Gray from tavern to tavern. As soon as the hour of liberty had struck he posted from place to place in quest of his last night's companions. He could find them, however, nowhere; so returned early to his rooms, went early to bed, and slept the sleep of the just.

At four in the morning he was awakened by the well known signal. Descending to the door, he was filled with astonishment to find Macfarlane with his gig, and in the gig one of those long and ghastly packages with which he was so well acquainted.

'What?' he cried. 'Have you been out alone? How did you manage?'

But Macfarlane silenced him roughly, bidding him turn to business. When they had got the body upstairs and laid it on the table, Macfarlane made at first as if he were going away. Then he paused and seemed to hesitate; and then, 'You had better look at the face,' said he, in tones of some constraint. 'You had better,' he repeated, as Fettes only stared at him in wonder.

'But where, and how, and when did you come by it?' cried the other.

'Look at the face,' was the only answer.

Fettes was staggered; strange doubts assailed him. He looked from the young doctor to the body, and then back again. At last, with a start, he did as he was bidden. He had almost expected the sight that met his eyes, and yet the shock was cruel. To see, fixed in the rigidity of death and naked on that coarse layer of sack-cloth, the man whom he had left well-clad and full of meat and sin upon the threshold of a tavern, awoke, even in the thoughtless Fettes, some of the terrors of the conscience. It was a *cras tibi* which re-echoed in his soul, that two whom he had known should have come to lie upon these icy tables. Yet these were only secondary thoughts. His first concern regarded Wolfe. Unprepared for a challenge so momentous, he knew not how to look his comrade in the face. He durst not meet his eye, and he had neither words nor voice at his command.

It was Macfarlane himself who made the first advance. He came up quietly behind and laid his hand gently but firmly on the other's shoulder.

'Richardson,' said he, 'may have the head.'

Now Richardson was a student who had long been anxious for that portion of the human subject to dissect. There was no answer, and the murderer resumed: 'Talking of business, you must pay me; your accounts, you see, must tally.'

Fettes found a voice, the ghost of his own: 'Pay you!' he cried. 'Pay you for that?'

'Why, yes, of course you must. By all means and on every possible account, you must,' returned the other. 'I dare not give it for nothing, you dare not take it for nothing; it would compromise us both. This is another case like Jane Galbraith's. The more things are wrong the more we must act as if all were right. Where does old K—— keep his money——'

'There,' answered Fettes hoarsely, pointing to a cupboard in the corner.

'Give me the key, then,' said the other, calmly, holding out his hand.

There was an instant's hesitation, and the die was cast. Macfarlane could not suppress a nervous twitch, the infinitesimal mark of an immense relief, as he felt the key turn between his fingers. He opened the cupboard, brought out pen and ink and a paper-book that stood in one compartment, and separated from the funds in a drawer a sum suitable to the occasion.

'Now, look here,' he said, 'there is the payment made – first proof of you good faith: first step to your security. You have now to clinch it by a second. Enter the payment in your book, and then you for your part may defy the devil.'

The next few seconds were for Fettes an agony of thought; but in balancing his terrors it was the most immediate that triumphed. Any future difficulty seemed almost welcome if he could avoid a present quarrel with Macfarlane. He set down the candle which he had been carrying all the time, and with a steady hand entered the date, the nature, and the amount of the transaction.

'And now,' said Macfarlane, 'it's only fair that you should pocket the lucre. I've had my share already. By-the-by, when a man of the world falls into a bit of luck, he has a few shillings extra in his pocket – I'm ashamed to speak of it, but there's a rule of conduct in the case. No treating, no purchase of expensive class-books, no squaring of old debts; borrow, don't lend.'

'Macfarlane,' began Fettes, still somewhat hoarsely. 'I have put my neck in a halter to oblige you.'

'To oblige me?' cried Wolfe. 'Oh, come! You did, as near as I can see the matter, what you downright had to do in self defence. Suppose I got into trouble, where would you be? This second little matter flows clearly from the first. Mr Gray is the continuation of Miss Galbraith. You can't begin and then stop. If you begin, you must keep on beginning; that's the truth. No rest for the wicked.'

A horrible sense of blackness and the treachery of fate seized hold upon the soul of the unhappy student.

'My God!' he cried, 'but what have I done? and when did I begin? To be made a class assistant – in the name of reason, where's the harm in that? Service wanted the position; Service might have got it. Would *he* have been where *I* am now?'

'My dear fellow,' said Macfarlane, 'what a boy you are! What harm *has* come to you? What harm *can* come to you if you hold your tongue? Why, man, do you know what this life is? There are two squads of us – the lions and the lambs. If you're a lamb, you'll come to lie upon these tables like Gray or Jane Galbraith; if you're a lion, you'll live and drive a horse like me, like K——, like all the world with any wit or courage. You're staggered at the first. But look at K——! My dear fellow, you're clever, you have pluck. I like you, and K—— likes you. You were born to lead the hunt: and I tell you, on my honour and my experience of life, three days from now you'll laugh at all these scarecrows like a high school boy at a farce.'

And with that Macfarlane took his departure and drove off up the wynd in his gig to get under cover before daylight. Fettes was thus left alone with his regrets. He saw the miserable peril in which he stood involved. He saw, with inexpressible dismay, that there was no limit to his weakness, and that, from concession to concession, he had fallen from the arbiter of Macfarlane's destiny to his paid and helpless accomplice. He would have given the world to have been a little braver at the time, but it did not occur to him that he might still be brave. The secret of Jane Galbraith and the cursed entry in the daybook closed his mouth.

Hours passed; the class began to arrive; the members of the unhappy Gray were dealt out to one and to another, and received without remark. Richardson was made happy with the head; and before the hour of freedom rang Fettes trembled with exultation to perceive how far they had already gone towards safety.

For two days he continued to watch, with increasing joy, the dreadful process of disguise.

On the third day Macfarlane made his appearance. He had been ill, he said; but he made up for lost time by the energy with which he directed the students. To Richardson in particular he extended the most valuable assistance and advice, and that student, encouraged by the praise of the demonstrator, burned high with ambitious hopes, and saw the medal already in his grasp.

Before the week was out Macfarlane's prophecy had been fulfilled. Fettes had outlived his terrors and had forgotten his baseness. He began to plume himself upon his courage, and had so arranged the story in his mind that he could look back on these events with an unhealthy pride. Of his accomplice he saw but little. They met, of course, in the business of the class; they received their orders together from Mr K——. At times they had a word or two in private, and Macfarlane was from first to last particularly kind and jovial. But it was plain that he avoided any reference to their common secret; and even when Fettes whispered to him that he had cast in his lot with the lions and forsworn the lambs, he only signed to him smilingly to hold his peace.

At length an occasion arose which drew the pair once more into a closer union. Mr K—— was again short of subjects; pupils were eager, and it was a part of this teacher's pretensions to be always well supplied. At the same time there came the news of a burial in the rustic graveyard of Glencorse. Time has little changed the place in question. It stood then, as now, upon the crossroad, out of call of human habitations, and buried fathom deep in the foliage of six cedar trees. The cries of the sheep upon the neighbouring hills, the streamlets upon either hand, one loudly singing among pebbles, the other dripping furtively from pond to pond, the stir of the wind in mountainous old flowering chestnuts, and once in seven days the voice of the bell and the old tunes of the precentor, were the only sounds that disturbed the silence around the rural church. The Resurrection Man – to use a by-name of the period – was not to be deterred by any of the sanctities of customary piety. It was part of his trade to despise and desecrate the scrolls and trumpets of old tombs, the paths worn by the feet of worshippers and mourners, and the offerings and the inscriptions of bereaved affection. To rustic neighbourhoods, where love is more than commonly tenacious, and where some bonds of blood or fellowship unite the entire society of a parish, the body-snatcher, far from being repelled by natural respect, was attracted by the ease and safety of the task. To bodies that had been laid in earth, in joyful expectation of a far different awakening, there came that hasty, lamp-lit, terror-haunted resurrection of the spade and mattock. The coffin was forced, the cerements torn, and the melancholy relics, clad in sackcloth, after being rattled for hours on moonless by-ways, were at length exposed to uttermost indignities before a class of gaping boys.

Somewhat as two vultures may swoop upon a dying lamb, Fettes and Macfarlane were to be let loose upon a grave in that green and quiet resting place. The wife of a farmer, a woman who had lived for sixty years, and been known for nothing but good butter and a godly conversation, was to be rooted from her grave at midnight and carried, dead and naked, to that far away city that she had always honoured with her Sunday best; the place beside her family was to be empty till the crack of doom; her innocent and almost venerable members to be exposed to that last curiosity of the anatomist.

Late one afternoon the pair set forth, well wrapped in cloaks and furnished with a formidable bottle. It rained without remission – a cold, dense, lashing rain. Now and again there blew a puff of wind, but these sheets of falling water kept it down. Bottle and all, it was a sad and silent drive as far as Penicuik, where they were to spend the evening. They stopped once, to hide their implements in a thick bush not far from the

churchyard, and once again at the Fisher's Tryst, to have a toast before
the kitchen fire and vary their nips of whisky with a glass of ale. When
they reached their journey's end the gig was housed, the horse was fed
and comforted, and the two young doctors in a private room sat down to
the best dinner and the best wine the house afforded. The lights, the fire,
the beating rain upon the window, the cold, incongruous work that lay
before them, added zest to their enjoyment of the meal. With every glass
their cordiality increased. Soon Macfarlane handed a little pile of gold
to his companion.

'A compliment,' he said. 'Between friends these little damned
accommodations ought to fly like pipe-lights.'

Fettes pocketed the money, and applauded the sentiment to the
echo. 'You are a philosopher,' he cried. 'I was an ass till I knew you. You
and K—— between you, by the Lord Harry! but you'll make a man of
me.'

'Of course we shall,' applauded Macfarlane. 'A man? I tell you, it
required a man to back me up the other morning. There are some big,
brawling, forty-year-old cowards who would have turned sick at the
look of the damned thing; but not you – you kept your head. I watched
you.'

'Well, and why not?' Fettes thus vaunted himself. 'It was no affair of
mine. There was nothing to gain on the one side but disturbance, and on
the other I could count on your gratitude, don't you see?' And he
slapped his pocket till the gold pieces rang.

Macfarlane somehow felt a certain touch of alarm at these unpleasant words. He may have regretted that he had taught his young
companion so successfully, but he had no time to interfere, for the other
noisily continued in this boastful strain:

'The great thing is not to be afraid. Now, between you and me, I
don't want to hang – that's practical; but for all cant, Macfarlane, I was
born with a contempt. Hell, God, Devil, right, wrong, sin, crime, and all
the old gallery of curiosities – they may frighten boys, but men of the
world, like you and me, despise them. Here's to the memory of Gray!'

It was by this time growing somewhat late. The gig, according to
order, was brought round to the door with both lamps brightly shining,
and the young men had to pay their bill and take the road. They
announced that they were bound for Peebles, and drove in that
direction till they were clear of the last houses of the town; then,
extinguishing the lamps, returned upon their course, and followed a by-
road towards Glencorse. There was no sound but that of their own
passage, and the incessant, strident pouring of the rain. It was pitch
dark; here and there a white gate or a white stone in the wall guided
them for a short space across the night; but for the most part it was at a
foot pace, and almost groping, that they picked their way through that

resonant blackness to their solemn and isolated destination. In the sunken woods that traverse the neighbourhood of the burying ground the last glimmer failed them, and it became necessary to kindle a match and re-illumine one of the lanterns of the gig. Thus, under the dripping trees, and environed by huge and moving shadows, they reached the scene of their unhallowed labours.

They were both experienced in such affairs, and powerful with the spade; and they had scarce been twenty minutes at their task before they were rewarded by a dull rattle on the coffin lid. At the same moment Macfarlane, having hurt his hand upon a stone, flung it carelessly above his head. The grave, in which they now stood almost to the shoulders, was close to the edge of the plateau of the graveyard; and the gig lamp had been propped, the better to illuminate their labours, against a tree, and on the immediate verge of the steep bank descending to the stream. Chance had taken a sure aim with the stone. Then came a clang of broken glass; night fell upon them; sounds alternately dull and ringing announced the bounding of the lantern down the bank, and its occasional collision with the trees. A stone or two, which it had dislodged in its descent rattled behind it into the profundities of the glen; and then silence, like night, resumed its sway; and they might bend their hearing to its utmost pitch, but naught was to be heard except the rain, now marching to the wind, now steadily falling over miles of open country.

They were so nearly at an end of their abhorred task that they judged it wisest to complete it in the dark. The coffin was exhumed and broken open; the body inserted in the dripping sack and carried between them to the gig; one mounted to keep it in its place, and the other, taking the horse by the mouth, groped along by the wall and bush until they reached the wider road by the Fisher's Tryst. Here was a faint disused radiancy, which they hailed like daylight; by that they pushed the horse to a good pace and began to rattle along merrily in the direction of the town.

They had both been wetted to the skin during their operations, and now, as the gig jumped among the deep ruts, the thing that stood propped between them fell now upon one and now upon the other. At every repetition of the horrid contact each instinctively repelled it with greater haste; and the process, natural although it was, began to tell upon the nerves of the companions. Macfarlane made some ill-favoured jest about the farmer's wife, but it came hollowly from his lips, and was allowed to drop in silence. Still their unnatural burthen bumped from side to side; and now the head would be laid, as if in confidence, upon their shoulders; and now the drenching sackcloth would flap icily about their faces. A creeping chill began to possess the soul of Fettes. He peered at the bundle, and it seemed somehow larger than at first. All over the countryside, and from every degree of distance, the farm dogs accompanied their passage with tragic ululations; and it grew and grew upon his mind that some unnatural miracle had been achieved, that some nameless change had befallen the dead body, and that it was in fear of their unholy burthen that the dogs were howling.

'For God's sake,' said he, making a great effort to arrive at speech, 'for God's sake, let's have a light!'

Seemingly Macfarlane was affected in the same direction; for though he made no reply, he stopped the horse, passed the reins to his companion, got down, and proceeded to kindle the remaining lamp. They had by that time got no farther than the crossroad down to Auchendinny. The rain still poured as though the deluge were returning, and it was no easy matter to make a light in such a world of wet and darkness. When at last the flickering blue flame had been transferred to the wick and began to expand and clarify, and shed a wide circle of misty brightness round the gig, it became possible for the two young men to see each other and the thing they had along with them. The rain had moulded the rough sacking to the outlines of the body underneath; the head was distinct from the trunk, the shoulders plainly modelled; something at once spectral and human riveted their eyes upon the ghastly comrade of their drive.

For some time Macfarlane stood motionless, holding up the lamp. A nameless dread was swathed, like a wet sheet, about the body, and tightened the white skin upon the face of Fettes; a fear that was meaningless, a horror of what could not be, kept mounting to his brain. Another beat of the watch, and he had spoken. But his comrade forestalled him.

'That is not a woman,' said Macfarlane, in a hushed voice.

'It was a woman when we put her in,' whispered Fettes.

'Hold that lamp,' said the other. 'I must see her face.'

And as Fettes took the lamp his companion untied the fastenings of the sack and drew down the cover from the head. The light fell very clear upon the dark, well-moulded features and smooth-shaven cheeks of a too familiar countenance, often beheld in dreams of both of these young men. A wild yell rang up into the night; each leaped from his own side into the roadway; the lamp fell, broke, and was extinguished; and the horse, terrified by this unusual commotion, bounded and went off towards Edinburgh at a gallop, bearing along with it, sole occupant of the gig, the body of the dead and long-dissected Gray.

Travelling Light
Bernard Taylor

'But you said you'd be arriving *tomorrow* . . .'

The little woman behind the reception desk looked more and more flustered and bewildered. Gideon turned to the stranger who stood nearby, shrugged helplessly, gave an ironic grin, then turned back to the woman. She looked at him anxiously through her thick-lensed spectacles.

'No,' Gideon said patiently. 'I wrote to say that *I* would be getting here *today*. My *wife* would be arriving *tomorrow*. But *I'd* be here *today*. I told you. I thought I made it perfectly clear . . .' His voice trailed off in the face of her helpless, wide-eyed inadequacy.

'I'm sorry,' she murmured. She seemed almost on the point of tears. 'I really am sorry. I don't know how there came to be such a mix-up.' She shook her head. 'And there's nothing at all available for tonight . . .'

At these last words the stranger took an anxious step forward, opening his mouth to speak. Quickly the woman forestalled him.

'Oh, we've got *your* room, Mr Travers . . .'

The man sighed, smiled, relaxing. The little woman went on:

'Though it seems they've given you a double room instead of the single you booked . . .' Weakly, she smiled away the inefficiency. 'Of course, we won't charge you the full rate . . .'

Gideon was stooping, picking up his suitcases. Now he'd have to start searching the hotels in the area. It was a bloody nuisance. And then the woman spoke again, her voice bright with inspiration.

'The room does have *two* beds in it . . .' Her suggestion hung in the air. She looked eagerly from one man to the other.

Travers at once took up the idea. He spoke for the first time, his voice, with its strong Scottish accent, taking Gideon by surprise.

'Now that's something to consider,' he said. He turned to Gideon. 'You'd be most welcome to share. After all, it's only for a night. And *I* certainly don't mind.'

Relief swept over Gideon. He beamed at the older man. 'That's very kind of you. Are you quite sure?'

'Perfectly.' Travers gave him a gap-toothed smile. 'I'm only too glad to help.'

A little while later, up in the room, Gideon sat on the edge of his bed clipping his fingernails and waiting for Travers to finish in the bathroom. Carefully he placed the nail-parings in a nearby ashtray. Already, from the bedside table, Beth smiled at him from the narrow leather frame of her photograph. Tomorrow, Gideon thought ... Tomorrow ...

Travers had left the bathroom door open, and now, as Gideon moved, he could see the other man as he stood at the wash-basin, a hotel towel around his naked waist. He was shaving with an old-fashioned cut-throat razor. Gideon watched, admiring the dexterity with which he handled the cruel-looking instrument.

'It's years since I saw anyone using one of those,' Gideon said, 'outside the barber's.'

'You can't beat it,' Travers said. Neatly he skimmed the blade over his prominent Adam's apple. 'It does the best job. By far.'

Gideon said, grimacing: 'It makes me think of those terrible murders that have been going on ...'

'The wife-slayings,' Travers said. 'Yes, very strange business.'

'Just imagine,' Gideon said, 'seven killings, all practically identical in pattern. All carried out in full view of reliable witnesses, and in each case by the victim's husband.' He shuddered. 'It's like some awful disease. Terrifying thought.' He shuddered. 'Imagine – seven of them.'

'You're wrong,' Travers said. 'Eight. There was another one this morning.' He carefully circumnavigated a large wart on his chin. 'Just like all the others. Her throat cut from ear to ear. Head almost severed from the body. Took place in the street this time. Brighton. Husband arrested again. There were plenty of witnesses. As usual.'

Gideon continued to watch as, with sensitive fingers, Travers tested the smoothness of his jaw. He was not a particularly attractive specimen, Gideon thought. The man's skin was unusually pallid, looking as though it was never exposed to the sun; it had a protected, preserved look about it. Over the white flesh of his chest grew a mat of short, spiky hair – like his eyebrows, eyelashes and the hair on his head, all of a light, sandy redness. And then, suddenly, Gideon was aware of Travers's pale eyes fixed upon him. Embarrassed, he looked away.

'So your wife's joining you tomorrow,' Travers said.

'Yes.' Gideon nodded happily. He and Beth had been apart for three months now, and these last days seemed never-ending. 'I'm doing this course,' he explained, when Travers asked the reason for their separation. 'It's not over yet, but at least we thought we could spend my holiday together – in a nice place.'

'You sound as if you're pretty close,' Travers said.

'We are.' Gideon thought of Beth, pictured her lovingly, her warm, soft features, her bright, clear blue eyes. Marrying her had been the best thing he had ever done. All pride, he shrugged, smiled. 'She's ... great ...'

'Well, that's good,' Travers said. 'Nice to hear.' He shook his razor dry and slipped it back into its case. 'Save me shaving in the morning,' he said. 'I'm not so fussy.' He put the razor-case into a plastic toilet bag. 'You people who go around with loads of suitcases,' he said, 'I believe in travelling light.' He came to the doorway, paused, his hand on the light switch. 'You want to come in here?'

'Yes.' Gideon rose from the bed. 'I think I'll have a shower.'

With the bathroom door closed behind him, Gideon stripped and stood before the mirror. Unlike Travers, he had a handsome body, tanned golden brown by the sun. His hair grew thick and richly black, its darkness contrasting with the whiteness of his smile. And today there was reason to smile: tomorrow he would see Beth again.

Later, when he emerged from the bathroom, he found Travers lying back smoking a cigarette. Gideon lay down on his own bed, a towelling robe around him. 'God, I'm tired,' he said. 'All that travelling ... the heat. I think I'll sleep for a while.'

'What time are you expecting your wife?' Travers asked. He was studying the small photograph of Beth. 'Early?'

'At ten tomorrow morning,' Gideon said. Somehow he resented Travers handling the framed picture. He watched him anxiously.

'She's very pretty,' Travers said.

'Yes ...'

'Are you meeting her at the station?'

'No. Here. Down in the foyer. She wasn't sure which train she'd manage, so ...' He paused. 'It was her idea.'

With some relief he watched as Travers replaced the photograph on the bedside table. He yawned.

'You do seem somewhat tired,' Travers said.

'Yes.' Gideon nodded, yawning again. He turned, smiling, stretching out full-length on the bed. Ten minutes later he was asleep.

When Travers leaned over him to clip from his head a lock of hair, Gideon almost awoke. For a moment he stirred uneasily, a frown creasing the smoothness of his tanned forehead. His mouth opened slightly in a silent, unknowing protest, and then he sank again, back into his slumber. Travers, standing above him, held the lock of hair in his hand. He added it to the little collection of nail-parings he had taken from the ash-tray. He smiled. It would be quite enough.

*   *   *

In the morning, when Gideon awoke, Travers was still asleep. The shape of him was just visible in the dim daylight as he lay bundled up under the bed-covers. Moving to the bathroom, Gideon turned on the water to wash. He felt odd, almost as if he were suffering from a hangover. But that couldn't be – he'd had nothing to drink last night.

The hot water gushed from the tap, clouding the glass. Yawning, Gideon switched on the light and rubbed a clear circle on the glass.

And then his heart turned over.

He looked at his white skin and the short, sandy-red hair that grew on his head and chest. He opened his mouth in a short cry of fear and horror and saw that two front teeth were missing. The hand that leapt to his face felt the ugly wart that stood out on his chin. Gasping for breath, he leaned over the basin, clutching at the rim for support. Dimly, from the bedroom, came the sounds of Travers stirring. After long moments he came in view.

Gideon raised his pale eyes and looked at him through sandy eyelashes. And he saw the dark, waving hair, the smooth, tanned cheek that Beth had so often kissed. Travers smiled at him, showing white, even teeth.

'Don't look like that,' he said. 'It won't be for long.' And he spoke with Gideon's own voice.

Gideon continued to stare, eyes wide with horror, uncomprehending and yet comprehending. Travers said, with a note of impatience: 'You're not going to stand there all day are you?'

'Oh God,' Gideon said – and spoke with a Scottish accent. 'Oh God, oh God, oh God, oh God . . .'

Travers smiled again, his cheek dimpling in the way that Beth had always loved. 'Come on,' he said. 'Time's getting on. And I've got an appointment at ten.' He opened the toilet bag and took from it the razor-case. Lifting out the razor he tested, on his thumb, the keenness of its shining blade.

'Come on,' he said. 'I've got to meet a lady. Down in the foyer.' He gave Gideon a grotesque wink. 'I mustn't keep her waiting.'

The Deathly Silence
Rosemary Timperley

He sits there, reading. The book lies open on the table before him. At regular intervals, he turns the page. Nothing distracts him. He has not spoken to me for weeks, not one word. I hate him.

When first we were married and he imposed these silences on the house, I would question him: 'What's the matter? Why aren't you speaking to me? What have I done?' Then, foolishly, I would start guessing: 'Is it that I mended your socks with the wrong colour wool? Or that I forgot to buy the marmalade? Or that your breakfast egg was overcooked? Or——' My list of sins and omissions as a wife was endless, I admit, but he'd never say which sin he was sulking *about*. So I stopped guessing and learned to stay silent myself.

The silences grew longer, with shorter intervals in between each. This latest one – I've lost count of its duration. It seems unbreakable. The longer it gets, the stronger it gets.

And *why*? I can only conclude that he simply regrets marrying the vast accumulation of faults which constitutes me, so is pretending to himself that he hasn't. Apart from accepting my services, albeit rather incompetent, he pretends I'm not there.

I suppose I could leave him – many women would – but I'm religious. At our wedding, I promised God I'd stick by my husband 'till death us do part', and breaking a promise to God is very dodgy. You never know what He might do to get His own back.

So there we are, night after night. He returns from work, has some supper, then sits at that table, reading. What does he read? Anything. Thrillers, biographies, travel books. As long as it's print. He removes himself from my presence mentally by absorbing himself in print.

The other night I thought: If only he really *did* remove himself from my presence. For the very sight of him sitting there was beginning to fill me with impotent rage. I wanted to bash him on the head with the frying-pan. But I didn't. I controlled such impulses, buried them inside me, let them boil, stew, bubble, ferment. I became full of mental poison.

It was thinking of this mental poison that turned my mind to real poison. Women had poisoned their husbands before now and got away with it – they must have done or we'd have heard more about them. Hundreds of them, surely. Thousands. And anything *they* could do...

Ideas are powerful creatures. However often you dismiss them, they come back. This particular idea came back again and again, then stayed for good and developed a mind of its own. It inhabited me. It even spoke inside my head, in a silent but perfectly articulated voice, heard with some inner ear. It said: If he died, you would be alone and free. You would get a widow's pension and be merry. You could even import a talking man if you felt like it. Wouldn't it be lovely? You take my advice – go ahead and poison him.

Apart from anything else, it was nice to be talked to again, even by an articulate idea sitting in one's own head.

Dare I? I said to it silently, and it silently answered: You can dare anything with me here. That's why I've come. It'll be easy. You can use your own stuff.

My 'own stuff' was sedative tablets prescribed for me by the doctor some time ago when *his* silences had been getting on my nerves, before I'd grown accustomed to them. I'd taken a few and kept the rest, the way people do. It was as if my unconscious had been preparing me for the coming of the idea. For here I was, fully equipped to kill. It seemed almost too easy to be true.

You know, men who are bloody to their wives take a great risk, since it's usually the wife who prepares the food. Does it never cross their tiny minds that the wife is often alone with that food before she bears it on a dish to her lord and master? Great men and nervous men have special food-tasters to have first nibble, or they try it on the dog, but most men go blithely on, eating whatever the wife provides, yet never bothering to keep on the right side of her. It would never cross *his* mind that I would poison him.

Moroccan women are said to stuff their men's food with aphrodisiacs, a slice from a donkey's ear being a particularly potent charm to excite husbandly love. But I don't want *his* love, thank you. I have enough of that. If you can call his occasional night-time acrobatics 'love'. The silence. The violence. He can 'make love' with hate. The bedroom fills with a miasma of evil particles, invisible, intangible, but inhaled. Poison gas. It makes me feel as if I can't breathe properly. If he were dead, I could breathe freely again. If he were dead, I could walk into this house without every nerve vibrating to the tension of the atmosphere. The mere idea of his death has a wonderfully tranquillizing effect on me. And what is an idea for if not to be acted upon?

Exactly, says the idea. You act upon me. Use your stuff.

Of course, I could use my stuff to kill myself – but I'd much rather get rid of him than me. It would be too galling to think of him still sitting here afterwards, reading, while I went through the unpleasant process of dying. I can just picture him behaving beautifully at my funeral, then coming home, heaving a sigh of relief, and getting on with his latest book. No, suicide is out. That would be his victory. Murder will be mine.

Murder! How interesting and dramatic it sounds. Only 'other people' commit murder. When I've done it, I shall be one of 'other people', then I suppose everyone else will be 'other people' instead – a grand change-around. When I'm one of Them, we'll become Us, and what's now Us will be Them. I wonder what it will be like. Will veils fall from my eyes so that I shall be able to identify other murderers at a glance, by some secret sign of identity that only killers know: a look in the eyes, a way of moving or speaking, so that they recognize each other – like those weird men called 'masons'? Perhaps I'll be able to go for walks and pick out murderers, the way young men go for walks and say they can pick out virgins.

But I am getting too far ahead. Fatal to waste thought on the delights of victory *before* the battle.

Yet I'm feeling so marvellous with these thoughts in my head. I've got hope again, that's what it is. I'd forgotten how it felt. Look at *him*, sitting there, reading, and thinking me so downcast and downtrodden, when all the time he's reading himself into his grave. Or into the fire. Yes, cremation, I think. I don't fancy the idea of him lounging about under a few feet of ground, reading. If he goes up in smoke there'll be none of that. He'll be nothing but a nothing, not a thing at all. Not even worth a worm's glance.

Suddenly he's looking at me. Hell, I hope there is no such thing as telepathy. If he's reading my mind...

No. My mistake. He's not looking at me but through me. He's a dab hand at that. He was looking at the clock, and my head is right in front of the clock face. He sees through my head, as if it weren't there, or as if I were a ghost. You wait, my lad, it's you who'll be the ghost. I'll bet they don't have any books in hell either. What will you do with yourself?

But I'm getting ahead again. I mustn't count my chickens. I have to carry out the killing first. And I'm having second thoughts about poisoning his food. He tends to leave a lot of food, just to be nasty to me. My guess is that he feeds himself to bursting when he's out so that he won't be hungry when he comes in; then he can put on that air of distaste when he faces what I give him and leave most of it, without a word, of course. Drink will be a better poison-base for lover-boy. His whisky nightcap. He swallows it down in one gulp the way a Russian knocks back vodka. No time to taste anything, but the effect is BDOING!

So that's settled. I'll mince up my tablets into finest powder and put them in his nightcap one evening.

Which evening? A shiver goes through me.

Don't start funking it, says the voice in my head.

I'm not, but I want to play fair. The condemned man should have a last chance.

How can he, without your telling him what you're up to?

I'll tell him if he speaks to me. That will be fair enough. But if he doesn't speak, why should I tell him anything? I know – I'll give him two weeks. If he speaks to me even once during the next two weeks, I'll remit the death sentence. I can't play fairer than that. If he speaks to me before the night of today fortnight, then he shall live...

Two weeks. Slowly they pass. Silently. I'm in a weird state, see-sawing between hope and dread. It's ironical – I'm going to kill him because he made me hate him by not speaking to me, yet now I don't want him to speak because if he does I shan't be able to kill him! If he suddenly speaks on the last day of his fortnight, I think I'll go mad ...

The last day. Silent breakfast. Good. Keep it up. Out he goes. Long hours passing. Waiting. Back he comes. Silent supper. Most of food left on plate. And now, in dead silence, he sits there, reading.

Now it is time for his nightcap. Silently, I prepare it for him as usual. Only not as usual. I slip the drug into the glass. I place it beside him. He doesn't look up. He goes on reading. Supposing he'd said 'Thank you'. Wouldn't that have been frustrating? I'd have had to whip the glass away and pretend to drop it. Wait. Yes, he's getting up. He picks up the glass and swallows the drink in one gulp, then plods over to the door. He's going to bed.

Suddenly he stops in the doorway and turns round.

'Thank you,' he says.

Too late.

He goes on up to bed. What shall I do now? There's a sense of anticlimax, an 'is that all?' feeling. By morning he will be dead. I shall never again have to see him sitting at that damned table, reading. He's left his current book open on the table, ready to continue reading over breakfast tomorrow. I never dare touch his books when he leaves them like that. Once, long ago, during a spell when he was speaking to me, he flew into a violent rate when I moved a book, so I never moved one again. Well, I can move it now. Now or tomorrow.

And suddenly, it hits me. It. I don't know what. It's not a physical blow, yet it feels like one. I'm struck by an intangible force of horror, and a voice in my head is silently bellowing: WHAT HAVE YOU DONE?

What have I done? Oh, God, oh, God, what have I done? I wasn't myself. I was mad. Possessed. I'm not a murderess. I'm not those 'other people' who commit crimes. I'm *me*! What have I done?

I hear him cough. There's still time. I rush up the stairs to the bedroom. 'Don't go to bed! Don't lie down! You've got to make yourself sick. You must drink salt and water. I poisoned your drink with my stuff. I haven't been taking it myself. I should have done. It was supposed to keep me "normal". You must be sick or you'll die. Please——' I'm in the bedroom, standing there shouting at him. I see myself in the long mirror. I look insane. He ignores me completely, but he looks smug. He's been aiming to drive me mad so he can have me put away, and now he thinks he's won. And he's gone back to not speaking. That 'Thank you' must have been a mistake. He must have forgotten it was me there and was thinking that a barmaid had served his drink. He was thanking her. For it's only me he not-speaks to. He's quite chatty with other people.

'I know I'm mad,' I say, 'and that's why you must believe me when I say I've killed you. I put poison in your nightcap. You've got to sick it up. I'll fetch you an emetic.'

I dash down to the kitchen and prepare the salt and water mixture. I come back with it. 'Please drink it. Please. I don't want to be a murderess after all. I only thought I did.'

He's in bed already, sitting up. I thrust the glass into his hand. He drops it, as if it doesn't really exist any more than I do. It smashes. The liquid is spilled, the life-saver seeping hopelessly into the bedside rug.

'You fool! You'll die if you don't believe me!' I tear down to the kitchen for another emetic, but by the time I'm back with it he has lain down and is asleep, snoring strangely. I shake him, but he won't wake. He'll never wake up again unless I can get help. The doctor – ring the doctor – what to say? 'Sorry to bother you, Doctor, but I've just murdered my husband, only he's not quite dead yet...' He won't believe me. Worse, he will believe me. There'd be a court case. Attempted murder. No provocation. All her husband did was not-speak. Some old judge: 'Many a wife would be grateful for such reticence; and I gather this unfortunate man read books. A worthy occupation, surely. Egg-headed instead of square-eyed, eh?' Chuckle, chuckle. 'No, I can find no justification for the conduct of this evil woman...'

I must lie. Telephone. Dial. 'Doctor? Oh, Doctor, hello. It's my husband. He's been rather depressed lately, and I think he's taken an overdose. I don't like the look of him.' The understatement of the year. I heartily loathe the look of him, but I don't want to be a murderess...

The doctor: 'I'll come round.'

And the doctor comes round, but *he* does not. He is dead.

Everyone is so sorry for me. Tragic, they say, that my poor dear

husband should have taken his own life. Some secret sorrow, perhaps?
Or the stress of modern life and all that? A shadow of suspicion in some
eyes – not suspicion of what really happened, but the look that anyone
receives who has lived with a suicide. Such a chatty, friendly man he
was, they imply; surely I could have kept him happy enough to stay
alive.

But I don't care. I've changed. I panicked at the thought of being a
murderess, went quite round the bend for a while as that black gale of
horror blew all about me. I behaved like a real nut – taking all that
trouble to do him in, and then trying to save him. Farcical. It was like a
farce. All that haring up and down stairs with glasses of salt and water.
Thank goodness he didn't believe me. For now that I am a murderess,
I've settled for it and I feel fine. I'm 'other people', and there are even
more of us than I suspected before. I see them in all sorts of ordinary
places – the supermarket, the bus queue, the underground, even the
post office – yes – I saw a murderess, middle-aged and wearing a boat
hat, collecting her widow's pension while I was collecting mine. We
knew immediately that we belonged to the same club. She winked at me
and I winked back.

And what of guilt? Shouldn't I be having a touch of the Lady
Macbeth? Not at all. I don't feel guilty. I gave him a fair chance. I even
tried to save him after he'd dug his own grave, or lighted his own pyre,
rather. For today he has been cremated. Gone for all eternity, every
dead silent particle of him, scattered over some defenceless roses.

A sensation of utter bliss came over me as I walked from the
crematorium and returned to the house – *my* house now. On a wave of
well-being, I flung open the front door.

Then I stopped. The atmosphere felt strange, like in the old days.
That feeling of tension, the poison gas catching my breath. Nonsense.
Imagination.

But I didn't imagine what I saw in the living-room: one of his books,
lying open on the table, exactly in the place where he used to sit and
read . . .

No – it can't be true – he's not still sitting there, reading——

As I stand staring in the dead still room, a page turns.

A Ghost Story
Mark Twain

I took a large room, far up New York's Broadway, in a huge old building whose upper storeys had been wholly unoccupied for years until I came. The place had long been given up to dust and cobwebs, to solitude and silence. I seemed groping among the tombs and invading the privacy of the dead, that first night I climbed up to my quarters. For the first time in my life a superstitious dread came over me; and as I turned a dark angle of the stairway and an invisible cobweb swung its slazy woof in my face and clung there, I shuddered as one who had encountered a phantom.

I was glad enough when I reached my room and locked out the mould and the darkness. A cheery fire was burning in the grate, and I sat down before it with a comfortable sense of relief. For two hours I sat there, thinking of bygone times; recalling old scenes, and summoning half-forgotten faces out of the mists of the past; listening, in fancy, to voices that long ago grew silent for all time, and to once familiar songs that nobody sings now. And as my reverie softened down to a sadder and sadder pathos, the shrieking of the winds outside softened to a wail, the angry beating of the rain against the panes diminished to a tranquil patter, and one by one the noises in the street subsided, until the hurrying footsteps of the last belated straggler died away in the distance and left no sound behind.

The fire had burned low. A sense of loneliness crept over me. I arose and undressed, moving on tiptoe about the room, doing stealthily what I had to do, as if I were environed by sleeping enemies whose slumbers it would be fatal to break. I covered up in bed, and lay listening to the rain and wind and the faint creaking of distant shutters, till they lulled me to sleep.

I slept profoundly, but how long I do not know. All at once I found myself awake, and filled with a shuddering expectancy. All was still. All but my own heart – I could hear it beat. Presently the bedclothes began to slip slowly towards the foot of the bed, as if some one were pulling them! I could not stir; I could not speak. Still the blankets slipped deliberately away, till my chest was uncovered. Then with a great effort I seized them and drew them over my head. I waited, listened, waited. Once more that steady pull began, and once more I lay torpid a century of dragging seconds till my chest was once more uncovered. At last I roused my energies and snatched the covers back to their place and held them with a strong grip. I waited. By and by I felt a faint tug, and took a fresh grip. The tug strengthened to a steady strain – it grew stronger and stronger. My hold parted, and for the third time the blankets slid away. I groaned. An answering groan came from the foot of the bed! Beaded drops of sweat stood upon my forehead. I was more dead than alive. Presently I heard a heavy footstep in my room – the step of an elephant, it seemed to me – it was not like anything human. But it was moving *from* me – there was relief in that. I heard it approach the door – pass out without moving bolt or lock – and wander away among the dismal corridors, straining the floors and joists till they creaked again as it passed – and then silence reigned once more.

When my excitement had calmed, I said to myself, 'This is a dream – simply a hideous dream.' And so I lay thinking it over until I convinced myself that it *was* a dream, and then a comforting laugh relaxed my lips and I was happy again. I got up and struck a light; and when I found that the locks and bolts were just as I had left them, another soothing laugh welled in my heart and rippled from my lips. I took my pipe and lit it, and was just sitting down before the fire, when – down went the pipe out of my nerveless fingers, the blood forsook my cheeks, and my placid breathing was cut short with a gasp! In the ashes on the hearth, side by side with my own bare footprint, was another, so vast that in comparison mine was but an infant's! Then I *had* had a visitor, and the elephantine tread was explained.

I put out the light and returned to bed, palsied with fear. I lay a long time, peering into the darkness, and listening. Then I heard a grating noise overhead, like the dragging of a heavy body across the floor; then the throwing down of the body, and the shaking of my windows in response to the concussion. In distant parts of the building I heard the muffled slamming of doors. I heard, at intervals, stealthy footsteps creeping in and out among the corridors, and up and down the stairs. Sometimes these noises approached my door, hesitated, and went away again. I heard the clanking of chains faintly, in remote passages, and listened while the clanking grew nearer – while it wearily climbed the stairways, marking each move by the loose surplus of chain that fell with an accented rattle upon each succeeding step as the goblin that bore it advanced. I heard muttered sentences; half uttered screams that seemed smothered violently; and the swish of invisible garments, the rush of invisible wings. Then I became conscious that my chamber was invaded

– that I was not alone. I heard sighs and breathings about my bed, and mysterious whisperings. Three little spheres of soft phosphorescent light appeared on the ceiling directly over my head, clung and glowed there a moment, and then dropped – two of them upon my face and one upon the pillow. They spattered liquidly and felt warm. Intuition told me they had turned to gouts of blood as they fell – I needed no light to satisfy myself of that. Then I saw pallid faces, dimly luminous, and white uplifted hands, floating bodiless in the air – floating a moment and then disappearing. The whispering ceased, and the voices and the sounds, and a solemn stillness followed. I waited and listened. I felt that I must have light or die. I was weak with fear. I slowly raised myself towards a sitting posture, and my face came in contact with a clammy hand! All strength went from me apparently, and I fell back like a stricken invalid. Then I heard the rustle of a garment – it seemed to pass to the door and go out.

When everything was still once more, I crept out of bed, sick and feeble, and lit the gas with a hand that trembled as if it were aged with a hundred years. The light brought some little cheer to my spirits. I sat down and fell into a dreamy contemplation of that great footprint in the ashes. By and by its outlines began to waver and grow dim. I glanced up and the broad gas-flame was slowly wilting away. In the same moment I heard that elephantine tread again. I noted its approach, nearer and nearer, along the musty halls, and dimmer and dimmer the light waned. The tread reached my very door and paused – the light had dwindled to a sickly blue, and all things about me lay in a spectral twilight. The door did not open, and yet I felt a faint gust of air fan my cheek, and presently was conscious of a huge, cloudy presence before me. I watched it with fascinated eyes. A pale glow stole over the Thing; gradually its cloudy folds took shape – an arm appeared, then legs, then a body, and last a great sad face looked out of the vapour. Stripped of its filmy housings, naked, muscular and comely, that petrified, prehistoric man, the so-called Cardiff Giant loomed above me!

All my misery vanished – for a child might know that no harm could come with that benignant countenance. My cheerful spirits returned at once, and in sympathy with them the gas flamed up brightly again. Never was a lonely outcast so glad to welcome company as I was to greet the friendly giant. I said:

'Why, is it nobody but you? Do you know, I have been scared to death for the last two or three hours? I am most honestly glad to see you. I wish I had a chair—— Here, here, don't try to sit down in that thing!'

But it was too late. He was in it before I could stop him, and down he went – I never saw a chair so shivered in my life.

'Stop, stop, you'll ruin ev——'

Too late again. There was another crash, and another chair was resolved into its original elements.

'Confound it, haven't you got any judgement at all? Do you want to ruin all the furniture in the place? Here, here, you petrified fool——'

But it was no use. Before I could arrest him he had sat down on the bed, and it was a melancholy ruin.

'Now what sort of a way is that to do? First you come lumbering about the place bringing a legion of vagabond goblins along with you to worry me to death, and when I overlook an indelicacy of costume, which would not be tolerated anywhere by cultivated people except in a respectable theatre, and not even there if the nudity were of *your* sex, you repay me by wrecking all the furniture you can find to sit down on. And why will you? You damage yourself as much as you do me. You have broken off the end of your spinal column, and littered up the floor with chips of your hams till the place looks like a marble yard. You ought to be ashamed of yourself – you are big enough to know better.'

'Well, I will not break any more furniture. But what am I to do? I have not had a chance to sit down for a century.' And the tears came into his eyes.

'Poor devil,' I said, 'I should not have been so harsh with you. And you are an orphan too, no doubt. But sit down on the floor here – nothing else can stand your weight – and besides, we cannot be sociable with you away up there above me; I want you down where I can perch on this high counting-house stool and gossip with you face to face.'

So he sat down on the floor, and lit a pipe which I gave him, threw one of my red blankets over his shoulders, inverted my hip-bath on his head, helmet fashion, and made himself picturesque and comfortable. Then he crossed his ankles, while I renewed the fire, and exposed the flat, honeycombed bottoms of his prodigious feet to the grateful warmth.

'What is the matter with the bottom of your feet and the back of your legs, that they are gouged up so?'

'Infernal chilblains – I caught them clear up to the back of my head, roosting out there under Newell's farm where they dug me up. But I love the place; love it as one loves his old home. There is no peace like the peace I feel when I am there.'

We talked along for half an hour, and then I noticed that he looked tired, and spoke of it.

'Tired?' said he. 'Well, I should think so. And now I will tell you all about it, since you have treated me so well. I am the spirit of the petrified man that lies across the street there in the museum. I am the ghost of the Cardiff Giant. I can have no rest, no peace, till they have given that poor body burial again. Now what was the most natural thing for me to do, to make men satisfy this wish? Terrify them into it! –

haunt the place where the body lay! So I haunted the museum night after night. I even got other spirits to help me. But it did no good, for nobody ever came to the museum at midnight. Then it occurred to me to come over the way and haunt this place a little. I felt that if I ever got a hearing I must succeed, for I had the most efficient company that perdition could furnish. Night after night we have shivered around through these mildewed halls, dragging chains, groaning, whispering, tramping up and down stairs, till, to tell you the truth, I am almost worn out. But when I saw a light in your room tonight I roused my energies again and went at it with a deal of the old freshness. But I'm tired out – entirely fagged out. Give me, I beseech you, give me some hope!'

I lit off my perch in a burst of excitement, and exclaimed:

'This transcends everything! Everything that ever did occur. Why, you poor blundering old fossil, you have had all your trouble for nothing – you have been haunting a *plaster cast* of yourself – the real Cardiff Giant is in Albany! Confound it, don't you know your own remains?'

It was a fact. The original fraud was ingeniously and fraudulently duplicated, and exhibited in New York as the 'only genuine' Cardiff Giant (to the unspeakable disgust of the owners of the real colossus) at the very same time that the latter was drawing crowds at a museum in Albany.

Well, when I explained all this, I never saw such an eloquent look of shame, of pitiable humiliation, overspread a countenance before.

The petrified man rose slowly to his feet, and said:

'Honestly, *is* that true?'

'As true as I am sitting here.'

He took the pipe from his mouth and laid it on the mantel, then stood irresolute a moment, dropping his chin on his chest, and finally said:

'Well – I *never* felt so absurd before. The petrified man has sold everybody else, and now the mean fraud has ended by selling its own ghost! My son, if there is any charity left in your heart for a poor friendless phantom like me, don't let this get out. Think how *you* would feel if you had made such an ass of yourself.'

I heard his stately tramp die away, step by step down the stairs and out into the deserted street, and felt sorry that he was gone, poor fellow – and sorrier still that he had carried off my red blanket and my bath-tub.

Guest Room
Tim Vicary

The steel sink shone, reflecting the sunlight to a pale, hovering glimmer on the ceiling. Three cereal bowls were drying neatly in the rack, together with one large dinner plate, two side plates, three mugs, and the usual heap of cutlery, which winked and glittered in the sunbeams.

She gazed at one of the side plates for a moment, bemused, and felt again the gentle tug at her memory, like the insistent tug of the breeze in the garden, tugging the sheets from under the clothes pegs.

It wasn't here, then, she thought. The plates were drying in the rack, the washing on the line. She looked around the kitchen, carefully. The surfaces were clear and immaculate; the cupboards closed; the mugs hung neatly from their hooks: no, she was not needed here. She looked through the hatch into the dining room. The table was polished, the floor clean, the chairs tidily in place. Looking left to the other half of the L-shaped room, she could see that the carpet had been hoovered, and the armchairs and sofa were grouped in their silent conference, as still as household megaliths.

Then what had she forgotten? She found herself in the hall, over the silent sheen of the parquet, staring at the frosted glass of the front door. It stood still, indifferent, as it always had; the latticed glass, the Yale lock. Watching, she saw something move, at the corner of her eye, tugging her vision to the left. But no, all was still as it should be; it was just the guest room door that hung half open, leaving a darker crack in the hallway of pale wallpaper and light wooden stairs.

The guest room! She went towards it, quickly, through the dark crack; yes, it was all clean, and still, in here, too. The bed was made, with clean sheets and counterpane, and stood tidily against the window; there was a vase of flowers, sweet williams, on the polished bedside cabinet; the window was slightly open to air the room. She had cleaned in here this morning; yes, this morning, she remembered. It was a different room now to the one she had been ill in, she thought, surveying it with careful satisfaction. The bed was in a different place, and the chest of drawers, the bookcase; she had even moved the carpet. She looked round the room again, carefully, establishing everything in its new position. Not a trace of that vanished time of flushed fever, medicine, dreams, and rumpled sheets...

Now a guest was to come and stay here. That was it, the memory. That would be why she had cleaned the room this morning, again. She had a vision of the guest, an indistinct figure in the sunshine, beginning the walk up the long drive. But who? She stared intently at the flowers, seeking their assistance. Sweet williams; who was it liked sweet williams? Their brilliance disturbed her. Red and white and crimson: as she stared they glowed in the vase like Van Gogh sunflowers ... but no, they were sweet williams, she had chosen them herself, especially, for the guest.

A confusing clatter of noises demanded attention from her ear. A door had banged; footsteps, running water – someone was in the kitchen! Flustered, she found herself moving towards the door. But she could not go until she knew who it was. That would be to show too much surprise. She must stay, calm.

She turned and moved slowly around the guest room again, quietly checking each article of furniture: the chest of drawers, the cabinet, the bed, the window, the flowers. Yes, it was all ready. The stillness, the inevitability of the objects reassured her. She moved back to the half-open door and looked past the light wooden staircase, over the quiet, shining parquet, to the kitchen door, where the noises were.

A schoolgirl came through the door. A tall girl of about fourteen, with long dark hair trailing to her waist, wearing a green school blazer, and carrying a satchel in one hand, a mug of coffee in the other, with a slice of lemon sponge balanced precariously on top of it. She watched as the girl climbed the staircase with practised caution and opened the door at the top by turning and pushing down the catch with her elbow.

Elizabeth, she thought. Of course. Time she was home. I should have remembered. 'Elizabeth!' she cried, as the door clicked shut at the top of the stairs. 'Hello, love.' But the words sounded strangely flat, sound-proofed, in her throat. She remembered, quickly – the fever had affected her voice. She heard Elizabeth's footsteps move across to her room, and the heavy movement of a chair being dragged over the floor.

She went back into the guest room, relieved. Elizabeth, of course! She came home every day at this time, and went upstairs to do her homework. She stared at the pale blue counterpane, which flowed so smooth and still over the contours of the silent bed. She had time to herself now; she must use it to find out who was the guest.

A letter! There must be a letter; how else did she know the guest was coming? Yes, she remembered quickly, she had seen a letter this morning; that was why she had tidied the guest room. The letter would be on the desk in the study. She began to form a picture of it: the torn envelope, the smudged postmark over the stamp. She could see its position too, precisely: in the study, on the desk, to the left of the table-lamp. But she could not see the writing; she would have to go to the study to read that.

As she moved into the hall she was confused by noises. A bang behind her, and footsteps overhead, as if Elizabeth was moving towards the top of the stairs. But if Elizabeth were upstairs, who was making those other noises in the kitchen? Noises identical to the earlier ones – running water, crockery, the slam of a fridge door. And then another bang behind her – they were too many, she could not place them.

'S'all right, I'll go, Lice!' Elizabeth was coming down the stairs, but another schoolgirl, smaller – her younger daughter, Jenny – rushed out of the kitchen, slid along the parquet the way she had always been told not to, and opened the front door to: a man, her husband, Christopher!

He caught Jenny up and kissed her, and then Elizabeth, who had come down the stairs. Jenny was looking indignant.

'Oh, Daddy! I thought it was a visitor! What's wrong with the back door, silly?'

'Sorry, Jinks, I forgot it was locked. Legs wouldn't take me any further,' he said, straightening up laboriously.

'Poor old man!' mocked Elizabeth, turning away to go back upstairs.

They had not noticed her. Jenny had walked straight past her; Chris had looked through her, and was now picking up his briefcase.

She rushed towards them, intending to push past Jenny, fling her arms around his neck and kiss him, welcome. But as she moved forward, the same three figures seemed to recede and shrink; there was a glass between her and them, she was rushing down a telescope that was pushing her further away. She saw them shiver, and stare at each other, startled; she heard Jenny shriek, a tiny sound, distant, as though heard through ear-muffs; saw Chris grab Jenny, and shove at the air with his arm, as though to ward something off ...

Furious, she clenched all her force on to the glass, the strong elusive surface of it, to burst through to her family. Their figures in the glass dimmed, and she could see and hear nothing: only, by concentrating all her force, could she feel the curved translucent tension of the glass itself. She was a physical body, she could feel the glass, she would break through. Slippery gloves of moisture began to condense on the surface, then a sudden crack slashed across it, then another, and another. Star-shaped crystals slit the surface, then the pressure burst a black gash across the mirror, a gash of black in which there was nothing, void.

*   *   *

Falling in a black void. Infinite void: no falling. Nothing; infinite space everywhere, night with no stars. Or ... one star, faint, a faint globe of light, a pale foetus containing figures, growing, nearer – she was falling

towards it. The black void rushed past her like a wind, and was shut out
suddenly, a door was closed on the night. Warmth and light and sound.

'Mummy? She athleep, da? Sssh.'

'No, go on. See, her eyes move. Touch. Gently.'

'Mummy?'

Eyes open, light, pastel, blurred. Little girl, curly hair, dimples,
blue anxious eyes. Man behind, anxious, young, so young – a lithe
Christopher?

Eyes closed, rest, listen.

'Karen. Love? Karen? It's me, love, Chris. Chris and Lithp.'

Eyes open. Weak, so weak. Something moving, in the corner of the
eye, across the eye, across the light a black shadow. The shadow dark,
with pale gaps, fingers – a hand. A hand across her face, forehead,
soothing; she should feel it.

She felt a hand gently soothe her forehead. Gently, but the skin was
rough. She felt the hand's rough skin brush against her hair, her
eyebrows. Her forehead felt clear, translucent, she could feel every
callous as the rough hand soothed.

'Karen?'

'Mummy? Ith me.'

The dimmed face, an anxious smile. She felt her cheeks quiver in
faint response. Below the face, she could feel another hand, chubby
fingers in her palm. She closed her fingers faintly on Elizabeth's hand,
felt the soft knuckles.

'Can you see me, love?' The young face, Chris, looking down at her.
'It's a girl.'

'Thyow her, da. Thyow her.'

She wanted to reach up, to touch Chris's young face above her, but
before he had noticed her limp hand moving, he had turned. And
returned. She had only shut her eyes for a moment, to rest, when he was
back; the rough hand soothed her forehead, his thrilled voice called her
softly.

'Karen! Look love, here, a little girl.'

A white bundle, red face, near hers. She wanted to move, to hold it,
but her arms would not rise. She looked at the face, but her weak eyes
would not focus, would not define what they saw. There was the picture,
the pastel light, the figures in front of her – the chubby Elizabeth, the
lithe Chris, the baby – but all blurred, distant; when she tried to focus on
the baby's face it became more blurred, and the rest, seen in the corner of
her eye, seemed clearer.

She could not control the picture. She glimpsed the snub nose of the
baby and had a sudden fear that it was a pig, it was turning into a pig,
and would run away screaming on its trotters; Chris was the ugly
Duchess and Elizabeth was Alice, the tall Alice with the long dark hair

who had stepped into the room through a crack in the mirror. She closed her eyes so as not to look.

'She's asleep, Lisp. Look, her eyes move under the lids. She's dreaming.'

The rough hand soothed her brow again gently, and she opened her eyes. No baby; just Chris and the chubby Elizabeth. She reached up and took her husband's hand in hers, felt the rough skin, the big veins, the long, knobbly fingers. She felt the bedclothes too; her body could feel the crisp of the sheets, the cool of the counterpane, and again Elizabeth's soft knuckles in her palm. She shut her eyes, listened, and felt. Christopher's soft voice reassured her.

'It's all right, love, you've made it. The second time. You're safe now, you both are. You've brought her to life. Sleep now, love, rest, you're safe now. We'll be here when you come back.'

*   *   *

She heard the murmur of words upstairs in the empty house, and she traced the sound to little Jenny's bedroom. Jenny was in bed, Chris was sitting beside her with his arm around her, and Elizabeth, her long red hair tied back in plaits over her nightie, was perched nervously on the other side of the bed. A small teddy lay, feet up, beside Jenny on the pillow.

They were talking, and her entry seemed to make no difference. Jenny looked as though she had been crying; her face was pale and her dark eyes stared intently at the wall by the door, or glanced suspiciously around her, at the cupboard, the curtains, at Chris and Elizabeth. There was a dark square on the wall where the mirror had been taken down.

'...mustn't worry, love,' Chris was saying. 'Mirrors can break from any number of causes ... the heat, the change of temperature ...'

'But Daddy, what about the cold? It felt all shivery and clammy,' Elizabeth broke in impatiently. 'You said you felt it too!'

Jenny shuddered and clung to her father, hiding her head against his chest. He rocked her softly, glancing reproachfully at Elizabeth.

'Yes, I did,' he said. 'But we were all a bit surprised when the mirror broke. It was probably just surprise ...'

'I don't think it was,' said Elizabeth firmly, with all the certainty of her fourteen years. 'I think it was Mother's spirit trying to reach us.'

'Woooooooer!' Jenny screamed with anger and fright, and glared at Elizabeth, then looked intently round the room. 'She's here! Now!' she said, holding tightly to Chris, but still staring, with wide eyes that were sensitive beyond fear.

Jenny was not looking at her but beside her. A long way back in her mind was the desire to comfort Jenny, but closer, stronger, was the urgent desire to be seen by her child and recognized. She began to move

– so slow it seemed, so difficult – nearer Jenny, into her line of sight. The three figures on the bed seemed still for a minute, almost stopped and staring, like a very very slow motion picture, while she herself threshed with all her weak force through the clinging air. But as she came nearer she had to fight also against a growing fear of the unnatural dark intensity of Jenny's eyes, that seemed to pull her towards the black world of their wide pupils ... Then the figures began to move again; Chris gathered Jenny into his arms, and she felt herself left immobile, helpless, outside.

'Daddy,' Elizabeth continued, with her own remorseless integrity, 'do you believe in ghosts?'

She saw Chris sigh, and she felt pale and helpless, fearing what he would say. She saw his face, tired and strained.

'All right, Lice, I'll tell you what I think,' he said. He looked at Jenny. 'Don't be frightened, Jinks, there's nothing to hurt you ... Nobody knows, of course, but this is what I think. When people die, it's just like falling asleep. Black and quiet and empty. There's no one to hurt you, nothing happens; just a long quiet sleep. See? Nothing to be frightened of. Only sometimes, when people die who aren't ready for it – they have an accident, or they are ill, like your mother was...'

Feebly, feebly she felt she should move, she should go, she should not listen. But she was helpless; as frozen still as they had been earlier, when she had tried to move towards them. She began to see what he saw in his mind: the stiff, contorted corpse on the bed in the guest room, and deep inside it, the weak worm of life still straining feebly to move. But she knew more than the truth he was telling; she must, or...

'... then they go into a sort of dream, like we do when we're asleep. Well, when you're dreaming, it seems real, doesn't it? Real as life sometimes, until the dream ends, or you wake up.' He looked at Jenny, who was watching him intently. 'Then you see there was nothing to be frightened of – it was all just a dream, gone, just like that!' He snapped his fingers in the air. Jenny shivered. He went on, uncomfortably: 'Well, perhaps your mother, after she died, did not go to sleep straight away, but dreamed she saw us in the hall this afternoon; and in a way, because we think we saw her, the dream came true. Like Jesus – his dream was so powerful that you remember people saw him and spoke to him after he was dead. But in the end, people say, he went up to heaven. That probably means that his dream ended and his spirit fell asleep. Just a quiet, peaceful sleep; and people didn't see him any more.'

'Miss Evans at school says she met a man once who told her Jesus came to him in the night,' said Elizabeth, the reply coming down swift and mechanical as a thrush's beak on a worm.

She stared at Elizabeth with sudden intense hope; yet Elizabeth seemed less real than either Chris or Jenny.

'Your Miss Evans would!' said Chris with an indignation that was also somehow grateful.

'So what's happened to Mummy? Is her spirit here?' asked Jenny impatiently, her voice still thrilling with tension.

'I don't know, love, really,' said Chris sadly. 'But if she is here, it's only because she's dreaming of us in her sleep. Soon she'll fall asleep and there'll be no more dreams, just peace and rest.'

'Did she hurt herself on the mirror? She might be hurt!' Jenny started up anxiously as though to go for help, but Chris held her back.

'No, Jinks, she can't hurt herself any more. She can't touch things any more. She's asleep now, where no one can hurt her.'

Jenny began to cry, and she watched as Chris comforted her. Elizabeth went to bed and still the father stayed with the little girl, talking to her, reading her a story, waiting with just a low nightlight on, until at last she fell asleep. He tiptoed out, leaving the hall light on, and, as he went out, she felt drawn after him as though she was tied, drawn into his room, away from her baby.

She watched as he undressed wearily. He sat for a moment by the bed and looked at a framed photo of the family at the seaside. Then he rolled into bed and some of her force returned. Inside her a memory stirred, and she knew he did not have the whole truth. How could he sleep if he did? She watched his body turn and restlessly ruckle the sheets, and his eyes move hastily under his eyelids.

* * *

Harsh spots and flashes of colour flared behind her eyelids, and when she opened her eyes they were scorched by the blue and white glare. She shielded them and squinted along the beach, where three small figures sprinted towards her through the haze. She watched as their legs ceased to bend and waver, and became firm and tall, and then they had faces and then their big brown bodies blocked out the sun and overwhelmed her, touching her with slippery cold or sandy hands and shouting, gasping and giggling and shouting loudly to themselves.

'Aah! Ooooh – No, Chris, don't!'

'Brr! Yow, Jenny, look!'

'Ha – ha! Ow! Jenny, you brat!'

'Have a good swim...?'

'I'm a seagull, you're a fish! Wheeeeee!'

'Gdoing, gdoing – gotcha, you little pest!'

'Oh, Daddy, don't Daddy...'

'Ghoooooooooooooost!'

'Oooooooh! Is that you, Lice? You horror!'

'Daddy, Daddy, someone's letting your tyres down!'

'Dig, dig, Mummy's in a pyramid!'

'Ha – ha! Fooled you! Oooops, look out!'

'Guess! Guess! Which hand! Which haa...'

'Guessst!'

The movement was too fast. She was bewildered, could not tell when it was her they spoke to. Every time she thought she had hold of one of them, a word, a face, a leg, it was gone, in a mad dance too swift and silly to follow. Then Chris and the kids would be tumbled together and she would be outside, forgotten yet belonging; then they would be all over her. Yet not with her; games and words were going through her, over her, around her...

'And who is this lady?'

'What? Oh, Daddy!'

'Who is this lady in the sand?'

'This is Mrs Christopher Hadley, if you please...'

'Silly Daddyman!'

'This lady is IT.'

'It?'

'She...?'

'I...?'

'It. She's it. Look out, she's got to catch us!'

'Catch – catch – catch – catch... Wooooooer, look out, here she comes!'

Running, stumbling, gleeful and desperate, across the sand after her children, her husband. Her heavy body hindered her; she enjoyed the movement of it, arms waving, legs heaving and tumbling in the cloying sand, yet she could not catch them. She wanted to go faster, flit after them over the sand.

They danced down to the sea and splashed her in the shallows. She almost caught Jenny but Chris dived between them to divert her, and then again, and then up in the dry sand they all fell in a heap and she held them all three in her arms.

'Gotcha! All my children! You've had it now! I'll eat you!'

'Wooooooer! It's a monster!'

'You're all slippery! Slippery little bodies! Thought you'd get away, did you? Well, here we are. One happy family!'

'We're slippery!'

'We'll slither!'

'We're mermaids!'

'We're eels!'

'We're seasnakes!'

They began to hiss at each other, and writhe in her arms, in an ectasy of recreation.

'You're children! I've got you!'

'We're dolphins!'

'We're sandworms!'

'We're seaweed!'

They leapt and danced in her arms. She could not hold them. She was not sure what she held. Wet fronds of hair, slippery black bodies, writhing sandy skin, enchanting chanting voices, the pulse of the surf.

'We're seals!'

'We're herrings!'

'We're water!'

'Water! Water! Wssssssh! Wssssssh!'

'No! No! Stop!' Her hands clasped and held, and she looked and looked at what she held, and it was Christopher, his naked arms gripped in her hands, his blue eyes looking at her quizzically and his fair hair tugged by the breeze that ruffled the surf beyond.

He did not understand. He must not understand.

'I'm ... a bit shaky, love,' she said softly, touching his cheek delicately with her hand. 'Let's go and have lunch.'

She turned and led the way back to the towels and the picnic hamper.

* * *

It seemed to be after a meal – after lunch, for it was midday – and an emptiness nagged as though it was Sunday. Christopher was in his armchair, talking to another man, but from where she was at the table she could not quite see the man's face. But the grey hair that curled down almost to his collar, and the heavy hand that reached out occasionally for the ashtray, reminded her of someone she should know, if only she could get closer. But the men's talk seemed to exclude her; she wondered for a moment if there was anything to do in the kitchen, but felt powerless to move even there.

'The end of the fever was the worst,' Chris was saying, 'she was always talking in her sleep, dreaming – hallucinating, almost.'

'Did she recognize you, or the children?' The man's voice spoke with almost professional tact.

'Sometimes. And then sometimes ... she'd look at me and I'd think she recognized me, until she started speaking, and then it wasn't me she was seeing at all ... or if it was me, it was in some sort of dream world of her own ... another time, another place ... and then sometimes you wouldn't know; she'd look, and talk, as though she were completely better ... we were convinced the first time ... then quarter of an hour later she'd be ... in some other dream...'

Chris's face sometimes looked intensely to the other, as if for some help, some hope; and then he would look away again, his face unseeing, as though absorbed in controlling a misery which no one could remove. She felt how confused and lonely he was, and knew she had some knowledge now that she could share with him, which would enlighten him, unseal his eyes from his own melancholy. But she could not reach him; the smoke around the grey man's head, the reverberation of their words, created a sort of charmed circle outside which she lay paralysed. If only he would look at her! But his eyes glanced desultorily around the room, or gazed for long periods at his fingernails, or out of the window, hardly noticing what they saw.

The girls rushed in. Jenny ran up to the grey-haired man and sat on his knee, twining her arms around his neck.

'Grandad! Grandad! Will you come and play French cricket? We've got the bat and ball all ready!'

Elizabeth was bouncing the ball up and down on a tennis racquet.

'All right, Jenny,' said the old voice, pleased. 'Just let me finish my cigar, eh?'

'You're a sooty old fireplace!' said Jenny, poking her face impudently into his. He blew smoke all over her and she tumbled on to the floor, coughing and giggling.

'Cheeky beggar!' chuckled the voice from behind the grey head. 'Now get outside and wait for us. But don't pester, or we won't come.' He made as if to get out of his chair and chase them, and she recognized the bent but strong figure of Chris's father, a doctor.

'Little beggars! That holiday seems to have done them some good, anyway,' Chris said wistfully.

'Chris,' said the grey-haired man, the compassionate professional tact returning to his voice, 'when she was feverish, was there any pattern that came out of her dreams?'

'No,' said Chris, dully. 'Not that I could see. It was just ... every incident seemed intensely real to her at the time, yet she never seemed to have ... any memory, from one to the other. They seemed much more real than ordinary dreams ... I mean, one didn't seem to just flow into another; they were distinct, separate. It made me think of when a ship sinks. You know, to try and save it, they seal off all the bulkheads, so that it's not a ship any more, a single entity, so much as a lot of little boxes, rooms, held together but with no communication. The water can be in one but not the other ...'

She stopped listening and tried again, with what feeble force she had left, to reach him; but a glass intervened, like one she remembered from somewhere before, and the two figures became smaller, more distant ...

As they rose to go into the garden they went past the table, and Chris absent-mindedly brushed some condensation from the mirror with his sleeve.

*   *   *

A rough hand was stroking her brow. The movement fretted her and she stirred, opening her eyes.

'Chris!'

His sad eyes watched her, glazed with weariness.

'I'm here. Rest, love. Gently.'

She raised her head and saw behind him the guest room, the medicines on the bedside cabinet, the drawn curtains keeping out a faint trace of daylight. Her head fell back on to the pillow, exhausted.

'You've been here a long time,' he said.

'Chris!' She clutched his hand. 'I'm better now. I know where I am.'

'Yes, love.' A smile broke through the exhaustion on his face. 'Rest now.'

She turned to look at him once more, but the effort irritated her, and she let herself drift, thinking only of the whiteness of the sheets.

In her dream she saw the guest room, the furniture clean and quiet, the bed rearranged under the window, the counterpane flowing smooth and still over the contours of the silent bed.

The Triumph of Death
H. Russell Wakefield

'Amelia,' said Miss Prunella Pendleham, 'I have received a most impertinent letter this morning.'

'Yes, Miss Pendleham?'

'It is from some Society, and it has the insolence to suggest that this house is haunted by ghosts. Now you know that to be false, utterly false.'

'Yes, Miss Pendleham,' said Amelia listlessly.

'Do I detect a hesitant note in your tone? You mean what you say, I trust?'

'Oh, yes, Miss Pendleham.'

'Very well. Now this Society actually wished to send down an investigator to examine and report on the house. I have replied that if any such person enters the grounds, he will be prosecuted for trespass. Here is my letter. Take it and post it at once.'

'Very well, Miss Pendleham.'

'You always seem so glad to get out of the house, Amelia! I wonder why. Now make haste there and back.'

A little later Miss Amelia Lornon was hurrying down the drive of Carthwaite Place. But as soon as she knew she was out of eyeshot from its upper windows, she slackened her pace. This she did for two reasons; she was feeling terribly frail and ill that morning, and to be out of that house, even for half an hour, meant a most blessed relief from that anguish which is great fear.

To reach the post office of the little hamlet she had to pass the rectory. Mrs Redvale, the rector's wife, was glancing out of the drawing-room window at the time.

'There's Amelia,' she said to her husband, 'I've never seen her looking so ill. Poor creature! It's time you did something about her, Claud, in my opinion.'

She was a handsome and determined-looking woman, quite obviously 'wearing the trousers', and her voice was sharply authoritative.

'What can I do, my dear?' replied the rector with the plaintive testiness of the conscience-moved weakling.

'You can and must do *something*. You can listen to me for one thing. I've been meaning to have this out with you for some time; ever since I realized what was going on. That sight of her convinces me it must be now, at once. If she dies without our having done a hand's turn to save her, I shall never know a minute's peace again; and I don't think you will either. Come quickly! Here she is going back.'

The rector reluctantly went to the window. What he saw brought a look of genuine distress to his kindly, diffident face. 'Yes,' he sighed, 'I can see what you mean only too well.'

'Now sit down,' ordered his spouse. 'I know we're in a difficult position; Miss Pendleham puts two pounds in the plate every Sunday, which is an enormous help to us. "There are my servant's wages," she seems to say, as she does it. But she is a very evil old woman; how evil, I don't think either of us fully realizes.'

'Yet she *does* come to church,' protested the rector.

'Yes, she comes to church,' replied his wife sardonically, 'and like a great many other people for a quite ulterior motive; she wants to keep *us quiet*, and she bribes us to do so – don't argue – I know I'm right! Now we've been here only six months, but we've learnt quite a lot in that time. We've learnt that the Pendleham family have always shown a vicious, inherited streak; drunkards, ruthless womanizers, and worse, even criminals – and just occasionally a brilliant exception. This old woman is the last of the line, and it'll be a very good thing when the horrid brood is extinct, in my opinion.'

'Of course,' said the rector, 'we have to trust Miles's opinion for all this, *really*. And we know he's utterly biased against her; he won't even speak to her.'

'He's been churchwarden here for forty years; so he ought to know,' replied Mrs Redvale. 'Besides, he loses financially by his attitude – she never buys a thing at his shop. He strikes me as a perfectly honest and sincere old man. Don't you think so?'

'I must say I do.'

'Well then, what's his story? That she was crossed in love when very young, some other woman, as she believes, stealing her man away. So she made up her mind to have revenge on her sex in her own stealthy, devilish way. He thinks her mind was permanently tainted at that time; that she is actually, if not technically, insane.'

'It all sounds so melodramatic!' murmured the rector.

'Melodramatic doesn't mean impossible,' answered his wife sharply; 'there's plenty of *real* melodrama in the world. Now Miles says she has had five companions since she marooned herself in that house thirty-five years ago. Three have died there and two escaped quickly, declaring

Miss Pendleham was a devil and the house hell. And now there's the sixth, Amelia; and she's dying, too.'

'Dying of what?' asked the rector.

'Of terror, if nothing else!'

'She could leave like those other two.'

'That's so easy to say! You might say it of a rabbit in a stoat's snare. When you're sufficiently frightened you can neither run nor struggle. And she's in a hopelessly weak position; ageing, penniless, naturally will-less and pliant. She'd never summon up courage to escape on her own.'

'But she seems, in a way, to like Miss Pendleham's company!'

'Simply because she dreads being alone in that *foul* house. Now you know it's haunted, Claud.'

'My dear Clara, you put me in a most difficult position, because, as you know, I agreed with Miss Pendleham, there were no such entities as ghosts.'

'Don't be a humbug, Claud! You said that only out of politeness and a desire to please. You knew it was a lie when you said it.'

'My dear!'

'No cant! You remember when we first went there what was looking out of the window on the first floor?'

'There seemed to be something for a moment.'

'Was it a small boy with his face covered with blood?'

'I got such a fleeting glimpse, my dear.'

'Was it Miss Pendleham or Amelia?'

'No, I suppose not.'

'They are the only people living in the house. And I told you what I saw when I went to powder my nose. I can see it now! Do you believe me?'

'I've never known you to tell a *pointless* lie. Yet a bush sometimes closely resembles a bear.'

'But a little dead girl doesn't resemble a bush! And you heard that scream!'

'I thought I heard something – a curious cry – it might have been a bird.'

'A bird! How would you like to live in that house with that sort of thing! You'd even – like Amelia – prefer Miss Pendleham's company to *Theirs*. It often makes me physically sick to think of her there. If we don't do something to save that poor woman, I shall be plagued by remorse till I die!'

'Do me the justice, Clara, to believe that is becoming true of me, also.'

'I wonder if you realize it as I do! I'm sensitive to places like that, and always have been. The very motes in the sunbeams there seem to make beastly patterns. I don't wonder Amelia is dying by inches, has been dying for years. She told me that when *They* are around her, the kettle will not boil. In other words, her brain is going as her body gives up the struggle!'

'Well, what can I do?' exclaimed the rector. 'Tell me, Clara! You are wiser than I in the affairs of this world, if I know more about the next.'

'And if there is such a place!' rapped Clara.

The rector sighed. 'I'm deeply grieved you're such a sceptic, Clara.'

'Nonsense! Every parson should have an agnostic wife; it keeps his mind alive. Well, we'll both think it over today and discuss it again tomorrow morning. I *mean* tomorrow. My mind is made up. As for that two pounds a week, could you go on taking it if Amelia died? Tomorrow at ten o'clock!'

* * *

'You were a long time, Amelia,' said Miss Pendleham.

'I was as quick as I could be, Miss Pendleham, but my heart was palpitating so.'

'Nonsense! You're perfectly well. Don't imagine things, Amelia!'

Miss Pendleham was one of those apparently timeless spinsters, so leisurely does the process of decay take its way with them. She was very tall and cylindrical in shape, an almost epicene, sexless body. She was invariably dressed in an iridescent grey garment of antique cut and rustling train. About her face, her nose in particular, the rector had made one of his rare jests, by adapting it to a Max Beerbohm pleasantry, 'Hints of the Iron Duke at most angles;' and, indeed, that ungainly, craggy feature dominated the rest. Her mouth was small, thin-lipped, dry. Her eyes were quite round – monkey's eyes – and an odd brimstone-yellow, a family stigma. Her hair was a dense grey mass. The face was a mask, as though modelled in wax from a corpse, quite colourless. Her age might have been anything from fifty-five to seventy.

Amelia was about forty-eight. Once upon a time she might have been a bonnie girl, for her features were well enough, but it required a sympathetic and perceptive eye so to scan and reconstruct the past. There are parasites which slowly devour and drain their hosts from within, till nothing is left but a thin, transparent envelope. A puff of wind and it disintegrates. Amelia might have been long entertaining some such greedy guest. Pounds underweight, gaunt and stooping, listless and lifeless of hair and eye, like a prisoner at long last delivered from a dungeon where she had lain neglected and forgotten. Death had his hand on her shoulder and was fast tightening his grip, but to give her her due it had taken nine hard years to bring her to this pass.

'I'll go and cook the luncheon,' she said.

'Yes; what is there?'

'Chops.'

'I'll have three. Are you hungry?'

'No, Miss Pendleham.'

'Then cook four, and let mine be red right through.'

Carthwaite Place rose on the northern slopes above Lake Windermere. It was unmistakably Elizabethan: a huge sombre pile of brick with a multitude of mullioned, transomed windows and a flat roof. It had thirty-five bedrooms and one bathroom. It required many thousands spent on it to make it habitable, but that money would never be found; and it was very slowly breaking up and passing. The grounds surrounding it had gone back to a wild, disorderly nature. Miss Pendleham never left it, save to attend matins on Sunday morning. Its one trace of modernity was a telephone, used for ordering her frugal wants from the market town six miles away.

Amelia dragged herself to the great stone vaulted kitchen and raked up the fire. She had begun to tremble again, and never did she glance behind her. Once she paused as though listening, her face revealing the greatest anxiety. Several times her mouth moved as though she were muttering something, but no sound came.

Presently she finished cooking and took the results to the dining-room where Miss Pendleham was already seated. The meal was eaten in dead silence and very quickly, for Miss Pendleham always attacked her food like a starving panther. On the wall facing Amelia was a tattered seventeenth century tapestry. It depicted a company of knights and ladies riding in pairs along a sinister serpentine path. On the left of the path were three rotting corpses in open coffins. The air above them was thronged with vile flying things. Amelia's eyes always flickered around the room trying not to see it. Miss Pendleham watched her covertly. At the end of the meal she said what she always said, 'Wash up quickly and come and read to me.'

'Very good, Miss Pendleham.'

When she got back to the drawing-room, Miss Pendleham handed her a book. It was a translation of the Abbé Boissard's life of Gilles de Rais, realistically illustrated. Amelia had already read it out endless times before. She read well, though the details of the abattoir ritual came oddly from her precise and virginal voice.

Presently Miss Pendleham stopped her. 'Something very similar,' she said in her high, metallic tone, 'is known to have been done here by an ancestor of my own. He killed by torture a number of children, chiefly young girls, and employed their bodies for some such curious ceremonies. It is owing to that, possibly, that the house has acquired its quite *false* repute of being a haunted place. Perhaps I have told you that before?'

'Yes, Miss Pendleham,' replied Amelia mechanically.

'I'm going to doze now. Wake me at five with the tea. Sit here till it is time to prepare it.'

This was an ordeal Amelia detested, but had long accepted as part of her daily calvary. Was Miss Pendleham asleep, or was she slyly watching her? Were her eyes quite closed?

It was a soaking afternoon, the small dense mountain rain streaming down the windows. There was just that steady rainpurr and the slow beat of the grandfather's clock to break the silence. Miss Pendleham never stirred nor did her breathing change. Slowly the light faded, and Amelia began to ache with stiffness and immobility. Suddenly there came from somewhere in the house a thin high cry of pain. Amelia's eyes went wild and she put her hand to her throat. Miss Pendleham opened her eyes wide and slowly leaned forward, staring at her. 'What's the matter, Amelia?' she said slowly.

'Nothing, Miss Pendleham,' gulped Amelia, 'I'll go and get the tea.'

Miss Pendleham glanced after her bowed back. For a moment the mask was raised and she smiled. But the smile merely contorted the lower part of her face, her yellow eyes took no share in it. There came again that remote, agonizing wail. The half-smile vanished, the yellow eyes flickered, the mask came down again.

After tea she played Patience and Amelia was left to her own devices till it was time to cook the supper. Anyone watching Miss Pendleham playing Patience, which is a stark test of virtue, would have decided that if he ever did business with her, he'd have kept a sharp lawyer at his elbow, for she always cheated when necessary, but never more than necessary.

Anyone who had watched Amelia presently preparing the supper by the light of two candles would have gleaned some understanding of the phrase 'mental torture'. Those candles threw strange shadows on the bare walls and arched roof. That observer might have caught himself imitating Amelia, glancing up fearfully and furtively at those crowding multi-formed shades, and learned her trick of flinching when she did so. Was that a small body lying prone and a tall figure with its hands to the small one's throat? And did that figure move? Just the flicker of the candle, of course. And yet that observer might well have wished himself away, but would he have had the heart to leave Amelia down there alone?

Supper was again a quite silent meal. Miss Pendleham scraped her well-piled plates tiger-clean. Amelia left half her sparse portions.

After supper Miss Pendleham said, 'Fetch my wrap from my bedroom, Amelia; I forgot to bring it down.' She said that almost every evening, perhaps because she knew how Amelia dreaded going up those dark stairs, ever since she had that fright four years ago.

Amelia fetched it, washed up, and returned again to the drawing-room. 'Now,' said Miss Pendleham, 'you can read to me for an hour. Get those stories by James.'

*   *   *

'Well, Claud,' said Clara next morning, 'have you been thinking it over?'

'Yes, my dear, but I can't see my way clear, I'm afraid. We say she tortures these women. But *how* does she torture them? She gives them board and lodging, pays them something, I suppose, a pittance, no doubt, but something. She is superficially kind to them. She does not – could not – legally compel them to stay. Who would call that torture, save ourselves?'

'And Mr Miles!'

'And Mr Miles, if you like. Suppose I did tackle her. If she didn't at once show me the door, she'd probably call in Amelia and ask her if she had anything to complain about. "No, Miss Pendleham," she'd certainly reply; and what sort of fool should I look!'

Mrs Redvale, like most women in the grip of logic, raised her voice. 'You've got to be firm, Claud, and not be fooled by that sort of thing. You must take the offensive. She can neither sack you nor eat you. Tell her straight that you are certain Amelia is dying and must have immediate attention. Remind her three of her companions have already died in the house, and, if there's a fourth, some very awkward questions are bound to be asked. There *is* Amelia again! I'll get her in.'

She hurried from the room and out into the street.

'How are you, Miss Lornon?' she asked kindly.

'All right, thank you, Mrs Redvale.'

'You don't look it! Come in a moment.'

'Oh, I can't! Miss Pendleham told me to hurry back with the stamps.'

'Never mind; it's only for a minute.'

Amelia hesitated and then reluctantly followed her in.

The rector scanned her closely as he greeted her.

Mrs Redvale now assumed her most forcible manner.

'Miss Lornon, you're in a very bad state, aren't you? Don't be afraid to tell me; it will go no further.'

Amelia began to cry in the most passive, hopeless way. 'I suppose so,' she murmured.

'That house is killing you, isn't it?'

'Oh, I can stand it, Mrs Redvale.'

'No, you can't! Have a good cry. You've *got* to get away from it!'

'I can't! Miss Pendleham would never let me go.'

'She'll have to! Look here, Amelia – I'm going to call you that –

we're determined to help you. In the meantime, remember nothing there can hurt you. They can frighten, they can't *hurt*.'

'They can!' she sobbed. 'They keep me awake nearly all night. In the summer it's not so bad, because they go away at dawn, but in the long nights it's terrible. I must go now.'

'You won't have to stand it much longer! Bear up until we can do something.'

'There's nothing to be done, thank you kindly, Mrs Redvale. Oh, I mustn't say any more. Miss Pendleham would be so cross if she knew I was talking like this!'

'Nonsense! Your health comes before everything!'

But Amelia had hurried from the room.

'You see!' exclaimed Clara. 'I could strangle that she-devil with my bare hands!'

'There's one thing I've never been sure about,' said the rector, 'does Miss Pendleham realize there's something the matter with the house? If not, the force of the charge against her is greatly weakened.'

'Of course she does!'

'How can you be so sure?'

'I watched her when we heard that ghastly cry. She heard it too, her demeanour showed it. But it doesn't worry her, she welcomes it as an instrument of that torture. She makes Amelia think, "I must be going mad if I see and hear things that aren't there." Can't you see what I mean? Her mind is diseased like that of her foul forbears. Those things are echoes of evil and she is utterly evil too. Did the "first murderer" frighten the other two? Of course not!'

'Clara, that is a fearful thing to say!'

'You've just seen that wretched woman, haven't you! Look here, Claud, if you don't do something about it I'll lose all respect for you! This is the test of your Christianity and courage. *I'm* an infidel, but I'd do it myself if I thought she'd take any notice of me, but she wouldn't for she hates and despises all women. But you are her spiritual adviser.'

'There's no need to be sarcastic, my dear.'

'There's need to be something to goad you to action! Will you, Claud?'

'Oh, I suppose so,' sighed the rector, 'but I wish I could consult the bishop first.'

'You'd get nothing but vague boomings. Is your courage at the sticking-point?'

'Yes, I'll do it.'

'Then go straight to the phone!'

He left the room and returned after a few moments. 'She will see me at half past nine tonight,' he said.

'Did you tell her what you wanted to see her about?'

'I just said something of importance.'

'And you were understanding – it's a matter of life and death, and we both know it!'

* * *

'Have you been crying, Amelia?'

'Oh no, Miss Pendleham, the cold wind caught my eyes.'

'It doesn't seem cold to me. Give me the book of stamps and get luncheon ready.'

During the meal Miss Pendleham said, 'You see that tapestry, Amelia?'

'Yes, Miss Pendleham.'

'You're not looking at it!'

Amelia glanced flinchingly up. She noticed that as each cavalier and his paramour reached the three open coffins, their smiles and lascivious glances changed to looks of loathing and horror. Because, she thought, they are young and happy and haven't learned to long for rest.

'It's called *The Triumph of Death*,' said Miss Pendleham.

'Yes, so you've told me.'

'That reminds me of something. Have you finished?'

'Yes, Miss Pendleham.'

Miss Pendleham led the way into the drawing-room. 'Today,' she said, 'is the anniversary of the death of Miss Davis. She was my companion before you came. She was a foolish, fanciful girl in some ways. Have I told you about her before?'

'Only a little, Miss Pendleham.'

'Yes, she was fanciful. She used to fancy she heard and saw strange things in the house and that shows her mind was tainted, does it not?'

'Yes, Miss Pendleham.'

'I mean, if the house were haunted, we should both of us see and hear such strange things, should we not?'

'Yes, Miss Pendleham.'

'Which we never do?'

'No, Miss Pendleham.'

'Of course not. Well, I should, perhaps, have dismissed Miss Davis earlier but I did not like to. Have I told you how she died?'

'No, Miss Pendleham.'

'I thought not. I had noticed she was getting thinner, and stranger in her manner, and she told me her sleep was disordered. I should have been warned when she came running to my room one day saying she had seen a child butchered in the kitchen – and she had other hallucinations which revealed her mind was in an abnormal state. One evening I sent her up to fetch my wrap, just as I sometimes send you and, as she did not reappear, I went in search of her. I found her lying dead in the powder-closet of my room. The doctor said she had died of a heart-attack and asked me if she could have had a fright of some kind. I said not to my knowledge. I think she must have supposed she had seen something displeasing. Look behind you, Amelia!'

Amelia started from her chair with a cry.

'What is the matter with you!' said Miss Pendleham severely. 'I merely wanted to draw your attention to the fact that the antimacassar was slipping from your chair. I hope *your* nerves are not giving way. Didn't you imagine you had a fright of some kind a month ago?'

'It was nothing, Miss Pendleham.'

'You screamed loudly enough. Bear Miss Davis in mind. Becoming *fanciful* is often the first symptom of brain disease, so the doctor told me; *hearing* things, *seeing* things when there is nothing to see or hear. Now you can read to me.'

And this Amelia did; Miss Pendleham presently telling her to stop and *seeming* to doze off, while the windows rattled disconcertingly and, as the light faded and the fire shook out its last flame and sank to its death-glow, something white seemed to dart across the Musicians' Gallery and something follow it as though in pursuit, and there came that thin wail of pain. Amelia went rigid with terror.

'What's the matter, Amelia?' said Miss Pendleham, leaning forward in her chair.

'Nothing, Miss Pendleham. I'll make up the fire and then get tea.'

While she was cooking the dinner that night she was thinking over what Miss Pendleham had said about Miss Davis. She had died of what was killing her, of course. She would die soon now, very soon. She knew it, and then Miss Pendleham would get someone else, and one day that someone would die too, for the same reason – unless ... Suddenly she paused in her work. What was that! Someone was crying in the servants' hall! That was something she'd never heard before. Her heart hammered in her throat, stopped horribly long, then raced away again. A piercing pain ran through her. Who was that crying! She must be brave. It might be someone *real* and not one of Them! She took a candle and tiptoed along the passage of the hall, a bare, desolate place reeking of dirt and vermin, which Amelia dreaded and seldom entered. There was no one there, but the sound of sobbing was louder. 'Oh, God,' moaned a voice, 'I cannot bear it! I cannot bear it!' Then came a laugh, a sly sinister chuckle and the wailing voice rose to a scream. 'Oh, God, I cannot bear it!'

*   *   *

As Amelia went back to the kitchen her face twitched violently and uncontrollably. Was that *real* or not? Was it just a sound in her head as

Miss Pendleham said it must be; just a *fancy*? If so, she was going mad like Miss Davis. What happened to mad people in that Other World? Were they mad *there* too, and forever? That didn't bear thinking about. She must die before that happened. She *was* dying; she knew that by the terrible pains in her heart. What would happen when she was dead? Miss Davis had died; she'd just heard her crying. No, that was just a sound in her head. Her face contorted again in the fearful effort to concentrate, to get it *straight* and clear in her mind. Well, she would die, like Miss Davis, and then Miss Pendleham would get someone else to look after her and it would all happen again with the new girl. No, it mustn't. It would not be right. Miss Pendleham was very kind, but she didn't understand about the house. It was all very curious and difficult, but it must not happen again. There was Miss Davis still crying, still crying in her head. But it would happen again unless – unless she was brave. If Miss Pendleham realized what sort of things happened to Miss Davis and her and what they saw and heard, she wouldn't let it happen, of course, but she didn't and so ... Did she hate Miss Pendleham? Of course not; why should she? Again St Vitus racked her face. But it wouldn't happen again. There was the man and the little girl! She flung up her hands to her ears. A red veil was drawn down before her eyes. She shook her hands from the wrist and stretched and curved her fingers. The expression on her face became at once hard and vacant, like that of a beast at bay. She retained that curious inhuman expression, and Miss Pendleham noticed it when she brought up the meal. It disturbed her and her own eyes went weasel-hard. Presently she said, 'Eat your dinner, Amelia; what's the matter with you?'

'Nothing, Miss Pendleham. I'm not very hungry.'

'Eat your food! By the way, you haven't been talking to the rector or his wife, have you?'

'I just said good morning to Mrs Redvale.'

'Are you sure that was all?'

'Yes, Miss Pendleham.'

And then there was silence for a time till Miss Pendleham rose and remarked, 'You can read to me for a while,' and Amelia read out a tale about some bed-clothes forming into a figure and frightening an old man in the other bed.

'What did you think of that, Amelia?' asked Miss Pendleham.

'Very nice, Miss Pendleham.'

'Nice! I don't believe you are paying attention. You read very badly again!'

'I'm sorry, Miss Pendleham. The old man was mad, wasn't he, Miss Pendleham? Like Miss Davis and *me*?'

Miss Pendleham stared at her. 'Get my wrap!' she said brutally.

Amelia got up slowly and went through the door leading to the stairs. As she started to climb them she crossed herself and stretched and curved her fingers. A fearful twitch convulsed her face.

Miss Pendleham went to the front door, opened it and left it ajar and went back to the drawing-room. Then, as the minutes passed, she cocked her head as though listening. There came that high torture-wail, and she straightened her head abruptly. The clock ticked, the windows throbbed and hammered in the gale. Presently she got up and went to the foot of the stairs. 'Amelia!' she called, her voice cracking oddly. There was no reply. She smiled and ran her thick tongue along her lips. She went up a few stairs and called again; then fetched a lighted candle from the drawing-room and ascended to the first landing. 'Amelia!' she called. A sudden fierce gust of wind spurted down the passage and blew out the candle, leaving her in pitch darkness. She began to grope her way down the corridor, her fingers sliding along the wall. They came to a gap and she turned in to the left, moving forward till her thighs met a bed. 'Amelia!' she called, and the echo was hurled hard back at her. She moved across the room, her hands groping out before her, till they found another gap – the powder-closet. This was crammed with her ancient and discarded clothes and stank of stale scent, sweat and decay. She touched a hanging frock and then another, her hands moving along. And then her right hand met something and she drew in her breath with a quickness. The next second she was twisting and writhing and from her lips came a choked scream. As she was ruthlessly drawn in among the reeking stuffs, swinging wildly on their hooks, she struck out blindly with her clenched fists again and again. At last she leaned forward, buckling at the knees, her arms fell quivering to her sides, there was a long vile rattle from her throat, and she was still.

*   *   *

'It's a quarter past nine,' said Clara, 'time you were off. You'd better have a drink before you go; it will help you to be firm, and you've got to be very firm.' She poured out a stiff whisky which the rector gulped down. Then he picked up his hat and coat and set out.

It had stopped raining, but it was still blowing a full gale and he had to fight his way against it. So soon as he entered the drive through the battered gates screeching on their hinges, he felt his nerves a-tingle. 'As one who on a lonely road doth walk in fear and dread.' The old lines leaped to his memory. He glanced fearfully up at the over-hanging boughs. Was that a footstep close behind him! He broke into a run. To his surprise he found the front door half open and went in. He saw a light in the drawing-room, entered and found it empty. He waited a few moments and then called timorously out, 'I'm here, Miss Pendleham!' Before the echo of his voice died away there came a long choked scream.

'Good God, what was that!' he muttered, and sweat broke out on him. 'It came from above. I must go up!'

He glanced distractedly around, picked up a candle-stick, lit the candle, and opened the door to the stairs with a quivering hand. As he hurried up the first flight, it seemed to him there was something astir in the house and that the shadows on the wall came from a company of persons following him up, and that others were awaiting him on the landing. He trembled and his breath came fast.

'Miss Pendleham!' he quavered. No sound. He lurched down the corridor till he came to an open door, through which he passed into a huge room. He raised the candle-stick and peered fearfully about him. Ah, there was another door – open – and there was Miss Pendleham.

'Here I am, Miss Pendleham!' he said. What was she doing? He could only see her body from the waist down, the rest was buried in some clothes. He tiptoed into the closet and gingerly pulled the clothes aside. And then he sprang back with a clipped cry, for he was gazing into the battered, dead face of Amelia Lornon. She was leaning back against the wall, and she had drawn Miss Pendleham's head down on her breast. Her hands clutched her neck so fiercely and the nails were driven in so deep, that the blood was seeping down over her lace collar. The last shred of self-control left him. The candle-stick fell from his hand, and he ran blunderingly from the room and down the stairs. The air seemed full of screams and laughter, something death-cold was pressed against his face, leaping figures ran beside him, till at last he staggered whimpering out into the night.

Mrs Lunt
Hugh Walpole

'Do you believe in ghosts?' I asked Runciman. I had to ask him this very platitudinous question more because he was so difficult a man to spend an hour with rather than for any other reason. You know his books, perhaps, or more probably you don't know them – *The Running Man*, *The Elm Tree*, and *Crystal and Candlelight*. He is one of those little men who are constant enough in this age of immense overproduction of books, men who publish every autumn their novel, who arouse by that publication in certain critics eager appreciation and praise, who have a small and faithful public, whose circulation is very small indeed, who, when you meet them, have little to say, are often shy and nervous, pessimistic and remote from daily life. Such men do fine work, are made but little of in their own day, and perhaps fifty years after their death are rediscovered by some digging critic and become a sort of cult with a new generation.

I asked Runciman that question because, for some unknown reason, I had invited him to dinner at my flat, and was now faced with a long evening filled with that most tiresome of all conversations, talk that dies every two minutes and has to be revived with terrific exertions. Being myself a critic, and having on many occasions praised Runciman's work, he was the more nervous and shy with me; had I abused it, he would perhaps have had plenty to say – he was that kind of man. But my question was a lucky one: it roused him instantly, his long, bony body became full of a new energy, his eyes stared into a rich and exciting reminiscence, he spoke without pause, and I took care not to interrupt him. He certainly told me one of the most astounding stories I have ever heard. Whether it was true or not I cannot, of course, say: these ghost stories are nearly always at second or third hand. I had, at any rate, the good fortune to secure mine from the source. Moreover, Runciman was not a liar: he was too serious for that. He himself admitted that he was not sure, at this distance of time, as to whether the thing had gained as the years passed. However, here it is as he told it.

'It was some fifteen years ago,' he said. 'I went down to Cornwall to stay with Robert Lunt. Do you remember his name? No, I suppose you do not. He wrote several novels; some of those half-and-half things that are not quite novels, not quite poems, rather mystical and picturesque, and are the very devil to do well. De la Mare's *Return* is a good example of the kind of thing. I had reviewed somewhere his last book, and reviewed it favourably, and received from him a really touching letter showing that the man was thirsting for praise, and also, I fancied, for company. He lived in Cornwall somewhere on the sea coast, and his wife had died some two years before; he said he was quite alone there, and would I come and spend Christmas with him; he hoped I would not think this impertinent; he expected that I would be engaged already, but he could not resist the chance. Well, I wasn't engaged; far from it. If Lunt was lonely, so was I; if Lunt was a failure, so was I; I was touched, as I have said, by his letter, and I accepted his invitation. As I went down in the train to Penzance I wondered what kind of a man he would be. I had never seen any photographs of him; he was not the sort of author whose picture the newspapers publish. He must be, I fancied, about my own age – perhaps rather older. I know when we're lonely how some of us are for ever imagining that a friend will somewhere turn up, that ideal friend who will understand all one's feelings, who will give one affection without being sentimental, who will take an interest in one's affairs without being impertinent – yes, the sort of friend one never finds.

'I fancy that I became quite romantic about Lunt before I reached Penzance. We would talk, he and I, about all those literary questions that seemed to me at that time so absorbing; we would, perhaps, often stay together and even travel abroad on those little journeys that are so swiftly melancholy when one is alone, so delightful when one has a perfect companion. I imagined him as sparse and delicate and refined, with a sort of wistfulness and rather childish play of fancy. We had both, so far, failed in our careers, but perhaps together we would do great things.

'When I arrived at Penzance it was almost dark, and the snow, threatened all day by an overhanging sky, had begun gently and timorously to fall. He had told me in his letter that a fly would be at the station to take me to his house; and there I found it – a funny old weather-beaten carriage with a funny old weather-beaten driver. At this distance of time my imagination may have created many things, but I fancy that from the moment I was shut into that carriage some dim suggestion of fear and apprehension attacked me. I fancy that I had some absurd impulse to get out of the thing and take the night train back to London again – an action that would have been very unlike me, as I had always a sort of obstinate determination to carry through anything that I had begun. In any case, I was uncomfortable in that carriage; it had, I remember, a nasty, musty smell of damp straw and stale eggs, and it seemed to confine me so closely as though it were determined that, once I was in, I should never get out again. Then, it was bitterly cold; I was colder during that drive than I have ever been before or since. It was that penetrating cold that seems to pierce your very brain, so that I could not think with any clearness, but only wish again and again that I hadn't come. Of course, I could see nothing – only feel the jolt over the uneven road – and once and again we seemed to fight our way through dark paths, because I could feel the overhanging branches of the trees knock against the cab with mysterious taps, as though they were trying to give me some urgent message.

'Well, I mustn't make more of it than the facts allow, and I mustn't see into it all the significance of the events that followed. I only know that as the drive proceeded I became more and more miserable: miserable with the cold of my body, the misgivings of my imagination, the general loneliness of my case.

'At last we stopped. The old scarecrow got slowly off his box, with many heavings and sighings, came to the cab door, and, with great difficulty and irritating slowness, opened it. I got out of it, and found that the snow was now falling very heavily indeed, and that the path was lightened with its soft, mysterious glow. Before me was a humped and ungainly shadow: the house that was to receive me. I could make nothing of it in that darkness, but only stood there shivering while the old man pulled at the doorbell with a sort of frantic energy as though he were anxious to be rid of the whole job as quickly as possible and return to his own place. At last, after what seemed an endless time, the door opened, and an old man, who might have been own brother to the driver, poked out his head. The two old men talked together, and at last my bag was shouldered and I was permitted to come in out of the piercing cold.

'Now this, I know, is not imagination. I have never at any period of my life hated at first sight so vigorously any dwelling-place into which I have entered as I did that house. There was nothing especially disagreeable about my first vision of the hall. It was a large, dark place, lit by two dim lamps, cold and cheerless; but I got no particular impression of it because at once I was conducted out of it, led along a passage, and then introduced into a room which was, I saw at once, as warm and comfortable as the hall had been dark and dismal. I was, in fact, so eagerly pleased at the large and leaping fire that I moved towards it at once, not noting, at the first moment, the presence of my host; and when I did see him I could not believe that it was he. I have told you the kind of man that I had expected; but, instead of the sparse, sensitive artist, I found facing me a large burly man, over six foot, I should fancy, as broad-shouldered as he was tall, giving evidence of great muscular strength, the lower part of his face hidden by a black, pointed beard.

'But if I was astonished at the sight of him, I was double amazed when he spoke. His voice was thin and piping, like that of some old woman, and the little nervous gestures that he made with his hands were even more feminine than his voice. But I had to allow, perhaps, for excitement, for excited he was; he came up to me, took my hand in both of his, and held it as though he would never let it go. In the evening, when we sat over our port, he apologized for this. 'I was so glad to see you,' he said; 'I couldn't believe that really you would come; you are the first visitor of my own kind that I have had here for ever so long. I was ashamed indeed of asking you, but I had to snatch at the chance – it means so much to me.''

'His eagerness, in fact, had something disturbing about it; something pathetic, too. He simply couldn't do too much for me: he led me through funny crumbling old passages, the boards creaking under us at every step, up some dark stairs, the walls hung, so far as I could see in the dim light, with faded yellow photographs of places, and showed me into my room with a deprecating agitated gesture as though he expected me at the first sight of it to turn and run. I didn't like it any more than I liked the rest of the house; but that was not my host's fault. He had done everything he possibly could for me: there was a large fire flaming in the open fireplace, there was a hot bottle, as he explained to me, in the big four-poster bed, and the old man who had opened the door to me was already taking my clothes out of my bag and putting them away. Lunt's nervousness was almost sentimental. He put both his hands on my shoulders and said, looking at me pleadingly: "If only you knew what it is for me to have you here, the talks we'll have. Well, well, I must leave you. You'll come down and join me, won't you, as soon as you can?"

'It was then, when I was left alone in my room, that I had my second impulse to flee. Four candles in tall old silver candlesticks were burning brightly, and these, with the blazing fire, gave plenty of light; and yet the room was in some way dim, as though a faint smoke pervaded it, and I remember that I went to one of the old lattice windows and threw it open for a moment as though I felt stifled. Two things quickly made me close it. One was the intense cold which, with a fluttering scamper of snow, blew into the room; the other was the quite deafening roar of the sea, which seemed to fling itself at my very face as though it wanted to knock me down. I quickly shut the window, turned round, and saw an old woman standing just inside the door. Now every story of this kind depends for its interest on its verisimilitude. Of course, to make my tale

convincing I should be able to prove to you that I saw that old woman;
but I can't. I can only urge upon you my rather dreary reputation of
probity. You know that I'm a teetotaller, and always have been, and,
most important evidence of all, I was not expecting to see an old
woman; and yet I hadn't the least doubt in the world but that it was an
old woman I saw. You may talk about shadows, clothes hanging on the
back of the door, and the rest of it. I don't know. I've no theories about
this story, I'm not a spiritualist. I don't know that I believe in anything
especially, except the beauty of beautiful things. We'll put it, if you like,
that I fancied that I saw an old woman, and my fancy was so strong that
I can give you to this day a pretty detailed account of her appearance.
She wore a black silk dress and on her breast was a large, ugly, gold
brooch; she had black hair, brushed back from her forehead and parted
down the middle; she wore a collar of some white stuff round her throat;
her face was one of the wickedest, most malignant, and furtive that I
have ever seen – very white in colour. She was shrivelled enough now,
but might once have been rather beautiful. She stood there quietly, her
hands at her side. I thought that she was some kind of housekeeper. "I
have everything I want, thank you," I said. "What a splendid fire!" I
turned for a moment towards it, and when I looked back she was gone.
I thought nothing of this, of course, but drew up an old chair covered
with green faded tapestry, and thought that I would read a little from
some book that I had brought down with me before I went to join my
host. The fact was that I was not very intent upon joining him before I
must. I didn't like him, I had already made up my mind that I would
find some excuse to return to London as soon as possible. I can't tell you
why I didn't like him, except that I was myself very reserved and had,
like many Englishmen, a great distrust of demonstrations, especially
from another man. I hadn't cared for the way in which he had put his
hands on my shoulders, and I felt perhaps that I wouldn't be able to live
up to all his eager excitement about me.

'I sat in my chair and took up my book, but I had not been reading
for more than two minutes before I was conscious of a most unpleasant
smell. Now, there are all sorts of smells – healthy and otherwise – but I
think the nastiest is that chilly odour that comes from bad sanitation
and stuffy rooms combined; you meet it sometimes at little country inns
and decrepit town lodgings. This smell was so definite that I could
almost locate it; it came from near the door. I got up, approached the
door, and at once it was as though I were drawing near to somebody
who, if you'll forgive the impoliteness, was not accustomed to taking too
many baths. I drew back just as I might had an actual person been
there. Then, quite suddenly, the smell was gone, the room was fresh,
and I saw, to my surprise, that one of the windows had opened and that
snow was again blowing in. I closed it and went downstairs.

'The evening that followed was odd enough. My host was not in himself an unlikeable man; he did his very utmost to please me. He had a fine culture and a wide knowledge of books and things. He became quite cheerful as the evening went on; gave me a good dinner in a funny little old dining-room hung with some admirable mezzotints. The old serving man looked after us – a funny old man, with a long white beard like a goat – and, oddly enough, it was from him that I first recaught my earlier apprehension. He had just put the dessert on the table, had arranged my plate in front of me, when I saw him give a start and look towards the door. My attention was attracted to this because his hand, as it touched the plate, suddenly trembled. My eyes followed, but I could see nothing. That he was frightened of something was perfectly clear, and then (it may, of course, very easily have been fancy) I thought that I detected once more that strange unwholesome smell.

'I forgot this again when we were both seated in front of a splendid fire in the library. Lunt had a very fine collection of books, and it was delightful to him, as it is to every book collector, to have somebody with him who could really appreciate them. We stood looking at one book after another and talking eagerly about some of the minor early English novelists who were my especial hobby – Bage, Godwin, Henry Mackenzie, Mrs Shelley, Mat Lewis, and others – when once again he affected me most unpleasantly by putting his arm round my shoulders. I have all my life disliked intensely to be touched by certain people. I suppose we all feel like this. It is one of those inexplicable things; and I disliked this so much that I abruptly drew away.

'Instantly he was changed into a man of furious and ungovernable rage; I thought that he was going to strike me. He stood there quivering all over, the words pouring out of his mouth incoherently, as though he were mad and did not know what he was saying. He accused me of insulting him, of abusing his hospitality, of throwing his kindness back into his face, and of a thousand other ridiculous things; and I can't tell you how strange it was to hear all this coming out in that shrill, piping voice as though it were from an agitated woman, and yet to see with one's eyes that big, muscular frame, those immense shoulders, and that dark bearded face.

'I said nothing. I am, physically, a coward. I dislike, above anything else in the world, any sort of quarrel. At last I brought out, "I am very sorry. I didn't mean anything. Please forgive me," and then hurriedly turned to leave the room. At once he changed again; now he was almost in tears. He implored me not to go; said it was his wretched temper, but that he was so miserable and unhappy, and had for so long now been alone and desolate that he hardly knew what he was doing. He begged me to give him another chance, and if I would only listen to his story, I would perhaps be more patient with him.

'At once, so oddly is man constituted, I changed in my feelings towards him. I was very sorry for him. I saw that he was a man on the edge of his nerves, and that he really did need some help and sympathy, and would be quite distracted if he could not get it. I put my hand on his shoulder to quieten him and to show him that I bore no malice, and I felt that his great body was quivering from head to foot. We sat down again, and in an odd, rambling manner he told me his story. It amounted to very little, and the gist of it was that, rather to have some sort of companionship than from any impulse of passion, he had married some fifteen years before the daughter of a neighbouring clergyman. They had had no very happy life together, and at the last, he told me quite frankly, he had hated her. She had been mean, overbearing, and narrow-minded; it had been, he confessed, nothing but a relief to him when, just a year ago, she had suddenly died from heart failure. He had thought, then, that things would go better with him, but they had not; nothing had gone right with him since. He hadn't been able to work, many of his friends had ceased to come to see him, he had found it even difficult to get servants to stay with him, he was desperately lonely, he slept badly – that was why his temper was so terribly on edge. He had no one in the house with him save the old man, who was, fortunately, an excellent cook, and a boy – the old man's grandson. "Oh, I thought," I said, "that that excellent meal tonight was cooked by your housekeeper." "My housekeeper?" he answered. "There's no woman in the house." "Oh, but one came to my room," I replied, "this evening – an old ladylike looking person in a black silk dress." "You were mistaken," he answered in the oddest voice, as though he were exerting all the strength that he possessed to keep himself quiet and controlled. "I am sure that I saw her," I answered. "There couldn't be any mistake." And I described her to him. "You were mistaken," he repeated again. "Don't you see that you must have been when I tell you there is no woman in the house?" I reassured him quickly lest there should be another outbreak of rage. Then there followed the oddest kind of appeal. Urgently, as though his very life depended upon it, he begged me to stay with him for a few days. He implied, although he said nothing definitely, that he was in great trouble, that if only I would stay for a few days all would be well, that if ever in all my life I had had a chance of doing a kind action I had one now, that he couldn't expect me to stop in so dreary a place, but that he would never forget it if I did. He spoke in a voice of such urgent distress that I reassured him as I might a child, promising that I would stay and shaking hands with him on it as though it were a kind of solemn oath between us.

*　　*　　*

'I am sure that you would wish me to give you this incident as it occurred, and if the final catastrophe seems to come, as it were, accidentally, I can only say to you that that was how it happened. It is since the event that I have tried to put two and two together, and that they don't altogether make four is the fault that mine shares, I suppose, with every true ghost story.

'But the truth is that after that very strange episode between us I had a very good night. I slept the sleep of all justice, cosy and warm, in my four-poster, with the murmur of the sea beyond the windows to rock my slumbers. Next morning, too, was bright and cheerful, the sun sparkling down on the snow, and the snow sparkling back to the sun as though they were glad to see one another. I had a very pleasant morning looking at Lunt's books, talking to him, and writing one or two letters. I must say that, after all, I liked the man. His appeal to me on the night before had touched me. So few people, you see, had ever appealed to me about anything. His nervousness was there and the constant sense of apprehension, yet he seemed to be putting the best face on it, doing his utmost to set me at my ease in order to induce me to stay, I suppose, and to give him a little of that company that he so terribly needed. I dare say if I had not been so busy about the books I would not have been so happy. There was a strange eerie silence about that house if one ever stopped to listen; and once, I remember, sitting at the old bureau writing a letter, I raised my head and looked up, and caught Lunt watching as though he wondered whether I had heard or noticed anything. And so I listened too, and it seemed to me as though someone were on the other side of the library door with their hand raised to knock; a quaint notion, with nothing to support it, but I could have sworn that if I had gone to the door and opened it suddenly someone would have been there.

'However, I was cheerful enough, and after lunch quite happy. Lunt asked me if I would like a walk, and I said I would; and we started out in the sunshine over the crunching snow towards the sea. I don't remember of what we talked; we seemed to be now quite at our ease with one another. We crossed the fields to a certain point, looked down at the sea – smooth now, like silk – and turned back. I remember that I was so cheerful that I seemed suddenly to take a happy view of all my prospects. I began to confide in Lunt, telling him of my little plans, of my hopes for the book that I was then writing, and even began rather timidly to suggest to him that perhaps we should do something together; that what we both needed was a friend of common taste with ourselves. I know that I was talking on, that we had crossed a little village street, and were turning up the path towards the dark avenue of trees that led to his house, when suddenly the change came.

'What I first noticed was that he was not listening to me; his gaze was fixed beyond me, into the very heart of the black clump of trees that fringed the silver landscape. I looked too, and my heart bounded. There was, standing just in front of the trees, as though she were waiting for us, the old woman whom I had seen in my room the night before. I stopped. "Why, there she is!" I said. "That's the old woman of whom I was speaking – the old woman who came to my room." He caught my shoulder with his hand. "There's nothing there," he said. "Don't you see that that's a shadow? What's the matter with you? Can't you see that there's nothing?" I stepped forward, and there was nothing, and I wouldn't, to this day, be able to tell you whether it was hallucination or not. I can only say that, from that moment, the afternoon appeared to become dark. As we entered into the avenue of trees, silently, and hurrying as though someone were behind us, the dusk seemed to have fallen so that I could scarcely see my way. We reached the house breathless. He hastened into his study as though I were not with him, but I followed and, closing the door behind me, said, with all the force that I had at command: "Now, what is this? What is it that's troubling you? You must tell me! How can I help you if you don't?" And he replied, in so strange a voice that it was as though he had gone out of his mind: "I tell you there's nothing! Can't you believe me when I tell you there's nothing at all? I'm quite all right . . . Oh, my God! – my God! . . . don't leave me! . . . This is the very day – the very night she said . . . But I did nothing, I tell you – I did nothing – it's only her beastly malice . . ." He broke off. He still held my arm with his hand. He made strange movements, wiping his forehead as though it were damp with sweat, almost pleading with me; then suddenly angry again, then beseeching once more, as though I had refused him the one thing he wanted.

'I saw that he was truly not far from madness, and I began myself to have a sudden terror of this damp, dark house, this great, trembling man, and something more that was worse than they. But I pitied him. How could you or any man have helped it? I made him sit down in the armchair beside the fire, which had now dwindled to a few glimmering red coals. I let him hold me close to him with his arm and clutch my hand with his, and I repeated, as quietly as I might: "But tell me; don't be afraid, whatever if is you have done. Tell me what danger it is you fear, and then we can face it together." "Fear! Fear!" he repeated; and then, with a mighty effort which I could not but admire, he summoned all his control. "I'm off my head," he said, "with loneliness and depression. My wife died a year ago on this very night. We hated one another. I couldn't be sorry when she died, and she knew it. When that last heart attack came on, between her gasps she told me that she would return, and I've always dreaded this night. That's partly why I asked you to come, to have anyone here, anybody, and you've been very kind – more kind than I had any right to expect. You must think me insane going on like this, but see me through tonight and we'll have splendid times together. Don't desert me now – now, of all times!" I promised that I would not. I soothed him as best I could. We sat there, for I know not how long, through the gathering dark; we neither of us moved, the fire died out, and the room was lit with a strange dim glow that came from the snowy landscape beyond the uncurtained windows. Ridiculous, perhaps, as I look back at it. We sat there, I in a chair close to his, hand in hand, like a couple of lovers; but, in real truth, two men terrified, fearful of what was coming, and unable to do anything to meet it.

'I think that that was perhaps the strangest part of it; a sort of paralysis that crept over me. What would you or anyone else have done – summoned the old man, gone down to the village inn, fetched the local doctor? I could do nothing, but see the snowshine move like trembling water about the furniture and hear, through the urgent silence, the faint hoot of an owl from the trees in the wood.

*　　*　　*

'Oddly enough, I can remember nothing, try as I may, between that strange vigil and the moment when I myself, wakened out of a brief sleep, sat up in bed to see Lunt standing inside my room holding a candle. He was wearing a night-shirt, and looked huge in the candle-light, his black beard falling intensely dark on the white stuff of his shirt. He came very quietly towards my bed, the candle throwing flickering shadows about the room. When he spoke it was in a voice low and subdued, almost a whisper. "Would you come," he asked, "only for half an hour – just for half an hour?" he repeated, staring at me as though he didn't know me. "I'm unhappy without somebody – very unhappy." Then he looked over his shoulder, held the candle high above his head, and stared piercingly at every part of the room. I could see that something had happened to him, that he had taken another step into the country of Fear – a step that had withdrawn him from me and from every other human being. He whispered: "When you come, tread softly; I don't want anyone to hear us." I did what I could. I got out of bed, put on my dressing-gown and slippers, and tried to persuade him to stay with me. The fire was almost dead, but I told him that we would build it up again, and that we would sit there and wait for the morning; but no, he repeated again and again: "It's better in my own room; we're safer there." "Safe from what?" I asked him, making him look at me. "Lunt, wake up! You're as though you were asleep. There's nothing to fear. We've nobody but ourselves. Stay here and let us talk, and have done with this nonsense." But he wouldn't answer; only drew me forward down the dark passage, and then turned into his room, beckoning me to follow. He got into bed and sat hunched up there, his hands holding his knees, staring at the door, and every once and again shivering with a little tremor. The only light in the room was that from the candle, now burning low, and the only sound was the purring whisper of the sea.

'It seemed to make little difference to him that I was there. He did not look at me, but only at the door, and when I spoke to him he did not answer me nor seem to hear what I had said. I sat down beside the bed and, in order to break the silence, talked on about anything, about nothing, and was dropping off, I think, into a confused doze, when I heard his voice breaking across mine. Very clearly and distinctly he said: "If I killed her, she deserved it; she was never a good wife to me, not from the first; she shouldn't have irritated me as she did – she knew what my temper was. She had a worse one than mine, though. She can't touch me; I'm as strong as she is." And it was then, as clearly as I can now remember, that his voice suddenly sank into a sort of gentle whisper, as though he were almost glad that his fears had been confirmed. He whispered: "She's there!" I cannot possibly describe to you how that whisper seemed to let fear loose like water through my body. I could see nothing – the candle was flaming high in the last moments of its life – I could see nothing; but Lunt suddenly screamed, with a shrill cry like a tortured animal in agony: "Keep her off me, keep her away from me, keep her off – keep her off!" He caught me, his hands digging into my shoulders; then, with an awful effect of constricted muscles, as though rigor had caught and held him, his arms slowly fell away, he slipped back on to the bed as though someone were pushing him, his hands fell against the sheet, his whole body jerked with a convulsive effort, and then he rolled over. I saw nothing; only, quite distinctly, in my nostrils was that same fetid odour that I had known on the preceding evening. I rushed to the door, opened it, shouted down the long passage again and again, and soon the old man came running. I sent him for the doctor, and then could not return to the room, but stood there listening, hearing nothing save the whisper of the sea, the loud ticking of the hall clock. I flung open the window at the end of the passage; the sea rushed in with its precipitant roar; some bells chimed the hour. Then at last, beating into myself more courage, I turned back towards the room ...'

'Well?' I asked as Runciman paused. 'He was dead, of course?'

'Dead, the doctor afterwards said, of heart failure.'

'Well?' I asked again.

'That's all.' Runciman paused. 'I don't know whether you can even call it a ghost story. My idea of the old woman may have been all hallucination. I don't even know whether his wife was like that when she was alive. She may have been large and fat. Lunt died of an evil conscience.'

'Yes,' I said.

'The only thing,' Runciman added at last, after a long pause, 'is that on Lunt's body there were marks – on his neck especially, some on his chest – as of fingers pressing in, scratches and dull blue marks. He may, in his terror, have caught at his own throat ...'

'Yes,' I said again.

'Anyway' – Runciman shivered – 'I don't like Cornwall – beastly country. Queer things happen there – something in the air ...'

'So I've heard,' I answered. 'And now have a drink. We both will.'

The Hollies and the Ivy
Elizabeth Walter

The house was called The Hollies, the name incised into the stone capping of the gatepost, but it looked as if The Ivies would have been more appropriate, for the word 'Hollies' was smothered under mantling green. Its removal was one of the many tasks the Pentecosts would have to tackle when at long last they moved in.

Gus and Judith Pentecost were a young couple with an interest in interior décor. Gus had recently opened a small shop selling such things as wallpaper, paint and curtain railing. He wanted his home to be an advertisement for his wares. The Hollies was a double fronted red-brick villa with the date 1873 on a stone shield above the porch. It had been empty for years, first owing to a dispute over the late owner's will and then because no building society would give a mortgage on it. It was in a very bad state of repair.

But it had presented a challenge which the young Pentecosts were only too eager to take on. When essential structural repairs had been dealt with, they moved in almost at once. It could not be said that removing ivy from a gatepost was high on their list of priorities, but they would get to it in due course. Meanwhile there was other ivy more loudly clamouring for attention, for the whole of one side of the house and much of the front was thickly covered with it. It was an exceptionally flourishing evergreen; its leaves had a glossy leathern look; its stems were as gnarled and twisted as the veins in an old man's hand. It even obscured several windows, which caused Gus to exclaim angrily that the builders might have cut it back while they were about it.

'They said they did,' Judith said. 'Mr Hardy mentioned it particularly because apparently they'd had such a job. The stems are terribly thick and hard. A knife wouldn't touch them. They even blunted an axe.'

Close inspection revealed that several stems had indeed been chopped through, but it seemed to make no difference. It was an ivy of singularly rampant growth. And near the front door was further evidence of its invasion: two holly bushes stood there, one dying, the other dead. Both were so completely covered with ivy that it was not at first apparent what they were. It was Judith who recognized them and saw in them the origin of the name The Hollies.

Gus surveyed the bushes. 'They've certainly had it now. Nothing for it but to dig them up – if we ever get round to it. The problem here is knowing where to start.'

Eventually they started on a sitting-room, ground floor, on the un-ivied side of the house. They stripped, plastered, papered, painted, laid the carpet and got the curtains up.

'You know,' said Judith, sitting in the middle of the new carpet, 'it's going to be rather lovely when we've got the furniture in.'

'Who says we're going to be able to afford furniture?'

'Of course we shall. We'll buy it second-hand.'

'I suppose you could go round the sale rooms——'

Gus was interrupted by a tapping at the windowpane.

'What was that?' Judith asked.

'Imagination, most likely.'

As if in contradiction, the tapping came again. Together they went to the window. There was nothing and no one to be seen. Yet barely had they turned their backs and resumed their conversation than the insistent, gentle tapping came again. This time Gus pushed back the catch and flung up the heavy sash window. The cold November air flooded in.

'Well, I'm damned! Come and look at this, Judy. It's our clinging friend ivy again. There's a bit growing up on this side and it's tapping against the window. Hand me that knife and I'll soon cut this one down to size.'

'"A rare old plant is the ivy green,"' Judith quoted softly.

'What's that you're saying?'

> *'A rare old plant is the ivy green*
> *That creepeth o're ruins old.*
> *Of right choice food are his meals, I ween,*
> *In his cell so lone and cold.'*

'Sounds cheerful.'

'Oh, it gets even better as it goes on. Something to the effect that he

> *'Joyously huggeth and crawleth around*
> *The rich mould of dead men's graves.'*

Gus closed the window with a bang. 'Shut up and put the light on.'

Judith took no notice. In the same soft, faraway voice she continued:

'*Creeping where Grim Death hath been,*
A rare old plant is the ivy green.'

Suddenly she shuddered. 'Oh, I'm cold, cold. You shouldn't have had that window open.'

Gus put an arm round her shoulders. 'You shouldn't have dredged up that lugubrious verse. Where on earth does it come from?'

'It's Dickens, believe it or not.'

'It makes one grateful for *David Copperfield*. Come on, let's call it a day and have a drink to celebrate our first victory over friend ivy.'

Next day the ivy was back, tapping on the pane.

*   *   *

Gus now decided on more drastic measures, and took an axe to the main stems all round the house. With great difficulty and several sharpenings of the axe he hacked through them, but two days later it was impossible to detect the cuts. Then he started from the upper windows, endeavouring to tear the plant down from above, but even the smallest tendrils seemed sunk deep into the brickwork, and the tiny roots clung like the suckers of a leech. Perhaps where force had failed, science would triumph. Gus determined to try weedkiller and sought the advice of the elderly man in the local seedsman's, who shook his head when he heard what the weedkiller was for.

'Won't have no effect on ivy,' he prophesied. 'Only thing to do with that is to cut it down.'

'I've tried that and it doesn't work,' Gus said sharply.

'Ah, got The Hollies, haven't you?'

'What's that got to do with it?'

'Quite a bit, I should say. Let's see, The Hollies is the old Dyer place, ain't it?'

'The last owner was a Mrs Dyer, yes.'

'Then you'd expect ivy to flourish rather than holly. It's the female principle, see. The holly and the ivy, like in the old carol. They've been fighting since before Christian times.'

'You seem to know a lot about it.'

'Plants are my business,' the old man said. 'There's a lot of interesting lore about plants if you take the trouble to learn it. The holly and the ivy's an example, see. Once in pagan times they was symbols – male and female, same as the sun and moon. And naturally –' he paused to chuckle – 'in any struggle the male – old holly – was the winner. Being evergreens, they got associated with Christmas, but there ain't nothing Christian about them two.'

'What's all that got to do with The Hollies?'

'Why, there it was the other way round. Mrs Dyer, she were the winner. The ivy beat the holly, see.'

'Not knowing Mrs Dyer, I don't.'

'She and her husband –' the old man laid one forefinger across the other – 'they was always at it like that, until one day he upped and left her.'

'I don't see much victory in that.'

'She had the house and she had the money, and he were never seen nor heard of again. That's why when she died they couldn't prove the will because he might be living. But I reckon he were dead long since. So did others. So did the police. At least they went round asking questions, but there was never anything anyone could prove. Only the ivy started growing over the holly. Try weedkiller if you like, but you'll never bring it down.'

            *   *   *

Gus did indeed try weedkiller, and proved the old man wrong in one respect. Far from having no effect, it seemed to make the ivy flourish more than ever. The normally slow-growing plant was spreading and thickening as if it were a Russian vine.

'It must like the smell of fresh paint,' Judith said despairingly. 'It's half over the back windows now.'

'Either that or it's an exceptionally fertile bit of ground,' Gus suggested. 'We'll have a fine garden some day when we get it clear.'

'*If* we ever get it clear.'

'We'll manage, don't you worry. Some of these weedkillers are slow to act.'

'You can say that again. Look at the way it's growing. I swear this tendril's lengthened while we've been standing here.'

'"A rare old plant is the ivy green,"' Gus quoted. 'Isn't that what your poem said?'

'Yes.' Judith suddenly turned and buried her head against him. 'Oh Gus, suppose it's true.'

'Suppose what's true?'

'That story you told me about Mrs Dyer doing away with her husband.'

'Nothing was ever proved, you know.'

'But perhaps that's why the ivy started growing. Perhaps she buried him here.'

'Seems to me that's a lot of perhapsing,' Gus said uneasily. 'How about: Perhaps you're tired. Perhaps you're letting your imagination run away with you.'

'I might have known you wouldn't understand.'

'Who says I don't?'

'It's obvious.'

'Not to me it isn't. What do you want me to do? Dig down to the foundations in search of a skeleton? Call in a parson to lay an imaginary ghost?'

'No.' Judith shook her head emphatically. 'Just let's get out of here.'

'We can't afford to. We've put everything we've got into The Hollies. You know that perfectly well.'

'You mean we're trapped?'

'Don't be silly, Judith. It's only for a year or two. Until the business gets on its feet. Then we can maybe sell The Hollies at a profit.'

'If it isn't an ivy-grown mound by then.'

Gus glanced at the sitting-room windows. The ivy was well above the sash. Surely it had been lower, much lower, a mere half hour ago?

'I'll have another go at chopping it down,' he said determinedly. 'And give it some more weedkiller too.'

'You won't do any good,' Judith said, half laughing, half crying. 'Mrs Dyer's going to win.'

*   *   *

It began to look as if she were right. Within a fortnight the ivy had spread to both sides of the house and the front windows were so darkened by it that even on the few bright days of winter, only a little sunlight got through. The Pentecosts slept with ear-plugs to deaden the tapping on the panes. Or rather, they lay awake with ear-plugs. Judith in particular was not sleeping well.

It is possible that others might have noticed the phenomenon of the ivy if The Hollies had not stood well back from the road, behind a brick wall which also had its cloak of ivy and was entered only through a heavy iron gate. Milk and papers the Pentecosts found it easiest to bring with them. Post was left in an old-fashioned postbox, though whether through laziness on the part of the postman or through superstition the Pentecosts were unable to decide. What was certain was that people on hearing their address would say, 'Oh, you've got The Hollies, have you? The old Dyer place ...' and their voices would tail away. No one seemed to have known the Dyers, and all enquiries about them proved vain. 'He disappeared,' people would say, 'and she went on living there. Sort of a recluse, she was.'

The Pentecosts, being newcomers, had few friends in the district, and those they had they were anxious not to invite to the house until such time as they had made it a show-place. So no one saw it but themselves.

'Tell you what,' Gus said halfway through December. 'The shop'll be closed for a week at Christmas. Let's have a blitz on the place then.

Finish painting the kitchen and lay the vinyl flooring, get the dining-room curtains hung, clear the ivy——'

'Clear the ivy!' Judith laughed hysterically. 'If you think you can do that, you must be mad.'

'OK, I'm mad,' Gus said cheerfully. 'Care to join me?'

Privately he thought Judith looked a little mad. She had lost weight and there were hollows round her eyes which he did not remember. It was more than time they got that ivy down.

On Christmas Eve, stocked up with food and drink for the festive season and with a notice 'Reopening January' on the shop, the Pentecosts rolled up their sleeves and got to work. Towards half past eight when they were at their paint-stained worst, there was a sudden scuffling of footsteps on the gravel.

Judith looked at Gus. 'Who on earth would come here now?'

A moment later a carol broke the stillness, young voices ringing fresh and true in the night air. Downing tools, the Pentecosts unbolted the front door and saw, framed in ivy, a group of carol-singers gathered round a lantern and muffled up as though on a Christmas card. The carol they had chosen was appropriately 'The Holly and the Ivy'. They had obviously been carefully rehearsed. The rendering was far better than Gus or Judith had anticipated. Gus began feeling in his pockets for change.

Realizing that he had left his money in his coat upstairs in the bedroom, he excused himself as the collecting box came round, leaving Judith to thank the singers and enquire their provenance.

'We're a mixed group from various churches,' explained the man with the lantern. 'We do this in aid of local charities every year. Funny thing is, we were just going home when someone remembered the old Dyer place was inhabited, so we thought we'd give you a call.'

'We're very glad you did,' Judith said warmly. 'You sang it awfully well. I suppose it's because you're tired that you suddenly went wrong in the last line.'

'Did we?' The lantern-bearer looked blank.

'You sang "the ivy bears the crown", not "the holly",'

'We didn't!' the singers cried indignantly.

'But I heard you. I heard you distinctly.'

They protested that Judith was the only one who had.

She turned as Gus came back with a generous contribution. 'Gus, didn't they sing "the ivy bears the crown" in the last line?'

Gus slipped an arm round her shoulders. 'My wife,' he explained, 'has ivy on the brain – not surprising when you see how much of it we have to contend with. But by this time next week it'll all be chopped down.'

The singers smiled understandingly, sympathetically. 'You've got

your work cut out,' they said. 'Rather you than me.' 'You'll need a
machete for that job.' And then, in a chorus of 'Merry Christmases',
they turned and went away.

Gus closed the door. Judith was white and shaking. 'They *did* sing it
wrong,' she said. 'I'm not imagining things. I heard them.' Her voice
was beginning to rise.

'What's it matter if they did?' Gus said reasonably. 'They'd hardly
admit they'd made a mistake. Holly or ivy – it makes no difference.
Have a drink, and then we'll get something to eat. I'm hungry.'

Judith allowed herself to be led away.

*   *   *

No doubt it was because they were tired, but that night the Pentecosts
slept unusually long and heavily. Yet when they awoke it was still dark.
For a time each lay silent, anxious not to disturb the other. Eventually
Judith spoke.

'Merry Christmas, darling. What time is it?'

'Merry Christmas, my sweet. I'll see.'

Without bothering to put the light on, Gus reached for his
luminous-dialled watch, a wedding present from Judith, shook it and
swore violently.

'What's the matter?'

'Damn thing's gone wrong, that's what. It must have stopped last
night at nine-fifteen. Funny I never noticed when I came to wind it up.'

'Well, we can't dial the time because we haven't got a telephone.
Does it really take three months to get a telephone installed?'

'Only God and the Post Office can tell you that. I'll go downstairs
and get the radio. Sooner or later there'll be a time signal on that.'

Gus struggled into dressing-gown and slippers and went towards the
bedroom door. As he passed the window, he stopped as though
transfixed, then said in a voice which he tried to make sound normal,
'Here, Judy, come and have a look at this.'

Judith joined him. The window seemed impenetrably dark. Then,
as she looked, she began to make out tiny chinks of brilliance, as though
there were irregular knot-holes in a shutter. The brillance suddenly
identified itself.

'It's sunlight!' she exclaimed unbelievingly.

With one accord, she and Gus rushed from the room into the
darkness of the landing. Frantically they opened door after door. The
whole house was crepuscular and tomblike, though it was a brilliant
day outside. Approaching a window, they stared out at a great mat of
ivy, its woody stems as thick as Gus's wrist, its dark, opaque leaves
overlapping like plate armour. Only very occasionally did a glimmer of
light get through.

Gus unbolted the front door. Where last night the carol-singers had stood framed in ivy, there was only dense greenery. Gus pushed at it, but the wall was solid, extending from ground to roof-height; perhaps over the roof as well. The back door was the same, and so were the french windows in the dining-room. The house was wrapped in ivy like a shroud.

It was Judith who put into words the thought they kept trying not to formulate. 'How are we going to get out?'

'Easy,' Gus said with forced cheerfulness. 'I'll have to chop a way through.'

'But the axe is in the shed.'

'There must be something in the house that'll cut it.'

'The bread knife, the carving knife ...'

But it was hopeless and they both knew it. The short day dimmed to dark. The ivy tapped at the window and scratched like a rat at the door. Towards morning (but of what day when all the days were darkness?) Gus said dreamily: 'Do you suppose that damn plant's getting thicker?'

'Yes,' Judith said. 'Thicker and thicker and thicker. Soon there'll be nothing left of us or of the house.' She began to sing in a cracked and broken voice:

> *'The Hollies and the ivy,*
> *When they are both well grown,*
> *Of all the trees that are in the wood,*
> *The ivy bears the crown.'*

'Shut up!' Gus said fiercely, but she went on singing and pretty soon he heard himself joining in. Their voices rose in mournful unison, echoing through the still, empty rooms of the house.

> *'The Hollies and the ivy,*
> *When they are both well grown ...'*

The ivy kept time with them, beating on the window-pane.

The Red Room
H. G. Wells

'I can assure you,' said I, 'that it will take a very tangible ghost to frighten me.' And I stood up before the fire with my glass in my hand.

'It is your own choosing,' said the man with the withered arm, and glanced at me askance.

'Eight-and-twenty years,' said I, 'I have lived, and never a ghost have I seen as yet.'

The old woman sat staring hard into the fire, her pale eyes wide open. 'Ah,' she broke in: 'and eight-and-twenty years you have lived and never seen the likes of this house, I reckon. There's a many things to see, when one's still but eight-and-twenty.' She swayed her head slowly from side to side. 'A many things to see and sorrow for.'

I half suspected the old people were trying to enhance the spiritual terrors of their house by their droning insistence. I put down my empty glass on the table and looked about the room, and caught a glimpse of myself, abbreviated and broadened to an impossible sturdiness, in the queer old mirror at the end of the room. 'Well,' I said, 'if I see anything tonight, I shall be so much the wiser. For I come to the business with an open mind.'

'It's your own choosing,' said the man with the withered arm once more.

I heard the sound of a stick and a shambling step on the flags in the passage outside, and the door creaked on its hinges as a second old man entered, more bent, more wrinkled, more aged even than the first. He supported himself by a single crutch, his eyes were covered by a shade, and his lower lip, half averted, hung pale and pink from his decaying yellow teeth. He made straight for an armchair on the opposite side of the table, sat down clumsily, and began to cough. The man with the withered arm gave this newcomer a short glance of positive dislike; the old woman took no notice of his arrival, but remained with her eyes fixed steadily on the fire.

'I said – it's your own choosing,' said the man with the withered arm, when the coughing had ceased for a while.

'It's my own choosing,' I answered.

The man with the shade became aware of my presence for the first time, and threw his head back for a moment and sideways, to see me. I caught a momentary glimpse of his eyes, small and bright and inflamed. Then he began to cough and splutter again.

'Why don't you drink?' said the man with the withered arm, pushing the beer towards him. The man with the shade poured out a glassful with a shaky arm that splashed half as much again on the deal table. A monstrous shadow of him crouched upon the wall and mocked his action as he poured and drank. I must confess I had scarce expected these grotesque custodians. There is to my mind something inhuman in senility, something crouching and atavistic; the human qualities seem to drop from old people insensibly day by day. The three of them made me feel uncomfortable, with their gaunt silences, their bent carriage, their evident unfriendliness to me and to one another.

'If,' said I, 'you will show me to this haunted room of yours, I will make myself comfortable there.'

The old man with the cough jerked his head back so suddenly that it startled me, and shot another glance of his red eyes at me from under the shade; but no one answered me. I waited a minute, glancing from one to the other.

'If,' I said a little louder, 'if you will show me to this haunted room of yours, I will relieve you from the task of entertaining me.'

'There's a candle on the slab outside the door,' said the man with the withered arm, looking at my feet as he addressed me. 'But if you go to the red room tonight——'

('This night of all nights!' said the old woman.)

'You go alone.'

'Very well,' I answered. 'And which way do I go?'

'You go along the passage for a bit,' said he, 'until you come to a door, and through that is a spiral staircase, and half-way up that is a landing and another door covered with baize. Go through that and down the long corridor to the end, and the red room is on your left up the steps.'

'Have I got that right?' I said, and repeated his directions. He corrected me in one particular.

'And are you really going?' said the man with the shade, looking at me again for the third time, with that queer, unnatural tilting of the face.

('This night of all nights!' said the old woman.)

'It is what I came for,' I said, and moved towards the door. As I did so, the old man with the shade rose and staggered round the table, so as to be closer to the others and to the fire. At the door I turned and looked at them, and saw they were all close together, dark against the firelight,

staring at me over their shoulders, with an intent expression on their
ancient faces.

'Goodnight,' I said, setting the door open.

'It's your own choosing,' said the man with the withered arm.

I left the door wide open until the candle was well alight, and then I
shut them in and walked down the chilly, echoing passage.

I must confess that the oddness of these three old pensioners in whose
charge her ladyship had left the castle, and the deep-toned, old-
fashioned furniture of the housekeeper's room in which they fore-
gathered, affected me in spite of my efforts to keep myself at a matter of
fact phase. They seemed to belong to another age, an older age, an age
when things spiritual were different from this of ours, less certain; an age
when omens and witches were credible, and ghosts beyond denying.
Their very existence was spectral; the cut of their clothing, fashions born
in dead brains. The ornaments and conveniences of the room about
them were ghostly – the thoughts of vanished men, which still haunted
rather than participated in the world of today. But with an effort I sent
such thoughts to the right-about. The long, draughty subterranean
passage was chilly and dusty, and my candle flared and made the
shadows cower and quiver. The echoes rang up and down the spiral
staircase, and a shadow came sweeping up after me, and one fled before
me into the darkness overhead. I came to the landing and stopped there
for a moment, listening to a rustling that I fancied I heard; then,
satisfied of the absolute silence, I pushed open the baize-covered door
and stood in the corridor.

The effect was scarcely what I expected, for the moonlight coming
in by the great window on the grand staircase picked out everything in
vivid black shadow or silvery illumination. Everything was in its place;
the house might have been deserted on the yesterday instead of eighteen
months ago. There were candles in the sockets of the sconces, and
whatever dust had gathered on the carpets or upon the polished flooring
was distributed so evenly as to be invisible in the moonlight. I was about
to advance, and stopped abruptly. A bronze group stood upon the
landing, hidden from me by the corner of the wall, but its shadow fell
with marvellous distinctness upon the white panelling and gave me the
impression of some one crouching to waylay me. I stood rigid for half a
minute perhaps. Then, with my hand in the pocket that held my
revolver, I advanced, only to discover a Ganymede and Eagle glistening
in the moonlight. That incident for a time restored my nerve, and a
porcelain Chinaman on a buhl table, whose head rocked silently as I
passed him, scarcely startled me.

The door to the red room and the steps up to it were in a shadowy
corner. I moved my candle from side to side, in order to see clearly the
nature of the recess in which I stood before opening the door. Here it

was, thought I, that my predecessor was found, and the memory of that story gave me a sudden twinge of apprehension. I glanced over my shoulder at the Ganymede in the moonlight, and opened the door of the red room rather hastily, with my face half-turned to the pallid silence of the landing.

I entered, closed the door behind me at once, turned the key I found in the lock within, and stood with the candle held aloft, surveying the scene of my vigil, the great red room of Lorraine Castle, in which the young duke had died. Or, rather, in which he had begun his dying, for he had opened the door and fallen headlong down the steps I had just ascended. That had been the end of his vigil, of his gallant attempt to conquer the ghostly tradition of the place, and never, I thought, had apoplexy better served the ends of superstition. And there were other and older stories that clung to the room, back to the half-credible beginning of it all, the tale of a timid wife and the tragic end that came to her husband's jest of frightening her. And looking around that large sombre room, with its shadowy window bays, its recesses and alcoves, one could well understand the legends that had sprouted in its black corners, its germinating darkness. My candle was a little tongue of light in its vastness, that failed to pierce the opposite end of the room, and left an ocean of mystery and suggestion beyond its island of light.

I resolved to make a systematic examination of the place at once, and dispel the fanciful suggestions of its obscurity before they obtained a hold upon me. After satisfying myself of the fastening of the door, I began to walk about the room, peering round each article of furniture, tucking up the valances of the bed, and opening its curtains wide. I pulled up the blinds and examined the fastenings of the several windows before closing the shutters, leant forward and looked up the blackness of the wide chimney, and tapped the dark oak panelling for any secret opening. There were two big mirrors in the room, each with a pair of sconces bearing candles, and on the mantelshelf, too, were more candles in china candlesticks. All these I lit one after the other. The fire was laid, an unexpected consideration from the old housekeeper – and I lit it, to keep down any disposition to shiver, and when it was burning well, I stood round with my back to it and regarded the room again. I had pulled up a chintz-covered armchair and a table, to form a kind of barricade before me, and on this lay my revolver ready to hand. My precise examination had done me good, but I still found the remoter darkness of the place, and its perfect stillness, too stimulating for the imagination. The echoing of the stir and crackling of the fire was no sort of comfort to me. The shadow in the alcove at the end in particular had that undefinable quality of a presence, that odd suggestion of a lurking, living thing, that comes so easily in silence and solitude. At last, to reassure myself, I walked with a candle into it, and satisfied myself that there was nothing tangible there. I stood that candle upon the floor of the alcove, and left it in that position.

By this time I was in a state of considerable nervous tension, although to my reason there was no adequate cause for the condition. My mind, however, was perfectly clear. I postulated quite unreservedly that nothing supernatural could happen, and to pass the time I began to string some rhymes together, Ingoldsby fashion, of the original legend of the place. A few I spoke aloud, but the echoes were not pleasant. For the same reason I also abandoned, after a time, a conversation with myself upon the impossibility of ghosts and haunting. My mind reverted to the three old and distorted people downstairs, and I tried to keep it upon that topic. The sombre reds and blacks of the room troubled me; even with seven candles the place was merely dim. The one in the alcove flared in a draught, and the fire's flickering kept the shadows and penumbra perpetually shifting and stirring. Casting about for a remedy, I recalled the candles I had seen in the passage, and, with a slight effort, walked out into the moonlight, carrying a candle and leaving the door open, and presently returned with as many as ten. These I put in various knick-knacks of china with which the room was sparsely adorned, lit and placed where the shadows had lain deepest, some on the floor, some in the window recesses, until at last my seventeen candles were so arranged that not an inch of the room but had the direct light of at least one of them. It occurred to me that when the ghost came, I could warn him not to trip over them. The room was now quite brightly illuminated. There was something very cheery and reassuring in these little streaming flames, and snuffing them gave me an occupation, and afforded a helpful sense of the passage of time.

Even with that, however, the brooding expectation of the vigil weighed heavily upon me. It was after midnight that the candle in the alcove suddenly went out, and the black shadow spring back to its place there. I did not see the candle go out; I simply turned and saw that the darkness was there, as one might start and see the unexpected presence of a stranger. 'By Jove!' said I aloud; 'that draught's a strong one!' and taking the matches from the table, I walked across the room in a leisurely manner to relight the corner again. My first match would not strike, and as I succeeded with the second, something seemed to blink on the wall before me. I turned my head involuntarily, and saw that the two candles on the little table by the fireplace were extinguished. I rose at once to my feet.

'Odd!' I said. 'Did I do that myself in a flash of absent-mindedness?'

I walked back, relit one, and as I did so, I saw the candle in the right sconce of one of the mirrors wink and go right out, and almost immediately its companion followed it. There was no mistake about it. The flame vanished, as if the wicks had been suddenly nipped between a finger and a thumb, leaving the wick neither glowing nor smoking, but black. While I stood gaping, the candle at the foot of the bed went out, and the shadows seemed to take another step towards me.

'This won't do!' said I, and first one and then another candle on the mantelshelf followed.

'What's up?' I cried, with a queer high note getting into my voice somehow. At that the candle on the wardrobe went out, and the one I had relit in the alcove followed.

'Steady on!' I said. 'These candles are wanted,' speaking with a half-hysterical facetiousness, and scratching away at a match the while for the mantel candlesticks. My hands trembled so much that twice I missed the rough paper of the matchbox. As the mantel emerged from darkness again, two candles in the remoter end of the window were eclipsed. But with the same match I also relit the larger mirror candles, and those on the floor near the doorway, so that for the moment I seemed to gain on the extinctions. But then in a volley there vanished four lights at once in different corners of the room, and I struck another match in quivering haste, and stood hesitating whither to take it.

As I stood undecided, an invisible hand seemed to sweep out the two candles on the table. With a cry of terror, I dashed at the alcove, then into the corner, and then into the window, relighting three, as two more vanished by the fireplace; then, perceiving a better way, I dropped the matches on the iron-bound deedbox in the corner, and caught up the bedroom candlestick. With this I avoided the delay of striking matches; but for all that the steady process of extinction went on, and the shadows I feared and fought against returned, and crept in upon me, first a step gained on this side of me and then on that. It was like a ragged storm-cloud sweeping out the stars. Now and then one returned for a minute, and was lost again. I was now almost frantic with the horror of the coming darkness, and my self-possession deserted me. I leaped panting and dishevelled from candle to candle in a vain struggle against that remorseless advance.

I bruised myself on the thigh against the table, I sent a chair headlong, I stumbled and fell and whisked the cloth from the table in my fall. My candle rolled away from me, and I snatched another as I rose. Abruptly this was blown out, as I swung it off the table by the wind of my sudden movement, and immediately the two remaining candles followed. But there was light still in the room, a red light that staved off the shadows from me. The fire! Of course I could still thrust my candle between the bars and re-light it!

I turned to where the flames were still dancing between the glowing coals, and splashing red reflections upon the furniture, made two steps towards the grate, and incontinently the flames dwindled and vanished, the glow vanished, the reflections rushed together and vanished, and as

I thrust the candle between the bars darkness close upon me like the shutting of an eye, wrapped about me in a stifling embrace, sealed my vision, and crushed the last vestiges of reason from my brain. The candle fell from my hand. I flung out my arms in a vain effort to thrust that ponderous blackness away from me, and, lifting up my voice, screamed with all my might – once, twice, thrice. Then I think I must have staggered to my feet. I know I thought suddenly of the moonlit corridor, and, with my head bowed and my arms over my face, made a run for the door.

But I had forgotten the exact position of the door, and struck myself heavily against the corner of the bed. I staggered back, turned, and was either struck or struck myself against some other bulky furniture. I have a vague memory of battering myself thus, to and fro in the darkness, of a cramped struggle, and of my own wild crying as I darted to and fro, of a heavy blow at last upon my forehead, a horrible sensation of falling that lasted an age, of my last frantic effort to keep my footing, and then I remember no more.

*   *   *

I opened my eyes in daylight. My head was roughly bandaged, and the man with the withered arm was watching my face. I looked about me, trying to remember what had happened, and for a space I could not recollect. I rolled my eyes into the corner, and saw the old woman, no longer abstracted, pouring out some drops of medicine from a little blue phial into a glass. 'Where am I?' I asked; 'I seem to remember you, and yet I cannot remember who you are.'

They told me then, and I heard of the haunted red room as one who hears a tale. 'We found you at dawn,' said he, 'and there was blood on your forehead and lips.'

It was very slowly I recovered my memory of my experience. 'You believe now,' said the old man, 'that the room is haunted?' He spoke no longer as one who greets an intruder, but as one who grieves for a broken friend.

'Yes,' said I; 'the room is haunted.'

'And you have seen it. And we, who have lived here all our lives, have never set eyes upon it. Because we have never dared ... Tell us, is it truly the old earl who——'

'No,' said I; 'it is not.'

'I told you so,' said the old lady, with the glass in her hand. 'It is his poor young countess who was frightened——'

'It is not,' I said. 'There is neither ghost of earl nor ghost of countess in that room, there is no ghost there at all; but worse, far worse——'

'Well?' they said.

'The worst of all the things that haunt poor mortal man,' said I;

'and that is, in all its nakedness – *Fear!* Fear that will not have light nor sound, that will not bear with reason, that deafens and darkens and overwhelms. It followed me through the corridor, it fought against me in the room——'

I stopped abruptly. There was an interval of silence. My hand went up to my bandages.

Then the man with the shade sighed and spoke. 'That is it,' said he. 'I knew that was it. A power of darkness. To put such a curse upon a woman! It lurks there always. You can feel it even in the daytime, even of a bright summer's day, in the hangings, in the curtains, keeping behind you however you face about. In the dusk it creeps along the corridor and follows you, so that you dare not turn. There is Fear in that room of hers – black Fear, and there will be – so long as this house of sin endures.'

All Souls'
Edith Wharton

Queer and inexplicable as the business was, on the surface it appeared fairly simple – at the time, at least; but with the passing of years, and owing to there not having been a single witness of what happened except Sara Clayburn herself, the stories about it have become so exaggerated, and often so ridiculously inaccurate, that it seems necessary that someone connected with the affair, though not actually present – I repeat that when it happened my cousin was (or thought she was) quite alone in her house – should record the few facts actually known.

In those days I was often at Whitegates (as the place had always been called) – I was there, in fact, not long before, and almost immediately after, the strange happenings of those thirty-six hours. Jim Clayburn and his widow were both my cousins, and because of that, and of my intimacy with them, both families think I am more likely than anybody else to be able to get at the facts, as far as they can be called facts, and as anybody can get at them. So I have written down, as clearly as I could, the gist of the various talks I had with cousin Sara, when she could be got to talk – it wasn't often – about what occurred during that mysterious weekend.

*　　*　　*

I read the other day in a book by a fashionable essayist that ghosts went out when electric light came in. What nonsense! The writer, though he is fond of dabbling, in a literary way, in the supernatural, hasn't even reached the threshold of his subject. As between turreted castles patrolled by headless victims with clanking chains, and the comfortable suburban house with a refrigerator and central heating where you feel, as soon as you're in it, *that there's something wrong*, give me the latter for sending a chill down the spine! And, by the way, haven't you noticed that it's generally not the high-strung and imaginative who see ghosts, but the calm matter-of-fact people who don't believe in them, and are sure they wouldn't mind if they did see one? Well, that was the case with

Sara Clayburn and her house. The house, in spite of its age – it was built, I believe, about 1780 – was open, airy, high-ceilinged, with electricity, central heating and all the modern appliances: and its mistress was – well, very much like her house. And, anyhow, this isn't exactly a ghost story and I've dragged in the analogy only as a way of showing you what kind of woman my cousin was, and how unlikely it would have seemed that what happened at Whitegates should have happened just there – or to her.

*   *   *

When Jim Clayburn died the family all thought that, as the couple had no children, his widow would give up Whitegates and move either to New York or Boston – for being of good Colonial stock, with many relatives and friends, she would have found a place ready for her in either. But Sally Clayburn seldom did what other people expected, and in this case she did exactly the contrary; she stayed at Whitegates.

'What, turn my back on the old house – tear up all the family roots, and go and hang myself up in a bird-cage flat in one of those new skyscrapers in Lexington Avenue, with a bunch of chickweed and a cuttlefish to replace my good Connecticut mutton? No, thank you. Here I belong, and here I stay till my executors hand the place over to Jim's next of kin – that stupid fat Presley boy ... Well, don't let's talk about him. But I tell you what – I'll keep him out of here as long as I can.' And she did – for being still in the early fifties when her husband died, and a muscular, resolute figure of a woman, she was more than a match for the fat Presley boy, and attended his funeral a few years ago, in correct mourning, with a faint smile under her veil.

Whitegates was a pleasant hospitable-looking house, on a height overlooking the stately windings of the Connecticut River; but it was five or six miles from Norrington, the nearest town, and its situation would certainly have seemed remote and lonely to modern servants. Luckily, however, Sara Clayburn had inherited from her mother-in-law two or three old stand-bys who seemed as much a part of the family tradition as the roof they lived under; and I never heard of her having any trouble in her domestic arrangements.

The house, in Colonial days, had been foursquare, with four spacious rooms on the ground floor, an oak-floored hall dividing them, the usual kitchen extension at the back, and a good attic under the roof. But Jim's grandparents, when interest in the 'Colonial' began to revive, in the early eighties, had added two wings, at right angles to the south front, so that the old 'circle' before the front door became a grassy court, enclosed on three sides, with a big elm in the middle. Thus the house was turned into a roomy dwelling, in which the last three generations of Clayburns had exercised a large hospitality; but the architect had respected the character of the old house, and the enlargement made it more comfortable without lessening its simplicity. There was a lot of land about it, and Jim Clayburn, like his fathers before him, farmed it, not without profit, and played a considerable and respected part in state politics. The Clayburns were always spoken of as a 'good influence' in the country, and the townspeople were glad when they learned that Sara did not mean to desert the place – 'though it must be lonesome, winters, living all alone up there atop of that hill' – they remarked as the days shortened, and the first snow began to pile up under the quadruple row of elms along the common.

Well, if I've given you a sufficiently clear idea of Whitegates and the Clayburns – who shared with their old house a sort of reassuring orderliness and dignity – I'll efface myself, and tell the tale, not in my cousin's words, for they were too confused and fragmentary, but as I built it up gradually out of her half-avowals and nervous reticences. If the thing happened at all – and I must leave you to judge of that – I think it must have happened in this way ...

*   *   *

The morning had been bitter, with a driving sleet – though it was only the last day of October – but after lunch a watery sun showed for a while through banked-up woolly clouds, and tempted Sara Clayburn out. She was an energetic walker, and given, at that season, to tramping three or four miles along the valley road, and coming back by way of Shaker's wood. She had made her usual round, and was following the main drive to the house when she overtook a plainly-dressed woman walking in the same direction. If the scene had not been so lonely – the way to Whitegates at the end of an autumn day was not a frequented one – Mrs Clayburn might not have paid any attention to the woman, for she was in no way noticeable, but when she caught up with the intruder my cousin was surprised to find that she was a stranger – for the mistress of Whitegates prided herself on knowing, at least by sight, most of her country neighbours. It was almost dark, and the woman's face was hardly visible, but Mrs Clayburn told me she recalled her as middle-aged, plain and rather pale.

Mrs Clayburn greeted her, and then added: 'You're going to the house?'

'Yes, ma'am,' the woman answered, in a voice that the Connecticut Valley in old days would have called 'foreign', but that would have been unnoticed by ears used to the modern multiplicity of tongues. 'No, I couldn't say where she came from,' Sara always said, 'What struck me as queer was that I didn't know her.'

She asked the woman, politely, what she wanted, and the woman answered: 'Only to see one of the girls.' The answer was natural enough,

and Mrs Clayburn nodded and turned off from the drive to the lower
part of the gardens, so that she saw no more of the visitor then or
afterwards. And, in fact, a half hour later something happened which
put the stranger entirely out of her mind. The brisk and light-footed
Mrs Clayburn, as she approached the house, slipped on a frozen
puddle, turned her ankle and lay suddenly helpless.

*   *   *

Price, the butler, and Agnes, the dour old Scottish maid whom Sara had
inherited from her mother-in-law, of course knew exactly what to do. In
no time they had their mistress stretched out on a lounge, and Dr
Selgrove had been called up from Norrington. When he arrived, he
ordered Mrs Clayburn to bed, did the necessary examining and
bandaging, and shook his head over her ankle, which he feared was
fractured. He thought, however, that if she would swear not to get up,
or even shift the position of her leg, he could spare her the discomfort of
putting it in plaster. Mrs Clayburn agreed, the more promptly as the
doctor warned her that any rash movement would prolong her
immobility. Her quick imperious nature made the prospect trying, and
she was annoyed with herself for having been so clumsy. But the
mischief was done, and she immediately thought what an opportunity
she would have for going over her accounts and catching up with her
correspondence. So she settled down resignedly in her bed.

'And you won't miss much, you know, if you have to stay there a few
days. It's beginning to snow, and it looks as if we were in for a good spell
of it,' the doctor remarked, glancing through the window as he gathered
up his implements. 'Well, we don't often get snow here as early as this;
but winter's got to begin some time,' he concluded philosophically. At
the door he stopped to add: 'You don't want me to send up a nurse from
Norrington? Not to nurse you, you know; there's nothing much to do till
I see you again. But this is a pretty lonely place when the snow begins,
and I thought maybe——'

Sara Clayburn laughed. 'Lonely? With my old servants? You forget
how many winters I've spent here alone with them. Two of them were
with me in my mother-in-law's time.'

'That's so,' Dr Selgrove agreed. 'You're a good deal luckier than
most people, that way. Well, let me see; this is Saturday. We'll have to
let the inflammation go down before we can X-ray you. Monday
morning, first thing, I'll be here with the X-ray man. If you want me
sooner, call me up.' And he was gone.

*   *   *

The foot, at first, had not been very painful; but towards the small hours
Mrs Clayburn began to suffer. She was a bad patient, like most healthy

and active people. Not being used to pain she did not know how to bear it, and the hours of wakefulness and immobility seemed endless. Agnes, before leaving her, had made everything as comfortable as possible. She had put a jug of lemonade within reach, and had even (Mrs Clayburn thought it odd afterwards) insisted on bringing in a tray with sandwiches and a thermos of tea. 'In case you're hungry in the night, madam.'

'Thank you; but I'm never hungry in the night. And I certainly shan't be tonight – only thirsty. I think I'm feverish.'

'Well, there's the lemonade, madam.'

'That will do. Take the other things away, please.' (Sara had always hated the sight of unwanted food 'messing about' in her room.)

'Very well, madam. Only you might——'

'Please take it away,' Mrs Clayburn repeated irritably.

'Very good, madam.' But as Agnes went out, her mistress heard her set the tray down softly on a table behind the screen which shut off the door.

'Obstinate old goose!' she thought, rather touched by the old woman's insistence.

Sleep, once it had gone, would not return, and the long black hours moved more and more slowly. How late the dawn came in November! 'If only I could move my leg,' she grumbled.

She lay still and strained her ears for the first steps of the servants. Whitegates was an early house, its mistress setting the example; it would surely not be long now before one of the women came. She was tempted to ring for Agnes, but refrained. The woman had been up late, and this was Sunday morning, when the household was always allowed a little extra time. Mrs Clayburn reflected restlessly: 'I was a fool not to let her leave the tea beside the bed, as she wanted to. I wonder if I could get up and get it?' But she remembered the doctor's warning, and dared not move. Anything rather than risk prolonging her imprisonment ...

Ah, there was the stable clock striking. How loud it sounded in the snowy stillness! One – two – three – four – five ...

What? Only five? Three hours and a quarter more before she could hope to hear the door handle turned ... After a while she dozed off again, uncomfortably.

Another sound aroused her. Again the stable clock. She listened. But the room was still in deep darkness, and only six strokes fell ... She thought of reciting something to put her to sleep; but she seldom read poetry, and being naturally a good sleeper, she could not remember any of the usual devices against insomnia. The whole of her leg felt like lead now. The bandages had grown terribly tight – her ankle must have swollen ... She lay staring at the dark windows, watching for the first glimmer of dawn. At last she saw a pale filter of daylight through the shutters. One by one the objects between the bed and the window recovered first their outline, then their bulk, and seemed to be stealthily regrouping themselves, after goodness knows what secret displacements during the night. Who that has lived in an old house could possibly believe that the furniture in it stays still all night? Mrs Clayburn almost fancied she saw one little slender-legged table slipping hastily back into its place.

'It knows Agnes is coming, and it's afraid,' she thought whimsically. Her bad night must have made her imaginative for such nonsense as that about the furniture had never occurred to her before ...

At length, after hours more, as it seemed, the stable clock struck eight. Only another quarter of an hour. She watched the hand moving slowly across the face of the little clock beside her bed ... ten minutes ... five ... only five! Agnes was as punctual as destiny ... in two minutes now she would come. The two minutes passed, and she did not come. Poor Agnes – she had looked pale and tired the night before. She had overslept herself, no doubt – or perhaps she felt ill, and would send the housemaid to replace her. Mrs Clayburn waited.

She waited half an hour; then she reached up to the bell at the head of the bed. Poor old Agnes – her mistress felt guilty about waking her. But Agnes did not appear – and after a considerable interval Mrs Clayburn, now with a certain impatience, rang again. She rang once; twice; three times – but still no one came.

Once more she waited; then she said to herself: 'There must be something wrong with the electricity.' Well – she could find out by switching on the bed lamp at her elbow (how admirably the room was equipped with every practical appliance!). She switched it on – but no light came. Electric current off; and it was Sunday, and nothing could be done about it till the next morning. Unless it turned out to be just a burnt-out fuse, which Price could remedy. Well, in a moment now some one would surely come to her door.

It was nine o'clock before she admitted to herself that something uncommonly strange must have happened in the house. She began to feel a nervous apprehension; but she was not the woman to encourage it. If only she had had the telephone put in her room, instead of out on the landing! She measured mentally the distance to be travelled, re-membered Dr Selgrove's admonition, and wondered if her broken ankle would carry her there. She dreaded the prospect of being put in plaster, but she had to get to the telephone, whatever happened.

She wrapped herself in her dressing-gown, found a walking-stick, and, resting heavily on it, dragged herself to the door. In her bedroom the careful Agnes had closed and fastened the shutters, so that it was not much lighter there than at dawn; but outside in the corridor the cold whiteness of the snowy morning seemed almost reassuring. Mysterious things – dreadful things – were associated with darkness; and here was the wholesome prosaic daylight come again to banish them. Mrs Clayburn looked about her and listened. A deep nocturnal silence in that day-lit house, in which five people were presumably coming and going about their work. It was certainly strange ... She looked out of the window, hoping to see someone crossing the court or coming along the drive. But no one was in sight, and the snow seemed to have the place to itself: a quiet steady snow. It was still falling, with a business-like regularity, muffling the outer world in layers on layers of thick white velvet, and intensifying the silence within. A noiseless world – were people so sure that absence of noise was what they wanted? Let them first try a lonely country house in a November snowstorm!

She dragged herself along the passage to the telephone. When she unhooked the receiver she noticed that her hand trembled.

She rang up the pantry – no answer. She rang again. Silence – more silence! It seemed to be piling itself up like the snow on the roof and in the gutters. Silence. How many people that she knew had any idea what silence was – and how loud it sounded when you really listened to it?

Again she waited: then she rang up 'Central'. No answer. She tried three times. After that she tried the pantry again ... The telephone was cut off, then; like the electric current. Who was at work downstairs, isolating her thus from the world? Her heart began to hammer. Luckily there was a chair near the telephone, and she sat down to recover her strength – or was it her courage?

Agnes and the housemaid slept in the nearest wing. She would certainly get as far as that when she had pulled herself together. Had she the courage——? Yes, of course she had. She had always been regarded as a plucky woman; and had so regarded herself. But this silence——

It occurred to her that by looking from the window of a neighbouring bathroom she could see the kitchen chimney. There ought to be smoke coming from it at that hour; and if there were she thought she would be less afraid to go on. She got as far as the bathroom and looking through the window saw that no smoke came from the chimney. Her sense of loneliness grew more acute. Whatever had happened below-stairs must have happened before the morning's work had begun. The cook had not had time to light the fire, the other servants had not yet begun their round. She sank down on the nearest chair, struggling against her fears. What next would she discover if she carried on her investigations?

The pain in her ankle made progress difficult; but she was aware of it now only as an obstacle to haste. No matter what it cost her in physical suffering, she must find out what was happening below-stairs – or had happened. But first she would go to the maid's room. And if that were empty – well, somehow she would have to get herself downstairs.

She limped along the passage, and on the way steadied herself by resting her hand on a radiator. It was stone-cold. Yet in that well-ordered house in winter the central heating, though damped down at night, was never allowed to go out, and by eight in the morning a mellow warmth pervaded the rooms. The icy chill of the pipes startled her. It was the chauffeur who looked after the heating – so he too was involved in the mystery, whatever it was, as well as the house-servants. But this only deepened the problem.

*   *   *

At Agnes's door Mrs Clayburn paused and knocked. She expected no answer, and there was none. She opened the door and went in. The room was dark and very cold. She went to the window and flung back the shutters; then she looked slowly around, vaguely apprehensive of what she might see. The room was empty but what frightened her was not so much its emptiness as its air of scrupulous and undisturbed order. There was no sign of anyone having lately dressed in it – or undressed the night before. And the bed had not been slept in.

Mrs Clayburn leaned against the wall for a moment; then she crossed the floor and opened the cupboard. That was where Agnes kept her dresses; and the dresses were there, neatly hanging in a row. On the shelf above were Agnes's few and unfashionable hats, rearrangements of her mistress's old ones. Mrs Clayburn, who knew them all, looked at the shelf, and saw that one was missing. And so also was the warm winter coat she had given to Agnes the previous winter.

The woman was out, then; had gone out, no doubt, the night before, since the bed was unslept in, the dressing and washing appliances untouched. Agnes, who never set foot out of the house after dark, who despised the movies as much as she did the wireless, and could never be persuaded that a little innocent amusement was a necessary element in life, had deserted the house on a snowy winter night, while her mistress lay upstairs, suffering and helpless! Why had she gone, and where had she gone? When she was undressing Mrs Clayburn the night before, taking her orders, trying to make her more comfortable, was she already planning this mysterious nocturnal escape? Or had something – the mysterious and dreadful Something for the clue of which Mrs Clayburn was still groping – occurred later in the evening, sending the maid downstairs and out of doors into the bitter night? Perhaps one of the men at the garage – where the chauffeur and gardener lived – had been suddenly taken ill, and someone had run up to the house for Agnes. Yes – that must be the explanation … Yet how much it left unexplained.

Next to Agnes's room was the linen room; beyond that was the housemaid's door. Mrs Clayburn went to it and knocked. 'Mary!' No one answered, and she went in. The room was in the same immaculate order as her maid's, and here too the bed was unslept in, and there were no signs of dressing or undressing. The two women had no doubt gone out together – gone where?

More and more the cold unanswering silence of the house weighed down on Mrs Clayburn. She had never thought of it as a big house, but now, in this snowy winter light, it seemed immense, and full of ominous corners around which one dared not look.

Beyond the housemaid's room were the back stairs. It was the nearest way down, and every step that Mrs Clayburn took was increasingly painful; but she decided to walk slowly back, the whole length of the passage, and go down by the front stairs. She did not know why she did this; but she felt that at the moment she was past reasoning, and had better obey her instinct.

More than once she had explored the ground floor alone in the small hours, in search of unwonted midnight noises; but now it was not the idea of noises that frightened her, but that inexorable and hostile silence, the sense that the house had retained in full daylight its nocturnal mystery, and was watching her as she was watching it; that in entering those empty orderly rooms she might be disturbing some unseen confabulation on which beings of flesh and blood had better not intrude.

The broad oak stairs were beautifully polished, and so slippery that she had to cling to the rail and let herself down tread by tread. And as she descended, the silence descended with her – heavier, denser, more absolute. She seemed to feel its steps just behind her, softly keeping time with hers. It had a quality she had never been aware of in any other silence, as though it were not merely an absence of sound, a thin barrier between the ear and the surging murmur of life just beyond, but an impenetrable substance made out of the world-wide cessation of all life and all movement.

Yes, that was what laid a chill on her: the feeling that there was no limit to this silence, no outer margin, nothing beyond it. By this time she had reached the foot of the stairs and was limping across the hall to the drawing-room. Whatever she found there, she was sure, would be mute and lifeless; but what would it be? The bodies of her dead servants, mown down by some homicidal maniac? And what if it were her turn next – if he were waiting for her behind the heavy curtains of the room she was about to enter? Well, she must find out – she must face whatever lay in wait. Not impelled by bravery – the last drop of courage had oozed out of her – but because anything, anything was better than to remain shut up in that snow-bound house without knowing whether she was alone in it or not, 'I must find that out, I must find that out,' she repeated to herself in a sort of meaningless sing-song.

The cold outer light flooded the drawing-room. The shutters had not been closed, nor the curtains drawn. She looked about her. The room was empty, and every chair in its usual place. Her armchair was pushed up by the chimney, and the cold hearth was piled with the ashes of the fire at which she had warmed herself before starting on her ill-fated walk. Even her empty coffee cup stood on a table near the armchair. It was evident that the servants had not been in the room since she had left it the day before after luncheon. And suddenly the conviction entered into her that, as she found the drawing-room, so she would find the rest of the house; cold, orderly – and empty. She would find nothing, she would find no one. She no longer felt any dread or ordinary human dangers lurking in those dumb spaces ahead of her. She knew she was utterly alone under her own roof. She sat down to rest her aching ankle, and looked slowly about her.

There were the other rooms to be visited, and she was determined to go through them all – but she knew in advance that they would give no answer to her question. She knew it, seemingly, from the quality of the silence which enveloped her. There was no break, no thinnest crack in it anywhere. It had the cold continuity of the snow which was still falling steadily outside.

She had no idea how long she waited before nerving herself to continue her inspection. She no longer felt the pain in her ankle, but was only conscious that she must not bear her weight on it, and therefore moved very slowly, supporting herself on each piece of furniture in her path. On the ground floor no shutter had been closed, no curtain drawn, and she progressed without much difficulty from room to room: the library, her morning-room, the dining-room. In each of them, every piece of furniture was in its usual place. In the dining-room, that table had been laid for the dinner of the previous evening, and the candelabra, with candles unlit, stood reflected in the dark mahogany. She was not the kind of woman to nibble a poached egg on a tray when she was alone, but always came down to the dining-room, and had what she called a civilized meal.

The back premises remained to be visited. From the dining-room she entered the pantry, and there too everything was in irreproachable order. She opened the door and looked down the back passage with its neat linoleum floor-covering. The deep silence accompanied her; she still felt it moving watchfully at her side, as though she were its prisoner and it might throw itself upon her if she attempted to escape. She limped on towards the kitchen. That of course would be empty too, and immaculate. But she must see it.

She leaned a minute in the embrasure of a window in the passage. 'It's like the *Marie Celeste* – a *Marie Celeste* on terra firma,' she thought, recalling the unsolved sea mystery of her childhood. 'No one ever knew what happened on board the *Marie Celeste*. And perhaps no one will ever know what happened here. Even I shan't know.'

At the thought her latent fear seemed to take on a new quality. It was like an icy liquid running through every vein, and lying in a pool about her heart. She understood now that she had never before known what fear was, and that most of the people she had met had probably never known either. For this sensation was something quite different . . .

It absorbed her so completely that she was not aware how long she remained leaning there. But suddenly a new impulse pushed her forward, and she walked on towards the scullery. She went there first because there was a service slide in the wall, through which she might peep into the kitchen without being seen; and some indefinable instinct told her that the kitchen held the clue to the mystery. She still felt strongly that whatever had happened in the house must have its source and centre in the kitchen.

In the scullery, as she had expected, everything was clean and tidy. Whatever had happened, no one in the house appeared to have been taken by surprise; there was nowhere any sign of confusion or disorder. 'It looks as if they'd know beforehand, and put everything straight,' she thought. She glanced at the wall facing the door, and saw that the slide was open. And then, as she was approaching it, the silence was broken. A voice was speaking in the kitchen – a man's voice, low but emphatic, and which she had never heard before.

She stood still, cold with fear. But this fear was again a different one. Her previous terrors had been speculative, conjectured, a ghostly emanation of the surrounding silence. This was a plain everyday dread of evil-doers. Oh, God, why had she not remembered her husband's revolver, which ever since his death had lain in a drawer in her room?

She turned to retreat across the smooth slippery floor but halfway her stick slipped from her, and crashed down on the tiles. The noise seemed to echo on and on through the emptiness, and she stood still, aghast. Now that she had betrayed her presence, flight was useless. Whoever was beyond the kitchen door would be upon her in a second . . .

But to her astonishment the voice went on speaking. It was as though neither the speaker nor his listeners had heard her. The invisible stranger spoke so low that she could not make out what he was saying, but the tone was passionately earnest, almost threatening. The next moment she realized that he was speaking in a foreign language, a language unknown to her. Once more her terror was surmounted by the urgent desire to know what was going on, so close to her yet unseen. She crept to the slide, peered cautiously through into the kitchen, and saw that it was as orderly and empty as the other rooms. But in the middle of the carefully scoured table stood a portable wireless, and the voice she heard came out of it . . .

She must have fainted then, she supposed; at any rate she felt so weak and dizzy that her memory of what happened next remained indistinct. But in the course of time she groped her way back to the pantry, and there found a bottle of spirits – brandy or whisky, she could not remember which. She found a glass, poured herself a stiff drink, and while it was flushing through her veins, managed, she never knew with how many shuddering delays, to drag herself through the deserted ground floor, up the stairs and down the corridor to her own room. There, apparently, she fell across the threshold, again unconscious . . .

When she came to, she remembered, her first care had been to lock herself in; then to recover her husband's revolver. It was not loaded, but she found some cartridges, and succeeded in loading it. Then she remembered that Agnes, on leaving her the evening before, had refused to carry away the tray with the tea and sandwiches, and she fell on them with a sudden hunger. She recalled also noticing that a flask of brandy had been put beside the thermos, and being vaguely surprised. Agnes's departure, then, had been deliberately planned, and she had known that her mistress, who never touched spirits, might have need of a stimulant before she returned. Mrs Clayburn poured some of the brandy into her tea, and swallowed it greedily.

After that (she told me later) she remembered that she had managed to start a fire in her grate, and after warming herself, had got back into her bed, piling on it all the coverings she could find. The afternoon passed in a haze of pain, out of which there emerged now and then a dim shape of fear – the fear that she might lie there alone and untended till she died of cold, and of the terror of her solitude. For she was sure by this time that the house was empty – completely empty, from garret to cellar. She knew it was so, she could not tell why; but again she felt that it must be because of the peculiar quality of the silence – the silence which had dogged her steps wherever she went, and was now folded down on her like a pall. She was sure that the nearness of any other human being, however dumb and secret, would have made a faint crack in the texture of that silence, flawed it as a sheet of glass is flawed by a pebble thrown against it . . .

*   *   *

'Is that easier?' the doctor asked, lifting himself from bending over her ankle. He shook his head disapprovingly. 'Looks to me as if you'd disobeyed orders – eh? Been moving about, haven't you? And I guess Dr Selgrove told you to keep quiet till he saw you again, didn't he?'

The speaker was a stranger, whom Mrs Clayburn knew only by name. Her own doctor had been called away that morning to the bedside of an old patient in Baltimore, and had asked this young man, who was beginning to be known at Norrington, to replace him. The newcomer was shy, and somewhat familiar, as the shy often are, and Mrs Clayburn decided that she did not much like him. But before she could convey this by the tone of her reply (and she was past mistress of the shades of disapproval) she heard Agnes speaking – yes, Agnes, the same, the usual Agnes, standing behind the doctor, neat and stern-looking as ever. 'Mrs Clayburn must have got up and walked about in the night instead of ringing for me, as she'd ought to.' Agnes intervened severely.

This was too much! In spite of the pain, which was now exquisite, Mrs Clayburn laughed. 'Ringing for you? How could I, with the electricity cut off?'

'The electricity cut off?' Agnes's surprise was masterly. 'Why, when was it cut off?' She pressed her finger on the bell beside the bed, and the call tinkled through the quiet room. 'I tried that bell before I left you last night, madam, because if there'd been anything wrong with it I'd have come and slept in the dressing-room sooner than leave you here alone.'

Mrs Clayburn lay speechless, staring up at her. 'Last night? But last night I was all alone in the house.'

Agnes's firm features did not alter. She folder her hands resignedly across her trim apron. 'Perhaps the pain's made you a little confused, madam.' She looked at the doctor, who nodded.

'The pain in your foot must have been pretty bad,' he said.

'It was,' Mrs Clayburn replied. 'But it was nothing to the horror of being left alone in this empty house since the day before yesterday, with the heat and the electricity cut off, and the telephone not working.'

The doctor was looking at her in evident wonder. Agnes's sallow face flushed slightly, but only as if in indignation at an unjust charge. 'But, madam, I made up your fire with my own hands last night – and look, it's smouldering still. I was getting ready to start it again just now, when the doctor came.'

'That's so. She was down on her knees before it,' the doctor corroborated.

Again Mrs Clayburn laughed. Ingeniously as the tissue of lies was being woven about her, she felt she could still break through it. 'I made up the fire myself yesterday – there was no one else to do it,' she said, addressing the doctor, but keeping her eyes on her maid. 'I got up twice to put on more coal, because the house was like a sepulchre. The central heating must have been out since Saturday afternoon.'

At this incredible statement Agnes's face expressed only a polite distress; but the new doctor was evidently embarrassed at being drawn into an unintelligible controversy with which he had no time to deal. He said he had brought the X-ray photographer with him, but the ankle was too much swollen to be photographed at present. He asked Mrs Clayburn to excuse his haste, as he had all Dr Selgrove's patients to visit besides his own, and promised to come back that evening to decide whether she could be X-rayed then, and whether, as he evidently feared, the ankle would have to be put in plaster. Then, handing his prescriptions to Agnes, he departed.

Mrs Clayburn spent a feverish and suffering day. She did not feel well enough to carry on the discussion with Agnes; she did not ask to see the other servants. She grew drowsy, and understood that her mind was confused with fever. Agnes and the housemaid waited on her as attentively as usual, and by the time the doctor returned in the evening her temperature had fallen; but she decided not to speak of what was on her mind until Dr Selgrove reappeared. He was to be back the following evening, and the new doctor preferred to wait for him before deciding to put the ankle in plaster – though he feared this was now inevitable.

*   *   *

That afternoon Mrs Clayburn had me summoned by telephone, and I arrived at Whitegates the following day. My cousin, who looked pale and nervous, merely pointed to her foot, which had been put in plaster, and thanked me for coming to keep her company. She explained that Dr Selgrove had been taken suddenly ill in Baltimore, and would not be back for several days, but that the young man who replaced him seemed fairly competent. She made no allusion to the strange incidents I have set down, but I felt at once that she had received a shock which her accident, however painful, could not explain.

Finally, one evening, she told me the story of her strange weekend, as it had presented itself to her unusually clear and accurate mind, and as I have recorded it above. She did not tell me this till several weeks after my arrival; but she was still upstairs at the time, and obliged to divide her days between her bed and a lounge. During those endless intervening weeks, she told me, she had thought the whole matter over: and though the events of the mysterious thirty-six hours were still vivid to her, they had already lost something of their haunting terror, and she had finally decided not to reopen the question with Agnes, or to touch on it in speaking to the other servants. Dr Selgrove's illness had been not only serious but prolonged. He had not yet returned, and it was reported that as soon as he was well enough he would go on a West Indian cruise, and not resume his practice at Norrington till the spring. Dr Selgrove, as my cousin was perfectly aware, was the only person who could prove that thirty-six hours had elapsed between his visit and that of his successor; and the latter, a shy young man, burdened by the heavy additional practice suddenly thrown on his shoulders, told me (when I risked a little private talk with him) that in the haste of Dr Selgrove's departure the only instructions he had given about Mrs Clayton were summed up in the brief memorandum: 'Broken ankle. Have X-rayed.'

Knowing my cousin's authoritative character, I was surprised at her decision not to speak to the servants of what had happened; but on thinking it over I concluded she was right. They were all exactly as they had been before that unexplained episode: efficient, devoted, respectful and respectable. She was dependent on them and felt at home with them, and she evidently preferred to put the whole matter out of her mind, as far as she could. She was absolutely certain that something strange had happened in her house, and I was more than ever convinced that she had received a shock which the accident of a broken ankle was not sufficient to account for; but in the end I agreed that nothing was to be gained by cross-questioning the servants or the new doctor.

I was at Whitegates off and on that winter and during the following summer, and when I went home to New York for good early in October I left my cousin in her old health and spirits. Dr Selgrove had been ordered to Switzerland for the summer, and this further postponement of his return to his practice seemed to have put the happenings of the strange weekend out of her mind. Her life was going on as peacefully and normally as usual, and I left her without anxiety, and indeed without a thought of the mystery, which was now nearly a year old.

I was living then in a small flat in New York by myself, and I had hardly settled into it when, very late one evening – on the last day of October – I heard my bell ring. As it was my maid's evening out, and I was alone, I went to the door myself, and on the threshold, to my amazement, I saw Sara Clayburn. She was wrapped in a fur cloak, with a hat drawn down over her forehead, and a face so pale and haggard that I saw something dreadful must have happened to her. 'Sara,' I gasped, not knowing what I was saying, 'where in the world have you come from at this hour?'

'From Whitegates. I missed the last train and came by car.' She came in and sat down on the bench near the door. I saw that she could hardly stand, and sat down beside her, putting my arm about her. 'For heaven's sake, tell me what happened.'

She looked at me without seeming to see me. 'I telephoned to Nixon's and hired a car. It took me five hours and a quarter to get here.' She looked about her. 'Can you take me in for the night? I've left my luggage downstairs.'

'For as many nights as you like. But you look so ill——'

She shook her head. 'No; I'm not ill. I'm only frightened – deathly frightened,' she repeated in a whisper.

Her voice was so strange, and the hands I was pressing between mine were so cold, that I drew her to her feet and led her straight to my little guest-room. My flat was in an old-fashioned building, not many stories high, and I was on more human terms with the staff than is possible in one of the modern Babels. I telephoned down to have my cousin's bags brought up, and meanwhile I filled a hot water bottle, warmed the bed, and got her into it as quickly as I could. I had never seen her as unquestioning and submissive, and that alarmed me even more than her pallor. She was not the woman to let herself be undressed and put to bed like a baby; but she submitted without a word, as though aware that she had reached the end of her tether.

'It's good to be here,' she said in a quieter tone, as I tucked her up and smoothed the pillows. 'Don't leave me yet, will you – not just yet.'

'I'm not going to leave you for more than a minute – just to get you a cup of tea,' I reassured her; and she lay still. I left the door open, so that she could hear me stirring about in the little pantry across the passage, and when I brought her the tea she swallowed it gratefully, and a little colour came into her face. I sat with her in silence for some time; but at last she began: 'You see it's exactly a year——'

I should have preferred to have her put off till the next morning whatever she had to tell me; but I saw from her burning eyes that she was determined to rid her mind of what was burdening it, and that until she had done so it would be useless to proffer the sleeping draft I had ready.

'A year since what?' I asked stupidly, not yet associating her precipitate arrival with the mysterious occurrences of the previous year at Whitegates.

She looked at me in surprise. 'A year since I met that woman. Don't you remember – the strange woman who was coming up the drive the afternoon when I broke my ankle? I didn't think of it at the time, but it was on All Souls' eve that I met her.'

Yes, I said, I remembered that it was.

'Well – all this is All Souls' eve, isn't it? I'm not as good as you are on Church dates, but I thought it was.'

'Yes. This is All Souls' eve.'

'I thought so ... Well, this afternoon I went out for my usual walk, I'd been writing letters, and paying bills, and didn't start till late; not till it was nearly dusk. But it was a lovely clear evening. And as I got near the gate, there was the woman coming in – the same woman ... going towards the house ...'

I pressed my cousin's hand, which was hot and feverish now. 'If it was dusk, could you be perfectly sure it was the same woman?' I asked.

'Oh, perfectly sure, the evening was so clear. I knew her and she knew me; and I could see she was angry at meeting me. I stopped her and asked: "Where are you going?" just as I had asked her last year. And she said, in the same queer half-foreign voice. "Only to see one of the girls", as she had before. Then I felt angry all of a sudden, and I said: "You shan't set foot in my house again. Do you hear me? I order you to leave." And she laughed: yes, she laughed – very low, but distinctly. By that time it had got quite dark, as if a sudden storm was sweeping up over the sky, so that though she was so near me I could hardly see her. We were standing by the clump of hemlocks at the turn of the drive, and as I went up to her, furious at her impertinence, she passed behind the hemlocks, and when I followed her she wasn't there ... No; I swear to you she wasn't there ... And in the darkness I hurried back to the house, afraid that she would slip by me and get there first. And the queer thing was that as I reached the door the black cloud vanished, and there was the transparent twilight again. In the house everything seemed as usual, and the servants were busy about their work; but I couldn't get it out of my head that the woman, under the shadow of that cloud, had somehow got there before me.' She paused for breath, and began again. 'In the hall I stopped at the telephone and rang up Nixon, and told him to send me a car at once to go to New York, with a man he knew to drive me. And Nixon came with the car himself ...'

Her head sank back on the pillow and she looked at me like a frightened child. 'It was good of Nixon,' she said.

'Yes; it was very good of him. But when they saw you leaving – the servants, I mean ...'

'Yes. Well, when I got upstairs to my room I rang for Agnes. She came, looking just as cool and quiet as usual. And when I told her I was starting for New York in half an hour – I said it was on account of a sudden business call – well, then her presence of mind failed her for the first time. She forgot to look surprised, she even forgot to make an objection – and you know what an objector Agnes is. And as I watched her I could see a little secret spark of relief in her eyes, though she was so on her guard. And she just said: "Very well, madam," and asked me what I wanted to take with me. Just as if I were in the habit of dashing off to New York after dark on an autumn night to meet a business engagement! No, she made a mistake not to show any surprise – and not even to ask me why I didn't take my own car. And her losing her head in that way frightened me more than anything else. For I saw she was so thankful I was going that she hardly dared speak, for fear she should betray herself, or I should change my mind.'

After that Mrs Clayburn lay a long while silent, breathing less unrestfully; and at last she closed her eyes, as though she felt more at ease now that she had spoken, and wanted to sleep. As I got up quietly to leave her, she turned her head a little and murmured: 'I shall never go back to Whitegates again.' Then she shut her eyes and I saw that she was falling asleep.

*　*　*

I have set down above, I hope without omitting anything essential, the record of my cousin's strange experience as she told it to me. Of what happened at Whitegates that is all I can personally vouch for. The rest – and of course there is a rest – is pure conjecture; and I give it only as such.

My cousin's maid, Agnes, was from the Isle of Skye, and the Hebrides, as everyone knows, are full of the supernatural – whether in the shape of ghostly presences, or the almost ghostlier sense of unseen watchers peopling the long nights of those stormy solitudes. My cousin, at any rate, always regarded Agnes as the – perhaps unconscious, at any rate irresponsible – channel through which communications from the other side of the veil reached the submissive household at Whitegates. Though Agnes had been with Mrs Clayburn for a long time without any peculiar incident revealing this affinity with the unknown forces, the power to communicate with them may all the while have been latent in the woman, only awaiting a kindred touch; and that touch may have been given by the unknown visitor whom my cousin, two years in succession, had met coming up the drive at Whitegates on the eve of All Souls'. Certainly the date bears out my hypothesis; for I suppose that, even in this unimaginative age, a few people still remember that All Souls' eve is the night when the dead can walk – and when, by the same token, other spirits, piteous or malevolent, are also freed from the restrictions which secure the earth to the living on the other days of the year.

If the recurrence of this date is more than a coincidence – and for my part I think it is – then I take it that the strange woman who twice came up the drive at Whitegates on All Souls' eve was either a 'fetch', or else, more probably, and more alarmingly, a living woman inhabited by a witch. The history of witchcraft, as is well known, abounds in such cases, and such a messenger might well have been delegated by the powers who rule in these matters to summon Agnes and her fellow servants to a midnight 'Coven' in some neighbouring solitude. To learn what happens at Covens, and the reason of the irresistible fascination they exercise over the timorous and superstitious, one need only address oneself to the immense body of literature dealing with these mysterious rites. Anyone who has once felt the faintest curiosity to assist at a Coven apparently soon finds the curiosity increase to desire, the desire to an uncontrollable longing, which, when the opportunity presents itself, breaks down all inhibitions; for those who have once taken part in a Coven will move heaven and earth to take part again.

* * *

Such is my – conjectural – explanation of the strange happenings at Whitegates. My cousin always said she could not believe that incidents which might fit into the desolate landscape of the Hebrides could occur in the cheerful and populous Connecticut Valley; but if she did not believe, she at least feared – such moral paradoxes are not uncommon – and though she insisted that there must be some natural explanation of the mystery, she never returned to investigate it.

'No, no,' she said with a little shiver, whenever I touched on the subject of her going back to Whitegates, 'I don't want ever to risk seeing that woman again ...' And she never went back.

The Case of the Long-Dead Lord
Dennis Wheatley

'Thank God you've come,' Bruce Hemmingway cried, as he gripped the hand of the little man for whom he'd been waiting on the platform at Inverness.

'Your wire interested me,' Neils Orsen replied with a gentle smile. 'What's this about my being a naturalist?'

'I'll tell you in a minute. Let's go over to the hotel.'

As the two men walked across the street they made an oddly assorted couple. Neils Orsen was small and lightly built, with transparently pale skin and large, luminous blue eyes. His domed head with a high intelligent brow and mass of soft fair hair appeared too large for his diminutive body. Hatless, dressed in pale grey, carrying a basket conspicuously labelled 'Live Cat', he made a striking contrast to the tall, dark-haired American by his side.

Over coffee in the hotel Bruce explained while the Siamese cat, Pāst, sat on a chair beside them, lapping cream.

'Arkon Clyde, a friend of mine from back home, has taken Castle Stuart for the shooting. I drew up the lease and as the Clydes have never been in Scotland before they asked me to see them settled in. At the moment there's just the old man, who is completely absorbed in books, and his glamorous daughter Fiona; their guests don't arrive for about a week. I've known the girl for some time; she's typical of her generation; sensible, a bit hard-boiled, but full of fun. Yet, when I arrived two days after them, I found her all shot to pieces.

'Well, that puzzled me quite a bit, but the only thing I could get out of her was that for the first time in her life she was suffering from the most appalling nightmares.

'The day before yesterday I took her a walk to explore the ruins of the old castle which are some two miles away. Leading to it there's a lovely avenue of old beeches. We'd only got half-way along it when suddenly she stopped dead, and a queer look came into her eyes. "I've been here before," she whispered to herself, then she began to mutter in what seemed to me like Gaelic. I took hold of her hands and shook her and she looked at me with wide, blinded eyes. As I called her name the spell seemed to snap. She just said she was tired of walking and wanted to go back.

'Maybe I'm wrong, but it didn't seem to me a case for an ordinary doctor, so I asked Arkon if I might have a friend of mine who was a naturalist to stay for a few days, because I didn't want them to know you are a ghost-hunter, and wired you that night.'

'Has anything happened since?' the little Swede asked in his careful English that held hardly a trace of accent.

'No, nothing; except that she never goes into her room if she can help it and spends most of her time wandering alone round the grounds.'

'Does she strike you as an imaginative young woman?'

'Far from it. She has brains as well as looks and graduated in Law at Columbus.'

Neils leaned back, placing the tips of his fingers together.

'So she doesn't like her room? Have you been into it?'

'Yes; I even spent the night before last there, but I slept like a top and yesterday she insisted on returning to it. I can't understand it – I'm sure she's terrified of it and yet she refuses to move.'

'The girl may be abnormally psychic; as neither you nor, apparently, her father are in the least disturbed.'

'Oh, one thing I forgot. She said that her door wouldn't stay shut. Well, the night I spent there it didn't budge an inch. I know, because I fixed a piece of cotton over the opening and it wasn't broken in the morning.'

'At certain phases of the moon, perhaps,' Neils hazarded, 'the Force – if there is a Force – might be stronger.'

'Maybe. But she didn't sleep any better in my room. It's killing her, Neils. A few days ago she was at least scared, and fighting it. Now she's just vague and won't talk. She looked like death at breakfast this morning, but of course her father didn't notice anything; he was buried in some book or other. I don't like leaving her alone. If only I could get that dog to stay with her.'

'What dog?'

'The boar-hound that belongs to the place. He liked her at first, but now he runs away as soon as she appears. Can people be possessed, Neils?'

'Certainly; but we've hardly enough evidence to pre-suppose such a thing in this case. Miss Clyde sounds like a girl suffering from a species of nervous collapse. Of course, a place having the history of Castle Stuart behind it would be filled with vibrations from the past, but apart from the dog's behaviour there is nothing to suggest that her condition is the result of psychic causes.'

'I know, Neils. But I'll swear something queer is going on. Ten days ago, in London, Fiona was a normal, healthy girl with bags of energy; now she's a nervous wreck and so washed out that one might – yes, one might even think that a vampire was sapping her vitality.'

Pāst closed his eyes and purred softly. 'Let us go,' said Neils, 'to Castle Stuart.'

*   *   *

As Bruce turned the car into the gateway the sun was brilliant over the Firth and mountain heads, and he felt a little ashamed at having summoned the famous psychic investigator for so nebulous a purpose. The Castle looked a mild architectural curiosity, but no more. There was nothing sinister here where the drive wound among the sun-burnished scrub and pines; Neils, with the cat upon his knees, glanced up at the brown stone battlements.

'But this is not very old,' he said, smiling.

'Oh, no, only about a hundred and fifty years. It's just a copy. The ruins of the original castle are about two miles away. It marks one boundary of the estate.'

In the great hall sunlight stabbed the worn surfaces of ancient flags that hung motionless, drooping long, twisted shadows across the stairway. While the servants were taking up Orsen's luggage the Swede stood very still, his head inclined as though he listened. Bruce had left him, to look for Fiona. He brought her through the garden door into the hall, where she stood, bathed in the dusty sunlight, her golden hair responding to its caresses; but her lovely green eyes were cold and distant as she shook hands with Orsen.

Her father rushed upon them from the library, American hospitality in every gesture. He was delighted to welcome Bruce's friend ... Pāst was cute ... He had found some interesting material on the bird-life of the island ... and the books were ready beside the sherry for the attention of Mr Orsen.

But Neils refused the wine, and Bruce said sadly, 'I'm afraid he never touches alcohol.'

Throughout luncheon Neils contrived to show a surprising know-ledge of his purported subject and Arkon Clyde took to him im-mediately; but Fiona obviously found it an effort to concentrate her attention sufficiently to appear barely civil, and directly the meal was over she excused herself abruptly.

''Fraid my girl doesn't take to this sort of life very easily,' Clyde said in apology as the door closed behind her. 'I guess she finds it a bit dull after New York.'

'I'll go and see if I can amuse her,' Bruce volunteered. Neils made no sign. His small, gnome-like figure remained bowed in contemplation; one hand was playing with a lock of hair.

Bruce found Fiona curled up on a garden seat behind the Castle. Sitting down, he said earnestly: 'Fiona, do tell me what's wrong. It's sticking out a mile that you've got something on your mind.'

'No! If I tell, you'll say I'm crazy.' She turned away from him and he saw the scarlet mouth tremble. 'I'm beginning to think I must be; no sane person could feel the way I do – could——' she spoke in a hard, strained voice – 'could feel *haunted*!'

As he remained silent she went on desperately: 'Dammit, Bruce, the Castle *is* haunted, and you know it. Why did you let Father bring me here?'

Bruce nodded. 'So I was right! Now listen, Fiona. My friend, Neils Orsen, is not really a naturalist but the world's greatest psychic investigator. I wired for him when I saw how things were with you, and I'm darned glad I did, because if anyone can help you, he can. Let me fetch him; then you can tell him all about it.'

'I don't think anyone can help me, but you can get him if you promise that Father shan't be worried about me.'

When Bruce returned with Orsen, she was sitting in the same position, staring at the ground. She turned her head slightly as they sat down. 'Give me a cigarette, please, Bruce.' Her hand shook as she held it. 'There's something after me in this place,' she began. 'It won't let me alone. I felt odd when I first saw the Castle as we came up the drive. I knew just how it would look. That gave me a kind of shock, and I didn't tell Father, but I wanted to run away. I oughtn't to go in or stay here. I lost the feeling a little until the evening – I was busy unpacking and getting the place straight. Then, when I was alone in my room before dinner, the door swung open suddenly and made me jump. It was perfectly light, and I could see nothing, but I was scared and ran out of the room. That damned door's been opening every night – except when Bruce slept there – and there's a queer, cold feeling in my head, as though I were forgetting how to think. All the time I have the idea that I know this place – that something is going to happen to me again. If only I could remember what – I might prevent it; but I can't. Wherever I go the air is full of whispers that I can't quite hear – and that was all – until last night.'

'Last night,' Bruce repeated.

She nodded. 'Yes; I was so frightened and wretched that I decided to sleep downstairs. I waited until you and Father were in your rooms. I thought perhaps the boar-hound would be sleeping in the hall; so I stood at the head of the stairs and whistled to him. And from my room – I'd left the door open – there came the most horrible chuckle, very hoarse and – and liquid. The Thing was there – it was watching me – laughing at me. I could feel it.'

'What did you do?' Orsen said quietly.

'I heard the dog growl and I ran down to him – but he was scared of something and wouldn't come near me. I stayed in the hall till about four o'clock. I couldn't sit still and I couldn't sleep, so when the light came I went for a walk. I got back about seven, had a bath and came down to breakfast. Oh, God! I'm frightened, Bruce – and I've never been frightened before. It'll get me and keep me for ever and ever. Don't let it! For God's sake don't let it!' She began to sob hysterically.

Neils stroked her hand soothingly. 'I'll do my very best to help you, I promise. Meanwhile, I suggest that you come and lie down in the hall. You have nothing to fear for the moment and you might be able to get some sleep.'

When they had made her comfortable Bruce offered to show Orsen his room. The man-servant had unpacked all the suitcases save one. 'I kept the key,' Neils smiled, 'and I'll see to it later. It contains my cameras.'

Bruce had already seen the cameras in Orsen's company on one strange adventure, but their process – Orsen's invention – was a mystery to him. Neils explained them only by saying that their plates were abnormally sensitive. He said the same thing of his sound-recorder, an instrument like a miniature dictaphone. Bruce wondered what his friend thought of Fiona's story but knew from past experience that he would have to wait until the little man chose to enlighten him.

'Where is Miss Clyde's room?' Orsen was asking.

'Across the passage, the second door; I'll sleep in it again if you like.' Neils shook his head. 'No, Pāst and I will occupy it tonight.'

He strayed towards the window and looked out across the Firth to where the blue hills melted into the horizon. 'What a history those moors could tell,' he said thoughtfully. 'Can you hear the skirl of pipes, Bruce, or see the kilted ghosts marching up across the heather?'

'No,' said Bruce uncomfortably. 'All the same, I'm jolly glad I asked you to come up here. I'll leave you now, as I expect you'd like to get your things straight.' Bruce was a normal practical person, but as he left his small friend, standing with arms folded, heavy head sunk forward, and eyes half closed, he thought – Neils himself gives me the creeps at times.

Fiona was no longer in the hall, and going outside he found her lying on the grass at the entrance to the wild garden. As he approached she sat up and said coldly: 'By the way, your friend is not thinking of spending the night in my room, is he?'

'He certainly is.'

'Well, he won't find anything. Tell him not to fuss.' She stretched her arms above her head. '*I'm* not worrying any more; I feel too tired to care.'

Bruce stared at her. He could hardly believe that this calm aloof creature had been sobbing hysterically on his shoulder half an hour before. 'Fiona,' he pleaded, 'there's one thing you must promise. Stick by me and Neils. We won't let any harm come to you.'

She smiled queerly. 'I think the harm has come to me already, and I'm living with it. Let me alone, Bruce; I'm not frightened any more.' She turned away from him towards the house; but half an hour later through sheer inertia she had consented to move into the other wing of the Castle for the coming night.

*   *   *

'Everything is ready,' Neils said to Bruce after dinner. 'I have the cameras fixed and I've taken other precautions.' He ran his fingers through his hair. 'By the way, where's the girl?'

'She's in the music-room; I'll go to her, I think.'

'Let me. Without her knowing it I may be able to strengthen her subconscious defences so that she gets some sleep. You go into the library and talk to Mr Clyde.' Neils was gone as quietly as a shadow.

On their way to bed he halted Bruce at the door of his own room. 'I'll come in here with you for half an hour in case the servants are about.' He shut the door and drew back the window curtains. Past watched him with colourless, unblinking eyes as he added quietly: 'There *is* something here.'

'What d'you think it is?'

'I can't say for certain. There are earth-bound spirits which can do great harm. You've heard me talk of such things before – of the dark places where those who have not yet passed over must lurk, and long to return. Alternatively, although this place is not old as castles go, it may have seen bloodshed. Torture or murder done for power cause vibrations and echoes that never die. If they can find some material thing to focus on they may become evil entities of great power, and even materialize at times. I have not felt any strong evil here, but when I was with Miss Clyde tonight I needed all my strength to resist a sense of bitterness, of seeking for justice, a cold and lost feeling at the heart. Perhaps that room——' he pointed across the passage – 'holds the secret. We shall see.'

'May I watch with you?'

'No. I want you to go to the other wing and stay beside her door until it is light.'

While the hours crept by and silence held Castle Stuart as though with a mighty hand, Bruce sat leaning his head against the lintels of Fiona's door. He had no sense of the ridiculous. At times he dozed. At times he watched the slowly gathering shadows that touched the angles of wall and stairway and crawled along the vaulted ceiling; swirling like an eddying tide around his feet. Twice the door at his cheek swung open and he heard Fiona come to shut it. Down in the well of the hall he heard the boar-hound whining in its sleep, but no sound of alarm came from Fiona's room and none came from the far side of the great staircase where Orsen kept vigil. By four o'clock the short northern night was over, and having seen the cold grey dawn begin to steal through the windows, Bruce sought his bed.

He slept late and found no opportunity to be alone with Neils until Clyde retired into the library and Fiona had set out on her morning walk.

Neils looked pale and weary; his eyelids drooped. 'There was nothing,' he said, 'nothing at all. And you?'

'Nothing. Her door opened twice, but she didn't look out.'

'Did she open it?'

'I don't know. I heard her come and shut it, but this morning when I asked her how she had slept she didn't complain of anything.'

'I have never passed a night in a room so free of vibrations,' the Swede said slowly. 'It is most perplexing. Pāst, too, felt nothing or he would certainly have shown it; and he is perhaps the severest of all tests. I think,' he added, 'I will spend tonight down in the hall.'

They passed an uneasy day and were glad when Fiona and her father retired to bed.

Again Bruce kept watch. Again, save for the opening and shutting of the door, he was not disturbed, and in the morning Neils, too, reported an untroubled night.

Fiona had now become so far withdrawn from the three men that, to Bruce's mind at least, she seemed to move among them like a spirit. She did not appear unhappy, but her wide green eyes were heavy and shadowed, contrasting violently with the transparent pallor of her face, and her lovely hair seemed to reflect the moon rather than the sun. She made polite conversation at meals, and escaped after them. Every effort that Bruce made to talk to her was coldly received.

At dinner on the third evening Neils spoke only when addressed. For the rest of the time he was silent, his gaze fixed on Fiona. She had not changed from the tweeds she had worn all day and sat calm and composed, her eyes staring vacantly at the table.

'Only six days to the twelfth,' Clyde said. 'I hope I shall have the pleasure of Bruce's company and yours, Mr Orsen, for the first few days at least.'

'Not mine, I fear,' Orsen said absently.

'But you won't be leaving us so soon?'

'Tomorrow, I'm afraid.'

Bruce checked his astonishment. By no look, by no lift of the eyebrow or whispered word had Neils given him a hint. Fiona heard of Orsen's projected departure without speaking. She ate practically nothing. Before coffee was served she got abruptly to her feet and left the room.

Her father stared after her with a worried frown creasing his forehead. 'I think Fiona must have gone *fey*,' he said, 'she looks mighty queer tonight.'

Orsen glanced quickly at his host. 'Why should she go *fey*? Only Scottish people are supposed to do that.'

'Well, she is Scotch – or anyway, a good half. Her mother was a McAin.'

Bruce saw that Orsen's enormous eyes were gleaming with suppressed excitement. But it was not until they had left the table and were alone that he whispered urgently:

'Her Scottish ancestry! I felt just now we should learn something important tonight. Quick! We must hunt the library for any books dealing with the history of Castle Stuart.'

For an hour the two men searched, dragging out volume after volume and frantically scanning their pages for a clue; they had almost despaired, when suddenly Orsen gave a cry of relief.

'This – this should give us the link we seek. It's the history of Castle Stuart, translated into English by the Reverend Father Cox, Chaplain to the Castle from 1698 to 1717.' He ran his finger down the index and turning to a page half-way through the book, began to read:

'Of all the Lordes of Castle Stuart, they do tell that Donald Stuart was the blackest of them all. He were fitter companie for men-at-arms in their drunken brawls than for the fair young maide he did bring to be his bryde.

'She was the Ladie Fiona McAin, own daughter to the McAin of Crath, a winsome lass of sixteen summers who did grieve most sorely to leave her mother's side.'

'Good God!' Bruce broke in. 'D'you realize Fiona's mother was a McAin and there's the extraordinary coincidence of the Christian names?'

'Of course,' Orsen nodded impatiently. 'It's something of this kind that I've been hunting for.' And he read on:

'It becometh us not to linger on that mating, for of a truth it was of an eagle and a dove, contrarie to the laws of nature and a thing offensive in the eyes of God. Poor maide how could she find happiness with such a spouse, and who shall caste blame upon her that she did welcome the young Lorde Ninan when fresh from the Court of France and full of the gracies of the French he did come as a guest for a while beneath Black Donald's roof?

'Lorde Ninan was a courtly, slender man, with smiling face and witty tongue. He did strum upon the lute for the Ladie Fiona's pleasure, write poesie for her and in the French fashion oft did kiss her hand.

'Some say that no more passed between the twain than this, for well did the Ladie Fiona know the jealous heart of her own dark Lorde. Yet on a night of feasting – so the tale is told – when the women had withdrawn and the men were in their cups, Black Donald did suddenlie miss the Lorde Ninan from his board and calling for his claymore he did stagger up the stairs to his Ladie's chamber.

'The lovers herde his loud approach, and knowing there to be murder in his drunken vengeful heart, the Ladie Fiona took Lorde Ninan's hande and guided him by a secret stair behind the tapestry down to the inner court.

'But Black Donald knew well the secret stair, and swift for all the liquor he had drunk, followed cursing upon their heels.

'They had but reached the postern gate when he espied them and shouting to his men-at-arms rushed after. Nearby the well Lorde Ninan turned at bay, but the Stuart clansmen fell upon him piercing him with a dozen pikes and skean dhus, so that he fell backwards over the well's rim, saving himself from plunging into its rockie depths onlie by the clutch of one stronge hand.

'The Ladie Fiona screamed for them to spare him but he knew his life was done, and as he hung there he cried aloud:

'"Fiona! I'll wait for thee, m'darling!" Then with one stroke did Black Donald slice off the clutching hande and the young Lorde fell to his death in the icie water sixty feet below.

'"Tis said that the Lorde Ninan's spirit doth wait there, uneasy stille, so that in passing the end of the avenue that leads up to that grim stronghold, the belated traveller yet may hear the last laugh of Black Donald when his bloodie wille was done, and that last heart-crye of the Lorde Ninan:

'"Fiona! I'll wait for thee, m'darling – I'll wait for thee."'

Orsen closed the book and stood up. 'The whole thing is clear now. It may be a case of re-incarnation or merely the McAin strain in Fiona's blood coupled with her given name. The restless spirit of Lord Ninan still waits for his love to join him. This world is a misty, timeless place to earth-bound spirits and that of Lord Ninan cannot distinguish between our Fiona and the Fiona who lived three hundred years ago; but it has become vaguely aware of her presence in the neighbourhood and is using all the power it can command to draw her to it.'

'Then her father must be told at once,' Bruce said quickly, 'and arrangements made for her to leave Scotland for good tomorrow.'

Neils nodded. 'Yes. It is she who is haunted; not the Castle or her room. That is why no manifestation occurs when she is not present. She must be got away as soon as possible, and in the meantime it's most important that she should not be allowed to go anywhere near the old ruin. The gravest possible danger awaits her there. If she were drawn to the place it's a virtual certainty that her mental resistance would be overcome and she'd feel herself compelled to throw herself down that well.'

'Right,' said Bruce. 'I'll go and tell her that you've found the root of the trouble and warn her not to leave the house.' He turned abruptly as Clyde came into the room, saying with a worried look:

'Bruce, I'm anxious about Fiona. The servants tell me she went out half an hour ago. She didn't even take a coat and it gets sharp at this time of night. I wish you'd go and ...'

Before he had time to complete his sentence Bruce leaped for the door and they heard his footsteps thunder across the hall.

Clyde had glimpsed the look of horror in Bruce's eyes and now he saw the strained expression on Orsen's face.

'What's this,' he exclaimed. 'What's happened?'

'We can only pray,' Orsen said quietly. 'Bruce can run faster than we can. Please God he will be in time.'

Up the rough track with the queer grey sky overhead and the lone moors hunched and darkening on either side, Bruce ran like a man possessed. A mist had risen off the sea; rags and rafes of it danced on the air. Here and there it came down solidly. He stumbled and fell over a tuft of heather. And now the mist came more shrouding and more white. A curlew sobbed its cry somewhere in the silence, and the trees at the roadside reared their great arms heavenwards in mockery.

He ran on, his breath coming in short gasps, knowing nothing but the blind necessity to be in time. As he topped the rise above the old castle, something told him he was too late. Down into the eerie mist he plunged and instantly felt a chill, as if a cold hand grasped his throat. He fell again, staggered to his feet, and ran on desperately across the turf. His footsteps dragged as though he was wading through a bog. A cold whiteness was all about him and with its physical desolation there bore upon his brain another darkness – a sense of evil, too sickening to be borne. He was crouched and groping. He muttered a prayer that died in his throat. Out of the gloom the stones reared, spectral and forbidding. 'Fiona!' he shouted. 'Fiona!'

The swathes of fog beat at his face. 'Fiona!' he called again. 'For God's sake answer.'

Cold, he thought suddenly. Cold – cold – cold. A faint wind whispered through the ruins. He passed his hand across his forehead. He did not know what thoughts they were which seized his brain and cramped it until no feeling came to him but one of intense fear. The wind whispered louder. Now he was up again and running forward. The evil mist was throttling him, but ahead he saw the figure of a girl – a girl who stayed at the edge of a dark, yawning pit. The mist had become a solid wall blocking his way; the wind rose to a shrill scream. He shut his eyes.

'Oh, Lord God, help me because——' strangely inspired the words came to his lips – 'because there is none other that fighteth for us but only Thou, oh God.' Then the mist was rent as though two great hands had torn it asunder and he was at Fiona's side, dragging her back. He felt her body fall limply against him; and now where the dark pit had gaped there was only the shallow, rock-filled ruin of an old well.

Lifting his head he saw that the mist had gone. Cool and grey under the evening sky lay the stones of old Castle Stuart. He stood there for a time holding Fiona in his arms. She stirred and smiled at him:

'What happened, Bruce ... Why are we here? ... He called me ... Why did he call me so urgently? ... Why did he want me?'

'He's gone.'

'Did you send him away?' she asked faintly. 'Thank you, Bruce.'

'I think,' he said, 'we should thank Neils Orsen.'